PRENTICE ALVIN

Alvin held the plow between his hands. He knew that he could turn it all to gold – he'd seen gold enough in his life to know the pattern, so he could show the bits of iron what they ought to be. But he also knew that it wasn't no ordinary gold that he wanted. No, he wanted something new . . . a living gold, a gold that could hold its shape and strength better than iron, better than the finest steel. Gold that was awake, aware of the world around it – a plow that knew the earth that it would tear, to lay it open to the fires of the sun.

So there he knelt, holding the shape of the gold inside his mind. 'Be like this,' he whispered to the iron.

He could feel how the atoms came from all around the plow and joined together with those already in the iron, forming bits much heavier that what the iron was, and lined up in different ways, until they fit the pattern that he showed them in his mind.

Between his hands he held a plow of gold. . . .

PRENTICE ALVIN
The Tales of Alvin Maker III

Orson Scott Card

A Legend Book
Published by Arrow Books Limited
20 Vauxhall Bridge Road, London SW1V 2SA

An imprint of the Random Century Group

London Melbourne Sydney Auckland
Johannesburg and agencies throughout
the world

First published by Legend 1989

This edition 1991

© Orson Scott Card 1989

Phototypeset by Input Typesetting Ltd, London

Printed and bound in Great Britain by
Courier International Ltd, Tiptree, Essex

ISBN 0 09 961210 0

For all my good teachers, especially:

Fran Schroeder,
fourth grade, Millikin Elementary, Santa Clara,
California,
for whom I wrote my first poems.

Ida Huber,
tenth-grade English, Mesa High School, Arizona,
who believed in my future more than I did.

Charles Whitman,
playwriting, Brigham Young University,
who made my scripts look better than they deserved.

Norman Council,
literature, University of Utah,
for Spenser and Milton, alive.

Edward Vasta,
literature, University of Notre Dame,
for Chaucer and for friendship.

and always François.

Acknowledgements

IN THE PREPARATION of this volume of the Tales of Alvin Maker I have, as always, depended on others for help. For immeasurable help on the opening chapters of this book, my thanks go to the gentlefolk of the second Sycamore Hill Writers Workshop, to wit: Carol Emshwiller, Karen Joy Fowler, Gregg Keizer, James Patrick Kelly, John Kessel, Nancy Kress, Shariann Lewitt, Jack Massa, Rebecca Brown Ore, Susan Palwick, Bruce Sterling, Mark L. Van Name, Connie Willis, and Allen Wold.

Thanks also to the Utah State Institute of Fine Arts for awarding a prize to my narrative poem "Prentice Alvin and the No-Good Plow." That encouragement led to my developing the story in prose and at greater length; this is the first volume to include part of the story recounted in that poem.

For details of frontier life and crafts, I have used John Seymour's wonderful book *The Forgotten Crafts* (New York City: Knopf, 1984) and Douglass L. Brownstone's *A Field Guide to America's History* (New York City: Facts On File, Inc., 1984).

I'm grateful that Gardner Dozois has kindly allowed pieces of the Tales of Alvin Maker to appear in the pages of *Isaac Asimov's Science Fiction Magazine*, allowing it to find an audience before the books appeared.

Beth Meacham at Tor is one of that vanishing breed of editors with a golden touch; her advice is never intrusive, always wise; and (rarest editorial trait of all) she returns my telephone calls. For that alone she may be sainted.

Thanks to my writing class in Greensboro in the winter and spring of 1988 for suggestions that led to important improvements in the book; and to my sister, friend, and editorial assistant, Janice, for her work on keeping story details fresh in mind.

Thanks most of all to Kristine A. Card, who listens to me ramble through the many versions of each as-yet-unwritten book, reads the dot-matrix printouts of the early drafts, and is my second self through every page of everything I write.

Contents

1

The Overseer

Let me start my history of Alvin's prenticeship where things first began to go wrong. It was a long way south, a man that Alvin had never met nor never would meet in all his life. Yet he it was who started things moving down the path that would lead to Alvin doing what the law called murder—on the very day that his prenticeship ended and he rightly became a man.

It was a place in Appalachee, in 1811, before Appalachee signed the Fugitive Slave Treaty and joined the United States. It was near the borders where Appalachee and the Crown Colonies meet, so there wasn't a White man but aspired to own a passel of Black slaves to do his work for him.

Slavery, that was a kind of alchemy for such White folk, or so they reckoned. They calculated a way of turning each bead of a Black man's sweat into gold and each moan of despair from a Black woman's throat into the sweet clear sound of a silver coin ringing on the money-changer's table. There was buying and selling of souls in that place. Yet there was nary a one of them who understood the whole price they paid for owning other folk.

Listen tight, and I'll tell you how the world looked from inside Cavil Planter's heart. But make sure the children are asleep, for this is a part of my tale that children ought not to hear, for it deals with hungers they don't understand too well, and I don't aim for this story to teach them.

Cavil Planter was a godly man, a church-going man, a tithepayer. All his slaves were baptized and given Christian names as soon as they understood enough English to be taught the gospel. He forbade them to practice their dark arts—he never allowed them to slaughter so much as a chicken themselves, lest they convert such an innocent act into a sacrifice to some hideous god. In all ways Cavil Planter served the Lord as best he could.

So, how was the poor man rewarded for his righteousness? His wife, Dolores, she was beset with terrible aches and pains, her wrists and fingers twisting like an old woman's. By the time she was twenty-five she went to sleep most nights crying, so that Cavil could not bear to share the room with her.

He tried to help her. Packs of cold water, soaks of hot water, powders and potions, spending more than he could afford on those charlatan doctors with their degrees from the University of Camelot, and bringing in an endless parade of preachers with their eternal prayers and priests with their hocum pocum incantations. All of it accomplished nigh onto nothing. Every night he had to lie there listening to her cry until she whimpered, whimper until her breath became a steady in and out, whining just a little on the out-breath, a faint little wisp of pain.

It like to drove Cavil mad with pity and rage and despair. For months on end it seemed to him that

2

he never slept at all. Work all day, then at night lie there praying for relief. If not for her, then for him.

It was Dolores herself who gave him peace at night. "You have work to do each day, Cavil, and can't do it unless you sleep. I can't keep silent, and you can't bear to hear me. Please—sleep in another room."

Cavil offered to stay anyway. "I'm your husband, I belong here"—he said it, but she knew better.

"Go," she said. She even raised her voice. "Go!"

So he went, feeling ashamed of how relieved he felt. He slept that night without interruption, a whole five hours until dawn, slept well for the first time in months, perhaps years—and arose in the morning consumed with guilt for not keeping his proper place beside his wife.

In due time, though, Cavil Planter became accustomed to sleeping alone. He visited his wife often, morning and night. They took meals together, Cavil sitting on a chair in her room, his food on a small side table, Dolores lying in bed as a Black woman carefully spooned food into her mouth while her hands sprawled on the bedsheets like dead crabs.

Even sleeping in another room, Cavil wasn't free of torment. There would be no babies. There would be no sons to raise up to inherit Cavil's fine plantation. There would be no daughters to give away in magnificent weddings. The ballroom downstairs—when he brought Dolores into the fine new house he had built for her, he had said, "Our daughters will meet their beaux in this ballroom, and first touch their hands, the way our hands first touched in your father's house." Now Dolores never saw the ballroom. She came downstairs only on Sundays to go

3

to church and on those rare days when new slaves were purchased, so she could see to their baptism.

Everyone saw her on such occasions, and admired them both for their courage and faith in adversity. But the admiration of his neighbours was scant comfort when Cavil surveyed the ruins of his dreams. All that he prayed for—it's as if the Lord wrote down the list and then in the margin noted "no, no, no" on every line.

The disappointments might have embittered a man of weaker faith. But Cavil Planter was a godly, upright man, and whenever he had the faintest thought that God might have treated him badly, he stopped whatever he was doing and pulled the small psaltery from his pocket and whispered aloud the words of the wise man.

> *In thee, O Lord, do I put my trust;*
> *Bow down thine ear to me;*
> *Be thou my strong rock.*

He concentrated his mind firmly, and the doubts and resentments quickly fled. The Lord was with Cavil Planter, even in his tribulations.

Until the morning he was reading in Genesis and he came upon the first two verses of chapter 16.

Now Sarai Abram's wife bare him no children: and she had an handmaid, an Egyptian, whose name was Hagar. And Sarai said unto Abram, Behold now, the Lord hath restrained me from bearing: I pray thee, go in unto my maid: it may be that I may obtain children by her.

At that moment the thought came into his mind,

4

Abraham was a righteous man, and so am I. Abraham's wife bore him no children, and mine likewise has no hope. There was an African slavewoman in their household, as there are such women in mine. Why shouldn't I do as Abraham did, and father children by one of these?

The moment the thought came into his head, he shuddered in horror. He'd heard gossip of White Spaniards and French and Portuguese in the jungle islands to the south who lived openly with Black women—truly they were the lowest kind of creature, like men who do with beasts. Besides, how could a child of a Black woman ever be an heir to him? A mix-up boy could no more take possession of an Appalachee plantation than fly. Cavil just put the thought right out of his mind.

But as he sat at breakfast with his wife, the thought came back. He found himself watching the Black woman who fed his wife. Like Hagar, this woman is Egyptian, isn't she? He noticed how her body twisted lithely at the waist as she bore the spoon from tray to mouth. Noticed how as she leaned forward to hold the cup to the frail woman's lips, the servant's breasts swung down to press against her blouse. Noticed how her gentle fingers brushed crumbs and drops from Dolores's lips. He thought of those fingers touching *him*, and trembled slightly. Yet it felt like an earthquake inside him.

He rushed from the room with hardly a word. Outside the house, he clutched his psaltery.

> *Wash me thoroughly from mine iniquity,*
> *And cleanse me from my sin.*
> *For I acknowledge my transgressions;*
> *And my sin is ever before me.*

5

Yet even as he whispered these words, he looked up and saw the field women washing themselves at the trough. There was the young girl he had bought only a few days before, six hundred dollars even though she was small, since she was probably breeding stock. So fresh from the boat she was that she hadn't learned a speck of Christian modesty. She stood there naked as a snake, leaning over the trough, pouring cups of water over her head and down her back.

Cavil stood transfixed, watching her. What had only been a brief thought of evil in his wife's bedroom now became a trance of lust. He had never seen anything so graceful as her blue-black thighs sliding against each other, so inviting as her shiver when the water ran down her body.

Was this the answer to his fervent psalm? Was the Lord telling him that it was indeed with him as it had been with Abraham?

Just as likely it was witchery. Who knew what knacks these fresh-from-Africa Blacks might have? She knows I'm here a-watching, and she's tempting me. These Blacks are truly the devil's own children, to excite such evil thoughts in me.

He tore his gaze from the new girl and turned away, hiding his burning eyes in the words of the book. Only somehow the page had turned—when did he turn it?—and he found himself reading in the Song of Solomon.

Thy two breasts are like two young roes
That are twins, which feed among the lilies.

"God help me," he whispered. "Take this spell from me."

6

Day after day he whispered the same prayer, yet day after day he found himself watching his slave-women with desire, particularly that newbought girl. Why was it God seemed to be paying him no mind? Hadn't he always been a righteous man? Wasn't he good to his wife? Wasn't he honest in business? Didn't he pay tithes and offerings? Didn't he treat his slaves and horses well? Why didn't the Lord God of Heaven protect him and take this Black spell from him?

Yet even when he prayed, his very confessions became evil imaginings. O Lord, forgive me for thinking of my newbought girl standing in the door of my bedroom, weeping at the caning she got from the overseer. Forgive me for imagining myself laying her on my own bed and lifting her skirts to anoint them with a balm so powerful the welts on her thighs and buttocks disappear before my eyes and she begins to giggle softly and writhe slowly on the sheets and look over her shoulder at me, smiling, and then she turns over and reaches out to me and— O Lord, forgive me, save me!

Whenever this happened, though, he couldn't help but wonder—why do such thoughts come to me even when I pray? Maybe I'm as righteous as Abraham; maybe it's the Lord who sent these desires to me. Didn't I first think of this while I was reading scripture? The Lord can work miracles— what if I went in unto the newbought girl and she conceived, and the Lord worked a miracle and the baby was born White? All things are possible to God.

This thought was both wonderful and terrible. If only it were true! Yet Abraham heard the voice of God, so he never had to wonder about what God

might want of him. God never said a word to Cavil
Planter.

And why not? Why didn't God just tell him right
out? Take the girl, she's yours! Or, Touch her not,
she is forbidden! Just let me hear your voice, Lord,
so I'll know what to do!

> *O Lord my rock;*
> *Unto thee will I cry,*
> *Be not silent to me:*
> *Lest, if thou be silent to me,*
> *I become like them*
> *That go down into the pit.*

On a certain day in 1810 that prayer was
answered.

Cavil was kneeling in the curing shed, which was
mostly empty, seeing how last year's burly crop was
long since sold and this year's was still a-greening in
the field. He'd been wrestling in prayer and confession and dark imaginings until at last he cried out,
"Is there no one to hear my prayer?"

"Oh, I hear you right enough," said a stern voice.

Cavil was terrified at first, fearing that some
stranger—his overseer, or a neighbor—had overheard some terrible confession. But when he looked,
he saw that it wasn't anyone he knew. Still, he knew
at once *what* the man was. From the strength in his
arms, his sun-browned face, and his open shirt—no
jacket at all—he knew the man was no gentleman.
But he was no White trash, either, nor a tradesman.
The stern look in his face, the coldness of his eye,
the tension in his muscles like a spring tight-bound
in a steel trap: He was plainly one of those men
whose whip and iron will keep discipline among the

8

Black fieldworkers. An overseer. Only he was stronger and more dangerous than any overseer Cavil had ever seen. He knew at once that *this* overseer would get every ounce of work from the lazy apes who tried to avoid work in the fields. He knew that whoever's plantation was run by *this* overseer would surely prosper. But Cavil also knew that he would never dare to hire such a man, for this overseer was so strong that Cavil would soon forget who was man and who was master.

"Many have called me their master," said the stranger. "I knew that you would recognize me at once for what I am."

How had the man known the words that Cavil thought in the hidden reaches of his mind? "Then you *are* an overseer?"

"Just as there was one who was once called, not *a* master, but simply Master, so I am not *an* overseer, but *the* Overseer."

"Why did you come here?"

"Because you called for me."

"How could I call for you, when I never saw you before in my life?"

"If you call for the unseen, Cavil Planter, then of course you will see what you never saw before."

Only now did Cavil fully understand what sort of vision it was he saw, there in his own burly curing shed. A man whom many called their master, come in answer to his prayer.

"Lord Jesus!" cried Cavil.

At once the Overseer recoiled, putting up his hand as if to fend off Cavil's words. "It is forbidden for any man to call me by that name!" he cried.

In terror, Cavil bowed his head to the dirt. "Forgive me, Overseer! But if I am unworthy to say your

9

name, how is it I can look upon your face? Or am I doomed to die today, unforgiven for my sins?"

"Woe unto you, fool," said the Overseer. "Do you really believe that you have looked upon my *face*?"

Cavil lifted his head and looked at the man. "I see your eyes even now, looking down at me."

"You see the face that you invented for me in your own mind, the body conjured out of your own imagination. Your feeble wits could never comprehend what you saw, if you saw what I truly am. So your sanity protects itself by devising its own mask to put upon me. If you see me as an Overseer, it is because that is the guise you recognize as having the greatness and power I possess. It is the form that you at once love and fear, the shape that makes you worship and recoil. I have been called by many names. Angel of Light and Walking Man, Sudden Stranger and Bright Visitor, Hidden One and Lion of War, Unmaker of Iron and Water-bearer. Today you have called me Overseer, and so, to you, that is my name."

"Can I ever know your true name, or see your true face, Overseer?"

The Overseer's face became dark and terrible, and he opened his mouth as if to howl. "Only one soul alive in all the world has ever seen my true shape, and that one will surely die!"

The mighty words came like dry thunder and shook Cavil Planter to his very root, so that he gripped the dirt of the shed floor lest he fly off into the air like dust whipped away in the wind before the storm. "Do not strike me dead for my impertinence!" cried Cavil.

The Overseer's answer came gentle as morning

sunlight. "Strike you dead? How could I, when you are a man I have chosen to receive my most secret teachings, a gospel unknown to priest or minister."

"Me?"

"Already I have been teaching you, and you understood. I know you desire to do as I command. But you lack faith. You are not yet completely mine."

Cavil's heart leapt within him. Could it be that the Overseer meant to give him what he gave to Abraham? "Overseer, I am unworthy."

"Of course you are unworthy. None is worthy of me, no, not one soul upon this earth. But still, if you obey, you may find favor in my eyes."

Oh, he will! cried Cavil in his heart, yes, he will give me the woman! "Whatever you command, Overseer."

"Do you think I would give you Hagar because of your foolish lust and your hunger for a child? There is a greater purpose. These Black people are surely the sons and daughters of God, but in Africa they lived under the power of the devil. That terrible destroyer has polluted their blood—why else do you think they are Black? I can never save them as long as each generation is born pure Black, for then the devil owns them. How can I reclaim them as my own, unless you help me?"

"Will my child be born White then, if I take the girl?"

"What matters to me is that the child will not be born pure Black. Do you understand what I desire of you? Not one Ishmael, but many children; not one Hagar, but many women."

Cavil hardly dared to name the secretest desire of his heart. "All of them?"

11

"I give them to you, Cavil Planter. This evil generation is your property. With diligence, you can prepare another generation that will belong to me."

"I will, Overseer!"

"You must tell no one that you saw me. I speak only to those whose desires already turn toward me and my works, the ones who already thirst for the water I bring."

"I'll speak no word to any man, Overseer!"

"Obey me, Cavil Planter, and I promise that at the end of your life you will meet me again and know me for what I truly am. In that moment I will say to you, You are mine, Cavil Planter. Come and be my true slave forever."

"Gladly!" cried Cavil. "Gladly! Gladly!"

He flung out his arms and embraced the Overseer's legs. But where he should have touched the visitor, there was nothing. He had vanished.

From that night on, Cavil Planter's slavewomen had no peace. As Cavil had them brought to him by night, he tried to treat them with the strength and mastery he had seen in the face of the fearful Overseer. They must look at me and see His face, thought Cavil, and it's sure they did.

The first one he took unto himself was a certain newbought slavegirl who had scarce a word of English. She cried out in terror until he raised the welts upon her that he had seen in his dreams. Then, whimpering, she permitted him to do as the Overseer had commanded. For a moment, that first time, he thought her whimpering was like Dolores's voice when she wept so quietly in bed, and he felt the same deep pity that he had felt for his beloved wife. Almost he reached out tenderly to the girl as he had once reached out to comfort Dolores. But then he

12

remembered the face of the Overseer and thought, this Black girl is His enemy; she is my property. As surely as man must plow and plant the land God gave to him, I must not let this Black womb lie fallow.

Hagar, he called her that first night. You do not understand how I am blessing you.

In the morning he looked in the mirror and saw something new in his face. A kind of fierceness. A kind of terrible hidden strength. Ah, thought Cavil, no one ever saw what I truly am, not even me. Only now do I discover that what the Overseer is, I also am.

He never felt another moment's pity as he went about his nightly work. Ashen cane in hand, he went to the women's cabin and pointed at the one who was to come with him. If any hung back, she learned from the cane how much reluctance cost. If any other Black, man or woman, spoke in protest, the next day Cavil saw to it that the Overseer took it out of them in blood. No White guessed and no Black dared accuse him.

The newbought girl, his Hagar, was the first to conceive. He watched her with pride as her belly began to grow. Cavil knew then that the Overseer had truly chosen him, and he took fierce joy in having such mastery. There would be a child, *his* child. And already the next step was clear to him. If his White blood was to save as many Black souls as possible, then he could not keep his mix-up babes at home, could he? He would sell them south, each to a different buyer, to a different city, and then trust the Overseer to see that they in turn grew up and spread his seed throughout all the unfortunate Black race.

And each morning he watched his wife eat her breakfast. "Cavil, my love," she said one day, "is something wrong? There's something darker in your face, a look of—rage, perhaps, or cruelty. Have you quarreled with someone? I would not speak except you—you frighten me."

Tenderly he patted his wife's twisted hand as the Black woman watched him under heavy-lidded eyes. "I have no anger against any man or woman," said Cavil gently. "And what you call cruelty is nothing more than mastery. Ah, Dolores, how can you look in my face and call me cruel?"

She wept. "Forgive me," she cried. "I imagined it. You, the kindest man I've ever heard of—the devil put such a vision in my mind, I know it. The devil can give false visions, you know, but only the wicked are deceived. Forgive me for my wickedness, Husband!"

He forgave her, but she wouldn't stop her weeping until he had sent for the priest. No wonder the Lord chose only men to be his prophets. Women were too weak and compassionate to do the work of the Overseer.

That's how it began. That was the first footfall on this dark and terrible path. Nor Alvin nor Peggy ever knew this tale until I found it out and told them both long after, and they recognized at once that it was the start of all.

But I don't want you to think this was the whole cause of all the evil that befell, for it wasn't. There were other choices made, other mistakes, other lies and other willing cruelties done. A man might have plenty of help finding the short path to hell, but no one else can make him set foot upon it.

14

2

Runaway

Peggy woke up in the morning with a dream of Alvin Miller filling her heart with all kinds of terrible desires. She wanted to run from that boy, and to stay and wait for him; to forget she knew him, and to watch him always.

She lay there on her bed with her eyes almost closed, watching the grey dawnlight steal into the attic room where she slept. I'm holding something, she noticed. The corners of it clenched into her hands so tight that when she let go her palm hurt like she been stung. But she wasn't stung. It was just the box where she kept Alvin's birth caul. Or maybe, thought Peggy, maybe she *had* been stung, stung deep, and only just now did she feel the pain of it.

Peggy wanted to throw that box just as far from her as she could, bury it deep and forget where she buried it, drown it underwater and pile rocks on so it wouldn't float.

Oh, but I don't mean that, she said silently, I'm sorry for thinking such a thing, I'm plain sorry, but he's coming now, after all these years he's coming to Hatrack River and he won't be the boy I see in all the paths of his future, he won't be the man I

15

see him turning into. No, he's still just a boy, just eleven years old. He's seen him enough of life that somewise maybe he's a man inside, he's seen grief and pain enough for someone five times his age, but it's still an eleven-year-old boy he'll be when he walks into this town.

And I don't want to see no eleven-year-old Alvin come here. He'll be looking for me, right enough. He knows who I am, though he never saw me since he was two weeks old. He knows I saw his future on the rainy dark day when he was born, and so he'll come, and he'll say to me, "Peggy, I know you're a torch, and I know you wrote in Taleswapper's book that I'm to be a Maker. So tell me what I'm supposed to be." Peggy knew just what he'd say, and every way he might choose to say it—hadn't she seen it a hundred times, a thousand times? And she'd teach him and he'd become a great man, a true Maker, and—

And then one day, when he's a handsome figure of twenty-one and I'm a sharp-tongued spinster of twenty-six he'll feel so *grateful* to me, so *obligated*, that he'll propose himself for marriage to me as his bounden duty. And I, being lovesick all these years, full of dreams of what he'll do and what we'll be together, I'll say yes, and saddle him with a wife he wished he didn't have to marry, and his eyes will hunger for other women all the days of our lives together—

Peggy wished, oh she wished so deep, that she didn't know for certain things would be that way. But Peggy was a torch right enough, the strongest torch she'd ever heard of, stronger even than the folk hereabouts in Hatrack River ever guessed.

She sat up in bed and did not throw the box or

16

hide it or break it or bury it. She opened it. Inside lay the last scrap of Alvin's birth caul, as dry and white as paper ash in a cold hearth. Eleven years ago when Peggy's mama served as midwife to pull baby Alvin out of the well of life, and Alvin first sucked for breath in the damp air of Papa's Hatrack River roadhouse, Peggy peeled that thin and bloody caul from the baby's face so he could breathe. Alvin, the seventh son of a seventh son, and the thirteenth child—Peggy saw at once what the paths of his life would be. Death, that was where he was headed, death from a hundred different accidents in a world that seemed bent on killing him even before he was hardly alive.

She was Little Peggy then, a girl of five, but she'd been torching for two years already, and in that time she never did a seeing on a birthing child who had so many paths to death. Peggy searched up all the paths of his life, and found in all of them but one single way that boy could live to be a man.

That was if she kept that birth caul, and watched him from afar off, and whenever she saw death reaching out to take him, she'd use that caul. Take just a pinch of it and grind it between her fingers and whisper what had to happen, see it in her mind. And it would happen just the way she said. Hadn't she held him up from drowning? Saved him from a wallowing buffalo? Caught him from sliding off a roof? She even split a roof beam once, when it was like to fall from fifty feet up and squash him on the floor of a half-built church; she split that beam neat as you please, so it fell on one side of him and the other, with just a space for him to stand there in between. And a hundred other times when she acted so early that nobody ever even guessed his life had been saved, even those times she saved him, using the caul.

How did it work? She hardly knew. Except that it was his own power she was using, the gift born right in him. Over the years he'd learned somewhat about his knack for making things and shaping them and holding them together and splitting them apart. Finally this last year, all caught up in the wars between Red men and White, he'd taken charge of saving his own life, so she hardly had to do a thing to save him anymore. Good thing, too. There wasn't much of that caul left.

She closed the lid of the box. I don't want to see him, thought Peggy. I don't want to know any more about him.

But her fingers opened that lid right back up, cause of course she had to know. She'd lived half her life, it seemed like, touching that caul and searching for his heartfire away far off in the northwest Wobbish country, in the town of Vigor Church, seeing how he was doing, looking up the paths of his future to see what danger lay in ambush. And when she was sure he was safe, she'd look farther ahead, and see him coming back one day to Hatrack River, where he was born, coming back and looking into her face and saying, It was you who saved me all those times, you who saw I was a Maker back afore a living soul thought such a thing was possible. And then she'd watch him learn the great depths of his power, the work he had to do, the crystal city he had to build; she saw him sire babies on her, and saw him touch the nursing infants she held in her arms; she saw the ones they buried and the ones that lived; and last of all she saw him—

Tears came down her face. I don't want to know,

18

she said. I don't want to know all the roads of the future. Other girls can dream of love, the joys of marriage, of being mothers to strong healthy babes; but all my dreams have dying in them, too, and pain, and fear, because my dreams are true dreams, I know more than a body can know and still have any hope inside her soul.

Yet Peggy *did* hope. Yes sir, you can be sure of it—she still clung to a kind of desperate hope, because even knowing what's likely to come down the pathways of a body's life, she still caught her some glimpses, some clear plain visions of certain days, certain hours, certain passing moments of joy so great it was worth the grief just to get there.

Trouble was those glimpses were so rare and small in the spreading futures of Alvin's life that she couldn't find a road that led there. All the pathways she could find easily, the plain ones, the ones most likely to become real, those all led to Alvin wedding her without love, out of gratitude and duty, a miserable marriage. Like the story of Leah in the Bible, whose beautiful husband Jacob hated her even though she loved him dear and bore him more babies than his other wives and would've died for him if he'd as much as asked her.

It's an evil thing God did to women, thought Peggy, to make us hanker after husband and children till it leads us to a life of sacrifice and misery and grief. Was Eve's sin so terrible, that God should curse all women with that mighty curse? You will groan and bear children, said Almighty Merciful God. You will be eager for your husband, and he will rule over you.

That was what was burning in her—eagerness for her husband. Even though he was only an eleven-year-old boy who was looking, not for a wife, but for a teacher. He may be just a boy, thought Peggy, but I'm a woman, and I've seen the man he'll be, and I yearn for him. She pressed one hand against her breast; it felt so large and soft, still somewhat out of place on her body, which used to be all sticks and corners like a shanty cabin, and now was softening, like a calf being fattened up for the return of the prodigal.

She shuddered, thinking what happened to the fatted calf, and once again touched the caul, and *looked*:

In the distant town of Vigor Church, young Alvin was breakfasting his last morning at his mother's table. The pack he was to carry on his journey to Hatrack River lay on the floor beside the table. His mother's tears flowed undisguised across her cheeks. The boy loved his mother, but never for a moment did he feel sorry to be leaving. His home was a dark place now, stained with too much innocent blood for him to hanker to stay. He was eager to be off, to start his life as a prentice boy to the blacksmith of Hatrack River, and to find the torch girl who saved his life when he was born. He couldn't eat another bite. He pushed back from the table, stood up, kissed his mama—

Peggy let go the caul and closed the lid of the box as tight and quick as if she was trying to catch a fly inside.

Coming to find me. Coming to start a life of misery together. Go ahead and cry, Faith Miller, but not because your little boy Alvin's on his way east. You cry for me, the woman whose life your boy will wreck. You shed your tears for one more woman's lonely pain.

20

Peggy shuddered, shook off the bleak mood of the grey dawn, and dressed herself quickly, ducking her head to avoid the low sloping crossbeams of the attic roof. Over the years she'd learned ways to push thoughts of Alvin Miller Junior clean out of her mind, long enough to do her duty as daughter in her parents' household and as torch for the people of the country hereabouts. She could go hours without thinking about that boy, when she set her mind to it. And though it was harder now, knowing he was about to set his foot on the road toward her that very morning, she still put thoughts of him aside.

Peggy opened the curtain of the south-facing window and sat before it, leaning on the sill. She looked out over the forest that still stretched from the roadhouse, down the Hatrack River and on to the Hio, with only a few pig farms here and there to block the way. Of course she wouldn't *see* the Hio, not that many miles from here, not even in the clear cool air of springtime. But what her natural eyes couldn't see, the burning torch in her could find easy enough. To see the Hio, she had only to search for a far-off heartfire, then slip herself inside that fellow's flame, and see out of his eyes as easy as she could see out of her own. And once there, once she had ahold of someone's heartfire, she could see other things, too, not just what he saw, but what he thought and felt and wished for. And even more: Flickering away in the brightest parts of the flame, often hidden by all the noise of the fellow's present thoughts and wishes, she could see the paths ahead of him, the choices coming to him, the life he'd make for himself if he chose this or that or another way in the hours and days to come.

Peggy could see so much in other people's heart-fires that she hardly was acquainted with her own.

She thought of herself sometimes like that lone lookout boy at the tip-top of a ship's mast. Not that she ever saw her a ship in her whole life, except the rafts on the Hio and one time a canal boat on the Irrakwa Canal. But she read some books, as many as ever she could get Doctor Whitley Physicker to bring back to her from his visits to Dekane. So she knew about the lookout on the mast. Clinging to the rigging, arms half-wrapped in the lines so he didn't fall if there was a sudden roll or pitch of the boat, or a gust of wind unlooked-for; froze blue in winter, burnt red in summer; and nothing to do all day, all the long hours of his watch, but look out onto the empty blue ocean. If it was a pirate ship, the lookout watched for victims' sails. If it was a whaler, he looked for blows and breaches. Most ships, he just looked for land, for shoals, for hidden sand bars; looked for pirates or some sworn enemy of his nation's flag.

Most days he never saw a thing, not a thing, just waves and dipping sea birds and fluffy clouds.

I am on a lookout perch, thought Peggy. Sent up aloft some sixteen years ago the day I was born, and kept here ever since, never once let down below, never once allowed to rest within the narrow bunk-space of the lowest deck, never once allowed to so much as close a hatch over my head or a door behind my back. Always, always I'm on watch, looking far and near. And because it isn't my natural eyes I look through, I can't shut them, not even in sleep.

No escape from it at all. Sitting here in the attic, she could see without trying:

Mother, known to others as Old Peg Guester,

known to herself as Margaret, cooking in the kitchen for the slew of guests due in for one of her suppers. Not like she has any particular knack for cooking, either, so kitchen work is hard, she isn't like Gertie Smith who can make salt pork taste a hundred different ways on a hundred different days. Peg Guester's knack is in womenstuff, midwifery and house hexes, but to make a good inn takes good food and now Oldpappy's gone she has to cook, so she thinks only of the kitchen and couldn't hardly stand interruption, least of all from her daughter who mopes around the house and hardly speaks at all and by and large that girl is the most unpleasant, ill-favored child even though she started out so sweet and promising, everything in life turns sour somehow. . . .

Oh, that was such a joy, to know how little your own mama cared for you. Never mind that Peggy also knew the fierce devotion that her mama had. Knowing that a portion of love abides in your mama's heart doesn't take away but half the sting of knowing her dislike for you as well.

And Papa, known to others as Horace Guester, keeper of the Hatrack River Roadhouse. A jolly fellow, Papa was, even now out in the dooryard telling tales to a guest who was having trouble getting away from the inn. He and Papa always seemed to have something more to talk about, and oh, that guest, a circuit lawyer from up Cleveland way, he fancied Horace Guester was just about the finest most upstanding citizen he ever met, if all folks was as good-hearted as old Horace there'd be no more crime and no more lawyering in the upriver Hio country. Everybody felt that way. Everybody loved old Horace Guester.

But his daughter, Peggy the torch, she saw into

his heartfire and knew how he felt about it. He saw those folks a-smiling at him and he said to himself, If they knew what I really was they'd spit in the road at my feet and walk away and forget they ever saw my face or knew my name.

Peggy sat there in her attic room and all the heartfires glowed, all of them in town. Her parents' most, cause she knew them best; the lodgers who stayed in the roadhouse; and then the people of the town.

Makepeace Smith and his wife Gertie and their three snot-nose children planning devilment when they weren't puking or piddling—Peggy saw Makepeace's pleasure in the shaping of iron, his loathing for his own children, his disappointment as his wife changed from a fascinating unattainable vision of beauty into a stringy-haired hag who screamed at the children first and then came to use the same voice to scream at Makepeace.

Pauley Wiseman, the sheriff, loving to make folks a-scared of him; Whitley Physicker, angry at himself because his medicine didn't work more than half the time, and every week he saw death he couldn't do a thing about. New folks, old folks, farmers and professionals, she saw through their eyes and into their hearts. She saw the marriage beds that were cold at night and the adulteries kept secret in guilty hearts. She saw the thievery of trusted clerks and friends and servants, and the honorable hearts inside many who were despised and looked down on.

She saw it all, and said nothing. Kept her mouth shut. Talked to no one. Cause she wasn't going to lie. She promised years before that she'd never lie, and kept her word by keeping still.

Other folks didn't have her problem. They could talk and tell the truth. But Peggy couldn't tell the

24

truth. She knew these folks too well. She knew what they all were scared of, what they all wanted, what they all had done that they'd kill her or theirself if they once got a notion that she knew. Even the ones who never done a bad thing, they'd be so ashamed to think she knew their secret dreams or private craziness. So she never could speak frankly to these folks, or something would slip out, not even a word maybe, it might be just the way she turned her head, the way she sidestepped some line of talk, and they'd know that she knew, or just fear that she knew, or just fear. Just fear alone, without even naming what it was, and it could undo them, some of them, the weakest of them.

She was a lookout all the time, alone atop the mast, hanging to the lines, seeing more than she ever wanted to, and never getting even a minute to herself.

When it wasn't some baby being born, so she had to go and do a seeing, then it was some folks in trouble somewhere that had to be helped. It didn't do her no good to sleep, neither. She never slept all the way. Always a part of her was looking, and saw the fire burning, saw it flash.

Like now. Now this very moment, as she looked out over the forest, there it was. A heartfire burning ever so far off.

She swung herself close in—not her body, of course, her flesh stayed right there in the attic—but being a torch she knew how to look *close* at far-off heartfires.

It was a young woman. No, a girl, even younger than herself. And strange inside, so she knew right off this girl first spoke a language that wasn't English, even though she spoke and thought in English

25

now. It made her thoughts all twisty and queer. But some things run deeper than the tracks that words leave in your brain; Little Peggy didn't need no help understanding that baby the girl held in her arms, and the way she stood at the riverbank knowing she would die, and what a horror waited for her back at the plantation, and what she'd done last night to get away.

See the sun there, three fingers over the trees. This runaway Black slave girl and her little bastard half-White boy-baby, see them standing on the shore of the Hio, half hid up in trees and bushes, watching as the White men pole them rafts on down. She a-scared, she know them dogs can't find her but very soon they get them the runaway finder, very worse thing, and how she ever cross that river with this boy-baby?

She cotch her a terrible thought: I leave this boy-baby. I hide him in this rotten log, I swim and steal the boat and I come back to here. That do the job, yes sir.

But then this Black girl who nobody never teach how to be a mama, she know a good mama don't leave this baby who still gots to suck two-hand times a day. She whisper, Good mama don't leave a little boy-baby where old fox or weasel or badger come and nibble off little parts and kill him dead. No ma'am not me.

So she just set down here a-hold of this baby, and watch the river flow on, might as well be the seashore cause she never get across.

Maybe some White folks help her? Here on the Appalachee shore the White folk hang them as help a slavegirl run away. But this runaway Black slavegirl hear stories in the plantation, about Whites who say nobody better be own by nobody else. Who say this Black girl better have that same right like the White lady, she say no to any man be not her true husband. Who say this Black girl better can keep her baby, not let them White boss promise he sell it on weaning day, they send this boy-baby to grow up into a house slave in Drydenshire, kiss a white man's feet if he say boo.

"Oh, your baby is so *lucky*," they say to this slavegirl. "He'll grow up in a fine lord's mansion in the Crown Colonies, where they still have a king—he might even *see* the King someday."

She don't say nothing, but she laugh inside. She don't set no store to see a king. Her pa a king back in Africa, and they shoot him dead. Them Portuguese slavers show her what it mean to be a king—it mean you die quick like everybody, and spill blood red like everybody, and cry out loud in pain and scared—oh, *fine* to be a king, and *fine* to see one. Do them White folk believe this lie?

I don't believe them. I say I believe them but I lie. I never let them take him my boy-baby. A king grandson him, and I tell him every day he growing up. When he the tall king, ain't nobody hit him with the stick or he hit them back, and nobody take his woman, spread her like a slaughterpig and stick this half-White baby in her but he can't do nothing, he sit in his cabin and cry. No ma'am, no sir.

So she do the forbidden evil ugly bad thing. She steal two candles and hot them all soft by the cook-fire. She mash them like dough, she mash in milk from her own teat after boy-baby suck, and she mash some of her spit in the wax too, and then she push it and poke it and roll it in ash till she see a poppet shape like Black slavegirl. Her very own self.

Then she hide this Black slavegirl poppet and she go to Fat Fox and beg him feathers off that big old blackbird he cotch him.

"Black slavegirl don't need her no feathers," say Fat Fox.

"I make a boogy for my boy-baby," she say.

Fat Fox laugh, he know she lie. "Ain't no black-feather boogy. I never heared of such a thing."

Black slavegirl, she say, "My papa king in Umba-wana. I know all secret thing."

Fat Fox shake his head, he laugh, he laugh. "What do you know, anyway? You can't even talk English. I'll give you all the blackbird feathers you want, but when that baby stops sucking you come to me and I'll give you another one, all Black this time."

She hate Fat Fox like White Boss, but he got him blackbird feathers so she say, "Yes sir."

Two hands she fill up with feathers. She laugh inside. She far away and dead before Fat Fox never put him no baby in her.

She cover Black slavegirl poppet with feathers till she little girl-shape bird. Very strong thing, this poppet with her own milk and spit in it, blackbird feathers on. Very strong, suck all her life out, but boy-baby, he never kiss no White Boss feet, White Boss never lay no lash on him.

Dark night, moon not showing yet. She slip out her cabin. Boy-baby suck so he make no sound. She tie that baby to her teat so he don't fall. She toss that poppet on the fire. Then all the power of the feather come out, burning, burning, burning. She feel this fire pour into her. She spread her wings, oh so wide, spread them, flap like she see that big old blackbird flap. She rise up into the air, high up in that dark night, she rise and fly, far away north she fly, and when that moon he come up, she keep him at her right hand so she get this boy-baby to land where White say Black girl never slave, half-White boy-baby never slave.

Come morning and the sun and she don't fly no more. Oh, like dying, like dying she think, walking her feet on the ground. That bird with her wing broke, she pray for Fat Fox to find her, she know that now. After you fly, make you sad to walk, hurt you bad to walk, like a slave with chains, that dirt under your feet.

But she walk with that boy-baby all morning and now she come to this wide river. This close I come, say runaway Black slavegirl. I fly this far, yes I fly this river across. But that sun come up and I come down before this river. Now I never cross, old finder find me somehow, whup me half dead, take my boy-baby, sell him south.

Not me. I trick them. I die first.

No, I die second.

Other folks could argue about whether slavery was a mortal sin or just a quaint custom. Other folks could bicker on about how Emancipationists were too crazy to put up with even though slavery was a real bad thing. Other folks could look at Blacks and feel sorry for them but still be somewhat glad they were mostly in Africa or in the Crown Colonies or in Canada or somewhere else far and gone. Peggy couldn't afford the luxury of having opinions on the subject. All she knew was that no heartfire ever was in such pain as the soul of a Black who lived in the thin dark shadow of the lash.

29

Peggy leaned out the attic window, called out: "Papa!"

He strode out from the front of the house, walked into the road, where he could look up and see her window. "You call me, Peggy?"

She just looked at him, said naught, and that was all the signal that he needed. He good-byed and fare-thee-welled that guest so fast the poor old coot was halfway into the main part of town before he knew what hit him. Pa was already inside and up the stairs.

"A girl with a babe," she told him. "On the far side of the Hio, scared and thinking of killing herself if she's caught."

"How far along the Hio?"

"Just down from the Hatrack Mouth, near as I can guess. Papa, I'm coming with you."

"No you're not."

"Yes I am, Papa. You'll never find her, not you nor ten more like you. She's too scared of White men, and she's got cause."

Papa looked at her, unsure what to do. He'd never let her come before, but usually it was Black men what ran off. But then, usually she found them this side the Hio, lost and scared, so it was safer. Crossing into Appalachee, it was prison for sure if they were caught helping a Black escape. Prison if it wasn't a quick rope on a tree. Emancipationists didn't fare well south of the Hio, and still less the kind of Emancipationist who helped run-off bucks and ewes and pickaninnies get north to French country up in Canada.

"Too dangerous across the river," he said.

"All the more reason you need me. To find her, and to spot if anyone else happens along."

30

"Your mother would kill me if she knew I was taking you."

"Then I'll leave now, out the back."

"Tell her you're going to visit Mrs. Smith—"

"I'll tell her nothing or I'll tell the truth, Papa."

"Then I'll stay up here and pray the good Lord saves my life by not letting her notice you leaving. We'll meet up at Hatrack Mouth come sundown."

"Can't we—"

"No we can't, not a minute sooner," he said. "Can't cross the river till dark. If they catch her or she dies afore we get there then it's just too bad, cause we can't cross the Hio in the daylight, bet your life on that."

Noise in the forest, this scare Black slavegirl very bad. Trees grab her, owls screech out telling where they find her, this river just laugh at her all along. She can't move cause she fall in the dark, she hurt this baby. She can't stay cause they find her sure. Flying don't fool them finders, they look far and see her even a hand of hands away off.

A step for sure. Oh, Lord God Jesus save me from this devil in the dark.

A step, and breathing, and branches they brush aside. But no lantern! Whatever come it see me in the dark! Oh, Lord God Moses Savior Abraham.

"Girl."

That voice, I hear that voice, I can't breathe. Can you hear it, little boy-baby? Or do I dream this voice? This lady voice, very soft lady voice. Devil got no lady voice, everybody know, ain't that so?

"Girl, I come to take you across the river and help you and your baby get north and free."

I don't find no words no more, not slave words or

31

Umbawa talk. When I put on feathers do I lose my words?

"We got a good stout rowboat and two strong men to row. I know you understand me and I know you trust me and I know you want to come. So you just set there, girl, you hold my hand, there, that's my hand, you don't have to say a word, you just hold my hand. There's some White men but they're my friends and they won't touch you. Nobody's going to touch you except me, you believe that, girl, you just believe it."

Her hand it touch my skin very cool and soft like this lady voice. This lady angel, this Holy Virgin Mother of God.

Lots of steps, heavy steps, and now lanterns and lights and big old White men but this lady she just hold on my hand.

"Scared plumb to death."

"Look at this girl. She's most wasted away to nothing."

"How many days she been without eating?"

Big men's voices like White Boss who give her this baby.

"She only left her plantation last night," said the Lady.

How this White lady know? She know everything, Eve the mama of all babies. No time to talk, no time to pray, move very quick, lean on this White lady, walk and walk and walk to this boat it lie waiting in the water just like I dream. O! here the boat little boy-baby, boat lift us cross the Jordan to the Promise Land.

They were halfway across the river when the Black girl started shaking and crying and chattering.

"Hush her up," said Horace Guester.

"There's nobody near us," answered Peggy. "No one to hear."

"What's she babbling about?" asked Po Doggly. He was a pig farmer from near Hatrack mouth and for a moment Peggy thought he was talking about *her*. But no, it was the Black girl he meant.

"She's talking in her African tongue, I reckon," said Peggy. "This girl is really something, how she got away."

"With a baby and all," agreed Po.

"Oh, the baby," said Peggy. "I've got to hold the baby."

"Why's that?" asked Papa.

"Because you're both going to have to carry her," she said. "From shore to the wagon, at least. There's no way this child can walk another step."

When they got to shore, they did just that. Po's old wagon was no great shakes for comfort—one old horseblanket was about as soft as it was going to get—but they laid her out and if she minded she didn't say so. Horace held the lantern high and looked at her. "You're plumb right, Peggy."

"What about?" she asked.

"Calling her a child. I swear she couldn't be thirteen. I swear it. And her with a baby. You sure this baby's hers?"

"I'm sure," said Peggy.

Po Doggly chuckled. "Oh, you know them guineas, just like bunny rabbits, the minute they can they do." Then he remembered that Peggy was there. "Begging your pardon, ma'am. We don't never have ladies along till tonight."

"It's *her* pardon you have to beg," said Peggy coldly. "This child is a mixup. Her owner sired this

boy without a by-your-leave. I reckon you understand me."

"I won't have you discussing such things," said
Horace Guester. His temper was hot, all right. "Bad
enough you coming along on this without you knowing all this kind of thing about this poor girl, it ain't
right telling her secrets like that."

Peggy fell silent and stayed that way all the ride
home. That was what happened whenever she spoke
frankly which is why she almost never did. The girl's
suffering made her forget herself and talk too much.
Now Papa was thinking on about how much his
daughter knew about this Black girl in just a few
minutes, and worrying how much she knew about
him.

Do you want to know what I know, Papa? I know
why you do this. You're not like Po Doggly, Papa,
who doesn't think much of Blacks but hates seeing
any wild thing cooped up. He does this, helping
slaves make their way to Canada, cause he's just got
that need in him to set them free. But you, Papa,
you do it to pay back your secret sin. Your pretty
little secret who smiled at you like heartbreak in
person and you could've said no but you didn't, you
said yes oh yes. While Mama was expecting me, it
was, and you were off in Dekane buying supplies,
you stayed there a week and had that woman must
be ten times in six days, I remember every one of
those times as clear as you do, I can feel you dreaming about her in the night. Hot with shame, hotter
with desire, I know just how a man feels when he
wants a woman so bad his skin itches and he can't
hold still. All these years you've hated yourself for
what you did and hated yourself all the more for
loving that memory, and so you pay for it. You risk

going to jail or getting hung up in a tree somewhere for the crows to pick, not because you love the Black man but because you hope maybe doing good for God's children might just set you free of your own secret love of evil.

And here's the funny thing, Papa. If you knew I knew your secret you would probably die, it might just kill you on the spot. And yet if I could tell you, just tell you that I know, then I could tell you something else on top of that, I could say, Papa, don't you see that it's your knack? You who thinks he never had no knack, but you got one. It's the knack for making folks feel loved. They come to your inn and they feel right to home. Well you saw her, and she was hungry, that woman in Dekane, she needed to feel the way you make folks feel, needed you so bad. And it's hard, Papa, hard not to love a body who loves you so powerful, who hangs onto you like clouds hanging onto the moon, knowing you're going to go on, knowing you'll never stay, but hungering, Papa. I looked for that woman, looked for her heartfire, far and wide I searched for her, and I found her. I know where she is. She ain't young now like you remember. But she's still pretty, pretty as you recall her, Papa. And she's a good woman, and you done her no harm. She remembers you fondly, Papa. She knows God forgave her and you both. It's you who won't forgive, Papa.

Such a sad thing, Peggy thought, coming home in that wagon. Papa's doing something that would make him a hero in any other daughter's eyes. A great man. But because I'm a torch, I know the truth. He doesn't come out here like Hector afore the gates of Troy, risking death to save other folks. He comes slinking like a whipped dog, cause he *is* a whipped dog inside. He runs out here to hide from a sin that the good Lord would have forgave long ago if he just allowed forgiveness to be possible.

Soon enough, though, Peggy stopped thinking it was sad about her Papa. It was sad about most *everybody*, wasn't it? But most sad people just keep right on being sad, hanging onto misery like the last keg of water in a drouth. Like the way Peggy kept waiting here for Alvin even though she knew he'd bring no joy to her.

It was that girl in the back of the wagon who was different. She had a terrible misery coming on her, going to lose the boy-baby, but she didn't just set and wait for it to happen so she could grieve. She said no. Plain no, just like that. I won't let you sell this boy south on me, even to a good rich family. A rich man's slave is still a slave, ain't he? And down south means he'll be even farther away from where he can run off and make it north. Peggy could feel those feelings in that girl, even as she tossed and moaned in the back of the wagon.

Something more, though. That girl was more a hero than Papa or Po Doggly either one. Because the only way she could think to get away was to use a witchery so strong that Peggy never even heard of it before. Never dreamed that Black folks had such lore. But it was no lie, it was no dream neither. That girl flew. Made a wax poppet and feathered it and burnt it up. Burnt it right up. It let her fly all this way, this long hard way till the sun came up, far enough that Peggy saw her and they took her across the Hio. But what a price that runaway had paid for it.

When they got back to the roadhouse, Mama was just as angry as Peggy ever saw her. "It's a crime you should have a whipping for, taking your sixteen-year-old daughter out to commit a crime in the darkness."

But Papa didn't answer. He didn't have to, once he carried that girl inside and laid her on the floor before the fire.

"She can't have ate a thing for days. For weeks!" cried Mama. "And her brow is like to burn my hand off just to touch her. Fetch me a pan of water, Horace, to mop her brow, while I heat up the broth for her to sip—"

"No, Mama," said Peggy. "Best you find some milk for the baby."

"The baby won't die, and this girl's likely to, don't you tell me my business, I know physicking for *this*, anyway—"

"No, Mama," said Peggy. "She did a witchery with a wax poppet. It's a Black sort of witchery, but she had the know-how and she had the power, being the daughter of a king in Africa. She knew the price and now she can't help but pay."

"Are you saying this girl's bound to die?" asked Mama.

"She made a poppet of herself, Mama, and put it on the fire. It gave her the wings to fly one whole night. But the cost of it is the rest of her life."

Papa looked sick at heart. "Peggy, that's plain crazy. What good would it do her to escape from slavery if she was just going to die? Why not kill herself there and save the trouble?"

Peggy didn't have to answer. The baby she was a-holding started to cry right then, and that was all the answer there was.

"I'll get milk," said Papa. "Christian Larsson's

37

bound to have a gill or so to spare even this time of the night."

Mama stopped him, though. "Think again, Horace," she said. "It's near midnight now. What'll you tell him you need the milk *for*?"

Horace sighed, laughed at his own foolishness. "For a runaway slavegirl's little pickaninny baby." But then he turned red, getting hot with anger. "What a crazy thing this Black girl done," he said. "She came all this way, knowing that she'd die, and now what does she reckon we'll do with a little pickaninny like that? We sure can't take it north and lay it across the Canadian border and let it bawl till some Frenchman comes to take it."

"I reckon she just figures it's better to die free than live slave," said Peggy. "I reckon she just knew that whatever life that baby found here had to be better than what it was there."

The girl lay there before the fire, breathing soft, her eyes closed.

"She's asleep, isn't she?" asked Mama.

"Not dead yet," said Peggy, "but not hearing us."

"Then I'll tell you plain, this is a bad piece of trouble," said Mama. "We can't have people knowing you bring runaway slaves through here. Word of that would spread so fast we'd have two dozen finders camped here every week of the year, and one of them'd be bound to take a shot at you sometime from ambush."

"Nobody has to know," said Papa.

"What are you going to do, tell folks you happened to trip over her dead body in the woods?"

Peggy wanted to shout at them. She ain't dead yet, so mind how you talk! But the truth was they had to get some things planned, and quick. What if

38

one of the guests woke up in the night and came downstairs? There'd be no keeping this secret then.

"How soon will she die?" Papa asked. "By morning?"

"She'll be dead before sunrise, Papa."

Papa nodded. "Then I better get busy. The girl I can take care of. You women can think of something to do with that pickaninny, I hope."

"Oh, we can, can we?" said Mama.

"Well I know I can't, so you'd better."

"Well then maybe I'll just tell folks it's my own babe."

Papa didn't get mad. Just grinned, he did, and said, "Folks ain't going to believe that even if you dip that boy in cream three times a day."

He went outside and got Po Doggly to help him dig a grave.

"Passing this baby off as born around here ain't such a bad idea," said Mama. "That Black family that lives down in that boggy land—you remember two years back when some slaveowner tried to prove he used to own them? What's their name, Peggy?"

Peggy knew them far better than any other White folks in Hatrack River did; she watched over them the same as everyone else, knew all their children, knew all their names. "They call their name Berry," she said. "Like a noble house, they just keep that family name no matter what job each one of them does."

"Why couldn't we pass this baby off as theirs?"

"They're poor, Mama," said Peggy. "They can't feed another mouth."

"We could help with that," said Mama. "We have extra."

"Just think a minute, Mama, how that'd look.

39

Suddenly the Berrys get them a light-coloured baby like this, you *know* he's half-White just to look at him. And then Horace Guester starts bringing gifts down to the Berry house."

Mama's face went red. "What do you know about such things?" she demanded.

"Oh, for heaven's sake, Mama, I'm a torch. And you know people would start to talk, you know they would."

Mama looked at the Black girl lying there. "You got us into a whole lot of trouble, little girl."

The baby started fussing.

Mama stood up and walked to the window, as if she could see out into the night and find some answer writ on the sky. Then, abruptly, she headed for the door, opened it.

"Mama," said Peggy.

"There's more than one way to pluck a goose," said Mama.

Peggy saw what Mama had thought of. If they couldn't take the baby down to the Berry place, they could maybe keep the baby here at the roadhouse and say they were taking care of it for the Berrys cause they were so poor. As long as the Berry family went along with the tale, it would account for a half-Black baby showing up one day. And nobody'd think the baby was Horace's bastard—not if his wife brought it right into the house.

"You realize what you're asking them, don't you?" said Peggy. "Everybody's going to think somebody else has been plowing with Mr. Berry's heifer."

Mama looked so surprised Peggy almost laughed out loud. "I didn't think Blacks cared about such things," she said.

Peggy shook her head. "Mama, the Berrys are just about the best Christians in Hatrack River. They have to be, to keep forgiving the way White folks treat them and their children."

Mama closed the door again and stood inside, leaning on it. "How *do* folks treat their children?"

It was a pertinent question, Peggy knew, and Mama had thought of it only just in time. It was one thing to look at that scrawny fussing little Black baby and say, I'm going to take care of this child and save his life. It was something else again to think of him being five and seven and ten and seventeen years old, a young buck living right there in the house.

"I don't think you have to fret about that," said Little Peggy, "not half so much as how *you* plan to treat this boy. Do you plan to raise him up to be your servant, a lowborn child in your big fine house? If that's so, then this girl died for nothing, she might as well have let them sell him south."

"I never hankered for no slave," said Mama. "Don't you go saying that I did."

"Well, what then? Are you going to treat him as your own son, and stand with him against all comers, the way you would if you'd ever borne a son of your own?"

Peggy watched as Mama thought of that, and suddenly she saw all kinds of new paths open up in Mama's heartfire. A son—that's what this half-White boy could be. And if folks around here looked cross-eyed at him on account of him not being all White, they'd have to reckon with Margaret Guester, they would, and it'd be a fearsome day for them, they'd have no terror at the thought of hell, not after what she'd put them through.

Mama hadn't felt such a powerful grim determination in all the years Peggy'd been looking into her heart. It was one of those times when somebody's whole future changed right before her eyes. All the old paths had been pretty much the same; Mama had no choices that would change her life. But now, this dying girl had brought a transformation. Now there were hundreds of new paths open, and all of them had a little boy-child in them, needing her the way her daughter'd never needed her. Set upon by strangers, cruelly treated by the boys of the town, he'd come to her again and again for protection, for teaching, for toughening, the kind of thing that Peggy'd never done.

That's why I disappointed you, wasn't it, Mama? Cause I knew too much, too young. You wanted me to come to you in my confusion, with my questions. But I never had no questions, Mama, cause I knew from childhood up. I knew what it meant to be a woman from the memories in your own head. I knew about married love without you telling me. I never had a tearful night pressed up against your shoulder, crying cause some boy I longed for wouldn't look at me; I never longed for any boy around here. I never did a thing you dreamed your little girl would do, cause I had a torch's knack, and I knew everything and need nothing that you wanted to give me.

But this half-Black boy, he'll need you no matter what his knack might be. I see down all those paths, that if you take him in, if you raise him up, he'll be more son to you than I ever was your daughter, though your blood is half of mine.

"Daughter," said Mama, "if I go through this door, will it turn out well for the boy? And for us, too?"

"Are you asking me to See for you, Mama?"

42

"I am, Little Peggy, and I never asked for that before, never on my own behalf."

"Then I'll tell you," Peggy hardly needed to look far down the paths of Mama's life to find how much pleasure she'd have in the boy. "If you take him in, and treat him like your own son, you'll never regret doing it."

"What about your papa? Will he treat him right?"

"Don't you know your own husband?" asked Peggy.

Mama walked a step toward her, her hand all clenched up even though she never laid a hand on Peggy. "Don't get fresh with me," she said.

"I'm talking the way I talk when I See," said Peggy. "You come to me as a torch. I talk as a torch to you."

"Then say what you have to say."

"It's easy enough. If you don't know how your husband will treat this boy, you don't know that man at all."

"So maybe I don't," said Mama. "Maybe I don't know him at all. Or maybe I do, and I want you to tell me if I'm right."

"You're right," said Peggy. "He'll treat him fair, and make him feel loved all the days of his life."

"But will he really love him?"

There wasn't no chance that Peggy'd answer that question. Love wasn't even in the picture for Papa. He'd take care of the boy because he ought to, because he felt a bounden duty, but the boy'd never know the difference, it'd feel like love to him, and it'd be a lot more dependable than love ever was. But to explain that to Mama would mean telling her how Papa did so many things because he felt so bad about his ancient sins, and there'd never be a time in Mama's life when she was ready to hear *that* tale.

So Peggy just looked at Mama and answered her the way she answered other folks who pried too deep into things they didn't really want to know. "That's for him to answer," Peggy said. "All you need to know is that the choice you already made in your heart is a good one. Already just deciding that has changed your life."

"But I haven't even decided yet," said Mama.

In Mama's heart there wasn't a single path left, not a single one, in which she didn't get the Berrys to say it was their boy, and leave him with her to raise.

"Yes you have," said Peggy. "And you're glad of it."

Mama turned and left, closing the door gentle behind her, so as not to wake the traveling preacher who was sleeping in the room upstairs of the door.

Peggy had just one moment's unease, and she wasn't even sure why. If she'd thought about it a minute, she'd have known it was on account of how she cheated her Mama without even knowing it. When Peggy did a Seeing for anybody else, she always took care to look far down the paths of their life, looking for darkness from causes not even guessed at. But Peggy was so sure she knew her Mama and Papa, she didn't even bother looking except at what was coming up right away. That's how it goes within a family. You think you know each other so well, and so you don't bother hardly getting to know each other at all. It wouldn't be years yet till Peggy would think back on this day, and try to figure why she didn't See what was coming. Sometimes she'd even imagine that her knack failed her. But it didn't. She failed her own knack. She wasn't the first to do so, nor the last, nor even the worst, but there's few ever lived to regret it more.

The moment of unease passed, and Peggy forgot it as her thoughts turned to the Black girl on the common-room floor. She was awake, her eyes open. The baby was still mewling. Without the girl saying a thing, Peggy knew she was willing for the babe to suckle, if she had anything in her breasts to suck on out. The girl hadn't even strength to open up her faded cotton shirt. Peggy had to sit beside her, cradling the child against her own thighs while she fumbled the girl's buttons open with her free hand. The girl's chest was so skinny, her ribs so stark and bare, that her breasts looked to be saddlebags tossed onto a rail fence. But the nipple still stood up for the baby to suck, and a white froth soon appeared around the baby's lips, so there was something there, even now, even at the very end of his mama's life.

The girl was far too weak to talk, but she didn't need to; Peggy heard what she wanted to say, and answered her. "My own mama's going to keep your boy," said Peggy. "And no wise is she going to let any man make a slave of him."

That was what the girl wanted most to hear—that and the sound of her greedy boy-baby slurping and humming and squealing at her breast.

But Peggy wanted her to know more than that before she died. "You boy-baby's going to know about you," she told the girl. "He's going to hear how you gave your life so you could fly away and take him here to freedom. Don't you think he'll ever forget you, cause he won't."

Then Peggy looked into the child's heartfire, searched there for what he'd be. Oh, that was a painful thing, because the life of a half-White boy in a White town was hard no matter which of the paths of his life he chose. Still, she saw enough to know the nature of the babe whose fingers scratched and clutched at his mama's naked chest. "And he'll be a man worth dying for, too, I promise you that."

The girl was glad to hear it. It brought her peace enough that she could sleep again. After a time the babe, satisfied, also fell asleep. Peggy picked him up, wrapped him in a blanket, and laid him in the crook of his mama's arm. Every last moment of your mama's life you'll be with her, she told the boychild silently. We'll tell you that, too, that she held you in her arms when she died.

When she died. Papa was out with Po Doggly, digging her grave; Mama was off at the Berrys, to persuade them to help her save the baby's life and freedom; and here was Peggy, thinking as if the girl was already dead.

But she wasn't dead, not yet. And all of a sudden it came to Peggy, with a flash of anger that she was too stupid to think of it before, that there was one soul she knew of who had the knack in him to heal the sick. Hadn't he knelt by Ta-Kumsaw at the battle of Detroit, that great Red man's body riddled with bullet holes, hadn't Alvin knelt there and healed him up? Alvin could save this girl, if he was here.

She cast off in the darkness, searching for the heartfire that burned so bright, the heartfire she knew better than any in the world, better even than her own. And there he was, running in the darkness, traveling the way Red men did, like he was asleep, and the land around him was his soul. He was coming faster than any White could ever come, even with the fastest horse on the best road between the

Wobbish and the Hatrack, but he wouldn't be here till noon tomorrow, and by then this runaway slave-girl would be dead and in the ground up in the family graveyard. By twelve hours at most she'd miss the one man in this country who could have saved her life.

Wasn't that the way of it? Alvin could save her, but he'd never know she needed saving. While Peggy, who couldn't do a thing, she knew all that was happening, knew all the things that might happen, knew the one thing that *should* happen if the world was good. It wasn't good. It wouldn't happen.

What a terrible gift it was, to be a torch, to know all these things a-coming, and have so little power to change them. The only power she'd ever had was just the words of her mouth, telling folks, and even then she couldn't be sure what they'd choose to do. Always there'd be some choice they could make that would set them down a path even worse than the one she wanted to save them from—and so many times in their wickedness or cantankerousness or just plain bad luck, they'd make that terrible choice and then things'd be worse for them than if Peggy'd just kept still and never said a thing. I wish I didn't know. I wish I had some hope that Alvin would come in time. I wish I had some hope this girl would live. I wish that I could save her life myself.

And then she thought of the many times she *had* saved a life. Alvin's life, using Alvin's caul. At that moment hope *did* spark up in her heart, for surely, just this once, she could use a bit of the last scrap of Alvin's caul to save this girl, to restore her.

Peggy leapt up and ran clumsily to the stairs, her legs so numb from sitting on the floor that she couldn't hardly feel her own footsteps on the bare wood. She tripped on the stairs and made some noise, but none of the guests woke up, as far as she noticed right off like that. Up the stairs, then up the attic ladderway that Oldpappy made into a proper stairway not three months afore he died. She threaded her way among the trunks and old furniture until she reached her room up against the west end of the house. Moonlight came in through her south-facing window, making a squared-off pattern on the floor. She pried up the floorboard and took the box from the place where she hid it whenever she left the room.

She walked too heavy or this one guest slept too light, but as she came down the ladderway, there he stood, skinny white legs sticking out from under his longshirt, a-gazing down the stairs, then back toward his room, like as if he couldn't make up his mind whether to go in or out, up or down. Peggy looked into his heartfire, just to find out whether he'd been downstairs and seen the girl and her baby—if he had, then all their thought and caution had been in vain.

But he hadn't—it was still possible.

"Why are you still dressed for going out?" he asked. "At this time of the morning, too?"

She gently laid her finger against his lips. To silence him, or at least that's how the gesture began. But she knew right away that she was the first woman ever to touch this man upon the face since his mama all those many years ago. She saw that in that moment his heart filled, not with lust, but with the vague longings of a lonely man. He was the minister who'd come day before yesterday morning, a traveling preacher—from Scotland, he said. She hardly paid him no mind, her being so preoccupied with knowing Alvin was on his way back. But now all that mattered was to send him back into his room, quick as could be, and she knew one sure way to do it. She put her hands on his shoulders, getting a strong grip behind his neck, and pulled him down to where she could kiss him fair on the lips. A good long buss, like he never had from a woman in all his days.

Just like she expected, he was back in his room almost before she let go of him. She might've laughed at that, except she knew from his heartfire it wasn't her kiss sent him back, like she planned. It was the box she still held in one hand, which she had pressed up against the back of his neck when she held him. The box with Alvin's caul inside.

The moment it touched him, he felt what was inside. It wasn't no knack of his, it was something else—just being so near something of Alvin's done it to him. She saw the vision of Alvin's face loom up inside his mind, with such fear and hatred like she never seen before. Only then did she realize that he wasn't just any minister. He was Reverend Philadelphia Thrower, who once had been a preacher back in Vigor Church. Reverend Thrower, who once had tried to kill the boy, except Alvin's pa prevented him.

The fear of a woman's kiss was nothing to him compared to his fear of Alvin Junior. The trouble was that now he was *so* afraid he was already thinking of leaving right this minute and getting out of this roadhouse. If he did that, he'd have to come downstairs and then he'd see all, just what she meant to fend off. This was how it went so often—she tried to stave off a bad thing and it turned out worse,

49

something so unlikely she didn't see it. How could she not have recognized who he was? Hadn't she seen him through Alvin's eyes all those many years past? But he'd changed this last year, he looked thin and haunted and older. Besides, she wasn't looking for him here, and anyhow it was too late to undo what she already done. All that mattered now was to keep him in his room.

So she opened his door and followed him inside and looked him square in the face and said, "He was born here."

"Who?" he said. His face was white as if he'd just seen the devil himself. He knew who she meant.

"And he's coming back. Right now he's on his way. You're only safe if you stay in your room tonight, and leave in the morning at first light."

"I don't know—know what you're talking about."

Did he really think he could fool a torch? Maybe he didn't know she was—no, he knew, he knew, he just didn't believe in torching and hexing and knacks and suchlike. He was a man of science and higher religion. A blamed fool. So she'd have to prove to him that what he feared most was so. She knew him, and she knew his secrets. "You tried to kill Alvin Junior with a butchery knife," she said.

That did it, right enough. He fell to his knees. "I'm not afraid to die," he said. Then he began to murmur the Lord's prayer.

"Pray all night, if you like," she said, "but stay in your room to do it."

Then she stepped through the door and closed it. She was halfway down the stairs when she heard the bar fall into place across the door. Peggy didn't even have time to care whether she caused him undue misery—he wasn't really a murderer in his heart. All she cared for now was to get the caul down to where she could use it to help the runaway, if by chance Alvin's power was really hers to use. So much time that minister had cost her. So many of the slavegirl's precious breaths.

She was still breathing, wasn't she? Yes. No. The babe lay sleeping beside her, but her chest didn't move even as much as him, her lips didn't make even so much as a baby's breath on Peggy's hand. But her heartfire still burned! Peggy could see that plain enough, still burned bright because she was so strong-hearted, that slavegirl was. So Peggy opened up the box, took out the scrap of caul, and rubbed a dry corner of it to dust between her fingers, whispering to her, "Live, get strong." She tried to do what Alvin did when he healed, the way he could feel the small broken places in a person's body, set them right. Hadn't she watched him as he did it so many times before? But it was different, doing it herself. It was strange to her, she didn't have the vision for it, and she could feel the life ebbing away from the girl's body, the heart stilled, the lungs slack, the eyes open but unlighted, and at last the heartfire flashed like a shooting star, all sudden and bright, and it was gone.

Too late. If I hadn't stopped in the hall upstairs, hadn't had to deal with the minister—

But no, no, she couldn't blame herself, it wasn't her power anyway, it was too late before she began. The girl had been dying all through her body. Even Alvin himself, if he was here, even he couldn't have done it. It was never more than a slim hope. Never even hope enough that she could see a single pathway where it worked. So she wouldn't do like so many did, she wouldn't endlessly blame herself when

51

after all she'd done her best at a task that had little hope in it from the start.

Now that the girl was dead, she couldn't leave the baby there to feel his mama's arm grow cold. She picked him up. He stirred, but slept on in the way that babies do. Your mama's dead, little half-White boy, but you'll have *my* mama, and my papa too. They got love enough for a little one; you won't starve for it like some children I seen. So you make the best of it, boy-baby. Your mama died to bring you here—you make the best of it, and you'll be something, right enough.

You'll be something, she heard herself whispering. You'll be something, and so will I.

She made her decision even before she realized there was even a decision to be made. She could feel her own future changing even though she couldn't see rightly what it was going to be.

That slave girl guessed at the likeliest future—you don't have to be a torch to see *some* things plain. It was an ugly life ahead, losing her baby, living as a slave till the day she dropped. Yet she saw just the faintest glimmer of hope for her baby, and once she saw it, she didn't hold back, no sir, that glimmer was worth paying her life for.

And now look at me, thought Peggy. Here I look down the paths of Alvin's life and see misery for myself—nowhere near as bad as that slavegirl's, but bad enough. Now and then I catch the shine of a bright chance for happiness, a strange and backward way to have Alvin and have him love me, too. Once I seen it, am I going to sit on my hands and watch that bright hope die, just because I'm not sure how to get to it from here?

If that beat-down child can make her own hope

out of wax and ash and feathers and a bit of herself, then I can make my own life, too. Somewhere there's a thread that if I just lay hold on it, it'll lead me to happiness. And even if I never find that particular thread, it'll be better than the despair waiting for me if I stay. Even if I never become a part of Alvin's life when he comes to manhood, well, that's still not as steep a price as that slavegirl paid for freedom.

When Alvin comes tomorrow, I won't be here.

That was her decision, just like that. Why, she could hardly believe she never thought of it before. Of all people in the whole of Hatrack River, she ought to have knowed that there's *always* another choice. Folks talked on about how they were forced into misery and woe, they didn't have no choice at all—but that runaway girl showed that there's always a way out, long as you remember even death can be a straight smooth road sometimes.

I don't even have to get no blackbird feathers to fly, neither.

Peggy sat there holding the baby, making bold and fearsome plans for how she'd leave in the morning afore Alvin could arrive. Whenever she felt a-scared of what she'd set herself to do, she cast her gaze down on that girl, and the sight of her was comfort, it truly was. I might someday end up like you, runaway girl, dead in some stranger's house. But better that unknown future than one I knew all along I'd hate, and then did nothing to avoid.

Will I do it, will I really do it in the morning, when the time's come and no turning back? She touched Alvin's caul with her free hand, just snaking her fingers into the box, and what she saw in Alvin's future made her feel like singing. Used to be most paths showed them meeting up and starting out her life of misery. Now only a few of those paths were there—in most of Alvin's futures, she saw him come to Hatrack River and search for the torch girl and find her gone. Just changing her mind tonight had closed down most of the roads to misery.

Mama came back with the Berrys before Papa came in from gravedigging. Anga Berry was a heavy-set woman with laughter lines outnumbering the lines of worry on her face, though both kinds were plain enough. Peggy knew her well and liked her better than most folks in Hatrack River. She had a temper but she also had compassion, and Peggy wasn't surprised at all to see her rush to the body of the girl and take up that cold limp hand and press it to her bosom. She murmured words almost like a lullaby, her voice was so low and sweet and kind.

"She's dead," said Mock Berry. "But that baby's strong I see."

Peggy stood up and let Mock see the baby in her arms. She didn't like him half so well as she liked his wife. He was the kind of man who'd slap a child so hard blood flowed, just cause he didn't like what was said or done. It was almost worse cause he didn't rage when he did it. Like he felt nothing at all, to hurt somebody or not hurt somebody made no powerful difference in his mind. But he worked hard, and even though he was poor his family got by; and nobody who knew Mock paid heed to them crude folks what said there wasn't a buck who wouldn't steal or a ewe you couldn't tup.

"Healthy," said Mock. Then he turned to Mama. "When he grow up to be a big old buck, ma'am, you still aim to call him your boy? Or you make him sleep out back in the shed with the animals?"

Well, he wasn't one to pussyfoot around the issue, Peggy saw.

"Shut your mouth, Mock," said his wife. "And you give me that baby, Miss. I just wished I'd knowed he was coming or I'd've kept my youngest on the tit to keep the milk in. Weaned that boy two months back and he's been nothing but trouble since, but you ain't no trouble, baby, you ain't no trouble at all." She cooed to the baby just like she cooed to his dead mama, and he didn't wake up either.

"I told you. I'll raise him as my son," said Mama.

"I'm sorry, ma'am, but I just never heard of no White woman doing such a thing," said Mock.

"What I say," said Mama, "that's what I do."

Mock thought on that a moment. Then he nodded. "I reckon so," he said. "I reckon I never heard you break your word, not even to Black folks." He grinned. "Most White folk allow as how lying to a buck ain't the same as *lying*."

"We'll do like you asked," said Anga Berry. "I'll tell anybody who asks me this is my boy, only we gave him to you cause we was too poor."

"But don't you ever go forgetting that it's a lie," said Mock. "Don't you ever go thinking that if it really was our own baby, we'd ever give him up. And don't you ever go thinking that my wife here ever would let some White man put a baby in her, and her being married to me."

Mama studied Mock for a minute, taking his measure in the way she had. "Mock Berry, I hope you come and visit me any day you like while this boy is in my house, and I'll show you how one White woman keeps her word."

Mock laughed. "I reckon you a regular Mancipationist."

Papa came in then, covered with sweat and dirt. He shook hands with the Berrys, and in a minute they told him the tale they all would tell. He made promises too, to raise the boy like his own son. He even thought of what never entered Mama's head— he said a few words to Peggy, to promise her that they wouldn't give no preference to the boy, neither. Peggy nodded. She didn't want to say much, cause anything she said would either be a lie or give her plans away; she knew she had no intention to be in this house for even a single day of this baby's future here.

"We go on home now, Mrs. Guester," said Anga. She handed the baby to Mama. "If one of my children wake up with a boogly dream I best be there or you hear them screams clear up here on the high road."

"Ain't you going to have no preacher say words at her grave?" said Mock.

Papa hadn't thought of it. "We do have a minister upstairs," he said.

But Peggy didn't let him hold that thought for even a moment. "No," she said, sharp as she could.

Papa looked at her, and knew that she was talking as a torch. Wasn't no arguing that point. He just nodded. "Not this time, Mock," he said. "Wouldn't be safe."

Mama fretted Anga Berry clear to the door. "Is there anything I ought to know?" said Mama. "Is there anything different about Black babies?"

"Oh, powerful different," said Anga. "But that baby, he half White I reckon, so you just take care

56

of that White half, and I reckon the Black half take care of hisself."

"Cow's milk from a pig bladder?" Mama insisted.

"You know all them things," said Anga. "I learnt everything I know from you, Mrs. Guester. All the women round here do. How come you asking me now? Don't you know I need my sleep?"

Once the Berrys were gone, Papa picked up the girl's body and carried her outside. Not even a coffin, though they would overlay the corpse with stones to keep the dogs off. "Light as a feather," he said when he first hoisted her. "Like the charred carcass of a burnt log."

Which was apt enough, Peggy had to admit. That's what she was now. Just ashes. She'd burnt herself right up.

Mama held the pickaninny boy while Peggy went up into the attic and fetched down the cradle. Nobody woke up this time, except that minister. He was *wide* awake behind his door, but he wasn't coming out for any reason. Mama and Peggy made up that little bed in Mama's and Papa's room, and laid the baby in it. "Tell me if this poor orphan baby's got him a name," said Mama.

"She never gave him one," said Peggy. "In her tribe, a woman never got her a name till she married, and a man had no name till he killed him his first animal."

"That's just awful," said Mama. "That ain't even Christian. Why, she died unbaptized."

"No," said Peggy. "She was baptized right enough. Her owner's wife saw to that—all the Blacks on their plantation were baptized."

Mama's face went sour. "I reckon she thought that made her a Christian. Well, I'll have a name

57

for you, little boy." She grinned wickedly. "What do you think your papa would do if I named this baby Horace Guester Junior?"

"Die," said Peggy.

"I reckon so," said Mama. "I ain't ready to be a widow yet. So for now we'll name him—oh, I can't think, Peggy. What's a Black man's name? Or should I just name him like any White child?"

"Only Black man's name I know is Othello," said Peggy.

"That's a queer name if I ever heard one," said Mama. "You must've got that out of one of Whitley Physicker's books."

Peggy said nothing.

"I know," said Mama. "I know his name. Cromwell. The Lord Protector's name."

"You might better name him Arthur, after the King," said Peggy.

Mama just cackled and laughed at that. "That's your name, little boy. Arthur Stuart! And if the King don't like such a namesake, let him send an army and I still won't change it. His Majesty will have to change his own name first."

Even though she got to bed so late, Peggy woke early next morning. It was hoofbeats woke her—she didn't have to go to the window to recognize his heartfire as the minister rode away. Ride on, Thrower, she said silently. You won't be the last to run away this morning, fleeing from that eleven-year-old boy.

It was the north-facing window she looked out of. She could see between the trees to the graveyard up the hill. She tried to see where the grave was dug last night, but there wasn't no sign her natural eyes could see, and in a graveyard there wasn't no heart-fires neither, nothing to help her. Alvin will see it though, she knew that sure. He'd head for that graveyard first thing he did, cause his oldest brother's body lay there, the boy Vigor, who got swept away in the Hatrack River saving Alvin's mother's life in the last hour before she gave birth to her seventh son. But Vigor hung on to life just long enough, in spite of the river's strongest pulling at him, hung on just long enough that when Alvin was born he was the seventh of seven living sons. Peggy herself had watched his heartfire flicker and die right after the babe was born. He would've heard that story a thousand times. So he'd come to that grave-yard, and *he* could feel his way through the earth and find what lay hidden there. He'd find that unmarked grave, that wasted body so fresh buried there.

Peggy took the box with the caul in it, put it deep in a cloth bag along with her second dress, a petticoat, and the most recent books Whitley Physicker had brought. Just because she didn't want to meet him face to face didn't mean she could forget that boy. She'd touch the caul again tonight, or maybe not till morning, and then she'd stand with him in memory and use his senses to find that name-less Black girl's grave.

Her bag packed, she went downstairs.

Mama had dragged the cradle into the kitchen and she was singing to the baby while she kneaded bread, rocking the cradle with one foot, even though Arthur Stuart was fast asleep. Peggy set her bag outside the kitchen door, walked in and touched her Mama's shoulder. She hoped a little that she'd see her Mama grieving something awful when she found out Peggy'd gone off. But it wasn't so. Oh, she'd carry on and rage at first, but in the times to come she'd miss Peggy less than she might've guessed. It was the baby'd take her mind off worrying about her daughter. Besides, Mama knew Peggy could take care of herself. Mama knew Peggy wasn't a one to need to hold a body's hand. While Arthur Stuart needed her.

If this was the first time Peggy noticed how her Mama felt about her, she'd have been hurt deep. But it was the hundredth time, and she was used to it, and looked behind it to the reasons, and loved her Mama for being a better soul than most, and forgave her for not loving Peggy more.

"I love you, Mama," said Peggy.

"I love you too, baby," said Mama. She didn't even look up nor guess what Peggy had in mind.

Papa was still asleep. After all, he dug a grave last night and filled it too.

Peggy wrote a note. Sometimes she took care to put in a lot of extra letters in the fancy way they did in books, but this time she wanted to make sure Papa could read it for hisself. That meant putting in no more letters than it took to make the sounds for reading out loud.

I lov you Papa and Mama but I got to leav I no its rong to lev Hatrak with out no torch but I bin torch sixtn yr. I seen my fewchr and ile be saf donte you fret on my acown.

She walked out the front door, carried her bag to the road, and waited on ten minutes before Doctor Whitley Physicker came along in his carriage, bound on the first leg of a trip to Philadelphia.

"You didn't wait on the road like this just to

hand me back that Milton I lent you," said Whitley Physicker.

She smiled and shook her head. "No sir, I'd like you take me with you to Dekane. I plan to visit with a friend of my father's, but if you don't mind the company I'd rather not spend the money for a coach."

Peggy watched him consider for a minute, but she knew he'd let her come, and without asking her folks, neither. He was the kind of man thought a girl had as much worth as any boy, and more than that, he plain liked Peggy, thought of her as something like a niece. And he knew that Peggy never lied, so he had no need to check with her folks.

And she hadn't lied to him, no more than she ever lied when she left off without telling all she knew. Papa's old lover, the woman he dreamed of and suffered for, she lived there in Dekane—widowed for the last few years, but her mourning time over so she wouldn't have to turn away company. Peggy knew that lady well, from watching far off for all these years. If I knock on her door, thought Peggy, I don't even have to tell her I'm Horace Guester's girl, she'd take me in as a stranger, she would, and care for me, and help me on my way. But maybe I *will* tell her whose daughter I am, and how I knew to come to her, and how Papa still lives with the aching memory of his love for her.

The carriage rattled over the covered bridge that Alvin's father and older brothers had built eleven years before, after the river drowned the eldest son. Birds nested in the rafters. It was a mad, musical, happy sound they made, at least to her ears, chirping so loud inside the bridge that it sounded like she imagined grand opera ought to be. They had opera

61

in Camelot, down south. Maybe someday she'd go and hear it, and see the King himself in his box.

Or maybe not. Because someday she might just find the path that led to that brief but lovely dream, and then she'd have more important things to do than look at kings or hear the music of the Austrian court played by lacy Virginia musicians in the fancy opera hall in Camelot. Alvin was more important than any of these, if he could only find his way to all his power and what he ought to do with it. And she was born to be part of it. That's how easily she slipped into her dreams of him. Yet why not? Her dreams of him, however brief and hard to find, were true visions of the future, and the greatest joy and the greatest grief she could find for herself both touched this boy who wasn't even a man yet, who had never seen her face to face.

But sitting there in the carriage beside Doctor Whitley Physicker, she forced those thoughts, those visions from her mind. What comes will come, she thought. If I find that path I find it, and if not, then not. For now, at least, I'm free. Free of my watch aloft for the town of Hatrack, and free of building all my plans around that little boy. And what if I end up free of him forever? What if I find another future that doesn't even have him in it? That's the likeliest end of things. Give me time enough, I'll even forget that scrap of a dream I had, and find my own good road to a peaceful end, instead of bending myself to fit his troubled path.

The dancing horses pulled the carriage along so brisk that the wind caught and tossed her hair. She closed her eyes and pretended she was flying, a runaway just learning to be free.

Let him find his path to greatness now without

me. Let me have a happy life far from him. Let some other woman stand beside him in his glory. Let another woman kneel a-weeping at his grave.

3

Lies

Eleven-year-old Alvin lost half his name when he came to Hatrack River. Back home in the town of Vigor Church, not far from where the Tippy-Canoe poured its waters into the Wobbish, everybody knowed his father was Alvin, miller for the town and the country round about. Alvin Miller. Which made his namesake, his seventh son, Alvin *Junior*. Now, though, he was going to live in a place where there wasn't six folks who so much as ever met his pa. No need for names like Miller and Junior. He was just Alvin, plain Alvin, but hearing that lone name made him feel like only half hisself.

He came to Hatrack River on foot, hundreds of miles across Wobbish and Hio territories. When he set out from home it was with a pair of sturdy broke-in boots on and a pack of supplies on his back. He did five miles that way, before he stopped up at a poor cabin and gave his food to the folk there. After another mile or so he met a poor traveling family, heading on west to the new lands of the Noisy River country. He gave them the tent and blanket in his pack, and because they had a thirteen-year-old boy about Alvin's size, he pulled off them new boots and gave them straight out, just like that, socks too. He kept only his clothes and the empty pack on his back.

Why, them folks were wide-eyed and silly-faced over it, worrying that Alvin's pa might be mad, him giving stuff away like that, but he allowed as how it was his to give.

"You sure I won't be meeting up with your pa with a musket and a possy-come-and-take-us?" asked the poor man.

"I'm sure he won't, sir," said young Alvin, "on account of I'm from the town of Vigor Church, and the folks there won't see you at all unless you force them."

It took them near ten seconds to realize where they'd heard the name of Vigor Church before. "Them's the folk of the Tippy-Canoe massacre," they said. "Them's the folk what got blood on their hands."

Alvin just nodded. "So you see they'll leave you be."

"Is it true they make every traveler listen to them tell that terrible gory tale of how they killed all them Reds in cold blood?"

"Their blood wasn't cold," said Alvin, "and they only tell travelers who come right on into town. So just you stay on the road, leave them be, ride on through. Once you cross the Wobbish, you'll be in open land again, where you'll be glad to meet up with settled folk. Not ten mile on."

Well, they didn't argue no more, nor even ask him how he came not to have to tell the tale hisself. The name of the Massacre of Tippy-Canoe was enough to put a silence on folks like setting in a church, a kind of holy, shameful, reverent attitude.

65

Cause even though most Whites shunned the bloody-handed folk who shed Red men's blood at Tippy-Canoe, they still knew that if they'd stood in the same place, they'd've done the same thing, and it'd be their hands dripping red till they told a stranger about the wretched deed they done. That guilty knowledge didn't make many travelers too keen on stopping in Vigor Church, or any homes in the upper Wobbish country. Them poor folks just took Alvin's boots and gear and moved on down the road, glad of a stretch of canvas over their heads and a slice of leather on their big boy's feet.

Alvin betook him off the road soon after, and plunged into woodland, into the deepest places. If he'd been wearing boots, he would've stumbled and crunched and made more noise than a rutting buffalo in the woods—which is about what most White folks did in the natural forest. But because he was barefoot, his skin touching the forest floor, he was like a different person. He had run behind Ta-Kumsaw through the forests of this whole land, north and south, and in that running young Alvin learned him how the Red man ran, hearing the greensong of the living woodland, moving in perfect harmony to that sweet silent music. When he ran that way, not thinking about where to step, the ground became soft under young Alvin's feet, and he was guided along, no sticks breaking when he stepped, no bushes swishing or twigs snapping off with his onward push. Behind him he left nary a footprint or a broken branch.

Just like a Red man, that was how he moved. And pretty soon his White man's clothing chafed on him, and he stopped and took it off, stuffed it into the pack on his back, and then ran naked as a jaybird, feeling the leaves of the bushes against his body. Soon he was caught up in the rhythm of his own running, forgetting anything about his own body, just part of the living forest, moving onward, faster and stronger, not eating, not drinking. Like a Red man, who could run forever through the deep forest, never needing rest, covering hundreds of miles in a single day.

This was the natural way to travel, Alvin knew it. Not in creaking wooden wagons, rattling over dry ground, sucking along on muddy roads. And not on horseback, a beast sweating and heaving under you, slave to your hurry, not on any errand of its own. Just a man in the woods, bare feet on the ground, bare face in the wind, dreaming as he ran.

All that day and all that night he ran, and well into the morning. How did he find his way? He could feel the slash of the well-traveled road off on his left, like a prickle or an itch, and even though that road led through many a village and many a town, he knew that after a while it'd fetch him up at the town of Hatrack. After all, that was the road his own folks followed, bridging every stream and creek and river on the way, carrying him as a newborn babe in the wagon. Even though he never traveled it before, and wasn't looking at it now, he knew where it led.

So on the second morning he fetched up at the edge of the wood, on the verge of a field of new green maize billowing over rolling ground. There was so many farms in this settled country that the forest was too weak to hold him in his dream much longer anyhow.

It took a while, just standing there, to remember who he was and where he was bound. The music of the greenwood was strong behind him, weak afore. All he could know for sure was a town ahead, and a river maybe five mile on, that's all he could *feel* for sure. But he knew it was the Hatrack River yonder, and so the town could be no other than the one he was bound for.

He had figured to run the forest right up to the edge of town. Now, though, he had no choice but to walk those last miles on White man's feet or not go at all. That was a thought he had never thought of—that there might be places in the world so settled that one farm butted right against the next, with only a row of trees or a rail fence to mark the boundary, farm after farm. Was this what the Prophet saw in his visions of the land? All the forest killed back and these fields put in their place, so a Red man couldn't run no more, nor a deer find cover, nor a bear find him where to sleep come wintertime? If that was so, no wonder he took all the Reds who'd follow him out west, across the Mizzipy. There was no living for a Red man here.

That made Alvin a little sad and a little scared, to leave behind the living lands he'd come to know as well as a man knows his own body. But he wasn't no philosopher. He was a boy of eleven, and he also hankered to see an eastern town, all settled up and civilized. Besides, he had business here, business he'd waited a year to take up, ever since he first learned there was such a body as the torch girl, and how she looked for him to be a Maker.

He pulled his clothes out of his pack and put them on. He walked the edge of the farmland till he came to a road. First time the road crossed a stream, there was proof it was the right road: a covered bridge stood over that little one-jump brooklet. His own pa and older brothers built that bridge, and others like it all the way along that road from Hatrack to Vigor Church. Eleven years ago they built it, when Alvin was a baby sucking on his mama while the wagon rattled west.

He followed the road, and it wasn't awful far. He'd just run hundreds of miles through virgin forest without harm to his feet, but the White man's road had no part of the greensong and it didn't yield to Alvin's feet. Within a couple of miles he was footsore and dusty and thirsty and hungry. Alvin hoped it wasn't too many miles on White man's road, or he'd sure be wishing he'd kept his boots.

The sign beside the road said, Town of Hatrack, Hio.

It was a good-sized town, compared to frontier villages. Of course it didn't compare to the French city of Detroit, but that was a foreign place, and this town was, well, American. The houses and buildings were like the few rough structures in Vigor Church and other new settlements, only smoothed out and growed up to full size. There was four streets that crossed the main road, with a bank and a couple of shops and churches and even a country courthouse and some places with shingles saying Lawyer and Doctor and Alchemists. Why, if there was professional folk here, it was a town *proper*, not just a hopeful place like Vigor Church before the massacre.

Less than a year ago he'd seen a vision of the town of Hatrack. It was when the Prophet, Lolla-Wossiky, caught him up in the tornado that he called down onto Lake Mizogan. The walls of the whirlwind turned to crystal that time, and in the crystal Alvin had seen many things. One of them was the town of Hatrack the way it was when Alvin was born. It was plain that things hadn't stayed the same in these eleven years. He didn't recognize a thing, walking through the town. Why, this place was so big now that not a soul even seemed to notice he was a stranger to give him howdy-do.

He was most of the way through the built-up part of town before he realized that it wasn't the town's bigness that made folks pay him no mind. It was the dust on his face, his bare feet, the empty pack on his back. They looked, they took him in at a glance, and then they looked away, like as if they were halfway scared he'd come up and ask them for bread or a place to stay. It was something Alvin never met up with before, but he knowed it right away for what it was. In the last eleven years, the town of Hatrack, Hio, had learned the difference between rich and poor.

The built-up part was over. He was through the town, and he hadn't seen a single blacksmith's shop, which was what he was supposed to be looking for, nor had he seen the roadhouse where he was born, which was what he was really looking for. All he saw right now was a couple of pig farms, stinking the way pig farms do, and then the road bent a bit south and he couldn't see more.

The smithy had to still be there, didn't it? It was only a year and a half ago that Taleswapper had carried the prentice contract Pa wrote up for Makepeace, the blacksmith of Hatrack River. And less than a year ago that Taleswapper hisself told Alvin that he delivered that letter, and Makepeace Smith was amenable—that was the word he used, *amenable*. Since Taleswapper talked in his halfway English manner, with the *R*s dropped off the ends of

70

words, it sounded to Alvin like old Taleswapper said Makepeace Smith was "a meaner bull," till Tale-swapper wrote it down for him. Anyway, the smith was here a year ago. And the torch girl in the road-house, the one he visioned in Lolla-Wossiky's crystal tower, she *must* be here. Hadn't she written in Tale-swapper's book, "A Maker is born"? When he looked at those words the letters burned with light like as if they been conjured, like the message writ by the hand of God on the wall in that Bible story: "Mean, mean, take all apart, son," and sure enough, it came to pass, Babylon was took all apart. Words of prophecy was what turned letters bright like that. So if that Maker was Alvin himself, and he knowed it was, then she must see more in her torchy way. She must know what a Maker really *is* and how to be one.

Maker. A name folks said with a hush. Or spoke of wistful, saying that the world had done with Makers, there'd be no more. Oh, some said Old Ben Franklin was a Maker, but he denied being so much as a wizard till the day he died. Taleswapper, who knew Old Ben like a father, he said Ben only made one thing in his life, and that was the Amer-ican Compact, that piece of paper that bound the Dutch and Swedish colonies with the English and Germany settlements of Pennsylvania and Suskwa-henny and, most important of all, the Red nation of Irrakwa, altogether forming the United States of America, where Red and White, Dutchman, Swede and Englishman, rich and poor, merchant and lab-orer, all could vote and all could speak and no one could say, I'm a better man than you. Some folks allowed as how that made Ben as true a Maker as

71

ever lived, but no, said Taleswapper, that made Ben a binder, a knotter, but not a Maker.

I am the Maker that torch girl wrote about. She touched me as I was a-borning, and when she did she saw that I had Maker-stuff in me. I've got to find that girl, growed up to be sixteen years old by now, and she's got to tell me what she saw. Cause the powers I've found inside me, the things that I can do, I know they've got a purpose bigger than just cutting stone without hands and healing the sick and running through the woods like any Red man can but no White man ever could. I've got a work to do in my life and I don't have the first spark of an idea how to get ready for it.

Standing there in the road, with a pig farm on either hand, Alvin heard the sharp *ching ching* of iron striking iron. The smith might as well have called out to him by name. Here I am, said the hammer, find me up ahead along the road.

Before he ever got to the smithy, though, he rounded the bend and saw the very roadhouse where he was born, just as plain as ever in the vision in the crystal tower. Whitewashed shiny and new with only the dust of this summer on it, so it didn't look quite the same, but it was as welcome a sight as any weary traveler could hope for.

Twice welcome, cause inside it, with any decent luck the torch girl could tell him what his life was supposed to be.

Alvin knocked at the door cause that's what you do, he thought. He'd never stayed in a roadhouse before, and had no notion of a public room. So he knocked once, and then twice, and then hallooed till finally the door opened. It was a woman with flour on her hands and her checked apron, a big

72

woman who looked annoyed beyond belief—but he knew her face. This was the woman in his crystal tower vision, the one what pulled him out of the womb with her own fingers around his neck.

"What in the world are you thinking of, boy, to knock my door like that and start hullaballooing like there was a fire? Why can't you just come on in and set like any other folk, or are you so powerful important that you got to have a servant come and open doors for you?"

"Sorry, ma'am," said Alvin, about as respectful as could be.

"Now what business could you have with us? If you're a beggar then I got to tell you we'll have no scraps till after dinner, but you're welcome to wait till then, and if you got a conscience, why, you can chop some wood for us. Except for look at you, I can't believe you're more than fourteen years old—"

"Eleven, ma'am."

"Well, then, you're right big for your age, but I still can't figure what business you got here. I won't serve you no liquor even if you got money, which I doubt. This is a Christian house, in fact more than mere Christian because we're true-blue Methodist and that means we don't touch a drop nor serve it neither, and even if we did we wouldn't serve children. And I'd stake ten pound of porkfat on a wager that you don't have the price of a night's lodging."

"No ma'am," said Alvin, "but—"

"Well then here you are, dragging me out of my kitchen with the bread half-kneaded and a baby who's bound to cry for milk any minute, and I reckon you don't plan to stand at the head of the table and explain to all my boarders why their dinner

73

is late, on account of a boy who can't open a door his own self, no, you'll leave me to make apologies myself as best I can, which is right uncivil of you if you don't mind my saying, or even if you do."

"Ma'am," said Alvin, "I don't want food and I don't want a room." He knew enough courtesy *not* to add that travelers had always been welcome to stay in his father's house whether they had money or not, and a hungry man didn't get afternoon scraps, he set down at Pa's own table and ate with the family. He was catching on to the idea that things were different here in civilized country.

"Well, all we deal with here is food and rooms," said the roadhouse lady.

"I come here, ma'am, cause I was born in this house almost twelve years ago."

Her whole demeanor changed at once. She wasn't a roadhouse mistress now, she was a midwife. "Born in this house?"

"Born on the day my oldest brother Vigor died in the Hatrack River. I thought as how you might even remember that day, and maybe you could show me the place where my brother lies buried."

Her face changed again. "You," she said. "You're the boy who was born to that family—the seventh son of—"

"Of a seventh son," said Alvin.

"Well what's become of you, tell me! Oh, it was a portentous thing. My daughter stood there and looked afar off and saw that your big brother was still alive as you came out of the womb—"

"Your daughter," said Alvin, forgetting himself so much that he interrupted her clean in the middle of a sentence. "She's a torch."

74

The lady turned cold as ice. "*Was*," she said. "She don't torch no more."

But Alvin hardly noticed how the lady changed. "You mean she lost her knack for it? I never heard of a body losing their knack. But if she's here, I'd like to talk to her."

"She ain't here no more," said the lady. Now Alvin finally caught on that she didn't much care to talk about it. "There ain't no torch now in Hatrack River. Babies will be born here without a body touching them to see how they lie in the womb. That's the end of it. I won't say another word about such a girl as that who'd run off, just run right off—"

Something caught in the lady's voice and she turned her back to him.

"I got to finish my bread," said the lady. "The graveyard is up the hill there." She turned around again to face him, with nary a sign of the anger or grief or what-all that she felt a second before. "If my Horace was here I'd have him show you the way, but you'll see it anyhow, there's a kind of path. It's just a family graveyard, with a picket fence around it." Her stern manner softened. "When you're done up there you come back and I'll serve you better than scraps." She hurried on into the kitchen. Alvin followed her.

There was a cradle by the kitchen table, with a babe asleep in it but wiggling somewhat. Something funny about the baby but Alvin couldn't say right off what it was.

"Thank you for your kindness, ma'am, but I don't ask for no handouts. I'll work to pay for anything I eat."

"That's rightly said, and like a true man—your

75

father was the same, and the bridge he built over the Hatrack is still there, strong as ever. But you just go now, see the graveyard, and then come back by and by."

She bent over the huge wad of dough on the kneading table. Alvin got the notion for just a moment that she was crying, and maybe he did and maybe he didn't see tears drop from her eyes straight down into the dough. It was plain she wanted to be alone.

He looked again at the baby and realized what was different. "That's a pickaninny baby, isn't it?" he said.

She stopped kneading, but left her hands buried to the wrist in dough. "It's a baby," she said, "and it's *my* baby. I adopted him and he's mine, and if you call him a pickaninny I'll knead your face like dough."

"Sorry, ma'am, I meant no harm. He just had a sort of cast to his face that he gave me the idea, I reckon—"

"Oh, he's half-Black all right. But it's the White half of him I'm raising up, just as if he was my own son. We named him Arthur Stuart."

Alvin got the joke of that right off. "Ain't nobody can call the King a pickaninny, I reckon."

She smiled. "I reckon not. Now get, boy. You owe a debt to your dead brother, and you best pay it now."

The graveyard was easy to find, and Alvin was gratified to see that his brother Vigor had a stone, and his grave was as well-tended as any other. Only a few graves here. Two stones with the same name— "Baby Missy"—and dates that told of children dying young. Another stone that said "Oldpappy" and then his real name, and dates that told of a long life. And Vigor.

He knelt by his brother's grave and tried to picture what he might have been like. The best he could do was imagine his brother Measure, who was his favorite brother, the one who was captured by Reds along with Alvin. Vigor must have been like Measure. Or maybe Measure was like Vigor. Both willing to die if need be, for their family's sake. Vigor's death saved my life before I was born, thought Alvin, and yet he hung on to the last breath so that when I was born I was still the seventh son of a seventh son, with all my brothers ahead of me alive. The same kind of sacrifice and courage and strength that it took when Measure, who hadn't killed a single Red man, who near died just trying to stop the Tippy-Canoe massacre from happening, took on himself the same curse as his father and his brothers, to have blood on his hands if he failed to tell any stranger the true story of the killing of all them innocent Reds. So when he knelt there at Vigor's grave, it was like he was kneeling at Measure's grave, even though he knew Measure wasn't dead.

Wasn't wholly dead, anyway. But like the rest of the folk of Vigor Church, he'd never leave that place again. He'd live out all his days where he wouldn't have to meet too many strangers, so that for days on end he could forget the slaughter on that day last summer. The whole family, staying together there, with all the folks in the country roundabout, living out their days of life until them as had the curse all died, sharing each other's shame and each other's loneliness like they was all kin, every one of them.

All them together, except for me. I didn't take no curse on me. I left them all behind.

Kneeling there, Alvin felt like an orphan. He might as well be. Sent off to be a prentice here, knowing that whatever he did, whatever he made, his kin could never come on out to see. He could go home to the bleak sad town from time to time, but that was more like a graveyard than this grassy living place, because even with dead folks buried here, there was hope and life in the town nearby, people looking forward instead of back.

Alvin had to look forward, too. Had to find his way to what he was born to be. You died for me, Vigor, my brother that I never met. I just haven't figured out yet why it was so important for me to be alive. When I find out, I hope to make you proud of me. I hope you'll think that I was worth dying for.

When his thoughts was all spent and gone, when his heart had filled up and then emptied out again, Alvin did something he never thought to do. He looked under the ground.

Not by digging, mind you. Alvin's knack was such that he could get the feel of underground without using his eyes. Like the way he looked into stone. Now it might seem to some folk like a kind of grave-robbing, for Al to peek inside the earth where his brother's body lay. But to Al it was the only way he'd ever see the man who died to save him.

So he closed his eyes and gazed under the soil and found the bones inside the rotted wooden box. The size of him—Vigor was a big boy, which is about what it would take to roll and yaw a full-sized tree in a river's current. But the soul of him, that wasn't there, and even though he knowed it wouldn't be Al was somewhat disappointed.

His hidden gaze wandered to the small bodies

barely clinging to their own dust, and then to the gnarled old corpse of Oldpappy, whoever that was, fresh in the earth, only a year or so buried.

But not so fresh as the other body. The unmarked body. One day dead at most, she was, all her flesh still on her and the worms hardly working at her yet.

He cried out in the surprise of it, and the grief at the next thought that came to mind. Could it be the torch girl buried there? Her mother said that she run off, but when folks run off it ain't unusual for them to come back dead. Why else was the mother grieving so? The innkeeper's own daughter, buried without a marker—oh, that spoke of terrible bad things. Did she run off and get herself shamed so bad her own folks wouldn't mark her burying place? Why else leave her there without a stone?

"What's wrong with you, boy?"

Alvin stood, turned, faced the man. A stout fellow who was right comfortable to look upon; but his face wasn't too easy right now.

"What are you doing here in this graveyard, boy?"

"Sir," said Alvin, "my brother's buried here."

The man thought a moment, his face easing. "You're one of that family. But I recall all their boys was as old as you even back then—"

"I'm the one what was born here that night."

At that news the man just opened up his arms and folded Alvin up inside. "They named you Alvin, didn't they," said the man, "just like your father. We call him Alvin Bridger around here, he's something of legend. Let me see you, see what you've become. Seventh son of a seventh son, come home to see your birthplace and your brother's grave. Of course you'll stay in my roadhouse. I'm Horace Guester, as you might guess, I'm pleased to meet

79

you, but ain't you somewhat big for—what, ten, eleven years old?"

"Almost twelve. Folks say I'm tall."

"I hope you're proud of the marker we made for your brother. He was admired here, even though we all met him in death and never in life."

"I'm suited," said Alvin. "It's a good stone." And then, because he couldn't help himself, though it wasn't a particularly wise thing to do, he up and asked the question most burning in him. "But I wonder, sir, why one girl got herself buried here yesterday, and no stone nor marker tells her name."

Horace Guester's face turned ashen. "Of course you'd see," he whispered. "Doodlebug or something. Seventh son. God help us all."

"Did she do something shameful, sir, not to have no marker?" asked Alvin.

"Not shame," said Horace. "As God is my witness, boy, this girl was noble in life and died a virtuous death. She stays unmarked so this house can be a shelter to others like her. But oh, lad, say you'll never tell what you found buried here. You'd cause pain to dozens and hundreds of lost souls along the road from slavery to freedom. Can you believe me that much, trust me and be my friend in this? It'd be too much grief, to lose my daughter and have this secret out, all in the same day. Since I can't keep the secret from you, you have to keep it with me, Alvin, lad. Say you will."

"I'll keep a secret if it's honourable, sir," said Alvin, "but what honorable secret leads a man to bury his own daughter without a stone?"

Horace's eyes went wide, and then he laughed like he was calling loony birds. When he got control of hisself, he clapped Alvin on the shoulder. "That

80

ain't my daughter in the ground there, boy, what made you think it was? It's a Black girl, a runaway slave, who died last night on her way north."

Now Alvin realized for the first time that the body was way too small to be no sixteen-year-old, anyhow. It was a child-size body. "That baby in your kitchen, it's her brother?"

"Her son," said Horace.

"But she's so small," said Alvin.

"That didn't stop her White owner from getting her with child, boy. I don't know how you stand on the question of slavery, or if you even thought about it, but I beg you do some thinking now. Think about how slavery lets a White man steal a girl's virtue and still go to church on Sunday while she groans in shame and bears his bastard child."

"You're a Mancipationist, ain't you?" said Alvin.

"Reckon I am," said the innkeeper, "but I reckon all good Christian folk are Mancipationists in their hearts."

"I reckon so," said Alvin.

"I hope *you* are, cause if word gets out that I was helping a slavegirl run off to Canada, there'll be finders and cotchers from Appalachee and the Crown Colonies a-spying on me so I can't help no others get away."

Alvin looked back at the grave and thought about the babe in the kitchen. "You going to tell that baby where his mama's grave is?"

"When he's old enough to know, and not to tell it," said the man.

"Then I'll keep your secret, if you keep mine."

The man raised his eyebrows and studied Alvin. "What secret *you* got, Alvin, a boy as young as you?"

81

"I don't have no partickler wish to have it known I'm a seventh son. I'm here to prentice with Makepeace Smith, which I reckon is the man I hear a-hammering at the forge down yonder."

"And you don't want folks knowing you can see a body lying in an unmarked grave."

"You caught my drift right enough," said Alvin. "I won't tell your secret, and you won't tell mine."

"You have my word on it," said the man. Then he held out his hand.

Took that hand and shook it, gladly. Most grownup folk wouldn't think of making a bargain like that with a mere child like him. But this man even offered his hand, like they were equals. "You'll see I know how to keep my word, sir," said Alvin.

"And anyone around here can tell you Horace Guester keeps a promise, too." Then Horace told him the story that they were letting out about the baby, how it was the Berrys' youngest, and they gave it up for Old Peg Guester to raise, cause they didn't need another child and she'd always hankered to have her a son. "And that part is true enough," said Horace Guester. "All the more, with Peggy running off."

"Your daughter," said Alvin.

Suddenly Horace Guester's eyes filled up with tears and he shuddered with a sob like Alvin never heard from a growed man in his life. "Just ran off this morning," said Horace Guester.

"Maybe she's just a-calling on somebody in town or something," said Alvin.

Horace shook his head. "I beg your pardon, crying like that, I just beg your pardon, I'm awful tired, truth to tell, up all night last night, and then this morning, her gone like that. She left us a note. She's gone all right."

"Don't you know the man she run off with?" asked Alvin. "Maybe they'll get married, that happened once to a Swede girl out in the Noisy River country—"

Horace turned a bit red with anger. "I reckon you're just a boy so you don't know better than to say such a thing. So I'll tell you now, she didn't run off with no *man*. She's a woman of pure virtue, and no one ever said otherwise. No, she run off alone, boy."

Alvin thought he'd seen all kinds of strange things in his life—a tornado turned into a crystal tower, a bolt of cloth with all the souls of men and women woven in it, murders and tortures, tales and miracles, Alvin knew more of life than most boys at eleven years of age. But this was the strangest thing of all, to think of a girl of sixteen just up and leaving her father's house, without no husband or nothing. In all his life he never saw a woman go *nowhere* by herself beyond her own dooryard.

"Is she—is she *safe*?"

Horace laughed bitterly. "Safe? Of course she's safe. She's a torch, Alvin, the best torch I ever heard of. She can see folks miles off, she knows their hearts, ain't a man born can come near her with evil on his mind without she knows exactly what he's planning and just how to get away. No, I ain't *worried* about her. She can take care of herself better than any man. I just—"

"Miss her," said Alvin.

"I guess it don't take no torch to guess that, am I right, lad? I miss her. And it hurt my feelings somewhat that she up and left with no warning. I could've given her God bless to send her on her way. Her mama could've worked up some good hex, not that Little Peggy'd need it, or anyhow just pack her a cold dinner for on the road. But none of that, no fare-thee-well nor God-be-with-you. It was like as if she was running from some awful boogly monster and had no time to take but one spare dress in a cloth bag and rush on out the door."

Running from some monster—those words stung right to Alvin's soul. She was such a torch that it might well be she saw Alvin coming. Up and ran away the morning he arrived. If she wasn't no torch then maybe it was just chance that took her off the same day he come. But she *was* a torch. She saw him coming. She knew he came all this way a-hoping to meet her and beg her to help him find his way into becoming whatever it was that he was born to be. She saw all that, and ran away.

"I'm right sorry that she's gone," said Alvin.

"I thank you for your pity, friend, it's good of you. I just hope it won't be for long. I just hope she'll do whatever she left to do and come on back in a few days or maybe a couple of weeks." He laughed again, or maybe sobbed, it was about the same sound. "I can't even go ask the Hatrack torch to tell a fortune about her, cause the Hatrack River torch is gone."

Horace cried outright again, for just a minute. Then he took Alvin by the shoulders and looked him in the eye, not even hiding the tears on his cheeks. "Alvin, you just remember how you seen me crying all unmanlike, and you remember that's how fathers feel about their children when they're gone. That's how your own pa feels right now, having you so far away."

"I know he does," said Alvin.

"Now if you don't mind," said Horace Guester, "I need to be alone here."

Alvin touched his arm just a moment and then he went away. Not down to the house to have his noon meal like Old Peg Guester offered. He was too upset to sit and eat with them. How could he explain that he was nigh on to being as heartbroke as them, to have that torch girl gone? No, he'd have to keep silence. The answers he was looking for in Hatrack, they were gone off with a sixteen-year-old girl who didn't want to meet him when he came.

Maybe she seen my future and she hates me. Maybe I'm as bad a boogly monster as anybody ever dreamed of on an evil night.

He followed the sound of the blacksmith's hammer. It led him along a faint path to a spring-house straddling a brook that came straight out of a hillside. And down the stream, along a clear meadow slope, he walked until he came to the smithy. Hot smoke rose from the forge. Around front he walked, and saw the blacksmith inside the big sliding door, hammering a hot iron bar into a curving shape across the throat of his anvil.

Alvin stood and watched him work. He could feel the heat from the forge clear outside; inside must be like the fires of hell. His muscles were like fifty different ropes holding his arm on under the skin. They shifted and rolled across each other as the hammer rose into the air, then bunched all at once as the hammer came down. Close as he was now, Alvin could hardly bear the bell-like crash of iron on iron, with the anvil like a sounding fork to make the sound ring on and on. Sweat dripped off the blacksmith's body, and he was naked to the waist, his white skin ruddy from the heat, streaked with soot from the forge and sweat from his pores. I've been sent here to be prentice to the devil, thought Alvin.

But he knew that was a silly idea even as he thought it. This was a hardworking man, that's all, earning his living with a skill that every town needed if it hoped to thrive. Judging from the size of the corrals for horses waiting to be shod, and the heaps of iron bars waiting to be made into plows and sickles, axes and cleavers, he did a good business, too. If I learn this trade, I'll never be hungry, thought Alvin, and folks will always be glad to have me.

And something more. Something about the hot fire and the ruddy iron. What happened in this place was akin somehow to making. Alvin knew from the way he'd worked with stone in the granite quarry, when he carved the millstones for his father's mill, he knew that with his knack he could probably reach inside the iron and make it go the way he wanted it to go. But he had something to learn from the forge and the hammer, the bellows and the fire and the water in the cooling tubs, something that would help him become what he was born to become.

So now he looked at the blacksmith, not as a powerful stranger, but as Alvin's future self. He saw how the muscles grew on the smith's shoulders and back. Alvin's body was strong from chopping wood and splitting rails and all the hoisting and lifting that he did earning pennies and nickels on neighbors' farms. But in that kind of work, your whole body went into every movement. You rared back with the axe and when it swung it was like your whole body was part of the axehandle, so that legs and hips and back all moved into the chop. But the smith, he held the hot iron in the tongs, held it so smooth and exact against the anvil that while his right arm swung the hammer, the rest of his body couldn't move a twitch, that left arm stayed as smooth and steady as a rock. It shaped the smith's body differently, forced the arms to be much stronger by themselves, muscles rooted to the neck and breastbone standing out in a way they never did on a farmboy's body.

Alvin felt inside himself, the way his own muscles grew, and knew already where the changes would have to come. It was part of his knack, to find his way within living flesh most as easily as he could chart the inner shapes of living stone. So even now he was hunkering down inside, teaching his body to change itself to make way for the new work.

"Boy," said the smith.

"Sir," said Alvin.

"Have you got business for me? I don't know you, do I?"

Alvin stepped forward, held out the note his father writ.

"Read it to me, boy, my eyes are none too good."

Alvin unfolded the paper. "From Alvin Miller of Vigor Church. To Makepeace, Blacksmith of Hatrack River. Here is my boy Alvin what you said could be your prentice till he be seventeen. He'll work hard and do what all you say, and you teach him what all a man needs to be a good smith, like in the articles I signed. He is a good boy."

The smith reached for the paper, held it close to his eyes. His lips moved as he repeated a few phrases. Then he slapped the paper down on the anvil. "This is a fine turn," said the smith. "Don't you know you're about a year late, boy? You was

87

supposed to come last spring. I turned away three offers for prentice cause I had your pa's word you was coming, and here I've been without help this whole year cause he *didn't* keep his word. Now I'm supposed to take you in with a year less on your contract, and not even a by-your-leave or beg-your-pardon."

"I'm sorry, sir," said Alvin. "But we had the war last year. I was on my way here but I got captured by Choc-Taw."

"Captured by—oh, come now, boy don't tell me tales like that. If the Choc-Taw caught you, you wouldn't have such a dandy head of hair now, would you! And like as not you'd be missing a few fingers."

"Ta-Kumsaw rescued me," said Alvin.

"Oh, and no doubt you met the Prophet hisself and walked on water with him."

As a matter of fact, Alvin done just that. But from the smith's tone of voice, he reckoned that it wouldn't be wise to say so. So Alvin said nothing.

"Where's your horse?" asked the smith.

"Don't have one," said Alvin.

"Your father wrote the date on this letter boy, two days ago! You must've rode a horse."

"I ran." As soon as Alvin said it, he knew it was a mistake.

"*Ran*?" said the smith. "With *bare feet*? It must be nigh four hundred mile or more to the Wobbish from here! Your feet ought to be ripped to rags clear up to your knees! Don't tell me tales, boy! I won't have no liars around me!"

Alvin had a choice, and he knew it. He could explain about how he could run like a Red man. Makepeace Smith wouldn't believe him, and so Alvin would have to show him some of what he could do. It would be easy enough. Bend a bar of iron just by stroking it. Make two stones mash together to form one. But Alvin already made up his mind he didn't want to show his knacks here. How could he be a proper prentice, if folks kept coming around for him to cut them hearthstones or fix a broken wheel or all the other fixing things he had a knack for? Besides, he never done such a thing, showing off just for the sake of proving what he could do. Back home he only used his knack when there was need.

So he stuck with his decision to keep his knack to himself, pretty much. Not tell what he could do. Just learn like any normal boy, working the iron the way the smith himself did, letting the muscles grow slowly on his arms and shoulders, chest and back.

"I was joking," Alvin said. "A man gave me a ride on his spare mount."

"I don't like that kind of joke," said the smith. "I don't like it that you lied to me so easy like that."

What could Alvin say? He couldn't even claim that he hadn't lied—he had, when he told about a man letting him ride. So he was as much a liar as the smith thought. The only confusion was about *which* statement was a lie.

"I'm sorry," said Alvin.

"I'm not taking you, boy. I don't have to take you anyway, a year late. And here you come lying to me the first thing. I won't have it."

"Sir, I'm sorry," said Alvin. "It won't happen again. I'm not known for a liar back home, and you'll see I'll be known for square dealing here, if you give me a chance. Catch me lying or not giving fair work all the time, and you can chuck me, no

89

questions asked. Just give me a chance to prove it, sir."

"You don't look like you're eleven, neither, boy."

"But I am, sir. You know I am. You yourself with your own arms pulled my brother Vigor's body from the river on the night that I was born, or so my pa told me."

The smith's face went distant, as if he was remembering. "Yes, he told you true, I was the one who pulled him out. Clinging to the roots of that tree even in death, so I thought I'd have to cut him free. Come here, boy."

Alvin walked closer. The smith poked and pushed the muscles of his arms.

"Well, I can see you're not a lazy boy. Lazy boys get soft, but you're strong like a hardworking farmer. Can't lie about *that*, I reckon. Still, you haven't seen what real work is."

"I'm ready to learn."

"Oh, I'm sure of that. Many a boy would be glad to learn from me. Other work might come and go, but there's always a need for a blacksmith. That'll never change. Well, you're strong enough in body, I reckon. Let's see about your brain. Look at this anvil. This here, the bick on the point, you see. Say that."

"Bick."

"And then the throat here. And this is the table— it ain't faced with blister steel, so when you ram a cold chisel into it the chisel don't blunt. Then up a notch onto the steel face, where you work the hot metal. And this is the hardie hole, where I rest the butt of the fuller and the flatter and the swage. And this here's the pricking hole, for when I punch holes

90

in strap iron—the hot punch shoots right through this space. You got all that?"

"I think so, sir,"

"Then name me the parts of the anvil."

Alvin named them as best he could. Couldn't remember the job each one did, not all of them, anyways, but what he did was good enough, cause the blacksmith nodded and grinned. "Reckon you ain't a half-wit, anyhow, you'll learn quick enough. And big for your age is good. I won't have to keep you on a broom and the bellows for the first four years, the way I do with smaller boys. But your age, that's a sticking point. A term of prentice work is seven year, but my written-up articles with your pa, they only say till you're seventeen."

"I'm almost twelve now, sir."

"So what I'm saying is, I want to be able to hold you the full seven years, if need be. I don't want you whining off just when I finally get you trained enough to be useful."

"Seven years, sir. The spring when I'm nigh on nineteen, then my time is up."

"Seven years is a long time, boy, and I mean to hold you to it. Most boys start when they're nine or ten, or even seven years old, so they can make a living, start looking for a wife at sixteen or seventeen years old. I won't have none of that. I expect you to live like a Christian, and no fooling with any of the girls in town, you understand me?"

"Yes sir."

"All right then. My prentices sleep in the loft over the kitchen, and you eat at table with my wife and children and me, though I'll thank you not to speak until spoken to inside the house—I won't have my prentices thinking they have the same rights as my own children, cause you don't."

"Yes sir."

"And as for now, I need to het up this strap again. So you start to work the bellows there."

Alvin walked to the bellows handle. It was T-shaped, for two-handed working. But Alvin twisted the end piece so it was at the same angle as the hammer handle when the smith lifted it into the air. Then he started to work the bellows with one arm.

"What are you doing, boy!" shouted Alvin's new master. "You won't last ten minutes working the bellows with one arm."

"Then in ten minutes I'll switch to my left arm," said Alvin. "But I won't get myself ready for the hammer if I bend over every time I work the bellows."

The smith looked at him angrily. Then he laughed. "You got a fresh mouth, boy, but you also got sense. Do it your way as long as you can, but see to it you don't slack on wind—I need a hot fire, and that's more important than you working up strength in your arms right now."

Alvin set to pumping. Soon he could feel the pain of this unaccustomed movement gnawing at his neck and chest and back. But he kept going, never breaking the rhythm of the bellows, forcing his body to endure. He could have made the muscles grow right now, teaching them the pattern with his hidden power. But that wasn't what Alvin was here for, he was pretty sure of that. So he let the pain come as it would, and his body change as it would, each new muscle earned by his own effort.

Alvin lasted fifteen minutes with his right hand, ten minutes with his left. He felt the muscles aching and liked the way it felt. Makepeace Smith seemed pleased enough with what he did. Alvin knew that he'd be changed here, that his work would make a strong and skillful man of him.

A man, but not a Maker. Not yet fully on the road to what he was born to be. But since there hadn't been a Maker in the world in a thousand years or more, or so folks said, who was he going to prentice himself to in order to learn *that* trade?

4

Modesty

Whitley Physicker helped Peggy down from the carriage in front of a fine-looking house in one of the best neighbourhoods of Dekane. "I'd like to see you to the door, Peggy Guester, just to make sure they're home to greet you," said he, but she knew he didn't expect her to allow him to do that. If anybody knew how little she liked to have folks fussing over her, it was Doctor Whitley Physicker. So she thanked him kindly and bid him farewell.

She heard his carriage rolling off, the horse clopping on the cobblestones, as she rapped the knocker on the door. A maid opened the door, a German girl so fresh off the boat she couldn't even speak enough English to ask Peggy's name. She invited her in with a gesture, seated her on a bench in the hall, and then held out a silver plate.

What was the plate *for*? Peggy couldn't hardly make sense at all of what she saw inside this foreign girl's mind. She was expecting something—what? A little slip of paper, but Peggy didn't have a notion why. The girl thrust the salver closer to her, insisting. Peggy couldn't do a thing but shrug.

Finally the German girl gave up and went away.

Peggy sat on the bench and waited. She searched for the heartfires in the house, and found the one she looked for. Only then did she realize what the plate was for—her calling card. Folks in the city, rich folks anyway, they had little cards they put their name on, to announce theirself when they came to visit. Peggy even remembered reading about it in a book, but it was a book from the Crown Colonies and she never thought folks in free lands kept such formality.

Soon the lady of the house came, the German girl shadowing her, peering from behind her fine day gown. Peggy knew from the lady's heartfire that she didn't think herself dressed in any partickler finery today, but to Peggy she was like the Queen herself.

Peggy looked into the heartfire and found what she had hoped for. The lady wasn't annoyed a bit at seeing Peggy there, merely curious. Oh, the lady was judging her, of course—Peggy never met a soul, least of all herself, what didn't make some judgment of every stranger—but the judgment was kind. When the lady looked at Peggy's plain clothes, she saw a country girl, not a pauper; when the lady looked at Peggy's stern, expressionless face, she saw a child who had known pain, not an ugly girl. And when the lady imagined Peggy's pain, her first thought was to try to heal her. All in all, the lady was *good*. Peggy made no mistake in coming here.

"I don't believe I've had the pleasure to meet you," said the lady. Her voice was sweet and soft and beautiful.

"I reckon not, Mistress Modesty," said Peggy. "My name is Peggy. I think you had some acquaintance with my papa, years ago."

"Perhaps if you told me his name?"

"Horace," said Peggy. "Horace Guester, of Hatrack, Hio."

Peggy saw the turmoil in her heartfire at the very sound of his name—glad memory, and yet a glimmer of fear of what this strange girl might intend. Yet the fear quickly subsided—her husband had died several years ago, and so was beyond hurt. And none of these emotions showed in the lady's face, which held its sweet and friendly expression with perfect grace. Modesty turned to the maid and spoke a few words of fluent German. The maid curtsied and was gone.

"Did your father send you?" asked the lady. Her unspoken question was: Did your father tell you what I meant to him, and he to me?

"No," said Peggy. "I come here on my own. He'd die if he found out I knew your name. You see I'm a torch, Mistress Modesty. He has no secrets, not from me. Nobody does."

It didn't surprise Peggy one bit how Modesty took the news. Most folks would've thought right off about all the secrets they hoped she wouldn't guess. Instead, the lady thought at once how awful it must be for Peggy, to know things that didn't bear knowing. "How long has it been that way?" she said softly. "Surely not when you were just a little girl. The Lord is too merciful to let such knowledge fill a child's mind."

"I reckon the Lord didn't concern himself much about me," said Peggy.

The lady reached out and touched Peggy's cheek. Peggy knew the lady had noticed she was somewhat dirty from the dust of the road. But what the lady mostly thought of wasn't clothes or cleanliness. A torch, she was thinking. That's why a girl so young wears such a cold, forbidding face. Too much knowledge has made this girl so hard.

"Why have you come to me?" asked Modesty. "Surely you don't mean harm to me or your father, for such an ancient transgression."

"Oh, no ma'am," said Peggy. Never in her life did her own voice sound so harsh to her, but compared to this lady she was squawking like a crow. "If I'm torch enough to know your secret, I'm torch enough to know there was some good in it as well as sin, and as far as the sin goes, Papa's paying for it still, paying double and treble every year of his life."

Tears came to Modesty's eyes. "I had hoped," she murmured, "I had hoped that time would ease the shame of it, and he'd remember it now with joy. Like one of those ancient faded tapestries in England, whose colors are no longer bright, but whose image is the very shadow of beauty itself."

Peggy might've told her that he felt more than joy, that he relived all his feelings for her like it happened yesterday. But that was Papa's secret, and not hers to tell.

Modesty touched a kerchief to her eyes, to take away the tears that trembled there. "All these years I've never spoken to a mortal soul of this. I've poured out my heart only to the Lord, and he's forgiven me; yet I find it somehow exhilarating to speak of this to someone whose face I can see with my eyes, and not just my imagination. Tell me, child, if you didn't come as the avenging angel, have you come perhaps as a forgiving one?"

Mistress Modesty spoke with such elegance that Peggy found herself reaching for the language of the books she read, instead of her natural talking voice.

"I'm a—a supplicant," said Peggy. "I come for help. I come to change my life, and I thought, being how you loved my father, you might be willing to do a kindness for his daughter."

The lady smiled at her. "And if you're half the torch you claim to be, you already know my answer. What kind of help do you need? My husband left me a good deal of money when he died, but I think it isn't money that you need."

"No ma'am," said Peggy. But what was it that she wanted, now that she was here? How could she explain why she had come? "I didn't like the life I saw for myself back in Hatrack. I wanted to—"

"Escape?"

"Somewhat like that, I reckon, but not exactly."

"You want to become something other than what you are," said the lady.

"Yes, Mistress Modesty."

"What is it that you wish to be?"

Peggy had never thought of words to describe what she dreamed of, but now, with Mistress Modesty before her, Peggy saw how simply those dreams might be expressed. "You, ma'am."

The lady smiled and touched her own face, her own hair. "Oh, my child, you must have higher aims than that. Much of what is best in me, your father gave me. The way he loved me taught me that perhaps—no, not *perhaps*—that I *was* worth loving. I have learned much more since then, more of what a woman is and ought to be. What a lovely symmetry, if I can give back to his daughter some of the wisdom he brought to me." She laughed gently. "I never imagined myself taking a pupil."

"More like a disciple, I think, Mistress Modesty."

"Neither pupil nor disciple. Will you stay here

as a guest in my home? Will you let me be your friend?"

Even though Peggy couldn't rightly see the paths of her own life, she still felt them open up inside her, all the futures she could hope for, waiting for her in this place, "Oh, ma'am," she whispered, "if you will."

5

Dowser

Hank Dowser'd seen him prentice boys a-plenty over the years, but never a one as fresh as this. Here was Makepeace Smith bent over old Picklewing's left forehoof, all set to drive in the nail, and up spoke his boy.

"Not that nail," said the blacksmith's prentice boy. "Not there."

Well, that was as fine a moment as Hank ever saw for the master to give his prentice boy a sharp cuff on the ear and send him bawling into the house. But Makepeace Smith just nodded, then looked at the boy.

"You think you can nail this shoe, Alvin?" asked the master. "She's a big one, this mare, but I can see you got you some inches since last I looked."

"I can," said the boy.

"Now just hold your horses," said Hank Dowser. "Picklewing's my only animal, and I can't just up and buy me another. I don't want your prentice boy learning to be a farrier and making his mistakes at my poor old nag's expense." And since he was already speaking his mind so frank like, Hank just rattled right on like a plain fool. "Who's the master here, anyway?" said he.

Well, that was the wrong thing to say. Hank knew it the second the words slipped out of his mouth. You don't says Who's the master, not in front of the prentice. And sure enough, Makepeace Smith's ears turned red and he stood up, all six feet of him, with arms like oxlegs and hands that could crush a bear's face, and he said, "I'm the master here, and when I say my prentice is good enough for the job, then he's good enough, or you can take your custom to another smith."

"Now just hold your horses," said Hank Dowser.

"I *am* holding your horse," said Makepeace Smith. "Or at least your horse's leg. In fact, your horse is leaning over on me something heavy. And now you start asking if I'm master of my own smithy."

Anybody whose head don't leak knows that riling the smith who's shoeing your horse is about as smart as provoking the bees on your way in for the honey. Hank Dowser just hoped Makepeace would be somewhat easier to calm down. "Course you are," said Hank. "I meant nothing by it, except I was surprised when your prentice spoke up so smart and all."

"Well that's cause he's got him a knack," said Makepeace Smith. "This boy Alvin, he can tell things about the inside of a horse's hoof—where a nail's going to hold, where it's going into soft hurting flesh, that kind of thing. He's a natural farrier. And if he says to me, Don't drive that nail, well I know by now that's a nail I don't want to drive, cause it'll make the horse crazy or lame."

Hank Dowser grinned and backed off. It was a

101

hot day, that's all. that's why tempers were so high. "I have respect for every man's knack," said Hank. "Just like I expect them to have respect for mine."

"In that case, I've held up your horse long enough," said the smith. "Here, Alvin, nail this shoe.

If the boy had swaggered or simpered or sneered, Hank would've had a reason to be so mad. But Prentice Alvin just hunkered down with nails in his mouth and hooked up the left forehoof. Picklewing leaned on him, but the boy was right tall, even though his face had no sign of beard yet, and he was like a twin of his master, when it come to muscle under his skin. It wasn't one minute, the horse leaning that way, before the shoe was nailed in place. Picklewing didn't so much as shiver, let alone dance the way he usually did when the nails went in. And now that Hank thought about it a little, Picklewing always *did* seem to favor that leg just a little as if something was a mite sore inside the hoof. But he'd been that way so long Hank hardly noticed it no more.

The prentice boy stepped back out of the way, still not showing any brag at all. He wasn't doing a thing that was the tiniest bit benoctious, but Hank still felt an unreasonable anger at the boy. "How old is he?" asked Hank.

"Fourteen," said Makepeace Smith. "He come to me when he was eleven."

"A mite old for a prentice, wouldn't you say?" asked Hank.

"A year late in arriving, he was, because of the war with the Reds and French—he's from out in the Wobbish country."

"Them was hard years," said Hank. "Lucky me I

was in Irrakwa the whole time. Dowsing wells for windmills the whole way along the railroad they were building. Fourteen, eh? Tall as he is, I reckon he lied about his age even so."

If the boy disliked being named a liar, he didn't show no sign of it. Which made Hank Dowser all the more annoyed. That boy was like a burr under his saddle, just made him mad whatever the boy did.

"No," said the smith. "We know his age well enough. He was born right here in Hatrack River, fourteen years ago, when his folks were passing through on their way west. We buried his oldest brother up on the hill. Big for his age though, ain't he?"

They might've been discussing a horse instead of a boy. But prentice Alvin didn't seem to mind. He just stood there, staring right through them as if they were made of glass.

"You got four years left of his contract, then?" asked Hank.

"Bit more. Till he's near nineteen."

"Well, if he's already this good, I reckon he'll be buying out early and going journeyman." Hank looked, but the boy didn't brighten up at this idea, neither.

"I reckon not," said Makepeace Smith. "He's good with the horses, but he gets careless with the forge. Any smith can do shoes, but it takes a *real* smith to do a plow blade or a wheel tire, and a knack with horses don't help a bit with that. Why, for my masterpiece I done me an anchor! I was in Netticut at the time, mind you. There ain't much call for anchors *here*, I reckon."

Picklewig snorted and stamped—but he didn't dance lively, the way horses do when their new shoes

103

are troublesome. It was a good set of shoes, well shod. Even *that* made Hank mad at the prentice boy. His own anger made no sense to him. The boy had put on Picklewig's last shoe, on a leg that might have been lamed in another farrier's hands. The boy had done him *good*. So why this wrath burning just under the surface, getting worse whatever the boy did or said?

Hank shrugged off his feelings. "Well, that's work well done," he said. "And so it's time for me to do my part."

"Now, we both know a dowsing's worth more than a shoeing," said the smith. "So if you need any more work done, you know I owe it to you, free and clear."

"I *will* come back, Makepeace Smith, next time my nag needs shoes." And because Hank Dowser was a Christian man and felt ashamed of how he disliked the boy, he added praise for the lad. "I reckon I'll be sure to come back while this boy's still under prentice bond to you, him having the knack he's got."

The boy might as well not've heard the good words, and the master smith just chuckled. "You ain't the only one who feels like that," he said.

At that moment Hank Dowser understood something that he might've missed otherwise. This boy's knack with hooves was good for trade, and Makepeace Smith was just the kind of man who'd hold that boy to every day of his contract, to profit from the boy's name for clean shoeing with no horses lost by laming. All a greedy master had to do was claim the boy wasn't good at forgework or something like, then use that as a pretext to hold him fast. In the meantime the boy'd make a name for this place as the best farriery in eastern Hio. Money in Makepeace Smith's pocket, and nothing for the boy at all, not money nor freedom.

The law was the law, and the smith wasn't breaking it—he had the right to every day of that boy's service. But the custom was to let a prentice go as soon as he had the skill and had sense enough to make his way in the world. Otherwise, if a boy couldn't hope for early freedom, why should he work hard to learn as quick as he could, work as hard as he could? They said even the slaveowners in the Crown Colonies let their best slaves earn a little pocket money on the side, so's they could buy their freedom sometime before they died.

No, Makepeace Smith wasn't breaking no law, but he was breaking the custom of masters with their prentice boys, and Hank thought ill of him for it; it was a mean sort of master who'd keep a boy who'd already learned everything the master had to teach.

And yet, even knowing that it was the boy who was in the right, and his master in the wrong—even knowing that, he looked at that boy and felt a cold wet hatred in his heart. Hank shuddered, tried to shake it off.

"You say you need a well," said Hank Dowser. "You want it for drinking or for washing or for the smithy?"

"Does it make a difference?" asked the smith.

"Well, I think so," said Hank. "For drinking you need pure water, and for washing you want water that got no disease in it. But for your work in the smithy, I reckon the iron don't give no never mind whether it cools in clear or murky water, am I right?"

"The spring up the hill is giving out, slacking off

105

year by year," said the smith. "I need me a well I can count on. Deep and clean and pure."

"You know why the stream's going slack," said Hank. "Everybody else is digging wells, and sucking out the water before it can seep out the spring. Your well is going to be about the last straw."

"I wouldn't be surprised," said the smith. "But I can't undig their wells, and I got to have my water, too. Reason I settled here was because of the stream, and now they've dried it up on me. I reckon I could move on, but I got me a wife and three brats up at the house, and I like it here, like it well enough. So I figure I'd rather draw water than move."

Hank went on down to the stand of willows by the stream, near where it came out from under an old springhouse, which had fallen into disrepair. "Yours?" asked Hank.

"No, it belongs to old Horace Guester, him who owns the roadhouse up yonder."

Hank found him a thin willow wand that forked just right, and started cutting it out with his knife. "Springhouse doesn't get much use now, I see."

"Stream's dying, like I said. Half the time in summer there ain't enough water in it to keep the cream jars cool. Springhouse ain't no good if you can't count on it all summer."

Hank made the last slice and the willow rod pulled free. He shaved the thick end to a point and whittled off all the leaf nubs, making it as smooth as ever he could. There was some dowsers who didn't care how smooth the rod was, just broke off the leaves and left the ends all raggedy, but Hank knew that the water didn't always want to be found, and then you needed a good smooth willow wand to find it. There

106

was others used a clean wand, but always the same one, year after year, place after place, but that wasn't no good neither. Hank knew, cause the wand had to be from willow or, sometimes, hickory that grew up sucking the water you were hoping to find. Them other dowsers were mountebanks, though it didn't do no good to say so. They found water most times because in most places if you dig down far enough there's *bound* to be water. But Hank did it right, Hank had the true knack. He could feel the willow wand trembling in his hands, could feel the water singing to him under the ground. He didn't just pick the first sign of water, either. He was looking for clear water, high water, close to the surface and easy to pull. He took *pride* in his work.

But it wasn't like that prentice boy—what was his name?—Alvin. Wasn't like him. Either a man could nail horseshoes without ever laming the horse, or he couldn't. If he *ever* lamed a horse, folks thought twice before they went to that farrier again. But with a dowser, it didn't seem to make no difference if you found water every time or not. If you called yourself a dowser and had you a forked stick, folks would pay you for dowsing wells, without bothering to find out if you had any knack for it at all.

Thinking that, Hank wondered if maybe that was why he hated this boy so much—because the boy already had a name for his good work, while Hank got no fame at all even though he was the only true dowser likely to pass through these parts in a month of Sundays.

Hank set down on the grassy bank of the stream and pulled off his boots. When he leaned to set the second boot on a dry rock where it wouldn't be so like to fill up with bugs, he saw two eyes blinking in the shadows inside a thick stand of bushes. It gave him such a start, cause he thought to see a bear, and then he thought to see a Red man hankering after dowser's scalp, even though both such was gone from these parts for years. No, it was just a little light-skinned pickaninny hiding in the bushes. The boy was a mixup, half-White, half-Black, that was plain to see once Hank got over the surprise. "What're you looking at?" demanded Hank.

The eyes closed and the face was gone. The bushes wiggled and whispered from something crawling fast.

"Never you mind him" said Makepeace Smith. "That's just Arthur Stuart."

Arthur Stuart! Not a soul in New England or the United States but knew that name as sure as if they lived in the Crown Colonies. "Then you'll be glad to hear that I'm the Lord Protector," said Hank Dowser. "Cause if the King be that partickler shade of skin, I got some news that'll get me three free dinners a day in any town in Hio and Suskwahenny till the day I die."

Makepeace laughed brisk at that idea. "No, that's Horace Guester's joke, naming him that way. Horace and Old Peg Guester, they're raising that boy, seeing how his natural ma's too poor to raise him. Curse I don't think that's the whole reason. Him being so light-skinned, her husband, Mock Berry, you can't blame him if he don't like seeing that child eat at table with his coal-black children."

Hank Dowser started pulling off his stockings. "You don't suppose old Horace Guester took him on account of he's the party responsible for causing the boy's skin to be so light."

"Hush your mouth with a pumpkin, Hank, before

108

you say such a thing," said Makepace. "Horace ain't that kind of a man."

"You're be surprised who I've known to turn out to be that kind of a man," said Hank. "Though I don't think it of Horace Guester, mind."

"Do you think Old Peg Guester'd let a half-Black bastard son of her husband into the house?"

"What if she don't know?"

"She'd know. Her daughter Peggy used to be torch here in Hatrack River. And everybody knowed that Little Peggy Guester never told a lie."

"I used to hear tell about the Hatrack River torch, afore I ever come here. How come I never seen her?"

"She's gone, that's why," said Makepeace. "Left three years ago. Just run off. You'd be wise never to ask about her up to Guester's roadhouse. They're a mite ticklish on the subject."

Barefoot now, Hank Dowser stood up on the bank of the stream. He happened to glance up, and there off in the trees, just a-watching him, stood that Arthur Stuart boy again. Well, what harm could a little pickaninny do? Not a bit.

Hank stepped into the stream and let the ice-cold water pour over his feet. He spoke silently to the water: I don't mean to block your flow, or slack you down even further. The well I dig ain't meant to do you no harm. It's like giving you another place to flow through, like giving you another face, more hands, another eye. So don't you hide from me, Water. Show me where you're rising up, pushing to reach the sky, and I'll tell them to dig there, and set you free to wash over the earth, you just see if I don't.

"This water pure enough?" Hank asked the smith.

109

"Pure as it can be," said Makepeace. "Never heard of nobody taking sick from it."

Hank dipped the sharp end of the wand into the water, upstream of his feet. Taste it, he told the wand. Catch the flavor of it, and remember, and find me more just this sweet.

The wand started to buck in his hands. It was ready. He lifted it from the stream; it settled down, calmer, but still shaking just the least bit, to let him know it was alive, alive and searching.

Now there was no more talking, no more thinking. Hank just walked, eyes near closed because he didn't want his vision to distract from the tingling in his hands. The wand never led him astray; to *look* where he was going would be as much as to admit the wand had no power to find.

It took near half an hour. Oh, he found a few places right off, but not good enough, not for Hank Dowser. He could tell by how sharp the wand bucked and dropped whether the water was close enough to the surface to do much good. He was so good at it now that most folks couldn't make no difference between him and a doodlebug, which was about as fine a knack as a dowser could ever have. And since doodlebugs were right scarce, mostly being found among seventh sons or thirteen children, Hank never wished anymore that he was a doodlebug instead of just a dowser, or not often, anyway.

The wand dropped so hard it buried itself three inches deep in the earth. Couldn't do much better than that. Hank smiled and opened his eyes. He wasn't thirty feet back of the smithy. Couldn't have found a better spot with his eyes open. No doodlebug could've done a nicer job.

110

The smith thought so, too. "Why, if you'd asked me where I wished the well would be, this is the spot I'd pick."

Hank nodded, accepting the praise without a smile, his eyes half-closed, his whole body still a-tingle with the strength of the water's call to him. "I don't want to lift this wand," said Hank, "till you've dug a trench all round this spot to mark it off."

"Fetch a spade!" cried the smith.

Prentice Alvin jogged off in search of the tool. Hank noticed Arthur Stuart toddling after, running full tilt on them short legs so awkward he was bound to fall. And fall he did, flat down on his face in the grass, moving so fast he slid a yard at least, and came up soaking wet with dew. Didn't pause him none. Just waddled on around the smithy building where Prentice Alvin went.

Hank turned back to Makepeace Smith and kicked at the soil just underfoot. "I can't be sure, not being a doodlebug," said Hank, as modest as he could manage, "but I'd say you won't have to dig ten feet till you strike water here. It's fresh and lively as I ever seen."

"No skin off my nose either way," said Makepeace. "I don't aim to dig it."

"That prentice of yours looks strong enough to dig it hisself, if he doesn't lazy off and sleep when your back is turned."

"He ain't the lazying kind," said Makepeace. "You'll be staying the night at the roadhouse, I reckon."

"I reckon not," said Hank. "I got some folks about six mile west who want me to find them some dry ground to dig a good deep cellar."

111

' "Ain't that kind of *anti*-dowsing?"

"It is, Makepeace, and it's a whole lot harder, too, in wettish country like this."

"Well, come back this way, then," said Make-peace, "and I'll save you a sip of the first water pulled up from your well."

"I'll do that," said Hank, "and gladly." That was an honor he wasn't often offered, that first sip from a well. There was power in that, but only if it was freely given, and Hank couldn't keep from smiling now. "I'll be back in a couple of days, sure as shooting."

The prentice boy come back with the spade and set right to digging. Just a shallow trench, but Hank noticed that the boy squared it off without measuring, each side of the hole equal, and as near as Hank could guess, it was true to the compass points as well. Standing there with the wand still rooted into the ground, Hank felt a sudden sickness in his stomach, having the boy so close. Only it wasn't the kind of sickness where you hanker to chuck up what you ate for breakfast. It was the kind of sickness that turns to pain, the sickness that turns to violence; Hank felt himself yearning to snatch the spade out of the boy's hands and smack him across the head with the sharp side of the blade.

Till finally it dawned on him, standing there with the wand a-trembling in his hand. It wasn't *Hank* who hated this boy, no sir. It was the *water* that Hank served so well, the *water* that wanted this boy dead.

The moment that thought entered Hank's head, he fought it down, swallowed back the sickness inside him. It was the plain craziest idea that ever entered his head. Water was water. All it wanted

112

was to come up out of the ground or down out of the clouds and race over the face of the earth. It didn't have no malice in it. No desire to kill. And anyway, Hank Dowser was a Christian, and a Baptist to boot—a natural dowser's religion if there ever was one. When he put folks under the water, it was to baptize them and bring them to Jesus, not to drown them. Hank didn't have murder in his heart, he had his Savior there, teaching him to love his enemies, teaching him that even to hate a man was like murder.

Hank said a silent prayer to Jesus to take this rage out of his heart and make him stop wishing for this innocent boy's death.

As if in answer, the wand leapt right out of the ground, flew clear out of his hands, and landed in the bushes most of two rods off.

That never happened to Hank in all his days of dowsing. A wand taking off like that! Why, it was as if the water had spurned him as sharp as a fine lady spurns a cussing man.

"Trench is all dug," said the boy.

Hank looked sharp at him, to see if he noticed anything funny about the way the wand took off like that. But the boy wasn't even looking at him. Just looking at the ground inside the square he'd just ditched off.

"Good work," said Hank. He tried not to let his voice show the loathing that he felt.

"Won't do no good to dig here," said the boy.

Hank couldn't hardly believe his ears. Bad enough the boy sassing his own master, in the trade he knew, but what in tarnation did this boy know about dowsing?

"What did you say, boy?" asked Hank.

113

The boy must have seen the menace in Hank's face, or caught the tone of fury in his voice, because he backed right down. "Nothing, sir," he said. "None of my business anyhow."

Such was Hank's built-up anger, though, that he wasn't letting the boy off so easy. "You think you can do my job too, is that it? Maybe your master lets you think you're as good as he is cause you got your knack with *hooves*, but let me tell you, boy, I am a true dowser and my wand tells me there's water here!"

"That's right," said the boy. He spoke mildly, so that Hank didn't really notice that the boy had four inches on him in height and probably more than that in reach. Prentice Alvin wasn't so big you'd call him a giant, but you wouldn't call him no dwarf, neither.

"That's *right*? It ain't for you to say right or wrong to what my wand tells me."

"I know it, sir, I was out of turn."

The smith came back with a wheelbarrow, a pick, and two stout iron levers. "What's all this?" he asked.

"Your boy here got smart with me," said Hank. He knew as he said it that it wasn't quite fair—the boy had already apologized, hadn't he?

Now at last Makepeace's hand lashed out and caught the boy a blow like a bear's paw alongside his head. Alvin staggered under the cuffing, but he didn't fall. "I'm sorry, sir," said Alvin.

"He said there was no water here, where I said the well should be." Hank just couldn't stop himself. "I had respect for *his* knack. You'd think he'd have respect for mine."

"Knack or no knack," said the smith, "he'll have

114

respect for my customers or he'll learn how long it takes to be a smith, oh sir! he'll learn."

Now the smith had one of the heavy iron levers in his hand, as if he meant to cane the boy across the back with it. That would be sheer murder, and Hank hadn't the heart for it. He held out his hand and caught the end of the lever. "No, Makepeace, wait, it's all right. He did tell me he was sorry."

"And is that enough for you?"

"That and knowing you'll listen to me and not to him," said Hank. "I'm not so old I'm ready to hear boys with hoof-knacks tell me I can't dowse no more."

"Oh, the well's going to be dug right here, you can bet your life. And this boy's going to dig it all himself, and not have a bite to eat until he strikes water."

Hank smiled. "Well, then, he'll be glad to discover that I know what I'm doing—he won't have to dig far, that's for sure."

Makepeace rounded on the boy, who now stood a few yards off, his hands slack at his side, showing no anger on his face, nothing at all, really. "I'm going to escort Mr. Dowser back to his newshod mare, Alvin. And this is the last I want to see of you until you can bring me a bucket of clean water from this well. You won't eat a bite or have a sip of water until you drink it from here!"

"Oh, now," said Hank, "have a heart. You know it takes a couple of days sometimes for the dirt to settle out of a new well."

"Bring me a bucket of water from the new well, anyway," said Makepeace. "Even if you work all night."

They headed back for the smithy then, to the

corral where Picklewing waited. There was some chat, some work at saddling up, and then Hank Dowser was on his way, his nag riding smoother and easier under him, just as happy as a clam. He could see the boy working as he rode off. There wasn't no flurry of dirt, just methodical lifting and dumping, lifting and dumping. The boy didn't seem to stop to rest, either. There wasn't a single break in the sound of his labor as Hank rode off. The *shuck* sound of the spade dipping into the soil, then the *swish-thump* as the dirt slid off onto the pile.

Hank didn't calm down his anger till he couldn't hear a sound of the boy, or even remember what the sound was like. Whatever power Hank had as a dowser, this boy was the enemy of his knack, that much Hank knew. He had thought his rage was unreasonable before, but now that the boy had spoke up, Hank knew he had been right all along. The boy thought he was a master of water, maybe even a doodlebug, and that made him Hank's enemy.

Jesus said to give your enemy your own cloak, to turn the other cheek—but what about when your enemy aims to take away your livelihood, what then? Do you let him ruin you? Not this Christian, thought Hank. I learned that boy something this time, and if it doesn't take, I'll learn him more later.

6

Masquerade

Peggy wasn't the belle of the Governor's Ball, but that was fine with her. Mistress Modesty had long since taught her that it was a mistake for women to compete with each other. "There is no single prize to be won, which, if one woman attains it, must remain out of reach for all the others."

No one else seemed to understand this, however. The other women eyed each other with jealous eyes, measuring the probable expense of gowns, guessing at the cost of whatever amulet of beauty the other woman wore; keeping track of who danced with whom, how many men arranged to be presented.

Few of them turned a jealous eye toward Peggy— at least not when she first entered the room in mid-afternoon. Peggy knew the impression she was making. Instead of an elegant coiffure, her hair was brushed and shining, pulled up in a style that looked well-tended, but prone to straying locks here and there. Her gown was simple, almost plain—but this was by calculation. "You have a sweet young body, so your gown must not distract from the natural litheness of youth." Moreover, the gown was unusually modest, showing less bare flesh than any

117

other woman's dress; yet, more than most, it revealed the free movement of the body beneath it.

She could almost hear Mistress Modesty's voice, saying, "So many girls misunderstand. The corset is not an end in itself. It is meant to allow old and sagging bodies to imitate the body that a healthy young woman naturally has. A corset on *you* must be lightly laced, the stays only for comfort, not containment. Then your body can move freely, and you can breathe. Other girls will marvel that you have the courage to appear in public with a natural waistline. But men don't measure the cut of a woman's clothes. Instead they pleasure in the naturalness of a lady who is comfortable, sure of herself, enjoying life on this day, in this place, in his company."

Most important, though, was the fact that she wore no jewelry. The other ladies all depended on beseemings whenever they went out in public. Unless a girl had a knack for beseemings herself, she had to buy—or her parents or husband had to buy—a hex engraven on a ring or amulet. Amulets were preferred, since they were worn nearer the face, and so one could get by with a much weaker—and therefore cheaper—hex. Such beseemings had no effect from far off, but the closer you came to a woman with a beseeming of beauty, the more you began to feel that her face was particularly beautiful. None of her features was transformed; you still saw what was actually there. It was your judgment that changed. Mistress Modesty laughed at such hexes. "What good does it do to fool someone, when he knows he's being fooled?" So Peggy wore no such hex.

All the other women at the ball were in disguise. Though no one's face was hidden, this ball was a

118

masquerade. Only Peggy and Mistress Modesty, of all the women here, were not in costume, were not pretending to some unnatural ideal.

She could guess at the other girls' thoughts as they watched her enter the room: Poor thing. How plain. No competition there. And their estimation was true enough—at least at first. No one took particular notice of Peggy.

But Mistress Modesty carefully selected a few of the men who approached her. "I'd like you to meet my young friend Margaret," she would say, and then Peggy would smile the fresh and open smile that was not artificial at all—her natural smile, the one that spoke of her honest gladness at meeting a friend of Mistress Modesty's. They would touch her hand and bow, and her gentle echoing courtesy was graceful and unmeasured, an honest gesture; her hand squeezed his as a friendly reflex, the way one greets a hoped-for friend. "The art of beauty is the art of truth," said Mistress Modesty. "Other women pretend to be someone else; you will be your love-liest self, with the same natural exuberant grace as a bounding deer or a circling hawk." The man would lead her onto the floor, and she would dance with him, not worrying about correct steps or keeping time or showing off her dress, but rather enjoying the dance, their symmetrical movement, the way the music flowed through their bodies together.

The man who met her, who danced with her, remembered. Afterward the other girls seemed stilted, awkward, unfree, artificial. Many men, themselves as artificial as most of the ladies, did not know themselves well enough to know they enjoyed Peggy's company more than any other young lady's. But then, Mistress Modesty did not introduce Peggy

119

to such men. Rather she only allowed Peggy to dance with the kind of man who could respond to her; and Mistress Modesty knew which men *they* were because they were genuinely fond of Mistress Modesty.

So as the hours passed by at the ball, hazy afternoon giving way to bright evening, more and more men were circling Peggy, filling up her dance card, eagerly conversing with her during the lulls, bringing her refreshment—which she ate if she was hungry or thirsty, and kindly refused if she was not—until the other girls began to take note of her. There were plenty of men who took no notice of Peggy, of course; no other girl lacked because of Peggy's plenty. But they didn't see it that way. What they saw was that Peggy was always surrounded, and Peggy could guess at their whispered conversations.

"What kind of spell does she have?"

"She wears an amulet under her bodice—I'm sure I saw its shape pressing against that cheap fabric."

"Why don't they see how thick-waisted she is?"

"Look how her hair is awry, as if she had just come in from the barnyard."

"She must flatter them dreadfully."

"Only a certain *kind* of man is attracted to her, I hope you notice."

Poor things, poor things. Peggy had no power that was not already born within any of these girls. She used no artifice that they would have to buy.

Most important to her was the fact that she did not even use her own knack here. All of Mistress Modesty's other teachings had come easily to her over the years, for they were nothing more than the extension of her natural honesty. The one difficult barrier was Peggy's knack. By habit, the moment she met someone she had always looked into his heartfire to see who he was; and, knowing more about him than she knew about herself, she then had to conceal her knowledge of his darkest secrets. It was this that had made her so reserved, even haughty-seeming.

Mistress Modesty and Peggy both agreed—she could not tell others how much she knew about them. Yet Mistress Modesty assured her that as long as she was concealing something so important, she could not become her most beautiful self—could not become the woman that Alvin would love for herself, and not out of pity.

The answer was simple enough. Since Peggy could not tell what she knew, and could not hide what she knew, the only solution was not to know it in the first place. That was the real struggle of these past three years—to train herself *not* to look into the heartfires around her. Yet by hard work, after many tears of frustration and a thousand different tricks to try to fool herself, she had achieved it. She could enter a crowded ballroom and remain oblivious to the heartfires around her. Oh, she *saw* the heart-fires—she could not blind herself—but she paid no attention to them. She did not find herself drawing close to see deeply. And now she was getting skilled enough that she didn't even have to *try* not to see into the heartfire. She could stand this close to someone, conversing, paying attention to their words, and yet see no more of his inner thoughts than any other person would.

Of course, years of torchery had taught her more about human nature—the kinds of thoughts that go behind certain words or tones of voice or expressions or gestures—that she was very good at guessing

121

others' present thoughts. But good people never minded when she seemed to know what was on their mind right at the moment. She did not have to hide that knowledge. It was only their deepest secrets that she could not know—and those secrets were now invisible to her unless she chose to see.

She did not choose to see. For in her new detachment she found a kind of freedom she had never known before in all her life. She could take other people at face value now. She could rejoice in their company, not knowing and therefore not feeling responsible for their hidden hungers or, most terribly, their dangerous futures. It gave a kind of exhilarating madness to her dancing, her laughter, her conversation; no one else at the ball felt so free as Modesty's young friend Margaret, because no one else had ever known such desperate confinement as she had known all her life till now.

So it was that Peggy's evening at the Governor's Ball was glorious. Not a *triumph*, actually, since she vanquished no one—whatever man won her friendship was not conquered, but liberated, even victorious. What she felt was pure joy, and so those who were with her also rejoiced in her company. Such good feelings could not be contained. Even those who gossiped nastily about her behind their fans nevertheless caught the joy of the evening; many told the governor's wife that this was the best ball ever held in Dekane, or for that matter in the whole state of Suskwahenny.

Some even realized who it was who brought such gladness to the evening. Among them were the governor's wife and Mistress Modesty. Peggy saw them talking once, as she turned gracefully on the floor, returning to her partner with a smile that made

122

him laugh with joy to be dancing with her. The governor's wife was smiling and nodding, and she pointed with her fan toward the dance floor, and for a moment Peggy's eyes met her. Peggy smiled in warm greeting; the governor's wife smiled and nodded back. The gesture did not go unremarked. Peggy would be welcome at any party she wanted to attend in Dekane—two or three a night, if she desired, every night of the year.

Yet Peggy did not glory in this achievement, for she recognized how small it really was. She had won her way into the finest events in Dekane—but Dekane was merely the capital of a state on the edge of the American frontier. If she longed for social victories, she would have to make her way to Camelot, to win the accolades of royalty—and from there to Europe, to be received in Vienna, Paris, Warsaw, or Madrid. Even then, though, even if she had danced with every crowned head, it would mean nothing. She would die, they would die, and how would the world be any better because she had danced?

She had seen true greatness in the heartfire of a newborn baby fourteen years ago. She had protected the child because she loved his future; she had also come to love the boy because of who he was, the kind of soul he had. Most of all, though, more important then her feelings for Prentice Alvin, most of all she loved the work that lay ahead of him. Kings and queens built kingdoms, or lost them; merchants made fortunes, or squandered them; artists made works that time faded or forgot. Only Prentice Alvin had in him the seeds of Making that would stand against time, against the endless wasting of the Unmaker. So as she danced tonight, she danced for him, knowing that if she could win the love of these strangers, she might also win Alvin's love, and earn a place beside him on his pathway to the Crystal City, that place in which all the citizens can see like torches, build like makers, and love with the purity of Christ.

With the thought of Alvin, she cast her attention to his distant heartfire. Though she had schooled herself not to see into nearby heartfires, she never gave up looking into his. Perhaps this made it harder for her to control her knack, but what purpose was it to learn anything, if by learning she lost her connection with that boy? So she did not have to search for him; she knew always, in the back of her mind, where his heartfire burned. In these years she had learned not to see him constantly before her, but still she could see him in an instant. She did so now.

He was digging in the ground behind his smithy. But she hardly noticed the work, for neither did he. What burned strongest in his heartfire was anger. Someone had treated him unfairly—but that could hardly be new, could it? Makepeace, once the most fair-minded of masters, had become steadily more envious of Alvin's skill at ironwork, and in his jealousy he had become unjust, denying Alvin's ability more fervently the further his prentice boy surpassed him. Alvin lived with injustice every day, yet never had Peggy seen such rage in him.

"Is something wrong, Mistress Margaret?" The man who danced with her spoke in concern. Peggy had stopped, there in the middle of the floor. The music still played, and couples still moved through the dance, but near her the dancers had stopped, were watching her.

"I can't—continue," she said. It surprised her to

124

find that she was out of breath with fear. What was she afraid of?

"Would you like to leave the ballroom?" he asked. What was his name? There was only one name in her mind: Alvin.

"Please," she said. She leaned on him as they walked toward the open doors leading onto the porch. The crowd parted; she didn't see them.

It was as if all the anger Alvin had stored up in his years of working under Makepeace Smith now was coming out, and every dig of his shovel was a deep cut of revenge. A dowser, an itinerant water-seeker, that's who had angered him, that's the one he meant to harm. But the dowser was none of Peggy's concern; nor was his provocation, however mean or terrible. It was Alvin. Couldn't he see that when he dug so deep in hatred it was an act of destruction? And didn't he know that when you work to destroy, you invite the Destroyer? When your labor is unmaking, the Unmaker can claim you.

The air outside was cooler in the gathering dusk, the last shred of the sun throwing a ruddy light across the lawns of the Governor's mansion. "Mistress Margaret, I hope I did nothing to cause you to faint."

"No, I'm not even fainting. Will you forgive me? I had a thought, that's all. One that I must think about."

He looked at her strangely. Any time a woman needed to part with a man, she always claimed to be near fainting. But not Mistress Margaret—Peggy knew that he was puzzled, uncertain. The etiquette of fainting was clear. But what was a gentleman's proper manner toward a woman who "had a thought"?

She laid her hand on his arm. "I assure you, my friend—I'm quite well, and I delighted in dancing with you. I hope we'll dance again. But for now, for the moment, I need to be alone."

She could see how her words eased his concern. Calling him "my friend" was a promise to remember him; her hope to dance with him again was so sincere that he could not help but believe her . He took her words at face value, and bowed with a smile. After that she didn't even see him leave.

Her attention was far away, in Hatrack River, where Prentice Alvin was calling to the Unmaker, not guessing what he was doing. Peggy searched and searched in his heartfire, trying to find something she might do to keep him safe. But there was nothing. Now that Alvin was being driven by anger, all paths led to one place, and that place terrified her, for she couldn't see what was there, couldn't see what would happen. And there were no paths out.

What was I doing at this foolish ball, when Alvin needed me? If I had been paying proper attention, I would have seen this coming, would have found some way to help him. Instead I was dancing with these men who mean less than nothing to the future of this world. Yes, they delight in me. But what is that worth, if Alvin falls, if Prentice Alvin is destroyed, if the Crystal City is unmade before its Maker begins to build it?

7

Wells

Alvin didn't need to look up when the dowser left. He could feel where the man was as he moved along, his anger like a black noise in the midst of the sweet green music of the wood. That was the curse of being the only White, man or boy, who could feel the life of the greenwood—it meant that he was also the only White who knew how the land was dying.

Not that the soil wasn't rich—years of forest growth had made the earth so fertile that they said the *shadow* of a seed could take root and grow. There was life in the fields, life in the towns even. But it wasn't part of the land's own song. It was just noise, whispering noise, and the green of the wood, the life of the Red man, the animal, the plant, the soil all living together in harmony, that song was quiet now, intermittent, sad. Alvin heard it dying and he mourned.

Vain little dowser. Why was he so mad? Alvin couldn't figure. But he didn't press it, didn't argue, because almost as soon as the dowser came along, Al could see the Unmaker shadowing the edges of his vision, as if Hank Dowser'd brought him along.

Alvin first saw the Unmaker in his nightmares as

a child, a vast nothingness that rolled invisibly toward him, trying to crush him, to get inside him to grind him into pieces. It was old Taleswapper who first helped Alvin give his empty enemy a name. The Unmaker, which longs to undo the universe, break it all down until everything is flat and cold and smooth and dead.

As soon as he had a name for it and some notion what it *was*, he started seeing the Unmaker in daylight, wide awake. Not right out in the open, of course. Look *at* the Unmaker and most times you can't see him. He goes all invisible behind all the life and growth and up-building in the world. But at the edges of your sight, as if he was sneaking up behind, that's where the sly old snake awaited, that's where Alvin saw him.

When Alvin was a boy he learned a way to make that Unmaker step back a ways and leave him be. All he had to do was use his hands to build something. It could be as simple as weaving grass into a basket, and he'd have some peace. So when the Unmaker showed up around the blacksmith's shop not long after Alvin got there, he wasn't too worried. There was plenty of chance for making things in the smithy. Besides, the smithy was full of fire—fire and iron, the hardest earth. Alvin knew from childhood on that the Unmaker hankered after water. Water was its servant, did most of its work, tearing things down. So it was no wonder that when a water man like Hank Dowser came along, the Unmaker freshened up and got lively.

Now, though, Hank Dowser was on his way, taking his anger and his unfairness with him, but the Unmaker was still there, hiding out in the meadow and the bushes, lurking in the long shadows of the evening.

Dig with the shovel, lever up the earth, hoist it to the lip of the well, dump it aside. A steady rhythm, a careful building of the pile, shaping the sides of the hole. Square the first three feet of the hole, to set the shape of the well house. Then round and gently tapered inward for the stonework of the finished well. Even though you know this well will never draw water, do it careful, dig as if you thought that it would last. Build smooth, as near to perfect as you can, and it'll be enough to hold that sly old spy at bay.

So why didn't Alvin feel a speck more brave about it?

Alvin knew it was getting on toward evening, sure as if he had him a watch in his pocket, cause here came Arthur Stuart, his face just scrubbed after supper, sucking on a horehound and saying not a word. Alvin was used to him by now. Almost ever since the boy could walk, he'd been like Alvin's little shadow, coming every day it didn't rain. Never had much to say, and when he did it wasn't too easy to understand his baby talk—he had trouble with his *R*s and *S*s. Didn't matter. Arthur never wanted nothing and never did no harm, and Alvin usually half-forgot the boy was around.

Digging there with the evening flies out, buzzing in his face, Alvin had nothing to do with his brain but think. Three years he been in Hatrack, and all that time he hadn't got him one inch closer to knowing what his knack was for. He hardly used it, except for a bit he done with the horses, and that was cause he couldn't bear to know how bad they suffered when it was so easy a thing for him to make the shoeing go right. That was a good thing to do, but it didn't amount to much up-building, compared to the ruination of the land all around him.

The White man was the Unmaker's tool in this forest land, Alvin knew that, better even than water at tearing things down. Every tree that fell, every badger, coon, deer, and beaver that got used up without consent, each death was part of the killing of the land. Used to be the Reds kept the balance of things, but now they were gone, either dead or moved west of the Missipy—or, like the Irrakwa and the Cherriky, turned White at heart, sleeves rolled up and working hard to unmake the land even faster than the White. No one left to try to keep things whole.

Sometimes Alvin thought he was the only one left who hated the Unmaker and wanted to build against him. And he didn't know how to do it, didn't have any idea what the next step ought to be. The torch who touched him at his birthing, she was the only one who might've taught him how to be a true Maker, but she was gone, run off the very morning that he came. Couldn't be no accident. She just didn't want to teach him aught. He had a destiny, he knew it, and not a soul to help him find the way.

I'm willing, thought Alvin. I got the power in me, when I can figure how to use it straight, and I got the desire to be whatever it is I'm meant to be, but somebody's got to teach me.

Not the blacksmith, that was sure. Profiteering old coot. Alvin knew that Makepeace Smith tried to teach him as little as he could. Even now Alvin reckoned Makepeace didn't know half how much Alvin had learned himself just by watching when his master didn't guess that he was alert. Old Makepeace never meant to let him go if he could help it. Here I got a destiny, a real honest-to-goodness Work to do in my life, just like the old boys in the Bible or Ulysses or Hector, and the only teacher I got is a smith so greedy I have to *steal* learning from him, even though it's mine by right.

Sometimes it burned Alvin up inside, and he got to hankering to do something spetackler to show Makepeace Smith that his prentice wasn't just a boy who didn't know he was being cheated. What would Makepeace Smith do if he saw Alvin split iron with his fingers? What if he saw that Al could straighten a bent nail as strong as before, or heal up brittle iron that shattered under the hammer? What if he saw that Al could beat iron so thin you could see sunlight through it, and yet so strong you couldn't break it?

But that was plain dumb when Alvin thought that way, and he knowed it. Makepeace Smith might gasp the first time, he might even faint dead away, but inside ten minutes he'd be figuring an angle how to make money from it, and Alvin'd be less likely than ever to get free ahead of time. And his fame would spread, yes sir, so that by the time he turned nineteen and Makepeace Smith had to let him go, Alvin would already have too much notice. Folks'd keep him busy healing and doodlebugging and fixing and stone shaping, work that wasn't even halfway toward what he was born for. If they brought him the sick and lame to heal, how would he ever have time to be aught but a physicker? Time enough for healing when he learned the whole way to be a Maker.

The Prophet Lolla-Wossiky showed him a vision of the Crystal City only a week before the massacre at Tippy-Canoe. Alvin knew that someday in the future it was up to him to build them towers of ice and light. That was his destiny, not to be a country fixit man. As long as he was bound to Makepeace Smith's service, he had to keep his real knack secret.

That's why he never ran off, even though he was big enough now that nobody'd take him for a runaway prentice. What good would freedom do? He had to learn first how to be a Maker, or it wouldn't make no difference if he went or stayed.

So he never spoke of what he could do, and scarce used his gifts, more than to shoe horses and feel the death of the land around him. But all the time in the back of his brain he recollected what he really was. A Maker. Whatever that is, I'm it, which is why the Unmaker tried to kill me before I was born and in a hundred accidents and almost-murders in my childhood back in Vigor Church. That's why he lurks around now, watching me, waiting for a chance to get me, waiting maybe for a time like tonight, all alone out here in the darkness, just me and the spade and my anger at having to do work that won't amount to nothing.

Hank Dowser. What kind of man won't listen to a good idea from somebody else? Sure the wand went down hard—the water was like to bust up through the earth at that place. But the reason it *hadn't* busted through was on account of a shelf of rock along there, not four feet under the soil. Why else did they think this was a natural meadow here? The big trees couldn't root, because the water that fell here flowed right off the stone, while the roots couldn't punch through the shelf of rock to get to the water underneath it. Hank Dowser could find water, but he sure couldn't find what lay *between*

132

the water and the surface. It wasn't Hank's fault he couldn't see it, but it sure was his fault he wouldn't entertain no notion it might be there.

So here was Alvin, digging as neat a well as you please, and sure enough, no sooner did he have the round side of the well defined than *clink, clank, clunk*, the spade rang against stone.

At the new sound, Arthur Stuart ran right up to the edge of the hole and looked in. "Donk donk,' he said. Then he clapped his hands.

"Donk donk is right," said Alvin. "I'll be donking on solid rock the whole width of this hole. And I ain't going in to tell Makepeace Smith about it, neither, you can bet on that, Arthur Stuart. He told me I couldn't eat nor drink till I got water, and I ain't about to go in afore dark and start pleading for supper just cause I hit rock, no sir."

"Donk," said the little boy.

"I'm digging every scrap of dirt out of this hole till the rock is bare."

He carefully dug out all the dirt he could, scraping the spade along the bumpy face of the rock. Even so, it was still brown and earthy, and Alvin wasn't satisfied. He wanted that stone to shine white. Nobody was watching but Arthur Stuart, and he was just a baby anyhow. So Alvin used his knack in a way he hadn't done since leaving Vigor Church. He made all the soil flow away from the bare rock, slide right across the stone and fetch up tight against the smooth-edge earthen walls of the hole.

It took almost no time till the stone was so shiny and white you could think it was a pool reflecting the last sunlight of the day. The evening birds sang in the trees. Sweat dripped off Alvin so fast it left little black spots where it fell on the rock.

Arthur stood at the edge of the hole. "Water," he said.

"Now you stand back, Arthur Stuart. Even if this ain't all that deep, you just stand back from holes like this. You can get killed falling in, you know."

A bird flew by, its wings rattling loud as could be. Somewhere another bird gave a frantic cry.

"Snow," said Arthur Stuart.

"It ain't snow, it's rock," said Alvin. Then he clambered up out of the hole and stood there, laughing to himself. "There's your well, Hank Dowser," Alvin said. "You ride on back here and see where your stick drove into the dirt."

He'd be sorry he got Al a blow from his master's hand. It wasn't no joke when a blacksmith hit you, specially one like his master, who didn't go easy even on a little boy, and sure not on a man-size prentice like Alvin.

Now he could go on up to the house and tell Makepeace Smith the well was dug. Then he'd lead his master back down here and show him this hole, with the stone looking up from the bottom, as solid as the heart of the world. Alvin heard himself saying to his master, "You show me how to drink that and I'll drink it." It'd be pure pleasure to hear how Makepeace'd cuss himself blue at the sight of it.

Except now that he could show them how wrong they were to treat him like they did, Alvin knew it didn't matter in the long run whether he taught them a lesson or not. What mattered was Makepeace Smith really did need this well. Needed it bad enough to pay out a dowser's cost in free ironwork. Whether it was dug where Hank Dowser said or somewhere else, Alvin knew he had to dig it.

That would suit Alvin's pride even better, now he

thought of it. He'd come in with a bucket, just like Makepeace ordered him to—but from a well of his own choosing.

He looked around in the ruddy evening light, thinking where to start looking for a diggable spot. He heard Arthur Stuart pulling at the meadow grass, and the sound of birds having a church choir practice, they were so loud tonight.

Or maybe they were plain scared. Cause now he was looking around, Alvin could see that the Unmaker was lively tonight. By rights digging the first hole should've been enough to send it headlong, kept it off for days. Instead it followed him just out of sight, ever step he took as he hunted for the place to dig the true well. It was getting more and more like one of his nightmares, where nothing he did could make the Unmaker go away. It was enough to send a thrill of fear right through him, make him shiver in the warm spring air.

Alvin just shrugged off that scare. He knew the Unmaker wasn't going to touch him. For all the years of his life till now, the Unmaker'd tried to kill him by setting up accidents, like water icing up where he was bound to step, or eating away at a riverbank so he slipped in. Now and then the Unmaker even got some man or other to take a few swipes at Alvin, like Reverend Thrower or them Choc-Taw Reds. In all his life, outside his dreams, that Unmaker never did anything direct.

And he won't now either, Alvin told hisself. Just keep searching, so you can dig the *real* well. The false one didn't drive that old deceiver off, but the real one's bound to, and I won't see him shimmering at the edges of my vision for three months after that.

With that thought in mind, Alvin hunkered down

and kept his mind on searching for a break in the hidden shelf of stone.

How Alvin searched things out underground wasn't like *seeing*. It was more like he had another hand that skittered through the soil and rock as fast as a waterdrop on a hot griddle. Even though he'd never met him a doodlebug, he figured doodling couldn't be much different than how he done it, sending his bug scout along under the earth, feeling things out all the way. And if he *was* doodlebugging, then he had to wonder if folks was right who allowed as how it was the doodlebug's very *soul* that slithered under the ground, and there were tales about doodlebugs whose souls got lost and the doodler never said another word or moved a muscle till he finally died. But Alvin didn't let such tales scare him off from doing what he ought to. If there was a need for stone, he'd find him the natural breaks to make it come away without hardly chipping at it. If there was a need for water, he'd find him a way to dig on down to get it.

Finally he found him a place where the shelf of stone was thin and crumbled. The ground was higher here, the water deeper down, but what counted was he could get through the stone to it.

This new spot was halfway between the house and the smithy—which would be less convenient for Makepeace, but better for his wife Gertie, who had to use the same water. Alvin set to with a will, because it was getting on to dark, and he was determined to take no rest tonight until the work was done. Without even thinking about it he made up his mind to use his power like he used to back on his father's land. He never struck stone with his spade; it was like the earth turned to flour and fair

136

to jumped out of the hole instead of him having to heft it. If any grownup happened to see him right then they'd think they was likkered up or having a conniption fit, he dug so fast. But nobody was looking, except for Arthur Stuart. It was getting nightward, after all, and Al had no lantern, so nobody'd ever even notice he was there. He could use his knack tonight without fear of being found out.

From the house came the sound of shouting, loud but not clear enough for Alvin to make out the words.

"Mad," said Arthur Stuart. He was looking straight at the house, as steady as a dog on point.

"Can you hear what they're saying?" said Alvin. "Old Peg Guester always says you got ears like a dog, perk up at everything."

Arthur Stuart closed his eyes. "You got no right to starve that boy," he said.

Alvin like to laughed outright. Arthur was doing as perfect an imitation of Gertie Smith's voice as he ever heard.

"He's too big to thrash and I got to learn him," said Arthur Stuart.

This time he sounded just like Alvin's master. "I'll be," murmured Alvin.

Little Arthur went right on. "Either Alvin eats this plate of supper Makepeace Smith or you'll wear it on your head. I'd like to see you try it you old hag I'll break your arms."

Alvin couldn't help himself, he just laughed outright. "Consarn it if you ain't a perfect mockingbird, Arthur Stuart."

The little boy looked up at Alvin and a grin stole across his face. Down from the house come the sound of breaking crockery. Arthur Stuart started to laugh and run around in circles. "Break a dish, break a dish, break a dish!" he cried.

"If you don't beat all," said Alvin. "Now you tell me, Arthur, you didn't really understand all them things you just said, did you? I mean, you were just repeating what you heard, ain't that so?"

"Break a dish on his *head*!" Arthur screamed with laughter and fell over backward in the grass. Alvin laughed right along, but he couldn't take his eyes off the little boy. More to him than meets the eye, thought Alvin. Or else he's plain crazy.

From the other direction came another woman's voice, a full-throated call that floated over the moist darkening air. "Ar*thur!* Arthur *Stuart!*"

Arthur sat right up. "Mama," he said.

"That's right, that's Old Peg Guester calling," said Alvin.

"Go to bed," said Arthur.

"Just be careful she don't give you a bath first, boy, you're a mite grimy."

Arthur got up and started trotting off across the meadow, up to the path that led from the spring-house to the roadhouse where he lived. Alvin watched him out of sight, the little boy flapping his arms as he ran, like as if he was flying. Some bird, probably an owl, flew right alongside the boy half-way across the meadow, skimming along the ground like as if to keep him company. Not till Arthur was out of sight behind the springhouse did Alvin turn back to his labor.

In a few more minutes it was full dark, and the deep silence of night came quick after that. Even the dogs were quiet all through town. It'd be hours before the moon came up. Alvin worked on. He didn't have to see; he could feel how the well was going, the earth under his feet. Nor was it the Red man's seeing now, their gift for hearing the greenwood song. It was his own knack he was using, helping him feel his way deeper into the earth.

He knew he'd strike rock twice as deep this time. But when the spade caught up on big chunks of rock, it wasn't a smooth plate like it was at the spot Hank Dowser chose. The stones were crumbly and broke up, and with his knack Al hardly had to press his lever afore the stones flipped up as easy as you please, and he tossed them out the well like clods.

Once he dug through that layer, though, the ground got oozy underfoot. If he wasn't who he was, he'd've had to set the work aside and get help to dredge it out in the morning. But for Alvin it was easy enough. He tightened up the earth around the walls of the hole, so water couldn't seep in so fast. It wasn't spadework now. Alvin used a dredge to scoop up the mucky soil, and he didn't need no partner to hoist it out on a rope, either, he just heaved it up and his knack was such that each scoop of ooze clung together and landed neat as you please outside the well, just like he was flinging bunny rabbits out the hole.

Alvin was master here, that was sure, working miracles in this hole in the ground. You tell me I can't eat or drink till the well is dug, thinking you'll have me begging for a cup of water and pleading for you to let me go to bed. Well, you won't see such a thing. You'll have your well, with walls so solid they'll be drawing water here after your house and smithy have crumbled into dust.

But even as he felt the sweet taste of victory, he saw that the Unmaker was closer than it had ever come in years. It flickered and danced, and not just at the edges of his vision anymore. He could see it right in front of him, even in the darkness, he could see it clearer than ever in daylight, cause now he couldn't see nothing real to distract him.

It was scary, all of a sudden, just like the nightmares of his childhood, and for a while Alvin stood in the hole, all froze with fear, as water oozed up from below, making the ground under him turn to slime. Thick slime a hundred feet deep, he was sinking down, and the walls of the well were getting soft, too, they'd cave in on him and bury him, he'd drown trying to breathe muck into his lungs, he knew it, he could feel it cold and wet around his thighs, his crotch; he clenched his fists and felt mud ooze between his fingers, just like the nothingness in all his nightmares—

And then he came to himself, got control. Sure, he was up to his waist in mud, and if he was any other boy in such a case he might have wiggled himself down deeper and smothered hisself, trying to struggle out. But this was Alvin, not some ordinary boy, and he was safe as long as he wasn't booglied up by fear like a child caught in a bad dream. He just made the slime under his feet harden enough to hold his weight, then made the hard place float upward, lifting him out of the mud until he was standing on gravelly mud at the bottom of the well.

Easy as breaking a rat's neck. If that was all the Unmaker could think of doing, it might as well go on home. Alvin was a match for him, just like he was a match for Makepeace Smith and Hank Dowser, both. He dug on, dredged up, hoisted, flung, then bent to dredge again.

He was pretty near deep enough now, a good six feet lower than the stone shelf. Why, if he hadn't

140

firmed up the earthen sides of the well, it'd be full of water over his head already. Alvin took hold of the knotted rope he left dangling and walked up the wall, pulling himself hand over hand up the rope.

The moon was rising now, but the hole was so deep it wouldn't shine into the well until near moon-noon. Never mind. Into the pit Alvin dumped a barrowload of the stones he'd levered out only an hour before. Then he clambered down after it.

He'd been working rock with his knack since he was little, and he was never more sure-handed with it than tonight. With his bare hands he shaped the stone like soft clay, making it into smooth square blocks that he placed all around the walls of the well from the bottom up, braced firm against each other so that the pushing of soil and water wouldn't cave it in. Water would seep easily through the cracks in the stones, but the soil wouldn't, so the well would be clean almost from the start.

There wasn't enough stone from the well itself, of course; Alvin made three trips to the stream to load the barrow with water-smoothed rocks. Even though he was using his knack to make the work easier, it was late at night and weariness was coming on him. But he refused to pay attention. Hadn't he learned the Red man's knack for running on long after weariness should have claimed him? A boy who followed Ta-Kumsaw, running without a rest from Detroit to Eight-Face Mound, such a boy had no need to give in to a single night of well-digging, and never mind his thirst or the pain in his back and thighs and shoulders, and ache of his elbows and his knees.

At last, at last, it was done. The moon past zenith, his mouth tasting like a horsehair blanket, but it was done. He climbed on out of the hole, bracing himself

141

against the stone walls he'd just finished building. As he climbed he let go of his hold on the earth around the well, unsealed it, and the water, now tame, began to trickle noisily into the deep stone basin he'd built to hold it.

Still Alvin didn't go inside the house, didn't so much as walk to the stream and drink. His first taste of water would be from this well, just like Makepeace Smith had said. He'd stay here and wait until the well had reached its natural level, and then clear the water and draw up a bucket and carry it inside the house and drink a cup of it in front of his master. Afterward he'd take Makepeace Smith outside and show him the well Hank Dowser called for, the one Makepeace Smith had cuffed him for, and then point out the one where you could drop a bucket and it was splash, not clatter.

He stood on the lip of the well, imagining how Makepeace Smith would sputter, how he'd cuss. Then he sat down, just to ease his feet, picturing Hank Dowser's face when he saw what Al had done. Then he lay right down to ease his aching back, and closed his eyes for just a minute, so he didn't have to pay no heed to the fluttering shadows of unmaking that kept pestering him out the corners of his eyes.

8

Unmaker

Mistress Modesty was stirring. Peggy heard her breathing change rhythm. Then she came awake and sat up abruptly on her couch. At once Mistress Modesty looked for Peggy in the darkness of the room.

"Here I am," Peggy murmured.

"What has happened, my dear? Haven't you slept at all?"

"I dare not," said Peggy.

Mistress Modesty stepped onto the portico beside her. The breeze from the southwest billowed the damask curtains behind them. The moon was flirting with a cloud; the city of Dekane was a shifting pattern of roofs down the hill below them. "Can you see him?" asked Mistress Modesty.

"Not him," said Peggy. "I see his heartfire; I can see through his eyes, as he sees; I can see his futures. But himself, no, I can't see him."

"My poor dear. On such a marvelous night, to have to leave the Governor's Ball and watch over this faraway child in grave danger." It was Mistress Modesty's way of asking what the danger was without actually *asking*. This way Peggy could answer or not, and neither way would any offense be given or taken.

"I wish I could explain," said Peggy. "It's his enemy, the one with no face—"

Mistress Modesty shuddered. "No face! How ghastly."

"Oh, he has a face for *other* men. There was a minister once, a man who fancied himself a scientist. He saw the Unmaker, but could not see him truly, not as Alvin does. Instead he made up a manshape for him in his mind, and a name—called him 'the Visitor', and thought he was an angel."

"An angel!"

"I believe that when most of us see the Unmaker, we can't comprehend him, we haven't the strength of intellect for that. So our minds come as close as they can. Whatever shape represents naked destructive power, terrible and irresistible force, that is what we see. Those who *love* such evil power, they make themselves see the Unmaker as beautiful. Others, who hate and fear it, they see the worst thing in the world."

"What does your Alvin see?"

"I could never see it myself, it's so subtle; even looking through his eyes I wouldn't have noticed it, if *he* hadn't noticed it. I saw that he was seeing something, and only then did I understand what it was he saw. Think of it as—the feeling when you think you saw some movement out of the corner of your eye, only when you turn there's nothing there."

"Like someone always sneaking up behind you," said Mistress Modesty.

"Yes, exactly."

"And it's sneaking up on Alvin?"

"Poor boy, he doesn't realize that he's calling to

144

it. He has dug a deep black pit in his heart, just the sort of place where the Unmaker flows."

Mistress Modesty sighed. "Ah, my child, these things are all beyond me. I never had a knack; I can barely comprehend the things you do."

"You? No knack?" Peggy was amazed.

"I know—hardly anyone ever admits to not having one, but surely I'm not the only one."

"You misunderstand me, Mistress Modesty," said Peggy. "I was startled, not that you had no knack, but that you *thought* you had no knack. Of course you have one."

"Oh, but I don't mind not having one, my dear—"

"You have the knack of seeing potential beauty as if it were already there, and by seeing, you let it come to be."

"What a lovely idea," said Mistress Modesty.

"Do you doubt me?"

"I don't doubt that you believe what you say."

There was no point in arguing. Mistress Modesty believed her, but was afraid to believe. It didn't matter, though. What mattered was Alvin, finishing his second well. He had saved himself once; he thought the danger was over. Now he sat at the edge of the well, just to rest a moment; now he lay down. Didn't he see the Unmaker moving closer to him? Didn't he realize that his very sleepiness opened himself wide for the Unmaker to enter him?

"No!" whispered Peggy. "Don't sleep!"

"Ah," said Mistress Modesty. "You speak to him. Can he hear you?"

"Never," said Peggy. "Never a word."

"Then what can you do?"

"Nothing. Nothing I can think of."

145

"You told me you used his caul—"

"It's a part of his power, that's what I use. But even his knack can't send away what came at his own call. I never had the knowledge to fend off the Unmaker itself, anyway, even if I had a yard of his caulflesh, and not just a scrap of it."

Peggy watched in desperate silence as Alvin's eyes closed. "He sleeps."

"If the Unmaker wins, will he die?"

"I don't know. Perhaps. Perhaps he'll disappear, eaten away to nothing. Or perhaps the Unmaker will own him—"

"Can't you see the future, torch girl?"

"All paths lead into darkness, and I see no path emerging."

"Then it's over," whispered Mistress Modesty.

Peggy could feel something cold on her cheeks. Ah, of course: her own tears drying in the cool breeze.

"But if Alvin were awake, *he* could fend off this invisible enemy?" Mistress Modesty asked. "Sorry to bother you with questions, but if I know how it works, perhaps I can help you think of something."

"No, no, it's beyond us, we can only watch—" Yet even as Peggy rejected Mistress Modesty's suggestion, her mind leapt ahead to ways of using it. I must waken him. I don't have to fight the Unmaker, but if I waken him, then he can do his fighting for himself. Weak and weary though he is, he might still find a way to victory. At once Peggy turned and rushed back into her room, scrabbled through her top drawer until she found the carven box that held the caul.

"Should I leave?" Mistress Modesty had followed her.

"Stay with me," said Peggy. "Please, for company. for comfort, if I fail."

"You won't fail," said Mistress Modesty. "*He* won't fail, if he's the man you say he is."

Peggy barely heard her. she sat on the edge of her bed, searching in Alvin's heartfire for some way to waken him. Normally she could use his senses even when he slept, hearing what he heard, seeing his memory of the place around him. But now, with the Unmaker seeping in, his senses were fading. She could not trust them. Desperately she cast about for some other plan. A loud noise? Using what little was left of Alvin's sense of the life around him, she found a tree, then rubbed a tiny bit of the caul and tried—as she had seen Alvin do it—to picture in her mind how the wood in the branch would come apart. It was painfully slow—Alvin did it so quickly!—but at last she made it fall. Too late. He barely heard it. The Unmaker had undone so much of the air around him that the trembling of sound could not pass through it. Perhaps Alvin noticed; perhaps he came a bit closer to wakefulness. Perhaps not.

How can I waken him, when he is so insensible that nothing can disturb him? Once I held this caul as a ridgebeam tumbled toward him; I burned a childsize gap in it, so that the hair of his head wasn't even touched. Once a millstone fell toward his leg; I split it in half. Once his own father stood in a loft, pitchfork in hand, driven by the Unmaker's madness until he had decided to murder his own most-beloved son; I brought Taleswapper down the hill to him, distracting the father from his dark purpose and driving off the Unmaker.

How? How did Taleswapper's coming drive off the Destroyer? Because he would have seen the

147

hateful beast and given the cry against it, that's why the Unmaker left when Taleswapper arrived. Taleswapper isn't anywhere near Alvin now, but surely there's someone I can waken and draw down the hill; someone filled with love and goodness, so that the Unmaker must flee before him.

With agonizing fear she withdrew from Alvin's heartfire even as the blackness of the Unmaker threatened to drown it, and searched in the night for another heartfire, someone she could waken and send to him in time. Yet even as she searched, she could sense in Alvin's heartfire a certain lightening, a hint of shadows within shadows, not the utter emptiness she had seen before where his future ought to be. If Alvin had any chance, it was from her searching. Even if she found someone, she had no notion how to waken them. But she would find a way, or the Crystal City would be swallowed up in the flood that came because of Alvin's foolish, childish rage.

9

Redbird

Alvin woke up hours later, the moon low in the west, the first scant light appearing in the east. He hadn't meant to sleep. But he was tired, after all, and his work was done, so of course he couldn't close his eyes and hope to stay awake. There was still time to take a bucketful of water and carry it inside.

Were his eyes open even now? The sky he could see, light grey to the left, light grey to the right. But where were the trees? Shouldn't they have been moving gently in the morning breeze, just at the fringes of his vision? For that matter, there was no breeze; and beyond the sight of his eyes, and touch on his skin, there were other things he could not feel. The green music of the living forest. It was gone; no murmur of life from the sleeping insects in the grass, no rhythm of the heartbeats of the dawn-browsing deer. No birds roosting in the trees, waiting for the sun's heat to bring out the insects.

Dead. Unmade. The forest was gone.

Alvin opened his eyes.

Hadn't they already been open?

Alvin opened his eyes again, and still he couldn't

149

see; without closing them, he opened them still again, and each time the sky seemed darker. No, not darker, simply farther away, rushing up and away from him, like as if he was falling into a pit so deep that the sky itself got lost.

Alvin cried out in fear, and opened his already-open eyes and saw:

The quivering air of the Unmaker, pressing down on him, poking itself into his nostrils, between his fingers, into his ears.

He couldn't feel it, no sir, except that he knew what *wasn't* there now; the outermost layers of his skin, wherever the Unmaker touched, his own body was breaking apart, the tiniest bits of him dying, drying, flaking away.

"No!" he shouted. The shout didn't make a sound. Instead, the Unmaker whipped inside his mouth, down into his lungs, and he couldn't close his teeth hard enough, his lips tight enough to keep that slimy uncreator from slithering on inside him, eating him away from the inside out.

He tried to heal himself the way he done with his leg that time the millstone broke it clean in half. But it was like the old story Taleswapper told him. He couldn't build things up half so fast as the Unmaker could tear them down. For every place he healed, there was a thousand places wrecked and lost. He was a-going to die, he was half-gone already, and it wouldn't be just death, just losing his flesh and living on in the spirit, the Unmaker meant to eat him body and spirit both alike, his mind and his flesh together.

A splash. He heard a splashing sound. It was the most welcome thing he ever heard in his life, to hear a sound at all. It meant that there *was* something beyond the Unmaker that surrounded and filled him.

Alvin heard the sound echo and ring inside his own memory, and with that to cling to, with that touch of the real world there to hang on to, Alvin opened his eyes.

This time for real, he knew, cause he saw the sky again with its proper fringe of trees. And there was Gertie Smith, Makepeace's missus, standing over him with a bucket in her hands.

"I reckon this is the first water from this well," she said.

Alvin opened his mouth, and felt cool moist air come inside. "Reckon so," he whispered.

"I never would've thought you could dig it all out and line it proper with stones, all in one night," she said. "That mixup boy, Arthur Stuart, he come to the kitchen where I was making breakfast biscuits, and he told me your well was done. I had to come and see."

"He gets up powerful early," said Alvin.

"And you stay up powerful late," said Gertie. "If I was a man your size I'd give my husband a proper licking, Al, prentice or no."

"I just did what he asked."

"I'm certain you did, just like I'm certain he wanted you to excavate that there circle of stone off by the smithy, am I right?" She cackled with delight. "That'll show the old coot. Sets such a store by that dowser, but his own prentice has a better dowsing knack than that old fraud—"

For the first time Alvin realized that the hole he dug in anger was like a signboard telling folks he had more than a hoof-knack in him. "Please, ma'am," he said.

"Please what?"

"My knack ain't dowsing, ma'am, and if you start saying so, I'll never get no peace."

She eyed him cool and steady. "If you ain't got the dowser's knack, boy, tell me how come there's clear water in this well you dug."

Alvin calculated his lie. "The dowser's stick dipped here, too, I saw it, and so when the first well struck stone, I tried here."

Gertie had a suspicious nature. "Do you reckon you'd say the same if Jesus was standing here judging your eternal soul depending on the truth of what you say?"

"Ma'am, I reckon if Jesus was here, I'd be asking forgiveness for my sins, and I wouldn't care two hoots about any old well."

She laughed again, cuffed him lightly on the shoulder. "I like your dowsing story. You just happened to be watching old Hank Dowser. Oh, that's a good one. I'll tell that tale to everybody, see if I don't."

"Thank you, ma'am."

"Here. Drink. You deserve first swallow from the first bucket of clear water from this well."

Alvin knew that the custom was for the owner to get first drinks. But she was offering, and he was so dry he couldn't have spit two bits' worth even if you paid him five bucks an ounce. So he set the bucket to his lips and drank, letting it splash out onto his shirt.

"I'd wager you're hungry, too," she said.

"More tired than hungry, I think," said Alvin.

"Then come inside to sleep."

He knew he should, but he could see the Unmaker not far off, and he was afeared to sleep again, that was the truth. "Thank you kindly, Ma'am, but anyhow, I'd like to be off by myself a few minutes."

"Suit yourself," she said, and went on inside.

The morning breeze chilled him as it dried off the water he spilled on his shirt. Was his ravishment by the Unmaker only a dream? He didn't think so. He was awake right enough, and it was real, and if Gertie Smith hadn't come along and dunked that bucket in the well, he would've been unmade. The Unmaker wasn't hiding out no more. He wasn't sneaking in backways nor roundabout. No matter where he looked, there it was, shimmering in the greyish morning light.

For some reason the Unmaker picked this morning for a face-to-face. Only Alvin didn't know how he was supposed to fight. If digging a well and building it up so fine wasn't making enough to drive off his enemy, he didn't know what else to do. The Unmaker wasn't like the men he wrestled with in town. The Unmaker had nothing he could take ahold of.

One thing was sure. Alvin'd never have a night of sleep again if he didn't take this Unmaker down somehow and wrestle him into the dirt.

I'm supposed to be your master, Alvin said to the Unmaker. So tell me, Unmaker, how do I undo *you*, when all you are is Undoing? Who's going to teach me how to win this battle, when you can sneak up on me in my sleep, and I don't have the faintest idea how to get to you?

As he spoke these words inside his head, Alvin walked to the edge of the woods. The Unmaker backed away from him, always out of reach. Al knew without looking that it also closed up behind him, so it had him on all sides.

This is the middle of the uncut wood where I ought to feel most at home, but the greensong, it's gone silent here, and all around me is my enemy from birth, and me here with no plan at all.

The Unmaker, though, he had a plan. He didn't need to waste no time a-dithering about what to do, Alvin found that out real quick.

Cause while Alvin was a-standing there in the cool heavy breeze of a summer morning, the air suddenly went chill, and blamed if snowflakes didn't start to fall. Right down on the green-leaf trees they came, settling on the tall thick grass between them. Thick and cold it piled up, not the wet heavy flakes of a warm snow, but the tiny icy crystals of a deep winter blizzard blow. Alvin shivered.

"You can't do this," he said.

But his eyes weren't closed *now*, he knew that. This wasn't no half-asleep dream. This was real snow, and it was so thick and cold that the branches of summer-green trees were snapping, the leaves were tearing off and falling to the ground in a tinkle of broken ice. And Alvin himself was like to freeze himself clear to death if he didn't get out of there somehow.

He started to walk back the way he came, but the snow was coming down so thick he couldn't see more than five or six feet ahead of him, and he couldn't feel his way because the Unmaker had deadened the greensong of the living woods. Pretty soon he wasn't walking, he was running. Only he didn't run sure-footed like Ta-Kumsaw taught him; he ran as noisy and stupid as any oaf of a White man, and like most Whites would've, he slipped on a patch of ice-covered stone and sprawled out face down across a reach of snow.

Snow that caught up in his mouth and nose and into his ears, snow that clung between his fingers, just like the slime last night, just like the Unmaker in his dream, and he choked and sputtered and cried out—

"I know it's a lie!"

His voice was swallowed up in the wall of snow.

"It's summer!" he shouted.

His jaw ached from the cold and he knew it'd hurt too much to speak again, but still he screamed through numb lips, "I'll make you stop!"

And then he realized that he could never make anything out of the Unmaker, could never make the Unmaker do or be anything because it was only Undoing and Unbeing. It wasn't the Unmaker he needed to call to, it was all the living things around him, the trees, the grass, the earth, the air itself. It was the greensong that he needed to restore.

He grabbed ahold of that idea and used it, spoke again, his voice scarce more than a whisper now, but he called to them, and not in anger.

"Summer," he whispered.

"Warm air!" he said.

"Leaves green!" he shouted. "Hot wind out of the southwest. Thunderheads in the afternoon, mist in the morning, sunlight hotting it up, burning off the fog!"

Did it change, just a little? Did the snowfall slacken? Did the drifts on the ground melt lower, the heaps on the treelimbs tumble off, baring more of the branch?

' "It's a hot morning, dry!" he cried. "Rain may drift in later like the gift of the Wise Men, coming from a long way off, but for now sunlight beating

155

on the leaves, waking you up, you're *growing*, putting out leaves, that's right! That's right!''

There was gladness in his voice because the snowfall was just a spatter of rain now, the snow on the ground was melted back to patches here and there, the broke-off leaves were sprouting on the branch again as quick as militia in a doubletime march.

And in the silence after his last shout, he heard birdsong.

Song like he'd never heard before. He didn't know this bird, this sweet melody that changed with every whistle and never played the same tune again. It was a weaving song, but one whose pattern you couldn't find, so you couldn't ever sing it again, but you also couldn't ravel it, spin it out and break it down. It was all of one piece, all of one single Making, and Alvin knew that if he could just find the bird with that song in his throat he'd be safe. His victory would be complete.

He ran, and now the greensong of the forest was with him, and his feet found the right places to step without him looking. He followed that song until he came to the clearing where the singing was.

Perched on an old log with a patch of snow still in the northwest shadow—a redbird. And sitting in front of that log, almost nose to nose as he listened to it sing—Arthur Stuart.

Alvin walked around the two of them real slow, walking a clean circle before he come much closer. Arthur Stuart like to never noticed he was there, he never took his eyes off that bird. The sunlight dazzled on the two of them, but neither bird nor boy so much as blinked. Alvin didn't say nothing, either. Just like Arthur Stuart, he was all caught up in the redbird song.

156

It wasn't no different from all the other redbirds, the thousand scarlet songbirds Alvin had seen since he was little. Except that from its throat came music that no other bird had ever sung before. This wasn't *a* redbird. Nor was it *the* redbird. There was no single bird had some gift the other redbirds lacked. It was just Redbird, the one picked for this moment to speak in the voice of all the birds, to sing the song of all the singers, so that this boy could hear.

Alvin knelt down on the new-grown grass not three feet from Redbird, and listened to its song. He knew from what Lolla-Wossiky once told him that Redbird's song was all the stories of the Red man, everything they ever done that was worth doing. Alvin halfway hoped to understand that ancient tale, or at least to hear how Redbird told of things that he took part in. The Prophet Lolla-Wossiky walking on water; Tippy-Canoe River all scarlet with Red folks' blood; Ta-Kumsaw standing with a dozen musketballs in him, still crying out for his men to stand, to fight, to drive the White thieves back.

But the sense of the song eluded him no matter how he listened. He might run the forest with a Red man's legs and hear the greensong with a Red man's ears, but Redbird's song wasn't meant for him. The saying told the truth: No one girl gets all the suitors, and no boy gets all the knacks. There was much that Alvin could do already, and much ahead of him to learn, but there'd be far more that was always out of his ken, and Redbird's song was part of that.

Yet Alvin was sure as shucks that Redbird wasn't here by accident. Come like this at the end of his first face-to-face with the Unmaker, Redbird had to have some purpose. He had to get some answers out of Redbird's song.

157

Alvin was just about to speak, just about to ask the question burning in him ever since he first learned what his destiny might be. But it wasn't his voice that broke into Redbird's song. It was Arthur Stuart's.

"I don't know days coming up," said the mix-up boy. His voice was like music and the words were clearer than any Alvin ever heard that three-year-old say before. "I only know days gone."

It took a second for Alvin to hitch himself to what was going on here. What Arthur said was the answer to Alvin's question. Will I ever be a Maker like the torch girl said? That was what Alvin would've asked, and Arthur's words were the answer.

But not Arthur Stuart's own answer, that was plain. The little boy no more understood what he was saying then he did when he was mimicking Makepeace's and Gertie's quarrel last night. He was giving Redbird's answer. Translating from birdsong into speech that Alvin's ears were fit to understand.

Alvin knew now that he'd asked the wrong question. He didn't need Redbird to tell him he was supposed to be a Maker—he knowed that firm and sure years ago, and knew it in spite of all doubts. The real question wasn't whether, it was *how* to be a Maker.

Tell me how.

Redbird changed his song to a soft and simple tune, more like normal birdsong, quite different from the thousand-year-old Red man's tale that he'd been singing up to now. Alvin didn't understand the sense of it, but he knew all the same what it was about. It was the song of Making. Over and over, the same tune repeating, only a few moments of it–but they were blinding in their brightness, a song so true that Alvin saw it with his eyes, felt it from his lips to his groin, tasted it and smelled it. The song of Making, and it was his own song, he knew it from how sweet it tasted on his tongue.

And when the song was at its peak, Arthur Stuart spoke again in a voice that was hardly human it piped so sharp, it sang so clear.

"The Maker is the one who is part of what he makes," said the mixup boy.

Alvin wrote the words in his heart, even though he didn't understand them. Because he knew that someday he *would* understand them, and when he did, he would have the power of the ancient Makers who built the Crystal City. He would understand, and use his power, and find the Crystal City and build it once again.

The Maker is the one who is part of what he makes.

Redbird fell silent. Stood still, head cocked; and then became, not Redbird, but any old bird with scarlet feathers. Off it flew.

Arthur Stuart watched the bird out of sight. Then he called out after it in his own true childish voice, "Bird! Fly bird!" Alvin knelt beside the boy, weak from the night's work, the grey dawn's fear, this bright day's birdsong.

"I flied," said Arthur Stuart. For the first time, it seemed, he took notice Alvin was there, and turned to him.

"Did you now?" whispered Alvin, reluctant to destroy the child's dream by telling him that folks don't fly.

"Big blackbird tote me," said Arthur. "Fly and fly." Then Arthur reached up his hands and pressed in on Alvin's cheeks. "Maker," he said. Then he laughed and laughed with joy.

So Arthur wasn't just a mimic. He really understood Redbird's song, some of it, at least. Enough to know the name of Alvin's destiny.

"Don't you tell anybody," Alvin said. "I won't tell anybody you can talk to birds, and you don't tell nobody I'm a Maker. Promise?"

Arthur's face grew serious. "Don't talk birds," he said. 'Birds talk *me*." And then: "I *flied*."

"I believe you," Alvin said.

"I beeve *you*," said Arthur. Then he laughed again.

Alvin stood up and so did Arthur. Al took him by the hand. "Let's go home," he said.

He took Arthur to the roadhouse, where Old Peg Guester was full of scold at the mixup boy for running off and bothering folks all morning. But it was a loving scold, and Arthur grinned like an idiot at the voice of the woman he called Mama. As the door closed with Arthur Stuart on the other side, Alvin told himself, I'm going to tell that boy what he done for me. Someday I'll tell him what this meant.

Alvin came home by way of the springhouse path and headed on down toward the smithy, where Makepeace was no doubt angry at him for not being ready for work, even though he dug a well all night.

The well. Alvin found himself standing by the hole that he had dug as a monument to Hank Dowser, with the white stone bright in the sunlight, bright and cruel as scornful laughter.

In that moment Alvin knew why the Unmaker came to him that night. Not because of the true well that he dug. Not because he had used his knack to hold the water back, not because he had softened the stone and bent it to his need. It was because he had dug that first hole down to the stone for one reason only—to make Hank Dowser look the fool.

To punish him? Yes sir, to make him a laughing-stock to any man who saw the stone-bottomed well on the spot that Hank had marked. It would destroy him, take away his name as a dowser—and unfairly so, because he *was* a good dowser who got hisself fooled by the lay of the land. Hank made an honest mistake, and Al had got all set to punish him as if he was a fool, which surely he was not.

Tired as he was, weak from labor and the battle with the Unmaker, Alvin didn't waste a minute. He fetched the spade from where it lay by the working well, then stripped off his shirt and set to work. When he dug this false well, it was a work of evil, to unmake an honest man for no reason better than spite. Filling it in, though, was a Maker's work. Since it was daylight, Alvin couldn't even use his knack to help—he did full labor on it till he thought he was so tired he might just die.

It was noon, and him without supper or breakfast either one, but the well was filled right up, the turves set back on so they'd grow back, and if you didn't look close you'd never know there'd been a hole at all. Alvin *did* use his knack a little, since no one was about, to weave the grassroots back together, knit them into the ground, so there'd be no dead patches to mark the spot.

All the time, though, what burned worse than the sun on his back or the hunger in his belly was his own shame. He was so busy last night being angry and thinking how to makc a fool of Hank Dowscr that it never once occurred to him to do the right thing and use his knack to break right through the shelf of stone in the very spot Hank picked. No one would've known save Alvin hisself that there'd be aught wrong with the place. That would've been the Christian thing, the charitable thing to do. When a man slaps your face, you answer by shaking his hand, that's what Jesus said to do, and Alvin just plain wasn't listening, Alvin was too cussed proud.

That's what called the Unmaker to me, thought Alvin. I could've used my knack to build up, and I used it to tear down. Well, never again, never again, never again. He made that promise three times, and even though it was a silent promise and no one'd ever know, he'd keep it better than any oath he might take before a judge or even a minister.

Well, too late now. If he'd thought of this before Gertie ever saw the false well or drew water from the true, he might've filled up the other well and made this one good after all. But now she'd seen the stone, and if he dug through it then all his secrets would be out. And once you've drunk water from a good new well, you can't never fill it up till it runs dry on its own. To fill up a living well is to beg for drouth and cholera to dog you all the days of your life.

He'd undone all he could. You can be sorry, and you can be forgiven, but you can't call back the futures that your bad decisions lost. He didn't need no philosopher to tell him that.

Makepeace wasn't a-hammering in the forge, and there wasn't no smoke from the smithy chimney, either. Must be Makepeace was up at the house, doing some chores there, Alvin figured. So he put the spade away back in the smithy and then headed on toward the house.

Halfway there, he come to the good well, and there was Makepeace Smith setting on the low wall of footing stones Al had laid down to be foundation for the wellhouse.

"Morning, Alvin," said the master.

"Morning, sir," said Alvin.

"Dropped me the tin and copper bucket right down to the bottom here. You must've dug like the devil hisself, boy, to get it so deep."

"Didn't want it to run dry."

"And lined it with stone already," said the smith. "It's a wonderment, I say."

"I worked hard and fast."

"You also dug in the right place, I see."

Alvin took a deep breath. "The way I figure it, sir, I dug right where the dowser said to dig."

"I saw another hole just yonder," said Makepeace Smith. "Stone as thick and hard as the devil's hoof all along the bottom. You telling me you don't aim for folks to guess why you dug there?"

"I filled that old hole up," said Alvin. "I wish I'd never dug such a well. I don't want nobody telling stories on Hank Dowser. There was water there, right enough, and no dowser in the world could've guessed about the stone."

"Except you," said Makepeace.

"I ain't no dowser, sir," said Alvin, and he told the lie again: "I just saw that his wand dipped over here, too."

Makepeace Smith shook his head, a grin just creeping out across his face. "My wife told me that tale already, and I like to died a-laughing at it. I cuffed your head for saying he was wrong. You telling me now you want him to get the credit?"

"He's a true dowser," said Alvin. "And I *ain't* no

163

dowser, sir, so I reckon since he *is* one, he ought to get the name for it."

Makepeace Smith drew up the copper bucket, put it to his lips, and drank a few swallows. Then he tipped back his head and poured the rest of the water straight onto his face and laughed out loud. "That's the sweetest water I ever drunk in my life, I swear."

It wasn't the same as promising to go along with his story and let Hank Dowser think it was his well, but Al knew it was the best he'd get from his master. "If it's all right, sir," said Al, "I'm a mite hungry."

"Yes, go eat, you've earned it."

Alvin walked by him. The smell of new water rose up from the well as he passed.

Makepeace Smith spoke again behind him. "Gertie tells me you took first swallow from the well."

Al turned around, fearing trouble now. "I did, sir, but not till she give it to me."

Makepeace studied on that notion awhile, as if he was deciding whether to make it reason for punishing Al or not. "Well," he finally said, "well, that's just like her, but I don't mind. There's still enough of that first dip in the wooden bucket for me to save a few swallows for Hank Dowser. I promised him a drink from the first bucket, and I'll keep my word when he comes back around."

"When he comes, sir," said Alvin, "and I hope you won't mind, but I think I'd like it best and so would he if I just didn't happen to be at home, if you see what I mean. I don't think he cottoned to me much."

The smith eyed him narrowly. "If this is just a way for you to get a few hours off work when that

164

dowser comes on back, why"—he broke into a grin—"why, I reckon that you've earned it with last night's labor."

"Thank you sir," said Alvin.

"You heading back to the house?"

"Yes sir."

"Well, I'll take these tools and put them away— you carry this bucket to the missus. She's expecting it. A lot less way to tote the water than the stream. I got to thank Hank Dowser special for choosing this very exact spot." The smith was still chuckling to himself at his wit when Alvin reached the house.

Gertie Smith took the bucket, set Alvin down, and near filled him to the brim with hot fried bacon and good greasy biscuits. It was so much food that Al had to beg her to stop. "We've already finished one pig," said Alvin. "No need to kill another just for my breakfast."

"Pigs are just corn on the hoof," said Gertie Smith, "and you worked two hogs' worth last night, I'll say that."

Belly full and belching, Alvin climbed the ladder into the loft over the kitchen, stripped off his clothes, and burrowed into the blankets on his bed.

The Maker is the one who is part of what he makes.

Over and over he whispered the words to himself as he went to sleep. He had no dreams or troubles, and slept clear through till suppertime, and then again all night till dawn.

When he woke up in the morning, just before dawn, there was a faint grey scarce brighter than moonlight sifting into the house through the windows. Hardly none of it got up into the loft where Alvin lay, and instead of springing up bright like he

165

did most mornings, he felt logey from sleep and a little sore from his labors. So he lay there quiet, a faint sort of birdsong chirping in the back of his mind. He didn't think on the phrase Arthur Stuart told him from Redbird's song. Instead he got to wondering how things happened yesterday. Why did hard winter turn to summertime again, just from him shouting?

"Summer," he whispered. "Warm air, leaves green." What was it about Alvin that when he said *summer*, summer came? Didn't always work that way, for sure—never when he was a-working the iron or slipping through stone to mend or break it. Then he had to hold the shape of it firm in his mind, understand the way things lined up, find the natural cracks and creases, the threads of the metal or the grain of the rock. And when he was a-healing, that was so hard it took his whole mind to find how the body ought to be, and mend it. Things were so small, so hard to see—well, not *see*, but whatever it was he did. Sometimes he had to work so hard to understand the way things were inside.

Inside, down deep, so small and fine, and always the deepest secrets of the way things worked skittered away like roaches when you bring a lamp into the room, always getting smaller, forming themselves up in strange new ways. Was there some particle that was smallest of all? Some place at the heart of things where what he saw was real, instead of just being made up out of lots of smaller pieces, and them out of smaller pieces still?

Yet he hadn't understood how the Unmaker made winter. So how did his desperate cries make the summer come back?

How can I be a Maker if I can't even guess how I do what I do?

The light came stronger from outside, shining through the wavering glass of the windows, and for a moment Alvin thought he saw the light like little balls flying so *fast*, that they was hit with a stick or shot from a gun, only even faster than that, bouncing around, most of them getting stuck in the tiny cracks of the wooden walls or the floor or the ceiling, so only a precious few got up into the loft where they got captured by Alvin's eyes.

Then that moment passed, and the light was just fire, pure fire, drifting into the room like the gentle waves washing against the shore of Lake Mizogan, and wherever they passed, the waves turned things warm—the wood of the walls, the massive kitchen table, the iron of the stove—so that they all quivered, they all danced with life. Only Alvin could see it, only Alvin knew how the whole room awoke with the day.

That fire from the sun, that's what the Unmaker hates most. The life it makes. Put that fire out, that's what the Unmaker says inside himself. Put all fires out, turn all water into ice, the whole world smooth with ice, the whole sky black and cold like night. And to oppose the Unmaker's desire, one lone Maker who can't do right even when he's digging a well.

The Maker is the one who is part of—part of what? What do I make? How am I part of it? When I work the iron, am I part of the iron? When I shiver stone, am I part of the stone? It makes no sense, but I got to make sense of it or I'll lose my war with the Unmaker. I could fight him all my days, every way I know how, and when I died the world would be farther along his downhill road than it was when I got born. There's got to be some secret, some key to everything, so I can build it all at once. Got to find that key, that's all, find the secret, and then I can speak a word and the Unmaker will shy back and cower and give up and die, maybe even die, so that life and light go on forever and don't fade.

Alvin heard Gertie begin to stir in the bedroom, and one of the children uttered a soft cry, the last noise before waking. Alvin flexed and stretched and felt the sweet delicious pain of sore muscles waking up, getting set for a day at the forge, a day at the fire.

10

Goodwife

Peggy did not sleep as long or as well as Alvin. His battle was over; he could sleep a victor's sleep. For her, though, it was the end of peace.

It was still midafternoon when Peggy tossed herself awake on the smooth linen sheets of her bed in Mistress Modesty's house. She felt exhausted; her head hurt. She wore only her shift, though she didn't remember undressing. She remembered hearing Redbird singing, watching Arthur Stuart interpret the song. She remembered looking into Alvin's heartfire, seeing all his futures restored to him—but she still did not find herself in any of them. Then her memory stopped. Mistress Modesty must have undressed her, put her to bed with the sun already nearing noon.

She rolled over; the sheet clung to her, and then her back went cold from sweat. Alvin's victory was won; the lesson was learned; the Unmaker would not find another such opening again. She saw no danger in Alvin's future, not soon. The Unmaker would doubtless lie in wait for another time, or return to working through his human servants. Perhaps the Visitor would return to Reverend Thrower,

169

or some other soul with a secret hunger for evil would receive the Unmaker as a welcome teacher. But that wasn't the danger, not the immediate danger, Peggy knew.

For as long as Alvin had no notion how to be a Maker or what to do with his power, then it made no difference how long they kept the Unmaker at bay. The Crystal City would never be built. And it must be built, or Alvin's life—and Peggy's life, devoted to helping him—both would be in vain.

It seemed so clear now to Peggy, coming out of a feverish exhausted sleep. Alvin's labor was to prepare himself, to master his own human frailties. If there was some knowledge somewhere in the world about the art of Making, or the science of it, Alvin would have no chance to learn it. The smithy was his school, the forge his master, teaching him— what?—to change other men only by persuasion and long-suffering, gentleness and meekness, unfeigned love and kindness. Someone else, then, would have to acquire that pure knowledge which would raise Alvin up to greatness.

I am done with all my schooling in Dekane.

So many lessons, and I have learned them all, Mistress Modesty. All so I would be ready to bear the title you taught me was the finest any lady could aspire to.

Goodwife.

As her mother had been called Goody Guester all these years, and other women Goody this or Goody that, any woman could have the name. But few deserved it. Few there were who inspired others to call her by the name in full: Goodwife, not just Goody; the way that Mistress Modesty was never called Missus. It would demean her name to be touched by a diminished, a common title.

Peggy got up from the bed. Her head swam for a moment; she waited, then got up. Her feet padded on the wooden floor. She walked softly, but she knew she would be heard; already Mistress Modesty would be coming up the stairs.

Peggy stopped at the mirror and looked at herself. Her hair was tousled by sleep, stringy with sweat. Her face was imprinted, red and white, with the creases of the pillowcase. Yet she saw there the face that Mistress Modesty had taught her how to see.

"Our handiwork," said Mistress Modesty.

Peggy did not turn. She knew her mentor would be there.

"A woman should know that she is beautiful," said Mistress Modesty. "Surely God gave Eve a single piece of glass, or flat polished silver, or at least a still pool to show her what it was that Adam saw."

Peggy turned and kissed Mistress Modesty on the cheek. "I love what you've made of me," she said.

Mistress Modesty kissed her in return, but when they drew apart, there were tears in the older woman's eyes. "And now I shall lose your company."

Peggy wasn't used to others guessing what *she* felt, especially when she didn't realize that she had already made the decision.

"Will you?" asked Peggy.

"I've taught you all I can," said Mistress Modesty, "but I know after last night that you need things that I never dreamed of, because you have work to do that I never thought that anyone could do."

171

"I meant only to be Goodwife to Alvin's Goodman."

"For me that was the beginning and the end," said Mistress Modesty.

Peggy chose her words to be true, and therefore beautiful, and therefore good. "Perhaps all that some men need from a woman is for her to be loving and wise and careful, like a field of flowers where he can play the butterfly, drawing sweetness from her blossoms."

Mistress Modesty smiled. "How kindly you describe me."

"But Alvin has a sturdier work to do, and what he needs is not a beautiful woman to be fresh and loving for him when his work is done. What he needs is a woman who can heft the other end of his burden."

"Where will you go?"

Peggy answered before she realized that she knew the answer. "Philadelphia, I think."

Mistress Modesty looked at her in surprise, as if to say, You've already decided? Tears welled in her eyes.

Peggy rushed to explain. "The best universities are there—free ones, that teach all there is to know, not the crabbed religious schools of New England or the effete schools for lordlings in the South."

"This isn't sudden," said Mistress Modesty. "You've been planning this for long enough to find out where to go."

"It *is* sudden, but perhaps I *was* planning, without knowing it. I've listened to others talk, and now there it is already in my mind, all sorted out, the decision made. There's a school for women there, but what matters is the libraries. I have no formal schooling, but somehow I'll persuade them to let me in."

"It won't take much persuasion," Mistress Modesty said, "if you arrive with a letter from the governor of Suskwahenny. And letters from other men who trust my judgment well enough."

Peggy was not surprised that Mistress Modesty still intended to help her, even though Peggy had determined so suddenly, so ungracefully to leave. And Peggy had no foolish notion of pridefully trying to do without such help. "Thank you, Mistress Modesty!"

"I've never known a woman—or a man, for that matter—with such ability as yours. Not your knack, remarkable as it is; I don't measure a person by such things. But I fear that you are wasting yourself on this boy in Hatrack River. How could any man deserve all that you've sacrificed for him?"

"Deserving it—that's his labor. Mine is to have the knowledge when he's ready to learn it."

Mistress Modesty was crying in earnest now. She still smiled—for she had taught herself that love must always smile, even in grief—but the tears flowed down her cheeks. "Oh, Peggy, how could you have learned so well, and yet make such a mistake?"

A mistake? Didn't Mistress Modesty trust her judgment, even now? " 'A woman's wisdom is her gift to women,' " Peggy quoted. " 'Her beauty is her gift to men. Her love is her gift to God.' "

Mistress Modesty shook her head as she listened to her own maxim from Peggy's lips. "So why do you intend to inflict your wisdom on this poor unfortunate man you say you love?"

"Because some men are great enough that they can love a whole woman, and not just a part of her."

"Is *he* such a man?"

How could Peggy answer? "He will be, or he won't have me."

Mistress Modesty paused for a moment, as if trying to find a beautiful way to tell a painful truth. "I always taught you that if you become completely and perfectly yourself, then good men will be drawn to you and love you. Peggy, let us say this man has great needs—but if you must become something that is *not* you in order to supply him, then you will not be perfectly yourself, and he will *not* love you. Isn't that why you left Hatrack River in the first place, so he would love you for yourself, and not for what you did for him?"

"Mistress Modesty, I want him to love me, yes. But I love the work he must accomplish even more than that. What I am today would be enough for the man. What I will go and do tomorrow is not for the man, it is for his work."

"But—" began Mistress Modesty.

Peggy raised an eyebrow and smiled slightly. Mistress Modesty nodded and did not interrupt.

"If I love his work more than I love the man, then to be perfectly myself, I must do what his work requires of me. Won't I, then, be even more beautiful?"

"To me, perhaps," said Mistress Modesty. "Few men have vision clear enough for *that* subtle beauty."

"He loves his work more than he loves his life. Won't he, then, love the woman who shares in it more than a woman who is merely beautiful?"

"You may be right," said Mistress Modesty, "for I have never loved work more than I have loved the person doing it, and I have never known a man who

174

truly loved his work more than his own life. All that I have taught you is true in the world I know. If you pass from my world into another one, I can no longer teach you anything."

"Maybe I can't be a perfect woman and also live my life as it must be lived."

"Or perhaps, Mistress Margaret, even the best of the world is not fit to recognize a perfect woman, and so will accept me as a fair counterfeit, while you pass by unknown."

That was more than Peggy could bear. She cast aside decorum and threw her arms around Mistress Modesty and kissed her and cried, assuring her that there was nothing counterfeit about her. But when all the weeping was done, nothing had changed. Peggy was finished in Dekane, and by next morning her trunk was packed.

Everything she had in the world was a gift from Mistress Modesty, except for the box Oldpappy gave her long ago. Yet what was in that box was a heavier burden by far than any other thing that Peggy carried.

She sat in the northbound train, watching the mountains drift by outside her east-facing window. It wasn't all that long ago that Whitley Physicker had brought her to Dekane in his carriage. Dekane had seemed the grandest place at first; at the time it seemed to her that she was discovering the world by coming here. Now she knew that the world was far too large for one person to discover it. She was leaving a very small place and going to another very small place, and perhaps from there to other small places. The same size heartfires blazed in every city, no brighter for having so much company.

I left Hatrack River to be free of you, Prentice

175

Alvin. Instead I found a larger, far more entangling net outside. Your work is larger than yourself, larger than me, and because I know of it I'm bound to help. If I didn't, I'd be a vile person in my own eyes.

So if you end up loving me or not, that doesn't matter all that much. Oh, yes, to *me* it matters, but the course of the world won't change one way or the other. What matters is that we both prepare you to do your work. Then if love comes, then if you can play Goodman to my Goodwife, we'll take that as an unlooked-for blessing and be glad of it as long as we can.

11

Wand

It was a week before Hank Dowser found his way back to Hatrack River. A miserable week with no profit in it, because try as he would he couldn't find decent dry ground for them folks west of town to dig their cellar. "It's all wet ground," he said. "I can't help it if it's all watery."

But they held him responsible just the same. Folks are like that. They act like they thought the dowser *put* the water where it sets, instead of just pointing to it. Same way with torches–blamed them half the time for *causing* what they saw, when all they did was see it. There was no gratitude or even simple understanding in most folks.

So it was a relief to be back with somebody half-decent like Makepeace Smith. Even if Hank wasn't too proud of the way Makepeace was dealing with his prentice boy. How could Hank criticize him? He himself hadn't done much better—oh, he was pure embarrassed now to think how he railed on that boy and got him a cuffing, and for nothing, really, just a little affront to Hank Dowser's pride. Jesus stood and took whippings and a crown of thorns in silence, but I lash out when a prentice mumbles a few silly words. Oh, thoughts like that put Hank Dowser in a dark mood, and he was aching for a chance to apologize to the boy.

But the boy wasn't there, which was too bad, though Hank didn't have long to brood about it. Gertie Smith took Hank Dowser up to the house and near jammed the food down his throat with a ramrod, just to get in an extra half-loaf of bread, it felt like. "I can't hardly walk," said Hank, which was true; but it was also true that Gertie Smith cooked just as good as her husband forged and that prentice boy shod and Hank dowsed, which is to say, with a true knack. Everybody has his talent, everybody has his gift from God, and we go about sharing gifts with each other, that's the way of the world, the best way.

So it was with pleasure and pride that Hank drank the swallows of water from the first clear bucket drawn from the well. Oh, it was fine water, sweet water, and he loved the way they thanked him from their hearts. It wasn't till he was getting mounted on his Picklewing again that he realised he hadn't seen the well. Surely he should've seen the well—

He rounded the smithy on horseback and looked where he thought he had dowsed the spot, but the ground didn't appear like it had been troubled in a hundred years. Not even the trench the prentice dug while he was standing there. It took him a minute to find where the well actually was, sort of halfway between smithy and house, a fine little roof over the windlass, the whole thing finished with smooth-worked stone. But surely he hadn't been so near the house when the wand dipped—

"Oh, Hank!" called Makepeace Smith. "Hank, I'm glad you ain't gone yet!"

Where was the man? Oh, there, back in the meadow just up from the smithy, near where Hank had first looked for the well. Waving a stick in his hand—a forked stick—

"Your wand, the one you used to dowse this well—you want it back?"

"No, Makepeace, no thanks. I never use the same wand twice. Doesn't work proper when it isn't fresh."

Makepeace Smith pitched the wand back over his head, walked back down the slope and stood exactly in the place where Hank *thought* he had dowsed the well to be. "What do you think of the well house we built?"

Hank glanced back toward the well. "Fine stonework. If you ever give up the forge, I bet there's a living for you in stonecutting."

"Why, thank you, Hank! But it was my prentice boy did it all."

"That's some boy you got," said Hank. But it left a bad taste in his mouth, to say those words. There was something made him uneasy about this whole conversation. Makepeace Smith meant something sly, and Hank didn't know rightly what it was. Never mind. Time to be on his way. "Good-bye, Makepeace!" he said, walking his nag back toward the road. "I'll be back for shoes, remember!"

Makepeace laughed and waved. "I'll be glad to see your ugly old face when you come!"

With that, Hank nudged old Picklewing and headed off right brisk for the road that led to the covered bridge over the river. That was one of the nicest things about the westbound road out of Hatrack. From there to the Wobbish the track was as sweet as you please, with covered bridges over every

179

river, every stream, every rush and every rivulet. Folks were known to camp at night on the bridges, they were so tight and dry.

There must've been three dozen redbird nests in the eaves of the Hatrack Bridge. The birds were making such a racket that Hank allowed as how it was a miracle they didn't wake the dead. Too bad redbirds were too scrawny for eating. There'd be a banquet on that bridge, it if was worth the trouble.

"Ho there, Picklewing, my girl, ho," he said. He sat astride his horse, a-standing in the middle of the bridge, listening to the redbird song. Remembering now as clear as could be how the wand had leapt clean out of his hands and flung itself up into the meadow grass. Flung itself northeast of the spot he dowsed. And that's just where Makepeace Smith picked it up when he was saying good-bye.

Their fine new well wasn't on the spot he dowsed at all. The whole time he was there, they all were lying to him, pretending he dowsed them a well, but the water they drank was from another place.

Hank knew, oh yes, he knew who chose the spot they used. Hadn't the wand as much as told him when it flew off like that? Flew off because the boy spoke up, that smart-mouth prentice. And now they made mock of him behind his back, not saying a thing to his face, of course, but he knew that Make-peace was laughing the whole time, figuring he wasn't smart enough to notice the switch.

Well, I noticed, yes sir. You made a fool of me, Makepeace Smith, you and that prentice boy of yours. But I noticed. A man can forgive seven times, or even seven times seven. But then there comes the fiftieth time, and even a good Christian can't forget.

'Gee-ap," he said angrily. Picklewing's ears twitched and she started forward in a gentle walk, new shoes clopping loud on the floorboards of the bridge, echoing from the walls and ceiling. "Alvin," whispered Hank Dowser. "Prentice Alvin. Got no respect for any man's knack except his own."

12

School Board

When the carriage pulled up in front of the inn, Old
Peg Guester was upstairs hanging mattresses half
out the windows to let them air, so she saw. She
recognized Whitley Physicker's rig, a new-fangled
closed car that kept the weather and most of the
dust out; Physicker could use a carriage like that,
now that he could afford to pay a man just to drive
for him. It was things like that carriage that had
most folks calling him *Dr. Physicker* now, instead
of just Whitley.

The driver was Po Doggly, who used to have a
farm of his own till he got to likkering up after his
wife died. It was a good thing, Physicker hiring him
when other folks just thought of old Po as a drunk.
Things like that made most plain folks think well of
Dr. Physicker, even if he did show off his money
more than was seemly among Christians.

Anyway, Po hopped down from his seat and
swung around to open the door of the carriage.
But it wasn't Whitley Physicker got out first—it was
Pauley Wiseman, the sheriff. If ever a man didn't
deserve his last name, it was Pauley Wiseman. Old
Peg felt herself wrinkle up inside just seeing him. It

was like her husband Horace always said—any man who *wants* the job of sheriff is plainly unfit for the office. Pauley Wiseman wanted his job, wanted it more than most folks wanted to breathe. You could see it in the way he wore his stupid silver star right out in the open, on the outside of his coat, so nobody'd forget they was talking to the man who had the keys to the town jail! As if Hatrack River needed a jail!

Then Whitley Physicker got out of the carriage, and Old Peg knew exactly what business they were here for. The school board had made its decision, and these two were come to make sure she settled for it without making any noise about it in public. Old Peg tossed the mattress she was holding, tossed it so hard it near to flew clean out the window; she caught it by a corner and pulled it back so it'd hang proper and get a good airing. Then she ran down the stairs—she wasn't so old yet she couldn't run a flight of stairs when she wanted. Downward, anyways.

She looked around a bit for Arthur Stuart, but of course he wasn't in the house. He was just old enough for chores, and he did them, right enough, but after that he was always off by himself, over in town sometimes, or sometimes bothering around that blacksmith boy, Prentice Alvin. "What you do that for, boy?" Old Peg asked him once. "What you always have to be with Prentice Alvin for?" Arthur just grinned and then put his arms out like a street rassler all set to grab and said, "Got to learn how to throw a man twice my size." What made it funny was he said it just exactly in Alvin's own voice, complete with the way Alvin would've said it—with a joke in his voice, so you'd know he didn't take

183

himself all that serious. Arthur had that knack, to mimic folks like as if he knew them right to the soul. Sometimes it made her wonder if he didn't have something of the torchy knack, like her runaway daughter, Little Peggy; but no, it didn't seem like Arthur actually understood what he was doing. He was just a mimic. Still, he was smart as a whip, and that's why Old Peg knew the boy deserved to be in school, probably more than any other child in Hatrack River.

She got to the front door just as they started to knock. She stood there, panting a little from her run down the stairs, waiting to open it even though she saw their shadows through the lace-curtain windows on the door. They were kind of shifting their weight back and forth, like they was nervous—as well they should be. Let 'em sweat.

It was just like them folks on the school board, to send Whitley Physicker of all people. It made Old Peg Guester mad just to see his shadow at her door. Wasn't he the one who took Little Peggy off six years ago, and then wouldn't tell her where the girl went? Dekane was all he said, to folks she seemed to know. And then Peg's husband Horace reading the note over and over, saying, If a torch can't see her own future safe, none of us can look out for her any better. Why, if it hadn't been for Arthur Stuart needing her so bad, Old Peg would have up and left. Just up and left, and see how they liked that! Take her daughter away and tell her it's all for the best— such a thing to tell a mother! Let's see what they think when *I* leave. If she hadn't had Arthur to look after, she would have gone so fast her shadow would've been stuck in the door.

And now they send Whitley Physicker to do it

again, to set her grieving over another child, just like before. Only worse this time, because Little Peggy really *could* take care of herself, while Arthur Stuart couldn't, he was just a six-year-old boy, a boy with no future at all unless Old Peg fought for it tooth and nail.

They knocked again. She opened the door. There was Whitley Physicker, looking all cheerful and dignified, and behind him Pauley Wiseman, looking all important and dignified. Like two masts on the same ship, with sails all puffed out and bossy-looking. All full of wind. Coming to tell me what's right and proper, are you? We'll see.

"Goody Guester," said Dr. Physicker. He doffed his hat proper, like a gentleman. That's what's wrong with Hatrack River these days, thought Old Peg. Too many folks putting on like gentlemen and ladies. Don't they know this is Hio? All the high-toned folks are down in the Crown Colonies with His Majesty, the other Arthur Stuart. The long-haired White king, as opposed to her own short-haired Black boy Arthur. Anybody in the state of Hio who thinks he's a gentleman is just fooling himself and nobody but the other fools.

"I suppose you want to come in," said Old Peg.

"I hoped you'd invite us," said Physicker. "We come from the school board."

"You can turn me down on the porch as easy as you can inside my house."

"Now see here," said Sheriff Pauley. He wasn't used to folks leaving him standing on porches.

"We didn't come to turn you down, Goody Guester," said the doctor.

Old Peg didn't believe it for a minute. "You telling me that stiff-necked bunch of high-collar

185

hypocrites is going to let a Black child into the new school?"

That set Sheriff Pauley off like gunpowder in a bucket. "Well, if you're so all-fired sure you know the answer, Old Peg, why'd you bother asking the question?"

"Cause I wanted you all down on record as being Black-hating slavers in your hearts! Then someday when the Emancipationists have their way and Black people have all their rights everywhere, you'll have to wear your shame in public like you deserve."

Old Peg didn't even hear her husband coming up behind her, she was talking so loud.

"Margaret," said Horace Guester. "No man stands on my porch without a welcome."

"*You* welcome them yourself, then," said Old Peg. She turned her back on Dr. Physicker and Sheriff Pauley and walked on into the kitchen. "I wash my hands of it," she shouted over her shoulder.

But once she was in the kitchen she realized that she wasn't cooking yet this morning, she was doing the upstairs beds. And as she stood there, kind of confused for a second, she got to thinking it was Pontius Pilate who did that first famous hand-washing. Why, she'd confessed herself unrighteous with her own words. God wouldn't look kindly on her if she once started in imitating someone as killed the Lord Jesus, like Pilate did. So she turned around and walked back into the common room and sat down near the hearth. It being August there wasn't no fire in it, which made it a cool place to sit. Not like the kitchen hearth, which was hot as the devil's privy on summer days like this. No reason she should sweat her heart out in the kitchen while these two

186

decided the fate of Arthur Stuart in the coolest spot in the house.

Her husband and the two visitors looked at her but didn't say a thing about her storming out and then storming back in. Old Peg knew what was said behind her back—that you might as well try to set a trap for a cyclone as to tangle with Old Peg Guester—but she didn't mind a bit if men like Whitley Physicker and Pauley Wiseman walked a little wary around her. After a second or two, waiting for her to settle down, they went right on with their talk.

"As I was saying, Horace, we looked at your proposal seriously," Physicker said. "It would be a great convenience to us if the new teacher could be housed in your roadhouse instead of being boarded here and there the way it usually happens. But we wouldn't consider having you do it for free. We have enough students enrolled and enough basis in the property tax to pay you a small stipend for the service."

"How much does a sty pen come to in money?" asked Horace.

"The details remain to be worked out, but the sum of twenty dollars for the year was mentioned."

"Well," said Horace, "that's a mite low, if you're thinking you're paying the actual cost."

"On the contrary, Horace, we know that we're underpaying you by considerable. But since you offered to do it free, we hoped this would be an improvement on the original offer."

Horace was all set to agree, but Peg wouldn't stand for all this pretending. "I know what it is, Dr. Physicker, and it's no improvement. We didn't offer to put up the schoolteacher for *free*. We offered to put up *Arthur Stuart*'s teacher for free. And if you

187

figure twenty dollars is going to make me change my mind about that, you better go back and do your figuring again."

Dr. Physicker got a pained look on his face. "Now, Goody Guester. Don't get ahead of yourself on this. There was not a man on the school board who had any personal objection to having Arthur Stuart attend the new school."

When Physicker said that, Old Peg took a sharp look at Pauley Wiseman. Sure enough, he squirmed in his chair like he had a bad itch in a place where a gentleman doesn't scratch. That's right, Pauley Wiseman, Dr. Physicker can say what he likes, but *I* know *you*, and there was one, at least, who had all kinds of objections to Arthur Stuart.

Whitley Physicker went on talking, of course. Since he was pretending that everybody loved Arthur Stuart dearly, he couldn't very well take notice of how uncomfortable Sheriff Pauley was. "We know Arthur has been raised by the two oldest settlers and finest citizens of Hatrack River, and the whole town loves him for his own self. We just can't think what benefit a school education would give the boy."

"It'll give him the same benefit it gives any other boy or girl," said Old Peg.

"Will it? Will his knowing how to read and write get him a place in a counting house? Can you imagine that even if they let him take the bar, any jury would listen to a Black lawyer plead? Society has decreed that a Black child will grow up to be a Black man, and a Black man, like ancient Adam, will earn his bread by the sweat of his body, not by the labors of his mind."

"Arthur Stuart is smarter than any child who'll be in that school and you know it."

"All the more reason we shouldn't build up young Arthur's hopes, only to have them dashed when he's older. I'm talking about the way of the world, Goody Guester, not the way of the heart."

"Well why don't you wise men of the school board just say, To hell with the rest of the world, we'll do what's right! I can't make you do what you don't want to do, but I'll be damned if I let you pretend it's for Arthur's own good!"

Horace winced. He didn't like to hear Old Peg swear. She'd only taken it up lately, beginning with the time she cussed Millicent Mercher right in public for insisting on being called "Mistress Mercher" instead of "Goody Mercher." It didn't sit well with Horace, her using those words, especially since she didn't seem to ken the time and place for it like a man would, or at least so he said. But Old Peg figured if you can't cuss at a lying hypocrite, then what was cussing invented for?

Pauley Wiseman started turning red, barely controlling a stream of his own favorite cusswords. But Whitley Physicker was now a gentleman, so he merely bowed his head for a moment, like as if he was saying a prayer—but Old Peg figured it was more likely he was waiting till he calmed down enough for his words to come out civil. "Goody Guester, you're right. We didn't think up that story about it being for Arthur's own good till after the decision was made."

His frankness left her without a word, at least for the moment. Even Sheriff Pauley could only give out a kind of squeak. Whitley Physicker wasn't sticking to what they all agreed to say; he sounded espe-

189

ciously close to telling the truth, and Sheriff Pauley didn't know what to do when people started throwing the truth around loose and dangerous. Old Peg enjoyed watching Pauley Wiseman look like a fool, it being something for which old Pauley had a particular knack.

"You see, Goody Guester, we want this school to work proper, we truly do," said Dr. Physicker. "The whole idea of public schools is a little strange. The way they do schools in the Crown Colonies, it's all the people with titles and money who get to attend, so that the poor have no chance to learn or rise. In New England all the schools are religious, so you don't come out with bright minds, you come out with perfect little Puritans who all stay in their place like God meant them to. But the public schools in the Dutch states and Pennsylvania are making people see that in America we can do it different. We can teach every child in every wildwood cabin to read and write and cipher, so that we have a whole population educated enough to be fit to vote and hold office and govern ourselves."

"All this is well and good," said Old Peg, "and I recollect hearing you give this exact speech in our common room not three months ago before we voted on the school tax. What I can't figure, Whitley Physicker, is why you figure my son should be the exception."

At this, Sheriff Pauley decided it was time to put an oar in. And since the truth was being used so recklessly, he lost control of himself and spoke truthfully himself. It was a new experience, and it went to his head a little. "Begging our pardon, Old Peg, but there isn't a drop of your blood in that boy, so

190

he's no-wise your son, and if Horace here has some part of him, it isn't enough to turn him White."

Horace slowly got to his feet, as if he was preparing to invite Sheriff Pauley outside to punch some caution into him. Pauley Wiseman must have known he was in trouble the second he accused Horace of maybe being the father of a half-Black bastard. And when Horace stood up so tall like that, Pauley remembered he wasn't no match for Horace Guester. Horace wasn't exactly a small man and Pauley wasn't exactly a large one. So old Pauley did what he always did when things got out of hand. He turned kind of sideways so his badge was facing straight at Horace Guester. Take a lick at me, that badge said, and you'll be facing a trial for assaulting an officer of the law.

Still, Old Peg knew that Horace wouldn't hit a man over a word; he hadn't even knocked down that river rat who accused Horace of unspeakable crimes with barnyard animals. Horace just wasn't the kind to lose control of himself in anger. In fact, Old Peg could see that as Horace stood there, he'd already forgotten about his anger at Pauley Wiseman and was thinking over an idea.

Sure enough, Horace turned to Old Peg as if Wiseman didn't even exist. "Maybe we should give it up, Peg. It was fine when Arthur was a sweet little baby, but . . ."

Horace, who was looking right at Old Peg's face, he knew better than to finish his sentence. Sheriff Pauley wasn't half so bright. "He just gets blacker every day, Goody Guester."

Well, what do you say to that kind of thing, anyway? At least now it was plain what was going on—that it was Arthur Stuart's color and nothing

191

else that was keeping him out of the new Hatrack River School.

Whitley Physicker sighed into the silence. Nothing that happened with Sheriff Pauley there ever went according to plan. "Don't you see?" said Physicker. He sounded mild and reasonable, which he was good at. "There's some ignorant and backward folks"— and at this he took a cool look at Sheriff Pauley— "who can't abide the thought of a Black child getting the same education as their own boys and girls. What's the advantage of schooling, they figure, if a Black has it the same as a White? Why, the next thing you know, Blacks would be wanting to vote or hold office."

Old Peg hadn't thought of that. It just never entered her mind. She tried to imagine Mock Berry being governor, and trying to give orders to the militia. There wasn't a soldier in Hio who'd take orders from a Black man. It'd be as unnatural as a fish jumping out of the river to kill him a bear.

But Old Peg wasn't going to give up so easy, just because Whitley Physicker made one point like that. "Arthur Stuart's a good boy," she said. "He wouldn't no more try to vote than I would."

"I know that," said Physicker. "The whole school board knows that. But it's the backwoods people who won't know it. They're the ones who'll hear there's a Black child in the school and they'll keep their children home. And here we'll be paying for a school that won't be doing its job of educating the citizenry of our republic. We're asking Arthur to forgo an education that will do him no good anyway, in order to allow others to receive an education that will do them and our nation a great deal of good."

It all sounded so logical. After all, Whitley Physicker was a doctor, wasn't he? He'd even been to college back in Philadelphia, so he had a deeper understanding than Old Peg would ever have. Why did she think even for a moment that she could disagree with a man like Physicker and not be wrong?

Yet even though she couldn't think of a single argument against him, she couldn't get rid of the feeling deep in her guts that if she said yes to Whitley Physicker, she'd be stabbing a knife right into little Arthur's heart. She could imagine him asking her, "Mama, why can't I go to school like all my friends?" And then all these fine words from Dr. Physicker would fly away like she'd never heard them, and she'd just sit there and say, "It's because you're Black, Arthur Stuart Guester."

Whitley Physicker seemed to take her silence as surrender, which it nearly was. "You'll see," said Physicker. "Arthur won't mind not going to school. Why, the White boys'll all be jealous of *him*, when he can be outside in the sun while they're cooped up in a classroom."

Old Peg Guester knew there was something wrong with all this, that it wasn't as sensible as it sounded, but she couldn't think what it was.

"And someday things might be different," said Physicker. "Someday maybe society will change. Maybe they'll stop keeping Blacks as slaves in the Crown Colonies and Appalachee. Maybe there'll be a time when . . ." His voice trailed off. Then he shook himself. "I get to wondering sometimes, that's all," he said. "Silly things. The world is the way the world is. It just isn't natural for a Black man to grow up like a White."

Old Peg felt a bitter hatred inside her when he

193

said those words. But it wasn't a hot rage, to make her shout at him. It was a cold, despairing hate, that said, Maybe I *am* unnatural, but Arthur Stuart is my true son, and I won't betray him. No I won't.

Again, though, her silence was taken to mean consent. The men all got up, looking relieved, Horace most of all. It was plain they never figured Old Peg would listen to reason so fast. The visitors' relief was to be expected, but why was Horace looking so happy? Old Peg had a nasty suspicion and she knew at once that it had to be the truth—Horace Guester and Dr. Physicker and Sheriff Pauley had already worked things out between them before they ever come a-calling today. This whole conversation was pretend. Just a show put on to make Old Peg Guester happy.

Horace didn't want Arthur Stuart in school any more than Whitley Physicker or anybody else in Hatrack River.

Old Peg's anger turned hot, but now it was too late. Physicker and Pauley was out the door, Horace following on out after them. No doubt they'd all pat each other on the back and share a smile out of Old Peg's sight. But Old Peg wasn't smiling. She remembered all too clear how Little Peggy had done a Seeing for her that last night before she run off, a Seeing about Arthur Stuart's future. Old Peg had asked Little Peggy if Horace would ever love little Arthur, and the girl refused to answer. That *was* an answer, sure enough. Horace might go through the motions of treating Arthur like his own son, but in fact he thought of him as just a Black boy that his wife had taken a notion to care for. Horace was no papa to Arthur Stuart.

So Arthur's an orphan all over again. Lost his

father. Or, rightly speaking, never had a father. Well, so be it. He's got two mothers: the one who died for him when he was born, and me. I can't get him in the school. I knew I couldn't, knew it from the start. But I can get him an education all the same. A plan for it sprung into her head all at once. It all depended on the schoolmistress they hired, this teacher lady from Philadelphia. With luck she'd be a Quaker, with no hate for Blacks and so the plan would work out just fine. But even if the schoolmistress hated Blacks as bad as a finder watching a slave stand free on the Canadian shore, it wouldn't make a bit of difference. Old Peg would find a way. Arthur Stuart was the only family she had left in the world, the only person she loved who didn't lie to her or fool her or do things behind her back. She wasn't going to let him be cheated out of anything that might do him good.

13

Springhouse

Alvin first knew something was up when he heard Horace and Old Peg Guester yelling at each other up at the old springhouse. It was so loud for a minute there that he could hear them clear over the sound of the forgefire and his own hammering. Then they quietened themselves down a mite, but by then Alvin was so curious he kind of laid off the hammer. Laid it right down, in fact, and stepped outside to hear better.

No, no, he wasn't *listening*. He was just going to the well to fetch more water, some to drink and some for the cooling barrel. If he happened to hear them somewhat, he couldn't be blamed, now, could he?

"Folks'll say I'm a bad innkeeper, making the teacher live in the springhouse instead of putting her up proper."

"It's just an empty building, Horace, and we'll put it to use. And it'll leave us the rooms in the inn for paying customers."

"I won't have that schoolmistress living off alone by herself. It ain't decent!"

"Why, Horace? Are you planning to make advances?"

Alvin could hardly believe his ears. Married people just didn't say such things to each other. Alvin half expected to hear the sound of a slap. But instead Horace must've just took it. Everybody said he was henpecked, and this was about all the proof a body'd need, to have his wife accuse him of hankering after adultery and him not hit her or even say boo.

"It doesn't matter, anyway," said Old Peg. "Maybe you'll have your way and she'll say no. But we'll fix it up, anyway, and offer it to her."

Horace mumbled something that Alvin couldn't hear.

"I don't care if Little Peggy *built* this springhouse. She's gone of her own free will, left without so much as a word to me, and I'm not about to keep this springhouse like a monument just because she used to come here when she was little. Do you hear me?"

Again Alvin couldn't hear what Horace said.

On the other hand, he could hear Old Peg right fine. Her voice just sailed right out like a crack of thunder. "You're telling *me* who loved who? Well let me tell you, Horace Guester, all your love for Little Peggy didn't keep her here, *did* it? But my love for Arthur Stuart is going to get him an education, do you understand me? And when it's all said and done, Horace Guester, we'll just see who does better at loving their children!"

There wasn't exactly a slap or nothing, but there was a slammed door which like to took the door of the springhouse off its hinges. Alvin couldn't help craning his neck a little to see who did the slamming. Sure enough, it was Old Peg stalking away.

197

A minute later, maybe even more, the door opened real slow. Alvin could barely make it out through the brush and leaves that had grown up between the well and the springhouse. Horace Guester came out even slower, his face downcast in a way Alvin had never seen him before. He stood there awhile, his hand on the door. Then he pushed it closed, as gentle as if he was tucking a baby into bed. Alvin always wondered why they hadn't tore down that springhouse years ago, when Alvin dug the well that finally killed the stream that used to go through it. Or at least why they never put it to some use. But now Alvin knew it had something to do with Peggy, that torch girl who left right before Alvin showed up in Hatrack River. The way Horace touched that door, the way he closed it, it made Alvin see for the first time how much a man might dote on a child of his, so that even when she was gone, the places that she loved were like holy ground to her old dad. For the first time Alvin wondered if he'd ever love a child of his own like that. And then he wondered who the mother of that child might be, and if she'd ever scream at him the way Old Peg screamed at Horace, and if he'd ever have at her the way Makepeace Smith had at his wife Gertie, him flailing with his belt and her throwing the crockery.

"Alvin," said Horace.

Well, Alvin like to died with embarrassment, to be caught staring at Horace like that. "I beg pardon, sir," said Alvin. "I shouldn't ought to've been listening."

Horace smiled wanly. "I reckon as you'd have to be a deaf mute not to hear that last bit."

"It got a mite loud," said Alvin, "but I didn't exactly go out of my way not to hear, neither."

"Well, I know you're a good boy, and I never heard of no one carrying tales from you."

The words "good boy" rankled a bit. Alvin was eighteen now, less than a year to being nineteen, long since ready to be a journeyman smith out on his own. Just because Makepeace Smith wouldn't release him early from his prenticeship didn't make it right for Horace Guester to call him a *boy*. I may be Prentice Alvin, and not a man yet afore the law, but no woman yells *me* to shame.

"Alvin," said Horace, "you might tell your master we'll be needing new hinges and fittings for the springhouse doors. I reckon we're fixing it up for the new schoolteacher to live here, if she wants."

So that was the way of it. Horace had lost the battle with Old Peg. He was giving in. Was that the way of marriage, then? A man either had to be willing to hit his wife, like Makepeace Smith, or he'd be bossed around like poor Horace Guester. Well, if that's the choices, I'll have none of it, thought Alvin. Oh, Alvin had an eye for girls in town. He'd see them flouncing along the street, their breasts all pushed up high by their corsets and stays, their waists so small he could wrap his great strong hands right around and toss them every which way, only he never thought of tossing or grabbing, they just made him feel shy and hot at the same time, so he looked down when they happened to look at him, or got busy loading or unloading or whatever business brought him into town.

Alvin knew what they saw when they looked at him, those town girls. They saw a man with no coat on, just in his shirt-sleeves, stained and wet from his labor. They saw a poor man who'd never keep them in a fine white clapboard house like their papa, who was no doubt a lawyer or a judge or a merchant. They saw him *low*, a mere prentice still, and him already more than eighteen years old. If by some miracle he ever married one such girl, he knew how it would be, her always looking down at him, always expecting him to give way for her because she was a lady.

And if he married a girl who was as low as himself, it would be like Gertie Smith or Old Peg Guester, a good cook or a hard worker or whatever, but a hellion when she didn't get her way. There was no woman in Alvin Smith's life, that was sure. He'd never let himself be showed up like Horace Guester.

"Did you hear me, Alvin?"

"I did, Mr. Horace, and I'll tell Makepeace Smith first off when I see him. All the fittings for the springhouse."

"And nice work, too," said Horace. "It's for the schoolmistress to live there." But Horace wasn't so whipped that he couldn't get a curl to his lip and a nasty tone to his voice as he said, "So she can give *private* lessons."

The way he said "private lessons" made it sound like it'd be a whorehouse or something, but Alvin knew right off, by putting things together, exactly who would be getting private lessons. Didn't everybody know how Old Peg had asked to have Arthur Stuart accepted at the school?

"Well, so long," said Horace.

Alvin waved him good-bye, and Horace ambled away along the path to the inn.

Makepeace Smith didn't come in that afternoon. Alvin wasn't surprised. Now that Alvin had his full mansize on him, he could do the whole work of the smithy, and faster and better than Makepeace. Nobody said aught about it, but Alvin noticed back last year that folks took to dropping in during the times when Makepeace *wasn't* at the forge. They'd ask Alvin to do their ironwork quick-like, while they was there waiting. "Just a little job" they'd say, only sometimes the job wasn't all that little. And pretty soon Alvin realized that it wasn't just chance brought them by. They wanted *Alvin* to do the work they needed.

It wasn't because Alvin did anything peculiar to the iron, either, except a hex or two where it was called for, and every smith did that. Alvin knew it wouldn't be right to best his master using some secret knack—it'd be like slipping a knife into a rassling match. It'd just bring him trouble anyway, if he used his knack to give *his* iron any peculiar strength. So he did his work natural, with his own strong arm and good eye. He'd earned every inch of muscle in his back and shoulders and arms. And if people liked his work better than Makepeace Smith's, why, it was because Alvin was a better blacksmith, not because his knack gave him the advantage.

Anyhow, Makepeace must've caught on to what was happening, and he took to staying away from the forge more and more. Maybe it was because he knew it was better for business, and Makepeace was humble enough to give way before his prentice's skill—but Alvin never quite believed that. More likely Makepeace stayed away so folks wouldn't see how he snuck a look over Alvin's shoulder now and then, trying to figure out what Al did better than his master. Or maybe Makepeace was plain jealous, and couldn't bear to watch his prentice at work. Could be, though, that Makepeace was just lazy, and since his prentice boy was doing the work just fine, why *shouldn't* Makepeace go out to drink himself silly with the river rats down at Hatrack Mouth?

Or perhaps, by some strange twist of chance, Makepeace was actually ashamed of how he kept Alvin to his prentice contract even though Alvin was plainly ready to take to the road as a journeyman. It was a low thing for a master to hold a prentice after he knew his trade, just to get the benefit of his labor without having to pay him a fair wage. Alvin brought good money into Makepeace Smith's household, everybody knew that, and all the while Alvin stayed dirt poor, sleeping in a loft and never two coins in his pocket to make a jingle when he walked to town. Sure, Gertie fed him proper—best food in town, Al knew well, having eaten a bite now and then with one of the town boys. But good food wasn't the same thing as a good wage. Food you ate and it was gone. Money you could use to buy things, or to do things—to have *freedom*. That contract Makepeace Smith kept in the cupboard up to the house, the one signed by Alvin's father, it made Alvin a slave as sure any Black in the Crown Colonies.

Except for one difference. Alvin could count the days till freedom. It was August. Not even a year left. Next spring he'd be free. No slave in the South ever knew such a thing; nary such a hope would ever enter their heads. Alvin had thought on that often enough over the years, when he was feeling most put upon; he'd think, if they can keep on living and working, having no hope of freedom, then I can hold out for another five years, three years, one year, knowing that it'll come to an end someday.

Anyway, Makepeace Smith didn't show up that afternoon, and when Alvin finished his assigned work, instead of doing chores and cleaning up, instead of getting ahead, he went on up to the spring-house and took the measure of the doors and windows. It was a place built to keep in the cool of the stream, so the windows didn't open, but the schoolmistress wouldn't cotton to *that*, never having a breath of air, so Alvin took the measure there, too. Not that he exactly decided to make the new window frames himself, seeing how he wasn't no carpenter particularly, except that woodworking skill any man learns. He was just taking the measure of the place, and when he got to the windows he kept going.

He took the measure of a lot of things. Where a little pot-bellied stove would have to go, if the place was going to be warm in the winter; and figuring that, he also figured how to lay in the right foundation under the heavy stove, and how to put the flaring around the chimney, all the things it'd take to make the springhouse into a tight little cabin, fit for a lady to live in.

Alvin didn't write down the measures. He never did. He just knew them, now that he'd put his fingers and hands and arms into all the places; and if he forgot, and took the measure wrong somehow, he knew that in a pinch he could make it fit even so. It was a kind of laziness, he knew, but he got precious little advantage from his knack these days, and there was no shame in such small fidging.

Arthur Stuart wandered along when Al was just about done at the springhouse. Alvin didn't say nothing, nor did Arthur; you don't greet somebody who belongs where you are, you hardly notice them. But when Alvin needed to get the measure of the roof, he just said so and then tossed Arthur up onto the roof as easy as Peg Guester tossed the feather mattresses from the inn beds.

Arthur walked like a cat on top of the roof, paying no heed to being up so high. He paced off the roof and kept his own count, and when he was done he didn't even wait to make sure Alvin was ready to catch him, he just took a leap into the air. It was like Arthur believed he could fly. And with Alvin there to catch him below, why, it might as well be true, since Alvin had such arms on him that he could catch Arthur easy and let him down as gentle as a mallard settling onto a pond.

When Al and Arthur was done with measuring, they went back to the smithy. Alvin took a few bars of iron from the pile, het up the forge, and set to work. Arthur set in to pumping the bellows and fetching tools—they'd been doing this so long that it was like Arthur was Alvin's own prentice, and it never occurred to either of them that there was anything wrong with it. They just did this together, so smooth that to other folks it looked like a kind of dance.

A couple of hours later, Alvin had all the fittings. It should've taken less time by half, only for some reason Alvin got it into his head that he ought to make a lock for the door, and then he got it into his head that it ought to be a real lock, the kind that a few rich folks in town ordered from back east in Philadelphia—with a proper key and all, and a catch that shut all by itself when you closed the door, so you'd never forget to lock the door behind you.

What's more, he put secret hexes on all the fittings, perfect six-point figures that spoke of safety, and no one with harm in his heart being about to turn the lock. Once the lock was closed and fastened in place on the door, nobody'd see those hexes, but they'd do the work sure, since when Alvin made a hex the measure was so perfect it cast a network of hexes like a wall for many yards on every side.

It occurred to Alvin to wonder why a hex should work at all. Of course he knew why it was such a magical shape, being twice three; and he knew how you could lay hexes down on a table and they'd fit snug together, as perfect as squares, only stronger, woven not with warp and weft, but with warp and weft and hax. It wasn't like squares, which were hardly ever found in nature, being too simple and weak; there was hexes in snowflakes and crystals and honeycombs. Making a single hex was the same as making a whole fabric of hexes, so that the perfect hexes he hid up inside the lock would wrap all the way around the house, sealing it from outside harm as surely as if he forged a net of iron and wove it right in place.

But that didn't answer the question *why* it worked. Why his hidden hexes should bar a man's hand, turn a man's mind away from entering. Why the hex should invisibly repeat itself as far as it could, the more perfect the hex, the farther the net it threw. All these years of puzzling things out, and he still knew so little. Knew so near to nothing that he despaired, and even now, holding the springhouse fittings in his hands, he wondered if in fact he shouldn't content himself to be a good smith and forget these tales of Makering.

With all his wondering and questioning, Alvin

never did ask himself what should have been the plainest question of all. Why would a schoolmistress need such a perfectly hexed, powerful lock? Alvin didn't even try to guess. He wasn't thinking like that. Instead he just knew that such a lock was something fine, and this little house had to be as fine as he could make it. Later on he'd wonder about it, wonder if he knew even then, before he met her, what this schoolmistress would mean to him. Maybe he already had a plan in the back of his mind, just like Old Peg Guester did. But he sure didn't know about it yet, and that was the truth. When he made all those fancy fittings, with patterns cut in them so the door would look pretty, he most likely was doing it for Arthur Stuart; maybe he was halfway thinking that if the schoolmistress had a right pretty little place to live, she'd be more inclined to give Arthur Stuart his private lessons.

It was time to quit for the day, but Alvin didn't quit. He pushed all the fittings up to the springhouse in a wheelbarrow, along with a couple of other tools he figured to need, and some scrap tin for the flaring of the chimney. He worked fast, and without quite meaning to, he used his knack to smooth the labor. Everything fit first time; the doors rehung as nice as could be, and the lock fitted exactly to the inside face of the door, bolted on so tight that it'd never come off. This was a door no man could force— easier to chop through the split-log wall than attack this door. And with the hexes inside, a man wouldn't dare to lift his axe against the house, or if he did, he'd be too weak to strike a telling blow—these were hexes that even a Red might not laugh at.

Al took another trip back to the shed outside the smithy and chose the best of the old broke-down pot-belly stoves that Makepeace had bought for the iron in them. Carrying a whole stove wasn't easy even for a man strong as a blacksmith, but it was sure the wheelbarrow couldn't handle such a load. So Alvin hefted it up the hill by main strength. He left it outside while he brought stones from the old streambed to make a foundation under the floor at the place where the stove would go. The floor of the springhouse was set on beams running the length of the house inside, but they hadn't planked over the strip where the stream used to go—it wouldn't have been much of a springhouse if they covered over the cold water. Anyway he put a tight stone foundation under an upstream corner where the floor was done but not too high off the ground, and then bolted sheets of thin-beat iron on top of the planks to make a fireproof floor. Then he hefted the stove into place and piped it up to the hole he knocked in the roof.

He set Arthur Stuart to work with a rasp, tearing the dead moss off the inside of the walls. It came off easy, but it mostly kept Arthur distracted so he didn't notice that Alvin was fixing things on that brokedown stove that couldn't be fixed by a natural man. Good as new, and all fittings tight.

"I'm hungry," said Arthur Stuart.

"Get on up to Gertie and tell her I'm working late and please send food down for both of us, since you're helping."

Arthur Stuart took off running. Alvin knew he'd deliver the message word for word, and in Alvin's own voice, so that Gertie'd laugh out loud and give him a good supper in a basket. Probably such a good supper that Arthur'd have to stop and rest three or four times on the way back, it'd be so heavy.

All this time Makepeace Smith never so much as showed his face.

When Arthur Stuart finally got back, Alvin was on the roof putting the final touches on the flaring, and fixing some of the shingles while he was up there. The flaring fit so tight water'd never get into the house, he saw to that. Arthur Stuart stood below, waiting and watching, not asking if he could go ahead and eat, not even asking how long till Alvin'd come down; he wasn't the type of child to whine or complain. When Alvin was done, he dropped over the edge of the roof, caught himself on the lip of the eaves, then dropped to the ground.

"Cold chicken be mighty good after a hot day's work," said Arthur Stuart, in a voice that was exactly Gertie Smith's, except pitched in a child's high voice.

Alvin grinned at him and opened the basket. They fell to eating like sailors who'd been on short rations for half the voyage, and in no time they was both lying there on their backs, bellies packed full, belching now and then, watching the white clouds move like placid cattle grazing across the sky.

The sun was getting low toward the west now. Definitely time to pack in for the day, but Alvin just couldn't feel good about that. "Best you get home," he said. "Maybe if you just run that empty basket back up to Gertie Smith's, you can get in without your Ma gets too upset at you."

"What you doing now?"

"Got windows to frame and re-hang."

"Well I got walls to finish rasping down," said Arthur Stuart.

Alvin grinned, but he also knew that what he planned to do to the windows wasn't a thing he

208

wanted witnesses for. He had no intention of actually doing a lot of carpentry, and he didn't ever let anybody watch him do something *obvious* with his knack. "Best you go home now," said Alvin.

Arthur sighed.

"You been a good help to me, but I don't want you getting in trouble."

To Alvin's surprise, Arthur just returned his own words back to him in his own voice. "You been a good help to me, but I don't want you getting in trouble."

"I mean it," said Alvin.

Arthur Stuart rolled over, got up, came over and sat down astride of Alvin's belly—which Arthur often did, but it didn't feel none too comfortable at the moment, there being about a chicken and a half inside that belly.

"Come on, Arthur Stuart," said Alvin.

"I never told nobody bout no redbird," said Arthur Stuart.

Well, that just sent a chill right through Alvin. Somehow he'd figured that Arthur Stuart was just too young that day more than three years ago to even remember that anything happened. But Alvin should've knowed that just because Arthur Stuart didn't talk about something didn't mean that he forgot. Arthur never forgot so much as a caterpillar crawling on a leaf.

If Arthur Stuart remembered the redbird, then he no doubt remembered that day when it was winter out of season, when Alvin's knack dug a well and made the stone come clean of dirt without using his hands. And if Arthur Stuart knew all about Alvin's knack, then what point was there in trying to sneak around and make it secret?

"All right then," said Alvin. 'Help me hang the windows." Alvin almost added, "as long as you don't tell a soul what you see." But Arthur Suart already understood that. It was just one of the things that Arthur Stuart understood.

They finished before dark, Alvin cutting into the wood of the window frames with his bare fingers, shaping what was just wood nailed into wood until it was windows that could slide free, up and down. He made little holes in the sides of the window frames and whittled plugs of wood to fit them, so the window would stay up as far as a body might want. Of course, he didn't quite whittle like a natural man, since each stroke of the knife took off a perfect arc. Each plug was done in about six passes of the knife.

Meantime Arthur Stuart finished the rasping, and then they swept out the house, using a broom of course, but Alvin helped with his knack so that every scrap of sawdust and iron filings and flakes of moss and ancient dust ended up outside the house. Only thing they didn't do was try to cover the strip of open dirt down the middle of the springhouse, where once the stream flowed. That'd take felling a tree to get the planks, and anyway Alvin was starting to get a little scared, seeing how much he'd done and how fast he'd done it. What if somebody came *tonight* and realized that all this work was done in a single long afternoon? There'd be questions. There'd be guesses.

"Don't tell anybody that we did this all in a day," said Alvin.

Arthur Stuart just grinned. He'd lost one of his front teeth recently, so there was a spot where his pink gums showed up. Pink as a White person's

210

gums, Alvin thought. Inside his mouth he's no different from a White. Then Alvin had this crazy idea of God taking all the people in the world who ever died and flaying them and hanging up their bodies like pigs in the butcher's shop, just meat and bones hanging there by the heel, even the guts and the head gone, just meat. And then God would ask folks like the Hatrack River School Board to come in and pick out which was Black folks and which was Red and which was White. They couldn't do it. Then God would say, "Well why in hell did you say that this one and this one and this one couldn't go to school with this one and this one and this one?" What answer would they have then? Then God would say, "You people, you're all the same rare meat under the skin. But I tell you, I don't like your flavor. I'm going to toss your beefsteaks to the dogs."

Well, that was such a funny idea that Alvin couldn't help but tell it to Arthur Stuart, and Arthur Stuart laughed just as hard as Alvin. Only after it was all said and the laughing was done did Alvin remember that maybe nobody'd told Arthur Stuart about how his ma tried to get him into the school and the school board said no. "You know what this is all about?"

Arthur Stuart didn't understand the question, or maybe he understood it even better than Alvin did. Anyways, he answered, "Ma's hoping the teacher lady'll learn me to read and write here in this springhouse."

"Right," said Alvin. No point in explaining about the school, then. Either Arthur Stuart already knew how some White folks felt about Blacks, or else he'd find out soon enough without Alvin telling him now.

"We're all the same rare meat," said Arthur Stuart. He used a funny voice that Alvin had never heard before.

"Whose voice was that?" asked Alvin.

"God, of course," said Arthur Stuart.

"Good imitation," said Alvin. He was being funny.

"Sure is," said Arthur Stuart. He wasn't.

Turned out nobody came to the springhouse for a couple of days and more. It was Monday of the next week when Horace ambled into the smithy. He came early in the morning, at a time when Makepeace was most likely to be there, ostentatiously "teaching" Alvin to do something that Alvin already knew how to do.

"*My* masterpiece was a ship's anchor," said Makepeace. "Course, that was back in Newport, afore I come west. Them ships, them whaling ships, they weren't like little bitty houses and wagons. They needed *real* ironwork. A boy like you, you do well enough out here where they don't know better, but you'd never make a go of it *there*, where a smith has to be a *man*."

Alvin was used to such talk. He let it roll right off him. But he was grateful anyway when Horace came in, putting an end to Makepeace's brag.

After all the *good-mornings* and *howdy-dos*, Horace got right to business. "I just come by to see when you'll have a chance to get started on the springhouse."

Makepeace raised an eyebrow and looked at Alvin. Only then did Alvin realize that he'd never mentioned the job to Makepeace.

"It's already done, sir," Alvin said to Make-

212

peace—for all the world as if Makepeace's unspoken question had been, "Are you finished yet?" and not, "What is this springhouse job the man's talking about?"

"Done?" said Horace.

Alvin turned to him. "I thought you must've noticed. I thought you were in a hurry, so I did it right off in my free time."

"Well, let's go see it," said Horace. "I didn't even think to look on my way down here."

"Yes, I'm dying to look at it myself," said the smith.

"I'll just stay here and keep working," said Alvin.

"No," said Makepeace. "You come along and show off this work you done in your *free time*." Alvin didn't hardly notice how Makepeace emphasized the last two words, he was so nervous to show off what he done at the springhouse. He only barely had sense enough to drop the keys he made into his pocket.

They made their way up the hill to the spring-house. Horace was the kind of man who could tell when somebody did real good work, and wasn't shy to say so. He fingered the fancy new hingework and admired the lock afore he put in the key. To Alvin's pride it turned smooth and easy. The door swung open quiet as a leaf in autumn. If Horace noticed the hexes, he didn't let on. It was other things he noticed, not hexery.

"Why, you cleaned off the walls," said Horace.

"Arthur Stuart did that," said Alvin. "Rasped it off neat as you please."

"And this stove—I tell you, Makepeace, I didn't figure the price of a new stove in this."

"It isn't a new stove," said Alvin. "I mean, beg-

213

ging your pardon, but it was a brokedown stove we kept for the scrap, only when I looked it over I saw we could fix it up, so why not put it here?"

Makepeace gave Alvin a cool look, then turned back to Horace. "That don't mean it's free, of course."

"Course not," said Horace. "If you bought it for scrap, though . . ."

"Oh, the price won't be too terrible high."

Horace admired how it joined to the roof. "Perfect work," he said. He turned around. To Alvin he looked a little sad, or maybe just resigned. "Have to cover the rest of the floor, of course."

"Not our line of work," said Makepeace Smith.

"Just talking to myself, don't mind me." Horace went over to the east window, pushed against it with his fingers, then raised it. He found the pegs on the sill and put them into the third hole on each side, then let the window fall back down to rest against the pegs. He looked at the pegs, then out the window, then back at the pegs, for a long time. Alvin dreaded having to explain how he, not trained as a fine carpenter, managed to hang such a fine window. Worse yet, what if Horace guessed that this was the original window, not a new one? That could only be explained by Alvin's knack—no carpenter could get inside the wood to cut out a sliding window like that.

But all Horace said was, "You did some extra work."

"Just figured it needed doing," said Alvin. If Horace wasn't going to ask about how he did it, Alvin was just as happy not to explain.

"I didn't reckon to have it done so fast," said Horace. "Nor to have so much done. The lock looks

214

to be an expensive one, and the stove—I hope I don't have to pay for all at once."

Alvin almost said, You don't have to pay for any of it, but of course that wouldn't do. It was up to Makepeace Smith to decide things like that.

But when Horace turned around, looking for an answer, he didn't face Makepeace Smith, he stood square on to Alvin. "Makepeace Smith here's been charging full price for your work, so I reckon I shouldn't pay you any less."

Only then did Alvin realize that he made a mistake when he said he did the work in his free time, since work a prentice did in his official free time was paid for direct to the prentice, and not the master. Makepeace Smith never gave Alvin free time— whatever work anyone wanted done, Makepeace would hire Alvin out to do, which was his right under the prentice contract. By calling it free time, Alvin seemed to be saying that Makepeace had given him time off to earn money for himself.

"Sir, I—"

Makepeace spoke up before Alvin could explain the mistake. "Full price wouldn't be right," said Makepeace. "Alvin getting so close to the end of his contract, I thought he should start trying things on his own, see how to handle money. But even though the work looks right to you, to me it definitely looks second rate. So half price is right. I figure it took at least twenty hours to do all this— right, Alvin?"

It was more like ten, but Alvin just nodded. He didn't know what to say, anyway, since his master was obviously not committed to telling the plain truth about this job. And the job he did would have been at least twenty hours—two full day's labor—for a smith without Alvin's knack.

"So," said Makepeace, "between Al's labor at half price and the cost of the stove and the iron and all, it comes to fifteen dollars."

Horace whistled and rocked back on his heels.

"You can have my labor free, for the experience," Alvin said.

Makepeace glared at him.

"Wouldn't dream of it," said Horace. "The Savior said the laborer is worthy of his hire. It's the sudden high price of iron I'm a little skeptical about.'

"It's a *stove*," said Makepeace Smith.

Wasn't till I fixed it, Alvin said silently.

"You bought it as scrap iron," said Horace. "As you said about Al's labor, full price wouldn't be right."

Makepeace sighed. "For old times's sake, Horace, cause you brought me here and helped set me up on my own when I came west eighteen years ago. Nine dollars."

Horace didn't smile, but he nodded. "Fair enough. and since you usually charge four dollars a day for Alvin's hire, I guess his twenty hours at *half* price comes to four bucks. You come by the house this afternoon, Alvin, I'll have it for you. And Makepeace, I'll pay you the rest when the inn fills up at harvest time."

"Fair enough," said Makepeace.

"Glad to see that you're giving Alvin free time now," said Horace. "There's been a lot of folks criticizing you for being so tight with a good prentice, but I always told them, Makepeace is biding his time, you'll see."

216

"That's right," said Makepeace. "I was biding my time."

"You don't mind if I tell other folks that the biding's done?"

"Alvin still has to do his work for me," said Makepeace.

Horace nodded wisely. "Reckon so," he said. "He works for you mornings, for himself afternoons—is that right? That's the way most fair-minded masters do it, when a prentice gets so near to journeyman."

Makepeace began to turn a little red. Alvin wasn't surprised. He could see what was happening—Horace Guester was being like a lawyer for him, seizing on this chance to shame Makepeace into treating Alvin fair for the first time in more than six years of prenticing. When Makepeace decided to pretend that Alvin really *did* have free time, why, that was a crack in the door, and Horace was muscling his way through by main force. Pushing Makepeace to give Alvin half days, no less! That was surely too much for Makepeace to swallow.

But Makepeace swallowed. "Half days is fine with me. Been meaning to do that for some time."

"So you'll be working afternoons yourself now, right, Makepeace?"

Oh, Alvin had to gaze at Horace with pure admiration. He wasn't going to let Makepeace get away with lazing around and forcing Alvin to do all the work at the smithy.

"When I work's my own business, Horace."

"Just want to tell folks when they can be sure to find the master in, and when the prentice."

"I'll be in *all day*."

"Why, glad to hear it," said Horace. "Well, fine work, I must say, Alvin. Your master done a good job teaching you, and you been carefuler than I ever seen before. You make sure to come by this evening for your four dollars."

"Yes sir. Thank you, sir."

"I'll just let you two get back to work now," said Horace. "Are these the only two keys to the door?"

"Yes sir," said Alvin. "I oiled them up so they won't rust."

"I'll keep them oiled myself. Thanks for the reminder."

Horace opened the door and pointedly held it open till Makepeace and Alvin came on out. Horace carefully locked the door, as they watched. He turned and grinned at Alvin. "Maybe first thing I'll have you do is make a lock this fine for *my* front door." Then he laughed out loud and shook his head. "No, I reckon not. I'm an innkeeper. My business is to let people in, not lock them out. But there's others in town who'll like the look of this lock."

"Hope so, sir. Thank you."

Horace nodded again, then took a cool gaze at Makepeace as if to say, Don't forget all you promised to do here today. Then he ambled off up the path to the roadhouse.

Alvin started down the hill to the smithy. He could hear Makepeace following him, but Alvin wasn't exactly hoping for a conversation with his master just now. As long as Makepeace said nothing, that was good enough for Alvin.

That lasted only until they were both inside the smithy.

"That stove was broke to hell and back," said Makepeace.

That was the last thing Alvin expected to hear,

and the most fearful. No chewing-out for claiming free time; no attempt to take back what he'd promised in the way of work schedule. Makepeace Smith had remembered that stove better than Alvin expected.

"Looked real bad, all right," said Alvin.

"No way to fix that without recasting," said Makepeace. "If I didn't know it was impossible, I would've fixed it myself."

"I thought so, too," said Alvin. "But when I looked it over—"

The look on Makepeace Smith's face silenced him. He knew. There was no doubt in Alvin's mind. The master knew what his prentice boy could do. Alvin felt the fear of being found out right down to his bones; it felt just like hide-and-go-find with his brothers and sisters when he was little, back in Vigor Church. The worst was when you were the last one still hid and unfound, all the waiting and waiting, and then you hear the footsteps coming, and you tingle all over, you feel it in every part of your body, like as if your whole self was awake and itching to move. It gets so bad you want to jump out and scream, "Here I am! I'm here!" and then run like a rabbit, not to the haven tree, but just anywhere, just run full out until every muscle of your body was wore out and you fell down on the earth. It was crazy—no good came of such craziness. But that's how it felt playing with his brothers and sisters, and that's how it felt now on the verge of being found out.

To Alvin's surprise, a slow smile spread across his master's face. "So that's it," said Makepeace. "That's it. Ain't you full of surprises. I see it now. Your pa said when you was born, he's the seventh son of a seventh son. Your way with horses, sure, I knew about that. And what you done finding that well, sense like a doodlebug, I could see *that*, too. But now." Makepeace grinned. "Here I thought you were a smith like never was born, and all the time you was fiddling with it like an alchemist."

"No sir," said Alvin.

"Oh, I'll keep your secret," said Makepeace. "I won't tell a soul." But he was laughing in the way he had, and Alvin knew that while Makepeace wouldn't tell straight out, he'd be dropping hints from here to the Hio. But that wasn't what bothered Alvin most.

"Sir," said Alvin, "all the work I ever done for *you*, I done honest, with my own arms and skill."

Makepeace nodded wisely, like he understood some secret meaning in Alvin's words. "I get it," he said. "Secret's safe with me. But I knew it all along. Knew you couldn't be as good a smith as you seemed."

Makepeace Smith had no idea how close he was to death. Alvin wasn't a murderous soul—any lust for blood that might have been born in him was driven out of him on a certain day inside Eight-Face Mound near seven years ago. But during all the years of his prenticeship, he had never heard one word of praise from this man, nothing but complaints about how lazy Alvin was, and how second-rate his work was, and all the time Makepeace Smith was lying, all the time he knew Alvin was good. Not till Makepeace was convinced Alvin had used hidden knackery to do his smithwork, not till now did Makepeace ever let Alvin know that he was, in fact, a good smith. Better than good. Alvin knew it, of course, knew he was a natural smith, but never having it said out loud hurt him deeper than he guessed. Didn't his master know how much a word might have meant, even half an hour ago, just a word like, "You've got some skill at this, boy," or, "You have a right good hand with that sort of work"? But Makepeace couldn't do it, had to lie and pretend Alvin had no skill until now, when Makepeace believed that he didn't have a smith's skill at all.

Alvin wanted to reach out and take hold of Makepeace's head and ram it into the anvil, ram it so hard that the truth would be driven right through Makepeace's skull and into his brain. I never used my Maker's knack in any of my smithwork, not since I got strong enough to do it with my own strength and skill, so don't smirk at me like I'm just a trickster, and no real smith. Besides, even if I used my Maker's art, do you think that's easy, either? Do you think I haven't paid a price for that as well?

All the fury of Alvin's life, all these years of slavery, all these years of rage at the unfairness of his master, all these years of secrecy and disguise, all his desperate longing to know what to do with his life and having no one in the world to ask, all this was burning inside Alvin hotter than the forge fire. Now the itching and tingling inside him wasn't a longing to run. No, it was a longing to do violence, to stop that smile on Makepeace Smith's face, to stop it forever against the anvil's beak.

But somehow Alvin held himself motionless, speechless, as still as an animal trying to be invisible, trying not to be where he is. And in that stillness Alvin heard the greensong all around him, and he let the life of the woodland come into him, fill his heart, bring him peace. The greensong wasn't loud

221

as it used to be, farther west in wilder times, when the Red man still sang along with the greenwood music. It was weak, and sometimes got near drowned out by the unharmonious noise of town life or the monotones of well-tended fields. But Alvin could still find the song at need, and sing silently along with it, and let it take over and calm his heart.

Did Makepeace Smith know how close he came to death? For it was sure he'd be no match of Alvin rassling, not with Al so young and tall and so much terrible righteous fire in his heart. Whether he guessed or not, the smile faded from Makepeace Smith's face, and he nodded solemnly. "I'll keep all I said, up there, when Horace pushed me so hard. I know you probably put him up to it, but I'm a fair man, so I'll forgive you, long as you still pull some weight here for me, till your contract's up."

Makepeace's accusation that Alvin conspired with Horace should have made Alvin angrier, but by now the greensong owned him, and Alvin wasn't hardly even in the smithy. He was in the kind of trance he learned when he ran with Ta-Kumsaw's Reds, where you forget who and where you are, and your body's just a far-off creature running through the woods.

Makepeace waited for an answer, but it didn't come. So he just nodded wisely and turned to leave. "I got business in town," he said. "Keep at it." He stopped at the wide doorway and turned back into the smithy. "While you're at it, you might as well fix those other brokedown stoves in the shed."

Then he was gone.

Alvin stood there a long time, not moving, not hardly even knowing he had a body to move. It was full moon before he came to himself and took a step. His heart was utterly at peace then, with not a spot of rage left in it. If he'd thought about it, he probably would've knowed that the anger was sure to come back, that he wasn't so much healed as soothed. But soothing was enough for now, it'd do. His contract would be up this spring, and then he'd be out of this place, a free man at last.

One thing, though. It never did occur to him to do what Makepeace Smith asked, and fix those other brokedown stoves. And as for Makepeace, he never brought it up again, neither. Alvin's knack wasn't a part of his prenticeship, and Makepeace Smith must've knowed that, deep down, must've knowed he didn't have the right to tell young Al what to do when he was a-Making.

A few days later Alvin was one of the men who helped lay the new floor in the springhouse. Horace took him aside and asked him why he never came by for his four dollars.

Alvin couldn't very well tell him the truth, that he'd never take money for work he did as a Maker. "Call it my share of the teacher's salary," said Alvin.

"You got no property to pay tax on," said Horace, "nor any children to go to the school, neither."

"Then say I'm paying you for my share of the land my brother's body sleeps in up behind the road-house," said Alvin.

Horace nodded solemnly. "That debt, if there *was* a debt, was paid in full by your father's and brothers' labor seventeen year gone, young Alvin, but I respect your wish to pay your share. So this time I'll consider you paid in full. But any other work you do for me, you take full wages, you hear me?"

"I will, sir," said Alvin. "Thank you sir."

"Call me Horace, boy. When a growed man calls me sir it just makes me feel old."

They went back to work then, and said nary another word about Alvin's work on the spring-house. But something stuck in Alvin's mind all the same: what Horace said when Alvin offered to let his wages be a share of the teacher's salary. "You got no property, nor any children to go to the school." There it was, right there, in just a few words. That was why even though Alvin had his full growth on him, even though Horace called him a growed man, he wasn't really a man yet, not even in his own eyes. Because he had no family. Because he had no property. Till he had those, he was just a big old boy. Just a child like Arthur Stuart, only taller, with some beard showing when he didn't shave.

And just like Arthur Stuart, he had no share in the school. He was too old. It wasn't built for the likes of him. So why did he wait so anxious for the schoolmistress to come? Why did he think of her with so all-fired much hope? She wasn't coming here for him, and yet he knew that he had done his work on the springhouse for her, as if to put her in his debt, or perhaps to thank her in advance for what he wanted her, so desperately, to do for him.

Teach me, he said silently. I got a Work to do in this world, but nobody knows what it is or how it's done. Teach me. That's what I want from you, Lady, to help me find my way to the root of the world or the root of myself or the throne of God or the Unmaker's heart, wherever the secret of Making lies, so that I can build against the snow of winter, or make a light to shine against the fall of night.

14

River Rat

Alvin was in Hatrack Mouth the afternoon the teacher came. Makepeace had sent him with the wagon, to fetch a load of new iron that came down the Hio. Hatrack Mouth used to be just a single wharf, a stop for riverboats unloading stuff for the town of Hatrack River. Now, though, as river traffic got thicker and more folks were settling out in the western lands on both sides of the Hio, there was a need for a couple of inns and shops, where farmers could sell provender to passing boats, and river travelers could stay the night. Hatrack Mouth and the town of Hatrack River were getting more important all the time, since this was the last place where the Hio was close to the great Wobbish Road—the very road that Al's own father and brothers cut through the wilderness west to Vigor Church. Folks would come downriver and unship their wagons and horses here, and then move west overland.

There was also things that folks wouldn't tolerate in Hatrack River itself: gaming houses, where poker and other games got played and money changed hands, the law not being inclined to venture much into the dens of river rats and other such scum. And upstairs of such houses, it was said there was women who wasn't ladies, plying a trade that decent folks scarcely whispered about and boys of Alvin's age talked of in low voices with lots of nervous laughter.

It wasn't the thought of raised skirts and naked thighs that made Alvin look forward to his trips to Hatrack Mouth. Alvin scarce noticed those buildings, knowing he had no business there. It was the wharf that drew him, and the porthouse, and the river itself, with boats and rafts going by all the time, ten going downstream for every one coming up. His favorite boats were the steamboats, whistling and spitting their way along at unnatural speeds. With heavy engines built in Irrakwa, these riverboats were wide and long, and yet they moved upstream against the current faster than rafts could float downstream. There was eight of them on the Hio now, going from Dekane down to Sphinx and back again. No farther than Sphinx, though, since the Mizzipy was thick with fog, and nary a boat dared navigate there.

Someday, thought Alvin, someday a body could get on such a boat as *Pride of the Hio* and just float away. Out to the West, to the wild lands, and maybe catch a glimpse of the place where Ta-Kumsaw and Tenskwa-Tawa live now. Or upriver to Dekane, and thence by the new steam train that rode on rails up to Irrakwa and the canal. From there a body could travel the whole world, oceans across. Or maybe he could stand on this bank and the whole world would someday pass him by.

But Alvin wasn't lazy. He didn't linger long at riverside, though he might want to. Soon enough he went into the porthouse and turned in Makepeace Smith's chit to redeem the iron packed in nine crates on the dock.

"Don't want you using my hand trucks to tote those, now," said the portmaster. Alvin nodded—it was always the same. Folks wanted iron bad enough, the portmaster included, and he'd be up to the smithy soon enough asking for this or that. But in the meantime, he'd let Alvin heft the iron all himself, and not let him wear out the portmaster's trucks moving such a heavy load. Nor did Makepeace ever give Alvin money enough to hire one of the river rats to help with the toting. Truth to tell, Alvin was glad enough of that. He didn't much like the sort of man who lived the river life. Even though the day of brigands and pirates was pretty much over, there being too much traffic on the water now for much to happen in secret, still there was thievery enough, and crooked dealing, and Alvin looked down hard on the men who did such things. To his way of thinking, such men counted on the trust of honest folks, and then betrayed them; and what could that do, except make it so folks would stop trusting each other at all? I'd rather face a man with raw fighting in him, and match him arm for arm, than face a man who's full of lies.

So wouldn't you know it, Alvin met the new teacher and matched himself with a river rat all in the same hour.

The river rat he fought was one of a gang of them lolling under the eaves of the porthouse, probably waiting for a gaming house to open. Each time Alvin came out of the porthouse with a crate of iron bars, they'd call out to him, taunting him. At first it was sort of good-natured, saying things like, "Why are you taking so many trips, boy? Just tuck one of those crates under each arm!" Alvin just grinned at remarks like that, since he knew that they knew just

227

how heavy a load of iron was. Why, when they unloaded the iron from the boat yesterday, the boatman no doubt hefted two men to a crate. So in a way, teasing him about being lazy or weak was a kind of compliment, since it was only a joke because the iron was heavy and Alvin was really very strong.

Then Alvin went on to the grocer's, to buy the spices Gertie had asked him to bring home for her kitchen, along with a couple of Irrakwa and New England kitchen tools whose purpose Al could only half guess at.

When he came back, both arms full, he found the river rats still loitering in the shade, only they had somebody new to taunt, and their mockery was a little ugly now. It was a middle-aged woman, some forty years old by Alvin's guess, her hair tied up severe in a bun and a plain hat atop it, her dark dress right up to the neck and down the wrist as if she was afraid sunlight on her skin might kill her. She was staring stonily ahead while the river rats had words at her.

"You reckon that dress is sewed on, boys?"

They reckoned so.

"Probably never comes up for no man."

"Why no, boys, there's nothing *under* that skirt, she's just a doll's head and hands sewed onto a stuffed dress, don't you think?"

"No way could she be a *real* woman."

"I can tell a real woman when I see one, anyway. The minute they lay eyes on me, *real* woman just naturally start spreading their legs and raising their skirts."

"Maybe if you helped her out a little, you could turn her into a real woman."

"This one? This one's carved out of wood. I'd get splinters in my oar, trying to row in such waters."

Well, that was about all Alvin could stand to hear. It was bad enough for a man to think such thoughts about a woman who invited it—the girls from the gaming houses, who opened their necklines down to where you could count their breasts as plain as a cow's teats and flounced along the streets kicking up their skirts till you could see their knees. But this woman was plainly a lady, and by rights oughtn't to have to hear the dirty thoughts of these low men. Alvin figured she must be waiting for somebody to fetch her—the stagecoach to Hatrack River was due, but not for a couple of hours yet. She didn't look fearful—she probably knew these men was more brag than action, so her virtue was safe enough. And from her face Alvin couldn't guess whether she was even listening, her expression was so cold and faraway. But the river rats' words embarrassed *him* so much he couldn't stand it, and couldn't feel right about just driving his wagon off and leaving her there. So he put the parcels he got from the port grocer into the wagon and then walked up to the river rats and spoke to the loudest and crudest talker among them.

"Maybe you'd best speak to her like a lady," said Alvin. "Or perhaps not speak to her at all."

Alvin wasn't surprised to see the glint these boys all got in their eyes the minute he spoke. Provoking a lady was one kind of fun, but he knew they were sizing him up now to see how easy he'd be to whup. They always loved a chance to teach a lesson to a town boy, even one built up as strong as Alvin was, him being a blacksmith.

"Maybe you'd best not speak to us at all," said

the loud one. "Maybe you already said more than you ought."

One of the river rats didn't understand, and thought the game was still talking dirty about the lady. "He's just jealous. He wants to pole her muddy river himself."

"I haven't said enough," said Alvin, "not while you still don't have the manners to know how to speak to a lady."

Only now did the lady speak for the first time. "I don't need protection, young man," she said. "Just go along, please." Her voice was strange-sounding. Cultured, like Reverend Thrower, with all the words clear. Like people who went to school in the East.

It would have been better for her not to speak, since the sound of her voice only encouraged the river rats.

"Oh, she's sweet on this boy!"

"She's making a move on him!"

"He wants to row our boat!"

"Let's show her who the real man is!"

"If she wants his little mast, let's cut it off and give it to him."

A knife appeared, then another. Didn't she know enough to keep her mouth shut? If they dealt with Alvin alone, they'd set up to have a single fight, one to one. But if they got to showing off for her, they'd be happy enough to gang up on him and cut him bad, maybe kill him, certainly take an ear or his nose or, like they said, geld him.

Alvin glared at her for a moment, silently telling her to shut her mouth. Whether she understood his look or just figured things out for herself or got plain scared to say more, she didn't offer any more conversation, and Alvin set to turning things in a direction he could handle.

"Knives," said Alvin, with all the contempt he could muster. "So you're afraid to face a blacksmith with bare hands?"

They laughed at him, but the knives got pulled back and put away.

"Blacksmith's *nothing* compared to the muscles we get poling the river."

"You don't pole the river no more, boys, and everybody knows that," said Alvin. "You just set back and get fat, watching the paddlewheel push the boat along."

The loudest talker got up and stepped out, pulling his filthy shirt off over his head. He was strongly muscled, all right, with more than a few scars making white and red marks here and there on his chest and arms. He was also missing an ear.

"From the look of you," said Alvin, "you've fought a lot of men."

"Damn straight," said the river rat.

"And from the look of you, I'd say most of them was better than you."

The man turned red, blushing under his tan clear down to his chest.

"Can't you give me somebody who's worth rassling? Somebody who mostly *wins* his fights?"

"I win my fights!" shouted the man—getting mad, so he'd be easy to lick, which was Al's plan. But the others, they started pulling him back.

"The blacksmith boy's right, you're no great shakes at rassling."

"Give him what he wants."

"Mike, you take this boy."

"He's yours, Mike."

From the back—the shadiest spot, where he'd been sitting on the only chair with a back to it—a man stood up and stepped forward.

"I'll take this boy," he said.

At once the loud one backed off and got out of the way. This wasn't what Alvin wanted at all. The man they called Mike was bigger and stronger than any of the others, and as he stripped his shirt off, Al saw that while he had a scar or two, he was mostly clean, and he had both his ears, a sure sign that if he ever lost a rassling match, he sure never lost *bad*.

He had muscles like a buffalo.

"My name is Mike Fink!" he bellowed. "And I'm the meanest, toughest son-of-a-bitch ever to walk on the water! I can orphan baby alligators with my bare hands! I can throw a live buffalo up onto a wagon and slap him upside the head until he's dead! If I don't like the bend of a river, I grab ahold of the end of it and give it a shake to straighten it out! Every woman I ever put down come up with triplets, if she come up at all! When I'm done with you, boy, your hair will hang down straight on both sides cause you won't have no more ears. You'll have to sit down to piss, and you'll never have to shave again!"

All the time Mike Fink was making his brag, Alvin was taking off his shirt and his knife belt and laying them on the wagon seat. Then he marked a big circle in the dirt, making sure he looked as calm and relaxed as if Mike Fink was a spunky seven-year-old boy, and not a man with murder in his eyes.

So when Fink was shut of boasting, the circle was marked. Fink walked to the circle, then rubbed it out with his foot, raising a dust. He walked all around the circle, rubbing it out. "I don't know who

232

taught you how to rassle, boy," he said, "but when you rassle *me*, there ain't no lines and there ain't no rules."

Once again the lady spoke up. "Obviously there are no rules when you speak, either, or you'd know that the word *ain't* is a sure sign of ignorance and stupidity."

Fink turned to the woman and made as if to speak. But it was like he knew he had nothing to say, or maybe he figured that whatever he said would make him sound more ignorant. The contempt in her voice enraged him, but it also made him doubt himself. At first Alvin thought the lady was making it more dangerous for him, meddling again. But then he realized that she was doing to Fink what Alvin had tried to do to the loudmouth – make him mad enough to fight stupid. Trouble was, as Alvin sized up the river man, he suspected that Fink didn't fight stupid when he was mad—it just made him fight meaner. Fight to kill. Act out his brag about taking off parts of Alvin's body. This wasn't going to be a friendly match like the ones Alvin had in town, where the game was just to throw the other man, or if they was fighting on grass, to pin him down.

"You're not so much," Alvin said, "and you know it, or you wouldn't have a knife hid in your boot."

Fink looked startled, then grinned. He pulled up his pantleg and took a long knife out of his boot, tossed it to the men behind him. "I won't need a knife to fight *you*," he said.

"Then why don't you take the knife out of the *other* boot?" asked Alvin.

Fink frowned and raised the other pantleg. "Ain't no knife here," he said.

Alvin knew better, of course, and it pleased him

that Fink was worried enough about this fight not to part with his most secret knife. Besides which, probably nobody else knew about that knife but Alvin, with his ability to see what others couldn't see. Fink didn't want to let on to the others that he had such a knife, or word would spread fast along the river and he'd get no advantage from it.

Still, Alvin couldn't afford to let Fink fight with the knife on him. "Then take off the boots and we'll fight barefoot," Alvin said. It was a good idea anyway, knife or no knife. Alvin knew that when the river rats fought, they kicked like mules with their boots. Fighting barefoot might take some of the spunk out of Mike Fink.

But if Fink lost any spunk, he didn't show it. Just sat down in the dust of the road and pulled off his boots. Alvin did the same, and his socks too—Fink didn't wear socks. So now the two of them had on nothing but their trousers, and already out in the sunlight there was enough dust and sweat that their bodies were looking a little streaked and cakey with clay.

Not so caked up, though, that Alvin couldn't feel a hex of protection drawn over Mike Fink's whole body. How could such a thing be? Did he have a hex on some amulet in his pocket? The pattern was strongest near his backside, but when Alvin sent his bug to search that pocket, there was nothing but the rough cotton canvas of Fink's trousers. He wasn't carrying so much as a coin.

But now a crowd was gathered. Not just the river rats who'd been resting in the porthouse shade, but a whole slew of others, and it was plain they all expected Mike Fink to win. He must be something of a legend on the river. Alvin realized, and no

234

surprise, with this mysterious hex he had. Alvin could imagine folks poking a knife at Fink, only to twist at the last moment, or lose their grip, or somehow keep the knife from doing harm. It was a lot easier to win all your wrassling if no man's teeth could bite into you, and if a knife couldn't do much more than graze your skin.

Fink tried all the obvious stuff first, of course, because it made the best show: Roaring, rushing at Alvin like a buffalo, trying to get a bear hug on him, trying to grab onto Alvin and give him a swing like a rock on a string. But Alvin wouldn't have none of that. He didn't even have to use knackery to get away, neither. He was younger and quicker than Fink, and the river man hardly so much as laid a hand on him. Al dodged away so sudden. At first the crowd hooted and called Alvin coward. But after a while of this, they began to laugh at Fink, since he looked so silly, rushing and roaring and coming up empty all the time.

In the meantime, Alvin was exploring to find the source of Fink's hex, for there was no hope of winning this fight if he couldn't get rid of that strong web. He found it soon enough—a pattern of dye embedded deep in the skin of Fink's buttock. It wasn't a perfect hex anymore, since the skin had changed shape somewhat as Fink grew over the years, but it was a clever pattern, with strong locks and links—good enough to cast a strong net over him, even if it was misshapen.

If he hadn't been in the middle of a rassling match with Fink, Alvin might have been more subtle, might have just weakened the hex a little, for he had no will to deprive Fink of the hex that had protected him for so long. Why, Fink might die of it, losing

235

his hex, especially if he had let himself get careless, counting on it to protect him. But what choice did Alvin have? So he made the dyes in Fink's skin start to flow, seeping into his bloodstream and getting carried away. Alvin could do without full concentration—just set it to happening and let it glide on, while he worked on dodging out of Fink's way.

Soon enough Al could sense the hex weakening, fading, finally collapsing completely. Fink wouldn't know it, but Alvin did—he could now be hurt like any other man.

By this time, though, Fink was no longer making those rough and stupid rushes at him. He was circling, feinting, looking to grapple in a square, then use his greater bulk to throw Alvin. But Alvin had a longer reach, and there was no doubt his arms were stronger, so whenever Fink reached to grab, Alvin batted the river man's arms out of the way.

With the hex gone, however, Alvin didn't slap him away. Instead, he reached inside Fink's arms, so that as Fink grasped his arms, Alvin got his hands hooked behind Fink's neck.

Alvin pulled down hard, bowing Fink down so his head was even with Alvin's chest. It was too easy—Fink was letting him, and Alvin guessed why. Sure enough, Fink pulled Alvin closer and brought his head up fast, expecting to catch Alvin on the chin with the back of his head. He was so strong he might've broke Alvin's neck doing that—only Alvin's chin wasn't where Fink thought it would be. In fact, Alvin had already rared his own head back, and when Fink came up hard and out of control, Alvin rammed forward and smashed his forehead into Fink's face. He could feel Fink's nose crumple under the blow, and blood erupted down both their faces.

It wasn't all that surprising, for a man's nose to get broke during a rassle like this. It hurt like blazes, of course, and it would've stopped a friendly match—though of course a friendly match wouldn't have included head butts. Any other river rat would've shook his head, roared a couple of times, and charged back into the fight.

Instead, Fink backed away, a look of real surprise on his face, his hands gripping his nose. Then he let out a howl like a whupped dog.

Everybody else fell silent. It was such a funny thing to happen, a river rat like Mike Fink howling at a broke-up nose. No, it wasn't rightly funny, but it was strange. It wasn't how a river rat was supposed to act.

"Come on, Mike," somebody murmured.

"You can take him, Mike."

But it was a half-hearted sort of encouragement. They'd never seen Mike Fink act hurt or scared before. He wasn't good at hiding it, either. Only Al knew why. Only Al knew that Mike Fink had never in his life felt such a pain, that Fink had never once shed his own blood in a fight. So many times he'd broke the other fellow's nose and laughed at the pain—it was easy to laugh, because he didn't know how it felt. Now he knew. Trouble was, he was learning what others learned at six years old, and so he was acting like a six-year-old. Not crying, exactly, but howling.

For a minute Alvin thought that maybe the match was over. But Fink's fear and pain soon turned to rage, and he waded back into the fight. Maybe he'd learned pain, but he hadn't learned caution from it.

So it took a few more holds, a few more wrenches and twists, before Alvin got Fink down onto the ground. Even as frightened and surprised as Fink was, he was the strongest man Alvin had ever rassled. Till this fight with Fink, Alvin had never really had occasion to find out just how strong he was; he'd never been pushed to his limit. Now he was, and he found himself rolling over and over in the dust, hardly able to breathe it was so thick. Fink's own hot panting breath now above him, now below, knees ramming, arms pounding and gripping, feet scrabbling in the dust, searching for purchase enough to get leverage.

In the end it came down to Fink's inexperience with weakness. Since no man could ever break a bone of his, Fink had never learned to tuck his legs, never learned not to expose them to where a man could stomp them. When Alvin broke free and scrambled to his feet, Fink rolled over quick and, for just a moment, lying there on the ground, he drew one leg across the other like a pure invitation. Alvin didn't even think, he just jumped into the air and came down with both feet onto Fink's top leg, jamming downward with all his weight, so the bones of the top leg were bowed over the lower one. So sharp and hard was the blow that it wasn't just the top leg that shattered, but the bottom one, too. Fink screamed like a child in the fire.

Only now did Alvin realize what he'd done. Oh, yes, of course he'd ended the fight—nobody's tough enough to fight on with two broken legs. But Alvin could tell at once, without looking—or at least without looking with his *eyes*—that these were not clean breaks, not the kind that can heal easy. Besides, Fink wasn't a young man now, and sure he wasn't a

238

boy. If these breaks healed at all, they'd leave him lame at best, outright crippled at worst. His livelihood would be gone. Besides, he must have made a lot of enemies over the years. What would they do now, with him broken and halt? How long would he live?

So Alvin knelt on the ground beside where Mike Fink writhed—or rather, the upper half of him writhed, while he tried to keep his legs from moving at all—and touched the legs. With his hands in contact with Fink's body, even through the cloth of his pants, Alvin could find his way easier, work faster, and in just a few moments, he had knitted the bones together. That was all he tried to do, no more—the bruise, the torn muscle, the bleeding, he had to leave that or Fink might get up and attack him again.

He pulled his hands away, and stepped back from Fink. At once the river rats gathered around their fallen hero.

"Is his legs broke?" asked the loudmouth river rat.

"No," said Alvin.

"They're broke to pieces!" howled Fink.

By then, another man had slit right up the pantleg. Sure enough he found the bruise, but as he felt along the bone, Fink screeched and pulled away. "Don't touch it!"

"Didn't feel broke to me," said the man.

"Look how he's moving his legs. They ain't broke."

It was true enough—Fink was no longer writhing with just the top half of his body, his legs were wiggling now as much as any other part of him.

One man helped Fink to his feet. Fink staggered, almost fell, caught himself by leaning against the loudmouth, smearing blood from his nose on the man's shirt. The others pulled away from him.

"Just a boy," muttered one.

"Howling like a puppydog."

"Big old baby."

"Mike *Fink*." And than a chuckle.

Alvin stood by the wagon, putting on his shirt, then sat up on the wagon seat to pull on his shoes and socks. He glanced up to find the lady watching him. She stood not six feet off, since the smith's wagon was pulled right up against the loading dock. She had a look of sour distaste. Alvin realized she was probably disgusted at how dirty he was. Maybe he shouldn't have put his shirt right back on, but then, it was also impolite to go shirtless in front of a lady. In fact, the town men, especially the doctors and lawyers, they acted ashamed to be out in public without a proper coat and waistcoat and cravat. Poor folks usually didn't have such clothes, and a prentice would be putting on airs to dress like that. But a shirt—he had to have his shirt on, whether he was filthy with dust or not.

"Beg pardon, Ma'am," he said. "I'll wash when I get home."

"Wash?" she asked. "And when you do, will your brutality also wash away?"

"I reckon I don't know, since I never heard that word."

"I daresay you haven't," she said. "Brutality. From the word *brute*. Meaning beast."

Alvin felt himself redden with anger. "Maybe so. Maybe I should've let them go on talking to you however they liked."

"I paid no attention to them. They didn't bother me. You had no need to protect me, especially not that way. Stripping naked and rolling around in the dirt. You're covered with blood."

Alvin hardly knew what to answer, she was so snooty and bone-headed. "I wasn't naked," Alvin said. Then he grinned. "And it was *his* blood."

"And are you proud of that?"

Yes, he was. But he knew that if he said so, it would diminish him in her sight. Well, what of that? What did he care what she thought of him? Still, he said nothing.

In the silence between them, he could hear the river rats behind him, hooting at Fink, who wasn't howling anymore, but wasn't saying much, either. It wasn't just Fink they were thinking about now, though.

"Town boy thinks he's tough."

"Maybe we ought to show him a *real* fight."

"Then we'll see how uppity his ladyfriend is."

Alvin couldn't rightly tell the future, but it didn't take no torch to guess at what was going to happen. Al's boots were on, his horse was full-hitched, and it was time to go. But snooty as she was, he couldn't leave the lady behind. He knew she'd be the river rats' target now, and however little she thought she needed protection, he knew that these river men had just watched their best man get whupped and humbled, and all on account of her, which meant she'd likely end up lying in the dirt with her bags all dumped in the river, if not worse.

"Best you get in," Alvin said.

"I wonder that you dare to give me instructions like a common—What are you doing?"

Alvin was tossing her trunk and bags into the back of the wagon. It seemed so obvious to him that he didn't bother answering her.

241

"I think you're robbing me, sir!"

"I am if you don't get in," said Alvin.

By now the river rats were gathering near the wagon, and one of them had hold of the horse's harness. She glanced around, and her angry expression changed. Just a little. She stepped from the dock onto the wagon seat. Alvin took her hand and helped her arrange herself on the seat. By now, the loudmouth river rat was standing beside him, leaning on the wagon, grinning wickedly. "You beat one of us, blacksmith, but can you beat us all?"

Alvin just stared at him. He was concentrating on the man holding the horse, making his hand suddenly tingle with pain, like he was being punctured with a hundred pins. The man cried out and let go the horse. The loudmouth looked away from Alvin, toward the sound of the cry, and in the moment Alvin kicked him in the ear with his boot. It wasn't much of a kick, but then, it wasn't much of an ear, either, and the man ended up sitting in the dirt, holding his head.

"Gee-yap!" shouted Alvin.

The horse obediently lunged forward—and the wagon moved about an inch. Then another inch. Hard to get a wagonload of iron moving fast, at least all of a sudden. Alvin made the wheels turn smooth and easy, but he couldn't do a thing about the weight of the wagon or the strength of the horse. By the time the horse got moving, the wagon was a good deal heavier, with the weight of river rats hanging on it, pulling back, climbing aboard.

Alvin turned around and swung his whip at them. The whip was for show—it didn't hit a one. Still, they all fell off or let go of the wagon as if it *had* hit them, or scared them anyway. What really happened was that all of a sudden the wood of the wagon got as slick as if it was greased. There was no way for them to hold onto it. So the wagon lurched forward as they collapsed back into the dust of the road.

They weren't done, though. After all, Alvin had to turn around and head back *up* the road right past them in order to get to Hatrack River. He was trying to figure what to do next when he heard a musket go off, loud as a cannonshot, the sound hanging on in the heavy summer air. When he got the wagon turned around, he saw the portmaster standing on the dock, his wife behind him. He was holding one musket, and she was reloading the one he had just fired.

"I reckon we get along well enough most of the time, boys," said the portmaster. "But today you just don't seem to know when you been beat fair and square. So I guess it's about time you settled down in the shade, cause if you make another move toward that wagon, them as don't die from buckshot'll be standing trial in Hatrack River, and if you think you won't pay dear for assaulting a local boy and the new schoolteacher, then you really are as dumb as you look."

It was quite a little speech, and it worked better than most speeches Alvin had heard in his life. Those river rats just settled right down in the shade, taking a couple of long pulls from a jug and watching Al and the lady with a real sullen look. The portmaster went back inside before the wagon even turned the corner onto the town road.

"You don't suppose the portmaster is in danger from having helped us, do you?" asked the lady. Alvin was pleased to hear that the arrogance was

243

gone from her voice, though she still spoke as clear and even as the ringing of a hammer on iron.

"No," said Alvin. "They all know that if ever a portmaster got harmed, them as did it would never work again on the river, or if they did, they wouldn't live through a night ashore."

"What about you?"

"Oh, I got no such guarantee. So I reckon I won't come back to Hatrack Mouth for a couple of weeks. By then all those boys'll have jobs and be a hundred miles up or downstream from here." Then he remembered what the portmaster had said. "You're the new schoolteacher?"

She didn't answer. Not directly, anyway. "I suppose there are men like that in the East, but one doesn't meet them in the open like this."

"Well, it's a whole lot better to meet them in the open than it is to meet them in private!" Al said, laughing.

She didn't laugh.

"I was waiting for Dr. Whitley Physicker to meet me. He expected my boat later in the afternoon, but he may be on his way."

"This is the only road, Ma'am," Alvin said.

"Miss," she said. "Not madame. That title is properly reserved for married women."

"Like I said, it's the only road. So if he's on his way, we won't *miss* him. Miss."

This time Alvin didn't laugh at his own joke. On the other hand, he thought, looking out of the corner of his eye, that he just might have caught a glimpse of her smiling. So maybe she wasn't as hoity-toity as she seemed, Alvin thought. Maybe she's almost human. Maybe she'll even consent to give private schooling to a certain little half-Black boy. Maybe she'll be worth the work I went to fixing up the springhouse.

Because he was facing forward, driving the wagon, it wouldn't be natural, let alone good manners, for him to turn and stare right at her like he wanted to. She he sent out his bug, his spark, that part of him that "saw" what no man or woman could rightly with their own eyes see. For Alvin this was near second nature by now, to explore people under the skin so to speak. Keep in mind, though, that it wasn't like he could see with his eyes. Sure enough he could tell what was under a body's clothes, but he still didn't see folks naked. Instead he just got a close-in experience of the surface of their skin, almost like he'd took up residence in one of their pores. So he didn't think of it like he was peeping in windows or nothing. It was just another way of looking at folks and understanding them; he wouldn't see a body's shape or color, but he'd see whether they was sweating or hot or healthy or tensed-up. He'd see bruises and old healed-up injuries. He'd see hidden money or secret papers—but if he was to read the papers, he had to discover the feel of the ink on the surface and then trace it until he could build up a picture of the letters in his mind. It was very slow. Not like seeing, no sir.

Anyhow, he sent his bug to "see" this high-toned lady that he couldn't exactly look at. And what he found caught him by surprise. Cause she was every bit as hexed-up as Mike Fink had been.

No, more. She was layers deep in it, from hexy amulets hanging around her neck to hexes stitched into her clothes, even a wire hex embedded in the bun of her hair. Only one of them was for protection, and it wasn't half so strong as Mike Fink's had

245

been. The rest were all—for what? Alvin hadn't seen such work before, and it took some thought and exploration to figure out what these hex-work webs that covered her were doing. The best he could get, riding along in the wagon, keeping his eyes on the road ahead, was that somehow these hexes were doing a powerful beseeming, making her look to be something that she wasn't.

The first thought he had, as I suppose was natural, was to try to discover what she really was, under her disguise. The clothes she wore were real enough—the hexery was only changing the sound of her voice, the hue and texture of the surface of her skin. But Alvin had little practice with beseemings, and none at all with beseemings wove from hexes. Most folks did a beseeming with a word and a gesture, tied up with a drawing of what they wanted to seem to be. It was a working on other folks' minds, and once you saw through it, it didn't fool you at all. Since Alvin always saw through it, such beseemings had no hold on him.

But hers was different. The hex changed the way light hit her and bounced off, so that you weren't fooled into thinking you saw what wasn't there. Instead you really saw her different, the light actually struck your eyes that way. Since it wasn't a change made on Alvin's mind, knowing the trickery didn't help him see the truth. And using his bug, he couldn't tell much about what was hidden away behind the hexes, except that she wasn't quite so wrinkled-up and bony as she looked, which made him guess she might be younger.

It was only when he gave up trying to guess at what lay under the disguise that he came to the real question: Why, if a woman had the power to disguise herself and seem to be anything she wanted, why would she choose to look like *that?* Cold, severe, getting old, bony, unsmiling, pinched-up, angry, aloof. All the things a woman ought to hope she never was, this teacher lady *chose* to be.

Maybe she was a fugitive in disguise. But she was definitely a woman underneath the hexes, and Alvin never heard of a woman outlaw, so it couldn't be that. Maybe she was just young, and figured other folks wouldn't take her serious if she didn't look older. Alvin knew about *that* right enough. Or maybe she was pretty, and men kept thinking of her the wrong way—Alvin tried to conjure up in his mind what might've happened with those river rats if she'd been real beautiful. But truth to tell, the rivermen probably would've been polite as they knew how, if she was pretty. It was only ugly women they felt free to taunt, since ugly women probably reminded them of their mothers. So her plainness wasn't exactly protection. And it wasn't designed to hide a scar, neither, cause Alvin could see her skin wasn't pocked or blemished or marred.

Truth was he couldn't guess at why she was all hid up under so many layers of lies. She could be anything or anybody. He couldn't even ask her, since to tell her he saw through her disguise was the same as to tell her of his knack, and how could he know she could be trusted with such a secret as *that*, when he didn't even know who she really was or why she chose to live inside a lie?

He wondered if he ought to tell somebody. Shouldn't the school board know, before putting the town's children into her care, that she wasn't exactly what she seemed to be? But he couldn't tell them, either, without giving himself away; and besides, maybe her secret was her own business and no harm to anyone. Then if he told the truth on her, it would ruin both him and her, with no good done for anybody.

No, best to watch her, real careful, and learn who she was the only way a body can ever truly know other folks: by seeing what they do. That's the best plan Alvin could think of, and the truth is, now that he knew she had such a secret, how could he *keep* from paying special attention to her? Using his bug to explore around him was such a habit for him that he'd have to work *not* to check up on her, especially if she was living up at the springhouse. He half hoped she wouldn't, so he wouldn't be bothered so much by this mystery; but he just as much hoped she would, so he could keep watch and make sure she was a rightful sort of person.

And I could watch her even better if I studied from her. I could watch her with her own eyes, ask her questions, listen to her answers, and judge what kind of person she might be. Maybe if she taught me long enough, she'd come to trust me, and I her, and then I'd tell her I'm to be a Maker and she'd tell her deep secrets to me and we'd help each other, we'd be true friends the way I haven't had no true friend since I left my brother Measure behind me in Vigor Church.

He wasn't pushing the horse too hard, the load being so heavy, what with her trunk and bags on top of the iron—and herself, to boot. So after all their talk, and then all this silence as he tried to figure out who she really was, they were still only about a half a mile out of Hatrack Mouth when Dr. Physicker's fancy carriage came along. Alvin recognized the carriage right off, and hailed Po Doggly, who was driving. It took all of a couple of minutes to move the teacher and her things from wagon to carriage. Po and Alvin did all the lifting—Dr. Physicker used all his efforts to help the teacher lady into the carriage. Alvin had never seen the doctor act so elegant.

"I'm terribly sorry you had to suffer the discomforts of a ride in that wagon," said the doctor. "I didn't think that I was late."

"In fact you're early," she said. And then, turning graciously to Alvin, she added, "And the wagon ride was surprisingly pleasant."

Since Alvin hadn't said a word for most of the journey, he didn't rightly know whether she meant it as a compliment for him being good company, or as gratitude that he kept his mouth shut and didn't bother her. Either way, though, it made him feel a kind of burning in his face, and not from anger.

As Dr. Physicker was climbing into the carriage, the teacher asked him, "What is this young man's name?" Since she spoke to the doctor, Alvin didn't answer.

"Alvin," said the doctor, settling into his seat. "He was born here. He's the smith's apprentice."

"Alvin," she said, now directing herself to him through the carriage window. "I thank you for your gallantry today, and I hope you'll forgive the ungraciousness of my first response. I had underestimated the villainous nature of our unwelcome companions."

Her words were so elegant-sounding if was like music hearing her talk, even though Alvin could only half-guess what she was saying. Her expression, though, was about as kindly as her forbidding face

249

could look, he reckoned. He wondered what her real visage might look like underneath.

"My pleasure, Ma'am," he said. "I mean Miss."

From the driver's bench, Po Doggly gee-ed the pair of mares and the carriage took off, still heading toward Hatrack Mouth, of course. It wasn't easy for Po to find a place on that road to turn around, either, so Alvin was well on his way before the carriage came back and passed him. Po slowed the carriage, and Dr. Physicker leaned over and tossed a dollar coin into the air. Alvin caught it, more by reflex than by thought.

"For your help for Miss Larner," said Dr. Physicker. Then Po gee-ed the horses again and they went on, leaving Alvin to chew on the dust in the road.

He felt the weight of the coin in his hand, and for a moment he wanted to throw it after the carriage. But that wouldn't do no good at all. No, he'd give it back to Physicker some other time, in some way that wouldn't get nobody riled up. But still it hurt, it stung deep, to be paid for helping a lady, like as if he was a servant or a child or something. And what hurt worst was wondering if maybe it was her idea to pay him. As if she thought he had earned a quarter-day's wages when he fought for her honor. It was sure that if he'd been wearing a coat and cravat instead of one filthy shirt, she'd have thought he done the service due a lady from any Christian gentleman, and she'd know she owed him gratitude instead of payment.

Payment. The coin burned in his hand. Why, for a few minutes there he'd almost thought she liked him. Almost he had hoped that maybe she'd agree to teach him, to help him work out some understand-

ing of how the world works, of what he could do to
be a true Maker and tame the Unmaker's terrible
power. But now that it was plain she despised him,
how could he even ask? How could he even pretend
to be worthy of teaching, when he knew that all she
saw about him was filth and blood and stupid pov-
erty? She knew he meant well, but he was still a
brute in her eyes, like she said first off. It was still
in her heart. Brutality.

Miss Larner. That's what the doctor called her.
He tasted the name as he said it. Dust in his mouth.
You don't take animals to school.

15

Teacher

Miss Larner had no intention of giving an inch to
these people. She had heard enough horror stories
about frontier school boards to know that they
would try to get out of keeping most of the promises
they made in their letters. It was beginning already.

"In your letters you represented to me that I
would have a residence provided as part of my
salary. I do not regard an inn as a private residence."

"You'll have your own private room," said Dr.
Physicker.

"And take all my meals at a common table? This
is not acceptable. If I stay, I will be spending all my
days in the company of the children of this town,
and when that day's work is over, I expect to be
able to prepare my own meals in private and eat
them in solitude, and then spend the evening in the
company of books, without distraction or annoyance. That is not possible in a roadhouse, gentlemen, and so a room in a roadhouse does *not* constitute a private residence."

She could see them sizing her up. Some were
abashed by the mere precision of her speech—she
knew perfectly well that country lawyers put on airs

in their own towns, but they were no match for someone of real education. The only real trouble was going to come from the sheriff, Pauley Wiseman. How absurd, for a grown man still to use a child's nickname.

"Now see here, young lady," said the sheriff.

She raised an eyebrow. It was typical of such a man that, even though Miss Larner seemed to be on the greying side of forty, he would assume that her unmarried status gave him the right to call her "young lady," as one addresses a recalcitrant girlchild.

"What is 'here' that I am failing to see?"

"Well, Horace and Peg Guester *did* plan to offer you a small house off by yourself, but we said no to it, plain and simple, we said no to them, and we say no to you."

"Very well, then. I see that you do not, after all, intend to keep your word to me. Fortunately, gentlemen, I am not a common schoolteacher, grateful to take whatever is offered. I had a good position at the Penn School, and I assure you that I can return there at will. Good day."

She rose to her feet. So did all the men except the sheriff—but they weren't rising out of courtesy.

"Please."

"Sit down."

"Let's talk about this."

"Don't be hasty."

It was Dr. Physicker, the perfect conciliator, who took the floor now, after giving the sheriff a steady look to quell him. The sheriff, however, did not seem particularly quelled.

"Miss Larner, our decision on the private house was not an irrevocable one. But please consider the

253

problems that worried us. First, we were concerned that the house would not be suitable. It's not really a house at all, but a mere room, made out of an abandoned springhouse – "

The old springhouse. "Is it heated?"

"Yes."

"Has it windows? A door that can be secured? A bed and table and chair?"

"All of that, yes."

"Has it a wooden floor?"

"A nice one."

"Then I doubt that its former service as a springhouse will bother me. Had you any other objections?"

"We damn well do!" cried Sheriff Wiseman. Then, seeing the horrified looks around the room, he added, "Begging the lady's pardon for my rough language."

"I am interested in hearing those objections," said Miss Larner.

"A woman alone, in a solitary house in the woods! It ain't proper!"

"It is the word *ain't* which is not proper, Mr. Wiseman," said Miss Larner. "As to the propriety of my living in a house to myself, I assure you that I have done so for many years, and have managed to pass that entire time quite unmolested. Is there another house within hailing distance?"

"The roadhouse to one side and the smith's place to the other," said Dr. Physicker.

"Then if I am under some duress or provocation, I can assure you that I will make myself heard, and I expect those who hear will come to my aid. Or are you afraid, Mr. Wiseman, that I may enter into some improper activity *voluntarily?*"

Of course that was exactly what he was thinking, and his reddening face showed it.

"I believe you have adequate references concerning my moral character," said Miss Larner. "But if you have any doubts on that score, it would be better for me to return to Philadelphia at once, for if at my age I cannot be trusted to live an upright life without supervision, how can you possibly trust me to supervise your young children?"

"It just ain't decent!" cried the sheriff. "Aren't."

"Isn't." She smiled benignly at Pauley Wiseman. "It has been my experience, Mr. Wiseman, that when a person assumes that others are eager to commit indecent acts whenever given the opportunity, he is merely confessing his own private struggle."

Pauley Wiseman didn't understand that she had just accused him, not until several of the lawyers started in laughing behind their hands.

"As I see it, gentlemen of the school board, you have only two alternatives. First, you can pay my boat passage back to Dekane and my overland passage to Philadelphia, plus the salary for the month that I will have expended in traveling."

"If you don't teach, you get no salary," said the sheriff.

"You speak hastily, Mr. Wiseman," said Miss Larner. "I believe the lawyers present will inform you that the school board's letters constitute a contract, of which you are in breach, and that I would therefore be entitled to collect, not just a month's salary, but the entire year's."

"Well, that's not *certain*, Miss Larner," began one of the lawyers.

"Hio is one of the United States now, sir," she

answered, "and there is ample precedent in other state courts, precedent which is binding until and unless the government of Hio makes specific legislation to the contrary."

"Is she a schoolteacher or a lawyer?" asked another lawyer, and they all laughed.

"Your second alternative is to allow me to inspect this—this springhouse—and determine whether I find it acceptable, and if I do, to allow me to live there. If you ever find me engaging in morally reprehensible behavior, it is within the terms of our contract that you may discharge me forthwith."

"We can put you in *jail*, that's what we can do," said Wiseman.

"Why, Mr. Wiseman, aren't we getting ahead of ourselves, talking of jail when I have yet to select which morally hideous act I shall perform?"

"Shut up, Pauley," said one of the lawyers.

"Which alternative do you choose, gentlemen?" she asked.

Dr. Physicker was not about to let Pauley Wiseman have at the more weak-willed members of the board. He'd see to it there was no further debate. "We don't need to retire to consider this, do we, gentlemen? We may not be Quakers here in Hatrack River, so we aren't used to thinking of ladies as wanting to live by themselves and engage in business and preach and whatnot, but we're open-minded and willing to learn new ways. We want your services, and we'll keep to the contract. All in favour?"

"Aye."

"Opposed? The ayes have it."

"Nay," said Wiseman.

"The voting's over, Pauley."

"You called it too damn fast!"

"Your negative vote has been recorded, Pauley."

Miss Larner smiled coldly. "You may be sure *I* won't forget it, Sheriff Wiseman."

Dr. Physicker tapped the table with his gavel. "This meeting is adjourned until next Tuesday afternoon at three. And now, Miss Larner, I'd be delighted to escort you to the Guesters' springhouse, if this is a convenient hour. Not knowing when you would arrive, they have given me the key and asked me to open the cottage for you; they'll greet you later."

Miss Larner was aware, as they all were, that it was odd, to say the least, for the landlord not to greet his guest in person.

"You see, Miss Larner, it wasn't certain whether you'd accept the cottage. They wanted you to make your decision when you saw the place—and not in their presence, lest you feel embarrassed to decline it."

"Then they have acted graciously," said Miss Larner, "and I will thank them when I meet them."

It was humiliating, Old Peg having to walk out to the springhouse all by herself to plead with this stuck-up snooty old Philadelphia spinster. Horace ought to be going out there with her. Talk man to man with her—that's what this woman seemed to think she was, not a lady but a lord. Might as well come from Camelot, she might, thinks she's a princess giving orders to the common folk. Well, they took care of it in France, old Napoleon did, put old Louis the Seventeenth right in his place. But lordly women like this teacher lady, Miss Larner, they never got their comeuppance, just went on through life think-

257

ing folks what didn't talk perfect was too low to take much account of.

So where was Horace, to put this teacher lady in her place? Setting by the fire. Pouting. Just like a four-year-old. Even Arthur Stuart never got such a pout on him.

"I don't like her," says Horace.

"Well like her or not, if Arthur's to get an education it's going to be from her or nobody," says Old Peg, talking plain sense as usual, but does Horace listen? I should laugh.

"She can live there and she can teach Arthur if she pleases, or not if she don't please, but I don't like her and I don't think she belongs in that springhouse."

"Why, is it holy ground?" says Old Peg. "Is there some curse on it? Should we have built a palace for her royal highness?" Oh, when Horace gets a notion on him it's no use talking, so why did she keep on trying?

"None of that, Peg," said Horace.

"Then what? Or don't you need reasons anymore? Do you just decide and then other folks better make way?"

"Because it's Little Peggy's place, that's why, and I don't like having that benoctious woman living there!"

Wouldn't you know? It was just like Horace, to bring up their runaway daughter, the one who never so much as wrote to them once she ran away, leaving Hatrack River without a torch and Horace without the love of his life. Yes ma'am, that's what Little Peggy was to him, the love of his life. If I ran off, Horace, or, God forbid, if I died, would you treasure my memory and not let no other woman take my place? I reckon not. I reckon there wouldn't be time for my spot on the sheet to get cold afore you'd have some other woman lying there. Me you could replace in a hot minute, but Little Peggy, we have to treat the springhouse as a *shrine* and make me come out here all by myself to face this high-falutin old maid and beg her to teach a little black child. Why, I'll be lucky if she doesn't try to buy him from me.

Miss Larner took her time about answering the door, too, and when she did, she had a handkerchief to her face—probably a perfumed one, so she wouldn't have to smell the odor of honest country folks.

"If you don't mind I've got a thing or two I'd like to discuss with you," said Old Peg.

Miss Larner looked away, off over Old Peg's head, as if studying some bird in a far-off tree. "If it's about the school, I was told I'd have a week to prepare before we actually registered students and began the autumn session."

From down below, Old Peg could hear the *ching-ching-ching* of one of the smiths a-working at the forge. Against her will she couldn't help thinking of Little Peggy, who purely hated that sound. Maybe Horace was right in his foolishness. Maybe Little Peggy haunted this springhouse.

Still, it was Miss Larner standing in the doorway now, and Miss Larner that Old Peg had to deal with. "Miss Larner, I'm Margaret Guester. My husband and I own this springhouse."

"Oh. I beg your pardon. You're my landlady, and I'm being ungracious. Please come in."

That was a bit more like it. Old Peg stepped up through the open door and stood there a moment to take in the room. Only yesterday it had seemed bare but clean, a place full of promise. Now it was almost homey, what with a doily and a dozen books on the armoire, a small woven rug on the floor, and two dresses hanging from hooks on the wall. The trunks and bags filled a corner. It looked a bit like somebody lived there. Old Peg didn't know what she'd expected. Of course Miss Larner had more dresses than this dark traveling outfit. It's just Old Peg hadn't thought of her doing something so ordinary as changing clothes. Why, when she's got one dress off and before she puts on another, she probably stands there in her underwear, just like anybody.

"Do sit down, Mrs. Guester."

"Around here we ain't much with Mr. and Mrs., except them lawyers, Miss Larner. I'm Goody Guester, mostly, except when folks call me Old Peg."

"Old Peg. What a—what an interesting name."

She thought of spelling out why she was called "Old" Peg—how she had a daughter what run off, that sort of thing. But it was going to be hard enough to explain to this teacher lady how she come to have a Black son. Why make her family life seem even more strange?

"Miss Larner, I won't beat around the bush. You got something that I need."

"Oh?"

"That is, not me, to say it proper, but my son, Arthur Stuart."

If she recognized that it was the King's proper name, she gave no sign. "And what might he need from me, Goody Guester?"

"Book-learning."

260

"That's what I've come to provide to all the children in Hatrack River, Goody Guester."

"Not Arthur Stuart. Not if those pin-headed cowards on the school board have their way."

"Why should they exclude your son? Is he over-age, perhaps?"

"He's the right age, Miss Larner. What he ain't is the right color."

Miss Larner waited, no expression on her face.

"He's Black, Miss Larner."

"Half-Black, surely," offered the teacher.

Naturally the teacher was trying to figure how the innkeeper's wife came to have her a half-Black boy-baby. Old Peg got some pleasure out of watching the teacher act polite while she must surely be cringing in horror inside herself. But it wouldn't do to let such a thought linger too long, would it? "He's adopted, Miss Larner," said Old Peg. "Let's just say that his Black mama got herself embarrassed with a half-White baby."

"And you, out of the goodness of your heart – "

Was there a nasty edge to Miss Larner's voice? "I wanted me a child. I ain't taking care of Arthur Stuart for pity. He's *my* boy now."

"I see," said Miss Larner. "And the good people of Hatrack River have determined that their children's education will suffer if half-Black ears should hear my words at the same time as pure White ears."

Miss Larner sounded nasty again, only now Old Peg dared to let herself rejoice inside, hearing the way Miss Larner said those words. "Will you teach him, Miss Larner?"

"I confess, Goody Guester, that I have lived in the City of Quakers too long. I had forgotten that there were places in this world where people of small

261

minds would be so shameless as to punish a mere child for the sin of being born with skin of a tropical hue. I can assure you that I will refuse to open school at all if your adopted son is not one of my pupils."

"No!" cried Old Peg. "No, Miss Larner, that's going too far."

"I am a committed Emancipationist, Goody Guester. I will not join in a conspiracy to deprive any Black child of his or her intellectual heritage."

Old Peg didn't know what in the world an intellectual heritage was, but she knew that Miss Larner was in too much sympathy. If she kept up this way, she'd be like to ruin everything. "You got to hear me out, Miss Larner. They'll just get another teacher, and I'll be worse off, and so will Arthur Stuart. No, I just ask that you give him an hour in the evening, a few days a week. I'll make him study somewhat in the daytime, to learn proper what you teach him quick. He's a bright boy, you'll see that. He already knows his letters—he can A and Z it better than my Horace. That's my husband, Horace Guester. So I'm not asking more than a few hours a week, if you can spare it. That's why we worked up this springhouse, so you could do it and none the wiser."

Miss Larner arose from where she sat on the edge of her bed, and walked to the window. "This is not what I ever imagined—to teach a child in secret, as if I were committing a crime."

"In *some* folks' eyes, Miss Larner – "

"Oh, I have no doubt of that."

"Don't you Quakers have silent meetings? All I ask is a kind of quiet meeting, don't you know – "

"I am not a Quaker, Goody Guester. I am merely

262

a human being who refuses to deny the humanity of others, unless their own acts prove them unworthy of that noble kinship."

"Then you'll teach him?"

"After hours, yes. Here in my home, which you and your husband so kindly provided, yes. But in secret? Never! I shall proclaim to all in this place that I am teaching Arthur Stuart, and not just a few nights a week, but daily. I am free to tutor such pupils as I desire—my contract is quite specific on that point—and as long as I do not violate the contract, they must endure me for at least a year. Will that do?"

Old Peg looked at the woman in pure admiration. "I'll be jiggered," she said, "you're mean as a cat with a burr in its behind."

"I regret that I've never seen a cat in such an unfortunate situation, Goody Guester, so that I cannot estimate the accuracy of your simile."

Old Peg couldn't make no sense of the words Miss Larner said, but she caught something like a twinkle in the lady's eye, so it was all right.

"When should I send Arthur to you?" she asked.

"As I said when I first opened the door, I'll need a week to prepare. When school opens for the White children, it opens for Arthur Stuart as well. There remains only the question of payment."

Old Peg was taken aback for a moment. She'd come here prepared to offer money, but after the way Miss Larner talked, she thought there'd be no cost after all. Still, teaching was Miss Larner's livelihood, so it was only fair. "We thought to offer you a dollar a month, that being most convenient for us, Miss Larner, but if you need more – "

"Oh, not cash, Goody Guester. I merely thought

263

to ask if you might indulge me by allowing me to hold a weekly reading of poetry in your roadhouse on Sunday evenings, inviting all in Hatrack River who aspire to improve their acquaintance with the best literature in the English language."

"I don't know as how there's all that many who hanker after poetry, Miss Larner, but you're welcome to have a go of it."

"I think you'll be pleasantly surprised at the number of people who wish to be thought educated, Goody Guester. We shall have difficulty finding seats for all the ladies of Hatrack River who compel their husbands to bring them to hear the immortal words of Pope and Dryden, Donne and Milton, Shakespeare and Gray and—oh, I shall be daring—Wordsworth and Coleridge, and perhaps even an American poet, a wandering spinner of strange tales named Blake."

"You don't mean old Taleswapper, do you?"

"I believe that is his most common sobriquet."

"You've got some of his poems wrote down?"

"Written? Hardly necessary, for that dear friend of mine. I have committed many of his verses to memory."

"Well, don't that old boy get around. Philadelphia, no less."

"He has brightened many a parlor in that city, Goody Guester. Shall we hold our first soiree this Sunday?"

"What's a swore raid?"

"Soiree. An evening gathering, perhaps with ginger punch – "

"Oh, you don't have to teach me nothing about hospitality, Miss Larner. And if that's the price for Arthur Stuart's education, Miss Larner, I'm sore afraid I'm cheating you, because it seems to me you're doing *us* the favor both ways."

"You're most kind, Goody Guester. But I must ask you one question."

"Ask away. Can't promise I'm too good at answers."

"Goody Guester," said Miss Larner. "Are you aware of the Fugitive Slave Treaty?"

Fear and anger stabbed right through Old Peg's heart, even to hear it mentioned. "A devilish piece of work!"

"Slavery is a devilish work indeed, but the treaty was signed to bring Appalachee into the Compact, and to keep our fragile nation from war with the Crown Colonies. Peace is hardly to be labeled devilish."

"It is when it's a peace that says they can send their damned finders into the free states and bring back captive Black people to be slaves!"

"Perhaps you're right, Goody Guester. Indeed, one could say that the Fugitive Slave Treaty is not so much a treaty of peace as it is an article of surrender. Nevertheless, it is the law of the land."

Only now did Old Peg realize what this teacher just done. What could it mean, her bringing up the Fugitive Slave Treaty, excepting to make sure Old Peg knew that Arthur Stuart wasn't safe here, that finders could still come from the Crown Colonies and claim him as the property of some family of White so-called Christians? And that also meant that Miss Larner didn't believe a speck of her story about where Arthur Stuart come from. And if she saw through the lie so easy-like, why was Old Peg fool enough to think everybody else believed it? Why, as far as Old Peg knew, the whole town of Hatrack

River had long since guessed that Arthur Stuart was a slave boy what somehow run off and got hisself a White mama.

And if everybody knew, what was to stop somebody from giving report on Arthur Stuart, sending word to the Crown Colonies about a runaway slave-child living in a certain roadhouse near the Hatrack River? The Fugitive Slave Treaty made her adoption of Arthur Stuart plain illegal. They could take the boy right out of her arms and she'd never have the right to see him again. In fact, if she ever went south they could arrest her and hang her under the slave-poaching laws of King Arthur. And thinking of that monstrous King in his lair in Camelot made her remember the unkindest thing of all—that if they ever took Arthur Stuart south, they'd change his name. Why, it'd be high treason in the Crown Colonies, having a slavechild named with the same name as the King. So all of a sudden poor Arthur would find hisself with some other name he never heard of afore. She couldn't help thinking of the boy all confused, somebody calling him and calling him, and whipping him for not coming, but how could he know to come, since nobody called him by his right name?

Her face must've painted a plain picture of all the thoughts going through her head, because Miss Larner walked behind her and put her hands on Old Peg's shoulders.

"You've nought to fear from me, Goody Guester. I come from Philadelphia, where people speak openly of defying that treaty. A young New Englander named Thoreau has made quite a nuisance of himself, preaching that a bad law must be defied, that good citizens must be prepared to go to

266

jail themselves rather than submit to it. It would do your heart good to hear him speak."

Old Peg doubted that. It only froze her to the heart to think of the treaty at all. Go to jail? What good would that do, if Arthur was being whipped south in chains? No matter what, it was none of Miss Larner's business. "I don't know why you're saying all this, Miss Larner. Arthur Stuart is the freeborn son of a free Black woman, even if she got him on the wrong side of the sheets. The Fugitive Slave Treaty means nothing to me."

"Then I shall think no more of it, Goody Guester. And now, if you'll forgive me, I'm somewhat weary from traveling, and I had hoped to retire early, though it's still light outside."

Old Peg sprang to her feet, mighty relieved at not talking anymore about Arthur and the Treaty. "Why, of course. But you ain't hopping into bed without taking a bath, are you? Nothing like a bath for a traveler."

"I quite agree, Goody Guester. However, I fear my luggage was not copious enough for me to bring my tub along."

"I'll send Horace over with my spare tub the second I get back, and if you don't mind hotting up your stove there, we can get water from Gertie's well yonder and set it to steaming in no time."

"Oh, Goody Guester, I fear you'll convince me before the evening's out that I'm in Philadelphia after all. It shall be almost disappointing, for I had steeled myself to endure the rigours of primitive life in the wilderness, and now I find that you are prepared to offer all the convivial blessings of civilization."

"I'll take it that what you said mostly means thank

you, and so I say you're welcome, and I'll be back in no time with Horace and the tub. And don't you dare fetch your own water, at least not today. You just set there and read or philosophate or whatever an educated person does instead of dozing off."

With that Old Peg was out of the springhouse. She like to flew along the path to the inn. Why, this teacher lady wasn't half so bad as she seemed at first. She might talk a language that Old Peg couldn't hardly understand half the time, but at least she was willing to talk to folks—and she'd teach Arthur at no cost and hold poetry readings in the roadhouse to boot. Best of all, though, best of all she might even be willing to talk to Old Peg sometimes and maybe some of that smartness might rub off on her. Not that smartness was all that much good to a woman like Old Peg, but then, what good was a jewel on a rich lady's finger, either? And if being around this educated eastern spinster gave Old Peg even a jigger more understanding of the great world outside Hatrack River, it was more than Old Peg had dared to hope for in her life. Like daubing just a spot of color on a drab moth's wing. It don't make the moth into a butterfly, but maybe now the moth won't despair and fly into the fire.

Miss Larner watched Old Peg walk away. Mother, she whispered. No, didn't even whisper. Didn't even open her mouth. But her lips pressed together a bit tighter with the *M*, and her tongue shaped the other sounds inside her mouth.

It hurt her, to deceive. She had promised never to lie, and in a sense she wasn't lying even now. The name she had taken, *Larner*, meant nothing more than *teacher*, and since she *was* a teacher, it was as truly her name as Father's name was Guester and Makepeace's name was Smith. And when people asked her questions, she never lied to them, though she did refuse to answer questions that might tell them more than they ought to know, that might set them wondering.

Still, despite her elaborate avoidance of an open lie, she feared that she merely deceived herself. How could she believe that her presence here, so disguised, was anything but a lie?

And yet surely even that deception was the truth, at its root. She was no longer the same person she had been when she was torch of Hatrack River. She was no longer connected to these people in the former ways. If she claimed to be Little Peggy, that would be a deeper lie than her disguise, for they would suppose that she was the girl they once knew, and treat her accordingly. In that sense, her disguise was a reflection of who she really was, at least here and now—educated, aloof, a deliberate spinster, and sexually unavailable to men.

So her disguise was not a lie, surely it was not; it was merely a way to keep a secret, the secret of who she used to be, but was no longer. Her vow was still unbroken.

Mother was long since out of sight in the woods between the springhouse and the inn, but still Peggy looked after her. And if she wanted, Peggy could have seen her even yet, not with her eyes, but with her torch sight, finding Mother's heartfire and moving close, looking tight. Mother, don't you know you have no secrets from your daughter Peggy?

But the fact was that Mother could keep all the secrets she desired. Peggy would not look into her heart. Peggy hadn't come home to be the torch of

Hatrack River again. After all these years of study, in which Peggy had read so many books so rapidly that she feared once that she might run out, that there might not be books enough in America to satisfy her—after all these years, there was only one skill she was certain of. She had finally mastered the ability *not* to see inside the hearts of other people unless she wanted to. She had finally tamed her torchy sight.

Oh, she still looked inside other people when she needed to, but she rarely did. Even with the school board, when she had to tame them, it took no more than her knowledge of human nature to guess their present thoughts and deal with them. And as for the futures revealed in the heartfire, she no longer noticed them.

I am not responsible for your futures, none of you. Least of all you, Mother. I have meddled enough in your life, in everyone's lives. If I know all your futures, all you people in Hatrack River, then I have a moral imperative to shape my own actions to help you achieve the happiest possible tomorrow. Yet in so doing, I cease to exist myself. My own future becomes the only one with no hope, and why should that be? By shutting my eyes to what *will* happen, I become like you, able to live my life according to my guesses at what *may* happen. I couldn't guarantee you happiness anyway, and this way at least I also have a chance of it myself.

Even as she justified herself, she felt the same sour guilt well up inside her. By rejecting her knack, she was sinning against the God that gave it to her. That great magister Erasmus, he had taught as much: Your knack is your destiny. You'll never know joy except through following the path laid out before you by what is inside you. But Peggy refused to submit to that cruel discipline. Her childhood had already been stolen from her, and to what end? Her mother disliked her, the people of Hatrack River feared her, often hated her, even as they came to her again and again, seeking answers to their selfish, petty questions, blaming her if any seeming ill came into their lives, but never thanking her for saving them from dire events, for they never knew how she had saved them because the evils never happened.

It wasn't gratitude she wanted. It was freedom. It was a lightening of her burden. She had started bearing it too young, and they had shown her no mercy in their exploitation. Their own fears always outweighed her need for a carefree girlhood. Did any of them understand that? Did any of them know how gratefully she left them all behind?

Now Peggy the torch was back, but they'd never know it. I did not come back for *you*, people of Hatrack River, nor did I come to serve your children. I came back for one pupil only, the man who stands even now at the forge, his heartfire burning so brightly that I can see it even in my sleep, even in my dreams. I came back having learned all that the world can teach, so I in turn can help that young man achieve a labor that means more than any one of us. *That* is my destiny, if I have one.

Along the way I'll do what other good I can—I'll teach Arthur Stuart. I'll try to fulfill the dreams his brave young mother died for; I'll teach all the other children as much as they're willing to learn, during those certain hours of the day that I've contracted for; I'll bring such poetry and learning into the town of Hatrack River as you're willing to receive.

Perhaps you don't desire poetry as much as you

would like to have my torchy knowledge of your possible futures, but I daresay poetry will do you far more good. For knowing the future only makes you timid and complacent by turns, while poetry can shape you into the kind of souls who can face any future with boldness and wisdom and nobility, so that you need not know the future at all, so that any future will be an opportunity for greatness, if you have greatness in you. Can I teach you to see in yourselves what Gray saw?

Some heart once pregnant with celestial fire,
Hands that the rod of empire might have swayed,
Or waked to ecstasy the living lyre.

But she doubted that any of these ordinary souls in Hatrack River were really mute, inglorious Miltons. Pauley Wiseman was no secret Caesar. He might wish for it, but he lacked the wit and self-control. Whitley Physicker was no Hippocrates, however much he tried to be a healer and conciliator—his love of luxury undid him, and like many other well-meaning physicians he had come to work for what the fee could buy, and not for joy of the work itself.

She picked up the water bucket that stood by the door. Weary as she was, she would not allow herself to seem helpless even for a moment. Father and Mother would come and find Miss Larner had already done for herself all that she could do before the tub arrived.

Ching-ching-ching. Didn't Alvin rest? Didn't he know the sun was boiling the western sky, turning it red before sinking out of sight behind the trees? As she walked down the hill toward the smithy, she felt as if she might suddenly begin to run, to fly down the hill to the smithy as she had flown the day that Alvin was born. It was raining that day, and Alvin's mother was stuck in a wagon in the river. It was Peggy who saw them all, their heartfires off in the blackness of the rain and the flooding river. It was Peggy who gave alarm, and then Peggy who stood watch over the birthing, seeing Alvin's future in his heartfire, the brightest heartfire she had ever seen or would ever see in all her life. It was Peggy who saved his life then by peeling the caul away from his face; and, by using bits of that caul, Peggy who had saved his life so many times over the years. She might turn her back on being torch of Hatrack River, but she'd never turn her back on *him*.

But she stopped herself halfway down the hill. What was she thinking of? She could not go to him, not now, not yet. He had to come to *her*. Only that way could she become his teacher; only that way was there a chance of becoming anything more than that.

She turned and walked across the face of the hill, slanting down and eastward toward the well. She had watched Alvin dig the well—both wells—and for once she was helpless to help him when the Unmaker came. Alvin's own anger and destructiveness had called his enemy, and there was nothing Peggy could do with the caul to save him that time. She could only watch as he purged the unmaking that was inside himself, and so defeated, for a time, the Unmaker who stalked him on the outside. Now this well stood as a monument both to Alvin's power and to his frailty.

She dropped the copper bucket into the well, and the windlass clattered as the rope unwound. A muffled splash. She waited a moment for the bucket to fill, then wound it upward. It arrived brimming. She meant to pour it out into the wooden bucket she brought with her, but instead she brought the copper bucket to her lips and drank from the cold heavy load of water that it bore. So many years she had waited to taste that water, the water that Alvin tamed the night he tamed himself. She had been so afraid, watching him all night, and when at last in the morning he filled up the first vengeful hole he dug, she wept in relief. This water wasn't salty, but still it tasted to her like her own tears.

The hammer was silent. As always, she found Alvin's heartfire at once, without even trying. He was leaving the smithy, coming outside. Did he know she was there? No. He always came for water when he finished his work for the day. Of course she could not turn to him, not yet, not until she actually heard his step. Yet, though she knew he was coming and listened for him, she couldn't hear him; he moved as silently as a squirrel on a limb. Not until he spoke did he make a sound.

"Pretty good water, ain't it?"

She turned around to face him. Turned too quickly, too eagerly—the rope still held the bucket, so it lurched out of her hands, splashed her with water, and clattered back down into the well.

"I'm Alvin, you remember? Didn't mean to frighten you, Ma'am. Miss Larner."

"I foolishly forgot the bucket was tied," she said. "I'm used to pumps and taps, I'm afraid. Open wells are not common in Philadelphia."

She turned back to the well to draw the bucket up again.

"Here, let me," he said.

"There's no need. I can wind it well enough."

"But why should you, Miss Larner, when I'm glad to do it for you?"

She stepped aside and watched as he cranked the windlass with one hand, as easily as a child might swing a rope. The bucket fairly flew to the top of the well. She looked into his heartfire, just dipped in, to see if he was showing off for her. He was not. He could not see how massive his own shoulders were, how his muscles danced under the skin as his arm moved. He could not even see the peacefulness of his own face, the same quiet repose that one might see in the face of a fearless stag. There was no watchfulness in him. Some people had darting eyes, as if they had to be alert for danger, or perhaps for prey. Others looked intently at the task at hand, concentrating on what they were doing. But Alvin had a quiet distance, as if he had no particular concern about what anyone else or he himself might be doing, but instead dwelt on inward thoughts that no one else could hear. Again the words of Gray's *Elegy* played out in her mind.

> *Far from the madding crowd's ignoble strife,*
> *Their sober wishes never learned to stray;*
> *Along the cool, sequestered vale of life*
> *They kept the noiseless tenor of their way.*

Poor Alvin. When I'm done with you, there'll be no cool sequestered vale. You'll look back on your prenticeship as the last peaceful days of your life.

He gripped the full, heavy bucket with one hand on the rim, and easily tipped it to pour it out into the bucket she had brought, which he held in his other hand; he did it as lightly and easily as a housewife pours cream from one cup into another. What if those hands as lightly and easily held my arms? Would he break me without meaning to, being so strong? Would I feel manacled in his irresistible grasp? Or would he burn me up in the white heat of his heartfire?

She reached out for her bucket.

"Please let me carry it, Ma'am. Miss Larner."

"There's no need."

"I know I'm dirted up, Miss Larner, but I can carry it to your door and set it inside without messing anything."

Is my disguise so monstrously aloof that you think I refuse your help out of excessive cleanliness? "I only meant that I didn't want to make you work anymore today. You've helped me enough already for one day."

He looked straight into her eyes, and now he lost that peaceful expression. There was even a bit of anger in his eyes. "If you're afraid I'll want you to pay me, you needn't have no fear of that. If this is your dollar, you can have it back. I never wanted it." He held out to her the coin that Whitley Physicker had tossed him from the carriage.

"I reproved Dr. Physicker at the time. I thought it insulting that *he* should presume to pay you for the service you did me out of pure gallantry. It cheapened both of us, I thought, for him to act as if the events of this morning were worth exactly one dollar."

His eyes had softened now.

Peggy went on in her Miss Larner voice. "But you must forgive Dr. Physicker. He is uncomfortable with wealth, and looks for opportunities to share it with others. He has not yet learned how to do it with perfect tact."

"Oh, it's no never mind now, Miss Larner, seeing how it didn't come from you." He put the coin back in his pocket and started to carry the full bucket up the hill toward the house.

It was plain he was unaccustomed to walking with a lady. His strides were far too long, his pace too quick, for her to keep up with him. She couldn't even walk the same route he took—he seemed oblivious to the degree of slope. He was like a child, not an adult, taking the most direct route even if it meant unnecessary clambering over obstacles.

And yet I'm barely five years older than he is. Have I come to believe my own disguise? At twenty-three, am I already thinking and acting and living like a woman of twice that age? Didn't I once love to walk just as he does, over the most difficult ground, for the sheer love of the exertion and accomplishment?

Nevertheless, she walked the easier path, skirting the hill and then climbing up where the slope was longer and gentler. He was already there, waiting at the door.

"Why didn't you open the door and set the bucket inside? The door isn't locked," she said.

"Begging your pardon, Miss Larner, but this is a door that asks not to be opened, whether it's locked or not."

So, she thought, he wants to make sure I know about the hidden hexes he put in the locks. Not many people could see a hidden hex—nor could she, for that matter. She wouldn't have known about them if she hadn't watched him put the hexes in the lock. But of course she couldn't very well tell him *that*. So she asked, "Oh, is there some protection here that I can't see?"

"I just put a couple of hexes into the lock. Nothing much, but it should make it fairly safe here. And there's a hex in the top of the stove, so I don't think you have to worry much about sparks getting free."

"You have a great deal of confidence in your hexery, Alvin."

"I do them pretty good. Most folks know a few hexes, anyway, Miss Larner. But not many smiths can put them into the iron. I just wanted you to know."

He wanted her to know more than that, of course. So she gave him the response he hoped for. "I take it, then, that you did some of the work on this springhouse."

"I done the windows, Miss Larner. They glide up and down sweet as you please, and there's pegs to hold them in place. And the stove, and the locks, and all the iron fittings. And my helper, Arthur Stuart, he scraped down the walls."

For a young man who seemed artless, he was steering the conversation rather well. For a moment she thought of toying with him, of pretending not to make the connections he was counting on, just to see how he handled it. But no—he was only planning to ask her to do what she came here to do. There was no reason to make it hard for him. The teaching itself would be hard enough. "Arthur Stuart," she said. "He must be the same boy that Goody Guester asked me to teach privately."

"Oh, did she already ask you? Or shouldn't I ask?"

"I have no intention of keeping it a secret, Alvin. Yes, I'll be teaching Arthur Stuart."

"I'm glad of that, Miss Larner. He's the smartest boy you ever knew. And a mimic! Why, he can hear

278

anything once and say it back to you in your own voice. You'll hardly believe it even when he's a-doing it."

"I only hope he doesn't choose to play such a game when I'm teaching him."

Alvin frowned. "Well, it isn't rightly a game, Miss Larner. It's just something he does without meaning to in particular. I mean to say, if he starts talking back to you in your own voice, he isn't making fun or nothing. It's just that when he hears something he remembers it voice and all, if you know what I mean. He can't split them up and remember the words without the voice that gave them."

"I'll keep that in mind."

In the distance, Peggy heard a door slam closed. She cast out and looked, finding Father's and Mother's heartfires coming toward her. They were quarreling, of course, but if Alvin was to ask her, he'd have to do it quickly.

"Was there something else you wanted to say to me, Alvin?"

This was the moment he'd been leading up to, but now he was turning shy on her. "Well, I had some idea of asking you—but you got to understand, I didn't carry the water for you so you'd feel obliged or nothing. I would've done that anyway, for anybody, and as for what happened today, I didn't rightly know that you were the teacher. I mean maybe I might've guessed, but I just didn't think of it. So what I done was just itself, and you don't owe me nothing."

"I think I'll decide how much gratitude I owe, Alvin. What did you want to ask me?"

"Of course you'll be busy with Arthur Stuart, so I can't expect you to have much time free, maybe just one day a week, just an hour even. It could be on Saturdays, and you could charge whatever you want, my master's been giving me free time and I've saved up some of my own earnings, and – "

"Are you asking me to tutor you, Alvin?"

Alvin didn't know what the word meant.

"Tutor you. Teach you privately."

"Yes, Miss Larner."

"The charge is fifty cents a week, Alvin. And I wish you to come at the same time as Arthur Stuart. Arrive when he does, and leave when he does."

"But how can you teach us both at once?"

"I daresay you could benefit from some of the lessons I'll be giving him, Alvin. And when I have him writing or ciphering, I can converse with you."

"I just don't want to cheat him out of his lesson time."

"Think clearly, Alvin. It would not be proper for you to take lessons with me alone. I may be somewhat older than you, but there are those who will search for fault in me, and giving private instruction to a young bachelor would certainly give cause for tongues to wag. Arthur Stuart will be present at all your lessons, and the door of the springhouse will stand open."

"We could go up and you could teach me at the roadhouse."

"Alvin. I have told you the terms. Do you wish to engage me as your tutor?"

"Yes, Miss Larner." He dug into his pocket and pulled out a coin. "Here's a dollar for the first two weeks."

Peggy looked at the coin. "I thought you meant to give this dollar back to Dr. Physicker."

"I wouldn't want to make him uncomfortable

about having so much money, Miss Larner." He grinned.

Shy he may be, but he can't stay serious for long. There'll always be a tease in him, just below the surface, and eventually it will always come out.

"No, I imagine not," said Miss Larner. "Lessons will begin next week. Thank you for your help."

At that moment, Father and Mother came up the path. Father carried a large tub over his head, and he staggered under the weight. Alvin immediately ran to help—or, rather, to simply take the tub and carry it himself.

That was how Peggy saw her father's face for the first time in more than six years—red, sweating, as he puffed from the labor of carrying the tub. And angry, too, or at least sullen. Even though Mother had no doubt assured him that the teacher lady wasn't half so arrogant as she seemed at first, still Father was resentful of this stranger living in the springhouse, a place that belonged only to his long-lost daughter.

Peggy longed to call out to him, call him Father, and assure him that it *was* his daughter who dwelt here now, and all his labor to make a home of this old place was really a gift of love to her. How it comforted her to know how much he loved her, that he had not forgotten her after all these years; yet it also made her heart break for him, that she couldn't name herself to him truly, not yet, not if she was to accomplish all she needed to. She would have to do with him what she was already trying to do with Alvin and with Mother—not reclaim old loves and debts, but win new love and friendship.

She could not come home as a daughter of this place, not even to Father, who alone would purely

281

rejoice at her coming. She had to come home as a stranger. For surely that's what she was, even if she had no disguise, for after three years of one kind of learning in Dekane and another three of schooling and study, she was no longer little Peggy, the quiet, sharp-tongued torch; she had long since become something else. She had learned many graces under the tutelage of Mistress Modesty; she had learned many other things from books and teachers. She was not who she had been. It would be as much a lie to say, Father, I am your daughter Little Peggy, as it was to say what she said now: "Mr. Guester, I am your new tenant, Miss Larner. I'm very glad to meet you."

He huffed up to her and put out his hand. Despite his misgivings, despite the way he had avoided meeting her when first she arrived at the roadhouse an hour or so past, he was too much the consummate innkeeper to refuse to greet her with courtesy—or at least the rough country manners that passed for courtesy in this frontier town.

"Pleased to meet you, Miss Larner. I trust your accommodation is satisfactory?"

It made her a little sad, to hear him trying fancy language on her, the way he talked to those customers he thought of as "dignitaries," meaning that he believed their station in life to be above his. I've learned much, Father, and this above all: that no station in life is above any other, if it's occupied by someone with a good heart.

As to whether Father's heart was good, Peggy believed it but refused to look. She had known his heartfire far too well in years past. If she looked too closely now, she might find things a daughter had no right to see. She'd been too young to control

282

herself when she explored his heartfire all those years ago; in the innocence of childhood she had learned things that made both innocence and childhood impossible. Now, though, with her knack better tamed, she could at last give him privacy in his own heart. She owed him and Mother that.

Not to mention that she owed it to herself not to know *exactly* what they thought and felt about everything.

They set up the tub in her little house. Mother had brought another bucket and a kettle, and now Father and Alvin both set to toting water up from the well, while Mother boiled some on the stove. When the bath was ready, she sent the men away; then Peggy sent Mother away as well, though not without considerable argument. "I am grateful for your solicitude," Peggy said, "but it is my custom to bathe in utter privacy. You have been exceptionally kind, and as I now take my bath, you may be sure I will think of you gratefully every moment."

The stream of high-sounding language was more than even Mother could resist. At last the door was closed and locked, the curtains drawn. Peggy removed her traveling gown, which was heavy with dust and sweat, and then peeled away her chemise and her pantalets, which clung hotly to her skin. It was one of the benefits of her disguise, that she need not trouble herself with corsetry. No one expected a spinster of her supposed age to have the perversely slender waist of those poor young victims of fashion who bound themselves until they could not breathe.

Last of all she removed her amulets, the three that hung around her neck and the one enwrapped with her hair. The amulets were hard-won, and not just because they were the new, expensive ones that

283

acted on what others actually saw, and not just on their opinion of it. It had taken four visits before the hexman believed that she really did want to appear ugly. "A girl so lovely as you, you don't need my art," he said it over and over again, until she finally took him by the shoulders and said, "That's why I need it! To make me *stop* being beautiful." He gave in, but kept muttering that it was a sin to cover what God created well.

God or Mistress Modesty, thought Peggy. I *was* beautiful in Mistress Modesty's house. Am I beautiful now, when no one sees me but myself, I who am least likely to admire?

Naked at last, herself at last, she knelt beside the tub and ducked her head to begin the washing of her hair. Immersed in water, hot as it was, she felt the same old freedom she had felt so long ago in the springhouse, the wet isolation in which no heartfires intruded, so she was truly herself alone, and had a chance of knowing what her self might actually be.

There was no mirror in the springhouse. Nor had she brought one. Nevertheless, she knew when her bath was done and she toweled herself before the stove, already sweating in the steamy room, in the early August evening—she knew that she *was* beautiful, as Mistress Modesty had taught her how to be; knew that if Alvin could see her as she really was, he would desire her, not for wisdom, but for the more casual and shallow love that any man feels for a woman who delights his eyes. So, just as she had once hidden from him so he wouldn't marry her for pity, now she hid from him so he wouldn't marry her for boyish love. This self, the smooth and youthful body, would remain invisible to him, so that her truer self, the sharp and well-filled mind, might entice the finest man in him, the man that would be, not a lover, but a Maker.

If only she could somehow disguise his body from her own eyes, so that she would not have to imagine his touch, as gentle as the touch of air on her skin as she moved across the room.

16

Property

The Blacks started in a-howling before the roosters got up. Cavil Planter didn't get up right away; the sound of it sort of fit into his dream. Howling Blacks figured in his dreams pretty common these days. Anyway it finally woke him, and he bounded up out of bed. Barely light outside; he had to open the curtain to get light enough to find his trousers. He could make out shadows moving down near the slave quarters, but couldn't see what all was going on. He thought the worst, of course, and pulled his shotgun down from the rack on his bedroom wall. Slave-owners, in case you didn't guess, always keep their firearms in the same room where they sleep.

Out in the hall, he nearly bumped into somebody. She screeched. It took Cavil a moment to realize it was his wife, Dolores. Sometimes he forgot she knew how to walk, seeing how she only left her room at certain times. He just wasn't used to seeing her out of bed, moving around the house without a slave or two to lean on.

"Hush now, Dolores, it's me, Cavil."

"Oh, what is it, Cavil! What's happening out

286

there!" She was clinging to his arm, so he couldn't move on.

"Don't you think I can tell you better if you let me go find out?"

She hung on tighter. "Don't do it, Cavil! Don't go out there alone! they might kill you!"

"Why would they kill me? Am I not a righteous master? Will the Lord not protect me?" All the same, he felt a thrill of fear. Could this be the slave revolt that every master feared but none spoke of? He realized now that this very thought had been lingering at the back of his mind since he first woke up. Now Dolores had put it into words. "I have my shotgun," said Cavil. "Don't worry about me."

"I'm afraid," said Dolores.

"You know what *I'm* afraid of? That you'll stumble in the dark and really hurt yourself. Go back to bed, so I don't have to worry about you while I'm outside."

Somebody started pounding at the door.

"Master! Master!" cried a slave. "We need you, Master!"

"Now see? That's Fat Fox," said Cavil. "If it was a revolt, my love, they'd strangle him first off, before they ever came after me."

"Is that supposed to make me feel better?" she asked.

"Master! Master!"

"To bed," said Cavil.

For a moment her hand rested on the hard cold barrel of the shotgun. Then she turned and, like a pale grey ghost in the darkness of the hall, she disappeared into the shadows toward her room.

Fat Fox was near to jumping up and down he was so agitated. Cavil looked at him, as always, with disgust. Even though Cavil depended on Fat Fox to let him know which slaves talked ugly behind his back, Cavil didn't have to like him. There wasn't a hope in heaven of saving the soul of any full-blood Black. They were all born in deep corruption, like as if they embraced original sin and sucked more of it with their mother's milk. It's a wonder their milk wasn't black with all the foulness that must be in it. I wish it wasn't such a slow process, turning the Black race White enough to be worth trying to save their souls.

"It's that Salamanda girl, Master," said Fat Fox.

"Is her baby coming early?" said Cavil.

"Oh no," said Fat Fox. "No, no, it ain't coming, no Master. Oh please come on down. It ain't that gun you needing, Master. It's your big old buck knife I think."

"I'll decide that," said Cavil. If a Black suggests you ought to put your gun away, that's when you hang onto it tightest of all.

He strode toward the slave women's quarters. It was getting light enough by now that he could see the ground, could see the Blacks all slinking here and there in the dark, watching him, white eyes watching. That was a mercy from the Lord God, making their eyes white, else you couldn't see them at all in the shadows.

There was a passel of women all outside the door to the cabin where Salamandy slept. Her being so close to her time, she didn't have to do any field work these days, and she got a bed with a fine mattress. Nobody could say Cavil Planter didn't take care of his breeding stock.

One of the women – in the darkness he couldn't tell who, but from the voice he thought it was maybe Coppy, the one baptized as Agnes but who chose to call herself after the copperhead rattler—anyway she cried out, "Oh, Master, you got to let us bleed a chicken on this one!"

"No heathen abominations shall be practiced on my plantation," said Cavil sternly. But he knew now that Salamandy was dead. Only a month from delivery, and she was dead. It stabbed his heart deep. One child less. One breeding ewe gone. O God have mercy on me! How can I serve thee aright if you take away my best concubine?

It smelled like a sick horse in the room, from her bowel opening up as she died. She'd hung herself with the bedsheet. Cavil damned himself for a fool, giving her such a thing. Here he meant it as a sign of special favor, her being on her sixth half-White baby, to let her have a sheet on her mattress, and now she turned around and answered him like this.

Her feet dangled not three inches from the floor. She must have stood on the bed and then stepped off. Even now, as she swayed slightly in the breeze of his movement in the room, her feet bumped into the bedstead. It took a second or two for Cavil to realize what that meant. Since her neck wasn't broke, she must have been a long time strangling, and the whole time the bed was inches away, and she *knew* it. The whole time, she could have stopped strangling at any time. Could have changed her mind. This was a woman who wanted to die. No, wanted to *kill*. Murder that baby she was carrying.

Proof again how strong these Blacks were in their wickedness. Rather than give birth to a half-White child with a hope of salvation, she'd strangle to death herself. Was there no limit to their perversity? How could a godly man save such creatures?

"She kill herself, Master!" cried the woman who

289

had spoke before. He turned to look at her, and now it was light enough to see for sure that it was Coppy talking. "She waiting for tomorrow night to kill somebody else, less we bleed a chicken on her!"

"It makes me ill, to think you'd use this poor woman's death as an excuse to roast a chicken out of turn. She'll have a decent burial, and her soul will *not* hurt anyone, though as a suicide she will surely burn in hell forever."

At his words Coppy wailed in grief. The other women joined in her keening. Cavil had Fat Fox set a group of young bucks digging a grave—not in the regular slaveyard, of course, since as a suicide she couldn't lie in consecrated ground. Out among the trees, with no marker, as befit a beast that took the life of her own young.

She was in the ground before nightfall. Since she was a suicide, Cavil couldn't very well ask the Baptist preacher or the Catholic priest to come help with it. In fact, he figured to say the words himself, only it happened that tonight was the night he'd already invited a traveling preacher to supper. That preacher showed up early, and the house slaves sent him around back where he found the burial in progress and offered to help.

"Oh, you don't need to do that," said Cavil.

"Let it never be said that Reverend Philadelphia Thrower did not extend Christian love to all the children of God—White or Black, male or female, saint or sinner."

The slaves perked up at that, and so did Cavil—for the opposite reason. That was Emancipationist talk, and Cavil felt a sudden fear that he had invited the devil into his own house by bringing this Presbyterian preacher. Nevertheless, it would probably do much to quiet the Blacks' superstitious fears as if he allowed the rites to be administered by a real preacher. And sure enough, when the words were said and the grave was covered, they all seemed right quiet—none of that ghastly howling.

At dinner, the preacher—Thrower, that was his name—eased Cavil's fears considerably. "I believe that it is part of God's great plan for the Black people to be brought to America in chains. Like the children of Israel, who had to suffer years of bondage to the Egyptians, these Blacks' souls are under the Lord's own lash, shaping them to His own purposes. The Emancipationists understand one truth—that God loves his Black children—but they misunderstand everything else. Why, if they had their way and freed all the slaves at once, it would accomplish the devil's purpose, not God's, for without slavery the Blacks have no hope of rising out of their savagery."

"Now, that sounds downright theological," said Cavil.

"Don't the Emancipationists understand that every Black who escapes from his rightful master into the North is doomed to eternal damnation, him and all his children? Why, they might as well have remained in Africa as go north. The Whites up north hate Blacks, as well they should since only the most evil and proud and stiffnecked dare to offend God by leaving their masters. But you here in Appalachee and in the Crown Colonies, you are the ones who truly love the Black man, for only you are willing to take responsibility for these wayward children and help them progress on the road to full humanity."

"You may be a Presbyterian, Reverend Thrower, but you know the true religion."

"I'm glad to know I'm in the home of a godly man, Brother Cavil."

"I hope I am your brother, Reverend Thrower."

And that's how the talk went on, the two of them liking each other better and better as the evening wore. By nightfall, when they sat on the porch cooling off, Cavil began to think he had met the first man to whom he might tell some part of his great secret.

Cavil tried to bring it up casual. "Reverend Thrower, do you think the Lord God speaks to any men today?"

Thrower's voice got all solemn. "I know He does."

"Do you think He might even speak to a common man like me?"

"You mustn't hope for it, Brother Cavil," said Thrower, "for the Lord goes where He will, and not where we wish. Yet I do know that it's possible for even the humblest man to have a—visitor."

Cavil felt a trembling in his belly. Why, Thrower sounded like he already knew Cavil's secret. But he didn't blurt it out all at once. "You know what I think?" said Cavil. "I think that the Lord God can't appear in his true form, because his glory would kill a natural man."

"Oh, indeed," said Thrower. "As when Moses craved a vision of the Lord, and the Lord covered his eyes with His hand, only letting Moses see His back parts as he passed by."

"I mean, what if a man like me saw the Lord Jesus himself, only not looking like any painting of him, but instead looking like an overseer. I reckon that a man sees only what will make him understand the power of God, not the true majesty of the Lord."

Thrower nodded wisely. "It may well be," he said.

"That's a plausible explanation. Or it might be that you only saw an angel."

There it was—that simple. From "what if a man like me" to Thrower saying "you saw an angel." That's how much alike these two men were. So Cavil told the whole story, for the first time ever, near seven years after it happened.

When he was done, Thrower took his hand and held it in a brotherly grip, looking him in the eye with a fierce-looking kind of expression. "To think of your sacrifice, mingling your flesh with that of these Black women, in order to serve the Lord. How many children?"

"Twenty-five that got born alive. You helped me bury the twenty-sixth inside Salamandy's belly this evening."

"Where are all these hopeful half-White youngsters?"

"Oh, that's half the labor I'm doing," said Cavil. "Till the Fugitive Slave Treaty, I used to sell them all south as soon as I could, so they'd grow up there and spread White blood throughout the Crown Colonies. Each one will be a missionary through his seed. Of course, the last few I've kept here. It ain't the safest thing, neither, Reverend Thrower. All my breeding-age stock is pure Black, and folks are bound to wonder where these mixup children come from. So far, though, my overseer, Lashman, he keeps his mouth shut if he notices, and nobody else ever sees them."

Thrower nodded, but it was plain his mind was on something else. "Only twenty-*five* of these children?"

"It's the best I could do," said Cavil. "Even a

Black woman can't make a baby right off after a birthing."

"I meant—you see, I also had a—visitation. It's the reason why I came here, came touring through Appalachee. I was told that I would meet a farmer who also knew my Visitor, and who had produced twenty-six living gifts to God."

"Twenty-*six*."

"Living."

"Well, you see—well, ain't that just the way of it, You see, I wasn't including in my tally the very first one born, because his mother run off and stole him from me a few days before he was due to be sold. I had to refund the money in cash to the buyer, and it was no good tracking, the dogs couldn't pick up her scent. Word among the slaves was that she turned into a blackbird and *flew*, but you know the tales they tell."

"So—twenty-six then. And tell me this—is there some reason why the name 'Hagar' should mean anything to you?"

Cavil gasped. "No one knows I called the mother by that name!"

"My Visitor told me that Hagar had stolen away your first gift."

"It's Him. You've seen Him, too."

"To me he comes as—not an overseer. More like a scientist—a man of unguessable wisdom. Because *I* am a scientist, I imagine, besides my vocation as a minister. I have always supposed that He was a mere angel—listen to me, a *mere* angel—because I dared not hope that He was—was the Master himself. But now what you tell me—could it be that we have both entertained the presence of our Lord? Oh, Cavil, how can I doubt it? Why else would the

294

Lord have brought us together like this? It means that I—that I'm forgiven."

"Forgiven?"

At Cavil's question, Thrower's face darkened.

Cavil hastened to reassure him. "No, you don't need to tell me if you don't want."

"I—it is almost unbearable to think of it. But now that I am clearly deemed acceptable—or at least, now that I've been given another chance—Brother Cavil, once I was given a mission to perform, one as dark and difficult and secret as your own. Except that where you have had the courage and strength to prevail, I failed. I tried, but I had not wit or vigor enough to overcome the power of the devil. I thought I was rejected, cast off. That's why I became a traveling preacher, for I felt myself unworthy to take a pulpit of my own. But now—"

Cavil nodded, holding the man's hands as tears flowed down his cheek.

At last Thrower looked up at him. "How do you suppose our—Friend—meant me to help you in your work?"

"I can't say," said Cavil. "But there's only one way I can think of, offhand."

"Brother Cavil, I'm not sure if I can take upon myself that loathsome duty."

"In my experience, the Lord strengthens a man, and makes it—bearable."

"But in my case, Brother Cavil—you see, I've never known a woman, as the Bible speaks of it. Only once have my lips touched a woman's, and that was against my will."

"Then I'll do my best to help you. How if we pray together good and long, and then I show you once?"

Well, that seemed like the best idea either of them

295

could think of right offhand, and so they did it, and it turned out Reverend Thrower was a quick learner. Cavil felt a great sense of relief to have someone else join in, not to mention a kind of peculiar pleasure at having somebody watch him and then watching the other fellow in turn. It was a powerful sort of brotherhood, to have their seed mingled in the same vessel, so to speak. Like Reverend Thrower said, "When this field comes to harvest, Brother Cavil, we shall not guess whose seed came unto ripeness, for the Lord gave us this field together, for this time."

Oh, and then Reverend Thrower asked the girl's name. "Well, we baptized her as 'Hepzibah,' but she goes by the name 'Roach.' "

"Roach!"

"They all take animal names. I reckon she doesn't have too high an opinion of herself."

At that, Thrower just reached over and took Roach's hand and patted it, as kindly a gesture as if Thrower and Roach was man and wife, an idea that made Cavil almost laugh right out. "Now, Hepzibah, you must use your Christian name," said Thrower, "and not such a debasing animal name."

Roach just looked at him wide-eyed, lying there curled up on the mattress.

"Why doesn't she answer me, Brother Cavil?"

"Oh, they never talk during this. I beat that out of them early—they always tried to talk me out of doing it. I figure better to have no words than have them say what the devil wants me to hear."

Thrower turned back to the woman. "But now I ask you to speak to me, Roach. You won't say devil words, will you?"

In answer, Roach's eyes wandered upward to where part of a bedsheet was still knotted around a

296

rafter. It had been raggedly hacked off below the knot.

Thrower's face got kind of sick-looking. "You mean this is the room where—the girl we buried—"

"This room has the best bed," said Cavil. "I didn't want us doing this on a straw pallet if we didn't have to."

Thrower said nothing. He just left the room, pretty quick, plunging outside into the darkness. Cavil sighed, picked up the lantern, and followed him. He found Thrower leaning over the pump. He could hear Roach skittering out of the room where Salamandy died, heading for her own quarters, but he didn't give no never mind to her. It was Thrower—surely the man wasn't so beside himself that he'd throw up on the drinking water!

"I'm all right," whispered Thrower. "I just—the same room—I'm not at all superstitious, you understand. It just seemed disrespectful to the dead."

These northerners. Even when they understood somewhat about slavery, they couldn't get rid of their notion of Blacks as if they was people. Would you stop using a room just because a mouse died there, or you once killed a spider on the wall? Do you burn down your stable just because your favorite horse died there?

Anyway, Thrower got himself together, hitched up his trousers and buttoned them up proper, and they went back into the house. Brother Cavil put Thrower in their guest room, which wasn't all that much used, so there was a cloud of dust when Cavil slapped the blanket. "Should have known the house slaves'd be slacking in this room," said Brother Cavil.

"No, matter," said Thrower. "On a night this warm, I'll need no blanket."

On the way down the hall to his bedroom, Cavil paused a moment to listen for his wife's breathing. As sometimes happened, he could hear her whimpering softly in her bedroom. The pain must be bad indeed. Oh Lord, thought Cavil, how many more times must I do Thy bidding before You'll have mercy and heal my Dolores? But he didn't go in to her—there was nothing he could do to help her, besides prayer, and he'd need his sleep. This had been a late night, and tomorrow had work enough.

Sure enough, Dolores had had a bad night—she was still asleep at breakfast time. So Cavil ended up eating with Thrower. The preacher put away an astonishingly large portion of sausage and grits. When his plate was clean for the third time, he looked at Cavil and smiled. "The Lord's service can give a man quite an appetite!" they both had a good laugh at that.

After breakfast, they walked outside. It happened they went near the woods where Salamandy had been buried. Thrower suggested looking at the grave, or else Cavil probably never would have known what the Blacks did in the night. There were footprints all over the grave itself, which was churned into mud. Now the drying mud was covered with ants.

"Ants!" said Thrower. "They can't possibly smell the body under the ground."

"No," said Cavil. "What they're finding is fresher and right on top. Look at that—cut-up entrails."

"They didn't—exhume her body and—"

"Not *her* guts. Reverend Thrower. Probably a squirrel or blackbird or something. They did a devil sacrifice last night."

Thrower immediately began murmuring a prayer.

"They know I forbid such things," said Cavil. "By evening, the proof of it would no doubt be gone. They're disobeying me behind my back. I won't have it."

"Now I understand the magnitude of the work you slaveowners have. The devil has an iron grip upon their souls."

"Well, never you mind. They'll pay for it today. They want blood dropped on her grave? It'll be their own. Mr Lashman! Where are you! Mr. Lashman!"

The overseer had only just arrived for the day's work.

"A little half-holiday for the Blacks this morning, Mr. Lashman," said Cavil.

Lashman didn't ask why. "Which ones you want whipped?"

"All of them. Ten lashes each. Except the pregnant women, of course. But even they—one lash for each of them, across the thighs. And all to watch."

"They get a bit unruly, watching it, sir," said Lashman.

"Reverend Thrower and I will watch also," said Cavil.

While Lashman was off assembling the slaves, Thrower murmured something about not really wanting to watch.

"It's the Lord's work," said Cavil. "I have stomach enough to watch any act of righteousness. I thought after last night that you did too."

So they watched together as each slave in turn was whipped, the blood dripping down onto Salamandy's grave. After a while Thrower didn't even flinch. Cavil was glad to see it—the man wasn't weak, after all, just a little soft from his upbringing in Scotland and his life in the North.

Afterward, as Reverend Thrower prepared to be on his way—he had promised to preach in a town a half-day's ride south—he happened to ask Cavil a question.

"I noticed that all your slaves seem—not old, you understand, but not young, either."

Cavil shrugged. "It's the Fugitive Slave Treaty. Even though my farm's prospering, I can't buy or sell any slaves—we're part of the United States now. Most folks keep up by breeding, but you know all my pickaninnies ended up south, till lately. And now I've lost me another breeder, so I'm down to five women now. Salamandy was the best. The others don't have so many years of babies left in them."

"It occurs to me," said Thrower. He paused in thought.

"What occurs to you?"

"I've traveled a lot in the North, Brother Cavil, and in most every town in Hio and Suskwahenny and Irrakwa and Wobbish, there's a family or two of Blacks. Now, you know and I know that they didn't grow on northern trees."

"All runaways."

"Some, no doubt, have their freedom legally. But many—certainly there are many runaways. Now, I understand that it's a custom for every slaveowner to keep a cachet of hair and nail clippings and—"

"Oh, yes, we take them from the minute they're born or the minute we buy them. For the Finders."

"Exactly."

"But we can't exactly send the Finders to walk every foot of ground in the whole North, hoping to run into one particular runaway buck. It'd cost more than the price of the slave."

"It seems to me that the price of slaves has gone up lately."

"If you mean that we can't buy one at any price—"

"That's what I mean, Brother Cavil. And what if the Finders don't have to go blindly through the North, relying on chance? What if you arranged to hire people in the North to scour the papers and take note of the name and age of every Black they see there? Then the Finders could go armed with information."

Well, that idea was so good that it stopped Cavil right short. "There's got to be something wrong with that idea, or somebody'd already be doing it."

"Oh, I'll tell you why nobody's done it so far. There's a good deal of ill-feeling toward slaveowners in the North. Even though northerners hate their Black neighbors, their misguided consciences won't let them cooperate in any kind of slave search. So any southerner who ever went north searching for a runaway soon learned that if he didn't have his Finder right with him, or if the trail was cold, then there was no use searching."

"That's the truth of it. Like a bunch of thieves up North, conspiring to keep a man from recovering his run-off stock."

"But what if you had northerners doing the searching for you? What if you had an agent in the North, a minister perhaps, who could enlist others in the cause, who could find people who could be trusted? Such an endeavor would be expensive, but given the impossibility of *buying* new slaves in Appalachee, don't you imagine people would be willing to pay enough to finance the work of recovering their runaways?"

301

"Pay? They'd pay double what you ask. They'd pay up front on the chance of you doing it."

"Suppose I charged twenty dollars to register their runaway—birthdate, name, description, time and circumstances of escape—and then charged a thousand dollars if I provide them with information leading to recovery?"

"Fifty dollars to register, or they won't believe you're serious. And another fifty whenever you send them information, even if it doesn't turn out to be the right one. And *three* thousand for runaways recovered healthy."

Thrower smiled slightly. "I don't wish to make an unfair profit from the work of righteousness."

"Profit! You got a lot of folks up there to pay if you're going to do a good job. I tell you, Thrower, you write up a contract, and then get the printer in town to run you off a thousand copies. Then you just go round and tell what you plan to one slaveowner in each town you come to in Appalachee. I reckon you'll have to get a new printing done within a week. We're not talking profit here, we're talking a valuable service. Why, I'll bet you get contributions from folks what *never* had a runaway. If you can make it so the Hio River stops being the last barrier before they get away clean, it'll not only return old runaways, it'll make the other slaves lose hope and stay home!"

Not half an hour later, Thrower was back outside and on his horse—but now he had notes written up for the contract and letters of introduction from Cavil to his lawyer and to the printer, along with letters of credit to the tune of five hundred dollars. When Thrower protested that it was too much, Cavil wouldn't even hear him out. "To get you started," said Cavil. "We both know whose work we're doing. It takes money. I have it and you don't, so take it and get busy."

"That's a Christian attitude," said Thrower. "Like the saints in the early Church, who had all things in common."

Cavil patted Thrower's thigh, where he sat stiff in the saddle—northerners just didn't know how to sit a horse. "We've had more in common than any other two men alive," said Cavil. 'We've had the same visions and done the same works, and if that don't make us peas in a pod, I don't know what will."

"When next I see the Visitor, if I should be so fortunate, I know that he'll be pleased."

"Amen," said Cavil.

Then he slapped Thrower's horse and watched him out of sight. My Hager. He's going to find my Hager and her little boy. Nigh on seven years since she stole my firstborn child from me. Now she'll come back, and this time she'll stay in chains and give me more children until she can't have no more. And as for the boy, he'll be my Ishmael. That's what I'll call him, too. Ishmael. I'll keep him right here, and raise him up to be strong and obedient and a true Christian. When he's old enough I'll hire him out to other plantations, and during the nights he'll go and carry on my work, spreading the chosen seed throughout Appalachee. Then my children will surely be as numberless as the sands of the sea, just like Abraham.

And who knows? Maybe then the miracle will happen, and my own dear wife will be healed, and she'll conceive and bear me a pure White child, my Isaac, to inherit all my land and all my work. Lord my Overseer, be merciful to me.

303

17

Spelling Bee

Early January, with deep snow, and a wind sharp
enough to slice your nose off—so of course that was
a day for Makepeace Smith to decide *he* had to work
in the forge all day, while Alvin went into town to
buy supplies and deliver finished work. In the
summer, the choice of jobs tended to go the other
way.

Never mind, thought Alvin. He *is* the master here.
But if I'm ever master of my own forge, and if I
have me a prentice, you can bet he'll be treated
fairer than I've been. A master and prentice ought
to share the work alike, except for when the prentice
plain don't know how, and then the master ought to
teach him. That's the bargain, not to have a slave,
not to always have the prentice take the wagon into
town through the snow.

Truth to tell, though, Alvin knew he wouldn't
have to take the wagon. Horace Guester's sleigh-
and-two would do the job, and he knew Horace
wouldn't mind him taking it, as long as Alvin did
whatever errands the roadhouse needed doing in
town.

Alvin bundled himself tight and pushed out into

the wind—it was right in his face, from the west, the whole way up to the roadhouse. He took the path up by Miss Larner's house, it being the closest way with the most trees to break the wind. Course she wasn't in. It being school hours, she was with the children in the schoolhouse in town. But the old springhouse, it was Alvin's schoolhouse, and just passing by the door got him to thinking about his studies.

She had him learning things he never thought to learn. He was expecting more of ciphering and reading and writing, and in a way that's what she had him doing, right enough. But she didn't have him reading out of those primers like the children—like Arthur Stuart, who plugged away at the studies by lamplight every night in the springhouse. No, she talked to Alvin about ideas he never would've thought of, and all his writing and calculating was about such things.

Yesterday:

"The smallest particle is an atom," she said. "According to the theory of Demosthenes, everything is made out of smaller things, until you come to the atom, which is smallest of all and cannot be divided."

"What's it look like?" Alvin asked her.

"I don't know. It's too small to see. Do *you* know?"

"I reckon not. Never saw anything so small but what you could cut it in half."

"But can't you *imagine* anything smaller?"

"Yeah, but I can split that too."

She sighed. "Well, now, Alvin, think again. If there *were* a thing so small it couldn't be divided, what would it be like?"

305

"*Real* small, I reckon."

But he was joking. It was a problem, and he set out to answer it the way he answered any practical problem. He sent his bug out into the floor. Being wood, the floor was a jumble of things, the broke-up once-alive hearts of living trees, so Alvin quickly sent his bug on into the iron of the stove, which was mostly all one thing inside. Being hot, the bits of it, the tiniest parts he ever saw clear, they were a blur of movement; while the fire inside, it made its own outward rush of light and heat, each bit of it so small and fine that he could barely hold the idea of it in his mind. He never really *saw* the bits of fire. He only knew that they had just passed by.

"Light," he said. "And heat. They can't be cut up."

"True. Fire isn't like earth—it can't be cut. But it can be changed, can't it? It can be extinguished. It can cease to be itself. And therefore the parts of it must become something else, and so they were not the unchangeable and indivisible atoms."

"Well, there's nothing smaller than those bits of fire, so I reckon there's no such thing as an atom."

"Alvin, you've got to stop being so empirical about things."

"If I knowed what that was, I'd stop being it."

"If I knew."

"Whatever."

"You can't always answer every question by sitting back and doodlebugging your way through the rocks outside or whatever."

Alvin sighed. "Sometimes I wish I never told you what I do."

"Do you want me to teach you what it means to be a Maker or not?"

"That's just *what* I want! And instead you talk about atoms and gravity and—I don't care what that old humbug Newton said, nor anybody else! I want to know how to make the—*place*." He remembered only just in time that there was Arthur Stuart in the corner, memorizing every word they said, complete with tone of voice. No sense filling Arthur's head with the Crystal City.

"Don't you understand, Alvin? It's been so long—thousands of years—that no one knows what a Maker really is, or what he does. Only that there were such men, and a few of the tasks that they could do. Changing lead or iron into gold, for instance. Water into wine. That sort of thing."

"I expect iron to gold'd be easier," said Alvin. "Those metals are pretty much all one thing inside. But wine—that's such a mess of different stuff inside that you'd have to be a—a—" He couldn't think of a word for the most power a man could have.

"Maker."

That was the word, right enough. "I reckon."

"I'm telling you, Alvin, if you want to learn how to do the things that Makers once did, you have to understand the nature of things. You can't change what you don't understand."

"And I can't understand what I don't see."

"Wrong! Absolutely false, Alvin Smith! It is what you *can* see that remains impossible to understand. The world you actually see is nothing more than an example, a special case. But the underlying principles, the order that holds it all together, *that* is forever invisible. It can only be discovered in the imagination, which is precisely the aspect of your mind that is most neglected."

Well, last night Alvin just got mad, which she said

would only guarantee that he'd stay stupid, which he said was just fine with him as he'd stayed alive against long odds by being as pure stupid as he was without any help from *her*. Then he stormed on outside and walked around watching the first flakes of this storm start coming down.

He'd only been walking a little while when he realized that she was right, and he knowed it all along. Knew it. He always sent out his bug to see what was *there*, but then when he got set to make a change, he first had to think up what he *wanted* it to be. He had to think of something that wasn't there, and hold a picture of it in his mind, and then, in that way he was born with and still didn't understand, he'd say, See this? this is how you ought to be! And then, sometimes fast, sometimes slow, the bits of it would move around until they lined up right. That's how he always did it: separating a piece off of living rock; joining together two bits of wood; making the iron line up strong and true; spreading the heat of the fire smooth and even along the bottom of the crucible. So I do see what isn't there, in my mind, and that's what makes it *come* to be there.

For a terrible dizzying moment he wondered if maybe the whole world was maybe no more than what he imagined it to be, and if that was true then if he stopped imagining, it'd just go away. Of course, once he got his sense together he knew that if he'd been thinking it up, there wouldn't be so many strange things in the world that he never could've thought of himself.

So maybe the world was all dreamed up in the mind of God. But no, can't be that neither, because if God dreamed up men like White Murderer Harrison then God wasn't too good. No, the best Alvin could think of was that God worked pretty much the way Alvin did—told the rocks of the earth and the fire of the sun and stuff like that, told it all how it was supposed to be and then let it be that way. But when God told *people* how to be, why, they just thumbed their noses and laughed at him, mostly, or else they pretended to obey while they still went on and did what they pleased. The planets and the stars and the elements, they all might be thought up from the mind of God, but people were just too can- tankerous to blame them on anybody but their own self.

Which was about the limit of Alvin's thinking last night, in the snow—wondering about what he could never know. Things like I wonder what God dreams about if he ever sleeps, and if all his dreams come true, so that every night he makes up a whole new world full of people. Questions that couldn't never get him a speck closer to being a Maker.

So today, slogging through the snow, pushing against the wind toward the roadhouse, he started thinking again about the original question—what an atom would be like. He tried to picture something so tiny that he couldn't cut it. But whenever he imagined something like that—a little box or a little ball or something—why, then he'd just up and imagine it splitting right in half.

The only way he couldn't split something in half was if it was so thin nothing could be thinner. He thought of it squished so flat it was thinner than paper, so thin that in that direction it didn't even *exist*, if you looked at it edge-on it would just plain not be there. But even then, he might not be able

309

to split it along the edge, but he could still imagine turning it and slicing it across, just like paper.

So—what if it was squished up in another direction, too, so it was all edge, going on like the thinnest thread you ever dreamed of? Nobody could see it, but it would still be there, because it would stretch from here to there. He sure couldn't split that along the edge, and it didn't have any flat surface like paper had. Yet as long as it stretched like invisible thread from one spot to another, no matter how short the distance was, he could still imagine snipping it right in half, and each half in half again.

No, the only way something could be small enough to be an atom is if it had no size at all in any direction, not length nor breadth nor depth. that would be an atom all right—only it wouldn't even *exist*, it'd just be *nothing*. Just a place without anything in it.

He stood on the porch of the roadhouse, stamping snow off his feet, which did better than knocking for telling folks he was there. He could hear Arthur Stuart's feet running to open the door, but all he was thinking about was atoms. Because even though he'd just figured out that there couldn't be no atoms, he was beginning to realize it might be even crazier to imagine there *not* being atoms, so things could always get cut into smaller bits and *those* things into smaller bits, and those into even *smaller* bits, forever and ever. And when you think about it, it's got to be one or the other. Either you get to the bit that can't be split, and it's an atom, or you never do, and so it goes on *forever*, which is more than Alvin's head could hold.

Alvin found himself in the roadhouse kitchen, with Arthur Stuart piggyback, playing with Alvin's hat and Scarf. Horace Guester was out in the barn stuffing straw into new bedticks, so Alvin asked Old Peg for use of the sleigh. It was hot in the kitchen, and Goody Guester didn't look to be in good temper. She allowed as how he could take the sled, but there was a price to pay.

"Save the life of a certain child, Alvin, and take Arthur Stuart with you," she said, "or I swear he'll do one more thing to rile me and end up in the pudding tonight."

It was true Arthur Stuart seemed to be in a mood to make trouble—he was strangling Alvin with his own scarf and laughing like a fool.

"Let's do some lessons, Arthur," said Alvin. "Spell 'choking to death.' "

"C-H-O-K-I-N-G," said Arthur Stuart. "T-W-O D-E-A-T-H."

Mad as she was, Goody Guester just had to break up laughing—not because he spelled "to" wrong, but because he'd spelled out the words in the most perfect imitation of Miss Larner's voice. "I swear. Arthur Stuart," she said, "you best never let Miss Larner hear you go on like that or your schooling days are over."

"Good! I hate school!" said Arthur.

"You don't hate school so much as you'd hate working with me in the kitchen every day," said Goody Guester. "All day every day, summer and winter, even swimming days."

"I might as well be a slave in Appalachee!" shouted Arthur Stuart.

Goody Guester stopped teasing and being mad, both, and turned solemn. "Don't even joke like that, Arthur. Somebody died once just to keep you from being such a thing."

"I know," said Arthur.

"No you don't, but you'd better just think before you—"

"It was my mama,' said Arthur.

Now Old Peg started looking scared. She took a glance at Alvin and then said, "Never mind about that, anyway."

"My Mama was a blackbird," said Arthur. "She flew so high, but then the ground caught her and she got stuck and died."

Alvin saw how Goody Guester looked at him, even more nervouslike. So maybe there was something to Arthur's story of flying after all. Maybe somehow that girl buried up beside Vigor, maybe somehow she got a blackbird to carry her baby somehow. Or maybe it was just some vision. Anyway, Goody Guester had decided to act like it was nothing after all—too late to fool Alvin, of course, but she wouldn't know that. "Well, that's a pretty story, Arthur," said Old Peg.

"It's true," said Arthur. "I remember."

Goody Guester started looking even more upset. But Alvin knew better than to argue with Arthur about this blackbird idea he had, and about him flying once. The only way to stop Arthur talking about it was to get his mind on something else. "Better come with me, Arthur Stuart," said Alvin. "Maybe you got a blackbird mama sometime in this kitchen is about to knead you like dough."

"Don't forget what I need you to buy for me," said Old Peg.

"Oh, don't worry. I got a list," said Alvin.

"I didn't see you write a thing!"

"Arthur Stuart's my list. Show her, Arthur."

Arthur leaned close to Alvin's ear and shouted so loud it like to split Alvin's eardrums right down to his ankles. "A keg of wheat flour and two cones of sugar and a pound of pepper and a dozen sheets of paper and a couple of yards of cloth that might do for a shirt for Arthur Stuart."

Even thought he was shouting, it was his mama's own voice.

She purely hated it when he mimicked her, and so here she came with the stirring fork in one hand and a big old cleaver in the other. "Hold still, Alvin, so I can stick the fork in his mouth and shave off a couple of ears!"

"Save me!" cried Arthur Stuart.

Alvin saved him by running away, at least till he got to the back door. Then Old Peg set down her instruments of boy-butchery and helped Alvin bundle Arthur Stuart up in coats and leggings and boots and scarves till he was about as big around as he was tall. Then Alvin pitched him out the door into the snow and rolled him with his foot till he was covered with snow.

Old Peg barked at him from the kitchen door. "That's right. Alvin Junior, freeze him to death before his own mother's eyes, you irresponsible prentice boy you!"

Alvin and Arthur Stuart just laughed. Old Peg told them to be careful and get home before dark, and then she slammed the door tight.

They hitched up the sleigh, then swept out the new snow that had blown in while they were hitching it and got in and pulled up the lap robe. They first went on down to the forge again to pick up the work Alvin had to deliver—mostly hinges and fittings and tools for carpenters and leatherworkers in town, who

313

were all in the midst of their busiest season of the year. Then they headed out for town.

They didn't get far before they caught up to a man trudging townward—and none too well dressed, either, for weather like this. When they were beside him and could see his face, Alvin wasn't surprised to see it was Mock Berry.

"Get on this sleigh, Mock Berry, so I won't have your death on my conscience," said Alvin.

Mock looked at Alvin like his words was the first Mock even noticed somebody was there on the road, even though he'd just been passed by the horses, snorting and stamping through the snow. "Thank you, Alvin," said the man. Alvin slid over on the seat to make room. Mock climbed up beside him—clumsy, cause his hands were cold. Only when he was sitting down did he seem to notice Arthur Stuart sitting on the bench. And then it was like somebody slapped him—he started to get right back down off the sleigh.

"Now hold on!" said Alvin. "Don't tell me you're just as stupid as the White folks in town, refusing to sit next to a mixup boy! Shame on you!"

Mock looked at Alvin real steady for a long couple of seconds before he decided how to answer. "Look here, Alvin Smith, you know me better than that. I know how such mixup children come to be, and I don't hold against them what some White man done to their mama. But there's a story in town about who's the real mama of this child, and it does me no good to be seen coming into town with this child nearby."

Alvin knew the story well enough—how Arthur Stuart was supposedly the child of Mock's wife Anga, and how, since Arthur was plainly fathered by some White man, Mock refused even to have the boy in his own house, which led to Goody Guester taking Arthur in. Alvin also knew the story wasn't true. But in a town like this it was better to have such a story believed than to have the true story guessed at. Alvin wouldn't put it past some folks to try to get Arthur Stuart declared a slave and shipped on south just to be rid of him so there'd be no more trouble about schools and such.

"Never mind about that," said Alvin. "Nobody's going to see you on a day like this, and even if they do. Arthur looks like a wad of cloth, and not a boy at all. You can hop off soon as we get into town." Alvin leaned out and took Mock's arm and pulled him onto the seat. "Now pull up the lap robe and snuggle close so I don't have to take you to the undertaker on account of having froze to death."

"Thank you kindly, you pernickety uppity prentice boy." Mock pulled the lap robe up so high that it covered Arthur Stuart completely. Arthur yelled and pulled it down again so he could see over the top. Then he gave Mock Berry such a glare that it might have burnt him to a cinder, if he hadn't been so cold and wet.

When they got into town, there was sleighs aplenty, but none of the merriment of the first heavy snowfall. Folks just went about their business, and the horses stood and waited, stamping their feet and snorting and steaming in the cold wind. The lazier sort of folks—the lawyers and clerks and such—they were all staying at home on a day like this. But the people with real work to do, they had their fires hot, their workshops busy, their stores open for business. Alvin made his rounds a-dropping off ironwork with the delivery book—one more slight, that he wouldn't

315

trust Alvin to take cash, like he was a nine-year-old prentice boy and not more than twice that age.

On those quick errands, Arthur Stuart stayed bundled up on the sleigh—Alvin never stayed indoors long enough to warm up from the walk between sleigh and front door. It wasn't till they got to Pieter Vanderwoort's general store that it was worth going inside and warming up for a spell. Pieter had his stove going right hot, and Alvin and Arthur wasn't the first to think of warming up there. A couple of boys from town were there warming their feet and sipping tea with a nip or two from a flask in order to keep warm. They weren't any of the boys Alvin spent much time with. He'd throwed them once or twice, but that was true of every male creature in town who was willing to rassle. Alvin knew that these two—Martin, that was the one with pimples, and the other one was Daisy—I know that sounds like a crazy name for anyone but a cow, but that was his name all right—anyway, Alvin knew that these two boys were the kind who like to set cats afire and make nasty jokes about girls behind their backs. Not the kind that Alvin spent much time with, but not any that he had any partickler dislike for, neither. So he nodded them good afternoon, and they nodded him back. One of them held up his flask to share, but Alvin said no thanks and that was that.

At the counter, Alvin pulled off some of his scarves, which felt good because he was so sweaty underneath; then he set to unwinding Arthur Stuart, who spun around like a top while Alvin pulled on the end of each scarf. Arthur's laughing brought Mr. Vanderwoort out from the back, and he set to laughing, too.

316

"They're so cute when they're little, aren't they," said Mr. Vanderwoort.

"He's just my shopping list today, aren't you, Arthur?"

Arthur Stuart spouted out his list right off, using his Mama's voice again. "A keg of wheat flour and two cones of sugar and a pound of pepper and a dozen sheets of paper and a couple of yards of cloth that might do for a shirt for Arthur Stuart."

Mr. Vanderwoort like to died laughing. "I get such a kick out of that boy, the way he talks like his mama."

One of the boys by the stove gave a whoop.

"I mean his adopted mama, of course," said Vanderwoort.

"Oh, she's probably his mama all right!" said Daisy. "I hear Mock Berry does a *lot* of work up to the roadhouse!"

Alvin just set his jaw against the answer that sprang to mind. Instead he hotted up the flask in Daisy's hand, so Daisy whooped again and dropped it.

"You come on back with me, Arthur Stuart," said Vanderwoort.

"Like to burned my hand off!" muttered Daisy.

"You just say the list over again, bit by bit, and I'll get what's wanted," said Vanderwoort. Alvin lifted Arthur over the counter and Vanderwoort set him down on the other side.

"You must've set it on the stove like the blamed fool you are, Daisy," said Martin. "What is it, whiskey don't warm you up less it's boiled?"

Vanderwoort led Arthur into the back room. Alvin took a couple of soda crackers from the barrel and pulled up a stool near the fire.

"I didn't set it anywheres near the stove," said Daisy.

"Howdy, Alvin," said Martin.

"Howdy, Martin, Daisy," said Alvin. "Good day for stoves."

"Good day for nothing," muttered Daisy. "Smart-mouth pickaninnies and burnt fingers."

"What brings you to town, Alvin?" asked Martin. "And how come you got that baby buck with you? Or did you buy him off Old Peg Guester?"

Alvin just munched on his cracker. It was a mistake to punish Daisy for what he said before, and a worse mistake to do it again. Wasn't it trying to punish folks that brought the Unmaker down on him last summer? No, Alvin was working on curbing his temper, so he said nothing. Just broke off pieces of the cracker with his mouth.

"That boy ain't for sale," said Daisy. "Everybody knows it. Why, she's even trying to educate him, I hear."

"I'm educating my dog, too," said Martin. "You think that boy's learnt him how to beg or point game or anything useful?"

"But you got yourself the advantage there, Marty," said Daisy. "A dog's got him enough brains to know he's a dog, so he don't try to learn how to read. But you get one of these hairless monkeys, they get to thinking they're people, you know what I mean?"

Alvin got up and walked to the counter. Vanderwoort was coming back now, arms full of stuff. Arthur was tagging along behind.

"Come on behind the counter with me, Al," said Vanderwoort. "Best if you pick out the cloth for Arthur's shirt."

"I don't know a thing about cloth," said Alvin.

"Well, I know about cloth but I don't know about what Old Peg Guester likes, and if she ain't happy with what you come home with, I'd rather it be your fault than mine."

Alvin hitched his butt up onto the counter and swung his legs over. Vanderwoort led him back and they spent a few minutes picking out a plaid flannel that looked suitable enough and might also be tough enough to make patches on old trousers out of the leftover scraps. When they came back, Arthur Stuart was over by the fire with Daisy and Martin.

"Spell 'sassafras,' " said Daisy.

"Sassafras," said Arthur Stuart, doing Miss Larner's voice as perfect as ever. "S-A-S-S-A-F-R-A-S."

"Was he right?" asked Martin.

"Beats hell out of me."

"Now don't be using words like that around a child," said Vanderwoort.

"Oh, never you mind," said Martin. "He's our pet pickaninny. We won't do him no harm."

"I'm not a pickaninny," said Arthur Stuart. "I'm a mixup boy."

"Well, ain't that the truth!" Daisy's voice went so loud and high that his voice cracked.

Alvin was just about fed up with them. He spoke real soft, so only Vanderwoort could hear him. "One more whoop and I'll fill that boy's ears with snow."

"Now don't get riled," said Vanderwoort. "They're harmless enough."

"That's why I won't kill him." But Alvin was smiling, and so was Vanderwoort. Daisy and Martin were just playing, and since Arthur Stuart was enjoying it, why not?

Martin picked something off a shelf and brought it over to Vanderwoort. "What's this word?" he asked.

"Eucalyptus," said Vanderwoort.

"Spell 'eucalipidus,' mixup boy."

"Eucalyptus," said Arthur. "E-U-C-A-L-Y-P-T-U-S."

"Listen to that!" cried Daisy. "That teacher lady won't give time of day to us, but here we got her own voice spelling whatever we say."

"Spell 'bosoms.' " said Martin.

"Now that's going too far," said Vanderwoort. "He's just a boy."

"I just wanted to hear the teacher lady's voice saying it," said Martin.

"I know what you wanted, but that's behind-the-barn talk, not in my general store."

The door opened and, after a blast of cold wind, Mock Berry came in, looking tired and half-froze, which of course he was.

The boys took no notice. "Behind the barn don't got a stove," said Daisy.

"Then keep that in mind when you decide how to talk," said Vanderwoort.

Alvin watched how Mock Berry took sidelong glances at the stove, but made no move to go over there. No man in his right mind would choose not to go to the stove on a day like this—but Mock Berry knew there was worse things than being cold. So instead he just walked up to the counter.

Vanderwoort must've known he was there, but for a while he just kept on watching Martin and Daisy play spelling games with Arthur Stuart, paying no mind to Mock Berry.

"Suskwahenny," said Daisy.

"S-U-S-K-W-A-H-E-N-N-Y," said Arthur.

"I bet that boy could win any spelling bee he ever entered," said Vanderwoort.

"You got a customer," said Alvin.

Vanderwoort turned real slow and looked at Mock Berry without expression. Then, still moving slow, he walked over and stood in front of Mock without a word.

"Just need me two pounds of flour and twelve feet of that half-inch rope," said Mock.

"Hear that?" said Daisy. "He's a-fixing to powder his face white and then hang himself, I'll bet."

"Spell 'suicide,' boy," said Martin.

"S-U-I-C-I-D-E," said Arthur Stuart.

"No credit," said Vanderwoort.

Mock laid down some coins on the counter. Vanderwoort looked at it a minute. "Six feet of rope."

Mock just stood there.

Vanderwoort just stood there.

Alvin knew it was more than enough money for what Mock wanted to buy. He couldn't hardly believe Vanderwoort was raising his price for a man about as poor but hard-working as any in town. In fact, Alvin began to understand a little about why Mock stayed so poor. Now, Alvin knew there wasn't much he could do about it—but he could at least do what Horace Guester had once done for him with his master Makepeace—make Vanderwoort put things out in the open and stop pretending he wasn't being as unfair as he was being. So Alvin laid down the paper Vanderwoort had just written out for him. "I'm sorry to hear there's no credit," Alvin said. "I'll go fetch the money from Goody Guester."

Vanderwoort looked at Alvin. Now he could either make Alvin go fetch the money or say right out that there was credit for the *Guesters*, just not for Mock Berry.

Of course he chose another course. Without a word he went into the back and weighed out the flour. Then he measured out twelve feet of half-inch rope. Vanderwoort was known for giving honest measure. But then, he was also known for giving a fair price, which is why it took Alvin to see him do otherwise with Mock Berry.

Mock took his rope and his flour and started out.

"You got change," said Vanderwoort.

Mock turned around, looking surprised though he tried not to. He came back and watched as Vanderwoort counted out a dime and three pennies onto the counter. Then, hesitating a moment, Mock scooped them off the counter and dropped them into his pocket. "Thank you sir," he said. then he went back out into the cold.

Vanderwoort turned to Alvin, looking angry or maybe just resentful. "I can't give credit to everybody."

Now, Alvin could've said something about at least he could give the same price to Blacks as Whites, but he didn't want to make an enemy out of Mr. Vanderwoort, who was after all a mostly good man. So Alvin grinned real friendly and said, "Oh, I know you can't. Them Berrys, they're almost as poor as me."

Vanderwoort relaxed, which meant it was Alvin's good opinions he wanted more than to get even for Alvin embarrassing him. "You got to understand, Alvin, it ain't good for trade if they come in here all the time. Nobody minds that mixup boy of yours — they're cute when they're little — but it makes folks

322

stay away if they think they might run into one of them here."

"I always knowed Mock Berry to keep his word," said Alvin. "And nobody ever said he stole or slacked or any such thing."

"No, nobody ever told such a tale on him."

"I'm glad to know you count us both among your customers," said Alvin.

"Well, lookit here, Daisy," said Martin. "I think *Prentice* Alvin's gone and turned preacher on us. Spell 'reverend,' boy."

"R-E-V-E-R-E-N-D."

Vanderwoort saw things maybe turning ugly, so of course he tried to change the subject. "Like I said, Alvin, that mixup boy's bound to be the best speller in the county, don't you think? What I want to know is, why don't he go on and get into the county spelling bee next week? I think he'd bring Hatrack River the championship. He might even get the *state* championship, if you want my opinion."

"Spell 'championship,' " said Daisy.

"Miss Larner never said me that word," said Arthur Stuart.

"Well figure it out," said Alvin.

"C-H-A-M-P," said Arthur. "E-U-N-S-H-I-P."

"Sounds right to me," said Daisy.

"Shows what *you* know," said Martin.

"Can you do better?" asked Vanderwoort.

"*I'm* not going to be in the county spelling bee," said Martin.

"What's a spelling bee?" asked Arthur Stuart.

"Time to go," said Alvin, for he knew full well that Arthur Stuart wasn't a regular admitted student in the Hatrack River Grammar School, and so it was a sure thing he wouldn't be in no spelling bee. "Oh, Mr Vanderwoort, I owe you for two crackers I ate."

"I don't charge my friends for a couple of crackers," said Vanderwoort.

"I'm proud to know you count me one of your friends," said Alvin. Alvin meant it, too—it took a good man to get caught out doing something wrong, and then turn around and treat the one that caught him as a friend.

Alvin wound Arthur Stuart back into his scarves, and then wrapped himself up again, and plunged back into the snow, this time carrying all that he bought from Vanderwoort in a burlap sack. He tucked the sack under the seat of the sleigh so it wouldn't get snowed on. Then he lifted Arthur Stuart into place and climbed up after. The horses looked happy enough to get moving again—they only got colder and colder, standing in the snow.

On the way back to the roadhouse they found Mock Berry on the road and took him on home. Not a word did he say about what happened in the store, but Alvin knew it wasn't cause he didn't appreciate it. He figured Mock Berry was plain ashamed of the fact that it took an eighteen-year-old prentice boy to get him honest measure and fair price in Vanderwoort's general store—only cause the boy was white. Not the kind of thing a man loves to talk about.

"Give a howdy to Goody Berry," said Alvin, as Mock hopped off the sleigh up the lane from his house.

"I'll say you said so," said Mock. "And thanks for the ride." In six steps he was clean gone in the blowing snow. The storm was getting worse and worse.

Once everything was dropped off at the road-house, it was near time for Alvin's and Arthur's schooling at Miss Larner's house, so they headed on down there and threw snowballs at each other all the way. Alvin stopped in at the forge to give the delivery book to Makepeace. But Makepeace must've laid off early cause he wasn't there; Alvin tucked the book onto the shelf by the door, where Makepeace would know to look for it. Then he and Arthur went back to snowballs till Miss Larner came back.

Dr. Whitley Physicker drove her in his covered sleigh and walked her right up to her door. When he took note of Alvin and Arthur waiting around, he looked a bit annoyed. "Don't you boys think Miss Larner shouldn't have to do any more teaching on a day like this?"

Miss Larner laid a hand on Dr. Physicker's arm. "Thank you for bringing me home, Dr. Physicker," she said.

"I wish you'd call me Whitley."

"You're kind to me, Dr. Physicker, but I think your honored title suits me best. As for these pupils of mine, it's in bad weather that I do my best teaching, I've found, for they aren't wishing to be at the swimming hole."

"Not me!" shouted Arthur Stuart. "How do you spell 'championship'?"

"C-H-A-M-P-I-O-N-S-H-I-P," said Miss Larner. "Wherever did you hear that word?"

"C-H-A-M-P-I-O-N-S-H-I-P," said Arthur Stuart— in Miss Larner's voice.

"That boy is certainly remarkable," said Physicker. "A mockingbird, I'd say."

"A mockingbird copies the song," said Miss

Larner, "but makes no sense of it. Arthur Stuart may speak back the spellings in my voice, but he truly knows the word and can read it or write it whenever he wishes."

"I'm not a mockingbird," said Arthur Stuart. "I'm a spelling bee championship."

Dr. Physicker and Miss Larner exchanged a look that plainly meant more than Alvin could understand just from watching.

"Very well," said Dr. Physicker. "Since I did in fact enroll him as a special student—at your insistence—he *can* compete in the county spelling bee. But don't expect to take him any farther, Miss Larner!"

"Your reasons were all excellent, Dr. Physicker, and so I agree. But *my* reasons—"

"Your reasons were overwhelming, Miss Larner. And I can't help but relish in advance the consternation of the people who fought to keep him out of school, when they watch him do as well as children twice his age."

"Consternation, Arthur Stuart," said Miss Larner.

"Consternation," said Arthur. "C-O-N-S-T-E-R-N-A-T-I-O-N."

"Good evening, Dr. Physicker. Come inside, boys. Time for school."

Arthur Stuart won the county spelling bee, with the word "celebratory." Then Miss Larner immediately withdrew him from further competition; another child would take his place at the state competition. As a result there was little note taken, except among the locals. Along with a brief notice in the Hatrack River newspaper.

Sheriff Pauley Wiseman folded up that page of the newspaper with a short note and put them in an envelope addressed to Reverend Philadelphia Thrower, The Property Rights Crusade, 44 Harrison Street, Carthage City, Wobbish. It took two weeks for that newspaper page to be spread open on Thrower's desk, along with the note, which said simply:

Boy turned up here summer 1811, only a few weeks old best guess. Lives in Horace Guester's roadhouse, Hatrack River. Adoption don't hold water I reckon if the boy's a runaway.

No signature — but Thrower was used to that, though he didn't understand it. Why should people try to conceal their identity when they were taking part in works of righteousness? He wrote his own letter and sent it south.

A month later, Cavil Planter read Thrower's letter to a couple of Finders. Then he handed them the cachets he'd saved all these years, those belonging to Hagar and her stole-away Ishmael-child. "We'll be back before summer," said the black-haired Finder. "If he's yourn, we'll have him."

"Then you'll have earned your fee and a fine bonus as well," said Cavil Planter.

"Don't need no bonus," said the white-haired finder. "Fee and costs is plenty."

"Well, then, as you wish," said Cavil. "I know God will bless your journey."

18

Manacles

It was early spring, a couple of months before Alvin's nineteenth birthday, when Makepeace Smith come to him and said, "About time you start working on a journeyman piece, Al, don't you think?"

The words sang like redbird song in Alvin's ears, so he couldn't hardly speak back except to nod.

"Well, what do you think you'll make?" asked the master.

"I been thinking maybe a plow," said Alvin.

"That's a lot of iron. Takes a perfect mold, and no easy one, neither. You're asking me to put a good bit of iron at risk, boy."

"If I fail, you can always melt it back."

Since they both knew that Alvin had about as much chance of failing as he did of flying, this was pretty much empty talk—just the last rags of Makepeace's old pretense about how Alvin wasn't much good at smithing.

"Reckon so," said Makepeace. "You just do your best, boy. Hard but not too brittle. Heavy enough to bite deep, but light enough to pull. Sharp enough to cut the earth, and strong enough to cast all stones aside."

"Yes sir." Alvin had memorized the rules of the tools back when he was twelve years old.

There were some other rules that Alvin meant to follow. He had to prove to himself that he was a good smith, and not just a half-baked Maker, which meant that he'd use none of his knack, only the skills that any smith has—a good eye, knowledge of the black metal, the vigor of his arms and the skill of his hands.

Working on his journeyman piece meant he had no other duties till it was done. He started from scratch on this one, as a good journeyman always does. No common clay for the mold—he went upriver on the Hatrack to the best white clay, so the face of the mold would be pure and smooth and hold its shape. Making a mold meant seeing things all inside-out, but Alvin had a good mind for shapes. He patted and stroked the clay into place on the wooden frame, all the time seeing how the different pieces of the mold would give the cooling iron its plow shape. Then he baked the mold dry and hard, ready to receive the iron.

For the metal, he took from the pile of scrap iron and then carefully filed the iron clean, getting rid of all dirt and rust. He scoured the crucible, too. Only then was he ready to melt and cast. He hotted up the coal fire, running the bellows himself, raising and lowering the bellows handle just like he done when he was a new prentice. At last the iron was white in the crucible—and the fire so hot he could scarce bear to come near it. But he came near it anyway, tongs in hand, and hoisted the crucible from the fire, then carried it to the mold and poured. The iron sparked and dazzled, but the mold held true, no buckling or breaking in the heat.

329

Set the crucible back in the fire. Push the other parts of the mold into place. Gently, evenly, getting no splash. He had judged the amount of liquid iron just right—when the last part of the form slipped into place, just a bit of iron squeezed out evenly all around the edges, showing there was just enough, and scarce any waste.

And it was done. Nothing for it but to wait for the iron to cool and harden. Tomorrow he'd know what he'd wrought.

Tomorrow Makepeace Smith would see his plow and call him a man—a journey man, free to practice at any forge, though not yet ready to take on his own prentices. But to Alvin—well, he'd reached that point of readiness years ago. Makepeace would have only a few weeks short of the full seven years of Alvin's service—that's what he'd been waiting for, not for this plow.

No, Alvin's real journeyman work was yet to come. After Makepeace declared the plow good enough, then Alvin had yet another work to perform.

"I'm going to turn it gold," said Alvin.

Miss Larner raised an eyebrow. "And what then? What will you tell people about a golden plow? That you found it somewhere? That you happened to have some gold lying about, and thought—this is just enough to make a plow?"

"You're the one what told me a Maker was the one who could turn iron to gold."

"Yes, but that doesn't mean it's wise to do it." Miss Larner walked out of the hot forge into the stagnant air of late afternoon. It was cooler, but not much—the first hot night of spring.

330

"More than gold," said Alvin. "Or at least not normal gold."

"Regular gold isn't good enough for you?"

"Gold is dead. Like iron."

"It isn't dead. It's simply—earth without fire. It never *was* alive, so it can't be dead."

"You're the one who told me that if I can imagine it, then maybe I can make it come to be."

"And you can imagine living gold?"

"A plow that cuts the earth with no ox to draw it."

She said nothing, but her eyes sparkled.

"If I could make such a thing, Miss Larner, would you consider as how I'd graduated from your school for Makers?"

"I'd say you were no longer a prentice Maker."

"Just what I thought, Miss Larner. A journeyman blacksmith and a journeyman Maker, both, if I can do it."

"And can you?"

Alvin nodded, then shrugged. "I think so. It's what you said about atoms, back in January."

"I thought you gave up on that."

"No ma'am. I just kept thinking—what is it you can't cut into smaller pieces? And then I thought— why, if it's got any size at all, it can be cut. So an atom, it's nothing more than just a place, one exact place, with no width at all."

"Euclid's geometric point."

"Well, yes ma'am, except that you said his geometry was all imaginary, and this is real."

"But if it has no size, Alvin—"

"That's what I thought—if it's got no size, then it's nothing. But it *isn't* nothing. It's a place. Only then I thought, it *isn't* a place—it just *has* a place.

331

If you see the difference. An atom can be in one place, one pure geometric point like you said, but then it can *move*. It can be somewhere else. So, you see, it not only has place, it has a past and a future. Yesterday it was there, today it's here, and tomorrow over yonder."

"But it isn't *anything*, Alvin."

"No, I know that, it isn't any*thing*. But it ain't *nothing*, neither."

"Isn't. Either."

"I know all that grammar, Miss Larner, but I'm not thinking about that right now."

"You won't have good grammar unless you use it even when you're not thinking about it. But never mind."

"See, I start thinking, if this atom's got no size, but can anybody tell where it is? It's not giving off any light, because it's got no fire in it to give off. So here's what I come up with: Just suppose this atom's got no *size*, but it's still got some kind of mind. Some kind of tiny little wit, just enough to know where it is. And the only power it has is to move somewhere else, and know where it is *then*."

"How could that be, a memory in something that doesn't exist?"

"Just suppose it! Say you got thousands of them just lying around, just going any which way. How can any of them tell where they are? Since all the others are moving any which way, nothing around it stays the same. But then suppose somebody comes along—and I'm thinking about God here—somebody who can show them a pattern. Show them some way to set still. Like he says—you, there, you're the center, and all the rest of you, you just stay the same

332

distance away from him all the time. Then what have you got?"

Miss Larner thought for a moment. "A hollow sphere. A ball. But still composed of nothing, Alvin."

"But don't you see? That's why I knew that this was true. I mean, if there's one thing I know from doodlebugging, it's that everything's mostly empty. That anvil, it looks solid, don't it? But I tell you it's mostly empty. Just little bits of ironstuff, hanging a certain distance from each other, all patterned there. But most of the anvil is the empty space between. Don't you see? Those bits are acting just like the atoms I'm talking about. So let's say the anvil is like a mountain, only when you get real close you see it's made of gravel. And then when you pick up the gravel, it crumbles in your hand, and you see it's made of dust. And if you could pick up a single fleck of dust you'd see that it was just like the mountain, made of even tinier gravel all over again."

"You're saying that what we see as solid objects are really nothing but illusion. Little nothings making tiny spheres that are put together to make your bits, and pieces made from bits, and the anvil made from pieces—"

"Only there's a lot more steps between, I reckon. Don't you see, this explains everything? Why is it that all I have to do is imagine a new shape or a new pattern or a new order, and show it in my mind, and if I think it clear and strong enough, and command the bits to change, why—they do. Because they're *alive*. They may be small and none too bright, but if I show them clear enough, they can do it."

"This is too strange for me, Alvin. To think that everything is really nothing."

"No, Miss Larner, you're missing the point. The point is that everything is *alive*. That everything is made out of living atoms, all obeying the commands that God gave them. And just following those commands, why, some of them get turned into light and heat, and some of them become iron, and some water, and some air, and some of them our own skin and bones. All those things are real—and so those atoms are real."

"Alvin, I told you about atoms because they were an interesting theory. The best thinkers of our time believe there are no such things."

"Begging your pardon, Miss Larner, but the best thinkers never saw the things I saw, so they don't know diddly. I'm telling you that this is the only idea I can think of that explains it all—what I see and what I do."

"But where did these atoms come from?"

"They don't come from anywhere. Or rather, maybe they come from everywhere. Maybe these atoms, they're just there. Always been there, always will be there. You can't cut them up. They can't die. You can't make them and you can't break them. They're forever."

"Then God didn't create the world."

"Of course he did. The atoms were nothing, just places that didn't even know where they were. It's God who put them all into places so he'd know where they were, and so *they'd* know where they were—and everything in the whole universe is made out of them."

Miss Larner thought about it for the longest time. Alvin stood there watching her, waiting. He knew

334

it was true, or at least truer than anything else he'd ever heard of or thought of. Unless she could think of something wrong with it. So many times this year she'd done that, point out something he forgot, some reason why his idea wouldn't work. So he waited for her to come up with something. Something wrong.

Maybe she would've. Only while she was standing there outside the forge, thinking, they heard the sound of horses cantering up the road from town. Of course they looked to see who was coming in such a rush.

It was Sheriff Pauley Wiseman and two men that Alvin never saw before. Behind them was Dr. Physicker's carriage, with old Po Doggly driving. And they didn't just pass by. They stopped right there at the curve by the forge.

"Miss Larner," said Pauley Wiseman. "Arthur Stuart around here?"

"Why do you ask?" said Miss Larner. "Who are these men?"

"He's here," said one of the men. The white-haired one. He held up a tiny box between his thumb and forefinger. Both the strangers looked at it, then looked up the hill toward the springhouse. "In there," said the white-haired man.

"You need any more proof than that?" asked Pauley Wiseman. He was talking to Dr. Physicker, who was now out of his carriage and standing there looking furious and helpless and altogether terrible.

"Finders," whispered Miss Larner.

"That's us," said the white-haired one. "You got a runaway slave up there, Ma'am."

"He is not," she said. "He is a pupil of mine, legally adopted by Horace and Margaret Guester—"

"We got a letter from his owner, giving his birth-

335

date, and we got his cachet here, and he's the very one. We're sworn and certified, Ma'am. What we Find is found. That's the law, and if you interfere, you're obstructing." The man spoke real nice and quiet and polite.

"Don't worry, Miss Larner," said Dr. Physicker. "I already have a writ from the mayor, and that'll hold him till the judge gets back tomorrow."

"Hold him in *jail*, of course," said Pauley Wiseman. "Wouldn't want anybody to try to run off with him, now, would we?"

"Wouldn't do much good if they tried," said the white-haired Finder. "We'd just follow. And then we'll probably shoot them dead, seeing how they was thieves escaping with stolen property."

"You haven't even told the Guesters, have you!" said Miss Larner.

"How could I?" said Dr. Physicker. "I had to stay with *them*, to make sure they didn't just take him."

"We obey the law," said the white-haired Finder.

"There he is," said the black-haired Finder.

Arthur Stuart stood in the open door of the spring-house.

"Just stay where you are, boy!" shouted Pauley Wiseman. "If you move a muscle I'll whip you to jelly!"

"You don't have to threaten him," said Miss Larner, but there wasn't nobody to listen, since they were all running up the hill.

"Don't hurt him!" cried Dr. Physicker.

"If he don't run, he won't get hurt," said the white-haired Finder.

"Alvin," said Miss Larner. "Don't do it."

"They ain't taking Arthur Stuart."

336

"Don't use your power like that. Not to hurt someone."

"I tell you—"

"Think, Alvin. We have until tomorrow. Maybe the judge—"

"Putting him in jail!"

"If anything happens to these Finders, then the nationals will be in it, to enforce the Fugitive Slave Treaty. Do you understand me? It's not a local crime like murder. You'd be taken off to Appalachee to be tried."

"I can't do *nothing*."

"Run and tell the Guesters."

Alvin waited just a moment. If it was up to him, he'd burn their hands right off before he let them take Arthur. But already the boy was between them, their fingers digging into Arthur's arms. Miss Larner was right. What they needed was a way to win Arthur's freedom for sure, not some stupid blunder that would end up making things worse.

Alvin ran for the Guesters' house. It surprised him how they took it—like they'd been expecting it all the time for the last seven years. Old Peg and Horace just looked at each other, and without a word Old Peg started in packing—her clothes *and* Arthur Stuart's.

"What's she packing *her* things for?" asked Alvin.

Horace smiled, a real tight smile. "She ain't going to let Arthur spend a night in jail alone. So she'll have them lock her up right alongside him."

It made sense—but it was strange to think of people like Arthur Stuart and Old Peg Guester in jail.

"What are *you* going to do?" asked Alvin.

"Load my guns," said Horace. "And when they're gone, I'll follow."

Alvin told him what Miss Larner had said about the nationals coming if somebody laid hand on a Finder.

"What's the worst they can do to me? Hang me. I tell you, I'd rather be hanged than live in this house a single day if they take Arthur Stuart away and I done nothing to stop them. And I can do it, Alvin. Hell, boy, I must've saved fifty runaway slaves in my time. Po Doggly and me, we used to pick them up this side of the river and send them on to safety in Canada. Did it all the time."

Alvin wasn't a bit surprised to hear of Horace Guester being an Emancipationist—and not a talker, neither.

"I'm telling you this, Alvin, cause I need your help. I'm just one man and there's two of them. I got no one I can trust—Po Doggly ain't gone with me on something like this in a week of Christmasses, and I don't know where he stands no more. But you—I know you can keep a secret, and I know you love Arthur Stuart near as much as my wife does."

The way he said it gave Alvin pause. "Don't *you* love him, sir?"

Horace looked at Alvin like he was crazy. "They ain't taking a mixup boy right out from under my roof, Al."

Goody Guester come downstairs then, with two bundles in homespun bags under her arms. "Take me into town, Horace Guester."

They heard the horses riding by on the road outside.

"That's probably them," said Alvin.

"Don't worry, Peg," said Horace.

"Don't *worry*?" Old Peg turned on him in fury. "Only two things are likely to happen out of this, Horace. Either I lose my son to slavery in the South, or my fool husband gets himself probably killed trying to rescue him. Of course I won't worry." Then she burst into tears and hugged Horace so tight it near broke Alvin's heart to see it.

It was Alvin drove Goody Guester into town on the roadhouse wagon. He was standing there when she finally wore down Pauley Wiseman so he'd let her spend the night in the cell—though he made her take a terrible oath about not trying to sneak Arthur Stuart out of jail before he'd do it.

As he led the way to the jail cell, Pauley Wiseman said, "You shouldn't fret none, Goody Guester. His master's no doubt a good man. Folks here got the wrong idea of slavery, I reckon."

She whirled on him. "Then you'll go in his place, Pauley? Seeing how it's so fine?"

"Me?" He was no more than amused at the idea. "I'm *White*, Goody Guester. Slavery ain't my natural state."

Alvin made the keys slide right out of Pauley's fingers.

"I'm sure getting clumsy," said Pauley Wiseman.

Goody Guester's foot just naturally ended up right on top of the key ring.

"Just lift up your foot, Goody Guester," said the sheriff, "or I'll charge you with aiding and abetting, not to mention resisting."

She moved her foot. The sheriff opened the door. Old Peg stepped through and gathered Arthur Stuart into her arms. Alvin watched as Pauley Wiseman closed and locked the door behind them. Then he went on home.

Alvin broke open the mold and rubbed away the clay that still clung to the face of the plow. The iron was smooth and hard, as good a plow as Alvin ever saw cast till then. He searched inside it and found no flaws, not big enough to mar the plow, anyway. He filed and rubbed, rubbed and filed till it was smooth, the blade sharp as if he meant to use it in a butcher shop instead of some field somewhere. He set it on top of the workbench. Then he sat there waiting while the sun rose and the rest of the world came awake.

In due time Makepeace came down from the house and looked at the plow. But Alvin didn't see him, being asleep. Makepeace woke him up enough to get him to walk back up to the house.

"Poor boy," said Gertie. "I bet he never even went to sleep last night. I bet he went on down and worked on that fool plow all night."

"Plow looks fair."

"Plow looks perfect, I'll bet, knowing Alvin."

Makepeace grimaced. "What do you know about ironwork?"

"I know Alvin and I know you."

"Strange boy. Ain't it the truth though? He does his best work when he stays up all night." Makepeace even had some affection in his voice, saying that. But Alvin was asleep in his bed by then and didn't hear.

"Sets such store by that mixup child," said Gertie. "No wonder he couldn't sleep."

"Sleeping now," said Makepeace.

"Imagine sending Arthur Stuart into slavery at his age."

"Law's the law," said Makepeace. "Can't say I

340

like it, but a fellow has to live by the law or what then?"

"You and the law," said Gertie. "I'm glad we don't live on the other side of the Hio, Makepeace, or I swear you'd be wanting slaves instead of prentices—if you know the difference."

That was as pure a declaration of war as they ever gave each other, and they were all set for one of their rip-snorting knockabout break-dish fights, only Alvin was snoring up in the loft and Gertie and Makepeace just glared at each other and let this one go. Since all their quarrels came out the same, with all the same cruel things said and all the same hurts and harms done, it was like they just got tired and said, Pretend I just said all the things you hate worst in all the world to hear, and I'll pretend you said the things I hate worst back to me, and then let be.

Alvin didn't sleep all that long, nor all too well, neither. Fear and anger and eagerness all played through his body till he could hardly hold still, let alone keep his brain drifting with the currents of his dreams. He woke up dreaming of a black plow turned to gold. He woke up dreaming of Arthur Stuart being whipped. He woke up again thinking of aiming a gun at one of them Finders and pulling the trigger. He woke up again thinking of aiming at a Finder and *not* pulling the trigger, and then watching them go away dragging Arthur after them, him screaming all the time, Alvin, where are you! Alvin, don't let them take me.

"Wake up or hush up!" shouted Gertie. "You're scaring the children."

Alvin opened his eyes and leaned over the edge of the loft. "Your children ain't even here."

"Then you're scaring *me*. I don't know what you

341

was dreaming, boy, but I hope that dream never comes even to my worst enemy—which happens to be my husband this morning, if you want to know the truth."

Her mentioning Makepeace made Alvin alert, yes sir. He pulled on his trousers, wondering when and how he got up to this loft and who pulled his pants and boots off. In just that little amount of time, Gertie somehow got food on the table—cornbread and cheese and a dollop of molasses. "I don't have time to eat, Ma'am," said Alvin. "I'm sorry, but I got to—"

"You got time."

"No Ma'am. I'm sorry—"

"Take the bread, then, you plain fool. You plan to work all day with an empty belly? After only a morning's sleep? Why, it ain't even noon yet."

So he was chewing on bread when he come down the hill to the forge. There was Dr. Physicker's carriage again, and the Finders' horses. For a second Alvin thought—they come here cause Arthur Stuart got away somehow, and the Finders lost him, and—

No. They had Arthur Stuart with them.

"Good morning, Alvin," said Makepeace. He turned to the other men. "I must be about the softest master I ever heard of, letting my prentice boy sleep till near noon."

Alvin didn't even notice how Makepeace was criticizing him and calling him a prentice *boy* when his journeyman piece stood there finished on the workbench. He just squatted down in front of Arthur Stuart and looked him in the eyes.

"Stand back now," said the white-haired Finder.

Alvin didn't hardly notice him. He wasn't really seeing Arthur Stuart, not with his eyes, anyhow. He was searching his body for some sign of harm. None. Not yet anyway. Just the fear in the boy.

"You haven't told us yet," said Pauley Wiseman. "Will you make them or not?"

Makepeace coughed. "Gentlemen, I once made a pair of manacles, back in New England. For a man convicted of treason, being shipped back to England in irons. I hope I never make a manacle for a seven-year-old boy who done no harm to a living soul, a boy who played around my forge and—"

"Makepeace," said Pauley Wiseman. "I told them that if you made the manacles, they wouldn't have to use this."

Wiseman held up the heavy iron-and-wood collar that he'd left leaning against his leg.

"It's the law," said the white-haired Finder. "We bring runaway slaves back home in that collar, to show the others what happens. But him being just a boy, and seeing how it was his mama what run away and not him, we agreed to manacles. But it don't make no difference to me. We get paid either way."

"You and your damned Fugitive Slave Treaty!" cried Makepeace. "You use that law to make slavers out of us, too."

"I'll make them," said Alvin.

Makepeace looked at him in horror. "You!"

"Better than that collar," said Alvin. What he didn't say was, I don't intend for Arthur Stuart to wear those manacles a minute longer than tonight. He looked at Arthur Stuart. "I'll make you some manacles as don't hurt much, Arthur Stuart."

"Wisely done," said Pauley Wiseman.

"Good to see somebody with sense here," said the white-haired Finder.

Alvin looked at him and tried to hold all his hatred

343

in. He couldn't quite do it. So his spittle ended up spattering the dust at the Finder's feet.

The black-haired Finder looked ready to throw a punch at him for that, and Alvin wouldn't've minded a bit to grapple with him and maybe rub his face in the dirt a minute or two. But Pauley Wiseman jumped right between them and he had sense enough to do his talking to the black-haired Finder, and not to Alvin. "You got to be a blame fool, setting to rassle with a blacksmith. Look at his arms."

"I could take him," said the Finder.

"You folks got to understand," said the white-haired Finder. "It's our knack. We can no more help being Finders than—"

"There's some knacks," said Makepeace, "where it'd be better to die at birth than grow up and use it." He turned to Alvin. "I don't want you using my forge for this."

"Don't make a nuisance of yourself, Makepeace," said Pauley Wiseman.

"Please," said Dr. Physicker. "You're doing the boy more harm than good."

Makepeace backed off, but none too graciously.

"Give me your hands, Arthur Stuart," Alvin said.

Alvin made a show of measuring Arthur's wrists with a string. Truth was, he could see the measure of him in his mind, every inch of him, and he'd shape the iron to fit smooth and perfect, with rounded edges and no more weight than needed. Arthur wouldn't feel no pain from these manacles. Not with his body, anyhow.

They all stood and watched Alvin work. It was the smoothest, purest job they'd ever see. Alvin used his knack this time, but not so it'd show. He hammered and bent the strap iron, cutting it exactly

344

right. The two halves of each manacle fit snug, so they wouldn't shift and pinch the skin. And all the time he was thinking how Arthur used to pump the bellows for him, or just stand there and talk to him while he worked. Never again. Even after they saved him tonight, they'd have to take him to Canada or hide him somehow—as if you could hide from a Finder.

"Good work," said the white-haired Finder. "I never saw me a better blacksmith."

Makepeace piped up from the dark corner of the forge. "You should be proud of yourself, Alvin. Why, let's make those manacles your journeyman piece, all right?"

Alvin turned and faced him. "My journeyman piece is that plow setting on the workbench, Make-peace."

It was the first time Alvin ever called his master by his first name. It was as clear as Alvin could let him know that the days of Makepeace talking to him like that were over now.

Makepeace didn't want to understand him. "Watch how you talk to me, boy! Your journeyman piece is what I say it is, and—"

"Come on, boy, let's get these on you." The white-haired Finder wasn't interested in Make-peace's talk, it seemed.

"Not yet," said Alvin.

"They're ready," said the Finder.

"Too hot," said Alvin.

"Well dip them in that bucket there and cool them off."

"If I do that, they'll change shape just a little, and then they'll cut the boy's arms so they bleed."

345

The black-haired Finder rolled his eyes. What did he care about a little blood from a mixup boy?

But the white-haired Finder knew that nobody'd stand for it if he didn't wait. "No hurry," he said. "Can't take too long."

They sat around waiting without a word. Then Pauley started in talking about nothing, and so did the Finders, and even Dr. Physicker, just jawing away like as if the Finders were any old visitors. Maybe they thought they were making the Finders feel more kindly so they wouldn't take it out on the boy once they had him across the river. Alvin had to figure that so he wouldn't hate them.

Besides, an idea was growing in his mind. It wasn't enough to get Arthur Stuart away tonight—what if Alvin could make it so even the Finders couldn't find him again?

"What's in that cachet you Finders use?" he asked.

"Don't you wish you knew," said the black-haired Finder.

"It's no secret," said the white-haired Finder. "Every slave-owner makes up a box like this for each slave, soon as he's bought or born. Scrapings from his skin, hair from his head, a drop of blood, things like that. Parts of his own flesh."

"You get his scent from that?"

"Oh, it ain't a scent. We ain't *bloodhounds*, Mr. Smith."

Alvin knew that calling him Mr. Smith was pure flattery. He smiled a little, pretending that it pleased him.

"Well then how does it help?"

"Well, it's our *knack*," said the white-haired Finder. "Who knows how it works? We just look at

346

it, and we—it's like we see the shape of the person we're looking for."

"It ain't like that," said the black-haired Finder.

"Well that's how it is for *me*."

"I just know where he is. Like I can see his soul. If I'm close enough, anyway. Glowing like a fire, the soul of the slave I'm searching for." The black-haired Finder grinned. "I can see from a long way off."

"Can you show me?" asked Alvin.

"Nothing to see," said the white-haired Finder.

"I'll show you, boy," said the black-haired Finder. "I'll turn my back and y'all move that boy around in the forge. I'll point to him over my shoulder, perfect all the time."

"Come on now," said the white-haired Finder.

"We got nothing to do anyway till the iron cools. Give me the cachet."

The black-haired Finder did what he bragged—pointed at Arthur Stuart the whole time. But Alvin hardly saw that. He was busy watching from the inside of that Finder, trying to understand what he was doing, what he was *seeing*, and what it had to do with the cachet. He couldn't see how seven-year-old dried-up bits of Arthur Stuart's newborn body could show them where he was *now*.

Then he remembered that for a moment right at first the Finder hadn't pointed at all. His finger had wandered a little, and only after just that pause had he started pointing right at Arthur Stuart. Like as if he'd been trying to sort out which of the people behind him in the smithy was Arthur. The cachet wasn't for Finding—it was for recognizing. The Finders saw everybody, but they couldn't tell who was who without a cachet.

347

So what they were seeing wasn't Arthur's mind, or Arthur's soul. They were just seeing a body, like every other body unless they could sort it out. And what they were sorting was plain enough to Alvin—hadn't he healed enough people in his life to know that people were pretty much the same, except for some bits at the center of each living piece of their flesh? Those bits were different for every single person, yet the same in every part of that person's flesh. Like it was God's way of naming them right in their flesh. Or maybe it was the mark of the beast, like in the book of Revelation. Didn't matter. Alvin knew that the only thing in that cachet that was the same as Arthur Stuart's body was that signature that lived in every part of his body, even the dead and cast-off parts in the cachet.

I can change those bits, thought Alvin. Surely I can change them, change them in every part of his body. Like turning iron into gold. Like turning water into wine. And then their cachet wouldn't work at all. Wouldn't help them at all. They could search for Arthur Stuart all they liked, but as long as they didn't actually see his face and recognize him the regular way, they'd never find him.

Best of all, they wouldn't even realize what happened. They'd still have the cachet, same as ever, and they'd know it hadn't been changed a bit because Alvin wouldn't change it. But they could search the whole world over and never find a body just like those specks in their cachet, and they'd never guess why.

I'll do it, thought Alvin. Somehow I'll figure a way to change him. Even though there must be millions of those signatures all through his body, I'll find a way to change everyone. Tonight I'll do it, and tomorrow he'll be safe forever.

The iron was cool. Alvin knelt before Arthur Stuart and gently put the manacles in place. They fit his flesh so perfectly he might have cast them in a mold taken from Arthur's own body. When they were locked into place, with a length of light chain strung between them, Alvin looked Arthur Stuart in the eye. "Don't be afraid," he said.

Arthur Stuart didn't say a thing.

"I won't forget you," said Alvin.

"Sure," said the black-haired Finder. "But just in case you get ideas about remembering him while he's on his way home to his rightful master, I ought to tell you square—we never both of us sleep at the same time. And part of being a Finder is, we know if anybody's coming. You can't sneak up on us. Least of all you, smith boy. I could see *you* ten miles away."

Alvin just looked at him. Eventually the Finder sneered and turned away. They put Arthur Stuart onto the horse in front of the white-haired Finder. But Alvin figured that as soon as they got across the Hio, they'd have Arthur walking. Not out of meanness, maybe—but it wouldn't do no good for Finders to show themselves being kindly to a runaway. Besides, they had to set an example for the other slaves, didn't they? Let them see a boy seven years old walking along, feet bleeding, head bowed, and they'd think twice about trying to run off with their children. They'd know that Finders have no mercy.

Pauley and Dr. Physicker rode away with them. They were seeing the Finders to the Hio River and watching them cross the river, to make sure they did no hurt to Arthur Stuart while he was in free territory. It was the best they could do.

Makepeace didn't have much to say, but what he said, he said plain. "A real man would never put manacles on his own friend," said Makepeace. "I'll go up to the house and sign your journeyman papers. I don't want you in my smithy or my house another night." He left Alvin alone by the forge.

He'd been gone no more than five minutes when Horace Guester got to the smithy.

"Let's go," he said.

"No," said Alvin. "Not yet. They can see us coming. They'll tell the sheriff if they're being followed."

"We got no choice. Can't lose their trail."

"You know something about what I am and what I can do," said Alvin. "I've got them even now. They won't get more than a mile from the Hio shore before they fall asleep."

"You can do that?"

"I know what goes on inside people when they're asleep. I can make that stuff start happening inside them the minute they're in Appalachee."

"While you're at it, why don't you kill them?"

"I can't."

"They aren't men! It wouldn't be murder, killing them!"

"They *are* men," said Alvin. "Besides, if I kill them, then it's a violation of the Fugitive Slave Treaty."

"Are you a lawyer now?"

"Miss Larner explained it to me. I mean she explained it to Arthur Stuart while I was there. He wanted to know. Back last fall. He said. 'Why don't my pa just kill them if some Finders come for me?'

350

and Miss Larner, she told him how there'd just be more Finders coming, only this time they'd hang you and take Arthur Stuart anyway."

Horace's face had turned red. Alvin didn't understand why for a minute, not till Horace Guester explained. "He shouldn't call me his pa. I never wanted him in my house." He swallowed. "But he's right. I'd kill them Finders if I thought it'd do good."

"No killing," said Alvin. "I think I can fix it so they'll never find Arthur again."

"I know. I'm going to ride him to Canada. Get to the lake and sail across."

"No sir," said Alvin. "I think I can fix it so they'll never find him *anywhere*. We just got to hide him till they go away."

"Where?"

"Springhouse, if Miss Larner'll let us."

"Why there?"

"I got it hexed up every which way from Tuesday. I thought I was doing it for the teacher lady. But now I reckon I was really doing it for Arthur Stuart."

Horace grinned. "You're really something, Alvin. You know that?"

"Maybe. Sure wish I knew *what*."

"I'll go ask Miss Larner if we can make use of her house."

"If I know Miss Larner, she'll say yes before you finish asking."

"When do we start, then?"

It took Alvin by surprise, having a grown man ask *him* when they should start. "Soon as it's dark, I reckon. Soon as those two Finders are asleep."

"You can really *do* that?"

"I can if I keep watching them. I mean sort of

351

watching. Keeping track of where they are. So I don't go putting the wrong people to sleep."

"Well, are you watching them now?"

"I know where they are."

"Keep watching, then." Horace looked a little scared, almost as bad as he did near seven years ago, when Alvin told him he knew about the girl buried there. Scared because he knew Alvin could do something strange, something beyond any hexings or knacks in Horace's ken.

Don't you know me, Horace? Don't you know that I'm still Alvin, the boy you liked and trusted and helped so many times? Finding out that I'm stronger than you thought, in ways you didn't think of, that don't mean I'm a whit more dangerous to you. No reason to be a-scared.

As if Horace could hear his words, the fear eased away from his face. "I just mean—Old Peg and I are counting on you. Thank God you ended up in this place, right at this time when we needed you so bad. The good Lord's looking out for us." Horace smiled, then turned and left the smithy.

What Horace said, it left Alvin feeling good, feeling sure of himself. But then, that was Horace's knack, wasn't it—to give folks the view of theirselves they most needed to see.

Alvin turned his thoughts at once to the Finders, and sent out his bug to stay with them, to keep track of the way their bodies moved like small black storms through the greensong around them, with Arthur Stuart's small song bright and clear between them. Black and White don't have nothing to do with bright and dark at heart, I reckon, thought Alvin. His hands stayed busy doing work at the forge, but for the life of him he couldn't pay real attention to it. He'd never watched somebody so far off before—except for that time he got helped by powers he didn't understand, inside Eight-Face Mound.

And the worst thing of all would be if he lost them, if they got away with Arthur Stuart, all because Alvin didn't pay attention close enough and lost that boy among all the beat-down souls of slaves in Appalachee and on beyond, in the deep South where all White men were servants to the other Arthur Stuart, King of England, and so all Blacks were slaves of slaves. Ain't going to lose Arthur in a place so bad. Going to hold on tight to him, like as if he got a thread to connect him to me.

Almost as soon as he thought of it, almost as soon as he imagined a thin invisible thread connecting him and that mixup boy, why, there it was. There was a thread in the air, a thread about as thin as what he imagined once trying to understand what an atom might be. A thread that only had size in one direction—the direction that led toward Arthur Stuart, connecting them heart to heart. Stay with him, Alvin told the thread, like as if it really was alive. And in answer it seemed to grow brighter, thicker, till Alvin was sure anybody who come along could see it.

But when he looked with his eyes, he couldn't see the thread at all; it only appeared to him again when he looked without eyes. It plain astonished him, that such a thing could come to be, created—not out of nothing—but created without pattern except the pattern found in Alvin's own mind. This is a Making. My first, thin, invisible Making—but it's real, and it's going to lead me to Arthur Stuart tonight, so I can set him free.

In her little house, Peggy watched Alvin and Arthur Stuart both, looking back and forth from one to the other, trying to find some pathway that led for Arthur's freedom without costing Alvin's death or capture. No matter how closely and carefully she looked, there was no such path. The Finders were too skilled with their terrible knack; on some paths, Alvin and Horace might carry Arthur off, but he'd only be found again and recaptured—at the cost of Alvin's blood or Alvin's freedom.

So she watched despairing as Alvin spun his almost nonexistent thread. Only then, for the first time, did she see some glimmer of a possibility of freedom in Arthur Stuart's heartfire. It came not from the fact that the thread would lead Alvin to the boy—on many paths before he spun the thread, she had seen Alvin finding the Finders and putting them to sleep. No, the difference now was that Alvin could make the thread at all. The possibility of it had been so small that there had been no path that showed it. Or perhaps—something she hadn't thought of before—the very act of Making was such a violation of the natural order that her own knack couldn't see paths that relied on it, not until it was actually accomplished.

Yet even at the moment of Alvin's birth, hadn't she seen his glorious future? Hadn't she seen him building a city made of the purest glass or ice? Hadn't she seen his city filled with people who spoke with the tongues of angels and saw with the eyes of God? The fact that Alvin would Make, that was always probable, provided he stayed alive. But any one particular act of Making, that was never likely, never natural enough for a torch—even an extraordinary torch like Peggy—to see it.

She saw Alvin put the Finders to sleep almost as soon as it was dark and they could find a stopping place on the far side of the Hio. She saw Alvin and Horace meet in the smithy, preparing to set out through the woods to the Hio, avoiding the road so they wouldn't meet the sheriff and Dr. Physicker coming back from Hatrack Mouth. But she paid little heed to them. Now that there was new hope, she gave her full attention to Arthur's future, studying how and where his slender new paths of freedom were rooted to the present action. She could not find the clear moment of choice and change. To her that fact was proof that all depended on Alvin becoming a Maker, truly, on this night.

"O God," she whispered, "if thou didst cause this boy to be born with such a gift, I pray thee teach him Making now, tonight."

Alvin stood beside Horace, masked by shadows at the riverbank, waiting for a well-lighted riverboat to pass. Out on the boat, musicians were playing, and people danced a fancy quadrille on the decks. It made Alvin angry, to see them playing like children when a real child was being carried off to slavery tonight. Still, he knew they meant no harm, and knew it wasn't fair to blame others for being happy while somebody they don't even know might be grieving. By that measure there'd be no happiness in all the world, Alvin figured. Life being how it is, Alvin thought, there's not a moment in the day when there ain't at least a few hundred people grieving about something.

The ship had no sooner passed around a bend than they heard a crashing in the woods behind them. Or rather, Alvin heard the sound, and it only seemed like crashing to *him* because of his sense of the right order of things in the greenwood song. It took more than a few minutes before Horace heard it at all. Whoever it was sneaking up on them, he was right stealthy for a White man.

"Now I'm wishing for a gun," whispered Horace.

Alvin shook his head. "Wait and watch," he whispered—so faint his lips barely moved.

They waited. After a while, they saw a man step out of the woods and slither down the bank to the muddy edge of the water, where the boat rocked on the water. Seeing nobody there, he looked around, then sighed and stepped out into the boat, turned around and sat down in the stern, glumly resting his chin on his hands.

Suddenly Horace started chuckling. "Play fetch with my bones when I'm dead, but I do think that's old Po Doggly."

At once the man in the boat leaned back and Alvin could finally see him clear in the moonlight. It *was* Dr. Physicker's driver, sure enough. But this didn't seem to bother Horace none. He was already slipping down the riverbank, to splash out to the boat, climb aboard and give Po Doggly such a violent hug the boat took on water. In only a second they both noticed that the boat was rocking out of kilter, and without a word they both shifted exactly right to balance the load, and then again without a word Po got the oars into the locks while Horace took a flat tin baling cup out from under his bench and commenced to dipping it and pouring it out overboard, again and again.

Alvin marveled for a moment at how smooth the two of them fit together. He didn't even have to ask—he knew from how they acted that they'd done this sort of thing a good many times before. Each knew what the other was going to do, so they didn't even have to think about it anymore. One man did his part, and the other his, and neither even had to check to make sure both parts were getting done.

Like the bits and pieces that made up everything in the world; like the dance of atoms Alvin had imagined in his mind. He'd never realized it before, but people could be like those atoms, too. Most of the time people were all disorganized, nobody knowing who anybody else was, nobody holding still long enough to trust or be trusted, just like Alvin imagined atoms might have been before God taught them who they were and gave them work to do. But here were two men, men that nobody'd ever figure even knew each other hardly, except as how everybody in a town like Hatrack River knows everybody else. Po Doggly, a one-time farmer reduced to driving for Dr. Physicker, and Horace Guester, the first settler in this place, and still prospering. Who'd've thought they could fit together so smooth? But it was because each one knew who the other was, knew it pure and true, knew it as sure as an atom might know the name God gave him; each one in his place, doing his work.

All these thoughts rushed through Alvin's mind so fast he hardly noticed himself thinking them, yet in later years he'd remember right enough that this was when he first understood: These two men, together, made something between them that was just as real and solid as the dirt under his feet, as the tree he was leaning on. Most folks couldn't see it—they'd look at the two of them and see nothing but two men who happened to be sitting in a boat together. But then, maybe to other atoms it wouldn't seem like the atoms making up a bit of a iron was anything more than two atoms as happened to be next to each other. Maybe you have to be far off, like God, or anyhow bigger by far in order to see what it is that two atoms make when they fit together in a certain way. But just because another atom don't see the connection don't mean it isn't real, or that the iron isn't as solid as iron can be.

And if I can teach these atoms how to make a string out of nothing, or maybe how to make iron out of gold, or even—let it be so—change Arthur's secret invisible signature all through his body so the Finders wouldn't know him no more—then why couldn't a Maker also do with people as he does with atoms, and teach them a new order, and once he finds enough that he can trust, build them together into something new, something strong, something as real as iron.

"You coming, Al, or what?"

Like I said, Alvin hardly knew what thought it was he had. But he didn't forget it, no, even sliding down the bank into the mud he knew that he'd never forget what he thought of just then, even though it'd take him years and miles and tears of blood before he really understood it all the way.

"Good to see you, Po," said Alvin. "Only I kind of thought we was doing something a mite secret."

Po rowed the boat closer in, slacking the rope and letting Alvin spider his way on board without getting his feet wet. Alvin didn't mind that. He had an aversion to water, which was natural enough seeing how often the Unmaker tried to use water to kill him. But the water seemed to be just water tonight; the Unmaker was invisible or far away. Maybe it was the slender string that still hooked Alvin to

Arthur—maybe that was such a powerful Making that the Unmaker plain hadn't the strength to turn even this much water against Alvin.

"Oh, it's still secret, Alvin," said Horace. "You just don't know. Afore you ever got to Hatrack River—or anyway I mean afore you came back—me and Po, we used to go out and fetch in runaway slaves and help them on to Canada whenever we could."

"Didn't the Finders ever get you?" asked Alvin.

"Any slave got this far, that meant the Finders wasn't too close behind," said Po. "A good number that reached us stole their own cachet."

"Besides, that was afore the Fugitive Slave Treaty," said Horace. "Long as the Finders didn't kill us outright, they couldn't touch us."

"And in those days we had a torch," said Po.

Horace said nothing, just untied the rope from the boat and tossed it back onto shore. Po started in rowing the first second the rope was free—and Horace had already braced himself for the first lurch of the boat. It was a miracle, seeing how smooth they knew each other's next move before the move was even begun. Alvin almost laughed out loud in the joy of seeing such a thing, knowing it was possible, dreaming of what it might mean—thousands of people knowing each other that well, moving to fit each other just right, working together. Who could stand in the way of such people?

"When Horace's girl left, why, we had no way of knowing there was a runaway coming through here." Po shook his head. "It was over. But I knowed that with Arthur Stuart put in chains and dragged on south, why, there wasn't no way in hell old Horace wasn't going to cross the river and fetch him back.

So once I dropped off them Finders and headed back away from the Hio a ways, I stopped the carriage and hopped on down."

"I bet Dr. Physicker noticed," said Alvin.

"Course he did, you fool!" said Po. "Oh, I see you're funning me. Well, he noticed. He just says to me, 'You be careful, them boys are dangerous.' And I said I'd be careful all right and then he says to me, 'It's that blame sheriff Pauley Wiseman. He didn't have to let them take him so fast. Might be we could've fought exerdiction if we could've held onto Arthur Stuart till the circuit judge come around. But Pauley, he did everything legal, but he moved so fast I just knew in my heart he wanted that boy gone, wanted him clean out of Hatrack River and never come back.' I believe him, Horace. Pauley Wiseman never did like that mixup boy, once Old Peg got the wind in her sails about him going to school."

Horace grunted; he turned the tiller just a little, exactly at the moment when Pauley slacked the oar on one side so the boat would turn slightly upstream to make the right landing on the far shore. "You know what I been thinking?" said Horace. "I been thinking your job just ain't enough to keep you busy, Po."

"I like my job good enough," said Po Doggly.

"I been thinking that there's a county election this fall, and the office of sheriff goes up for grabs. I think Pauley Wiseman ought to get turned out."

"And me get made sheriff? You think that's likely, me being a known drunk?"

"You ain't touched a drop the whole time you been with the doctor. And if we live through this and get Arthur back safe, why, you're going to be a hero."

"A hero hell! You crazy, Horace? We can't tell a soul about this or there'll be a reward out for our brains on rye bread from the Hio to Camelot."

"We ain't going to print up the story and sell copies, if that's what you mean. But you know how word spreads. Good folks'll know what you and me done."

"Then *you* be sheriff, Horace."

"Me?" Horace grinned. "Can you imagine me putting a man in jail?"

Po laughed softly. "Reckon not."

When they reached the shore, again their movements were swift and fit together just right. It was hard to believe it had been so many years since they worked together. It was like their bodies already knew what to do, so they didn't even have to think about it. Po jumped into the water—ankle deep is all, and he leaned on the boat so as not to splash much. The boat rocked a bit at *that*, of course, but without a bit of wasted motion Horace leaned against the rocking and calmed it down, hardly even noticing he was doing it. In a minute they had the bow dragged up onto the shore—sandy here, not muddy like the other side—and tied to a tree. To Alvin the rope looked old and rotten, but when he sent his bug inside to feel it out, he was sure it was still strong enough to hold the boat against the rocking of the river against the stern.

Only when all their familiar jobs was done did Horace present himself like militia on the town square, shoulders squared and eyes right on Alvin. "Well, now, Al, I reckon it's up to you to lead the way."

"Ain't we got to track them?" asked Po.

"Alvin knows where they are," said Horace.

"Well ain't that nice," said Po. "And does he know whether they got their guns aimed at our heads?"

"Yes," said Alvin. He said it in such a way as to make it plain that he didn't want no more questions.

It wasn't plain enough for Po. "You telling me this boy's a torch, or what? Most I heard was he got him a knack for shoeing horses."

Here was the bad part about having somebody else along. Alvin didn't have no wish to tell Po Doggly what all he could do, but he couldn't very well tell the man that he didn't trust him.

It was Horace came to the rescue. "Po, I got to tell you, Alvin ain't part of the story of this night."

"Looks to me like he's the biggest part."

"I tell you, Po, when this story gets told, it was you and me came along and happened to find the Finders asleep, you understand?"

Po wrinkled his brow, then nodded. "Just tell me this, boy. Whatever knack you got, you a Christian? I don't even ask that you be a Methodist."

"Yes sir," said Alvin. "I'm a Christian, I reckon. I hold to the Bible."

"Good then," said Po. "I just don't want to get myself all mixed up in devil stuff."

"Not with me," said Alvin.

"All right then. Best if I don't know what you do, Al. Just take a care not to get me killed because I don't know it."

Alvin stuck out his hand. Po shook it and grinned. "You blacksmiths got to be strong as a bear."

"Me?" said Alvin. "A bear gets in my way. I beat on his head till he's a wolverine."

"I like your brag, boy."

A moment's pause, and then Alvin led them off, following the thread that connected him to Arthur Stuart.

It wasn't all that far, but it took them an hour cutting through the woods in the dark—with all the leaves out, there wasn't much moonlight got to the ground. Without Alvin's sense of the forest around them, it would've taken three times as long and ten times the noise.

They found the Finders asleep in a clearing with a campfire dying down between them. The white-haired Finder was curled up on his bedroll. The black-haired Finder must've been left on watch; he was snoring away leaning against a tree. Their horses were asleep not far off. Alvin stopped them before they got close enough to disturb the animals.

Arthur Stuart was wide awake, sitting there staring into the fire.

Alvin sat there a minute, trying to figure how to do this. He wasn't sure how smart the Finders might be. Could they find scraps of dried skin, fallen-off hairs, something like that, and use it for a new cachet? Just in case, it wouldn't do no good to change Arthur right where he was; nor would it be too smart to head on out into the clearing where they might leave bits of their own selves, as proof of who stole Arthur away.

So from a distance, Alvin got inside the iron of the manacles and made cracks in all four parts, so they fell away to the ground at once, with a clank. The noise bothered the horses, who nickered a bit, but the Finders were still sleeping like the dead. Arthur, though, it didn't take him a second to figure out what was happening. He jumped to his feet all

363

at once and started looking around for Alvin at the clearing's edge.

Alvin whistled, trying to match the song of a red-bird. It was a pretty bad imitation, as birdcalls go, but Arthur heard it and knew that it was Alvin calling him. Without a moment's waiting or worrying, Arthur plunged right into the woods and not five minutes later, with a few more bad birdcalls to guide him, he was face to face with Alvin.

Of course Arthur Stuart made as if to give Alvin a big old hug, but Alvin held up a hand. "Don't touch anybody or anything," he whispered. "I've got to make a change in you, Arthur Stuart, so the Finders can't catch you again."

"I don't mind," said Arthur.

"I don't dare have a single scrap of the old way you used to be. You got hairs and skin and such all over in your clothes. So strip them off."

Arthur Stuart didn't hesitate. In a few moments his clothes were in a pile at his feet.

"Excuse me for not knowing a bit about this," said Po, "but if you leave those clothes a-lying there, them Finders'll know he come this way, and that points north to them sure as if we painted a big white arrow on the ground."

"Reckon you're right," said Alvin.

"So have Arthur Stuart bring them along and float them down the river," said Horace.

"Just make sure you don't touch Arthur or nothing," said Alvin.

"Arthur, you just pick up your clothes and follow along slow and careful. If you get lost, give me a redbird whistle and I'll whistle back till you find us."

"I knew you was coming, Alvin," said Arthur Stuart. "You too, Pa."

"So did them Finders," said Horace, "and much as I wish we could arrange it, they ain't going to sleep forever."

"Wait a minute anyway," said Alvin. He sent his bug back into the manacles and drew them back together, fit them tight, joined the iron again as if it had been cast that way. Now they lay on the ground unbroken, fastened tight, giving no sign of how the boy got free.

"I don't suppose you're maybe breaking their legs or something, Alvin," said Horace.

"Can he *do* that from here?" asked Po.

"I'm doing no such thing," said Alvin. "What we want is for the Finders to give up searching for a boy who as far as they can tell doesn't exist no more."

"Well that makes sense, but I still like thinking of them Finders with their legs broke," said Horace.

Alvin grinned and plunged off into the forest, deliberately making enough noise and moving slow enough that the others could follow him in the near-darkness; if he wanted to, he could've moved like a Red man through the woods, making not a sound, leaving no whiff of a trail that anyone could follow.

They got to the river and stopped. Alvin didn't want Arthur getting into the boat in his present skin, leaving traces of himself all over. So if he was going to change him, he had to do it here.

"Toss them clothes, boy," said Horace. "Far as you can."

Arthur took a step or two into the water. It made Alvin scared, for with his inward eye he saw it as if Arthur, made of light and earth and air, suddenly got part of himself disappeared into the blackness of the water. Still, the water hadn't harmed them

365

none on the trip here, and Alvin saw as how it might even be useful.

Arthur Stuart pitched his wad of clothes out into the river. The currents wasn't all that strong; they watched the clothes turn lazily and float downstream, gradually drifting apart. Arthur stood there, up to his butt in water, watching the clothes. No, not watching them—he didn't turn a speck when they drifted far to the left. He was just looking at the north shore, the free side of the river.

"I been here afore," he said. "I seen this boat."

"Might be," said Horace. "Though you was a mite young to remember it. Po and I, we helped your mama into this very boat. My daughter Peggy held you when we got to shore."

"My sister Peggy," said Arthur. He turned around and looked at Horace, like as if it was really a question.

"I reckon so," said Horace, and that was the answer.

"Just stand there, Arthur Stuart," said Alvin. "When I change you, I got to change you all over, inside and out. Better to do that in the water, where all the dead skin with your old self marked in it can wash away."

"You going to make me White?" asked Arthur Stuart.

"Can you *do* that?" asked Po Doggly.

"I don't know what all is going to change," said Alvin. "I hope I don't make you White, though. That'd be like stealing away from you the part of you your mama gave you."

"They don't make White boys be slaves," said Arthur Stuart.

"They ain't going to make this partickler mixup

366

boy a slave anyhow," said Alvin. "Not if I can help it. Now just stand there, stand right still, and let me figure this out."

They all stood there, the men and the boy, while Alvin studied inside Arthur Stuart, finding that tiny signature that marked every living bit of him.

Alvin knew he couldn't just go changing it willy-nilly, since he didn't rightly understand what all that signature was *for*. He just knew that it was somehow part of what made Arthur himself, and you don't just change that. Maybe changing the wrong thing might strike him blind, or make his blood turn to rainwater or something. How could Alvin know?

It was seeing the string still connecting them, heart to heart, that gave Alvin the idea—that and remembering what the Redbird said, using Arthur Stuart's own lips to say it. "The Maker is the one who is part of what he Makes." Alvin stripped off his own shirt and then stepped out into the water and knelt down in it, so he was near eye-to-eye with Arthur Stuart, cool water swirling gently around his waist. Then he put out his hands and pulled Arthur Stuart to him and held him there, breast to breast, hands on shoulders.

"I thought we wasn't supposed to touch the boy," said Po.

"Hush up you blame fool," said Horace Guester. "Alvin knows what he's doing."

I wish that was true, thought Alvin. But at least he had an idea what to do, and that was better than nothing. Now that their living skin was pressed together, Alvin could look and compare Arthur's secret signature with his own. Most of it was the same, exactly the same, and the way Alvin figured, that's the part that makes us both human instead of

367

cows or frogs or pigs or chickens. That's the part I don't dare change, not a bit of it.

The rest—I can change that. But not any old how. What good to save him if I turn him bright yellow or make him stupid or something?

So Alvin did the only thing as made sense to him. He changed bits of Arthur's signature to be just like Alvin's own. Not *all* that was different—not all that much, in fact. Just a little. But even a little meant that Arthur Stuart had stopped being completely himself and started being partly Alvin. It seemed to Alvin that what he was doing was terrible and wonderful at the same time.

How much? How much did he have to change till the Finders wouldn't know the boy? Surely not all. Surely just *this* much, just *these* changes. There was no way to know. All that Alvin could do was guess, and so he took his guess and that was it.

That was only the beginning, of course. Now he started in changing all the other signatures to match the new one, each living bit of Arthur, one by one, as fast as he could. Dozens of them, hundreds of them; he found each new signature and changed it to fit the new pattern.

Hundreds of them, and hundreds more, and still he had changed no more than a tiny patch of skin on Arthur's chest. How could he hope to change the boy's whole body, going so slow?

"It hurts," whispered Arthur.

Alvin drew away from him. "I ain't doing nothing to hurt you, Arthur Stuart."

Arthur looked down at his chest. "Right here," he said, touching the spot where Alvin had been working.

Alvin looked in the moonlight and saw that indeed

that spot seemed to be swollen, changed, darkened. He looked again, only not with his eyes, and saw that the rest of Arthur's body was attacking the part that Alvin changed, killing it bit by bit, fast as it could.

Of course. What did he expect? The signature was the way the body recognized itself—that's why every living bit of a body had to have that signature in it. If it wasn't there, the body knew it had to be a disease or something and killed it. Wasn't it bad enough that changing Arthur was taking so long? Now Alvin knew that it wouldn't do no good to change him at all—the more he changed him, the sicker he'd get and the more Arthur Stuart's own body would try to kill itself until the boy either died or shed the new changed part.

It was just like Taleswapper's old story, about trying to build a wall so big that by the time you got halfway through building it, the oldest parts of it had already crumbled to dust. How could you build such a wall if it was getting broke down faster than you could build it up?

"I can't," said Alvin. "I'm trying to do what can't be done."

"Well if you can't do it," said Po Doggly, "I hope you can fly, cause that's the only way you can get that boy to Canada before the Finders catch up with you."

"I can't," said Alvin.

"You're just tired," said Horace. "We'll all just hush up so you can think."

"Won't do any good," said Alvin.

"My mama could fly," said Arthur Stuart.

Alvin sighed in impatience at this same old story coming back again.

"It's true, you know," said Horace. "Little Peggy told me. That little black slave girl, she diddled with some ash and blackbird feathers and such, and flew straight up here. That's what killed her. I couldn't believe it the first time I realized the boy remembers, and we always kept our mouths shut about it hoping he'd forget. But I got to tell you, Alvin, it'd be a pure shame if that girl died just so you could give up on us at this same spot in the river seven years later."

Alvin closed his eyes. "Just shut your mouth and let me think," he said.

"I *said* that's what we'd do," said Horace.

"So *do* it," said Po Doggly.

Alvin hardly even heard them. He was looking back inside Arthur's body, inside that patch that Alvin changed. The new signature wasn't bad in itself – only where it bordered on the skin with the old signature, that was the only place the new skin was getting sick and dying. Arthur'd be just fine if Alvin could somehow change him all at once, instead of bit by bit.

The way that the string came all at once, when Alvin thought of it, pictured where it started and where it ended and what it *was*. All the atoms of it moving into place at the same time. Like the way Po Doggly and Horace Guester fit together all at once, each doing his own task yet taking into account all that the other man did.

But the string was clean and simple. This was hard—like he told Miss Larner, turning water into wine instead of iron into gold.

No, can't think of it that way. What I did to make the string was teach all the atoms what and where to be, because each one of them was alive and each one could obey me. But inside Arthur's body I ain't dealing with atoms, I'm dealing with these living bits, and each one of *them* is alive. Maybe it's even the signature itself that makes them alive, maybe I can teach them all what they ought to be—instead of moving each part of them, one at a time, I can just say—Be like this—and they'll do it.

He no sooner thought of it than he tried it. In his mind he thought of speaking to all the signatures in Arthur's skin, all over his chest, all at once; he showed them the pattern he held in his mind, a pattern so complex he couldn't even understand it himself, except that he knew it was the same pattern as the signatures in this patch of skin he had changed bit by bit. And as soon as he showed them, as soon as he commanded them—Be like this! This is the way!—they changed. It all changed, all the skin on Arthur Stuart's chest, all at once.

Arthur gasped, then howled with pain. What had been a soreness in a patch of skin was now spread across his whole chest.

"Trust me," Alvin said. "I'm going to change you sure now, and the pain will stop. But I'm doing it under the water, where all the old skin gets carried off at once. Plug your nose! Hold your breath!"

Arthur Stuart was panting from the pain, but he did what Alvin said. He pinched his nose with his right hand, then took a breath and closed his mouth. At once Alvin gripped Arthur's wrist in his left hand and put his right hand behind the boy and plunged him under the water. In that instant Alvin held Arthur's body whole in his mind, seeing all the signatures, not one by one, but all of them; he showed them the pattern, the new signature, and this time

371

thought the words so strong his lips spoke them. "This is the way! Be like this!"

He couldn't feel it with his hands—Arthur's body didn't change a whit that he could sense with his natural senses. But Alvin could still see the change, all at once, all in an instant, every signature in the boy's body, in the organs, in the muscles, in the blood, in the brain; even his hair changed, every part of him that was connected to himself. And what wasn't connected, what didn't change, that was washed away and gone.

Alvin plunged himself under the water, to wash off any part of Arthur's skin or hair that might have clung to him. Then he rose up and lifted Arthur Stuart out of the water, all in one motion. The boy came up shedding waterdrops like a spray of cold pearls in the moonlight. He stood there gasping for breath and shaking from the cold.

"Tell me it don't hurt no more," said Alvin.

"Any more," said Arthur, correcting him just like Miss Larner always did. "I feel fine. Except cold."

Alvin scooped him up out of the water and carried him back to the bank. "Wrap him in my shirt and let's get out of here."

So they did. Not a one of them noticed that when Arthur imitated Miss Larner, he didn't use Miss Larner's voice.

Peggy didn't notice either, not right away. She was too busy looking inside Arthur Stuart's heartfire. How it changed when Alvin transformed him! So subtle a change it was that Peggy couldn't even tell what it was Alvin was changing—yet in the moment that Arthur Stuart emerged from the water, not a single path from his past remained—not a single path leading southward into slavery. And all the new paths, the new futures that the transformation had brought to him—they led to such amazing possibilities.

During all the time it took for Horace, Po, and Alvin to bring Arthur Stuart back across the Hio and through the woods to the smithy, Peggy did nothing more than explore in Arthur Stuart's heartfire, studying possibilities that had never before existed in the world. There was a new Maker abroad in the land; Arthur was the first soul touched by him, and everything was different. Moreover, most of Arthur's futures were inextricably tied with Alvin. Peggy saw possibilities of incredible journeys—on one path a trip to Europe where Arthur Stuart would be at Alvin's side as the new Holy Roman Emperor Napoleon bowed to him; on another path a voyage into a strange island nation far to the south where Red men lived their whole lives on mats of floating seaweed; on another path a triumphant crossing into westward lands where the Reds hailed Alvin as the great unifier of all the races, and opened up their last refuge to him, so perfect was their trust. And always by his side was Arthur Stuart, the mixup boy—but now trusted, now himself gifted with some of the Maker's own power.

Most of the paths began with them bringing Arthur Stuart to her springhouse, so she was not surprised when they knocked at her door.

"Miss Larner," called Alvin softly.

She was distracted; reality was not half so interesting as the futures revealed now in Arthur Stuart's heartfire. She opened the door. There they stood, Arthur still wrapped in Alvin's shirt.

"We brought him back," said Horace.

373

"I can see that," said Peggy. She *was* glad of it, but that gladness didn't show up in her voice. Instead she sounded busy, interrupted, annoyed. As she was. Get on with it, she wanted to say. I've seen this conversation as Arthur overheard it, so get on with it, get it over with, and let me get back to exploring what this boy will be. But of course she could say none of this—not if she hoped to remain disguised as Miss Larner.

"They won't find him," said Alvin, "not as long as they don't actually see him with their eyes. Something—their cachet don't work no more."

"Doesn't work anymore," said Peggy.

"Right," said Alvin. "What we come for—came for—can we leave him with you? Your house, here, Ma'am, I've got it hexed up so tight they won't even think to come inside, long as you keep the door locked."

"Don't you have any more clothes for him than this? He's been wet—do you want him to take a chill?"

"It's a warm night," said Horace, "and we don't want to be fetching clothes from the house. Not till the Finders come back and give up and go away again."

"Very well," said Peggy.

"We'd best be about our business," said Po Doggly. "I got to get back to Dr. Physicker's."

"And since I told Old Peg that I'd be in town, I'd better be there," said Horace.

Alvin spoke straight to Peggy. "I'll be in the smithy, Miss Larner. If something goes wrong, you give a shout, and I'll be up the hill in ten seconds."

"Thank you. Now—please go on about your business."

She closed the door. She didn't mean to be so abrupt. But she had a whole new set of futures. No one but herself had ever been so important in Alvin's work as Arthur was going to be. But perhaps that would happen with everyone that Alvin actually touched and changed—perhaps as a Maker he would transform everyone he loved until they all stood with him in those glorious moments, until they all looked out upon the world through the lensed walls of the Crystal City and saw all things as God must surely see them.

A knock on the door. She opened it.

"In the first place," said Alvin, "don't open the door without knowing who it is."

"I knew it was you," she said. Truth was, though, she didn't. She didn't even think.

"In the second place, I was waiting to hear you lock the door, and you never did."

"Sorry," she said. "I forgot."

"We went to a lot of work to save this boy tonight, Miss Larner. Now it's all up to you. Just till the Finders go."

"Yes, I know." She really was sorry, and let her voice reveal her regret.

"Good night then."

He stood there waiting. For what?

Oh, yes. For her to close the door.

She closed it, locked it, then returned to Arthur Stuart and hugged him until he struggled to get away. "You're safe," she said.

"Of course I am," said Arthur Stuart. "We went to a lot of work to save this boy tonight, Miss Larner."

She listened to him, and knew there was something wrong. What was it? Oh yes, of course. Alvin had just said exactly those words. But what was wrong? Arthur Stuart was always imitating people.

Always imitating. But this time Arthur Stuart had repeated Alvin's words in his own voice, not Alvin's. She had never heard him do that. She thought it was his knack, that he was so natural a mimic he didn't even realize he was doing it.

"Spell 'cicada,' " she said.

"C-I-C-A-D-A," he answered. In his own voice, not hers.

"Arthur Stuart," she whispered. "What's wrong?"

"Ain't nothing wrong, Miss Larner," he said. "I'm home."

He didn't know. He didn't realize it. Never having understood how perfect a mimic he had been, now he didn't realize when the knack was gone. He still had the near-perfect memory of what others said—he still had all the words. But the voices were gone; only his seven-year-old voice remained.

She hugged him again, for a moment, more briefly. She understood now. As long as Arthur Stuart remained himself, the Finders could have found him and taken him south into slavery. The only way to save him was to make him no longer completely himself. Alvin hadn't known, of course he hadn't, that in saving Arthur, he had taken away his knack, or at least part of it. The price of Arthur's freedom was making him cease to be fully Arthur. Did Alvin understand that?

"I'm tired, Miss Larner," said Arthur Stuart.

"Yes, of course," she said. "You can sleep here— in my bed. Take off that dirty shirt and climb in under the covers and you'll be warm and safe all night."

376

He hesitated. She looked into his heartfire and saw why; smiling, she turned her back. She heard a rustle of fabric and then a squeak of bedsprings and the swish of a small body sliding along her sheets into bed. Then she turned around, bent over him where he lay upon her pillow, and kissed him lightly on the cheek.

"Good night, Arthur," she said.

"Good night," he murmured.

In moments he was asleep. She sat at her writing table and pulled up the wick on her lamp. She would do some reading while she waited for the Finders to return. Something to keep her calm while she waited.

No, she wouldn't. The words were there on the page, but she made no sense of them. Was she reading Descartes or Deuteronomy? It didn't matter. She couldn't stay away from Arthur's new heartfire. Of course all the paths of his life changed. He wasn't the same person anymore. No, that wasn't quite true. He was still Arthur. Mostly Arthur.

Almost Arthur. Almost what he was. But not quite.

Was it worth it? To lose part of who he had been in order to live free? Perhaps this new self was better than the old; but that old Arthur Stuart was gone now, gone forever, even more surely than if he had gone south and lived the rest of his life in bitter slavery, with his time in Hatrack as a memory, and then a dream, and then a mythic tale he told the pickaninnies in the years just before he died.

Fool! she cried to herself in her heart. No one is the same person today that he was yesterday. No one had a body as young as it was, or a heart so naive, or a head so ignorant as it was. He would have been far more terribly transformed—mal-formed—by life in bondage than by Alvin's gentle changes. Arthur Stuart was more surely himself now that he would have been in Appalachee. Besides, she had seen all the dark paths that once dwelt in his heartfire, the taste of the lash, the stupefying sun beating down on him as he labored in the field, or the hanging rope that awaited him on the many paths that led to his leading or taking part in a slave revolt and slaughtering dozens of Whites as they lay in their beds. Arthur Stuart was too young to under-stand what had happened to him; but if he were old enough, if he could choose which future he'd prefer, Peggy had no doubt that he would choose the sort of future Alvin had just made possible.

In a way, he lost some of himself, some of his knack, and therefore some of the choices he might have had in life. But in losing those, he gained so much more freedom, so much more power, that he was clear winner in the bargain.

Yet as she remembered his bright face when he spelled words to her in her own voice, she could not keep herself from shedding a few tears of regret.

19

The Plow

The finders woke up not long after Arthur Stuart's rescuers took him across the river.

"Look at this. Manacles still fastened tight. Good hard iron."

"Don't matter. They got them a good spell for sleeping and a good spell for slipping out of chains, but don't they know us Finders always find a runaway, once we got his scent?"

If you could've seen them, you'd think they was glad Arthur Stuart got loose. Truth was, these boys loved a good chase, loved showing folks that Finders just couldn't be shook loose. And if it so happened they put a fistful of leadshot through somebody's belly before the hunt was done, well, ain't that just the way of it? Like dogs on the trail of a bleeding deer.

They followed Arthur Stuart's path through the forest till they came to the water's edge. Only then did their cheerful looks give way to a kind of frown. They lifted up their eyes and looked across the water, searching for the heartfires of men abroad at this time of night, when all honest folk was bound to be asleep. The white-haired one, he just couldn't see far enough; but the black-haired one, he said, "I see a few, moving about. And a few not moving. We'll pick up the scent again in Hatrack River."

Alvin held the plow between his hands. He knew that he could turn it all to gold—he'd seen enough in his life to know the pattern, so he could show the bits of iron what they ought to be. But he also knew that it wasn't no ordinary gold that he wanted. That would be too soft, and as cold as any ordinary stone. No, he wanted something new, not just iron to gold like any alchemist could dream of, but a living gold, a gold that could hold its shape and strength better than iron, better than the finest steel. Gold that was awake, aware of the world around it—a plow that knew the earth that it would tear, to lay it open to the fires of the sun.

A golden plow that would know a man, that a man could trust, the way Po Doggly knew Horace Guester and each trusted the other. A plow that wouldn't need no ox to draw, nor added weight to force it downward into the soil. A plow that would know which soil was rich and which was poor. A sort of gold that never had been seen in all the world before, just like the world had never seen such a thin invisible string as Alvin spun between Arthur Stuart and himself today.

So there he knelt, holding the shape of the gold inside his mind. "Be like this," he whispered to the iron.

He could feel how atoms came from all around the plow and joined together with those already in the iron, forming bits much heavier than what the iron was, and lined up in different ways, until they fit the pattern that he showed them in his mind.

Between his hands he held a plow of gold. He rubbed his fingers over it. Gold, yes, bright yellow in the firelight from the forge, but still dead, still cold. How could he teach it to be alive? Not by showing it the pattern of his own flesh—that wasn't the kind of life it needed. It was the living atoms that he wanted to waken, to show them what they were compared to what they *could* be. To put the fire of life in them.

The fire of life. Alvin lifted the golden plow—much heavier now—and despite the heat of the slacking fire, he set it right amid the glowing charcoal of the forge.

They were back on their horses now, them Finders, walking them calmly up the road to Hatrack River, looking into every house and hut and cabin, holding up the cachet to match it with the heartfires that they found within. But nary a match did they find, nary a body did they recognize. They passed the smithy and saw that a heartfire burned inside, but it wasn't the runaway mixup boy. It was bound to be the smith what made the manacles, they knew it.

"I'd like to kill him," whispered the black-haired Finder. "I know he put that spell in the manacles, to make them so that boy could slip right out."

"Time enough for that after we find the pickaninny," said the white-haired Finder.

They saw two heartfires burning in the old springhouse, but neither one was like what they had in the cachet, so they went on, searching for a child that they might recognize.

The fire was deep within the gold now, but all it was doing was melting it. That wouldn't do at all—it was life the plow needed, not the death of metal in the fire. He held the plowshape in his mind and showed it plain as can be to every bit of metal in the plow; cried out silently to every atom, It ain't enough to be lined up in the little shapes of gold—you need to hold this larger shape yourselves, no matter the fire, no matter what other force might press or tear or melt or try to maim you.

He could sense that he was heard—there was movement in the gold, movement against the downward slipping of the gold as it turned to fluid. But it wasn't strong enough, it wasn't *sure* enough. Without thinking, Alvin reached his hands into the fire and clung to the gold, showing it the plowshape, crying to it in his heart, Like this! Be like this! This is what you are! Oh, the pain of it burned something fierce, but he knew that it was right for his hands to be there, for the Maker is a part of what he makes. The atoms heard him, and formed themselves in ways that Alvin never even thought of, but the result of it all was that the gold now took the heat of the fire into itself without melting, without losing shape. It was done; the plow wasn't alive, exactly, not the way he wanted—but it could stand in the forgefire without melting. The gold was more than gold now. It was gold that knew it was a plow and meant to stay that way.

Alvin pulled his hands away from the plow and saw flames still dancing on his skin, which was charred in places, peeling back away from the bone. Silent as death, he plunged his hands into the water barrel and heard the sizzle of the fire on his flesh as it went out. Then, before the palm could come in full force, he set to healing himself, sloughing away the dead skin and making new skin grow.

He stood there, weakened from all his body had to do to heal his hands, looking into the fire at the gold plow. Just setting there, knowing its shape and holding to it—but that wasn't enough to make the plow alive. It had to know what a plow was for. It had to know why it lived, so it could act to fulfill that purpose. That was Making, Alvin knew it now; that was what Redbird came to say three years ago. Making wasn't like carpentry or smithy work or any such, cutting and bending and melting to force things into new shapes. Making was something subtler and stronger—making things *want* to be another way, a new shape, so they just naturally flowed that way. It was something Alvin had done for years without knowing what it was he was doing. When he thought he was doing no more than finding the natural cracks in stone, he was really making those cracks; by imagining where he wanted them to be, and showing it to the atoms within the bits within the pieces of the rock, he taught them to want to fulfill the shape he showed them.

Now, with this plow, he had done it, not by accident, but on purpose; and he'd taught the gold to be something stronger, to hold better to its shape than anything he'd ever Made before. But how could he teach it more, teach it to act, to move in ways that gold was never taught to move?

In the back of his mind, he knew that his golden plow wasn't the real problem. The real problem was the Crystal City, and the building blocks of *that* weren't going to be simple atoms in a metal plow. The atoms of a city are men and women, and they don't believe the shape they're shown with the simple faith that atoms have, they don't understand with such pure clarity, and when they act, their

383

actions are never half so pure. But if I can teach his gold to be a plow and to be alive, then maybe I can make a Crystal City out of men and women; maybe I can find people as pure as the atoms of this gold, who come to understand the shape of the Crystal City and love it the way I did the moment I saw it when I climbed the inside of that twister with Tenskwa-Tawa. Then they'll not only hold that shape but also make it act, make the Crystal City a living thing much larger and greater than any one of us who are its atoms.

The Maker is the one who is part of what he makes.

Alvin ran to the bellows and pumped up the fire till the charcoal was glowing hot enough to drive any regular smith outside into the night air to wait till the fire slacked. But not Alvin. Instead he walked right up to the forge and climbed right into the heat and the flame. He felt the clothes burning right off his body, but he paid no mind. He curled himself around that plow and then commenced to healing himself, not piecemeal, not bit by bit, but healing himself by telling his whole body, all at once, Stay alive! Put the fire that burns you into this plow!

And at the same time, he told the plow, Do as my body does! Live! Learn from every living bit of me how each part has its purpose, and acts on it. I can't show you the shape you've got to be, or how it's done, cause I don't know. But I can show you what it's like to be alive, by the pain of my body, by the healing of it, by the struggle to stay alive. Be like this! Whatever it takes, however hard it is for you to learn, this is you, be like me!

It took forever, trembling in the fire as his body struggled with the heat, finding ways to channel it the way a river channels water, pouring it out into the plow like it was an ocean of gold fire. And within the plow, the atoms struggled to do what Alvin asked, wanting to obey him, not knowing how. But his call to them was strong, too strong not to hear; and it was more than a matter of hearing him, too. It was like they could tell that what he wanted from them was good. They trusted him, they wanted to be the living plow he dreamed of, and so in a million flecks of time so small that a second seemed like eternity to them, they tried this, they tried that, until somewhere within the golden plow a new pattern was made that knew itself to be alive exactly as Alvin wanted it to be; and in a single single moment the pattern passed throughout the plow and it was alive.

Alive. Alvin felt it moving within the curve of his body as the plow nestled down into the coals of the fire, cutting into it, plowing it as if it were soil. And because it was a barren soil, one that could bear no life, the plow rose quickly out of it and slipped outward, away from the fire toward the lip of the forge. It moved by deciding to be in a different place, and then being there; when it reached the brink of the forge it toppled off and tumbled to the smithy floor.

In agony Alvin rolled from the fire and also fell, also lay pressed against the cold dirt of the floor. Now that the fire no longer surrounded him, his body gained against the dream of his skin, healing him as he had taught it to do, without him having to tell it what to do, without need of direction at all. Become yourself, that had been Alvin's command, and so the signature within each living bit of him obeyed the pattern it contained, until his body was whole and perfect, the skin new, uncallused, and unburned.

What he couldn't remove was the memory of pain, or the weakness from all the strength his body had given up. But he didn't care. Weak as he was, his heart was jubilant, because the plow that lay beside him on the ground was living gold, not because he made it, but because he taught it how to make itself.

The Finders found nothing, nowhere in town—yet the black-haired Finder couldn't see anyone running away, neither, not within the farthest distance that any natural man or horse could possibly have gone since the boy got taken back. Somehow the mixup boy was hiding from them, a thing they knew full well was pure impossible—but it must be so.

The place to look was where the boy had lived for all those years. The roadhouse, the springhouse, the smithy—places where folks were up unnatural late at night. They rode to near the roadhouse, then tied up their horses just off the road. They loaded their shotguns and pistols and set off on foot. Passing by the roadhouse they searched again, accounting for every heartfire; none of them was like the cachet.

"That cottage, with that teacher lady," said the white-haired Finder. "That's where the boy was when we found him before."

The black-haired Finder looked over that way. Couldn't see the springhouse through the trees, of course, but what he was looking for he could see, trees or not. "Two people in there," he said.

"Could be a mixup boy, then," said the white-haired Finder.

"Cachet says not." Then the black-haired Finder grinned nastily. "Single teacher lady, living alone, got a visitor this time of night? I know what kind of company she's keeping, and it ain't no mixup boy."

"Let's go see anyhow," said the white-haired Finder. "If'n you're right, she won't be putting out any complaint on how we broke in her door, or we'll just tell what we saw going on inside when we done it."

They had a good little laugh about that, and set off through the moonlight toward Miss Larner's house. They meant to kick in the door, or course, and have a good laugh when the teacher lady got all huffy about it and made her threats.

Funny thing was, when they actually got near the cottage, that plan just clean went out of their heads. They forgot all about it. Just looked again at the heartfires within and compared them to the cachet.

"What the hell are we doing up here?" asked the white-haired Finder. "Boy's bound to be at the roadhouse. We *know* he ain't here!"

"You know what I'm thinking?" said the black-haired one. "Maybe they killed him."

"That's plain crazy. Why save him, then?"

"How else do you figure they made it so we can't see him, then?"

"He's in the roadhouse. They got some hex that hides him up, I'll bet. Once we open the right door there, we'll see him and that'll be that."

For a fleeting moment the black-haired Finder thought—well, why not look in this teacher lady's cottage, too, if they got a hex like that? Why not open *this* door?

But he no sooner had that thought than it just slipped away so he couldn't remember it, couldn't even remember *having* a thought. He just trotted

387

away after the white-haired Finder. Mixup boy's bound to be in the roadhouse, that's for sure.

She saw their heartfires, of course, as the Finders came toward her cottage, but Peggy wasn't afraid. She had explored Arthur Stuart's heartfire all this time, and there was no path there which led to capture by these Finders. Arthur had dangers enough in the future—Peggy could see that—but no harm would come to the boy tonight. So she paid them little heed. She knew when they decided to leave; knew when the black-haired Finder thought of coming in; knew when the hexes blocked him and drove him away. But it was Arthur Stuart she was watching, searching out the years to come.

Then, suddenly, she couldn't hold it to herself any longer. She had to tell Alvin, both the joy and sorrow of what he had done. Yet how could she? How could she tell him that Miss Larner was really a torch who could see the million newborn futures in Arthur Stuart's heartfire? It was unbearable to keep all this to herself. She might have told Mistress Modesty, years ago, when she lived there and kept no secrets.

It was madness to go down to the smithy, knowing that her desire was to tell things she couldn't tell without revealing who she was. Yet it would surely drive her mad to stay within these walls, alone with all this knowledge that she couldn't share.

So she got up, unlocked the door, and stepped outside. No one around. She closed the door and locked it; then again looked into Arthur's heartfire and again found no danger for the boy. He would be safe. She would see Alvin.

Only then did she look into Alvin's heartfire; only

388

then did she see the terrible pain that he had suffered only minutes ago. Why hadn't she noticed? Why hadn't she seen? Alvin had just passed through the greatest threshold of his life; he had truly done a great Making, brought something new into the world, and she hadn't seen. When he faced the Unmaker while she was in far-off Dekane, she had seen his struggle—now, when she wasn't three rods off, why hadn't she turned to him? Why hadn't she known his pain when he writhed inside the fire?

Maybe it was the springhouse. Once before, near nineteen years ago, the day that Alvin was born, the springhouse had damped her gift and lulled her to sleep till she was almost too late. But no, it couldn't be that—the water didn't run through the springhouse anymore, and the forgefire was stronger than that.

Maybe it was the Unmaker itself, come to block her. But as she cast about with her torchy sight, she couldn't see any unusual darkness amid the colors of the world around her, not close at hand, anyway. Nothing that could have blinded her.

No, it had to be the nature of what Alvin himself was doing that blinded her to it. Just as she hadn't seen how he would extricate himself from his confrontation with the Unmaker years ago, just as she hadn't seen how he would change young Arthur at the Hio shore tonight, it was just the same way she hadn't seen what he was doing in the forge. It was outside the futures that her knack could see, the particular Making he performed tonight.

Would it always be like that? Would she always be blinded when his most important work was being done? It made her angry, it frightened her—what good is my knack, if it deserts me just when I need it most!

No. I didn't need it most just now. Alvin had no need of me or my sight when he climbed into the fire. My knack has never deserted me when it was *needed*. It's only my desire that's thwarted.

Well, he needs me now, she thought. She picked her way carefully down the slope; the moon was low, the shadows deep, so the path was treacherous. When she rounded the corner of the smithy, the light from the forgefire, spilling out onto the grass, was almost blinding; it was so red it made the grass look shiny black, not green.

Inside the smithy Alvin lay curled on the ground, facing toward the forge, away from her. He was breathing heavily, raggedly. Asleep? No. He was naked; it took a moment to realize that his clothing must have burned off him in the forge. He hadn't noticed it in all his pain, and so had no memory of it; therefore she hadn't seen it happen when she searched for memories in his heartfire.

His skin was shockingly pale and smooth. Earlier today she had seen his skin a deep brown from the sun and the forgefire's heat. Earlier today he had been callused, with here and there a scar from some spark of searing burn, the normal accidents of life beside a fire. Now, though, his skin was as unmarked as a baby's, and she could not help herself; she stepped into the smithy, knelt beside him, and gently brushed her hand along his back, from his shoulder down to the narrow place above the hip. His skin was so soft it made her own hands feel coarse to her, as if she marred him just by touching him.

He let out a long breath, a sigh. She withdrew her hand.

390

"Alvin," she said. "Are you all right?'

He moved his arm; he was stroking something that lay within the curl of his body. Only now did she see it, a faint yellow in the double shadow of his body and of the forge. A golden plow.

"It's alive," he murmured.

As if in answer, she saw it move smoothly under his hand.

Of course they didn't knock. At this time of night? They would know at once it couldn't be some chance traveler—it could only be the Finders. Knocking at the door would warn them, give them a chance to try to carry the boy farther off.

But the black-haired Finder didn't so much as try the latch. He just let fly with his foot and the door crashed inward, pulling away from the upper hinge as it did. Then, shotgun at the ready, he moved quickly inside and looked around the common room. The fire there was dying down, so the light was scant, but they could see that there was no one there.

"I'll keep watch on the stairs," said the white-haired Finder. "You go out the back to see if anybody's trying to get out that way."

The black-hired Finder immediately made his way past the kitchen and the stairs to the back door, which he flung open. The white-haired Finder was halfway up the stairs before the back door closed again.

In the kitchen, Old Peg crawled out from under the table. Neither one had so much as paused at the kitchen door. She didn't know who they were, of course, but she hoped—hoped it was the Finders, sneaking back here because somehow, by some

391

miracle, Arthur Stuart got away and they didn't know where he was. She slipped off her shoes and walked as quietly as she could from the kitchen to the common room, where Horace kept a loaded shotgun over the fireplace. She reached up and took it down, but in the process she knocked over a tin teakettle that someone had left warming by the fire earlier in the evening. The kettle clattered; hot water spilled over her bare feet; she gasped in spite of herself.

Immediately she could hear footsteps on the stairs. She ignored the pain and ran to the foot of the stairs, just in time to see the white-haired Finder coming down. He had a shotgun pointed straight at her. Even though she'd never fired a gun at a human being in her life, she didn't hesitate a moment. She pulled the trigger; the gun kicked back against her belly, driving the breath out of her and slamming her against the wall beside the kitchen door. She hardly noticed. All she saw was how the white-haired Finder stood there, his face suddenly relaxing till it looked as stupid as a cow's face. Then red blossoms appeared all over his shirt, and he toppled over backward.

You'll never steal another child away from his mama, thought Old Peg. You'll never drag another Black into a life of bowing under the whip. I killed you, Finder, and I think the good Lord rejoices. But even if I go to hell for it, I'm glad.

She was so intent on watching him that she didn't even notice that the door out back stood open, held in place by the barrel of the black-haired Finder's gun, pointed right at her.

Alvin was so intent on telling Peggy what he had done that he hardly noticed he was naked. She

392

handed him the leather apron hanging from a peg on the wall, and he pulled it on by habit, without a thought. She hardly heard his words; all that he was telling her, she already knew from looking in his heartfire. Instead she was looking at him, thinking, Now he's a Maker, in part because of what I taught him. Maybe I'm finished now, maybe my life will be my own—but maybe not, maybe now I've just begun, maybe now I can treat him as a man, not as a pupil or a ward. He seemed to glow with an inner fire; and every step he took, the golden plow echoed, not by following him or tangling itself in his feet, but by slipping along on a line that could have been an orbit around him, well out of the way but close enough to be of use; as if it were a part of him, though unattached.

"I know," Peggy told him. "I understand. You *are* a Maker now."

"It's more than that!" he cried. "It's the Crystal City. I know how to build it now, Miss Larner. See the city ain't the crystal towers that I saw, the city's the people inside it, and if I'm going to build the place I got to find the kind of folks who ought to be there, folks as true and loyal as this plow, folks who share the dream enough to want to build it, and keep on building it even if I'm not there. You see, Miss Larner? The Crystal City isn't a thing that a single Maker can make. It's a city of Makers; I got to find all kinds of folk and somehow make Makers out of them."

She knew as he said it that this was indeed the task that he was born for—and the labour that would break his heart. "Yes," she said. "That's true, I know it is." And in spite of herself, she couldn't sound like Miss Larner, calm and cool and distant.

She sounded like herself, like her true feelings. She was burning up inside with the fire that Alvin lit there.

"Come with me, Miss Larner," said Alvin. "You know so much, and you're such a good teacher—I need your help."

No, Alvin, not those words. I'll come with you for those words, yes, but say the words, the ones I need so much to hear. "How can I teach what only you know how to do?" she asked him—trying to sound quiet, calm.

"But it ain't just for the teaching, either—I can't do this alone. What I done tonight, it's so hard—I need to have you with me." He took a step toward her. The golden plow slipped across the floor toward her, behind her; if it marked the outer border of Alvin's largest self, then she was now well within that generous circle.

"What do you need me for?" asked Peggy. She refused to look within his heartfire, refused to see whether or not there was any chance that he might actually—no, she refused even to name to herself what it was she wanted now, for fear that somehow she'd discover that it couldn't possibly be so, that it could never happen, that somehow tonight all such paths had been irrevocably closed. Indeed, she realized, that was part of why she had been so caught up in exploring Arthur Stuart's new futures; he would be so close to Alvin that she could see much of Alvin's great and terrible future through Arthur's eyes, without ever having to know what she would know if she looked into Alvin's own heartfire: Alvin's heartfire would show her whether, in his many futures, there were any in which he loved her, and married her, and put that dear and perfect body into her arms to give her and get from her that gift that only lovers share.

"Come with me," he said. "I can't even think of going on out there without you, Miss Larner. I—" He laughed at himself. "I don't even know your first name, Miss Larner."

"Margaret," she said.

"Can I call you that? Margaret—will you come with me? I know you ain't what you seem to be, but I don't care what you look like under all that hexery. I feel like you're the only living soul who knows me like I really am, and I—"

He just stood there, looking for the word. And she stood there, waiting to hear it.

"I love you," he said. "Even though you think I'm just a boy."

Maybe she would've answered him. Maybe she would've told him that she knew he was a man, and that she was the only woman who could love him without worshipping him, the only one who could actually be a helpmeet for me. But into the silence after his words and before she could speak, there came the sound of a gunshot.

At once she thought of Arthur Stuart, but it only took a moment to see that his heartfire was undisturbed; he lay asleep up in her little house. No, the sound came from farther off. She cast her torchy sight to the roadhouse, and there found the heartfire of a man in the last moment of death, and he was looking at a woman standing down at the foot of the stairs. It was Mother, holding a shotgun.

His heartfire dimmed, died. At once Peggy looked into her mother's heartfire and saw, behind her thoughts and feelings and memories, a million paths of the future, all jumbling together, all changing

395

before her eyes, all becoming one single path, which led to one single place. A flash of searing agony, and then nothing.

"Mother!" she cried. "Mother!"

And then the future became the present; Old Peg's heartfire was gone before the sound of the second gunshot reached the smithy.

Alvin could hardly believe what he was saying to Miss Larner. He hadn't known until this moment, when he said it, how he felt about her. He was so afraid she'd laughed at him, so afraid she'd tell him he was far too young, that in time he'd get over how he felt.

But instead of answering him, she paused for just a moment, and in that moment a gunshot rang out. Alvin knew at once that it came from the roadhouse; he followed the sound with his bug and found where it came from, found a dead man already beyond all healing. And then a moment later, another gunshot, and then he found someone else dying, a woman. He knew that body from the inside out; it wasn't no stranger. It had to be Old Peg.

"Mother!" cried Miss Larner. "Mother!"

"It's Old Peg Guester!" cried Alvin.

He saw Miss Larner tear open the collar of her dress, reach inside and pull out the amulets that hung there. She tore them off her neck, cutting herself bad on the breaking strings. Alvin could hardly take in what he saw—a young woman, scarce older than himself, and beautiful, even though her face was torn with grief and terror.

"It's my mother!" she cried. "Alvin, save her!"

He didn't wait a second. He just tore on out of the smithy, running barefoot on the grass, in the road, not caring how the rough dirt and rocks tore into his soft, unaccustomed feet. The leather apron caught and tangled between his knees; he tugged it, twisted it to the side, out of his way. He could see with his bug how Old Peg was already past saving, but still he ran, because he had to *try*, even though he knew there was no reason in it. And then she died, and still he ran, because he couldn't bear not to be running to where that good woman, his friend was lying dead.

His good friend and Miss Larner's mother. The only way that could be is if she was the torch girl what run off seven years ago. But then if she was such a torch as folks around her said, why didn't she see it coming? Why didn't she look into her own mother's heartfire and forsee her death? It made no sense.

There was a man in front of him on the road. A man running down from the roadhouse toward some horses tied to trees just over yonder. It was the man who killed Old Peg, Alvin knew that, and cared to know no more. He sped up, faster than he'd ever run before without getting strength from the forest around him. The man heard him coming maybe thirty yards off, and turned around.

"You, smith!" cried the black-haired Finder. "Glad to kill you too!"

He had a pistol in his hand, he fired.

Alvin took the bullet in his belly, but he didn't care about that. His body started work at once fixing what the bullet tore, but it wouldn't've mattered a speck if he'd been bleeding to death. Alvin didn't even slow down; he flew into the man, knocking him down, landing on him and skidding with him ten feet across the dirt of the road. The man cried out in fear and pain. That single cry was the last sound he made; in his rage, Alvin caught the man's head in such a grip that it took only one sharp jab of his other hand against the man's jaw to snap his neck-bone clean in half. The man was already dead, but Alvin hit his head again and again with his fists, until his arms and chest and his leather apron was all covered with the black-haired Finder's blood and the man's skull was broke up inside his head like shards of dropped pottery.

Then Alvin knelt there, his head stupid with exhaustion and spent anger. After a minute or so he remembered that Old Peg was still lying there on the roadhouse floor. He knowed she was dead, but where else did he have to go? Slowly he got to his feet.

He heard horses coming down the road from town. That time of night in Hatrack River, gunshots meant only trouble. Folk'd come. They'd find the body in the road—they'd come on up the roadhouse. No need for Alvin to stay to greet them.

Inside the roadhouse, Peggy was already kneeling over her mother's body, sobbing and panting from her run up to the house. Alvin only knew for sure it was her from her dress—he'd only seen her face but once before, for a second there in the smithy. She turned when she saw Alvin come inside. "Where were you! Why didn't you save her! You could have saved her!"

"I never could," said Alvin. It was wrong of her to say such a thing. "There wasn't time."

"You should have looked! You should have seen what was coming."

Alvin didn't understand her. "I can't see what's coming," he said. "That's *your* knack."

398

Then she burst out crying, not the dry sobs like when he first came in, but deep, gut-wrenching howls of grief. Alvin didn't know what to do.

The door opened behind him.

"Peggy," whispered Horace Guester. "Little Peggy."

Peggy looked up at her father, her face so streaked with tears and twisted up and reddened with weeping that it was a marvel he could recognize her. "I killed her!" she cried. "I never should have left, Papa! I killed her!"

Only then did Horace understand that it was his wife's body lying there. Alvin watched as he started trembling, groaning, then keening loud and high like a hurt dog. Alvin never seen such grieving. Did my father cry like that when my brother Vigor died? Did he make such a sound as this when he thought that me and Measure was tortured to death by Red men?

Alvin reached out his arms to Horace, held him tight around the shoulders, then led him over to Peggy and helped him kneel there beside his daughter, both of them weeping, neither giving a sign that they saw each other. All they saw was Old Peg's body spread out on the floor; Alvin couldn't even guess how deeply, how agonizingly each one bore the whole blame for her dying.

After a while the sheriff came in. He'd already found the black-haired Finder's corpse outside, and it didn't take him long to understand exactly what happened. He took Alvin aside. "This is pure self-defence if I ever saw it," said Pauley Wiscman, "and I wouldn't make you spend three seconds in jail for it. But I can tell you that the law in Appalachee don't take the death of a Finder all that easy, and the treaty lets them come up here and get you to take back there for trial. What I'm saying, boy, is you better get the hell out of here in the next couple of days or I can't promise you'll be safe."

"I was going anyway," said Alvin.

"I don't know how you done it," said Pauley Wiseman, "but I reckon you got that half-Black pickaninny away from them Finders tonight and hid him somewhere around here. I'm telling you, Alvin, when you go, you best take the boy with you. Take him to Canada. But if I see his face again. I'll ship him south myself. It's that boy caused all this— makes me sick, a good White woman dying cause of some half-Black mixup boy."

"You best never say such a thing in front of me again, Pauley Wiseman."

The sheriff only shook his head and walked away. "Ain't natural," he said. "All you people set on a monkey like it was folks." He turned around to face Alvin. "I don't much care what you think of me, Alvin Smith, but I'm giving you and that mixup boy a chance to stay alive, I hope you have brains to take it. And in the meantime, you might go wash off that blood and fetch some clothes to wear."

Alvin walked on back to the road. Other folks was coming by then—he paid them no heed. Only Mock Berry seemed to understand what was happening. He led Alvin on down to his house, and there Anga washed him down and Mock gave him some of his own clothes to wear. It was nigh onto dawn when Alvin got him back to the smithy.

Makepeace was setting there on a stool in the smithy door, looking at the golden plow. It was resting on the ground, still as you please, right in front of the forge.

"That's one hell of a journeyman piece," said Makepeace.

"I reckon," said Alvin. He walked over to the plow and reached down. It fairly leapt into Alvin's hands—not heavy at all now— but if Makepeace noticed how the plow moved by itself just before Alvin touched it, he didn't say.

"I got a lot of scrap iron," said Makepeace. "I don't even ask you to go halves with me. Just let me keep a few pieces when you turn them into gold."

"I ain't turning no more iron into gold," said Alvin.

It made Makepeace angry. "That's *gold*, you fool! That there plow you made means never going hungry, never having to work again, living fine instead of in that rundown house up there! It means new dresses for Gertie and maybe a suit of clothes for me! It means folks in town saying Good morning to me and tipping their hats like I was a gentleman. It means riding in a carriage like Dr. Physicker, and going to Dekane or Carthage or wherever I please and not even caring what it costs. And you're telling me you ain't making no more *gold*?"

Alvin knew it wouldn't do no good explaining, but still he tried. "This ain't no common gold, sir. This is a living plow—I ain't going to let nobody melt it down to make coins out of it. Best I can figure, nobody could melt it even if they wanted to. So back off and let me go."

"What you going to do, plow with it? You blame fool, we could be kings of the world together!" But when Alvin pushed on by, headed out of the smithy, Makepeace stopped his pleading and started getting ugly. "That's my iron you used to make that golden plow! That gold belongs to *me*! A journeyman piece always belongs to the master, less'n he gives it to the journeyman and I sure as hell don't! Thief! You're stealing from me!"

"You stole five years of my life from me, long after I was good enough to be a journeyman," Alvin said. "And this plow—making it was none of your teaching. It's alive, Makepeace Smith. It doesn't belong to you and it doesn't belong to me. It belongs to itself. So let me just set it down here and we'll see who gets it."

Alvin set down the plow on the grass between them. Then he stepped back a few paces. Makepeace took one step toward the plow. It sank down into the soil under the grass, then cut its way through the dirt till it reached Alvin. When he picked it up, it was warm. He knew what that had to mean. "Good soil," said Alvin. The plow trembled in his hands.

Makepeace stood there, his eyes bugged out with fear. "Good Lord, boy, that plow *moved*."

"I know it," said Alvin.

"What are you, boy? The devil?"

"I don't think so," said Alvin. "Though I might've met him once or twice."

"Get on out of here! Take that thing and go away! I never want to see your face around here again!"

"You got my journeyman paper," said Alvin. "I want it."

Makepeace reached into his pocket, took out a folded paper, and threw it onto the grass in front of the smithy. Then he reached out and pulled the smithy doors shut, something he hardly ever did, even in winter. He shut them tight and barred them on the inside. Poor fool, as if Alvin couldn't break down them walls in a second if he really wanted to get inside. Alvin walked over and picked up the paper. He opened it and read it—signed all proper. It was legal. Alvin was a journeyman.

The sun was just about to show up when Alvin got to the springhouse door. Of course it was locked, but locks and hexes couldn't keep Alvin out, specially when he made them all himself. He opened the door and went inside. Arthur Stuart stirred in his sleep. Alvin touched his shoulder, brought the boy awake. Alvin knelt there by the bed and told the boy most all that happened in the night. He showed him the golden plow, showed him how it moved. Arthur laughed in delight. Then Alvin told him that the woman he called Mama all his life was dead, killed by the Finders, and Arthur cried.

But not for long. He was too young to cry for long. "You say she kilt one herself afore she died?"

"With your pa's own shotgun."

"Good for her!" said Arthur Stuart, his voice so fierce Alvin almost laughed, him being so small.

"I killed the other one myself. The one that shot her."

Arthur reached out and took Alvin's right hand and opened it. "Did you kill him with this hand?"

Alvin nodded.

Arthur kissed his open palm.

"I would've fixed her up if I could," said Alvin. "But she died too fast. Even if I'd been standing right there the second after the shot hit her, I couldn't've fixed her up."

Arthur Stuart reached out and hung onto Alvin around his neck and cried some more.

It took a day to put Old Peg into the ground, up on the hill with her own daughters and Alvin's brother

403

Vigor and Arthur's mama who died so young. "A place for people of courage," said Dr. Physicker, and Alvin knew that he was right, even though Physicker didn't know about the runaway Black slave girl.

Alvin washed away the bloodstains from the floor and stairs of the roadhouse, using his knack to pull out what blood the lye and sand couldn't remove. It was the last gift he could give to Horace or to Peggy. Margaret. Miss Larner.

"I got to leave now," he told them. They were sitting on chairs in the common room of the inn, where they'd been receiving mourners all day. "I'm taking Arthur to my folks' place in Vigor Church. He'll be safe there. And then I'm going on."

"Thank you for everything," said Horace. "You been a good friend to us. Old Peg loved you." Then he broke down crying again.

Alvin patted him on the shoulder a couple of times, and then moved over to stand in front of Peggy. "All that I am, Miss Larner, I owe to you."

She shook her head.

"I meant all I said to you. I still mean it."

Again she shook her head. He wasn't surprised. With her mama dead, never even knowing that her own daughter'd come home, why, Alvin didn't expect she could just up and go. Somebody had to help Horace Guester run the roadhouse. It all made sense. But still it stabbed him to the heart, because now more than ever he knew that it was true—he loved her. But she wasn't for him. That much was plain. She never had been. A woman like this, so educated and fine and beautiful—she could be his teacher, but she could never love him like he loved her.

'Well then, I guess I'm saying good-bye," said Alvin. He stuck out his hand, even though he knew it was kind of silly to shake hands with somebody grieving the way she was. But he wanted so bad to put his arms around her and hold her tight the way he'd held Arthur Stuart when he was grieving, and a handshake was as close as he could come to that.

She saw his hand, and reached up and took it. Not for a handshake, but just holding his hand, holding it tight. It took him by surprise. He'd think about that many times in the months and years to come, how tight she held to him. Maybe it meant she loved him. Or maybe it meant she only cared for him as a pupil, or thanked him for avenging her mama's death—how could he know what a thing like that could mean? But still he held onto that memory, in case it meant she loved him.

And he made her a promise then, with her holding his hand like that; made her a promise even though he didn't know if she even wanted him to keep it. "I'll be back," he said. "And what I said last night, it'll always be true." It took all his courage then to call her by the name she gave him permission last night to use. "God be with you, Margaret."

"God be with you, Alvin," she whispered.

Then he gathered up Arthur Stuart, who'd been saying his own good-byes, and led the boy outside. They walked out back of the roadhouse to the barn, where Alvin had hidden the golden plow deep in a barrel of beans. He took off the lid and held out his hand, and the plow rose upward until it glinted in the light. Then Alvin took it up, wrapped it double in burlap and put it inside a burlap bag, then swung the bag over his shoulder.

Alvin knelt down and held out his hand the way

he always did when he wanted Arthur Stuart to climb up onto his back. Arthur did, thinking it was all for play—a boy that age, he can't be grieving for more than an hour or two at a time. He swung up onto Alvin's back, laughing and bouncing.

"This time it's going to be a long ride, Arthur Stuart," said Alvin. "We're going all the way to my family's house in Vigor Church."

"Walking the whole way?"

"*I'll* be walking. *You're* going to ride."

"Gee-yap!" cried Arthur Stuart.

Alvin set off at a trot, but before long he was running full out. He never set foot on that road, though. Instead he took off across country, over fields, over fences, and on into the woods, which still stood in great swatches here and there across the states of Hio and Wobbish between him and home. The greensong was much weaker than it had been in the days when the Red men had it all to themselves. But the song was still strong enough for Alvin Smith to hear. He let himself fall into the rhythm of the greensong, running as the Red men did. And Arthur Stuart—maybe he could hear some of the greensong too, enough that it could lull him to sleep, there on Alvin's back. The world had gone. Just him, Arthur Stuart, the golden plow—and the whole world singing around him. I'm a journeyman now. And this is my first journey.

20

Cavil's Deed

Cavil Planter had business in town. He mounted his horse early on that fine spring morning, leaving behind wife and slaves, house and land, knowing all were well under his control, fully his own.

Along about noon, after many a pleasant visit and much business well done, he stopped in at the postmaster's store. There were three letters there. Two were from old friends. One was from Reverend Philadelphia Thrower in Carthage, the capital of Wobbish.

Old friends could wait. This would be news about the Finders he hired, though why the letter should come from Thrower and not from the Finders themselves, Cavil couldn't guess. Maybe there was trouble. Maybe he'd have to go north to testify after all. Well, if that's what it takes, I'll do it, thought Cavil. Gladly I'll leave the ninety and nine sheep, as Jesus said, in order to reclaim the one that strayed.

It was bitter news. Both Finders dead, and so also the innkeeper's wife who claimed to have adopted Cavil's stolen firstborn son. Good riddance to her, thought Cavil, and he spared not a second's grief for the Finders—they were hirelings, and he valued them less than his slaves, since they weren't *his*. No, it was the last news, the worst news, that set Cavil's hands trembling and his breath to stop. The man who killed one of the Finders, a prentice smith named Alvin, he ran off instead of standing trial—and took with him Cavil's son.

He took my son. And the worst words from Thrower were these: "I knew this fellow Alvin when he was a mere child, and already he was an agent of evil. He is our mutual Friend's worst enemy in all the world, and now he has your most valued property in his possession. I wish I had better news. I pray for you, lest your son be turned into a dangerous and implacable foe of all our Friend's holy work."

With such news, how could Cavil go about the rest of the day's business? Without a word to the postmaster or to anybody, Cavil stuffed the letters into his pocket, went outside, mounted his horse, and headed home. All the way his heart was tossed between rage and fear. How could those northerner Emancipationist scum have let his slave, his son, get stolen right out from under them, by the worst enemy of the Overseer? I'll go north, I'll make them pay, I'll find the boy, I'll—and then his thoughts would turn all of a sudden to what the Overseer would say, if ever he came again. What if he despises me now, and never comes again? Or worse what if He comes and damns me for a slothful servant? Or what if He declares me unworthy and forbids me to take any more Black women to myself? How could I live if not in His service—what else is my life *for*?

And then rage again, terrible blasphemous rage, in which he cried out deep within his soul, O my

Overseer! Why did You let this happen? You could have stopped it with a word, if You are truly Lord!

And then terror: Such a thing, to doubt the power of the Overseer! No, forgive me, I am truly Thy slave, O Master! Forgive me, I've lost everything, forgive me!

Poor Cavil. He'd find out soon enough what losing everything could mean.

He got himself home and turned the horse up that long drive leading to the house, only the sun being hot he stayed under the shade of the oaks along the south side of the road. Maybe if he'd rode out in the middle of the lane he would've been seen sooner. Maybe then he wouldn't have heard a woman cry out inside the house just as he was coming out from under the trees.

"Dolores!" he called. "Is something wrong?"

No answer.

Now, that scared him. It conjured up pictures in his mind of marauders or thieves or such, breaking into the house while he was gone. Maybe they already killed Lashman, and even now were killing his wife. He spurred his horse and raced around the house to the back.

Just in time to see a big old Black running from the back door of the house down toward the slave quarters. He couldn't see the Black man's face, on account of his trousers, which he didn't have on, nor any other clothing either—no, he was holding those trousers like a banner, flapping away in front of his face as he ran down toward the sheds.

A Black, no pants on, running out of my house, in which a woman was crying out. For a moment Cavil was torn between the desire to chase down the Black man and kill him with his bare hands and the

409

need to go up and see Dolores, make sure she was all right. Had he come in time? Was she undefiled?

Cavil bounded up the stairs and flung open the door to his wife's room. There lay Dolores in bed, her covers tight up under her chin, looking at him through wide-open, frightened eyes.

"What happened!" cried Cavil. "Are you all right?"

"Of course I am!" she answered sharply. "What are you doing home?"

That wasn't the answer you get from a woman who's just cried out in fear. "I heard you call out," said Cavil. "Didn't you hear me answer?"

"I hear everything up here," said Dolores. "I got nothing to do in my life but lie and listen. I hear everything that's said in this house and everything that's done. Yes, I heard you call. But you weren't answering *me*."

Cavil was astonished. She sounded angry. He'd never heard her sound angry before. Lately he'd hardly heard a word from her at all—she was always asleep when he took breakfast, and their dinners together passed in silence. Now this anger—why? Why now?

"I saw a Black man running away from the house," said Cavil. "I thought maybe he—"

"Maybe he what?" She said the words like a taunt, a challenge.

"Maybe he hurt you."

"No, he didn't *hurt* me."

Now a thought began to creep into Cavil's mind, a thought so terrible he couldn't even admit he was thinking it. "What *did* he do, then?"

"Why, the same holy work that you've been doing, Cavil."

410

Cavil couldn't say a thing to that. She knew. She knew it all.

"Last summer, when your friend Reverent Thrower came, I lay here in my bed as you talked, the two of you."

"You were asleep. Your door was—"

"I heard everything. Every word, every whisper. I heard you go outside. I heard you talk at breakfast. Do you know I wanted to kill you? For years I thought you were the loving husband, a Christ-like man, and all this time you were rutting with these Black women. And then sold all your own babies as slaves. You're a monster, I thought. So evil that for you to live another minute was an abomination. But my hands couldn't hold a knife or pull the trigger on a gun. So I lay here and thought. And you know what I thought?"

Cavil said nothing. The way she told it, it made him sound so bad. "It wasn't like that, it was holy."

"It was adultery!"

"I had a vision!"

"Yes, your vision. Well, fine and dandy, Mr. Cavil Planter, you had a vision that making half-White babies was a good thing. Here's some news for you. I can make half-White babies, too!"

It was all making sense now. "He raped you!"

"He didn't rape me, Cavil. I invited him up here. I told him what to do. I made him call me his vixen and say prayers with me before and after so it would be as *holy* as what you did. We prayed to your damned Overseer, but for some reason he never showed up."

"It never happened."

"Again and again, every time you left the plantation, all winter, all spring."

411

"I don't believe it. You're lying to hurt me. You *can't* do that—the doctor said—it hurts you too bad."

"Cavil, before I found out what you done with those Black women, I thought I knew what pain was, but all that suffering was nothing, do you hear me? I could live through that pain every day forever and call it a holiday. I'm pregnant, Cavil."

"He raped you. That's what we'll tell everybody, and we'll hang him as an example, and—"

"Hang *him*? There's only one rapist on this plantation, Cavil, and don't think for a moment that I won't tell. If you lay a hand on my baby's father, I'll tell the whole country what you've been doing. I'll get up on Sunday and tell the church."

"I did it in the service of the—"

"Do you think they'll believe that? No more than I do. The word for what you done isn't holiness. It's concupiscence. Adultery. Lust. And when word gets out, when my baby is born Black, they'll turn against you, all of them. They'll run you out."

Cavil knew she was right. Nobody would believe him. He was ruined. Unless he did one simple thing.

He walked out of her room. She lay there laughing at him, taunting him. He went to his bedroom, took the shotgun down from the wall, poured in the powder, wadded it, then dumped in a double load of shot and rammed it tight with a second wad.

She wasn't laughing when he came back in. Instead she had her face towards the wall, she was crying. Too late for tears, he thought. She didn't turn to face him as he strode to the bed and tore down the covers. She was naked as a plucked chicken.

"Cover me!" she whimpered. "He ran out so fast, he didn't dress me. It's cold! Cover me, Cavil—"

Then she saw the gun.

Her twisted hand flailed in the air. Her body writhed. She cried out in pain of trying to move so quickly. Then he pulled the trigger and her body just flopped right down on the bed, a last sigh of air leaking from the top of her neck.

Cavil went back to his room and reloaded the gun.

He found Fat Fox fully dressed, polishing the carriage. He was such a liar, he thought he could fool Cavil Planter. But Cavil didn't even bother listening to his lies. "Your vixen wants to see you upstairs," he said.

Fat Fox kept denying it all the way until he got into the room and saw Dolores on the bed. Then he changed his tune. "She made me! What could I do, Master! It was like you and the women, Master! What choice a Black slave got? I got to obey, don't I? Like the women and you!"

Cavil knew devil talk when he heard it, and he paid no mind. "Strip off your clothes and do it again," he said. Fat Fox howled and Fat Fox whined, but when Cavil jammed him in the ribs with the barrel, he did what he was told. He closed his eyes so he didn't have to see what Cavil's shotgun done to Dolores, and he did what he was told. Then Cavil fired the gun again.

In a little while Lashman came in from the far field, all a-lather with running and fearing when he heard the gunshots. Cavil met him downstairs. "Lock down the slaves, Lashman, and then go fetch me the sheriff."

When the sheriff came, Cavil led him upstairs and

showed him. The sheriff went pale. "Good Lord," he whispered.

'Is it murder, Sheriff? I did it. Are you taking me to jail?"

"No sir," said the sheriff. "Ain't nobody going to call this murder." Then he looked at Cavil with this twisted kind of expression on his face. "What kind of man are you, Cavil?"

For a moment Cavil didn't understand the question.

"Letting me see your wife like that. I'd rather die before I let somebody see my wife like that."

The sheriff left. Lashman had the slaves clean up the room. There was no funeral for either one. They both got buried out where Salamandy lay. Cavil was pretty sure a few chickens died over the graves, but by then he didn't care. He was on his tenth bottle of bourbon and his ten-thousandth muttered prayer to the Overseer, who seemed powerful standoffish at a time like this.

Along about a week later, or maybe longer, here comes the sheriff again, with the priest and the Baptist preacher both. The three of them woke Cavil up from his drunken sleep and showed him a draught for twenty-five thousand dollars. "All of your neighbors took up a collection," the priest explained.

"I don't need money," Cavil said.

"They're buying you out," said the preacher.

"Plantation ain't for sale."

The sheriff shook his head. "You got it wrong, Cavil. What happened here, that was bad. But you letting folks see your wife like that—"

"I only let *you* see."

"You ain't no gentleman, Cavil."

"Also, there's the matter of the slave children,"

414

said the Baptist preacher. "They seem remarkably light-skinned, considering you have no breeding stock but what's black as night."

"It's a miracle from God," said Cavil. "The Lord is lightening the Black race."

The sheriff slid a paper over to Cavil. "This is the transfer of title of all your property—slaves, buildings, and land— to a holding company consisting of your former neighbors."

Cavil read it. "This deed says all the slaves here on the land," he said. "I got rights in a runaway slave boy up north."

"We don't care about that. He's yours if you can find him. I hope you noticed this deed also includes a stipulation that you will never return to this county or any adjoining county for the rest of your natural life."

"I saw that part," said Cavil.

"I can assure you that if you break that agreement, it will be the end of your natural life. Even a conscientious, hardworking sheriff like me couldn't protect you from what would happen."

"You said no threats," murmured the priest.

"Cavil needs to know the consequences," said the sheriff.

"I won't be back," said Cavil.

"Pray to God for forgiveness," said the preacher.

"That I will." Cavil signed the paper.

That very night he rode out on his horse with a twenty-five-thousand-dollar draught in his pocket and a change of clothes and a week's provisions and a pack horse behind him. Nobody bid him farewell. The slaves were singing jubilation songs in the sheds behind him. His horse manured the end of the drive. And in Cavil's mind there was only one thought.

The Overseer hates me, or this all wouldn't have happened. There's only one way to win back his love. That's to find that Alvin Smith, kill him, and get back my boy, my last slave who still belongs to me.

Then, O my Overseer, will You forgive me, and heal the terrible stripes Thy lash has torn upon my soul?

21

Alvin Journeyman

Alvin stayed home in Vigor Church all summer, getting to know his family again. Folks had changed, more than a little—Cally was mansize now, and Measure had him a wife and children, and the twins Wastenot and Wantnot had married them a pair of French sisters from Detroit, and Ma and Pa was both grey-haired mostly, and moving slower than Alvin liked to see. But some things didn't change— there was playfulness in them all, the whole family, and the darkness that had fallen over Vigor Church after the massacre at Tippy-Canoe, it was—well, not *gone*—more like it had changed into a kind of shadow that was behind everything, so the bright spots in life seemed all the brighter by contrast.

They all took to Arthur Stuart right off. He was so young he could hear all the men of the town tell him the tale of Tippy-Canoe, and all that he thought of it was to tell them his own story—which was really a mish-mash of his real mama's story, and Alvin's story, and the story of the Finders and how his White mama killed one afore she died.

Alvin pretty much let Arthur Stuart's account of things stand uncorrected. Partly it was because why should he make Arthur Stuart out to be wrong, when he loved telling the tale so? Partly it was out of sorrow, realizing bit by bit that Arthur Stuart never spoke in nobody else's voice but his own. Folks here would never know what it was like to hear Arthur Stuart speak their own voice right back at them. Even so, they loved to hear the boy talk, because he still remembered all the words people said, never forgetting a scrap it seemed like. Why should Alvin mar what was left of Arthur Stuart's knack?

Alvin also figured that what he never told, nobody could ever repeat. For instance, there was a certain burlap parcel that nobody ever saw unwrapped. It wouldn't do no good for word to get around that a certain golden object had been seen in the town of Vigor Church—the town, which hadn't had many visitors since the dark day of the massacre at Tippy-Canoe, would soon have more company than they wanted, and all the wrong sort, looking for gold and not caring who got harmed along the way. So he never told a soul about the golden plow, and the only person who even knew he was keeping a secret was his close-mouthed sister Eleanor.

Alvin went to call on her at the store she and Armor-of-God kept right there on the town square, ever since before there *was* a town square. Once it had been a place where visitors, Red and White, came from far away to get maps and news, back when the land was still mostly forest from the Mizzipy to Dekane. Now it was still busy, but it was all local folks, come to buy or hear gossip and news of the outside world. Since Armor-of-God was the only grown-up man in Vigor Church who wasn't cursed with Tenskwa-Tawa's curse, he was also the only one who could easily go outside to buy goods and hear news, bringing it all back in to the farmers and tradesmen of Vigor Church. It happened that today Armor-of-God was away, heading up to the town of Mishy-Waka to pick up some orders of glass goods and fine china. So Alvin found only Eleanor and her oldest boy, Hector, there, tending the store.

Things had changed a bit since the old days. Eleanor, who was near as good a hexmaker as Alvin, didn't have to conceal her hexes in the patterns of hanging flower baskets and arrangements of herbs in the kitchen. Now some of the hexes were right out in the open, which meant they could be much clearer and stronger. Armor-of-God must've let up a little on his hatred of knackery and hidden powers. That was a good thing—it was a painful thing, in the old days, to know how Eleanor had to pretend not to be what she was or know what she knew.

"I got something with me," said Alvin.

"So I see," said Eleanor. "All wrapped in a burlap bag, as still as stone, and yet it seems to me there's something living inside."

"Never you mind about that," said Alvin. "What's here is for no other soul but me to see."

Eleanor didn't ask any questions. She knew from those words exactly why he brought his mysterious parcel by. She told Hector to wait on any customers as came by, and then led Alvin out into the new ware-room, where they kept such things as a dozen kinds of beans in barrels, salt meat in kegs, sugar in paper cones, powder salt in waterproof pots, and spices all in different kinds of jars. She went straight to the fullest of the bean barrels, filled with a kind of green-speckle bean that Alvin hadn't seen before.

"Not much call for these beans," she said. "I reckon we'll never see the bottom of this barrel."

Alvin set the plow, all wrapped in burlap, on top of the beans. And then he made the beans slide out of the way, flowing around the plow smooth as molasses, until it sank right down to the bottom. He didn't so much as ask Eleanor to turn away, since she knew Alvin had power to do *that* much since he was just a little boy.

"Whatever's living in there," said Eleanor, "it ain't going to die, being dry down at the bottom of the barrel, is it?"

"It won't ever die," said Alvin, "at least not the way folks grow old and die."

Eleanor gave in to curiosity just enough to say, "I wish you could promise me that if anybody ever knows what's in there, so will I."

Alvin nodded to her. That was a promise he could keep. At the time, he didn't know how or when he'd ever show that plow to anybody, but if anybody could keep a secret, silent Eleanor could.

So anyway he lived in Vigor Church, sleeping in his old bedroom in his parents' house, lived there a good many weeks, well on toward July, and all the while he kept most of what happened in his seven-year prenticeship to himself. In fact he talked hardly more than he had to. He went here and there, a-calling on folks with his Pa or Ma, and without much fuss healing such toothaches and broken bones and festering wounds and sickness as he found. He helped at the mill; he hired out to work in other farmers' fields and barns; he built him a small forge and did simple repairs and solders, the kind a smith can do without a proper anvil. And all that time, he pretty much spoke when people spoke to him, and said little more than what was needed to do business or get the food he wanted at table.

420

He wasn't glum—he laughed at a joke, and even told a few. He wasn't solemn, neither, and spent more than a few afternoons down in the square, proving to the strongest farmers in Vigor Church that they weren't no match for a blacksmith's arms and shoulders in a rassling match. He just didn't have any gossip or small talk, and he never told a story on himself. And if you didn't keep a conversation going, Alvin was content to let it fall into silence, keeping at his work or staring off into the distance like as if he didn't even remember you were there.

Some folks noticed how little Alvin talked, but he'd been gone a long time, and you don't expect a nineteen-year-old to act the same as an eleven-year-old. They just figured he'd grown up to be a quiet man.

But a few knew better. Alvin's mother and father had some words between the two of them, more than once. "The boy's had some bad things happen to him," said his mother; but his father took a different view. "I reckon maybe he's had bad and good mixed in together, like most folks—he just doesn't know us well enough yet, after being gone seven years. Let him get used to being a man in this town, and not a boy anymore, and pretty soon he'll talk his leg off."

Eleanor, she also noticed Alvin wasn't talking, but since she also knew he had a marvelous secret living thing hidden in her bean barrel, she didn't fuss for a minute about something being *wrong* with Alvin. It was like she said to her husband, Armor-of-God, when he mentioned about how Alvin just didn't seem to have five words altogether for nobody. "He's thinking deep thoughts," said Eleanor. "He's working out problems none of us knows enough to help him with. You'll see—he'll talk plenty when he figures it all out."

And there was Measure, Alvin's brother who got captured by Reds when Alvin was; the brother who had come to know Ta-Kumsaw and Tenskwa-Tawa near as well as Alvin himself. Of course Measure noticed how little Alvin had told them about his prentice years, and in due time he'd surely be one Alvin could talk to—that was natural, seeing how long Alvin had trusted Measure and all they'd been through together. But at first Alvin felt shy even around Measure, seeing how he had his wife, Delphi, and any fool could see how they hardly could stand to be more than three feet apart from each other; he was so gentle and careful with her, always looking out for her, turning to talk to her if she was near, looking for her to come back if she was gone. How could Alvin know whether there was room for him anymore in Measure's heart? No, not even to Measure could Alvin tell his tale, not at first.

One day in high summer, Alvin was out in a field building fences with his younger brother Cally, who was man-size now, as tall as Alvin though not as massive in the back and shoulders. The two of them had hired on for a week with Martin Hill. Alvin was doing the rail splitting—hardly using his knack at all, either, though truth to tell he could've split all the rails just by asking them to split themselves. No, he set the wedge and hammered it down, and his knack only got used to keep the logs from splitting at bad angles that wouldn't give full-length rails.

They must have fenced about a quarter mile before Alvin realized that it was peculiar how Cally never fell behind. Alvin split, and Cally got the posts and rails laid in place, never needing a speck of help to set a post into soil too hard or soft or rocky or muddy.

So Alvin kept his eye on the boy—or, more exactly, used his knack to keep watch on Cally's work—and sure enough, Alvin could see that Cally had something of Alvin's knack, the way it was long ago when he didn't half understand what he was doing with it. Cally would find just the right spot to set a post, then make the ground soft till he needed it to be firm. Alvin figured Cally wasn't exactly planning it. He probably thought he was finding spots that were naturally good for setting a post.

Here it is, thought Alvin. Here's what I know I've got to do: teach somebody else to be a Maker. If ever there was someone I should teach, it's Cally, seeing how he's got something of the same knack. After all, he's seventh son of a seventh son same as me, since Vigor was still alive when I was born, but long dead when Cally came along.

So Alvin just up and started talking as they worked, telling Cally all about atoms and how you could teach them how to be, and they'd be like that. It was the first time Alvin tried to explain it to anybody since the last time he talked to Miss Larner—Margaret—and the words tasted delicious in his mouth. This is the work I was born for, thought Alvin. Telling my brother how the world works, so he can understand it and get some control over it.

You can bet Alvin was surprised, then, when Cally all of a sudden lifted a post high above his head and threw it on the ground at his brother's feet. It had so much force—or Cally had so ravaged it with his knack—that it shivered into kindling right there where it hit. Alvin couldn't hardly even guess why, but Cally was plain filled with rage.

"What did I say?" asked Alvin.

"My name's Cal," said Cally. "I ain't been Cally since I was ten years old."

"I didn't know," said Alvin. "I'm sorry, and from now on you're Cal to me."

"I'm *nothing* to you," said Cal. "I just wish you'd go away!"

It was only right at this minute that Alvin realized that Cal hadn't exactly invited him to go along on this job—it was Martin Hill what asked for Alvin to come, and before that, the job had been Cal's alone.

"I didn't mean to butt into your work here," said Alvin. "It just never entered my head you wouldn't want my help. I know I wanted your company."

Seemed like everything Alvin said only made Cal seethe inside till now his face was red and his fists were clenched tight enough to strangle a snake. "I had a place here," said Cal. "Then you come back. All fancy school taught like you are, using all them big words. And *healing* people without so much as touching them, just walking into their house and talking a spell, and when you leave everybody's all healed up from whatever ailed them—"

Alvin didn't even know folks had noticed he was doing it. Since nobody said a thing about it, he figured they all thought it was natural healing. "I can't think how that makes you mad, Cal. It's a good thing to make folks better."

All of a sudden there were tears running down Cal's cheeks. "Even laying hands on them, I can't always fix things up," said Cal. "Nobody even asks me no more."

It never occurred to Alvin that maybe Cal was

424

doing his own healings. But it made good sense. Ever since Alvin left, Cal had pretty much been what Alvin used to be in Vigor Church, doing all his works. Seeing how their knacks were so much alike, he'd come close to taking Alvin's place. And then he'd done things Alvin never did when he was small, like going about healing people as best he could. Now Alvin was back, not only taking back his old place, but also besting Cat at things that only Cal had ever done. Now who was there for Cal to be?

"I'm sorry," said Al. "But I can teach you. That's what I was starting to do."

"I never seen them bits and what-not you're talking about," said Cal. "I didn't understand a thing you talked about. Maybe I just ain't got a knack as good as yours, or maybe I'm too dumb, don't you see? All I can be is the best I figure out for myself. And I don't need you proving to me that I can't never measure up. Martin Hill asking for you on this job, cause he knows you can make a better fence. And there you are, not even using your knack to split the rails, though I know you can, just to show me that *without* your knack you're a match for me."

"That's not what I meant," said Alvin. "I just don't use my knack around—"

"Around people as dumb as *me*," said Cal.

"I was doing a bad job explaining," said Alvin, "but if you'll let me, Cal, I can teach you how to change iron into—"

"Gold," said Cal, his voice thick with scorn. "What do you think I am? Trying to fool me with an alchemist's tales! If you knew how to do *that*, you wouldn't've come home poor. You know I once used to think you were the beginning and end of the world. I thought, when Al comes home, it'll be like old times, the two of us playing and working together, talking all the time, me tagging on, doing everything together. Only it turns out you still think I'm just a little boy, you don't say nothing to me except 'here's another rail' and 'pass the beans, please.' You took over all the jobs folks used to look to me to do, even one as simple as making a stout rail fence."

"Job's yours," said Alvin, shouldering his hammer. There was no point in trying to teach Cal anything—even if he *could* learn it, he could never learn it from Alvin. "I got other work to do, and I won't detain you any longer."

"*Detain* me," said Cal. "Is that a word you learned in a book, or from that ugly old teacher lady in Hatrack River that your ugly little mix-up boy talks about?"

Hearing Miss Larner and Arthur Stuart so scornfully spoken of, that made Alvin burn inside, especially since he had in fact learned to use phrases like "detain you any longer" from Miss Larner. But Alvin didn't say anything to show his anger. He just turned his back and walked off, back down the line of the finished fence. Cal could use his own knack and finish the fence himself; Alvin didn't even care about collecting the wages he'd earned in most of a day's work. He had other things on his mind— memories of Miss Larner, partly, but mostly he was upset about how Cal hadn't wanted Alvin to teach him. Here he was the person in the whole world who had the best chance to learn it all as easy as a baby learning to suck, since it was his natural knack—only he didn't want to learn it, not from Alvin. It was something Alvin never would have

426

thought possible, to turn down the chance to learn something, just because the teacher was somebody you didn't like.

Come to think of it, though, hadn't Alvin hated going to school with Reverend Thrower, cause of how Thrower always made him feel like he was somehow bad or evil or stupid or something? Could it be that Cal hated Alvin the way Alvin had hated Reverend Thrower? He just couldn't understand why Cal was so angry. Of all people in the world, Cal had no reason to be jealous of Alvin, because he could come closest to doing all that Alvin did; yet for that very reason, Cal was so jealous he'd never learn it, not without going through every step of figuring it out for himself.

At this rate, I'll never build the Crystal City, cause I'll never be able to teach Making to another soul.

It was a few weeks after that when Alvin finally tried again to talk to somebody, to see if he really could teach Making. It was on a Sunday, in Measure's house, where Alvin and Arthur Stuart had gone to take their dinner. It was a hot day, so Delphi laid a cold table—bread and cheese and salt ham and smoked turkey—and they all went outside to take the afternoon in the shade of Measure's north-facing kitchen porch.

"Alvin, I invited you and Arthur Stuart here today for a reason," said Measure. "Delphi and me, we already talked it over, and said a few things to Pa and Ma, too."

"Sounds like it must be pretty terrible, if it took that much talking."

"Reckon not," said Measure. "It's just—well, Arthur Stuart, here, he's a fine boy, and a good hard worker, and good company to boot."

427

Arthur Stuart grinned. "I sleep solid, too," he said.

"Fine sleeper," said Measure. "But Ma and Pa ain't exactly young no more. I think Ma's used to doing things in the kitchen all her own way."

"That she is," sighed Delphi, as if she had more than a little reason for knowing exactly how set in her ways Goody Miller was.

"And Pa, well, he's tiring out. When he gets home from the mill, he needs to lie down, have plenty of quiet around him."

Alvin thought he knew where the conversation was heading. Maybe his folks just weren't the quality of Old Peg Guester or Gertie Smith. Maybe they couldn't take a mix-up boy into their home or their heart. It made him sad to think of such a thing about his own folks, but he knew right off that he wouldn't even complain about it. He and Arthur Stuart would just pack up and set out on a road leading—nowhere in particular. Canada, maybe. Somewhere that a mix-up boy'd be full welcome.

"Mind you, they didn't say a thing like that to *me*," said Measure. "In fact, I sort of said it all to them. You see, me and Delphi, we got a house somewhat bigger than we need, and with three small ones Delphi'd be glad of a boy Arthur Stuart's age to help with kitchen chores like he does."

"I can make bread all myself," said Arthur Stuart. "I know Mama's recipe by heart. She's dead."

"You see?" said Delphi. "If he can make bread himself sometimes, or even just help me with the kneading, I wouldn't end up so worn out at the end of the week."

"And it won't be long before Arthur Stuart could help out in my work in the fields," said Measure.

"But we don't want you to think we're looking to hire him on like a servant," said Delphi.

"No, no!" said Measure. "No, we're thinking of him like another son, only growed up more than my oldest Jeremiah, who's only three and a half, which makes him still pretty much useless as a human being, though at least he isn't always trying to throw himself into the creek to drown like his sister Shiphrah—or like you when you were little, I might add."

Arthur Stuart laughed at that. "Alvin like to drowned *me* one time," said Arthur Stuart. "Stuck me right in the Hio."

Alvin felt pure ashamed. Ashamed of lots of things: The fact that he never told Measure the whole story of how he rescued Arthur Stuart from the Finders; the fact that he even thought for a minute that Measure and Ma and Pa might be trying to get rid of a mix-up boy, when the truth was they were squabbling over who got to have him in their home.

"It's Arthur Stuart's choice where to live, once he's invited," said Alvin. "He came home along with me, but I don't make such choices for him."

"Can I live here?" asked Arthur Stuart. "Cal doesn't much like me."

"Cal's got troubles of his own," said Measure, "but he likes you fine."

"Why didn't Alvin bring home something useful, like a horse?" said Arthur Stuart. "You eat like one, but I bet you can't even pull a two-wheel shay."

Measure and Delphi laughed. They knew Arthur Stuart was repeating something Cal had said, word for word. Arthur Stuart did it so often folks came to expect it, and took delight in his perfect memory.

But it made Alvin sad to hear it, because he knew that only a few months ago, Arthur Stuart would have said it in Cal's own voice, so even Ma couldn't've known without looking that it wasn't Cal himself.

"Is Alvin going to live down here too?" asked Arthur Stuart.

"Well, see, that's what we're thinking," said Measure. "Why don't you come on down here, too, Alvin? We can put you up in the main room here, for a while. And when the summer work's done, we can set to fixing up our old cabin – it's still pretty solid, since we ain't moved out of it but two years now. You can be pretty much on your own then. I reckon you're too old now to be living in your pa's house and eating at your ma's table."

Why, Alvin never would've reckoned it, but all of a sudden he found his eyes full of tears. Maybe it was the pure joy of having somebody notice he wasn't the same old Alvin Miller Junior anymore. Or maybe it was the fact that it was Measure, looking out for him like in the old days. Anyway, it was at that moment that Alvin first felt like he'd really come home.

"Sure I'll come down here, if you want me," Alvin said.

"Well there's no reason to cry about it," said Delphi. "I already got three babies crying every time they think of it. I don't want to have to come along and dab your eyes and wipe your nose like I do with Keturah."

"Well at least he don't wear diapers," said Measure, and he and Delphi both laughed like that was the funniest thing they ever heard. But actually they were laughing with pleasure at how Alvin had gotten so sentimental over the idea of living with them.

So Alvin and Arthur Stuart moved on down to Measure's house, and Alvin got to know his best-loved brother all over again. All the old things that Alvin once loved were still in Measure as a man, but there were new things, too. The tender way Measure had with his children, even after a spanking or a stiff talking to. The way Measure looked after his land and buildings, seeing all that needed doing, and then doing it, so there was never a door that squeaked for a second day, never an animal that was off its feed for a whole day without Measure trying to account for what was wrong.

Above all, though, Alvin saw how Measure was with Delphi. She wasn't a noticeably pretty girl, though not particular ugly either; she was strong and stout and laughed loud as a donkey. But Alvin saw how Measure had a way of looking at her like the most beautiful sight he ever could see. She'd look up and there he'd be, watching her with a kind of dreamy smile on his face, and she'd laugh or blush or look away, but for a minute or two she'd move more graceful, walking partly on her toes maybe like she was dancing, or getting set to fly. Alvin wondered then if he could ever give such a look to Miss Larner as would make *her* so full of joy that she couldn't hardly stay connected to the earth.

Then Alvin would lie there in the night, feeling all the subtle movements of the house, knowing without even using his doodlebug what the slow and gentle creaking came from; and at such times he remembered the face of the woman named Margaret who had been hiding inside Miss Larner all those months, and imagined her face close to his, her lips parted,

431

and from her throat those soft cries of pleasure Delphi made in the silence of the night. Then he would see her face again, only this time twisted with grief and weeping. At such times his heart ached inside him, and he yearned to go back to her, to take her in his arms and find some place inside her where he could heal her, take her grief away, make her whole.

And because Alvin was in Measure's house, his wariness slipped away from him, so that his face again began to show his feelings. It happened, then, that once when Measure and Delphi exchanged such a look as they had between them, Measure happened to look at Alvin's face. Delphi was gone out of the room by then, and the children were long since in bed, so Measure was free to reach out a hand and touch Alvin's knee.

"Who is she?" Measure asked.

"Who?" asked Alvin, confused.

"The one you love till it takes your breath away just remembering."

For a moment Alvin hesitated, by long habit. But then the gateway opened, and all his story spilled out. He started with Miss Larner, and how she was really Margaret, who was the same girl who once was the torch in Taleswapper's stories, the one that looked out for Alvin from afar. But telling the story of his love for her led to the story of all she taught him, and by the time the tale was done, it was near dawn. Delphi was asleep on Measure's shoulder— she'd come back in sometime during the tale, but didn't last long awake, which was just as well, with her three children and Arthur Stuart sure to want breakfast on time no matter how late she stayed up in the night. But Measure was still awake, his eyes

432

sparkling with the knowledge of what the Redbird said, of the living golden plow, of Alvin in the forge-fire, of Arthur Stuart in the Hio. And also a deep sadness behind that light in Measure's eyes, for the murder Alvin had done with his own hands, however much it might have been deserved; and for the death of Old Peg Guester, and even for the death of a certain runaway Black slave girl Arthur Stuart's whole lifetime ago.

"Somehow I got to go out and find people I can teach to be Makers," said Alvin. "But I don't even know if somebody without a knack like mine can learn it, or how much they ought to know, or if they'd even want to know it."

"I think," said Measure, "that they ought to love the dream of your Crystal City before they ever know that they might learn to help in the making of it. If word gets out that there's a Maker who can teach Making, you'll get the sort of folks as wants to rule people with such power. But the Crystal City—ah, Alvin, think of it! Like living inside that twister that caught you and the Prophet all those years ago."

"Will you learn it, Measure?" asked Alvin.

"I'll do all I can to learn it," said Measure. "But first I make you a solemn promise, that I'll only use what you teach me to build up the Crystal City. And if it turns out I just can't learn enough to be a Maker, I'll help you any other way I can. Whatever you ask me to do, Alvin, that I'll do—I'll take my family to the ends of the Earth, I'll give up everything I own, I'll die if need be—anything to make the vision Tenskwa-Tawa showed you come true.'

Alvin held him by both hands, held him for the longest time. Then Measure leaned forward and

433

kissed him, brother to brother, friend to friend. The movement woke Delphi. She hadn't heard most of it, but she knew that something solemn was happening, and she smiled sleepily before she got up and let Measure take her off to bed for the last few hours till dawn.

That was the beginning of Alvin's true work. All the rest of that summer, Measure was his pupil and his teacher. While Alvin taught Making to Measure, Measure taught fatherhood, husbanding, manliness to Alvin. The difference was that Alvin didn't half realize what he was learning, while Measure won each new understanding, each tiny shred of the power of Makery, only after terrible struggle. Yet he *did* understand, bit by bit, and he did learn more than a little bit of Making; and Alvin began to understand, after many failed efforts, how to go about teaching someone else to "see" without eyes, to "touch" without hands.

And now, when he lay awake at night, he did not yearn so often for the past, but rather tried to imagine the future. Somewhere out there was the place where he should build the Crystal City; and out there, too, were the folks he had to find and teach them to love that dream and show them how to make it real. Somewhere there was the perfect soil that his living plow was meant to delve. Somewhere there was a woman he could love and live with till he died.

Back in Hatrack River, that fall there was an election, and it happened that because of certain stories floating around about who was a hero and who was a snake, Pauley Wiseman lost his job and Po Doggly got him a new one. Along about that time, too,

Makepeace Smith come in to file a complaint about how back last spring his prentice run off with a certain item that belonged to his master.

"That's a long time waiting to file such a charge," said Sheriff Doggly.

"He threatened me," said Makepeace Smith. "I feared for my family."

"Well, now, you just tell me what it was he stole."

"It was a plow," said Makepeace Smith.

"A common plow? I'm supposed to find a common plow? And why in tarnation would he steal such a thing?'

Makepeace lowered his voice and said it all secret-like. "The plow was made of gold."

Oh, Po Doggly just laughed his head off, hearing that.

"Well, it's true, I tell you," said Makepeace.

"Is it, now? Why, I think that I believe you, my friend. But if there was a gold plow in your smithy, I'll lay ten to one that it was Al's, not yours."

"What a prentice makes belongs to the master!"

Well, that's about when Po started getting a little stern. "You start telling tales like that around Hatrack River, Makepeace Smith, and I reckon other folks'll tell how you kept that boy when he long since was a better smith than you. I reckon word'll get around about how you wasn't a fair master, and if you start to charging Alvin Smith with stealing what only he in all this world could possibly make, I think you'd find yourself laughed to scorn."

Maybe he would and maybe he wouldn't. It was sure that Makepeace didn't try no legal tricks to try to get that plow back from Alvin—wherever he was. But he told his tale, making it bigger every time he told it—how Alvin was always stealing from him,

435

and how that golden plow was Makepeace Smith's inheritance, made plowshape and painted black, and how Alvin uncovered it by devil powers and carried it off. As long as Gertie Smith was alive she scoffed at all such tales, but she died not too long after Alvin left, from a blood vein popping when she was a-screaming at her husband for being such a fool. From then on, Makepeace had the story his own way, even allowing as how Alvin killed Gertie herself with a curse that *made* her veins pop open and bleed to death inside her head. It was a terrible lie, but there's always folks as like to hear such tales, and the story spread from one end of the state of Hio to the other, and then beyond. Pauley Wiseman heard it. Reverend Thrower heard it. Cavil Planter heard it. So did a lot of other folks.

Which is why when Alvin finally ventured forth from Vigor Church, there was plenty of folks with an eye for strangers carrying bundles about the size of a plowshare, looking for a glint of gold under burlap, measuring strangers to see if they might be a certain run-off prentice smith who stole his master's inheritance. Some of those folks even meant to take it back to Makepeace Smith in Hatrack River, if it happened they ever laid their hands upon the golden plow. On the other hand, with some of those folks such a thought never crossed their minds.

MURDER AND MENDELSSOHN

A Phryne Fisher Mystery

Kerry Greenwood

ALLEN&UNWIN
SYDNEY·MELBOURNE·AUCKLAND·LONDON

First published in 2013

Copyright © Kerry Greenwood 2013

Allen & Unwin
83 Alexander Street
Crows Nest NSW 2065 Australia
Phone: (61 2) 8425 0100
Email: info@allenandunwin.com
Web: www.allenandunwin.com

Cataloguing-in-Publication details are available
from the National Library of Australia
www.trove.nla.gov.au

ISBN 978 1 74237 956 2

Set in 11.5/14 pt Adobe Garamond by Bookhouse, Sydney

Printed and bound in Australia by the SOS Print + Media Group.

10 9 8

MIX
Paper from
responsible sources
FSC® C011217

The paper in this book is FSC® certified.
FSC® promotes environmentally responsible,
socially beneficial and economically viable
management of the world's forests.

This book is for Michael Warby,
peerless researcher, dear friend, il magnifico

With thanks to David Greagg (Duty Wombat and reason for existing); Ben Pryor, Shelley Robinson, Mark Pryor, Jade King, Patrizia di Biase, Themetrula Gardner, Helen Gordon-Clark, Mark Dolahenty, Patrick Burns, Vanessa Craigie, Cathy Collopy, Rita Battaglin, Daniel Barfoot, Winston B Todd, Tom Lane, Bill Collopy, Katie Purvis, Frank Mattea, Susan Tonkin, Woody, Marie Eleanor, Simon Johnson, Hugh Hunt and all my choral friends who sang rude pub songs with me and oratorios and masses and endless Christmas Carols and Laudate and 'Wild Mountain Thyme'; my folk heroes Danny Spooner and Judy Small; and my mother, who sang my earliest song to me, to the percussion accompaniment of her heart.

CHAPTER ONE

As from the pow'r of Sacred Lays
The Spheres began to move;
And sung the great Creator's praise
To all the bless'd above;
So, when the last and dreadful Hour
This crumbling Pageant shall devour,
The TRUMPET shall be heard on high,
The dead shall live, the living die,
And MUSICK shall untune the Sky.

John Dryden
'A Song for St Cecilia's Day'

It was a quiet St Kilda morning in the summer of 1929. The
Hon. Miss Phryne Fisher was sitting in her jasmine bower,
drenched in scent. She was wearing a pale green silk gown
embroidered with golden phoenixes, the symbol of the empress.
Flaming pearls of longevity burned their way, comet-like, upon
her fluttering sleeves. Her hair was as shiny as patent leather,
cut in a neat bob which swung forward as she read. She was
nibbling a croissant and drinking cafe au lait. With her pink
cheeks and red lips and green eyes, she looked like a hand-
coloured French fashion plate.

Sitting on the table in a pose made famous by Basht, goddess of cats, was her black cat Ember. He was waiting for the tidbits that her fellow breakfaster would undoubtedly award such a beautiful cat who had not even ventured a paw towards that luscious stack of crispy bacon, though if a suitable offering wasn't made fairly soon, was contemplating pre-emptive action.

Phryne ought to have been reading *Vogue*, or perhaps some yellow-backed scandalous French novel, occasionally making arch comments to her lover, who would be exhausted from a night of passion. Instead, to ruin the picture, she was reading an autopsy report, and her companion was a tired-out police detective, eating one of Mrs Butler's breakfasts and absorbing very strong tea as a corrective to not getting any sleep.

Dot, Phryne's companion, was embroidering waratahs on her hope chest table linen. She fully intended to marry Detective Sergeant Hugh Collins in due course, and had no wish to be found unprepared for that happy event. Tinker and Jane were playing chess in the arbour. Ruth was in the kitchen with Mrs Butler, cook to the household, shelling peas and discussing ways to cook pineapple. The black and white sheepdog Molly was lying under the table with her head on the inspector's foot, confident that he would drop bacon rind before his toes went numb. This trick had always worked for Molly, and if it didn't on this occasion, she had a way of laying her head confidingly in a male lap with just a hint of teeth that invariably produced results.

A steady hum of useful activity serenaded Mr Butler as he sat down on his comfortable chair and sipped his after-breakfast cup of coffee. Fortunately, he could not hear the topic of conversation.

'All right,' said Phryne, putting down the report and pouring her favourite policeman another cup of the stewed licorice black tea. Just the way he liked it: enough tannic acid to dye a cauldron full of stockings. To which he then added milk and three lumps of sugar. Generations of tea aficionados rolled in their graves. 'I've read it. Someone has stifled an orchestral conductor with really quite a lot of sheets of Mendelssohn's *Elijah* stuffed down his throat.'

'Right,' said the detective inspector.

'Seems excessive, even as musical criticism,' commented Phryne. 'Your doctor has done a competent examination. Taken samples of blood, urine and stomach contents. Noted no signs of struggle, no scratches or bruises except those on his shoulders, which seem to mean that the murderer knelt on him while suffocating him. I think those are kneecap marks. And he didn't struggle because he had a tummy full of—' her eyebrows lifted '—enough opiates to knock out a small-ish rhinoceros. In fact, enough to kill him, which makes the added sheet music supererogatory. Baroque, verging on rococo. A flamboyant murderer, Jack dear, with a point to prove.'

'Yes,' said Jack. 'But what point? I don't know anything about music. And I don't know anything about these . . . these sort of people. I thought . . .' His voice trailed off and he took a strengthening gulp of the tar-water tea.

Phryne smiled. She knew how much Jack Robinson hated asking for her unofficial and potentially world-shattering help. She volunteered.

'I have always liked Mendelssohn,' she told him. 'Who is performing it?'

'The Melbourne Harmony Choir, with the Occasional Orchestra. Amateurs but with professional soloists and a professional conductor,' Jack read from his notebook. 'The dead man was called Hedley Tregennis. Forty-five, born in

Richmond, separated from his wife, no children. Bit of a reputation for being loud, insulting and impatient.'

'That applies to most conductors,' said Phryne.

'See? I don't know all this stuff. They're having a rehearsal tonight at the Scots Church Assembly Hall, just before the lantern lecture. Can you come along with me? You're sure to notice things that I won't. Just as long,' added Jack Robinson anxiously, noticing the bright interest in those green eyes, 'you don't get the idea that it's your case, or anything silly like that.'

'Of course not,' cooed Phryne. 'What time? Can I pick you up?'

'Mr Butler driving?' asked Jack Robinson. Miss Fisher drove like a demon and he had to keep his eyes shut the whole journey, in case he saw how many breaches of the traffic laws she committed, and closing his eyes in a moving car made him queasy.

'Yes, there will be nowhere to leave the car in Collins Street.'

'Right, then, five thirty at the police station,' he told her.

'What's the lantern lecture?' she asked, as he dropped bacon rinds to Molly, fed Ember a large piece of the same, and wiped his mouth preparatory to facing the world again.

'Some bloke called Rupert Sheffield,' he said. 'On the science of deduction. Ought to ask him to help,' he added, and left, thanking Mrs Butler on the way out through the kitchen.

Phryne was unexpectedly stung. Science of deduction? What did any man called Rupert know about deduction that the Hon. Miss Phryne Fisher didn't know?

Ridiculous. She shook herself into order like an affronted cat and ate the rest of her croissant with a sharp snap of her white teeth.

'We got a case, Guv?' asked Tinker. A Queenscliff fisher

boy, he had attached himself at heel, like a small scruffy terrier, and Phryne had decided that he might be useful. As well as being endearingly intelligent. And devoted to Sexton Blake. He had fitted in well. Phryne's adopted daughter Jane found him clever and was teaching him chess. Her other adopted daughter Ruth liked his appetite, which was reliably voracious, even for cooking experiments which had slightly failed. Mr and Mrs Butler appreciated the supply of fresh fish and Dot liked having someone sleeping in the back garden, which made her feel more secure. Molly liked accompanying him on fishing expeditions. Ember tolerated him with his usual amused disdain. Ember was utterly uninterested in any other humans apart from his own family (Phryne, Ruth and Jane), whom he considered to be under his protecting paw. Others might be awarded some passing notice if they came bearing food. Possibly. Tinker was bearable, and pleasantly free with his fish.

That meant that Tinker was enveloped in a glow of approval from the entire household, which in turn had meant that Tinker could be easy in their company. He adored Phryne with his whole heart. And, together with Dot, he worried about her. She was far too bold for someone who was only five foot two and weighed in at about seven stone in a wringing wet army overcoat.

However, he thought, as he returned to Phryne's briefing on this odd murder, even the Guv'nor couldn't get into too much trouble at a choir rehearsal and a lantern lecture.

Could she?

As he often did, Tinker felt uneasy, and shared a glance with Dot. She was concerned, too.

'Any ideas?' Phryne asked her household.

'Must be very angry,' offered Jane.

'Why angry?'

'Didn't just want Mr Tregennis dead,' said Jane, who was destined to be a doctor. 'He would have died with that overdose. He was dying, in fact, wasn't he, when the music was stuffed into his mouth?'

'Probably,' agreed Phryne.

'If the murderer just wanted to get rid of the bloke, then the morphine would have done the trick,' said Tinker, with the callousness of fourteen. 'But that wasn't enough.'

'And if the murderer wanted him to suffer, he went the wrong way about it,' said Dot. 'The poor man can't have felt a thing.'

'Yes, and isn't that odd?' commented Phryne. 'The music stuffed into the mouth is, as my learned colleague says, an act of rage. But the method of death, as my other learned colleague observes, is peaceful and painless. Not a mark on him, no struggle, no bruises. And from this we can surmise . . .'

'Well,' said Jane, 'either the murderer is mad, a person of moods . . .'

'Yes,' said Phryne. 'Or?'

'Or the murderer is two people,' said Dot. 'One who just wants him dead and one who's real furious at him.'

'Yes,' said Phryne, 'or . . . ?'

'The murderer's weak,' said Tinker. 'Not strong enough to hold the bloke down and suffocate him without drugging him first.'

Phryne continued, reading from her notes. Jack had rather meanly taken his file with him. 'Now, stomach contents disclose that he had eaten a rather expensive snack just before he died. Half a dozen fresh oysters, a slice or two of smoked salmon, a small piece of stilton and water biscuits.'

'Expensive is right,' commented Ruth. 'Stilton has to be

specially imported, oysters are really unsafe to eat unless you buy the ones from select fishmongers, and smoked salmon comes from Scotland.'

'Correct. As last meals go, it is a rather lavish one. He seems to have drunk . . .'

'Champagne?' suggested Ruth, who knew which wines were appropriate for shellfish. Mr Butler was a mine of information on the subject.

'No, oddly enough, a sweet dessert wine. Muscat, perhaps, or Imperial Tokay,' replied Phryne. 'Which is costly, but in my opinion has a tawdry taste and is far too sugary.'

'But I bet it would cover up the taste of the poison,' said Dot. 'Like putting bitter medicine into syrup.'

'Never fooled me,' said Phryne, brooding darkly on the cough medicines of her youth. She particularly had it in for Buckley's Canadiol Mixture, which tasted like rendered-down pine trees. 'But a good notion, Dot dear. Presumably Mr Tregennis had a sweet tooth, his poisoner knew that, and instead of providing a light dry sparkling wine with his after-rehearsal amuse-bouche, gave him a glass of some noxious wine which would hide the poison. Morphine is extremely bitter. Only other way to hide it would be in a naturally bitter drink or food. Keep that in mind next time you are contemplating murder.'

'Six months ago, Miss, I would have been shocked at that comment,' said Dot.

Phryne beamed at her. 'See how you've been coming along, Dot dear? Well done!'

Dot was not sure whether this was a sign of growing sophistication or an indication of moral degeneracy, and decided to confess it to her local priest in due course. He was an old priest. He would cope.

7

'The body was found on the floor of the conductor's room. He had been dead for some time. The cleaning lady found him when she came in to sweep at six this morning. He was last seen—by everyone else—retreating there and slamming the door after an unusually fraught rehearsal. He seems to have been a short-tempered bully, and one wonders if the entire choir—or perhaps only the basses—decided to remove him.'

She looked up to see if the joke had registered. No one smiled. She decided that she really must see to the musical education of her minions, and went on.

'No sign of any plates, glasses or cutlery,' she told them. 'Whoever brought the food took all evidence away with them. The usual police search found no suicide note, no useful calling cards, matchbooks, foreign coins, obscure words written on the walls or scales of rare venomous reptiles.'

'Oh.' Tinker was disappointed.

'The choir departed in a body and caught the tram into Carlton, where they went to a sly-grog pub and sang very rude songs until at least three in the morning.'

'But they can't have been in full view all the time,' objected Dot. 'Some of them must have, you know, visited the conveniences, gone out for a breath of air—any one of them could have come back to poison Mr Tregennis.'

'Yes, Dot, true,' said Phryne. 'That is why Jack wanted me to come and look at his choristers. In case something leaps to mind.'

'Where did the food come from?' asked Ruth, who had been thinking deeply. 'That's not ordinary pie cart stuff, that's expensive hotel food.'

'Another thing which the overworked constabulary are even now trying to ascertain.' Phryne leafed through her notes. 'Questions?'

'Any sign that he had . . . been with a lady?' asked Dot, even more convinced of her eventual destination. 'No lipstick marks, things like that?'

'I am not going to harrow your innocent ears with the ghastly details, Dot, but he certainly hadn't had any close communion with anyone for some days, and only Jane can ask me how I know that, and only if she looks up the anatomy text first on seminal vesicles. And asks me in private. No lipstick, greasepaint, love bites or other indelicate things, but long blonde hairs on his coat. Blondes are being asked pointed questions as we speak.'

'Because it is the sort of intimate supper they describe in *Larousse Gastronomique*,' added Ruth. 'Oysters, smoked salmon, wine. Even though it's the wrong wine.' Ruth was aggrieved. Anyone who could afford smoked salmon ought to know that it went with champagne.

'It might have been a love affair gone wrong,' said Jane.

'Then why stuff music down the poor bloke's throat?' asked Tinker.

Phryne patted his shoulder.

'We need, as Sherlock Holmes would say, more data. So I shall go out this evening and get some, and I would rather go alone, darlings. Then I shall come back and we shall discuss it. All right?'

'If you say so, Guv,' said Tinker, on behalf of them all.

'Good. Very good, all of you.' Phryne smiled general approval. 'You have all done very well. Science of deduction, indeed,' she added, and swept into the house to bathe and dress.

'It's just a choir rehearsal,' said Jane to Tinker. 'How much trouble can she get into at a choir rehearsal?'

'She's Miss Phryne,' said Dot. 'She could get into trouble in heaven. God forgive me,' she added, and crossed herself.

CHAPTER TWO

All things shall perish from under the sky,
Music alone shall live, music alone shall live,
Music alone shall live, never to die.

Traditional round

Phryne remembered the stairs up to the Scots Church Assembly
Hall. She put on a low-heeled pair of shoes, as she had slightly
sprained her ankles dancing the Charleston two nights before.
Not wishing to overawe the choir, she dressed in a decently
quiet turquoise dress, jacket and hat and took a large handbag.
As usual her petticoat pocket contained emergency requisites:
a spare lighter, a banknote, cigarettes, a pearl-handled .22
Beretta. One never knew what the exigencies of rehearsal
might entail. Mr Butler drove Phryne and her policeman
with calm and dignity into the city, left them at the corner
of Collins and Russell streets, and took the car to the garage
where it had been built. He had instructions to come back at
nine. Phryne had decided to watch the lantern lecture. It might
even be instructive.

She was making suggestions to Jack Robinson as she felt her way, a little gingerly, up the stairs. Hugh Collins waited at the door.

'You need to find out who brought that food, Jack dear, and I suggest you start with the hotel just across the road. That was, as Ruth pointed out, expensive provender, not available from just any soup kitchen. Then you need to find the conductor's lover.'

'His lover?' asked Jack.

'Well, yes, that aphrodisiac little supper was an invitation of sorts. Then you need talk to the choir's librarian.'

'Why?' asked Jack.

At that moment someone caught Phryne around the waist and dragged her into a close embrace. He never knew how close he was to a knee where it would not have been appreciated because, fortunately for him, Phryne recognised him and flung her arms around his neck.

'John!' she exclaimed. 'John Wilson, how can you possibly be here? One moment.' She turned in his arms and said to Jack Robinson, 'The librarian has all the scores, numbered. Get her to call them all in. That music had to come from somewhere. I'll be in directly.'

Jack Robinson shook his head, collected his detective sargent, and entered the hall. John Wilson chuckled.

'Still the same Phryne, eh?' he asked. 'And it's Dr John, now.'

'Oh, excellent, so you went back after . . . afterwards?'

John Wilson had been a medical student in 1918 when he had been dragged from his residency and dropped into the Battle of the Somme. He had run a forward casualty clearing station, dipped deep in blood and death. Horrified, shell-shocked and twenty-two years old, he had met Phryne, bringing in the wounded. There, in her ambulance, under

11

bombardment, he and Phryne had mutually ripped the clothes off each other and mated fiercely, deaf from shelling, desperate to find a warm living body to hang on to while the world bled and fractured and blew up around them. Thereafter Phryne had invited him into her ambulance frequently. He had always been delighted to accept her invitation, alone of the women in the world, for John Wilson's heart was given to men. Phryne seemed to be in a different category. He had often puzzled about it. However, she was exceptional.

And then, near the end of the war, in November, for God's sake, a sniper had been amusing himself shooting at the red cross on John's tent, and only Phryne jamming her ambulance into gear, forcing it up and over a trench and covering him, meant that he got a bullet in the leg, not a number of them in head and heart. He had been standing just behind the red cross. He had been carried off by his own stretcher-bearers, and somehow he had never seen Phryne again.

She looked just the same, a little plumper than the starveling he had known, still the same black hair, red lips and green eyes that cut through all pretence. She smelt bewitchingly of clean hair and Jicky. She was waiting for his reassurance so he gave it.

'It was just my leg, dear girl, not my hands. And it isn't too bad. I can get along. And if it hadn't been for you—' he tightened his embrace '—it wouldn't be anything at all.'

Phryne kissed him on the cheek. He smelt the same as he had when she had last kissed him. Coffee, pipe tobacco, his own warm, earthy scent. No faint overscent of ether; not practising medicine, then. His kindly blue eyes were still the same, his skin more weathered, his military haircut greying a little at the temples. His body, under her hands, was muscular and stocky. She would not at all mind hauling John Wilson into her ambulance again—and this time she had a house and a comfortable bed. Definitely today's Good Thought.

'What are you doing here, John darling?' she asked. 'Can you dine with me?'

He smiled gently. He had always smiled at her like that. As though her energy amused him. He had always been quiet and kind, a stalwart presence, as the young soldiers died under his hands and he and Phryne wept in each other's arms over the death of hope and innocence, kisses tainted with high-explosive smoke. How had she lost touch with this admirable John? He had gone back to university and she had stayed in Paris. She had heard that he was living with his young man, what was his name . . . Galahad? Lancelot? Something like that. And she had assumed he was happy. From the sad shadows under his eyes, she had been wrong. She patted his cheek with one scented hand. He took this as a cue.

'Do you mean here in Australia, Phryne love, or here on the steps of the assembly hall, where we are making exhibitions of ourselves?'

'I always liked your voice,' she said. 'So deep and pleasant, it made the poor boys feel better just to hear you. Here in all senses, please.'

'I came to Australia with Rupert Sheffield, who was a code-breaker and mathematician. Did something very hush-hush. In Greece, you know. He's a dear fellow but a tad accident-prone. We had barely arrived in your fine country when a whole net of cargo just missed flattening us. Careless. We are in Melbourne for him to give his mathematical wisdom to the masses. I'm here on the steps because he is giving a lecture tonight and wanted me to test the apparatus. It flickered too much last night.'

'Sheffield the Science of Deduction man? Oh, and are you and he . . . ?'

'No,' he said quickly. 'Not at all.'

'And Arthur?' She had remembered the name.

'Arthur died,' he said steadily. 'A long time ago. Heart failure. Never knew he had anything wrong with him and even I didn't diagnose it.'

'John dear,' she said softly. He leaned his forehead into her shoulder a moment, then she felt his spine straighten, the military manner reassumed like a coat. Or a mask.

'Now, I must go and see about that projector,' he said. 'Are you helping the police with their enquiries, Phryne?'

'Oh, yes, just with the choir. My policeman doesn't know anything about "these sorts of people" and I do.'

'Madame.' He bowed her through the door.

'And dinner? Dr MacMillan is here, too. She'd be delighted to see you again.'

'I'd love to, Phryne, but I'd have to find out what Sheffield . . .'

'All right, I see,' said Phryne, who knew a case of raging unrequited love when she saw it, even if John ignored his own clinical indications. 'I'll stay for the show, and you can talk to me afterwards.'

'Thanks,' he murmured, and kissed her cheek.

Phryne went towards what sounded like a full-scale choral riot in a mixed frame of mind. On the one hand, her old friend Dr Wilson was in Melbourne. On the other hand, her chances of resuming their former relations seemed increasingly unlikely.

'Drat,' she murmured, and plunged into the fray.

•

Approximately thirty singers were gathered around approximately one librarian, who was trying to order her scores by their accession numbers. She was not assisted by the voices, which were explaining that they'd left their score 1) at home, 2) in the dressing room, 3) on the bus or 4) had never had one to begin with, despite that signature in the book; yes, it was their signature, but they couldn't remember being issued a score and had been looking over Matt's shoulder. Phryne had sung in many a chorus and saw this as situation normal, but Jack Robinson was disconcerted. Disconcerted policemen have a tendency to shout.

'Silence!' he bellowed, in tones which had frozen spines in darkest Little Lon and compelled instant obedience from Fitzroy hooligans. The choir didn't precisely fall silent, as any choir has been yelled at by experts, but the squabbling abated enough for him to make himself heard.

'Hedley Tregennis has been murdered,' he announced. 'Show some respect. I need to talk to all of you. Who wants to be first?'

There was a noticeable lack of volunteers. Phryne had taken a seat on stage and was scanning faces in her usual manner. She nodded towards a stocky lad with blond hair and blue eyes. That was the leader of this group. The collection of singers were all keeping him in sight. Jack beckoned and he came forward, tripping over a piece of string and having to be helped to his feet by a large economy-size bass.

'Name?' barked the policeman.

'Smith,' he said. 'Matthew. Tenor.'

'Collins, are you writing this down?' demanded Robinson.

Hugh licked his indelible pencil and nodded.

'When was the last time you saw Hedley Tregennis?'

'Last night,' said Matthew Smith. 'He slammed off stage

in a filthy temper and told us to bugger off and not come back until today, so—' he shrugged '—we buggered off as requested.'

'Where did you go from here?'

'Most of us went to the pub,' the young man answered. 'I went home. They stayed until quite late at the pub.'

'More like early morning,' observed the large bass. 'I didn't get home till four. My landlady had locked me out and I had to sleep in the laundry. Lucky it's summer.'

'I got home at three thirty, but I live in Carlton; you must have had to walk home,' commented another bass.

'Well, yes, Tom, I spent all my money at the Cr—' said the bass, and shut up abruptly as a small fierce alto slapped a hand across his mouth.

'I am not interested in sly grog,' said Jack Robinson with deteriorating patience. 'I am interested in the last time you saw Hedley Tregennis. And if you don't tell me everything you know about it, I shall arrange a raid on the Criterion and you will have nowhere to drink. Line up and give names, addresses and the time you last saw Hedley Tregennis to the constable at the table over there. Anyone who has something particular to say, talk to my sergeant. I'm going to sit over there and wait until someone tells me something interesting.'

He found a seat. Phryne stayed where she was, watching. Robinson admired the way she did not seem to watch; inspecting her nails, running a finger up her calf as though to check for a run in her stocking, fussing with her hair. She looked perfectly harmless, unless you caught her eye, in which case you felt that you were stripped down to component molecules, weighed in the balance, and found wanting. She examined the choir as they returned from giving their details and lined up on stage, beginning to sing rounds as a warm-up as soon as there were more than four of them. Led by Tom, the bass, they started the charming and absurd 'Life is But a Melancholy Flower' to the tune of 'Frère Jacques' and sang along quite tunefully until a soprano clutched her hands dramatically to her bosom and wailed, 'We shouldn't be doing this!' in a voice trained to carry. The singing died down.

'Why not, Julia?' asked Matthew Smith. 'We're a choir and we're stuck here and the concert's on in two weeks.'

'But we should have some respect, like the policeman said,' she declaimed.

'Why?' asked a tall, affected tenor with sleek brown hair and a determined pair of spectacles. 'He didn't have any respect for us. Or for the work. Poor old Mendelssohn, taken at a breakneck gallop like that.'

'What about the poor old dead man?' asked a redheaded alto.

'It's all right for you, you're a med student, Bones,' protested Julia, who unlike the stereotype was thin, dark, and would be scraggy when she was forty. 'You're used to dead people. He was just lying on the floor like a bundle of old . . . old music. That's upsetting!'

'Dead people are dead,' said Bones, shrugging again.

'You're disgusting!' protested Julia.

The interaction was interesting. Phryne listened carefully, then cut Julia out as she lined up for a cup of the choir's thin tea.

'Talk to me,' she said politely.

Julia bridled. The temperament, however, was canonical. 'Why?'

'Me or the cop,' said Phryne.

Julia tried a half-hearted flounce. Phryne had seen flounces before. She raised an eyebrow. Julia surrendered.

'Oh, all right, who are you?'

'I'm Phryne Fisher,' said Phryne. 'Come and sit down over

here. Now, tell me how you knew what the deceased Hedley Tregennis looked like.'

'I was guessing,' said Julia.

'Like a bundle of old music,' persisted Phryne. 'He could have been flat on his back or on his front or sitting in a chair, but he was, as it happens, lying curled up and there was music involved. How did you know that?'

Julia looked around wildly for rescue. No one interrupted.

'Woman's intuition?' she ventured.

Phryne chuckled. 'Have a heart. When did you see the body?'

'Oh, all right,' said Julia crossly. 'I wasn't going to the pub, I was going home, then when I was halfway there I remembered I had left my score behind. I knew the caretaker wouldn't lock up until after ten because of the lantern lecture so I came back and went backstage to the conductor's room.'

'Why there?' asked Phryne.

'It has a lock; the librarian stashes the scores there when someone leaves one behind. Scores are expensive. That's why she carries on so much if someone loses one.'

'Then how were you intending to retrieve your score?' asked Phryne. 'Do you have a key?'

'No, but there's one hung up in the locker. In case we forget. No one knows it's there.'

'Except thirty singers, their friends and hangers-on, and the pianist,' observed Phryne. Julia bit her lip.

'Oh, yes, them. Us. I suppose. I unlocked the door and he was lying on the floor all dead and I was so scared I just ran away.'

'Locking the door behind you,' said Phryne evenly.

'Yes,' said Julia.

'And taking your score.'

'Yes, well, it was just on the desk—I didn't have to step over

18

him or anything,' explained Julia. 'And I needed to rehearse. I've got a quartet. It's "Holy, Holy, Holy." Everyone says I'm ready to sing it.'

'Right,' said Phryne. Singers. She had forgotten what they were like. 'I'm sure you'll be good. Now, I want you to close your eyes. Think for me. You're back in the conductor's office. You're not looking at the dead man. You're looking at the room. Are you there?'

'Yes,' breathed Julia, who would have been an ideal hypnotic subject.

'Look around. What can you see?' prompted Phryne in a soft, gentle voice.

'Desk, chair, scores on the desk, teapot, teacup. Coat hung behind the door. Wastepaper basket full of torn-up paper.'

'Music paper?' asked Phryne.

'No, just writing paper, white, with black ink on it. That's all, really. Dead man on the floor. Mr Tregennis. Horrible man.'

'Why was he horrible?' Phryne enquired, taking advantage of Julia's trance.

'Hands,' said Julia. 'All over us. Any girl. He'd pinch and poke and grab. Like an octopus. Nasty hot hands. And he'd yell and stamp and call us all tarts and whores if we sang a note wrong. I'm not sorry he's dead,' said Julia, coming out of her fugue state. 'What have I been saying?'

'Nothing at all worrying,' said Phryne. 'Tell me, did Mr Tregennis have a girlfriend in the choir? Someone special?'

The pink mouth made a creditable moue of distaste.

'Not us,' she said loudly. 'None of us would go within arm's reach of him.'

'Right,' agreed the redheaded alto. She held out a hand.

'Annie,' she said. 'You're Phryne Fisher, aren't you? Seen you before. Detecting?'

'Just here to help my favourite policeman arrest the right person.'

'Good, because it wasn't us. Not that we're weeping buckets,' confessed Annie. 'Because we aren't. He was a pig. And that's being unkind to pigs. But you want to tell your policeman to look for the mystery woman.'

Her voice had a portentous tone with an edge of irony.

Phryne grinned. 'And who would this mystery woman be?'

'I don't know,' said Annie crossly. 'If we knew that she wouldn't be a mystery woman. She always came to see him after a rehearsal in this hall. Tommy said he saw her but he's not a reliable person. Loves practical jokes. Leg pulls. You know. You could ask him,' she said, suddenly smiling at some wicked thought.

'Do you think he will try to pull my leg?' asked Phryne.

'No, probably not, but it would be nice to watch when you demolish him,' said Annie. 'Tommy's been getting on our nerves lately.'

'You do me too much credit,' murmured Phryne. 'I shall sic my policeman on him. That ought to be sufficient.'

'Thank you,' said Annie.

'Now, Julia, you left the hall with your score and went home—at what time?' asked Phryne.

'Must have been about nine,' said Julia. 'Was it really awful of me to leave him there?' she asked pathetically.

'Nothing could have done him the slightest good at that point,' Phryne reassured her. Annie took Julia back to the tea queue and Phryne drifted over to Jack Robinson.

'He was dead by about nine, and the tray was gone as well,' she told him. 'Rehearsal finished at eight when the lantern lecture started and most of the choir were out of the hall by eight thirty. Some would have gone to the facilities and some stayed to wait for those who had done so, but apart from the caretaker and one soprano the place would have been empty of this choir by eight thirty. The lantern lecture finished at nine and Tregennis was dead by then.'

'I'm not even going to ask how you know that,' Jack Robinson replied.

'Good, because I'm not going to tell you. I suggest that you have a word with that big dark-haired bruiser over there. Name of Tommy. Practical joker. If he found Tregennis dead, he might have thought it amusing to stuff music down his throat.'

'Might he?' asked Robinson. 'Sense of humour, eh? And he's a big bloke, he could have done it.'

Phryne nodded. 'Anything interesting from the interviews?'

'The ones who didn't go to the pub went blamelessly home, some to their doting parents in South Yarra and some to their digs in Carlton,' said Robinson. 'The piano bloke lives in Collins Street at eighty-eight, so just had to totter. Must have been a good piano player before the grog got him, though. Says he played with Beecham. Called Tregennis a butcher.'

'Only musically, Jack dear, just an expression. Right, you get Tommy, and we'd better clear these people backstage—it's time for the lantern lecture on the science of deduction.'

'That sounds like it might be useful,' said Jack Robinson, and went off to apprehend the bass. Phryne snorted. Deduction was not a science. It was an art, and she was very good at it.

•

Phryne slid out into the auditorium and slipped into a seat at the back. The hall was half full, not bad for a summer weekend, when most people would be at the beach. But the Melbourne craze for self-improvement apparently continued. She could see the solid, comfortable outline of Wilson sitting next to the lantern slide projector. And she could hear the speaker. A beautiful voice. A voice that was English, educated without being shrill, deep, rich and perfectly pitched. A voice which could only be compared to Irish coffee with chocolate on top.

She looked at the speaker.

Oh, my.

He was tall and slender. He moved with the assurance of a dancer, occasionally flinging out a hand for emphasis or to point out an equation on the lantern slide. He had a mop of dark curls and a long, pale, sculptured face. Greek? If so, Ancient Greek. Strong. Disdainful, as though he knew that his audience couldn't possibly be bright enough to really appreciate him. And the oddest eyes that Phryne had ever seen. Liquid, quick, set at a cat-like angle, chillingly observant and, Phryne could swear, in some lights lavender or silver.

John Wilson's devotion was instantly explained. Not so the lecture. Phryne knew that she had one flaw (she admitted to one, apart from an occasional nostalgic plunge into the foods of her youth, such as dried apricots): she had no head for mathematics. Smitten young physicists had poured explanations into her ears, and she had or had not seduced them, but she had never understood any physics or mathematics except the Newtonian, because they were the ones which got you shot. Words were being used, concepts explained, that she did not even begin to comprehend.

'When estimating the interpolation error, carefully select the interpolative points and use Tchebyshev polynomials.'

The lecture ended with the last slide. The lights came up. The audience rose, stretched, filtered out. Phryne went to the projector to stand beside John as the lecturer leapt lightly down off the stage and walked forward.

He moves like a cat, she thought. A big cat. Panther,

perhaps. Phryne put a hand on John's arm. 'Introduce me?' she asked.

He smiled at her. 'Of course. This is Rupert Sheffield. The Hon. Miss Phryne Fisher,' he said. 'An old friend of mine whom I have not seen since the war.'

'Delighted,' said Rupert, taking Phryne's hand and bowing a little.

'As am I,' she replied.

'Apart from the fact that you are wealthy, have a black cat in the house, use Jicky and have slightly sprained your ankles dancing, I know little about you,' he told her.

Tit for tat, Phryne thought, and you started it. She smiled up into the amazing lavender—they really were lavender—eyes and said, 'And apart from the fact that you went to Winchester and Cambridge, spent the war breaking codes, have your shoes made by Loeb and your suits in Savile Row—and I think that tie is from Westford's in Soho—use coconut dressing on your hair, are right-handed and a friend of my dear John Wilson, I know very little about *you*.'

John chuckled.

Rupert stiffened and touched his tie. 'Halligen's,' he corrected.

'My mistake,' said Phryne amiably.

'My dear,' said John, 'you have always been exceptional.'

'In many ways,' agreed Phryne. 'What I don't know is whether you would like to come to dinner tomorrow night?'

'You may have John,' conceded the beautiful man, 'since you have a prior claim. I shall be busy. Thinking,' he threw in, as he paced off down the aisle like a panther to whom an indecent suggestion has been made by a gutter cat of no breeding.

'Right,' said Phryne, desperately trying not to laugh. 'It

is offended, see, it stalks away,' she added. The outer door slammed and she giggled helplessly.

'He's a good fellow really,' rumbled John. 'You shouldn't tease him, Phryne.'

'He started it,' Phryne reminded him.

'Phryne, you were in Intelligence, weren't you? After the war?' he asked.

'Yes, for a while. Why?'

'I don't like these . . . accidents. Someone may wish to harm Rupert. Could you . . . ask around?'

'Of course,' said Phryne, patting his cheek. 'Seven, at my house? Here's my card. Try to soothe the poor dear. I don't want to steal you from him, John.'

'You don't . . . no, Phryne, you've got it wrong,' he called after her receding figure.

'Wouldn't be the first time,' she answered, her hand on the backstage door. 'Must go, I've got choristers to grill.'

And then she was gone. John packed up his lantern slides with the slight breathlessness that close contact with Phryne had always given him. It occurred to him that, for the very first time in his life, Rupert Sheffield might have met his match.

Then he chuckled, too.

•

Jack Robinson was not managing the massed choir very well. They milled about. They talked all the time. They wanted to go home. They fretted.

'Herding cats, Jack dear.' Phryne patted him on the arm. 'Watch.'

She stood on a chair with a fine flourish of silk-clad legs, which riveted all the male eyes, and clapped her hands twice. More or less instant silence fell.

'Everyone who went to the pub, take the hand of a person that you know was in the pub with you and walk to the right. Only a person whom you know accompanied you to the pub. To the tune of "Life is But a Melancholy Flower" divided by sop, alto, tenor and bass,' she said, and they began to sing and move like little lambkins.

'*Life is but a, life is but a,*' sang the basses.

'*Melancholy flower, Melancholy flower,*' sang the tenors.

'*Life is butter melon, life is butter melon,*' sang the altos.

'*Cauliflower, cauliflower,*' sang the sopranos.

Silly sort of song, reflected Jack, but it was working. Most of the choir were grouped together, still singing their nonsensical round. Eleven of them remained, those who had gone blamelessly home. Apart from the ineffable Julia, they named themselves as Jenny Leaper, soprano; Helen Burke, alto; and one Tabitha Willis, a vibrant young woman with black curls who exuded such an air of health and well-being that Phryne found herself smiling at her. You could cure a migraine just by leaning on her shoulder. She, of course, was also an alto. The other soprano was Chloe McMahon, who had the heft and force of a woman destined for Wagner, an armoured brassiere and a horned helmet. Formidable. The others were all male, the pianist, tenors and basses. Which rather cut down their chances of being the mystery woman, although Miss Fisher knew some very strange people. Mr Tregennis was probably not a candidate for one of Krafft-Ebing's studies, as he had been molesting the female choir members exclusively. She led them away in a group to allow Detective Inspector Robinson to question the ladies. He shot her a resentful look. She blew him a kiss.

'Well,' she said, perching on a table and again displaying

silk stockings, 'what can you tell me about this regrettable occurrence?'

'Define regrettable,' said a skinny young man with overlong hair and a handful of written notes.

'Oh, do shut up, Len,' said Matthew, the placid blond with the beginnings of a beard. When he grew up he was definitely going to play Father Christmas with conviction and no need for padding. Tasty. Phryne's mind was rather running to men with a certain embonpoint. If only as a contrast to the beautiful Lin Chung, away in Hong Kong on business, drat it all. She restrained herself, as Jack would not look kindly on her seducing the suspects.

'Introduce yourselves,' she told them, and shook hands with, successively, Leonard, tenor and nuisance, he of the notes; Oliver, another economy-size bass, with red hair and a gorgeous smile; a tall and rather languid medical student called Bones; and a palpable gigolo called Luigi. He lingered over her hand, bent to kiss it, and gave her his practised flash of white teeth and a waft of bay rum. She awarded him a glance which smouldered. He preened. That was quite enough of that, she thought.

'Tell me about the conductor,' she said.

'Why are you just talking to us?' demanded Len suspiciously.

'Because, my pet, you have no alibi. You could have doubled back and . . . caused his death. Show me your scores.'

They were produced from bags and satchels. Phryne flicked through them. Every one was complete.

'Good. Now, you were saying?'

'He wasn't a very nice man,' said Matthew.

'He was a pig,' riposted Oliver, blushing with annoyance. 'He couldn't keep his hands off the ladies of the choir. Some of them were threatening to leave.'

'I was in favour of speaking very severely to him,' said Matthew. 'But the others wouldn't let me.'

'Because he came cheap, you see,' said Bones the medical student. 'We're only semi-professional, we haven't got a lot to spend on conductors when we have to pay the orchestra.'

'Tell me,' said Phryne to him, 'do you work in a hospital?'

'Not yet, they aren't going to loose us on the wards, not even in a free clinic,' he replied. 'Why?'

'Drugs,' said Phryne mysteriously.

'Oh,' exclaimed Oliver. 'He was poisoned?'

'Among other things. Anyone drug in your choir?'

'Us? How could we afford drugs? And they affect the voice,' Matthew told her. 'We might drink a bit much sometimes . . .'

'Most times . . .' said Oliver.

'When we have a chance . . .' put in Leonard.

'Or when someone else is buying . . .' agreed Bones.

'But we don't take drugs,' concluded Matthew. Fugues, thought Phryne; they were obviously contagious. Like singing in harmony. The main choir was still buttering melons.

'And what about this mystery woman?' she asked.

'Tommy said he saw her,' said Matthew.

'But you don't altogether believe him,' said Phryne.

They gazed at her, astonished.

'How did you know that? No, never mind, let's get on—I want to get home before morning or I'll be sleeping in the back garden again,' grumbled Len. 'No, we don't. We were curious about her. I even hung about one night hoping to catch sight of her. But I didn't. Can we go home now?'

'Who's taking over as concert master until you get a new conductor?' asked Phryne.

'Me,' said Matthew. 'I'll do, in a pinch.'

'You don't want to be a conductor?' asked Phryne.

'No,' said Matthew. 'I want to be a diplomat. Languages.'

'My card,' said Phryne, handing them out. 'Telephone if you remember anything you don't quite want to tell a policeman without a little . . . filtering.'

She gave them a comprehensive smile, and wandered over to join the ladies. Who were reducing Robinson to spluttering fury. They seemed incapable of speaking one at a time or keeping to a subject.

'This way, ladies.' Phryne led Chloe away by one smooth, pearly, dimpled hand and the others followed as if towed. She formed them into a neat half-circle and scanned every face.

'All right, you have ten minutes to tell me about the mystery woman, one at a time, or I'll give you back to that poor detective inspector and he can lock you up for the night. He's about three, perhaps two and a half inches from the end of his tether. Right? Then we all get to go home.'

'Right,' said the alto Tabitha, shaking her dark curls. 'The mystery woman wasn't one of us.'

'Very well,' said Phryne, who knew how interconnected choirs were, and how impossible it was to keep a secret among them. 'Who is she?'

'Not sure,' said Chloe in her creamy voice. 'Tommy said he saw her but . . .'

'You don't believe Tommy, yes, I know. Any more clues?'

'She was tall,' offered Julia. 'I heard her walking down the corridor and she had flat shoes on.'

'And that makes her tall?' questioned Tabitha.

'Yes, Tab, because you know how he hated any woman being taller than him and you know how he loved high heels,' explained Julia. Phryne thought about it. It made a certain kind of sense. Julia sense, in fact.

'She brought him food,' said Helen. 'When I went into

the conductor's room the next day, I could always smell food. Expensive food. My mother is a very good cook.'

'Hotel food,' said Jenny, who was small and dynamic. 'He didn't offer to share it with us!'

'And he was secretive about her,' said Chloe.

'I think she might have been a musician,' said Tabitha.

'Why?' asked Phryne.

'The orchestral score was always open on the desk when she had been there the night before,' said Tabitha, thinking about it. 'If she had been a singer it would have been the score for voice.'

'And Tommy said she had black hair,' said Chloe, 'but we don't—'

'All right. Scores.'

They were produced. Phryne flicked through them. No pages missing but some rather good cartoons of a pig in a suit, waving a conductor's baton. That would be Miss Willis. Phryne checked the name pencilled in the front. Right. She glanced at Miss Willis and she grinned.

'Cards.' Phryne distributed them. 'Call me if you remember anything which you need to tell the cops without attribution. Clear?' She scanned the faces again. They nodded.

Phryne dismissed them. The rest of the choir was sent out, singing a new round. '*London's burning, London's burning . . .*'

'The mystery woman,' Phryne told Jack, 'probably has black hair or blonde hair, is probably taller than the conductor, might be a musician, and always brings him food. Best I could do, Jack dear.'

'Better than I did,' snarled Jack. 'You going home?'

'And that right speedily,' agreed Phryne, and wafted out to Collins Street, where Mr Butler was patiently awaiting her.

'Did you have an agreeable evening, Miss Fisher?' he asked, putting the Hispano-Suiza into gear.

'Most intriguing,' said Phryne, leaning back into the butter-soft upholstery. 'I met an old friend, heard an incomprehensible lecture, and talked to a lot of singers.'

'And a nice murder,' said Mr Butler comfortably. 'Cocktails when you get home.'

'Mr Butler, you are an ornament to your profession,' commented Phryne, and smiled.

CHAPTER THREE

What Passion cannot Musicke raise and quell?

John Dryden
'A Song for St Cecilia's Day'

Phryne had related all the details she had gleaned about the case of the murdered conductor to her family at a late supper. They all liked supper, because they had been given a high tea at five o'clock to prevent hunger—Mrs Butler abhorred hunger and would not have it in her house—so they were only peckish by nine thirty. Nevertheless, it was fine to sit up late, and grown-up, though by half past ten they were all yawning.

'To bed,' announced Dot.

'Miss Phryne? Can I go and see that mathematical lantern lecture?' asked Jane.

'Certainly. Tomorrow, if you like. Do you want to take Ruth?'

'No,' said Jane. 'She'd be bored. Tink, you want to come?'

'If you like,' said Tinker. He enjoyed being an escort. It made him feel brave. Not that Phryne's children would be in any danger from the actual villains in the city. News like Phryne got around. The fate of previous unwise attackers had also been quite the topic of conversation in Little Lon. It was whispered that certain sharks had a well-fed look and would come to her hand for tidbits of dissected enemy. But there were always larrikins and dolts and drunks. And a young girl on her own was, by default, prey. Not with Sir Edward the Brave in attendance. Tinker had been a small thin boy in a very tough seaside town. What he didn't know about dirty fighting, gouging, biting, kicking and squirrel grips wasn't worth knowing. And this lecture might be interesting. He had discovered a fine natural talent for mathematics. Another way of looking at the world. Anyway, the Guv'nor was having a private dinner with her old friends, and he would have been eating in the kitchen anyway. This way he and Jane could go to Little Bourke Street for a Chinese meal—Lin Chung's family owned several restaurants—go to the lecture and come home in a taxi in the dark. Tinker had never got over being able to just summon up a cab and ride home in luxury. Jane loved them, too. Ruth would like having Mrs Butler to herself, to talk endlessly about food, free of Jane and Tinker imploring them to find another topic of conversation. Good-o all round, he thought.

•

Phryne slept soundly all night, dreaming of Mendelssohn. GBS had been rude about him, and he did tend to write the musical equivalent of fairy floss, but some of the choruses in *Elijah* were superb. 'He Shall Give His Angels Charge Over Thee', for instance. She was singing '*Take all the prophets of Baal, let none of them escape you*' as she came downstairs.

'Good morning, Dot, lovely day—where is everyone?' she

asked. The house seemed strangely quiet. Only Ember and Dot sat in the parlour, Dot embroidering and Ember watching for a chance to stitch himself into the pattern.

'They've gone swimming and taken that dratted dog with them,' said Dot. 'Imagine, she barked at poor Ember!'

'What did Ember do to her?' asked Phryne, speaking from long experience.

'I don't know—it was all over by the time we got to the kitchen,' Dot told her. Phryne inspected Ember. Even for a male black cat, he looked smug.

'I shouldn't be concerned, Dot, I expect that Ember started it. He usually does. Now, I have to send a telegram—anything you want in town?'

'You can just telephone, Miss,' said Dot.

'Not this sort of telegram,' said Phryne. 'I have to send it from the GPO. Fancy a little walk?'

'Oh, yes, please.'

'And we can have lunch in Coles, if you like,' said Phryne generously. For the impoverished Dot, Coles Cafeteria was the height of luxury, and even after having been introduced to raspberry and champagne sorbet made with, as it might be, real fruit, she preferred lime green jelly with artificial cream on top. A concoction which can never have seen an actual lime. Or a real cow. But Phryne could take a few smooths with the rough, and a lunch at Coles would really make her appreciate the delicate cuisine which Mrs Butler had planned for her dinner with Dr MacMillan and Dr Wilson. She could smell the leeks and potatoes cooking. Vichyssoise. Delicious. Since Phryne had encountered both of her guests in France, Mrs Butler had decided on a French menu. Could not be better.

Phryne dressed in a violet suit and dove grey blouse—those eyes, those strange eyes of that annoying man! She had never known that eyes could be that colour. She wondered what they might be like, close, gazing into her own.

That was beyond unlikely. If Phryne was any judge of men, and she was, having intimately encountered many, he was frigid. Probably a virgin. Uninterested in women; probably uninterested in sex. And, thus, uninterested in poor John Wilson, sterling fellow as he undoubtedly was.

Phryne tutted, tilted her shady hat at an attractive angle, took up her bag and gloves and her draft coded message, and left the house. Mr Butler drove Dot and Phryne decorously into the city and left them at the General Post Office, which was the only place in Melbourne where one could send a coded telegram.

The GPO had been erected in Marvellous Melbourne days, when if it wasn't huge, turreted and requiring the same amount of stone as Mycerinus's pyramid, it wasn't a state building. Phryne had always liked it. It was so shiny, so clean, smelling of beeswax and paste, always hurrying to get the mail out on time, to send those vital messages to and from. Commerce, romance, sad news, good news. Testaments and sonnets and love letters and news about the sinking of ships and the landing of cargos; good terms and bad debts and secrets scribbled in darkness. Long wooden counters lined one wall. Rows of cubicles were opposite, and one of them was marked in severe lettering CODING CLERK. In keeping with the opulence of the building, however, the lettering was in gold leaf.

'Coding clerk?' asked Dot. She was a little out of breath after all those steps.

'I am concerned about the company my old friend John is keeping,' said Phryne. 'Rupert Sheffield was in Intelligence in Greece, therefore he was under the command of my friend Compton Mackenzie. Amazing man. An actor from a whole lineage of actors. Has only one subject, which is himself, but an excellent section head and as sharp as a needle. He retired and bought an island in the Hebrides. I am going to ask him about—'

'Mr Sheffield. Is he dangerous? Should we have kept Jane and Tinker away from him?' asked Dot, worried.

'No, I don't think he's dangerous,' said Phryne, trying to analyse her reaction to Sheffield. 'But he might attract danger. I don't know, Dot, but it does no harm to enquire. John Wilson asked me. He is uneasy. So I will. And I can't just send a telegram to Compton in clear. Not if there is something covert going on. I just hope he remembers that alphanumeric. It must be out of date by now.'

'I see,' said Dot. She suppressed a shiver and wandered over to look at a display of postage stamps of all nations. They were very pretty. She wondered where Magyar Posta was.

'Destination, please?' asked the coding clerk, a thin young man who appeared to have been carved out of soap. Phryne wondered if he ever left the building and went into the sun. Perhaps coding clerks were required to live in the cellars, existing on post office glue and old stamps and lost parcels. That explained all those lost Christmas cakes . . .

'The Island of Barra, Outer Hebrides, Scotland, United Kingdom,' said Phryne, sitting down.

He shoved a form across the desk for her to fill in, which she did with commendable patience. He blotted it thoroughly. Then he read it through, stamped one side, turned it over and counter-stamped the other side, and put out his hand for her draft.

'Mr Compton Mackenzie?' he asked.

'The very same,' agreed Phryne, and tried smiling at him.

It had no effect. Another impervious young man! Was she losing her charm?

'And you are the Hon. Miss Phryne Fisher?' he asked.

'Indeed,' said Phryne, handing over her passport. He inspected it carefully and eyed her and the picture narrowly. A very careful young man. Fairly soon Phryne would lose her fight to contain the impulse to swipe him with that elaborate *Post Office Guide* with the red cover. She wondered if the King's monogram would be embossed on his cheek.

Just in time to prevent a breach of regulations, the young man handed back Phryne's passport.

'Two shillings and sixpence,' said the coding clerk, and Phryne paid.

With a twiddle of the fingers, the young man sent the message. His hands were very deft and expressive, unlike the rest of him. In a trice or two, the telegram was off across the world. Phryne wondered what Compton would make of hearing from her after all these years. The answer should be interesting.

Now for a little wander through the city. Dot usually wanted to go to Georges, although she never bought anything there. And, of course, the promised lunch at Coles Cafeteria.

Georges would be amusing, anyway.

•

Phryne and Dot returned home with an armload of bags (Phryne), a small packet of embroidery silk (Dot), a sense of a good morning's work (Dot) and a mild case of heartburn (Phryne, who did not like lunching on one slice of orange, one slice of tomato, one slice of canned beetroot, one slice of onion, one transparent slice of ham, a leaf of lettuce and salad cream). Next time, thought Phryne, I shall miss the lunch and just drink the tea, which was very good. That salad cream would kill slugs. Hasn't done me any good, either. And it really is getting hot. Me for a soothing cool swim and then a soothing cool, scented bath and I fancy lounging around for the rest of the day reading those library books, which will be overdue soon.

Though Phryne was neither mouse nor man, her plan went agley as soon as she walked inside and found that she had visitors. Three choristers, Mr Butler informed her, were waiting for her in the smaller parlour, where they were drinking lemonade and picking out tunes on the piano.

'Leave them to it for a while, Mr B; I need a bath and a change of clothes and some milk of magnesia.'

'I will bring a draught up directly, Miss Fisher,' he told her, and she ascended to her own apartments, where she drew and wallowed in a cool, scented bath. She dressed in a loose silken purple gown patterned with dragons, drank her milk of magnesia ('Coles lunch, Miss Fisher?' sympathised Mr Butler) and sailed down to the smaller parlour, where three voices were extemporising on a Sanctus, as there weren't enough people to sing four-part harmony.

'Sa-a-a-a-an-ctus,' sang a bass.

'S-a-a-a-anctus,' sang a tenor.

'S-a-a-a-anctus,' sang an alto.

'Dominus Deus Sabaoth,' concluded Phryne as she walked in. 'I do like plainchant. A considering cocktail, Mr Butler, if you please. Would you like a drink?' she asked them.

'What a silly question,' said the tenor, the Father Christmas Matthew.

'Foolish indeed,' said the black-haired alto, Tabitha.

'But extremely generous,' said the large economy-sized redhead, Oliver. 'Thank you!'

Mr Butler provided gins and tonics all round. Phryne waited until they had all sipped and then asked, 'Is there a reason for this musical visit?'

'Yes,' said Matthew. He was appreciating Phryne's gown and her delicate bare feet in her sandals. Phryne felt relieved. She hadn't lost 'it', after all. She was gratified, and the young man had a mouth which just needed to be kissed, but she wasn't supposed to be seduced by the suspects, either.

'And that would be?' asked Phryne.

'The mystery woman,' said Tabitha. 'I pinned that idiot Julia down and made her tell me everything she remembered about seeing Mr Tregennis dead. He had sheets of music stuffed down his throat, didn't he?' she demanded.

'He did,' said Phryne. Today's considering cocktail was lemony and sharp, flecked with shaved ice. Delicious.

'Which is why that cop thinks it's us,' said Oliver in his deep rumble.

'Got it in one,' said Phryne.

'The cop called in all the scores,' said Tabitha.

'His name,' Phryne reminded her, 'is Detective Inspector Robinson, and he didn't detain the lot of you last night, so it might be sensible to be polite. Also, he is a friend of mine.'

'Sorry,' Tabitha said conventionally. 'We're a bit upset. Anyway, there are two scores missing. Two choral scores, that is. Was it choral music in his . . . er . . . mouth?'

'I shall find out,' said Phryne. 'Do you know if he was writing anything? A journal, perhaps, a lot of letters? His wastepaper basket was full of torn paper when your Julia saw it. It was empty when he was found.'

'No idea.' Tabitha consulted her colleagues and received head shakes all round.

'She saw a teapot and cup. They were also gone,' said Phryne. 'Any ideas?'

'He always had a teapot and cup,' said Matthew. 'Insisted on not drinking our tea, which is fair enough, that urn leaves a copper deposit on the teeth. I've tried to scour it but it really needs sandblasting. Or mining. It was an institution teapot, made of stainless steel, and his cup was a Coles china cup, thick, with a blue ring around the edge. It's missing?'

'It is,' said Phryne.

'Odd,' said Matthew.

Tabitha retrieved the conversation.

'Anyway, the missing scores belong to Oliver and Chloe. And we didn't do it.'

'No?' asked Phryne.

'No, really not,' Matthew assured her. 'He was a nasty man and definitely deserved a thump or two, but not death. Not for being grabby with sopranos and unpleasant to the tenors. That's not uncommon. Chloe really only cares about music. She wants to sing the Ring Cycle, and she might. She never even listened to what Tregennis was saying about the sopranos. She knows how good she is. And he didn't grab her much.'

'All right, where were the scores left?' asked Phryne.

'Last I saw mine I left it on the piano,' rumbled Oliver. 'Then I had to rush off to my father's office, and I forgot it. That was two weeks ago. Haven't been able to find it since.'

'Did you tell the librarian?' asked Phryne.

'No, because she'd fine me and I haven't even so much as a split pea until next week,' confessed Oliver, blushing red to match his hair.

'And Chloe put hers down on a chair. She put her straw hat on top,' Tabitha told her. 'When she came back the hat was there but the score was gone. She didn't think anything of it, because scores get mixed up. We're not supposed to permanently mark them so someone who ripped pages out of theirs might have taken hers and rubbed out the pencilling and substituted their own.'

'So they might, but that assumes that the score stealer is a chorister, and the chorister is also the murderer. We really don't know that. Besides, you told me that the choir didn't do it. It is a capital mistake,' quoted Phryne from Conan Doyle—her mind really was running on the Science of Deduction lately, for some reason—'to theorise ahead of one's data. All we know is that someone pinched your scores. Tell me what you have gleaned about the mystery woman.'

'We don't think she's a singer. She might be a violinist. Jenny remembered seeing a bow in the conductor's room—more than once.'

'How well do you know your orchestra?' asked Phryne.

'They don't mix with us,' said Matthew. 'Professionals, you know, where we're just amateurs.'

'And your répétiteur?' asked Phryne. Eyes widened.

'Professor Szabo?' boomed Oliver. 'He's an old darling. Was a great pianist once.'

'Before the grog got him?' asked Phryne. They boggled at her acumen.

'Yes, poor old man. But he likes us and he plays well enough for a rehearsal. He lives in one room in that seedy apartment house and likes to get out occasionally.'

Matthew clearly had a soft spot for Professor Szabo. Possibly he had a soft spot for anything weak or damaged. He definitely had a house full of ailing kittens and three-legged dogs and probably lame ducks, too.

'Tell me about yourselves. Are you all students?'

'Yes,' said Tabitha. 'I'm vet sci. That means I get to fix all of Matthew's wretched pets. Matt's arts and languages. Oliver's commerce. His father's a capitalist. Not that you'd know from Oliver. He's as poor as a church mouse.'

'I say, Tab,' murmured Oliver.

'And his brother's a famous actor,' added Tabitha. 'Oliver lives with his father in Kew. I live with my family in Yarraville. Matthew lives with his aged evil grandmother in Carlton. We all attend the University of Melbourne. Is that enough for you?' she demanded.

'Oh, no,' cooed Phryne. 'Not nearly enough—but enough for now.'

Mr Butler entered. 'Detective Inspector Robinson, Miss Fisher.'

'Oh, help,' said Tabitha.

'Very well, Mr Butler, I shall be there directly. Could you put him in the parlour, and then take these young persons out through the kitchen? After they have written their names and addresses on this piece of paper. Drink up, darlings,' said Phryne. 'I decline to get involved in a French farce. Mr B, while you're in the kitchen, I suspect Mr Robinson would like a few sandwiches, if there are some left over from your lunch, which must have been better than mine. Au revoir,' said Phryne, and floated out after the butler.

The choristers exchanged glances.

'Strewth,' said Oliver.

They all agreed.

•

'Jack dear, you look hot,' she observed, as she sat down near the sweat-drenched policeman who was wiping his forehead with his handkerchief.

'More Science of Deduction, eh?' snarled Robinson.

Phryne was taken aback. Jack did not usually snarl at her without a reason.

'Whatever is wrong?' she asked, patting the hand not holding the handkerchief.

'I'm so sorry, Phryne,' he said, grasping her hand. 'I shouldn't snap at you when all I want to do is deck that snobby Englishman.'

'Oh, Rupert Sheffield has been helping you, has he?' asked Phryne maliciously. Jack had clearly brought this dreadful fate upon himself.

'Helping! Stalking around making observations! Telling us that we were idiots!'

'Ah,' said Phryne, pleased. 'The very intelligent quite often have no manners. And no tact,' she added. 'Come, here's Mr Butler with a pint of iced soda water, a nice bottle of beer and a selection of dainties, as I expect that you have not had lunch.'

'Thanks, and sorry,' said Robinson, grabbing the soda water and draining it in a draught, then starting on the beer and sandwiches as though he was starving. With his mouth full, he directed Phryne's attention to a file on the table, and she took it up and leafed through it as he methodically cleared the tray of anything edible in a manner made famous by the Sunshine Harvester Factory's best-selling machine. Mr Butler, almost raising one eyebrow, took the tray away and brought it back, reloaded. That American Refrigerating Machine kept leftovers nice and cool and moist, but if this demand continued he might have to wake Mrs B from her after-lunch nap and request more food, and that would not be conducive to domestic harmony. Mrs Butler valued her rest, having earned it.

Fortunately, halfway through the replenished sandwiches, Jack Robinson was slowing down.

'So, no breakfast, either?' asked Phryne.

'Y'know, we don't appreciate you,' said Robinson, fingers hovering over the selection of sandwiches. Egg next, or perhaps ham? He took both. He was not up to complex decisions at the moment. The presence of Rupert Sheffield had left bruises on his amour-propre.

'You don't?' asked Phryne, collecting a potted shrimp sandwich for herself. Her insides had quite settled.

'No,' said Jack. 'You could do the same as that . . . bloke. You're as clever as him. Cleverer, probably. You could make me feel like a dolt, easy. But you don't.'

'No, because I like you, and you are not and have never been a dolt. Dismiss the thought from your mind,' said Phryne, making a fluttering motion with her fingers which mimed the thought flying off like a butterfly. 'And do not let some up-jumped overeducated mannequin tell you otherwise. What did he see that we didn't see?'

'Made the point about the scores,' said Jack. 'About the missing teapot and cup, the missing tray, the mystery woman.'

'Nothing new really,' said Robinson. 'It was just the way he said it all.'

'Good. Now drink your beer and we'll summarise. The music in the conductor's mouth was indeed from a choral score of Mendelssohn's *Elijah*. That is on open sale. Easy to find. Might not have anything to do with the actual Harmony Choir. There are two scores missing, one belonging to Chloe McMahon and the other to that large red-haired chap, Oliver. Neither seem to have a reason to kill the conductor. They are not romantically involved and, in any case, Miss McMahon was only occasionally the subject of the conductor's unwelcome attentions. Matthew, their friend, professed a desire to thump the victim, but by the sound of him that would not be a rare impulse.'

'Yes,' said Robinson, bolstered by the beer, the food, and Miss Fisher's decorative and comforting company. 'I always like cases when the victim's been practically begging to be killed. It means I don't have to be sorry for him.'

'Oh, I do know what you mean, Jack dear.' Phryne beamed on her favourite policeman. For the first time since Rupert Sheffield had entered his life, Jack Robinson smiled. Phryne went on.

'The scribbled pages have been collected by a cardboard manufacturer and you don't think that there's a chance of finding them—and neither do I. You have very sensibly secured the conductor's residence. When it is searched I think you will find love letters—I think that is what he was writing. Either a love letter, or a letter breaking off the relationship. Attempts to write those sort of letters tend to fill the wastepaper basket with failed drafts. Not letters to banks or creditors. This feels like a personal murder, Jack dear, does it not? A domestic murder.'

'With added music,' Jack reminded her.

'Might be an afterthought. Might even be a different person.'

'Don't,' groaned Robinson.

'Do we know where the food came from?' Phryne reminded him.

'Still asking,' said Jack, heaving himself to his feet.

'And did anyone happen to to look out of their window and notice a woman walk into the hall? Any person, in fact. The mystery woman was supposed to be black-haired, but there are blonde hairs on his coat.'

'We got that one,' he said. 'The victim tried to . . . embrace Miss Chloe. He grabbed her and some of her hair got on his coat. She kicked herself free, which explains the bruise on the victim's shin.'

'Odious man,' commented Phryne.

'Too right,' said Jack. 'Thanks,' he said, taking her hand. 'You've been . . . kind. And we really do appreciate you. Thanks,' he said again, and Mr Butler let him out.

Phryne sat down and requested another cocktail. Jack had quite forgotten that he had left the file on Phryne's table. She would read it again before he remembered and sent someone to fetch it. Things like files and scores did get misplaced, she thought. Now for a nice drink, and a nap. She had guests to dinner, and as they were old friends, it might be a long night. Phryne accepted her drink, carried it and the file upstairs to her boudoir, and lay down on her sumptuous couch, sipping and reading, until she was sleepy enough to close her eyes and rest.

CHAPTER FOUR

There must be spirits willing to be driven
To that immeasurable blackness, or
To those old landscapes, endlessly regiven,
Whence Hell and Heaven itself were both begotten.

Wallace Stevens
'For an Old Woman in a Wig'

Ruth had seen Jane and Tinker off to catch the train into the city and had returned to the kitchen, where Mrs Butler was perfecting her French dinner. It was a lovely menu, delicate and light, as befitted the close, humid weather. Cold leek and potato soup. Little pastry boats filled with minced chicken or fish in a white sauce. A large green salad, a tomato and spring onion salad, a cold roast of beef with horseradish or port wine jelly to taste, cold roasted chickens with sage and onion stuffing, with a variety of crisp cold vegetables, each with their proper sauces. Fruit salad. A marmalade-filled roulade with slices of sugared oranges and crème Chantilly which was even now rolling in its damp tea towel as though there were no such things as culinary accidents in the world. Cheeses and fruits and coffee or tea. Ember had been fed, and was now licking leftover whipped cream off Ruth's finger. Molly had been fed and shut out in the back garden, where she would not get underfoot. Molly was of the opinion that a sufficiently distracted cook dropped things. This was true. She had caught a pastry bateau, a scrap of chicken skin and a lump of codfish roe. But the last one had been an empty saucepan which had narrowly missed her head, so she had been gagged with a large bone and sent out to recover her wits in peace. Mrs Butler directed Ruth to slice the rye bread which would accompany the soup. Ruth dipped the big carving knife in hot water and sliced with extreme concentration.

'Good,' said the cook, stretching and massaging the small of her back. 'You've been a real help, dear. I reckon that's all done. Just fill the coffee percolator for me, will you? And have a bateau. I'm not sure about that pastry in this dratted weather.'

Ruth nibbled. 'Flaky, light and crisp,' she reported. 'As if it would dare to be anything else.'

'That American Refrigerating Machine is so useful,' admitted Mrs Butler. 'Not only nice cold drinks but proper butter pastry—at this temperature! Now, how about a glass of something cold and a nice sit-down? I shall ask Mr Butler to make us a shandy.'

Feeling very grown up, Ruth took off her apron, pulled off her scarf, and accompanied Mrs Butler into the garden. The orchids were doing well, and the scent of jasmine was almost a taste. Presently Mr Butler brought out a tray on which reposed three tall glasses, frosty with cold, in which a delightful golden liquid tinkled. Dot put down her library book.

'Oh, lovely,' she said, taking a glass. 'Thank you so much. It's just getting hotter,' she added.

'And your aspirin, Mrs B,' said Mr Butler.

'Thunderstorms give me a headache,' said Mrs Butler, taking the tablets and swallowing them with the first sip of her shandy.

'Going to storm,' said Dot. 'We'll know as soon as poor Ember dives for the wardrobe.'

'He just can't stand thunderstorms, can you, my darling?' asked Ruth in a besotted voice. Ember, who was sitting on the wrought-iron table, allowed her to stroke his whiskers, which were quivering unpleasantly. Fairly soon it would be time to seek the safe haven of a good thick mahogany wardrobe between him and the weather.

'I hope Jane will be all right,' said Ruth.

'She's got Tinker with her,' said Mrs Butler comfortably. 'He's reliable. And he knows that Mr Lin's people will be keeping an eye out. They seem to think it's their duty, God bless them. Tinker knows the way home. He's smart. And he's probably really nasty to get hold of in a fight. They've got the money for a taxi. All they can get tonight is bored and wet.'

'Of course,' said Dot.

'And this is a buffet dinner, so we can lay it out and then we can all sit down to a nice supper in the kitchen, just us,' said Ruth. She was very fond of Jane and she liked Tinker, but it was nice to have a small gathering. And Dot was interested in food, too.

Ruth sipped at her very first grown-up shandy with contentment in her heart and flour on her plaits.

•

Phryne woke in good time to bathe again, put on an even more silky costume, and take the autopsy report downstairs with her. After all, she had two doctors to dinner. Mr Butler showed her the buffet, covered for the moment with a muslin cloth. He poured her a champagne cocktail. Perfect. Just the right combination of sour and sweet.

'The bottles of Glen Sporran are on the sideboard, Miss, with the ice bucket and the soda. What will the gentleman drink?'

'Good, my dear Dr MacMillan doesn't really drink anything else. And I don't know what John Wilson prefers to drink.'

'You do not know the gentleman well, Miss Fisher?'

'I know him very well. But on a battlefield you drink what you can get. Including a dreadful pastis made, I swear, out of licorice allsorts soaked in medicinal alcohol. And British Army brandy, than which there is none worse.'

She paused, seeing that she was shocking Mr Butler. He shuddered lightly.

'Whatever the gentleman would actually prefer, Miss Fisher, we have it. From very good red wine or white wine or sweet wine or dry wine or sparkling wine to beer or brandy, indeed, though not that British Army liquid, which I have tasted.'

'You have?' Phryne was surprised. She hadn't known that Mr Butler was interested in the mortification of the flesh. He gave a small butlerine wince.

'And it gave me no pleasure. Indeed, I do not think it could actually be called brandy. I would call it rectified spirit with a spoonful of molasses in every bottle. But we have nothing made of licorice. Though he might like real pastis? I shall bring in a bottle in case.'

'Your cellar does you credit, Mr Butler,' Phryne told him. Ah, champagne. There were few situations which the divine drink could not improve. 'In victory, one requires champagne,' a short dark corporal with dreams of empire had declared. 'In defeat, one needs it.'

'*J'ai besoin de toi*,' thought Phryne. John Wilson had said that to her, one freezing lice-ridden night on the Western

Front. 'I have need of you.' In that case, it was to stop the both of them from dying of hypothermia. They were both alive in the morning. A lot of soldiers weren't, had frozen where they lay, curled up like embryos, sunk back into the Great Mother's womb. She recalled the first bath she took, after she left the front, in the Hotel Splendide in Paris. It had taken one scalding disinfectant bath just to kill the lice, body lice and head lice, and another to soothe the myriad bites on her white skin. And a third, highly scented, to take the stench of dead men and high explosive and mud out of her nostrils.

Phryne drank more champagne. It was fine to be alive. And in Australia, where such things did not come.

Dr MacMillan was shown into the parlour and proceeded to shed clothes. Phryne watched, fascinated, wondering how far this naturist urge would go. She stopped at shirt and trousers and bare feet.

'Would you like to change into a gown, Elizabeth?' asked Phryne. 'I've got lots. Silk? Cotton?'

'No, my hinny, just get me a lot of soda water and a triple whisky,' said the doctor. 'I've had the devil of a walk in air that feels like the tropics and the thunder is itching in my head.'

Mr Butler materialised at her side with a miraculous pint of water, a triple whisky on ice, and a paper of aspirins. Dr MacMillan stared at him in amazement.

'Thank you,' she said, taking all three. 'You are a remarkable man.'

'Mrs Butler gets thunderstorm headaches,' he said, explaining his deductions. 'I always have some aspirin in my pocket in this weather. Perhaps a refill?' he asked, as the whisky had unaccountably vanished.

'Indeed,' said Dr MacMillan. She added in Gaelic, '*Moran taing agus beannachdan leat*,' and sipped at her second drink.

'What's been happening with you, my dear doctor?' asked Phryne.

'Oh, women trying to die, staff falling sick, outbreak of measles—the usual things,' said the doctor. 'But your mention of John Wilson has caused me to recall . . . many things which I thought I had forgotten.'

'Me, too,' said Phryne. 'The Somme has been in my mind ever since I met him again.'

'Ach, weel,' said Elizabeth. 'I wonder if he will still call me Lisbet? He said his mother was called Elizabeth and he didn't see me as a Liz. He was a very good man.' She sipped again. 'Like this is very good whisky. I never asked you,' she said, changing the subject, 'where does it come from?'

'Specially made to a secret recipe on the island of Mull,' said Phryne. 'They only make it for me and the Gentlemen's Studio in Carnaby Street.'

'I can taste the peat,' said Dr MacMillan.

'That's how I found Compton Mackenzie again,' explained Phryne. 'He's moved to Barra and is a Highland laird.'

Elizabeth chuckled. 'I did not know him, but they say he puts his whole heart intae whatever the man is being,' she said.

'He does indeed, and I expect he is the most Scottish of all possible Scots, even though he was born in West Hartlepool. I've just sent him a coded telegram.'

'You have, hinny? Why?'

'He was head of Intelligence in Athens, and a very strange man, who is now accompanying our John Wilson, was also there. I wanted to ask about him.'

'His name?'

'Rupert Sheffield. He detested me on sight.'

'And the feeling was returned in full measure?' Dr MacMillan knew Phryne very well.

'I'm not at all sure,' said Phryne slowly, holding out her glass and receiving another champagne cocktail from the attentive Mr Butler. 'He is very beautiful, but alien, an angel or a demon.'

'Fey?' Elizabeth MacMillan was from the highlands, herself.

'Yes, that's what's worrying me. That neck-or-nothing, tare-an'-hounds drawling Cambridge courage which is a cover for despair. The ones who rush into the frontlines and win medals for bravery because they don't care if they live or die. And some not only die, but they are the cause of death in others. I don't like it. He's here doing a lantern show on the Science of Deduction. Ostensibly. And he's insulted my favourite policeman.'

'The good Jack Robinson?' clucked Elizabeth.

'The same.'

'I've never heard of the man,' said the doctor. 'But I stayed in France and then went home to Scotland and I didn't meet you, m'dear, until the flu epidemic. But I knew John Wilson. He wasn't even a doctor then—did he qualify?' Phryne nodded. 'Well, iphm, I would have expected it. I received the patients from his clearing station—ay, and they were well cared for, held together, stitched in lantern light, even emergency amputations. Most of them lived, which argues skill, and most of them thanked him, which argues compassion. I myself plugged up the hole in his leg when they brought him back to me, thankful that he had a Blighty wound, after some Hun sniper had targeted his Red Cross tent.'

'And I only got to you, Lisbet, my dear, because Phryne drove her ambulance between me and said Hun,' said a voice from the door. 'At serious risk of her irreplaceable life, might I add.'

'John Wilson,' exclaimed Elizabeth MacMillan, rising to

her feet and embracing him. 'I wondered how you got on, my hinny! You never wrote. I feared that . . . I was feared. But here you are.'

'Here I am,' he said, and kissed her on the cheek. 'And you look just the same, short hair and trousers, just as you were.'

'Did that bad girl really drive her ambulance in front of a sniper?' asked Elizabeth.

'She did. Ruined his day and saved my skin.'

'You still got shot,' Phryne pointed out. 'It didn't work. And I stripped the gears, such as they were. You were wounded.'

'But not shot dead,' said John, dragging her into his arms. She kissed him cordially on the mouth. He tasted tired and discouraged.

'She's always been a wild child,' said Elizabeth. 'Wait till I tell you about her landing a plane on a Hebridean beach during the flu epidemic. Now, sit, man, what will you drink?'

'What have you got?' asked John, limping towards a solid chair and leaning his cane against it. He tried to conceal his sigh of relief when he sat down and the weight was off his wounded leg.

'Knowing the admirable Mr Butler, my man, anything your heart desires,' said Elizabeth.

'Really anything?' asked John. He was in pain, Phryne noticed, chronic pain, the little wrinkles around the eyes, the careful movements. Stoic, that was John. I bet he arrived at Elizabeth's field hospital making the stretcher-bearers laugh at his jokes. He needs amusement and distraction. We can do that.

'Really,' Phryne assured him. 'I would trust Mr Butler's cellar against any request. Wine? Beer? Cider? Brandy? Gin? Dr Mac's Glen Sporran whisky? Name your poison, my dear. I'm drinking a champagne cocktail and about to venture on a glass or two of wine to go with the cold supper.'

'Pastis?' asked John hopefully.

Mr Butler unbent enough to smile. 'Sir,' he said, and produced the bottle, a glass of ice and a little jug of water.

'Amazing,' said John. He poured and diluted the spirit until it was as white as milk. He sipped. It tasted much better than ethanol and liquorice allsorts. 'I've been thinking about France all day,' he confessed, and Phryne and Dr Mac laughed.

'So have we,' said Phryne. 'Ever since I saw you again. And we have a French dinner. Mrs Butler is a gem amongst cooks. Another drink, or are you hungry?'

'Starved,' he said.

'Ravenous,' said Dr Mac.

'Then we shall dine,' said Phryne. 'Here are comestibles of the best; do you remember that Gascon who sold cakes? He used to say that.'

'Very superior comestibles,' said John. 'Much better than those sawdust brioche he used to sell, the rascal.'

'Sit, and I shall serve you,' said Phryne. When John protested, Mr Butler murmured in his ear, 'If you would indicate your preference, sir, it would be my pleasure to serve you.'

'A bit of everything, especially roast beef with jelly,' said John helplessly. He was staying in a good hotel but this was a lavish feast even by hotel standards. Mr Butler brought him a small bowl of vichyssoise, and a plate laden with a selection of the available food. It looked lovely and he was very hungry. Sheffield never had time for lunch. It was a meal to which John was rather attached. The pastis had sharpened his appetite and it didn't actually need sharpening.

'Some hae meat and cannae eat,' began Elizabeth, 'and some can eat and want it: but we hae meat and we can eat and so the Lord be thankit.'

'Amen,' said John, and picked up his cutlery. He drank

his vichyssoise first, and it was very good, and then attacked a mound of rare roast beef of such quality that he tried not to whimper in gratitude. Phryne ate petits bateaux and talked amusingly about her home and her family and her profession. He gathered that she was a private detective, had three adopted children and some connection with Chinatown which he could not quite fathom. One piece of news made him swallow and attempt to speak.

'Good gracious, Phryne, your sister Eliza is in Australia?'

'All of the outsiders end up exiled to Australia,' she told him airily. 'She's a Sapphic and her beloved came here. Actually, it was rather exciting for a while. It was just like one of Ruth's romances with more sacks and guns and fewer roses. And a mummified man from a funfair. And they went on to do Fabian good works in St Kilda. Father isn't speaking to either of us, thank God.'

'I am never going to get this straight,' said John, not at all cast down. He ate some more roast beef and handed his plate to Mr Butler for a refill.

Really, thought that admirable functionary, Miss Fisher's friends have all been starving today. Luckily it is a generous house. There is no lack, thought Mr Butler complacently, and supplied John with more rare beef and potato salad. The doctor's preferred drink, apart from pastis, was a robust red wine. Very suitable. Mr Butler refilled his glass. This friend of Miss Fisher's was a war hero. He should have the best that the Fisher ménage had to offer. Who knew how many young men lived because of Dr John Wilson? And nearly at the cost of himself. It was like Miss Fisher to think of a solution to a sniper in time to save a friend's life. Bold but not really reckless. Those ambulances had armoured sides.

Mr Butler decided he should create another cocktail for her

on the morrow. He would call it 'Phryne'. Sour, certainly, with a lime juice base, perhaps, and . . . Cointreau? Cherry brandy? Noyau? This would require study.

Meanwhile, there was dinner to serve. The doctor was underfed. This would be remedied.

'Wonderful food,' said Dr MacMillan. 'What's in that little pastry thing?'

'Minced cooked chicken with *sauce blanc* and chives,' Phryne replied. 'Have another.'

'I shall,' said Dr MacMillan, and did. John tried the roast chicken. He tried the carrots in Vichy water. He nibbled at celery with cream cheese. It was all delicious.

'I feel like a python who has been given his very own water buffalo,' he said, finally laying down his knife and fork. 'No, Mr Butler, I couldn't eat another bite. Thank you very kindly.'

Mr Butler bowed and withdrew. Dessert and coffee were all prepared. Now he could go to the kitchen, loosen his braces, take off his shoes, and dine lavishly on extras and have a few glasses of that red, which was really very palatable. There were at least ten more bottles of it in the cellar.

'John dear, you were famished,' commented Phryne. 'What have you been doing all day?'

'Had to go along with Sheffield to see some people, and he walks very fast on those long shanks; it's hard for him to remember that I'm an old crock. Then he got into an argument with a policemen. Then more visits to various people. I missed lunch.'

'There's a lot of that about,' said Phryne. Walks too fast for a war-damaged man, *un mutilé de guerre*, to keep up, does he? The hound. Rupert was going down in her estimation like a rock in seawater.

'I've got an interesting case from that same policeman,' she said lightly. 'I'll ask you about it after dessert.'

'Oh, yes, you're a private eye, aren't you? How very enterprising of you, Phryne,' said John. He felt contented. That had been a very good dinner and here were two people who unaffectedly liked and approved of him. It was a change from his usual company. He relaxed and his scarred leg began to hurt less. Both women noticed this and resolved to keep him in that condition.

'This weather,' grumbled Dr MacMillan. 'How anyone knows what to expect is beyond me. This very week it has been hot, cold, wet, windy and sunny.'

'And that was only Wednesday,' laughed Phryne. 'You'll become accustomed, Elizabeth. You'll know that you've settled in when you reach for your umbrella and your sunhat together.'

'It's better than London,' said John. 'Rain, cold, more rain, occasional bursts of spring so beautiful that it breaks the heart, and then—for a change—rain.'

'And then days when it is so hot that you swelter, just in time to catch pneumonia because the weather changes and you're out in a storm in insufficient clothing,' agreed Phryne. 'How about a little more wine?'

'A little more,' said John. His kindly blue eyes surveyed Phryne and Elizabeth sitting side by side on the sofa, looking innocuous, which was not like them at all, either of them. It would be very pleasant to allow them to continue being considerate of his feelings. It had been a long time since anyone had worried about what he felt. A very long time since he had sat in a comfortable parlour with two people who knew him from the war and still liked him. But it would not do. He straightened up a little.

'All right, lovely ladies,' he said, and smiled. 'Ask me

whatever you like, and I'll tell you. And I'll ask whatever I like, and you will tell me. Deal?'

'Are you sure, sweetheart?' asked Phryne.

'I am,' he told her. She leaned forward and patted his shoulder.

'I put on the tourniquet and got you loaded up,' said Phryne. 'We were all shocked. Young Ginger was crying.'

'You kissed me,' he said.

'Of course I did,' responded Phryne. 'Then they took you off and there was a bombardment. Almost the last one of the war. You arrived at Elizabeth's hospital. Go on from there.'

'Lisbet knows better than I,' he told her. 'I only remember the jolting of the stretcher. I heard someone shout, "The doc's copped it!" My leg burned like fire. Then I woke up, days later.'

'I took out the bullet,' reported Elizabeth, 'but it had done a good deal of damage. Missed the main arterial structure, but smashed the femur and ripped through muscle and tendon. I put him back together again as best I could, dealt with the inevitable fever, and—'

'You used to sit by my bed,' he said to her, tenderly. 'You held my hand. Once you even fell asleep, your head on my arm. I remember the nurses tiptoeing around you. They said you'd been awake and operating for forty-nine hours. You were absolutely soaked in blood.'

'And none of it mine.' Elizabeth wiped her eyes. 'Lord, yes, I recall those two days; they brought in four transports, one after another. I couldnae tell them to bring no more, with them dyin' in heaps. And I thought I had a hard day today.' She laughed briefly.

'I've always wondered,' said John. 'With the femur in that condition, and a reasonable stump left, why didn't you amputate?'

'Because it was you, my mannie.' Elizabeth wiped her eyes with the back of her hand. 'I thought, if I could save one, if I could only save one limb, it would be yours. Outsiders must stick together. I wanted you to go home to your young man with both legs.'

'I never knew that,' John told her. 'Thank you.'

'It almost didn't work. You seemed obstinately set on dyin'.'

'But you wouldn't let me,' he said gently.

'I would not. When we discharged you to the convalescent home you were expecting to go back to university and finish your degree. Was your young man not waiting for you?'

John smiled sadly. 'Oh, yes, he was. We got digs together and never slept apart one night for three years. Art was a sweet, gentle boy. And then he died, and I couldn't seem to care about anyone else. I qualified and worked in the Royal Free in London. In Accident and Emergency.'

'But that wasn't enough,' hinted Phryne.

'No,' said John. He drank more wine. 'I was quite comfortable, had my room in the doctors' lodgings, but I was slowly going mad. Dreams. Nightmares. And this confounded leg. Working on the wards always aggravated it. I decided that I would emigrate, to New Zealand, perhaps—that was far enough away from my memories. Then I thought, no, that's foolish, the memories were part of me, I couldn't escape them by running away. So I went looking for a service flat, found that Rupert Sheffield had a very good two-bedroom place, and needed a fellow lodger. That's when Sheffield came into my life.'

'Ah,' said Phryne. 'So you live together?'

'Yes, but not like that, Phryne.'

'I understand,' she replied. 'I know the sort. The body is just a machine to support the mind.'

'The mind/brain hypothesis is very interesting,' said Elizabeth, picking at her marmalade roulade. It was superb.

'He needs someone to look after him,' said Phryne relentlessly. 'To make sure he eats and sleeps occasionally. To soothe people after he has insulted them. He needs you, though I bet he hasn't noticed that he does, or thanks you for your care.'

'No, he hasn't,' said John, reddening a little. 'But I wouldn't have expected him to notice.'

'And you, my mannie, need someone to look after,' said Elizabeth. 'I can comprehend that.'

'And he is gorgeous,' said Phryne.

'And blazingly intelligent,' said John. 'He really can do some of the things which Sherlock Holmes could do. After all, Sherlock was based on Dr Joseph Bell, Conan Doyle's mentor at Edinburgh Medical School.'

'And still a legend when I was there.' Elizabeth felt that she could possibly manage just one more mouthful of roulade.

'Was he, Lisbet?' asked John.

'Och, yes. The professors all told stories about him. Observation, that was his watchword. "You must see everything, or why did the good Lord give you eyes?" He used to run diagnosis classes—they still do. A person comes in and sits down and the students are allowed to look as much as they like, but not to ask questions. So my own Professor McIver, as a student, diagnosed the subject as an alcoholic. Bell challenged him, and he said, alcoholic skin, tremor, unfocused eyes, and so on, and Bell told him he was right, very good, "You see but you do not observe," and directed him to look at the man's coat pocket. Which contained a half-empty bottle of cheap whisky.'

John and Phryne laughed.

'What do you know about Rupert, then?' asked Phryne. 'Family? Background?'

'Oh, Winchester, his father's a life peer.'

'Oh, good,' said Phryne. 'I outrank him.'

'Phryne!' exclaimed Elizabeth.

'Sorry,' said Phryne unconvincingly. Usually she never thought her father's title to a minor and unimportant barony at all significant. But it was pleasant to have something which Rupert Sheffield, for all his aristocratic airs, didn't have.

'He volunteered for Intelligence, he was finishing a maths degree at Cambridge, and went out to Greece to break codes. He's never talked much about it.'

'That is as it should be,' said Phryne. 'I did a little Intelligence work too, as you know, but I have never spoken of it. Besides, it was messy.'

'When you say "messy", my dear, are you referring to . . .' Phryne waited for the end of Elizabeth's question. 'On second thought, do not answer that. Even if I ask again, I must beg you never to tell me what you meant. As you say, it should not be spoken of.'

Phryne nodded. 'You know, the war did terrible things to us,' she said, toying with her glass of wine.

'Ay, it did,' said Elizabeth. 'I learned the meaning of despair, and I have never forgotten it.'

'It made me, at least, quite ruthless and willing to kill,' said Phryne.

'Indeed,' agreed John. 'I saw you shoot that trench raider with a smile on your lips. I would have done it, too, but you had my Webley.'

'You wouldn't have reacted fast enough,' Phryne replied. 'You are essentially a very good man and you are a doctor: doctors don't want to kill things. Whereas I . . . don't mind. If I have to, to prevent injury to the people I am protecting.'

'And how did you get my Webley, anyway?' asked John. 'I was so relieved I never thought to ask.'

'I picked your holster,' answered Phryne. 'If that is the right term. I gave it back,' she protested. 'Ginger found me one a couple of days later. There was no shortage of abandoned weapons at your place, John dear.'

'That's true,' he said, remembering.

'And the Webley Mark VI is a good solid weapon, though heavy, getting on for three pounds; I had to use two hands to hold the thing. And a large calibre at .455. Now my little Beretta is only a .22, but has quite enough punch for anything I might need it for. Threats, mostly,' said Phryne.

'Even your Detective Inspector Robinson might find it hard to ignore you shooting someone in Melbourne, Phryne,' said Elizabeth.

'Yes, so I shall try very hard not to do that. Poor man is harrowed enough. Your Sheffield gave him the rounds of the assembly hall and called him an idiot.'

'I know. I was there. I'm so sorry,' said John dotingly. 'He really has no manners at all.'

'And yet "manners makyth man", that's the motto of his school,' Phryne told him.

'The only things from school that seem to have stuck are quadratic equations and a very acute clothes sense,' said John. 'Now you, Lisbet, how did you come to this far-flung place?'

'I was restless and bored and Europe was ruined,' Elizabeth replied. 'There was an appeal for female doctors from the Queen Victoria Hospital. I got passage on a ship and there was Phryne. She was coming here to investigate a suspected poisoning. Then I went to work, and now I have a little house, a friend, and a lot of roses.'

'A friend? Or a lover?' asked John.

'Both,' Elizabeth smiled. 'Her name is Marie, she's Scots from Inverness, and she just wants to stay home and keep house, which is why I had to get a house. But I do like growing roses.'

'Not a sane one amongst the three of us,' murmured John.

Phryne laughed and kissed him. 'We shall be happy lunatics,' she told him. 'Sanity is overrated. Let's move into the parlour. There are liqueurs and coffee and tea and things like that. I am having . . . let me see.'

They did not assist John in rising, finding his cane, or moving to another room, for which he was very grateful. He sank down onto a soft aquamarine leather sofa in a cool green and blue room. A life-size nude painting of Phryne pouring water from an amphora riveted his attention.

'You were an artists' model, Phryne?' he asked.

'Certainly. It's called *La Source*. Isn't she beautiful?'

'Too thin,' said Dr MacMillan. 'You were all bones at that age, girrl, I can count them.'

'But that's how I remember you,' said John, accepting a small glass of the whisky. 'Just like that. Smudgier, perhaps, dirtier. We were always grimy.'

'You too, darling; the only clean things about you were your hands,' teased Phryne.

'But you always smelt lovely,' said John. 'Now I come to think of it, how on earth did you manage that? I remember burying my face in your neck and smelling that spicy, flowery, utterly unlikely scent.'

'The only cosmetics I took with me to war were cold cream and a large flask of Stephanotis. Still one of my favourites. Here,' said Phryne, perching on the arm of the sofa and allowing his head to incline into her neck, under the swinging hair.

John took a deep breath, and was flooded with obscene reminiscences.

'So you do,' he stammered. 'Delightful.'

Phryne released him and took her own chair. She had a glass of ice, in which a very small amount of green chartreuse puddled. He wondered if she had chosen the drink to match the room. Phryne was wearing evening pyjamas of pearly, undersea silk. She might easily have had some mermaid in her ancestry. He suspected as much. She could probably swim like a fish.

The conversation roved over Australia (extraordinary), international affairs (ghastly as ever) and medical practice (innovations in infection control). John and Elizabeth talked about Edinburgh and John talked about Rupert Sheffield's remarkable intelligence. They both read the autopsy report on the late Hedley Tregennis.

'It's a toss-up, Phryne,' Elizabeth told her. 'The opiates would have killed him, anyway.'

'But there might have been two murderers, the poisoner and the music stuffer,' said Phryne. 'I need a cause of death.'

'Och, I see the difficulty. What do you think, John?'

John had been thinking how extraordinarily foolish he had been not to find Phryne earlier. She was so beautiful she hurt his eyes. He recalled his wits.

'Petechial haemorrages in the eyes, Lisbet, swollen trachea—I think he actually died of suffocation, though you are correct that a massive dose like that would have killed anyone. So that makes the second person the killer.'

'Not legally,' said Phryne. 'The first one left the victim in a state which allowed the second one to kill him. If they knew each other it's a felony murder. If they didn't it will be one serve of attempted murder and one serve of actual murder. Oh, well, thank you for your expert opinions—that will be very helpful.'

Finally the hand-painted art deco Lamia clock chimed eleven.

'Well, it's been fine to see you again, John,' said Elizabeth, levering herself to her feet. 'I'll be asking Mr Butler to call me a taxi, I'm thinking. I've babies to deliver tomorrow. Will I see you again? Can I show you my roses?'

'Of course—we're here for another week,' said John. 'So good to see you again, Lisbet dear.'

Mr Butler summoned a cab, and Phryne and John saw her off with her bundle of discarded clothes. The air was thick with heat; there were ominous grumblings in the east. John took Phryne's hand. Strong hands, he remembered.

'I suppose I should be going too,' said John Wilson with absolutely no sense of urgency.

'Not unless you wish to, in which case Mr Butler will call you a car. It's too hot to walk anywhere tonight and the hot weather makes the local criminals positively cranky. Your choice, darling. I'm not dragging you into my ambulance anymore.'

'What if I ask really nicely to be dragged?' he said, and Phryne kissed him on the mouth. John Wilson's fate was, at that point, sealed.

CHAPTER FIVE

There must be spirits wandering in the valleys
And on green-planed hills, that find forgotten

Beggars of earth intent
On maids with aprons lifted up to carry
Red-purples home—beggars that cry out sallies

Of half-remembered songs . . . sing 'Tarry,
Tarry, are you gone?' . . . Such spirits are the
fellows.
In heaven, of those whom hell's illusions harry.

Wallace Stevens
'For an Old Woman in a Wig'

Tinker liked Chinese food. It was tasty, if a bit unidentifiable. A child of semi-starvation, he could eat anything that wasn't actively poisonous, and didn't even blench when the chicken soup with the actual chicken's feet sticking out of the bowl had been put before him. Actually it had been really good chicken soup. Mrs Hoong of the Golden Lotus cafe liked feeding these western children who seemed to appreciate her cuisine. And they were of the inner chamber of Miss Fisher, concubine to the master of the Lin family, Lin Chung. She would, of course, never let them pay, but they always left a tip, sixpence under the teapot. Mrs Hoong thought that was an indication of very good breeding.

If she had been aware of Jane and Tinker's actual breeding, it would not have changed her views. Tinker liked the Golden Lotus because the Chinese tarts who inhabited it between transactions were so beautiful and so strange. When they caught him looking at them, they would smile and blow him kisses.

Jane just adored lacquered duck, steamed pork buns and a uniquely glutinous rice cake wrapped in banana leaf. It had black sesame seeds in it. Only Mrs Hoong knew how to make it. Jane was picking up quite a lot of Cantonese, just by hearing it spoken, and could thank Mrs Hoong fittingly for her excellent dinner.

'*Do jeh, Ayi,*' Jane said, putting her hands together politely.

'What does *ayi* mean?' asked Tinker, also making the correct gesture.

'Aunty,' Jane replied. 'A title of affectionate respect.'

'*Ng-sai ng-goi, biu jie mui.* Very welcome, little cousins,' said Mrs Hoong, and they left their sixpence and went out into the dark of Little Bourke Street, which was electric with noises, quarrels, laughter and scents. Familiar and really exotic, thought Jane, taking a deep sniff of rice wine, roasting meat, exhaust smoke, asafoetida, pork fat frying, melon tea, starch from the big laundry and the sweet, pervasive underlay of the opium pipes that some of the old men still smoked.

A couple of intoxicated Chinese sailors almost jostled them off the pavement into the path of an oncoming truck. Tinker seized Jane and they scrambled back to safety. Ahead they saw that the mariners had been hustled into Celestial Way by a couple of blue-clad men who were addressing them in very strong tones.

'*Jang jang dei jou ng-ho chung chong Lum-gar ching-fu Phryne geh siu pun yau.*'

'It is unwise to jostle, hustle or otherwise endanger the children of the Lin concubine Phryne's house,' translated Jane.

'I didn't know you spoke that much Chinese,' commented Tinker, as the two blue-clad men elevated the sailors by their collars and banged their heads together.

'I don't, I just speak Mr Lin,' said Jane. 'Come along, we don't want to be late for the lecture.'

They paused to bow courteously to their avengers, then went up Little Bourke Street, were stunned briefly by a wave of cooking from the Imperial Hotel on the corner, then turned into Collins Street and walked down to the Scots Church Assembly Hall. This was the long way, of course. Tinker and Jane could have got to their destination in three minutes by ducking down alleys. But Jane loved walking in the city after dark, and Tinker distrusted alleys and lanes, even when he knew that he had guardians. By daylight he was happy to explore. By night, he preferred to stick to streets with street-lights. And, even though it pained him to admit it, strolling policemen.

It was a hot night, pregnant with storms. Tinker was pleased that they had an umbrella. He was carrying it and the satchel with a notebook and several pencils. If Tinker did not have charge of it, Jane would leave it behind when she became engrossed in her own theories. Retracing her own steps had become something of a specialty of Jane's until Tinker had arrived. He seemed to be able to find anything. Perhaps he had learned this valuable skill scavenging along the beaches and docks in Queenscliff. He didn't mind accompanying Jane.

She liked him. Anyway, Jane always wanted to go to interesting places. The Medical Museum at the University of Melbourne, for instance. And because she was terribly clever, she had no room in her head for unimportant information, which was why Tinker and Ruth often had to remind her of the way home and the location of her other shoe and the fact that it was dinner time.

The lecture room was about half full, good attendance for such a hot night in the middle of the week. The speaker was introduced by a small, old professor of mathematics from the university of Cambridge. Jane wondered how much esoteric knowledge was hidden under that bald scalp. Tinker wondered why he had come. The introduction was close to inaudible but Jane got the idea that Rupert Sheffield was a prodigy, a coming man, an amazing mathematician of whom great things were expected in his field. Which was what such persons always, to Jane's knowledge, said.

But Rupert Sheffield was another thing altogether. He was tall and graceful and extremely well dressed. Jane had not tried to acquire any knowledge about clothes while in Miss Phryne's house, but some of her visitors had worn suits like that, and she had heard them described by such terms as handmade, Savile Row and (by the charming old tailor Mr Rosenberg, who always had a pocket full of barley sugar for good children) as high-class schmutter. The suit was dark grey, the shirt pale blue, the tie from some public school (she would ask Miss Phryne when she got home) and he moved like a dancer. Very smooth.

His voice made the audience fall in love with him. Rich, educated, seductive. Jane thought that he could read out the phone book in that voice and they would all sit there riveted. He began by talking about deduction, a process of rendering the world predictable and understandable by observation. 'If this, then this.' That was easy enough; everyone did that, to some degree. But Sheffield explained that by using various mathematical methods, he could give a value to every piece of information, greater or less depending on importance, and discover patterns, parallels and connections not noticeable to the ordinary person.

He was a magician, thought Jane, instantly suspicious. He was like the man at the Tivoli who made the lady disappear and then reappear, who made flowers fall out of the air, who poured milk into the bowl and revealed swimming goldfish.

Tinker felt the same. 'I reckon this bloke's got a bridge to sell,' he whispered.

Jane nodded, and gestured for her notebook and pencil. Rupert was beginning to expound his deductive method.

Tinker parted company with the lecture at the mention of 'non-linear integrals'. There followed by Tchebyshev polynomials, roots, nodes, and one sentence which went 'points in range in which error converges to zero'—at which the speaker flung out a triumphant hand in a very graceful gesture, Jane scribbled furiously, and Tinker wondered if they were handing out tea at this bunfight. Probably not.

Instead, he examined the other people in the hall. Tinker would have bet the cuppa for which his soul longed that most of the crowd didn't understand this maths gibberish any more than Tinker did. Jane might, of course. She was now frowning and biting the end of her pencil. If not fed at intervals by her doting sister, Jane might subsist entirely on tea and pencils. And all that graphite couldn't be good for her.

The speaker continued, speaking of lattices. Not the sort you grow roses on, but some strange way of looking at facts. Tinker realised that this was not maths, it was philosophy. He cheered up immediately. He was a sailor's son from Queenscliff. No one would expect him to understand philosophy. And this had to be over soon.

At last, the speaker concluded his remarks, the projector was turned off, and Jane shut her notebook. She was in that euphoric state which Tinker had last seen when she discovered simultaneous equations. He picked up the umbrella, shoved both notebooks into the satchel and took Jane's hand. He slid it into the crook of his elbow and guided her out of the hall, down the steps and into the hot night.

Thereafter, all the way home in the taxi, she didn't say a word. By the time they were both in the kitchen and Ruth was making tea, Jane had calmed down enough to babble about variants and reflexives. Ruth looked at Tinker. He shrugged.

'I dunno. We had dinner at Mrs Hoong's, then this bloke with a voice like red velvet started talking, and that's the last I understood.'

'Oh,' said Ruth. 'That's all right, you did well. It's just a state. She gets into them. She'll come out of it. Tea, Janey,' she said into her sister's ear. 'Orange biscuits. Eat. Drink. Now.'

Jane did as requested. A blessed silence fell in which the word 'deduction' was not mentioned, which was all right with Tinker. He drank his second cup of tea and grabbed another orange bikkie. And one more for Molly. It was late, he was tired. He went to his bachelor quarters to read Sexton Blake.

Numbers, concepts, they spun in her head in a fascinating cloud. Ruth put Jane and herself to bed.

'Better in the morning, Jane,' she said, and returned to her romance. Jane closed her eyes, the better to appreciate the glories of the lattice.

•

John Wilson managed the stairs to Phryne's boudoir quite well. Of course, he had incentive. He could smell Phryne's scent, taste her mouth, and largely forgot about his damaged leg as she moved up before him, her rear elevation almost as enchanting as her front view. And blessing of blessings, her bedroom was not only provided with green silk sheets and a drinks trolley, but an arrangement comprising an electric fan and a block of ice which cooled the air to liveable temperature. He sat down and almost groaned with relief.

'Oh, lovely,' he said. Phryne looked at his honest kindly face and his beautiful blue eyes. There were plenty of pretty men—indeed, she rather had a penchant for them—but this was an old friend, as precious as a childhood teddy bear. Phryne still had Lambie, her childhood stuffed toy. She did not mind that Lambie was partially bald and more than a little battered. This man needed to be loved and cosseted and soothed, and Phryne was in the mood for those things and also in the mood for a different body in her arms.

Therefore, time to extract the doctor from his clothes. She knelt down and removed his shoes, peeled off his socks, unbuttoned his shirt. Ember, who was expecting thunder and appreciated cool air, left his post on the bed. He knew from experience that once Phryne started undressing gentlemen, it would be no place for a cat of delicate sensibilities. Besides, his wardrobe called. The thunder was getting close.

'Hello, cat,' said John. Ember gave him a dismissive sniff and walked to the wardrobe. Phryne opened the door and he jumped inside.

'Why does he do that?' asked John, removing his own shirt and beginning on his trousers.

'He was abandoned in a thunderstorm when he was just a slip of a kitten,' Phryne told him, allowing the top of her pyjamas to fall to the floor. She loosed the drawstrings and kicked off her trousers. 'We think he was shell-shocked. Come here,' she purred, extending her arms.

John slid forward into her embrace. She smelt bewitching and his lips found the hollow in the base of her throat, the cleft between her breasts, the slight curve of a belly which had always been concave. He liked her with more flesh on her bones. More Phryne was definitely an improvement. Satiny, smooth, warm flesh, in the cool wash of scented air. And so profoundly unlike his own desire that she was alien and marvellous. He found names for her; Circe, mermaid, nymph.

She assessed his state of health quickly. That scarred thigh would possibly not take his weight, but, then, it didn't have to. She gently pushed him down onto his back and slipped between his legs, rubbing like an amorous beast, while he shivered under her touch, and found all those pleasure points which he remembered Phryne to have; since she was the only woman he had ever lain with, he recalled them perfectly. She murmured his name, John sweetheart, John darling, as his fingers found the right places and he felt her convulse above him. Then she straddled his hips, taking care not to touch the scar. He was embraced in a wet heat which belied the icy air, and he dissolved in fire, an orgasm so strong that he nearly fainted.

'Phryne,' he murmured.

'Oh, that was *so* nice,' she said, disentangling herself and then sitting up a little so that he could rest his head upon her breast. 'And it's better when no one is shooting at us, isn't it?'

'Infinitely,' he agreed. A small breast was under his cheek. Strange feeling, reminding him of no one else, for his mother had been a cushiony, comfortable sort of woman, and Phryne was his only female lover. She was thin but not as skinny as she had been, the smoke-stained scarecrow hauling stretchers out of that wretched ambulance with surprising strength. '*Point d'appui*,' she had explained. 'It's just finding the balance. Then everything slides into place.' She had found John's point of balance, all right. When first seized and kissed by that fierce mouth, he had briefly thought of trying to explain that actually he was 'so', a player on the other team and uninterested in her gender, but then decided not to, because 1) she wouldn't have listened, and in any case, 2) it suddenly wasn't true. He had seesawed down into heterosexuality, to his great astonishment. And here he was again, while the object of his profound adoration slept—if he slept—in his room at the Windsor and had probably not noticed that John had not come back.

'You really do love him, don't you?' asked Phryne. It was not an interrogation, she was affectionately curious, so he answered.

'Yes,' said John.

She stroked his hair. 'And he doesn't love you?' she asked.

'He doesn't love anyone,' explained John. 'He doesn't have any idea of the concept. He's all mind. All intellect.'

'Nothing is all intellect,' said Phryne. 'Unless he is supernatural. I agree that he is as beautiful as a succubus, no, incubus, but he is made of flesh.'

'He detests the flesh,' said John. 'I have to make him sleep, remind him to eat. When he's not thinking, he enjoys gourmet foods and fine wine. Then he doesn't eat for days. If he didn't have me to mind him . . .'

'He would have burned out by now,' concluded Phryne crossly. She had seen this before. The tyranny of weakness. The means by which the heartless gained all that they wanted without giving one solitary kiss in return. 'But what would happen to him without me?' was the cry of many an abused spouse, sister, mother about husbands and widowed mothers and frightful siblings. And Rupert Sheffield had managed it without any emotional involvement. Without the concurrent statement from the bruised wife: 'He really does love me.' Ingenious. He might just be as intelligent as John thinks he is, damn him.

'It's not his fault,' said John, sensing tension in the breast upon which he was reposing.

That was the third thing they always said.

'So what do you get out of this . . . partnership?' she asked. 'Just the right to stare at his gorgeous face all day?'

'No, he needs me,' said John. 'He relies on me to watch his back. People dislike him, there have been attempts to silence him, when he knows something about people, and he says it—he always says it. And I was so bored, Phryne, after Arthur died. I was sinking down into grey fog, and then Sheffield came along and it was all sparkling and bright again.'

'I see,' said Phryne. She did. Regrettably. A nectar trap, like those of the sundew or the pitcher plant. Brilliant in conception, beautiful to the sight, ruthless in execution, and the fly gets digested alive all the same. Nice petals, though.

'As it is here,' John continued, drawing a callused finger down her thigh. 'Here, with you. All sparkling.'

He kissed the breast he was lying on, then down Phryne's body, lingering over her belly, licking with interest at her navel, into which it might be nice to pour wine. It was amazing some passing sultan hadn't offered her an emerald or a ruby for that navel. His clever mouth moved down until he found the sweet spot and Phryne arched her back. He forgot his damaged leg as he moved above her and inside her, belly to belly.

Phryne was pleased, assuaged and holding him around the neck while he shuddered into another climax.

He recovered his breath, realised that his leg was registering a complaint, and lay on his back, panting. Phryne fetched a cool wet cloth and washed him with precise licks, like that of a mother cat. Then she stretched out beside him and sighed a sated sigh.

'I should go,' John murmured. Storms gave him bad dreams. It would be the height of ill manners to scream and cry and remember the war in a lady's bed.

'Why?' asked Phryne.

'I . . .' he began.

She suppressed his attempt to rise with a firm hand on his chest. 'He won't notice you have gone,' she told him. 'And it might do him some good to know that you aren't always there. Lie down, it's going to storm. I . . . would like some company. Thunderstorms make me remember . . .'

'Oh, God, Phryne, and me. Of course I'll stay.'

'All right. If I have a nightmare, you wake me, and I'll do the same for you. Deal?'

He took her hand and kissed it.

'Deal,' he said.

•

John fell asleep like a man falling down a well. Phryne considered him as his features relaxed. You could tell a lot about a person if you watched them as they slept. The face they wore for the world was gone; the face they actually owned was on display, vulnerable and soft. John was sad, even in sleep. Unloved since Arthur died, she guessed. That scent of wormwood had been strong. He was still a young man. The semen of young men was lightly scented. He had been without a lover, possibly without even release, for a long time. That could be remedied, at least while he was in Melbourne. He was a considerate and comfortable lover. Not exciting, but Phryne could always find excitement. Excitement, indeed, had a way of finding her.

She snuggled down beside him in the wash of the cool air and tried not to listen to the noise of the electric fan, which emitted an intensely irritating 'cluck' every seven minutes.

The storm hit at three am. From inside his wardrobe, Ember wailed his discomfort and outrage. Molly gave the thunder her usual remedy for anything strange: a good solid barking. Phryne heard big guns and smelt the reek of trenches. She was endeavouring to coax another m.p.h out of her baulky ambulance, trying to outrun the creeping barrage. Her patients in the back moaned and screamed and young Audrey beside her was praying. Every bounce of the ambulance brought a massed shriek of agony. She'd done this before, grimy hands white-knuckled on the wheel, trying by main force to shove the gears into place, hearing the explosions coming nearer. But this time she was not going to get out of range. She struggled, stamping and slapping the engine into a lower gear as it shuddered and whined. But this time, they were all going to die . . .

John Wilson, not even yet a doctor, despaired. He was standing in a pool of fresh blood. The last patient had bled to death in his hands as he tried to staunch too many wounds with too few swabs, with no disinfectant and no morphine and no help. The creeping barrage was coming closer, and suddenly he laid his head down on the ruined chest of the dead soldier and waited, almost happy, almost peaceful, thinking that it would be all right to die now, because it would take away the pain . . .

And felt hands flailing, a voice screaming. His dead man wasn't quite dead. He closed his arms around the soldier, clasping him in a close embrace, and soothed him. 'There, there,

I'm here,' he told the corpse. 'I won't leave you, and it will all be better soon. We'll all be safely dead soon.'

'John?' asked the dead man, and he found he was awake and pinning Phryne Fisher down. He had flung himself across her as he had during an artillery bombardment, to protect her from shrapnel with his own body.

'Get off,' she squeaked, poking him in the ribs. 'You're heavy.'

'I was dreaming,' he explained, rolling aside and gathering her into his arms.

'So was I,' she told him. Her eyes in the actinic light were huge, dilated black with shock. She was shivering. 'Creeping barrage?' he asked.

'Yes. I used to outrun them. But this time, I . . . didn't.'

'I had just watched one too many lads die,' said John, tears running down his face and dripping onto Phryne's shoulder. 'Just the one too many. I despaired. I always knew that there would be one too many deaths.'

'And then you'd lie down and die too?' asked Phryne, recovering her courage.

'Yes,' he said simply.

'I didn't let you then, and neither did Elizabeth, and I won't let you now,' said Phryne. 'Sweetheart,' she added, kissing him soundly. He tasted bitterly of tears.

'I'm cold,' said John, releasing her as she got up to turn off the fan and pull on her pyjamas and robe. She rummaged and threw him an extravagant red silk gentleman's dressing gown. He put it on, still shaking, wiping his wet cheeks.

'Downstairs, my dearest John, there is cocoa made with your actual chocolate, and that's where my household will be. Come along,' she said, and preceded him out the door. John found his cane and followed. Perhaps he really was still dreaming.

But in a spacious kitchen, he was introduced to Mrs Butler, who nodded affably, and Jane, Ruth and Tinker, who shook hands like good children. Dot smiled at him. Molly, who was bouncing up and down, was the picture of a Good Dog, sure that she had seen that presumptuous storm off all by herself.

There was indeed cocoa. It was made with fresh creamy milk, demerara sugar and chocolate from a tin with a Dutch lady on it, and it was sweet, hot and heartening.

'Miss Phryne's got shell shock,' Jane informed him, as he sat for the first time in his life in a warm kitchen surrounded by accepting faces, wearing some other gentleman's gown. It was a splendid one, agreed, but it wasn't something in which retired army doctor John would normally be seen dead. He stroked it appreciatively. It had padded lapels and golden dragons on it.

'Indeed?' he asked. He was not used to children. This blonde one had eyes like a hawk. She knew all about John, she also knew what he had been doing in Miss Fisher's bed, and was not remotely bothered by any fact. She disconcerted him.

'And so have you,' Jane continued. 'We always have cocoa on thundery nights. Cocoa feels more real than tea.'

'So it does,' agreed John.

'The Guv'nor always puts rum in hers,' suggested Tinker, hefting a bottle of Queensland OP. 'You want some too?'

John extended his mug. Tinker was generous with his rum. The sip went right down into John's memories and warmed them to the cockles. Ruth offered him his own pipe and tobacco. Phryne must have sent her upstairs by another stair. She thought of everything.

'Miss Phryne thinks you need a smoke,' she explained. 'She'll be back soon. She's in the garden.'

'Then I shall join her,' said John, and took his cup and

his smoking materials and went into the small garden, where Phryne stood under the verandah and scanned the sky.

'Looking for Very lights?' he asked. She did not jump but leaned back into his side, as though he was a tree. He found this extremely touching.

'Yes,' she answered. He put his mug of cocoa down on the small table and began to fill his pipe. Phryne found a gasper, lit it, and offered him her box of matches.

'Three lights from one match will draw a sniper,' she said.

'I know,' he told her.

They smoked companionably. Phryne had scanned the whole horizon. There were no Very lights, sent up to guide a barrage or an assault. In fact, there were few lights of any kind. In the silence, the sea made itself heard. John smelt rain-battered jasmine flowers and cocoa. He puffed. The fear began to subside. He could feel his heart slowing down, his respiration improving. Phryne, leaning against him, was drawing in long breaths of sweet air.

'We'll never really forget, will we?' she asked him.

'No,' he said. 'But it's better with company. You dragged me out of my dream, Phryne dear. I was quite happy to die in it. One day, I'll die in it for real.'

'No, you won't,' she said fiercely. 'A solution will be found,' she told him.

'If anyone can find it,' he replied, 'it would be you.'

Presently they went back to bed. Tinker, it seemed, lived in a shed in the garden. He took Molly with him, saying that he was going fishing early. 'Fish rise after a storm,' he told John. 'It's the fresh water.'

The household took its leave. Phryne dissuaded Jane from attempting to interrogate John about his injured leg, and led him back up the stairs, which had roughly doubled in height and gradient.

Usually after one of those dreams he felt utterly exhausted. This one, dreamed in company, had had a reduced effect. Another thing for which he had to thank Phryne Fisher.

'Pyjamas,' she said, throwing him a pair of flannelette garments in his size. 'Let's get warm,' she added, leaping into bed and drawing up the blanket and comforter. 'I will never get used to this weather. You can get sunburn and frostbite on the same day, while not moving so much as an inch. Come along, John,' she chided. He took off the dressing gown. He put on the pyjamas. He got into bed and was embraced. And he fell asleep again.

It really had been an astonishing night.

CHAPTER SIX

Of the milk within the saltiest spurge, heard, then,
The sea unfolding in the sunken clouds?
Oh! C'était mon extase et mon amour.

Wallace Stevens
'Sea Surface Full of Clouds'

Dr John Wilson woke in luxury. Green silk sheets. Cool morning light. The Hon. Miss Phryne Fisher curled up beside him, snuggled into the curve of his arm. And a black tomcat seated on his chest, tail wrapped around paws, staring censoriously into his eyes. He was just withdrawing the paw which he had used to pat John's cheek. John got the impression that if he did not respond he could find himself short an eye. An extremely male fellow mammal was making a claim to Miss Fisher. What that paw on Phryne's shoulder said was *mine!*

'Very well, old chap,' murmured John. His body felt lax and full of ease. He leaned down and kissed Phryne on the forehead.

'Mmm?' she asked.

'It's dawn and your cat seems to be suggesting breakfast,' he told her. Phryne never woke up easily. She shut her eyes again and replaced herself in his embrace, snuggling emphatically. Ember waited until she had settled and then patted John's cheek again.

'I'm sorry, old chap, but ladies will be ladies,' John told him. 'You of all creatures ought to know that.'

Ember thought about clawing him, glanced at Phryne again, then got down off John's chest and curled up beside Phryne, putting nose on paws.

'That's a sensible cat,' John told him, and went back to sleep.

•

When he woke again it was full light, Phryne was sitting up in bed, and she directed him to the bathroom because it was breakfast time and she wanted to feed him properly.

'When are you due back at the hotel?' she asked.

'Not until eleven,' he said.

'Good. I shall escort you down,' said Phryne, in defiance of all custom, and went into the lavish bathroom—a malachite bath, he had never even heard of such a thing—to bathe and dress. John had only the clothes in which he had gone to dinner last night. He felt quite raffish. He started to wonder why Phryne owned a pair of striped flannelette pyjamas in just his size, and who owned the splendid red dressing gown, and then stopped wondering about it. She had her mysteries. And at this hour he might not be able to cope with the answers. If at all.

If breakfast at Miss Phryne's had been the last meal of a condemned man, he would have gone to his execution whistling. Phryne bade him return whenever he wished. Would tonight be too soon? he wondered. After the lantern lecture?

Phryne kissed him and consented.

Regretfully, he took his leave. He passed the telegraph boy on his bike at the gate.

As Phryne received the telegram and paid the boy his penny from a jar kept on the hall table, the phone rang and she answered it.

'Your appointment with Dr Fanshawe is for two o'clock this afternoon,' said a nasal female voice.

'Have you got the right number?' Phryne was extremely healthy.

'Miss Phryne Fisher, *chatte noire*, two o'clock, Dr Fanshawe, 123 Collins Street,' intoned the female voice.

'Oh, very well,' replied Phryne. Black Cat. That had been her code name when she had done a little light espionage for Compton, many years ago. He must have telegraphed the local branch of MI6. Must be about Rupert Sheffield. Could be interesting. 'I'll be there.'

The phone went dead without further comment. Phryne opened her telegram. In code, of course.

'I'll be a little while,' she called to her family, ascending the stairs again.

Ten minutes work and she had decoded the flimsy. She laughed as she read it. She had sent 'who is Rupert Sheffield query' and the reply had come back, recalling Compton's voice and his signalling eyebrows, 'Idiot Savant stop Emphasis savant stop Emphasis idiot stop regards C.'

She could just hear him saying it. She laughed again.

'Miss?' Dot's voice. Telegrams worried her, and all her generation. Mostly they came to announce the death of another brother, son, lover.

Intelligence habits are not easily abandoned. Phryne tore her ciphering across and shoved it into her fireplace along with the telegram, set a match to it and watched it burn to ash. Then she crushed the ash with the poker.

'Best thing to do with them,' agreed Dot. 'Bad news, Miss?'

'No, just confusing. Well, I haven't anything to do until this afternoon, when I have to go into the city again. Have we heard from Jack Robinson?'

Dot blushed. 'He's sent Hugh with the choral people's statements, and he wants him to stay here until you've read them all, because he can't just lend them to you.'

'Well, you can entertain Hugh and I can read the file—that ought to take up the time until my doctor's appointment.'

'Oh, Miss—you aren't feeling well?' Dot clasped her hands to her bosom.

'I feel in top form, Dot dear. What did you make of Dr Wilson?'

'Seemed a nice man. The girls liked him. Jane says he's sad.'

'She is very acute,' commented Phryne. 'Hand me those shoes, will you? The glacé kid. Ember's been chewing my slippers, the naughty puss.'

She cast a reproachful glance at Ember. He turned his head elegantly, shedding all reproof. They were of an interesting texture. He liked chewing them. No further correspondence would be entered into.

'I thought he was sad too,' said Dot. 'But he's sad and kind, not sad and bitter. What happened to him?'

'His lover died of a heart attack after only three years,' Phryne told her truthfully, not mentioning the gender of the lover because this could only get more confusing. 'And he had a bad war.'

'Mr Butler said you saved his life.'

'I did, and Dr MacMillan saved his leg. But we couldn't save his heart, Dot dear.'

'You're on the way to patching it up again, then, Miss. That's a good deed,' said Dot, who had clear views on the Cardinal Virtue of Charity. It took strange forms. Especially when Miss Phryne was dispensing it.

Meanwhile, there was Hugh Collins sitting in the garden, sipping a shandy and guarding the file. Dot felt that her embroidery needed to be inspected in sunlight to make sure that the colours balanced, and went with it to keep it company.

Jane was in the parlour, attempting to improve her under-standing of a sentence which began, 'The conditioning of problems: perturbations in input data can have large changes in output. If this is not so, the problem is well conditioned. If it is so, the problem is ill conditioned.'

She had almost understood that. The next heading was 'Homoscedasticity'. She started to read about multiple regression models. She blinked. She rubbed her temples. Ruth took the book firmly out of her hands and shut it with a slap. *Pure Mathematics* was placed on the table. Jane was hauled to her feet.

'We're going swimming,' stated Ruth. 'But first, a nice glass of lemonade and an aspirin.'

Jane went quietly.

•

Phryne spread the statements out over the dining table. She compared all of the available manuscripts to the master list of choristers which Jack had provided. There seemed to have been nine sopranos, twelve altos, four tenors, six basses and the répétiteur, Professor Arnold Szabo, present at the fatal rehearsal. Phryne decided to sort them by first names and by presence or absence after rehearsal was finished, as every statement insisted that the unlamented and very late Tregennis had been offensively present until he had stormed off to the conductor's room and bidden them all begone at about eight. She made two lists.

AT THE PUB IN EACH OTHER'S COMPANY
Were sopranos Millicent, Miriam, Caterina, Isabelle, Calliope and Josephine. Of the tenors only Daniel Smith had managed the journey. Almost all of the altos, comprising Annie, Irene, Maisie, Lydia, Mary, Emmeline, Lobelia, Alison, Geneva and Ophelia were there. And basses: Tom, David, Aaron and Luke.

UNACCOUNTED FOR
Julia, left hall at nine, by her account, soprano.

Jenny Leaper went on to her job in a bakery, soprano.

Helen Burke went home to mind her little sisters, alto.

Tabitha Willis went home to finish an essay on distemper (duly handed in), alto.

Chloe McMahon went home to wash her hair, (Wagnerian) soprano. Score missing.

Leonard Match went home and has now got on a train to Albury to visit relatives and is still there, bass.

Matthew, the Father Christmas blond, went home to his grandmother and cooked a late dinner, tenor.

Mike aka Bones, the languid medical student, went to a cramming session on anatomy with two others, tenor.

Luigi had an assignation with a lady whom he would not name [of *course* he did, thought Phryne], tenor.

Oliver went to work filing in his father's office, bass. Score missing.

Professor Szabo went home to his room in 88 Collins

Street, drank the rest of his bottle of ruby port, and fell asleep. The poor old man.

It looked all very organised set out like that, of course, but it didn't really help much. Phryne, with the help of a considering cocktail, read rapidly through all the statements, collating times and places (as far as could be dredged up from multiple inebriated reminiscences) and decided, after two hours, that she was amply provided with information and completely clueless about the murder.

The doctors Wilson and MacMillan had agreed that the actual cause of death was choking. He must have died between eight and nine, when Julia saw the corpse complete with music, and although Julia was vague about anything which did not involve singing, Phryne had scared her and, thought Phryne, she had told the truth. As she saw it. Therefore, the conductor barrels his way out of the hall, flinging epithets at the choir, and stomps into his room at about eight. There someone brings him sweet poisoned wine and an intimate little supper. They find him writing something incriminating—a love letter? Worse, a letter dismissing a lover? But surely whoever brought those exquisite little suppers wouldn't ask him to drink Tokay. As Ruth said, it didn't match. And Hedley Tregennis was an unpleasant man, but no one had accused him of lack of taste. Perhaps she needed to look at this another way.

Phryne pulled a clean sheet of paper and wrote a time line which did not rely on any assumptions.

1. Eight o'clock. Tregennis is in his room. Writing and tearing up letters.
2. Someone—mystery woman?—brings him supper and the correct glass of champagne. She goes or is

sent away, taking the tray or basket with her. At this point Tregennis is alive and well fed.

3. Another person brings him tea in his teapot, and a glass of Imperial Tokay improved with morphine. This person may just wait to see him drink it, and then leave.
4. He collapses to the floor. He is dying. A third person enters, stuffs music down his throat (thus killing him) and departs.
5. Nine o'clock. Julia enters, picks up her score, and leaves again, locking the door behind her and not mentioning it to anyone.
6. Someone removes the wastepaper and the crockery.

So far, so good. This schematic made sense of all the information. She estimated that a small supper such as the one Tregennis had eaten would only occupy fifteen minutes, even if he lingered over the smoked salmon. And it was possible that the papers, the teapot and the cup had been removed by the assembly hall staff collecting dishes for washing, though he or she would surely have noticed a dead conductor on the floor. Then again, caretakers were underpaid and overworked, also under-appreciated. The caretaker might have thought that it wasn't any of their business if the choir slaughtered the conductor. Or might not have noticed the body on the floor.

She searched through the statements. One from Mrs Elsie Cook, caretaker. Yes, she had removed the teapot and the cup. And the paper. And she had not observed any corpse. Observing corpses wasn't her job. For which she didn't get paid enough anyway.

Well, then, that paper was gone. The tea things had been washed. Other clues must be considered.

It had been choral music stuffed into Tregennis's mouth. So it could have come from Oliver's score, abandoned on the piano, or from Chloe's score, pinched one rehearsal from under her summer hat. Or even bought for the purpose. *Elijah* was a popular oratorio and often performed; the music would be readily available. She giggled as she remembered a list of scores for sale. And the Lord Gave Mendelssohn fourpence.

Well, this had all been illuminating, but she needed to go and see the local representative of MI6 as personified by one Dr Fanshawe, and she decided to lunch in town.

She returned the file to Hugh Collins's custody, elaborately did not notice that he had actually put his blue-clad arm around Dot's virgin waist, and sauntered out into the sunshine.

•

The nearest hotel with a reputation for haute cuisine to the Scots Church was probably the Imperial Hotel. It stood right across from Parliament House, in Spring Street. It was a plush hostelry, catering as it did for patrons with very high standards: politicians and prostitutes. The Ladies of the Night needed sustenance and it wasn't going to come from the pie cart, not if someone else was paying for the pleasure of their company.

The verandahs had been removed, Phryne knew, by a censorious city council, because said ladies were sheltering under them while plying their trade. This had not driven the ladies further away than the very comfortable precincts of the Maj theatre. Which also sold chocolates. The Imperial was still a notorious place, but its ladies' lounge had twice the acreage of the average drinking hole.

Phryne strolled in and found a seat at the bar. She bought a gin and tonic and then remembered that unaccompanied ladies could not lunch at the Imperial. She smiled at the barman, a middle-aged man with world-weary eyes and thinning hair. 'Just mind my drink for a moment, will you? I've got to go and get a man.'

'Plenty on offer,' he said, grinning. 'I can introduce you, if you like. No pollies, it's holidays.'

'That's a mercy,' commented Phryne.

'Well, there's cops in that corner,' said the barman, laying out his wares like a showman. 'Tarts over there, theatre people over there, and that bunch I'm not too sure about. Hanging round here more than a bit. Had to throw 'em out last Tuesday for singing. Or there's me.' He waved a bar towel at himself. 'I'm yours, anytime. I get off work at six.'

'So kind, but I can't wait, I want some lunch,' Phryne told him, blowing him a kiss.

She carried her drink over to two choristers.

'But Aunty is coming soon,' Oliver was protesting. 'And that friend of his, Gawain, isn't that his name? You know how cross he gets when the choir isn't up to speed.'

'Well, we'll just have to tell Aunty it wasn't our fault that our conductor got murdered, and it wasn't us, so we'll just have to get on with it,' stated Matthew.

'Hello.' Phryne subsided into a chair. 'Might I ask you both to lunch with me?'

'Miss Fisher!' gasped Oliver, blushing a pretty pink which clashed with his hair. 'We'd be delighted. But . . . We'd be . . .'

'Honoured,' said Matthew. 'But we just about afforded a beer . . .'

'Each,' concluded Oliver.

Phryne fleetingly wondered if choristers were always fugual, and in which circumstances this could be really intriguing. She slapped her imagination down. It really was most indelicate, bless it.

'My treat. I want to lunch here but I can't without a gentleman, and I have always been a fan of excess, so I shall greedily help myself to two.'

They went quietly.

Phryne looked at the folio-sized menu and said to the maître d', 'Shucked oysters, six, if you please, with lemon juice. A little smoked salmon. Then something light—a cheese soufflé would be perfect. Later we can talk about dessert. Gentlemen?'

Matthew was fighting down the urge to say, 'One of each, please,' but ordered soup and roast beef, and Oliver ordered soup and roast chicken, one of his favourite dishes. Phryne ordered wine for all of them.

'This is very kind of you, Miss Fisher,' Matthew began. 'Is there anything that we can . . . er . . . do for you?'

Phryne could think of lots of things, but was supposed to be 1) solving a murder, and 2) engaging in espionage, and 3) seducing an old army friend, and decided with regret that her life had enough divertissements at present. Matthew would probably keep. Therefore she gave him a wicked smile and said, 'Talk to me about the choir, about Mendelssohn's *Elijah*, and any other thing which enters your heads.'

'Matt, don't turn round,' said Oliver urgently. 'It's that deduction bloke. The Pommy.'

'Is anyone with him?' asked Phryne, seeing Rupert Sheffield in the pub mirror, artfully angled so that diners could catch sight of avenging wives, angry constituents and process servers and have time to escape out the back way. Phryne could not see John Wilson in attendance.

'How do you feel about lunching with him?' asked Phryne.

'Ponce,' said Oliver. 'He was real rude. To everyone.'

'Yes, that does seem to be his trademark,' answered Phryne.

She raised a finger and a waiter was instantly at her side. She beckoned him to lean down, whispered in his ear, and dropped a ten-shilling note on his tray. He nodded soberly, trousered the note, and flickered away—clearly another graduate of the Mr Butler school of evanescence.

'Do either of you speak French?' asked Phryne.

'No,' said Oliver.

'Yes,' said Matthew.

Of course, he was going to be a diplomat. Phryne smiled at him. He really was very attractive.

'In that case, Matthew, I must ask you to stay silent about anything you hear—and for the purposes of this conversation, you don't speak a word of French, right? *Tais-toi*,' she said, and tapped him on the lips with one forefinger. He nodded mutely.

'Miss Fisher?' asked Rupert Sheffield, alone and without his minder. The waiter stood to one side, eyes averted, waiting for orders. Sheffield really could move like Ember. She had not heard his approach.

'*Bonjour*,' said Phryne. '*Tu es venu à propos du petit souper?*' You are here about the little supper?

'*Bien sûr. C'était clair.*' Of course. It is obvious.

'*Il est venu de cette cuisine*,' said Phryne. It came from this kitchen.

'*Évidemment, tout le monde pourrait le voir.*' He snapped. Clearly, anyone could see that.

'*Alors, ça va rendre l'Inspecteur principal Robinson très heureux*,' Phryne told him. So that will make Detective Inspector Robinson very happy.

'*Tant pis*,' said Rupert. Too bad.

Rupert was still standing, looming over Phryne, who had a limited tolerance for being loomed over. The waiter delivered the first course, and she invited him to sit with an imperious wave. Reluctantly, he obeyed. The waiter brought him a glass of wine. Phryne gave him an oyster fork and pushed over the plate.

'*Je pense qu'elles sont très bonnes*,' she said. I believe they're very good.

Ungraciously, Rupert took up a shell and drank down an oyster.

'*Assez passable*,' he said. Quite passable. '*Vous avez appris le français à l'école, puis vous avez vécu à Paris.*' You learned your French at school then you lived in Paris.

'*Et tu l'as appris d'une nurse francophone, ou bien, peut-être de ta mère*,' Phryne replied—And you learned yours from a French-speaking nanny, or maybe, yes, your mother—eating an oyster. It was very good, creamy and tasting of the sea.

'*Ma mère*,' confirmed Sheffield.

'*Tu parles un français soigné et correct*,' said Phryne, tu-toi-ing him shamelessly. You speak very formal and correct French.

'*Et vous parlez un français pitoyable de les rues de Montparnasse*,' snapped Sheffield. And you speak Parisian French from the gutters of Montparnasse.

'*Comme de juste, Auguste*,' agreed Phryne, with a cheeky grin. '*Dis donc, ce n'est pas la peine de t'en prendre à moi. Je vais parler à la femme aux cheveux noir, et je dirai à mon policier que tu m'as tout expliqué*,' she said condescendingly. But let us not become too personal. I shall speak to the woman with black hair, and I shall tell my policeman that you explained it all to me.

Sheffield glared at her.

It was a very good glare, she thought, dark, brooding, very Heathcliff. Phryne had been glared at by angry people before, and on one occasion an affronted tiger. This was about five on the 'I'll skin you alive, gnaw your beating heart and dance on your bones' ten-stage Glare Scale. Though a ten was only briefly seen before a necromancer sacrificed you to the demon Astrophel. Phryne smiled sunnily.

Sheffield was nervous. He shifted in his chair, his long, elegant fingers drummed the white-clothed table. He caught the eyes of both singers, who looked away. At least the glare worked on them, thought Sheffield. The detestable Miss Fisher seemed immune to glares as well as all decency. Phryne did not speak further, though she offered him another oyster. Finally, he could not stand it any longer. He had to know what she had done with him.

'*Où est Jean Wilson?*' he demanded. Where is John Wilson?

'*Jl'ai renvoyé chez lui il y a trois heures,*' I sent him home about three hours ago, said Phryne. '*Tu ne le mérites pas, tu sais.*' You do not deserve him, you know.

Rupert gave her a sudden, piercing flick of his violet eyes, said '*Je sais*', I know, and left with hardly a whisk of his beautiful suit.

'*Nom de dieu! En effet, merde!*' said Phryne, and fanned herself. Bloody hell.

'*Le souper?*' Supper? asked Matthew. '*Tu veux dire que la femme mystère l'a acheté ici?*' You mean that the mystery woman got it from here?

'*Oui, et je suis sur le point de la retrouver. Mange.*' Yes, and I'm about to find her. Keep eating, Phryne told Matthew, and beckoned the waiter again. He bent, she whispered, a note flickered in the air.

'Have an oyster?' Phryne asked Oliver. 'So rude of us to speak another language. I'm sure that Matthew won't tell you all about it later. How is the soup?'

'Wonderful,' said Oliver. He could see a trolley with a whole baron of beef on it, accompanied by every possible vegetable. This morning he had scraped up the threepence for one pot of beer and had been expecting not to eat again until supper. He didn't care what French plotting had taken place over his head, though from the stunned expression on Matt's face, it had been juicy stuff.

He ate the oyster. It was very good.

As the choristers were ploughing into amazing quantities of roasted beasts and Phryne ate her cheese soufflé with delicate licks of her fork, an aproned woman was escorted in by the waiter and sat down beside her. Phryne ordered wine with the crook of an eyebrow.

'I'm so sorry,' Phryne told her.

Reddened eyes looked into hers. The woman scraped back her long black hair, which she had tugged out of its bun.

'He wasn't a good man,' she whispered.

'I have never found that that makes the slightest difference,' said Phryne.

'No,' said the woman.

'You'll have to tell the cops you were there,' Phryne said gently. 'You haven't done anything wrong.'

'But was it the oysters?' The question burst out of the scratched throat in a fierce whisper. 'Was it my food that killed him?'

'If I thought it was, would I be eating them?' asked Phryne, exhibiting six empty oyster shells.

The woman with black hair was on the verge of tears of relief. Phryne gave her a napkin and bade her drink her wine.

'It was someone else,' Phryne told her. 'You brought him his little supper and a glass of what—champagne?'

'Yes, of course, what else would you drink with smoked salmon?' asked the cook, outraged.

'What is your name? I'm Phryne Fisher.' Phryne offered her hand and the waiter poured more wine at her signal.

'Genevieve Upton,' replied the woman, sipping at her second glass. 'How do you know it wasn't . . .'

'Because someone came along afterwards and gave him a glass of something really sweet—probably Imperial Tokay—which was poisoned,' said Phryne.

'Tokay? We don't keep it here,' said Genevieve.

'Good thing too, it's ghastly, like white port with sugar in it. How long did you know Tregennis?'

Genevieve raked her hands through her hair again. She sniffed.

'Oh, it's been four months. Came in here and I thought he was . . .'

'Quite,' said Phryne.

Matthew and Oliver were listening with their ears flapping, but that hadn't hindered their consumption of a truly heroic number of calories. The ghostly waiter had refilled their plates several times. Ah, to be young again, he thought, rubbing his ulcer.

'I took him his basket at eight as usual,' Genevieve said. 'I stayed while he ate. He said he'd see me that night, but he never came . . . He never came.'

'When did you leave the assembly hall?'

'About twenty past eight. I had to get back here—there was a private party.'

'And you were at work all that evening?'

'Oh, yes, Miss. With about twenty witnesses.'

'Then you just need to go and tell your tale to Detective Inspector Robinson, who is a very nice man. He will understand why you fibbed to him. Your work is your livelihood. You were terrified that it was your food that had killed him. He'll comprehend. Then it will be all over,' said Phryne, and patted Genevieve's work-hardened hand.

Dark eyes looked into Phryne's green ones. Then Genevieve emptied her glass in one gulp, got up, straightened her apron, and went out.

'So she's the mystery woman!' marvelled Matthew.

'She is, but she isn't the murderer,' Phryne told them.

'Good,' said Oliver. 'I liked her.'

'So did I,' said Phryne. 'Now, how about some dessert? And you need to tell me about Mendelssohn's *Elijah*. About your choir. And many other beautiful things.'

Dessert was a trifle so rich, so creamy, so fruity, that Matthew groaned.

'We're going to have to go home and sleep off this lunch,' he told Phryne. 'Can we talk to you again?'

'Of course,' said Phryne indulgently. 'Telephone my house when you have recovered. Thank you for your company,' she said, dropped some notes on the ever-present waiter's tray, and sailed out.

'All right,' said Oliver. 'I want you to tell me everything they said.'

'It's printed on my eardrums,' said Matthew, and began to recount it.

CHAPTER SEVEN

Let the wind blow high, let the wind blow low
Through the streets in me kilt I go
All the lasses say 'Hello!
Donald, where's your troosers?'

Folk song, sung to the tune of
'Johnnie Cope'

So this was 123 Collins Street. What an excellent place for an intelligence cell, thought Phryne. A hairdresser's establishment, a pharmacy with bow windows, each one exhibiting the curved jeroboam of coloured liquid which had fascinated her as a child, a flower shop and doctor's offices. She would bet that the three-storey red-brick buildings backed onto Flinders Lane, a quick exit into a world of buttons, braid and schmutter, always busy at any hour, as fine tailoring waits for no man. It looked ultimately respectable. And a café which served little cakes and rather good coffee, by the scent. What could be more comfortable? It reminded her of Paris.

Phryne consulted brass plates and opened the heavy wooden door of number 123 into a small atrium with a staircase and a modern lift, without attendant. There were also stairs. Dr Fanshawe was on the second floor. Phryne did not like lifts, so she climbed the stairs. There was no one around. Her heels clicked on wooden boards. The place smelt of coffee and brass polish. She was wondering if this might be a trap, and had her little gun under her hand as she continued. After all, her telegram had not mentioned this Fanshawe. Rupert Sheffield might have brought all manner of enemies—the man had a positive genius for making them, after all—and one of them might decide that Phryne was part of his ménage. Not while she was still breathing, but John might be in danger. Therefore she kept going.

The second floor showed her a row of doors, all firmly shut. She searched for and found Fanshawe, went in, and was greeted by a plump motherly receptionist, who was knitting a tiny pale blue garment, probably for a grandson. A cup of tea steamed at her elbow.

'Hello, dear,' she said. 'Miss Fisher?'

'That's me,' said Phryne, hand still on gun. One never knew.

'Go right in, dear, Mr Fanshawe's waiting for you.' As Phryne drew near to her desk, she whispered, 'He's a bit put out, to be honest. That loathsome man was here yesterday and upset him. See if you can cheer him up a bit.'

'Let me make a wild guess—would that be Rupert Sheffield?' asked Phryne sotto voce.

The plump woman's face crumpled into a grimace.

'That's him. Beautiful as a devil. My gran always said the devil was beautiful. In you go, dear,' she added, waving her knitting at the door into the inner office.

Phryne knocked on the glass and was bidden to enter. A youngish, baldish man stood up from behind a desk stacked with files. He had a sharp face and bright eyes. He beckoned

Phryne to a seat, said, 'Excuse me for a moment, Miss Fisher,' and started rummaging for his notes.

Phryne looked around. Public school. Cricket trophies on the shelves. Textbooks, Glaister on Toxicology, *Gray's Anatomy*. Journals. Doctor's bag. Drugs in a locked cabinet. Medical background, so he could convincingly imitate a doctor if he had to do so. No framed degree, so he probably wasn't an actual doctor, at least under the name Fanshawe. Pictures of a good-looking wife and two good-looking children. Nice office, with the sun streaming in the window. Local. Army. Had a photo of a graduating class for officers—now, could she pick him out? Too difficult from where she was sitting. With an 'Aha!' Mr Fanshawe found what he was looking for.

'I've a set of questions to ask,' he said. 'You know the drill, Miss Fisher.'

'I just hope I remember the answers,' said Phryne. 'It's been a long time since I did this. All right, fire away.'

'What was your name?' asked Mr Fanshawe.

'*Chatte Noire. Je suis la chatte,*' said Phryne.

He inclined his head. 'In England, who was your contact?'

'Major Russell.'

'In France?'

'Georges Santain.'

'Is there no help for . . .'

'The widow's son?' asked Phryne. 'I always thought that unwise. I can hardly be a Master Mason.'

'Er, possibly. I believe that they don't say that now. I might be out of date. I mean, we are out in the colonies, you know, Miss Fisher.'

'I like it here,' declared Phryne. Mr Fanshawe had that bruised, harried look Phryne was beginning to recognise. Victim of Rupert Sheffield. She seemed fated to follow him around, trying to glue his subjects back together with food and praise. Phryne was intending, if the occasion offered, to take this out of Rupert Sheffield's very decorative hide. She could think of lots of ways in which he could compensate her. 'Is that it?' she asked.

Mr Fanshawe consulted his paper. 'What was your first coding phrase?'

'Precious stone set in a silver sea.'

'And the second?'

'Earth hath not anything to show more fair.'

'What phrase meant "Come at once"?'

'It wasn't a phrase. It was a word. Lucknow.'

'Right. I'm Peter Fanshawe. Nice to meet you, Miss Fisher.' He stood up and shook her hand. Phryne wondered what he would have done if she had failed to remember her code words. She refrained from scanning those innocent walls for hidden machine guns.

'And nice to meet you. Now, what can I do for you? I've been entirely out of any Intelligence work for years and years.'

'Mr Compton Mackenzie sent a special telegram,' said Mr Fanshawe. He had a pleasant voice, definitely a local, and Phryne could just see his children rushing up to hug him as he came home. He was bright and quick, and essentially nice. How could Sheffield have ballyragged him?

'How is good old Compton? Apparently he's quite the laird these days,' said Phryne warmly.

The young man blushed a little. 'I've never met him,' he confessed. 'We're not important here, Miss Fisher, as has recently been pointed out.'

'Might I make a broad intuitive leap and tell you that whatever Rupert Sheffield said to you is to be completely ignored? Just cut him out of your remembrance.'

'Miss Fisher!' exclaimed Fanshawe. 'Are you another mathematician?' Two of you, he managed to convey, would be too much for one lifetime.

Phryne patted his hand. 'No, no, I'm not going to lecture you on the Science of Deduction, I've just been meeting his victims a lot lately. So let me apply some balm to your feelings because I would like this to be a pleasant meeting and I really need you to trust me. Right?'

Fanshawe nodded. 'Mr Compton Mackenzie said to trust you.'

'This is how it went: he swanned in here, sneered lightly, pinned you with his violet eyes, told you that Australia was the end of the universe and any attempts at espionage here must be utterly pitiful. Right?'

Fanshawe nodded.

'He then told you that only fools played cricket, as he had seen your trophies. He insulted your school, as even though you went to Melbourne Grammar and were in the First Eleven, that would not compare to Eton, Harrow or Winchester.'

'Right.'

'He sneered at your suit, though it is a bespoke, hand-finished one from . . . probably Mr Merrydale—he favours those slightly wider lapels—in Flinders Lane, and entirely as good as anything from Savile Row.'

'Right again.'

'Then he told you that he had no intention of allowing you to know what he was doing in Australia. Then he swept out. Right?'

'Yes,' said Fanshawe.

Phryne jumped up and began to pace. Fanshawe watched. She was small but she was exceedingly fierce. Mr Compton

Mackenzie had told him not to underestimate Phryne. He wouldn't.

'The person who was waiting for him outside your door was an old and dear friend of mine called Dr John Wilson, and this Sheffield is such an idiot that if he is doing anything odd in Australia, he might get John Wilson killed. And I do not—emphatically do not—care about Rupert, but I really do care about John. Someone has already tried to kill him. Hence my telegram to Compton, and your summons to me. Right?'

'Right,' murmured Fanshawe. He felt immediately better. He tapped a bell and sent Mrs Thomas for tea and cakes.

'Did you really make one hundred and sixty-seven against the Scotch oafs?' she asked, looking at the trophy. 'That must have been a long day.'

'It was,' said Fanshawe. 'I was so tired that I stumbled and was run out on the one hundred and sixty-seventh. But we won.'

'Yes, cricket matches between Scotch and Grammar are always something of a tribal feud,' she said. 'Now, let's have a nice cup of tea and you can tell me what you want of me.'

'Right-o, Miss Fisher,' said Peter Fanshawe. 'Head Office has sent names, everyone that Sheffield might have offended. He was quite a good agent, you know, brilliant code-breaker. He did a little fieldwork. He was in a group that broke up a gun-running ring. He located some missing children. He did a few police-type things.'

'By deduction,' said Phryne dryly.

Fanshawe grinned at her tone. 'Yes—he's a pig, but he's awfully good at deduction.'

'So am I,' Phryne told him, 'and I am not a pig. All right. Any of them likely to be here?'

'I really can't find anyone at present,' said Peter Fanshawe.

'Most of the gun-runners are still in jail, except the ones whom the Albanians shot.'

'Those Albanians,' sighed Phryne. 'So hot-tempered.'

'And the Turks shot some of the others,' continued Fanshawe.

'Ditto,' said Phryne.

'There was a man called Mitchell, an Englishman, who they never could lay hands on. Still trying to trace him. No record of him entering Australia. And the rest of the files are still on their way. We have a dedicated telegraph but it all has to be decoded.'

'All right,' said Phryne. 'I'll look out for stray gun-runners. Meanwhile, I shall keep an eye on the repulsive Rupert for you. And—' she leaned closer to him '—if I need help, if I need a few agents and some firepower, can you command it?'

'Yes, Miss Fisher,' said Peter Fanshawe. 'Here's the telephone number. There will be someone at the end of that line at any time, day or night. Just say your name and state your wish. You shall have everything I've got.'

'Wonderful. Of course, perhaps Sheffield is just as he seems,' said Phryne. 'Accident-prone. But I like to be careful.'

With this patently untrue statement, she allowed Mrs Thomas to pour her a cup of tea and began to talk to Peter Fanshawe about his children.

'Little Alice is such a sweet girl,' said Peter. 'And Norman is going to be a good athlete. Right reflexes.'

'You still play with the Grammar Old Boys, don't you?' asked Phryne. 'Do you take Norman to your games?'

'Of course . . . how did you know?' he asked nervously. Deduction was going to make this poor man jumpy for a good while, Phryne thought.

'You dote on your children and you still have batting

calluses on your right hand,' said Phryne. 'Sorry, didn't mean to sound like Sheffield.'

'Not in one million years could you ever sound like that . . . person,' said Mrs Thomas. 'Well, I'd better get on with my decoding.' She went out.

'She's your code-breaker?' asked Phryne, chuckling.

Peter Fanshawe grinned. The grin lit up his whole face. 'Yes. She's brilliant. Never guess from looking at her, would you?' he asked, delighted. 'It's the knitting, I think.'

'Great cover,' agreed Phryne. 'And Rupert didn't deduce it?'

'No, just told her that her grandchild was going to be a girl. Which he isn't, because he is already born. How I disliked that man! Now, Miss Fisher, let me show you the way out. You can't come in the front door if you're pursued,' he told her, as he led the way downstairs. 'But if you need to sneak in, then the Flinders Lane entrance is your best bet. This way.'

The offices had been modified. The red-brick buildings actually shared internal walls. One of these had been holed and a door installed, masked by a hanging curtain. This led to a narrow stairwell, down into what seemed to be a tailor's shop. Phryne smelt steam and starch and tweed. Peter turned a handle on a blank bit of wall, and Phryne emerged into a changing room.

'When you come in, just pull on this clothing hook and turn it to the left,' explained Peter Fanshawe, smiling at her. 'This way.'

'Very pretty,' said Phryne. The tailor's shop was busy. Several ladies worked there. They gave Phryne an uninterested once-over and went back to their tasks, sewing on buttons and neatening seams.

'And here you are in Flinders Lane.' Peter waved as though to make a present of the scene. Phryne took his hand again, shook it, and left. Nice. A good little niche, excellent organisation, and Mrs Thomas to break the codes. Rupert Sheffield had altogether missed the intelligence in Mrs Thomas's eyes. He had a huge—in fact, a bloody enormous—blind spot. Women.

That could be useful, thought Phryne. Her diabolical grin caused a lounging gentleman to choke on his afternoon beer.

•

When she got home she found the household peaceful. Jane, having been dragged out for a swim and aware that no more exertion would be demanded of her, was placidly playing chess with Tinker. He had brought in the fish for dinner and was feeling gratified by Mrs Butler's praise. It was not every passing fisher boy who could haul in a snapper on a cheap, light rig. Tinker had done it. Mrs Butler was already talking about roast *poisson a Nivelles*. Tinker was sure it would taste fine.

'So, what did you make of Mr Sheffield's lecture?' asked Phryne, as Tinker sadly tipped his king onto its side.

'Not a thing, Guv,' confessed Tinker. 'I was lost after he said "the science of deduction".'

'I was too,' said Phryne. 'Jane?'

'The mathematics are beyond me,' said Jane, biting her forefinger. 'At least, at present. I think they might be sound enough. The problem is that giving each element of a situation a value is not a mathematical judgment, but a personal one.'

Phryne and Tinker looked at each other. Tinker shrugged.

'I mean,' said Jane, 'say there is a crime scene at which there is a flannel soaked in ether and a pelican. You have to give a value to the flannel and the pelican. So you believe that the anaesthetic is more important than the pelican, so you give the pelican a one and the flannel a six.'

'I begin to see what you mean,' said Phryne.

'Yes, Miss Phryne, because what if it turns out—'

'That the rag was being used to clean stains off an overcoat, and the pelican was the key to all of it?' asked Ruth, coming in from the kitchen bearing a plate. 'Would anyone like to try some slightly-not-quite-right gingerbread? It's made with treacle,' she added. 'Which is probably why it hasn't quite worked.'

'So,' said Jane, 'if it's a pelican-smuggling ring, or the pelican has swallowed the gold watch that proves who the murderer is, then giving them numbers just confuses things.'

'Interesting,' said Phryne, trying a corner of the treacly gingerbread. It was good, but heavy. This was not a ginger-bread to drop on your foot. But it would probably feed the poor for weeks. 'And giving them values is not a matter of logic or scientific reasoning. It's up to the detective to say, this is important, this isn't, for no better reason than his own experience.'

'Yes,' said Jane.

'Or intuition,' said Phryne. 'Which is another way of saying a good informed guess.'

They all laughed.

•

Phryne was roused from a decadent afternoon snooze by Dot, coming in with an armload of ironed garments and the news that choristers had been visited upon her. Six of them, it appeared. Phryne brushed her hair and washed her face and went down to the garden, where Mr Butler had corralled them and supplied them with drinks.

They seemed perfectly happy to sit and sing and drink for the foreseeable future. Phryne was greeted with a shout of welcome by Oliver and Matthew. Tabitha smiled at her and raised a glass. A stunningly beautiful young woman, with a rope of chestnut hair and eyes like agate, turned a perfect profile to her.

'Caterina,' she introduced herself. 'Soprano.'

'And are you a soprano, too?' Phryne asked the remaining woman.

'Of course,' she replied. 'Calliope, they call me Cally.' Calliope had the sort of bosom on which one could repose with perfect confidence. She was born to nurture.

And another bass, presumably. This one appeared to be called Tommy and was very big. Probably a rugby player, employed for crushing opposing wings to death. And he was clumsy. Phryne saw Mr Butler's point. Loose Tommy in a drawing room and there would be breakage. Sooner introduce a buffalo into a china shop. Even now he was struggling to subdue a perfectly solid wrought-iron chair.

'Oh, do stop it,' said Matthew wearily. 'Just sit down and fold your hands in your lap, Tommy, like a good boy. We've got enough trouble without you going five rounds with the garden furniture.'

Tommy sat down with a thump. He folded his hands. Matthew, it seemed, had some sort of moral suasion over these people. That could be very useful.

'All right,' said Phryne. 'To what do I owe the honour of this visit?'

'You found the mystery woman,' Matthew said. 'She didn't kill him.'

'No,' said Phryne. 'And you weren't supposed to tell anyone about that, Matthew.'

'Oh, but I didn't think you meant *us*,' protested Matthew.

Choristers, thought Phryne. 'All right, I forgive you, as long as only the choir knows. What brings you here?'

'You wanted to talk about Mendelssohn,' said Matthew, 'and choirs and conductors and so on. I brought Tommy and Cally and Tab and Cat and Oliver. We know a lot about *Elijah*. Cat's brother is a famous pianist. And Tab has sung *Elijah* eight times.'

'Right,' said Phryne. 'I appreciate your expertise. Tell me all.'

'That might take awhile,' said Caterina, 'and I have to be home by seven.'

'Start telling me all,' said Phryne. 'I, too, have company coming tonight.' She smiled at the thought. More John Wilson, yum. 'We can continue this conversation at another time if needs be. But first, who is Aunty? You were talking about her at lunch.'

They all giggled, except the deeper voices, who chortled.

Tabitha explained. 'He's Mark Henty, a very good soloist with the Sydney Opera company. Known as Aunty Mark for reasons which—'

'Are apparent,' said Phryne.

'He's going to sing the role of Elijah for us,' explained Tabitha. 'He's bringing Gawain, his accompanist. But he is going to go mental at the state of readiness of the chorus. You have to get Mendelssohn right, you see. You can fudge the edges with really strong composers, and everyone gets lost sooner or later in Bach, but Mendelssohn's so delicate and light, a blurry sound ruins him. And when Aunty Mark is cross, we all smart for it.'

'Especially me,' said Matthew ruefully. 'Because I'm choirmaster now. I've called extra rehearsals. We're not far off getting it right. Not really all that far off,' he said hopefully.

'Possibly,' said Tabitha. 'At least Leonard is in Albury and will be missing for a couple of days. One day I'm going to slaughter him when he stands up with two pages of notes and cross-questions the conductor.'

'Now if it had been good old Len who was poisoned, we would all be suspects,' agreed Calliope. 'But as it happened, it wasn't.' She sounded regretful.

'What was wrong with Tregennis as a conductor?' asked Phryne.

'Hard to know where to start,' said Matthew.

'Oh, I know where to start,' said Caterina through clenched (white) teeth. 'I could show you the bruises.'

'Would you, Cat?' begged Tommy.

'No,' she said, quite without malice. 'Cally's seen them. He pinched.'

'And he groped,' said Calliope. 'Horrible man.'

'And not only that,' protested Oliver. 'I mean, sorry, ladies, but just being a disgusting old lecher isn't too uncommon. But he was rude to everyone. He hated sopranos—well, that isn't that uncommon, either . . .' He ducked as Caterina clipped at his ears. 'They mostly carry the tune, and you can really hear it when they are flat.' Oliver became aware that even the delightful Calliope was glaring at him and coughed himself into silence.

'But, as my tragically tactless colleague is trying to say,' put in Matthew hastily, 'Tregennis also screamed at the altos, yelled at the basses, and was exceptionally nasty to the tenors. Instead of making us go back and trying over a whole chunk again, he would concentrate on a few notes, and after awhile you can't sing six notes correctly without the rest of the piece. Then he would swell up, scream at the accompanist, and reduce everyone to tears or impotent fury.'

'That sounds like a very bad way to get the best out of a choir,' said Phryne.

'Oh, it was,' agreed Tabitha. 'The sops were scared to sing out, the basses growled, the tenors lost their places and the altos all wanted to kill him.'

'And then someone did. Or several someones,' Phryne reminded them.

'I spent an hour trying to talk Professor Szabo out of leaving, poor old man,' said Calliope. 'He was so distressed. All he would say is that Tregennis was a butcher and that when he played with Beecham, Mendelssohn sounded like Mendelssohn would have wanted.' Of course, one would apply Calliope to the wounded souls. She was an emollient, like cream. But in defence of the weak and the oppressed, Phryne felt that Calliope could surprise the oppressors.

'Poor old prof,' said Tommy. 'He did play with Beecham, you know. He's still got the concert programs. Showed them to me when I carried him up all those creaky old steps one night.'

'That was nice of you,' said Caterina.

'Oh, he wasn't heavy,' said Tommy.

'Of course not,' agreed Caterina. 'Not for you.'

Tommy glowed.

'What should Mendelssohn sound like?' asked Phryne.

'He's called flimsy,' said Tabitha. 'I've sung *Elijah* a lot, it's very popular. I prefer Handel's *Messiah*, actually, lots of big strong fugues, solid music. But this is a bit fugitive if badly conducted. His recits are extremely boring if they aren't well sung, and they're usually not, because the soloists are used to opera.'

'And the old Felix was a conductor himself. I wish they'd had recording back in 1846. First performance was in Birmingham and it's been a favourite ever since,' said Matthew.

'He's a romantic, his works are poetic. Not a hammer, hammer, hammer on the majors like your Handel.'

'He's not my Handel,' protested Tabitha. 'I just like singing him. As do you.'

Matthew conceded that this was so.

'Did you say someones?' asked Oliver. 'More than one person killed him?'

'Yes, at least two of them,' replied Phryne. 'The mystery woman brought him his supper. He ate it and she took away the basket. She was gone in twenty minutes. Then someone brought in his teacup and pot. And a glass of poisoned wine. And someone else stuffed music in his mouth while he was dying.'

'Erk,' said Caterina, summing up the feelings of the gathering.

'Then the caretaker collected the crockery and took away the wastepaper. Can any of you tell me what he might have been writing? He was scrawling a draft, screwing it up and throwing it away and starting on another,' said Phryne.

They all looked blank.

'That sounds like love letters,' offered Calliope.

'I thought so too,' said Tommy. 'The bl— dratted things are so hard to write. A man might go through a hundred sheets of paper and still not get it right.'

Phryne had no doubt as to the intended recipient of Tommy's love letters. Neither had the others. The only one who wasn't grinning was Caterina.

'You're wrong about the number of someones,' stated Calliope.

'Oh?' asked Phryne. 'Why?'

'Because Tregennis used to make poor Professor Szabo bring him his tea,' said Calliope, her voice warm with sympathy. 'I tried to take over a couple of times, but Tregennis told me that women couldn't prepare tea properly and it was Szabo's duty, and he made such a fuss that it was doing more harm than good, so I stopped. So the prof brought in the tea, and then someone else brought in the poisoned wine.'

'Why not Professor Szabo?' asked Phryne.

'If there was any wine around,' said Calliope sadly, 'he would have drunk it. He's a soak, the poor old dear.'

'No, couldn't trust him with a glass of anything, up to and including battery acid,' agreed Tommy.

'In any case, didn't you say that the poisoned wine was Imperial Tokay?' asked Matthew.

'What, in that conversation you weren't supposed to be quoting?' asked Phryne. He blushed. 'But, yes, it was something like that.'

'Then it couldn't be the prof. Where would he get his hands on expensive wine? He can just about afford cheap port.'

'Well, there we are. When is your next rehearsal?' asked Phryne.

'Thursday,' said Matthew. 'Do come along. Can you sing?'

'I've sung this before,' Phryne informed him. 'See you then, thank you for visiting.' She ushered the young people out of the garden and shut the back gate on them.

'Very nice young people,' observed Mr Butler, gathering glasses.

'Indeed, and I do hope one of them isn't a murderer,' said Phryne.

•

The evening was quiet, as Jane was attempting to understand higher mathematics, Dot was at the pictures with Hugh Collins, Tinker had gone out for a spot of twilight fishing and Ruth was reading her favourite recipe book. The roast fish had been delicious.

Phryne took her glass up to her boudoir and stared out her window at the sea. Very comforting, a seascape. It was eternal, and completely unaffected by humans and human wars and human cruelty. She could see Tinker on the pier. Molly was lying next to him, paws in the air, tail stretched out to trip passing anglers. Darkness was creeping over the bay.

Australia did not have the long, delicious twilights of Europe. Nor the fast passing of light to dark of the tropics. Phryne had always enjoyed twilight, the gentle transition from being able to see to being in the dark. The thud with which the night fell in the equatorial bits of the world she found disconcerting.

But with the darkening of the sky came John Wilson limping valiantly up the stairs. Mr Butler shimmered up behind him, carrying a tray of drinks. Both of them seemed a little out of breath when they arrived.

John sank down into a plush armchair, panting a little.

Mr Butler set down the tray. 'A telephone message from Inspector Robinson, Miss,' he announced.

'Indeed? And what does Jack have to say?' asked Phryne, still staring out the window.

'The mystery woman is confirmed to be innocent of any wrongdoing, Miss.'

'Good.'

'And he has a mass of papers which he would like you to inspect, Miss Fisher. He suggests tomorrow morning?'

'Yes, tell him to bring it all here at about ten. Also tell him that the person with the tea and the person with the wine are two different people.'

'As you wish, Miss Fisher. Will there be anything else?'

Phryne looked at John, who shook his head.

'No, thank you, Mr Butler.'

Mr Butler vanished in his usual way.

'John dear, have a drink. Whatever is wrong?' she asked. He took the whisky, gulped it down, and held out his glass for a refill.

'Sheffield,' he gasped.

'What's happened to him?' asked Phryne, hoping that it might be humiliating or at least involve loss of underwear.

'Nearly run down by a car,' said John. 'Just now, as we were leaving the assembly hall. Big black car, fast.'

'In Collins Street?' asked Phryne. Usually that street was far too busy to get up any speed. She should know. She had tried.

'Came out of one of the lanes like a bat out of hell. Just when Sheffield stepped off the kerb. I barely managed to drag him back.'

'Which hasn't done your leg any good,' diagnosed Phryne.

'Just gave my knee a bit of a bang,' he said dismissively. 'No lasting damage. Not asking you to nurse me, Phryne.'

'Spiffy, because I am not going to,' she said. 'However, you are dusty and grimy and in need of a bath, so I shall run one in my new malachite bath, and I shall watch you take it, and I shall sit on the edge and amuse you. Does that sound good?'

'Good? It sounds wonderful,' he replied.

She rumpled his greying fair hair. 'And if you merit it, I might join you,' she told him, and went to run the bath. 'If you get out of that suit, I shall have someone brush it. I think Dot's back now.'

He got out of the suit, putting on that same beautiful dragon-emblazoned dressing gown. Phryne spoke on the house telephone. Presently Dot arrived, smiled at him, and picked up the clothes. She was so patently a Good Girl that he felt less uncomfortable about the way that Phryne had wrapped her establishment around him like a greatcoat around a chilled soldier.

'Hello, Miss Williams,' he said. 'Sorry to be a trouble.'

'No trouble,' said Dot. 'Miss Phryne says you nearly got run over!'

'Yes, but I'm not hurt, just a bit shocked,' he said, as her beautiful brown eyes beamed compassion at him.

'Nasty things,' said Dot, 'motor cars. I always keep my eyes closed when Miss Phryne's driving.'

'Oh, so did I,' John told her.

Dot examined him. 'What was she like when she was driving that ambulance?' she asked quietly.

'Skinny and fierce,' John told her. 'Wild. Feral, perhaps. Always untamed and unfazed.'

'Just like now, then,' said Dot. 'I'll have to get the oil stains on these out with petrol,' she told him, 'and leave them out to air until the morning. Did you take all your things out of your pockets?' John nodded. 'Good night, then,' she said, and went out.

'Well, now you're here for the night,' said Phryne, emerging from the bathroom. 'I have your trousers hostage. Always a position of strength. And you will allow me to assist you into the bath,' she told him.

Since she had removed most of her clothes in order to do so, John felt it was only fair to allow himself to be helped. Besides, that knee was developing a really impressive bruise. It hurt. Also, he was still shaking. That metal monster had come so close to Sheffield, it had brushed the front of his coat. So close to obliterating John Wilson's reason for living.

And, just for that moment, he had grappled Sheffield in his arms, his face against Sheffield's neck; he had inhaled that expensive cologne, that scent of honeysuckle. That keen, strange herbal smell of his skin. Just for a moment. And Sheffield, to keep his balance, had embraced John. Just for a moment.

No wonder John was still shaking.

Phryne, losing patience with his slowness, had stripped him and was conducting him to a massive bath, fully large enough for two. There were steps up and steps down and he managed them with care. Then he lay down, slowly, in green pine-smelling water, just this side of too hot. Phryne lowered his head to rest on a little rubber travelling pillow and he closed his eyes.

'And since it is inadvisable to fall asleep in a bath, I shall tell you all about a strange case in which I am involved. You've seen some of it already.' Phryne's voice was close. He opened his eyes. She was sitting on the edge of the bath, quite naked, with her feet in the water. Phryne was more comfortable without a stitch on than many people John knew who were wearing a full bathing costume.

'The dead conductor?' asked John. The hot water was soothing his nerves. His knee, however, was enpurpling a treat. It would be his bad leg that took the knock. 'Rupert thought it was the woman who brought the food.'

'It wasn't,' Phryne assured him, a little smugly. 'I found her. Just before Rupert did. Cook at the Imperial Hotel.'

'Oh dear,' said John, stirring a little to get the bad knee underwater. 'He wouldn't have liked that.'

'No, he didn't. We had a brief but blistering conversation, fortunately in French. I don't think he likes me,' said Phryne. 'He speaks beautiful French, though. It was worth being insulted to hear such a lovely accent.'

'His mother was French,' John murmured. 'Pity she didn't like him.'

'Oh?' asked Phryne.

'No, she hated his father,' John responded. 'So she hated her son, too. He was fobbed off on nannies as a child, then sent to school as soon as he was old enough. And he must have had a bad time there, too.'

'Indeed?' insinuated Phryne. 'Know thine enemy' had always been her watchword.

'Yes. He's very clever. But he tells people that he's very clever. He can't see that a little modesty might be a good idea. At least Winchester didn't have fags, didn't beat him too badly, because he was so bright and willing to learn. He wanted, he says, to know everything. So they could characterise him as a swot and leave him alone. He had a maths master who understood him, and he was always very good at languages.'

'I could hear that,' agreed Phryne. She splashed the water with her toes.

'When they took him out of Cambridge, like they took me out of medical school, he was too young to cope with a war.'

'Yes, darling,' said Phryne, picking up one of John's hands and stroking it. 'We were all too young.'

'They sent him to Athens. I think that they were fairly kind to him. He broke codes, he's a shark at codes. And he learned Turkish and Greek and so on, just by being around speakers. I don't know if he ever left Athens, he's never said. He read the Koran in a Turkish translation. Just to practise his Turkish.'

'Not religious, then?' coaxed Phryne.

'No, poor chap. I always found faith a great comfort. Otherwise it is too much, Phryne. Too cruel. To think that all the lads, all those boys, were just gone, blown out like candles. Don't you agree?'

'I do,' said Phryne. 'I like to think of them sitting down with all their mates to a serious drinking session, washed clean of mud and stench, all shiny and jolly. And if that doesn't constitute heaven, I'm not going; though, of course, I might not have the option.'

'Don't be silly,' murmured John. 'All of those dead boys and quite a lot of the living ones will petition the deity for your presence. And me too,' he added, kissing the hand which lingered over his.

'Very kind,' she said. 'And your voice ought to be heard; you are one of the truly good people I know. Not a long list, either.'

'Don't be silly, Phryne, I'm an—'

'Invert?' said Phryne. 'Of course you are.' She said this as though he had just claimed to have blue eyes, as something utterly ordinary.

'And that means,' John persisted, 'that I am a sinner.'

'Rubbish,' said Phryne sharply. 'No one can help whom they love. I am positive that your God doesn't care a fig.'

'This from a woman who isn't going to heaven,' said John, and chuckled.

'Not for that reason,' Phryne replied. 'I can prove it to you.'

'You can prove that Leviticus isn't God's word?' asked John.

'Certainly. Leviticus was a series of rules for a nomadic desert-dwelling culture, where it was sensible not to eat bacteria-enhanced shellfish or terrine of unclean creeping things, where you needed to isolate people who might have leprosy, granted. But consider: if you wish to condemn yourself to hell for Leviticus 18:22, then you need to carry out all the rest of the laws—stoning blasphemers, buying foreign slaves, killing witches, making burnt offerings and slaying those who twist thread of two types, which means you have to rise from this bath and slaughter Dot, who uses twined cotton and silk thread to embroider her hope chest table linen.'

'I have never had scripture explained to me by a naked woman before,' said John, somewhat startled.

'All the better to concentrate your attention,' said Phryne, reaching down and taking a handful of his attention and squeezing gently.

'I'm listening,' he assured her. Fervently.

'It's not Christ's law,' she said. 'I would draw your attention to Galatians, where my absolutely least-favourite saint—and it hurts me to to admit this—made the point. The Apostle Paul—he of the "women should shut up in church and obey their husbands", *that* Apostle Paul—says that Christ redeemed us from the laws. We are no longer under Old Testament law. Galatians, in fact, chapter three. Look it up, though not immediately.'

Her fingers stroked a little. John, who had thought himself exhausted, found that he wasn't. Not really.

'And do you know what your Christ thought of male lovers?' asked Phryne.

'No,' breathed John.

'Read Luke. I like the Book of Luke, he's a good writer and he wrote in Greek, so it went through fewer translations. In Luke a centurion called Longinus comes to Jesus and asks him to heal his boy who is dear to him. The Greek word is *pais*. That means lover. Not servant, not slave. He tells Jesus he doesn't even need to come to his house, just to—'

'Speak the word only, and he is healed,' remembered John.

'Quite.'

'But, Phryne, Christ healed lepers, he ate with tax gatherers and talked to prostitutes.'

'Your point?' asked Phryne. 'He liked stimulating company? Those pharisees must have been extremely boring, even at dinner.'

'No, he was merciful to the sinners,' said John, aware that he was on shaky theological ground. He remembered Longinus, a Roman, going to a Jewish faith healer on behalf of a 'boy who was dear to him'. He had wondered at the time. It seemed like extreme action for a Roman to take on behalf of a slave.

The hand under the water became a little more insistent.

'So, if the reason that you are not leaping on Sheffield is because you do not want to drag him into your sin, dismiss it,' urged Phryne.

'All right, all right, I'm convinced.' John grinned at her. 'You have remarkably effective debating methods, Phryne! Where did you learn all this theology, anyway?'

'When I was at school they made me sit for hours in a freezing church and listen to sermons which were the epitome of the word "tedious",' she explained. 'So I read the nearest book, which was the Bible. I found it fascinating. But occasionally contradictory.'

'But doesn't St Paul say something about homosexuality being wicked?' asked John, as lessons came back to him.

'Yes, but there he is being an idiot,' rejoined Phryne.

'You must have been a frightful child,' commented John, sliding a wet hand down her thigh.

'Oh, I was,' said Phryne proudly.

'But the other reason I am not leaping on Sheffield is that he doesn't want me,' explained John.

'Ah,' said Phryne, sliding down into the bath beside him. 'But I do.'

Henceforward, John found that making love in a warm bath put no strain whatsoever on his injured leg. And he would emerge cleaner than one whose sins had been scarlet, but now were washed as white as wool.

He woke at about dawn and looked out across the sea from Phryne's bed. The sun was rising, the darkness lifting. Phryne was asleep beside him, snuggled into his side. She slept like a cat sleeps, neat and elegant, making every place a subtle background to the picture of utter relaxation. No nightmares tonight, he thought, and lay back down, closing his eyes. Even if he wanted to slip away, his trousers were still unransomed.

Striving and failing to force down a smug smile, John Wilson went back to sleep.

CHAPTER EIGHT

> *But joy incessant palls the sense*
> *And love unchanged will cloy*
> *And she became a bore intense unto her love-*
> *sick boy.*
> *With fitful glimmer burned my flame and I*
> *grew cold and coy.*
> *At last one morning I became*
> *Another's love-sick boy!*

Gilbert and Sullivan
Trial By Jury

Phryne woke, slid out from under John Wilson's embrace as a
cat slides out of an importunate grasp, and went to dress. Dot
knocked at the boudoir door with her coffee and croissant.

'Nice day, Miss. Detective Inspector Robinson is coming
at ten.'

'Then we had better give John back his clothes,' said
Phryne, sipping. 'All well?'

'Yes, Miss. Tinker got knocked into the sea by one of those
horrible old men, but no harm done, he can swim.'

'Then why are you looking so worried?' asked Phryne,
nibbling her croissant.

'Because Molly bit the old man and Tinker thinks he's coming to complain,' said Dot, shifting from foot to foot. 'He might complain about her and get her shot.'

'No, that won't happen,' said Phryne. 'Every dog is allowed one bite, and we didn't know that Molly bit people before, did we?'

Dot looked down and tugged the end of her plait. 'Well, actually, Miss, we did, because—'

'No, we didn't,' said Phryne firmly. 'Suppress your incurable honesty, Dot. If the old child-beater has the nerve to come here, escort him in to see me. Anything else?'

'No, Miss.' Dot was delighted. She was very fond of Molly. 'Though you might rinse poor Molly's mouth—she might have caught something, biting such bitter flesh. Right, I'd better get dressed.'

'I brought the doctor's suit,' said Dot.

Phryne dropped it quietly on the end of her bed, where John Wilson was sleeping like a child, and donned suitable clothing to inspect documents. While Dot informed Tinker that he didn't have to spirit Molly away, Phryne sat down in her parlour with her policeman and a large cardboard box full of Hedley Tregennis's papers.

'Tip them all out on the table, Jack dear, and we shall sort. Bills here, correspondence here, all the rest of the stuff here. He was quite well off,' she said, looking at a passbook. 'More than a hundred quid in the bank. Cheques mostly drawn to cash, took out ten quid a week for usual expenses. No large withdrawals, nothing odd that I can see. Some sort of salary paid in every month.'

'His rent was paid up until the end of the month,' said Jack.

'He favoured French food; this is a menu from Le Perroquet in Prahran. Expensive.'

'He was negotiating for a conducting job with the Sydney Opera chorus,' said Jack. 'They didn't seem to want him, even though he reduced his usual fee.'

'Choristers gossip,' said Phryne. 'Almost as much as policemen. Someone would have asked about him, and whole fistfuls of black balls would have gone into the hat. More bills, all docketed, all paid. A neat life, so far. Right. What about all this crumpled, scribbled and torn stuff? What do you have there, Jack?'

The detective inspector's eyebrows were rising towards his hair.

'Love letters,' he said faintly. 'Should be handled with tongs.'

Phryne read a few smouldering sentences and giggled. 'I shall have Mr Butler fetch you a set of oven gloves. Speaking of which, here is the very man. Yes, Mr B?'

Mr Butler's utter lack of expression indicated extreme displeasure.

'A Mr Brown, Miss Fisher. A person from the pier, I believe. Come to complain about—'

'Send him in, and send in Tinker, too. I'm so glad you're here, Jack dear. I may need some official backing.'

Jack Robinson felt uneasy. He would have to support Phryne, no matter what she did. He hoped it wouldn't mean his badge, or the infliction of serious injuries. On anyone. By anyone.

Mr Butler ushered in a crabbed, shabby old man who stank so strongly of old fish that Mr Butler took it upon himself to open the parlour window.

Mr Brown, failing to remove his cap in the presence of a lady, stared at Phryne and snarled, 'That mongrel of yours bit me. I want it shot.'

'Then want must be your master, I'm afraid,' said Phryne.

'I had no notion that she would bite. Suppose you tell the detective inspector what you were doing to make the previously friendly dog bite you?'

'Jeez,' said Mr Brown. 'Cops?'

'I'm Detective Inspector Robinson,' snapped Jack, who didn't like the look of this old reprobate. He also had a soft spot for Molly. 'Well? What happened?'

'I was just sitting there fishing and the mongrel bit me,' protested Mr Brown. 'See? Here. Look, there's blood.'

Robinson inspected an undoubted dog bite on his insanitary calf. He hoped Molly hadn't been poisoned.

'All right, I see there's blood. Now, why did the dog bite you?'

Greater criminals than Mr Brown had broken down and confessed under Jack Robinson's relentless regard.

'I might'a, I say I might'a given the young bloke a bit of a shove with me foot,' he stammered.

'Tinker?' asked Jack Robinson.

Tinker peeled back his shirt to show the clear mark of a boot sole. He had been kicked off the pier into the water.

'You're lucky you didn't break his ribs,' said Robinson. 'You want to charge him with assault and battery, Tinker?'

Tinker shook his head. 'As long as Molly's all right,' he bargained.

Robinson favoured Mr Brown with a long, slow, considering stare, as though he was memorising his features and would know him if he saw him again.

'Get out, and if I hear of you abusing boys again, I'll have you. All right?' he said very quietly. Mr Brown looked as though shortly Mr Butler might have to call someone to scrub the carpet.

'Yair, all right, boss, don't go crook.'

Mr Butler escorted the cringing Mr Brown out of the room

and subsequently out of the house. Tinker grinned at him. Molly, from where she was tethered in the back garden, gave him a valedictory snarl.

'Better watch out for him in future, Tink, I don't think he likes you,' said the policeman.

'I catch more fish than him. I can stay out of his way,' said Tinker, who had never got used to having allies. It was a strange and intoxicating sensation. And Molly was safe. How had she known that Brown was in the house? Musta smelt the old bastard, thought Tinker. Good old Molly. Just wanted another go at him, despite the way he must have tasted.

'All right, Tink, ask Mrs B for some arnica and get Jane to put it on,' Phryne ordered. 'That's going to be a nasty bruise.'

'Can I help with the paperwork, Guv?' asked Tinker.

'No fear,' said Robinson. 'I don't think *I'm* old enough to read these letters, much less you. Arnica and a bandage, and you can play hero for the rest of the day.'

'Grouse,' said Tinker.

He left to be attended by his female housemates. Jane was very good at first aid. Her hands were sure and she was not crippled by Ruth's empathy with the pain of the sufferer. Phryne remembered poor John Wilson and his damaged leg. She would attend to him when he woke up. They read in silence for some time.

'All right, the person who signs herself "Aspasia" is clearly besotted with Hedley Tregennis,' said Phryne. 'And we know she's not Genevieve Upton because of the dates. Aspasia's been with Tregennis for three years.'

'A woman of strong feelings . . .' said Robinson.

'And no taste whatsoever,' concluded Phryne, fanning herself with a handful of inflammatory correspondence. 'Interesting epistolary style, though. Could write erotica for a living. Anaïs Nin would be intrigued. She seems to have been a musician. Jenny saw a violin bow in the conductor's room on one occasion.'

'Right, female violinists of the orchestra,' said Jack, rummaging for his file.

Mr Butler had returned with Jane. Jane looked excited and smelt strongly of rubbing liniment.

'Miss Phryne, can I go and put arnica on the doctor's knee? He's up now. I've already got arnica on my hands. And I can look at his leg,' said Jane. 'Might make it easier for him to get down the stairs, poor man,' she added, belatedly remembering that doctors were supposed to be compassionate. She was trying to acquire this skill.

'Take Dot with you to preserve the poor man's modesty, Jane dear, and try not to hurt him,' said Phryne absently.

'I don't want to hurt him,' Jane told her. 'I want to make him feel better.'

'So do we all,' agreed Phryne, reading a few more lines of Aspasia's impassioned prose. My, my, Hedley Tregennis must have had hidden talents. The writer was describing something which Phryne had not only never tried but never even thought of, which was a vanishingly small number of things . . .

She heard Jane and Dot go up the stairs. Jack ran a finger down the list of musicians and found the female violinists.

'No Aspasia, of course. There's an Anne,' offered Robinson. 'So you're . . . looking after that doctor bloke?' he asked abruptly.

'He's a very old friend of mine, Jack; he incurred a back full of shrapnel on my account, and I am very fond of him,' said Phryne. 'Would you like to see the scars?' She dragged up her blouse and showed him her smooth side, pitted with small scars. 'Creeping barrage got us. I would have been eviscerated if not for John Wilson.'

'I owe him a thankyou, then,' said Jack, trying not to touch that soft skin. 'I thought, because he was with that Sheffield . . .'

'Sheffield is not John's fault,' stated Phryne. 'And yesterday someone nearly ran him down.'

'I can understand that,' said Robinson, and grinned.

'Oh, so can I. Fortunately I have an alibi, so it wasn't me. But poor John saved Sheffield's life, and I bet he never even noticed. And John's banged his already injured leg, which is why Jane has gone to apply arnica to him. And to get a good look at the scar—she loves scars. Dot will make sure that John doesn't feel like an anatomy specimen.'

'Well, poor bloke just stood there and looked embarrassed when that Sheffield was mouthing off at us,' said Robinson. 'I reckon you're right, Sheffield isn't his doing. All right, and it was nice of him to save your life, too. Makes a bit of a habit of it.'

'So he does,' agreed Phryne. 'Have you got descriptions of the female violinists?'

'I have. Why?'

'From some of her letters, it is clear that Tregennis called her the Queen of Sheba, who is popularly pictured as dark-skinned. At another point she mentions that he adores her dark eyes. So you want a dark-complexioned woman, rather tending to the embonpoint. Plump,' said Phryne. 'She rather goes on about how much he likes pillowing his head on her . . . never mind. Dark. Plump.'

'Only one,' said Jack. 'Mrs Horace Reagan. Given name Alice.'

'Ah,' said Phryne. 'Right, mark her down and let's look at all the rubbish.'

She placed the love letters in a pile with a snow globe on

top, which might cool their ardour, and began straightening out and laying flat the screwed-up pages.

'Oh dear,' said Robinson, fitting together two ripped pieces.

'Yes, I've got the same thing,' said Phryne.

'*I never want to see you again, you traitorous bitch?*' asked Jack.

'I hope that's a quote,' said Phryne, a little taken aback.

'Of course it's a quote.' Jack touched the back of her hand. 'What have you got?'

'And I quote, *get out of my life you . . .* well, *bitch* is the nicest thing he says. I don't know why he threw these away; they all seem to be variants on a theme. Surely there are only so many ways of calling a woman names that begin with a "c"?' asked Phryne.

'You'd think so, wouldn't you?' murmured Jack. 'Oh, wait one moment. Here's one that isn't just abuse. *How is Horry going to feel when I show him the letters?* Now there's a nice motive for murder.'

'Nifty,' said Phryne. 'I wonder if he was blackmailing her, as well? I am having the greatest difficulty feeling sorry for this murder victim, Jack.'

'Me too,' said Jack. 'But a policeman's lot is not a happy one, you know.'

Phryne smiled at him with great affection. There was a discreet cough (Butler's Instruction Manual lesson 7: attracting attention without causing offence).

'Yes, Mr Butler?' asked Phryne.

'Mr Rupert Sheffield, Miss Fisher.'

'Show him in,' said Phryne.

'He is just enquiring for Dr Wilson, Miss Fisher,' said the butler.

'Send him up to the boudoir, then. I don't need to speak to him. Jane should be almost finished with her ministrations by now,' said Phryne, and turned back to Jack, hearing feet pacing up her staircase. She hid a private smile. Making Rupert jealous in a good cause was too diverting. Another reason why Phryne would not be entering heaven. There were already far too many, but she was not sorry about any of them. And that trench raider had really merited it.

•

Rupert Sheffield paused at the door to Phryne's boudoir. It was a beautiful room in the art deco style. Miss Fisher liked green and purple, clearly; there was even a vase of irises on her table. He caught sight of his own face in an elaborate mirror with pinkish glass, wreathed in ceramic vine leaves. Anyone invited into this room was invited to a bacchanal, that was plain.

He looked ivory-pale and alien in all that luxury, and the vine leaves crowned a face which might have belonged to Apollo in one of his world-shattering, plague-spreading moods, but not Pan or even Dionysus.

He was looking at John Wilson sitting with his trouser leg rolled up almost to the hip. His bare foot was on a hassock and a blonde girl was kneeling by his side. A sharp scent of arnica hit Rupert's nose. Not a scent common in Miss Fisher's boudoir, he was sure. A plain young woman was seated in the other chair, hands folded over a rolled bandage, a safety pin stuck into her cardigan.

Miss Fisher does not even attend John herself, thought Sheffield, but orders a servant to look after him. She did not deserve him either. The girl was talking to John, and John was replying.

'Yes, shattered the femur,' he told the girl, who was massaging liniment into a red bruise on John's knee and shin. Recent. Must have been sustained when he pushed Sheffield out of the way of that car. Unnecessary. Sheffield had been in no danger at all. He would have been able to leap back to the kerb. John had injured himself without reason. Illogical reaction. 'My surgeon wouldn't take the leg off, fought to save it. I was picking slivers of bone out of the scar for weeks.'

'But the bone must have regrown,' observed the girl. 'And at least some of the muscles and tendons reattached. Otherwise you would not be able to walk and you walk quite well.'

'Yes, the human body has remarkable regenerative qualities,' John agreed.

She was too bold to be a servant. Must be a daughter of the house. And the plain woman would be Miss Fisher's companion, who would cast a cloak of respectability over her mistress's affairs. She did look very respectable. By the crucifix, a Catholic, too. She loved all the shades of autumn; her dress was beige and her cardigan dark brown. Good but subdued clothes, sensible house shoes, clean hands with pinpricks in one forefinger—an embroiderer, then. Long hair in a plait, no cosmetics, scent of roses—an old-fashioned person. No rings on the hands. But she was easy in the presence of a strange man in a boudoir, therefore was probably engaged. Then again, the girl was comfortable in her situation, and she rewarded Rupert's interest.

Her hands were assured and skilled. Her massage was firm but John was not in pain. She knew where the bones and muscles attached, where the pressure points were, and how to produce the right effect. And the questions she was asking John were very intelligent. Her accent was educated young female Australian. She was dressed in a blue linen shift, covered with an oversized gardening smock, so as not to get liniment on her clothes. Her hair was clipped short. She was not interested in her appearance, though the person who had chosen the dress had done so because she had quite unusual dark blue eyes. She had raised them, summed up Sheffield with a long glance, then had dismissed him as of no importance to her task at hand and returned her attention to John. She had extended her massage from the bruise to the complex scar on John's thigh. She seemed to find it fascinating. So did Rupert, who had never seen it before. The bullet had shattered the bone and mangled the flesh, and the medical attendant had only been able to reorder it as best he could, extract the missile, and stitch the remnants together in a purse-string suture, open to allow drainage of the inevitable infection.

'Why didn't Dr MacMillan amputate?' the girl asked in her clear, dispassionate voice.

The plain young woman exclaimed, 'Jane! Miss Phryne told you not to hurt the doctor, and that includes his feelings!'

'No, no,' soothed John. 'She's gathering information. I'm familiar with that look. Sort of sharpens the face . . .'

Where could he have seen such a look before? Rupert asked himself. Oh, of course. Me. Do I look like that?

'There's enough thigh to make a suitable stump,' said Jane, shaking off the plain woman's objection.

'Yes, but she said she wanted to send me home to my . . . to my . . . to someone who was waiting for me, with both legs,' explained John. 'And here I am, still bipedal, you see. That feels very nice,' he added, as the tight scar tissue eased under Jane's fingers.

'So, wasn't your lover waiting for you?' asked Jane.

The plain woman was about to object again, but John raised a hand. 'Yes, but it's not a story with a happy ending, Jane. I don't want to talk about it, if you don't mind.'

'All right,' said Jane equably. There were many other interesting things about Dr Wilson which she could explore instead. 'The car hit you here,' she observed, putting a finger on the centre of the bruise. 'That's the round boss of a hub cap. You must have been right beside it. Did Mr Sheffield thank you for saving his life?' she asked, and Sheffield was aware that Jane knew he was watching.

'Didn't need to,' said John valiantly.

'That will do for now,' said Jane. 'I can bandage it again tomorrow morning if you are here.'

'Thank you, Jane, you are very kind,' responded John.

She took the bandage from the plain woman, wound it and secured it expertly, and then pulled the hem of the trouser down. Then she put on a sock and John's shoe, tying the laces neatly.

'Up you come,' said Jane, offering a hand. The contrast of the small girl and tall, stocky John was piquant.

Rupert stepped into the room. The plain woman jumped. Jane assessed him coldly.

'Might I be of assistance?' he asked.

John flushed red. But he took Rupert's hand and was lifted to his feet. Jane held out his stick. Rupert took it.

'I believe I should thank you for saving my life,' said Rupert. John flicked him an amazed upward glance which for some reason made Rupert feel briefly ashamed.

'No trouble, my dear chap,' said John.

'But it would only be polite to thank you. After all, you were injured. I didn't realise that it was significant. Can I give you an arm down the stairs?' asked Rupert, his voice at full Irish coffee with extra cream and chocolate liqueur.

Greatly wondering, John leaned his full weight on Sheffield's arm and they went down the marble stairs together. Phryne, catching sight of them from her parlour, suppressed a chortle and came out to bid farewell to her guests.

'Thank you for lending me Jane,' John said to her. 'And for everything else.'

Phryne leaned across Rupert's immaculate chest to kiss John on the cheek. 'Pleasure, in every sense,' she said. 'Can't you stay for breakfast?'

'He's breakfasting with me,' said Sheffield flatly. 'Good morning, Miss Fisher.'

Phryne waited until the door was safely shut before she collapsed into helpless laughter. Jane, going back to the kitchen to replace her smock, gave her a piercing look just as she was calming down and set her off again.

'What was all that about?' asked Jack Robinson. 'No, on second thought, don't tell me. Come back here, Miss Phryne Fisher. We've got a murder to solve and we are finally getting somewhere.'

'As you wish,' murmured Phryne, and returned to the Case of the Vengeful Violinist.

Presently, Jack took his evidence and went to interview the epistolary Mrs Horace Reagan. Phryne had nothing to do and was full of energy. She called to Molly, put on her lead, and took her for a brisk walk along the foreshore. There was always a chance she would meet Mr Brown, and get another chance to remonstrate with him for kicking Tinker.

The picture of John leaning on Sheffield's arm with a look of schoolgirl adoration, however, worried Phryne as much as it amused her. She had better not get this wrong.

Therefore, she wouldn't. It was as simple as that.

And now it must be time for lunch. She turned for home. Molly romped beside her, full of the consciousness of being a Good Dog. Phryne shared it.

Phryne was engaged in a fitting for a new dress, which was trying. That was because it was for Jane, and Jane thought that clothes were tedious and being fitted for them even more tedious. She did not wriggle, precisely, but she was never still. Madame Fleuri's best fitter was getting cross. Cross fitters have ways to punish annoying subjects.

'If you talked to me, Miss Phryne, I wouldn't feel like I had pins and needles,' she said.

The fitter, Mlle Galle, sent Phryne a look of heartfelt pleading. This was going to be a very nice little dress but it had to drape correctly, and she had another child to fit before she got that cup of tea that Mrs Butler always made her. Phryne did not want to see Jane perforated.

'Fine. Your topic?' asked Phryne, perching on the arm of a chair.

'Will you answer anything?' asked Jane cunningly.

'Probably,' said Phryne, who was never an easy touch.

'Why are you trying to drive Dr Wilson into that unpleasant Mr Sheffield's arms?' asked Jane.

Occasionally Jane's questions dropped onto the listener with the approximate weight and impact of a falling piano. Phryne blinked.

'Your perspicacity never ceases to astound me,' Phryne told her. 'Because that's where he wants to be, Jane dear. I am not forcing John into Sheffield's arms. I want Sheffield to recognise John's devotion.'

'But I really do not like Mr Sheffield,' Jane told her. 'He is rude and I don't think he cares for anyone. Isn't that an unkind thing to do to nice Dr Wilson?'

'No, because that is nice Dr Wilson's dearest wish.'

'People,' sighed Jane. 'I'll never understand them.'

'They are not logical,' agreed Phryne.

Mlle Galle patted Jane's shoulder and unpinned the marked basque. Jane sped off down the stairs. Ruth stood up in her sensible undergarments. Mademoiselle smiled at her. This one would be no trouble at all. And then there would be *thé anglaise*, for which she had acquired a passion.

•

Four o'clock brought a very pleased Jack Robinson.

'Got her,' he said. 'She stole the morphine out of her husband's medical bag, and the Tokay out of his wine cellar. You know what he was angriest about? Not the affair—apparently she has lots of them. It was the wine. "I don't know why she had to use my Tokay," he grumbled. "I've only got three bottles left." Thank you for all the help,' said the policeman.

'My pleasure, Jack dear.' Phryne hugged him briefly. 'But . . .'

'Yair, I know. Cause of death is choking, and we still don't know who choked him.'

'I might be able to assist,' said Phryne, steering him to a chair. Jack Robinson sat. Phryne was about to land something frightful upon him, and he liked to be sitting when she did so. It was hard to stagger while sitting down.

'How?' he asked, really wanting to know.

'I might join the choir,' she told him.

'That sounds like it might be all right,' he said, on a breath of relief.

'I have sung *Elijah* before,' she told him. 'Choirs can always do with a new soprano. The person who stuffs music into a dying man's mouth isn't bold or dangerous. I won't be in any peril.'

'You create your own peril,' grumbled Jack. 'All right, that sounds good.'

'Excellent—there's a rehearsal tonight, I'm going to volunteer.'

Jack Robinson had to say it, even though he knew it would be useless. Phryne defined 'precipitate'.

'Just don't get into . . . don't put yourself . . .' He stumbled over his warnings. Phryne had heard them all before, anyway, and had never taken a blind bit of notice.

She smiled at him brightly. 'I won't,' she said.

He didn't believe a word of it.

•

Bidding Mr Butler to return for her later, Phryne climbed the Scots Church Assembly Hall steps one more time and found a gaggle of choristers just inside the door.

'Scores,' announced the librarian.

Phryne smiled at Matthew, who was looking rather harried, and at the embraceable Calliope and the elegant Caterina. She signed for a score with her flamboyant pen and looked around for fellow sopranos. Julia was there, already mouthing over her quartet. So was the Wagnerian Chloe.

'Come along,' urged Matthew, waving his arms in broad, shooing gestures, as if he was herding goats. 'Think of what Aunty Mark is going to say to us if we can't get through "Oh Lord Thou Hast Overthrown" without getting lost again.'

'Ouch,' commented Oliver. 'That's the entry to his big recit.'

'Right,' agreed Daniel grimly.

They flurried and moved, shedding hats, until they were lined up in the proper order. A small man, bald, shabby, muttering, confronted Phryne as she stood in the front row.

'You're new. Who are you?' he demanded in a thick Mittel-European accent.

'I am Phryne Fisher,' she said with a beaming smile, as though he was a favourite uncle. 'And you?'

'Just a poor strummer of keys,' he muttered. 'When I was with Beecham . . .'

Phryne could smell the cheap port on his breath, see the damage that the alcohol had done: reddened eyes, jaundiced skin, tremor, chapped lips. He might have been a good-looking man once, before, as the policeman had said, the grog got him. Tommy, who seemed to have a sympathy for the old man, led him away from Phryne, patting him on the shoulder. Poor creature. Not likely to last much longer. But his hands, as he laid them on the keys, were as steady as a rock.

The choir began to sing scales and exercises. Voices eased, high or low notes were reached without strain. They sang the absurd lament that life was but a melancholy flower to warm up.

'Basses and altos,' said Matthew. 'From A, if you please.'

'*Open the heavens,*' boomed the basses, '*and send us relief.*'

'Sops and tenors,' said Matthew. His beat was clear. This was a relief. Phryne had sung with conductors who waved their arms around as though they were flinging away armloads of rotten fish. She had sung with ones whose delicacy and economy of movement had been called 'mouse-milking'. Both were equally hard to follow and both would scream at the choir for not following the unfollowable. Then there were the ones who forgot that the choir did not speak, as it were, Hungarian, and who roared at them for not following instructions in a foreign tongue. At least Matthew wouldn't do that. He pushed his wheat-coloured hair back from his brow. Phryne reminded herself he was off limits, drat it all.

However, she could not imagine him stuffing music into anyone's mouth, unless they asked very nicely. But he was still a suspect and she was in the middle of a murder investigation, so she told her libido to lie down and tackled her notes again. The piece was almost correct but colourless and lacklustre.

'No, look,' pleaded Matthew. 'There's a drought, you're begging for rain, you're representing the people—put some emotion into it! Imagine your children dying.' The choir looked at him. He made a wild gesture. 'All right, imagine your favourite sheep dying! Now put your backs into it. Boy, you ready?'

'Ready,' said Caterina. Anyone less like a boy would be hard to imagine.

They sang it again. Matthew seemed pleased.

'Right, that was all right, we'll run on. Tommy, you do Elijah. Some passion, please!' demanded Matthew, and raised his hands again.

Just as the prophet Tommy was asking his boy if there was a cloud in the sky, the door banged open. A large man whisked inside and stood with his hands on his hips. He listened for a moment. Then he sang a challenge, in a baritone voice with a tenor quality clear as a bell and rich as plum pudding.

'*I am a Pirate King!*' he sang, and the whole choir forgot Mendelssohn.

'*Hurrah, hurrah, hurrah for the Pirate King!*' they chorused. He walked down the aisle, a big man with a bony face and closely cropped brown hair. He had immense presence.

'*It is, it is, a glorious thing to be a Pirate King!*' he sang.

Everyone seemed to agree. They flocked offstage to embrace him. Phryne caught his eye, and he took her hand to kiss it.

'Hello, Miss Fisher!' he exclaimed.

'Hello,' replied Phryne. Up close, he was a bit intimidating, being so very large and strong and totally immune to her charms, charm she never so wisely. She was never wrong about the team for which any person played. And Aunty Mark's was not Phryne's, though they probably had a lot of friends in common. His lips were warm and soft. No wonder several male persons were staring at him as though they had been recently gaffed. He was very attractive. He really needed the ruffled shirt. Or a cloak. Or a feathered hat. Or all of the above.

'Do I know you?' she asked. She was sure that she hadn't seen him before. He had a way of being noticed.

'You were kind to a friend of mine and got him out of trouble,' he replied, and leaned close to whisper a name. Phryne nodded. A simple matter of paying off a blackmailer, following him home and burgling his house, stealing a whole safe full of secrets and, more importantly, the photographic plates which would have ruined Gawain's life.

She had also given him back all of his money. Phryne liked neat solutions. Which was why she had burned the personal secrets of the innocent and given all the politicians' dreadful transgressions to Jack Robinson, who had prosecuted with a certain decently suppressed glee.

She had lost touch with Gawain, but there he was, following this magnificent presence up the aisle, grabbing her hand and squeezing it.

'So you moved to Sydney?' asked Phryne.

'It seemed best,' he replied. He was not much taller than Phryne, with pale blue eyes, and he was already losing his hair, but the look which the Pirate King directed at him was very affectionate. 'Fell on my feet,' he murmured.

'You call that Mendelssohn?' Aunty Mark was demanding. 'You're praying for rain from a parched land, not asking someone to pass you the sugar!'

'Sorry,' said Matthew. 'But our conductor got murdered.'

'Really? Do tell!' He intercepted Matthew's wounded look.

'No, sorry, Matt—your rehearsal. Suppose I just take over Elijah, and you get on?'

'All right,' conceded Matthew, and the choristers moved back to their places. The tempo picked up, the voices quickened. Aunty Mark was listening. Mourning for their dying children or perhaps sheep, the people sang, '*Open the heavens and send us relief*,' as though they meant it. '*Help thy servant now, O God.*'

'*Go up now, child, and look towards the sea,*' sang Mark, and Caterina replied in a boyish pipe which belied her womanly stature, '*There is nothing. The heavens are as brass.*'

Australians would know what that looked like, Phryne thought. Nowhere in Europe could one see those bleached skies, that coppery, shining, unbearable light. Elijah enjoined the choir to pray and confess and sent the child up again to look for a cloud.

'*There is nothing. The earth is iron under me.*'

Matthew waved at Caterina to skip to the end of her piece. She obediently sang, '. . . *the storm rushes louder and louder.*'

'*Thanks be to God for all his mercies,*' sang the people.

Phryne had sung this before, but now began to realise how tense the situation was. Elijah had boasted that his god was the best. The prophets of Baal had been bested (and horribly executed). But then Elijah had to make good on his promise. In the Bible he sent the boy to the mountain seven—or was it nine?—times. Here it was only thrice, but the music rang with strain. Elijah was trusting in the Lord, and so was everyone else, but what if it didn't work?

He'd be down there on the bank of the brook Cherith minus a head, of course. In company with the prophets of Baal. When she had been a child, Phryne had relished the violent bits of the Old Testament. As a grown woman, she was beginning to think that gentleness had something going for it.

A brief discussion broke out about the next piece, and Phryne had leisure to inspect the choir. It was fairly easy to pick out the couples. It was even easier to identify the one-mind-one-body-one-heart couple, who appeared to be called DavidandLobelia. They were alto and bass, and David had moved through the tenors to be near his beloved. They were presently entwined in an embrace so close that fairly soon David would be wearing Lobelia's dark blue dress. Every choir had one of them. The established couples just kept an eye on each other. The rest were circling, considering, snatching glances. Caterina was the cynosure of at least four sets of eyes, the most ox-like being Tommy. The giraffe boy Daniel was intercepting and apparently failing to notice ardent passion being directed at him from the sops. Tiny dark Josephine clearly thought he was gorgeous, perhaps hoping to breed some legs back into her bloodline. He, on the other hand, was gazing at tall, fair and dismissive Isabelle, who was a legal secretary and not interested in anyone at present.

Any chorus is a hotbed of emotion, of course, but Phryne had previously sung with older people, who were more experienced at hiding their reactions. This was at white-heat, dangerous and visible on the surface for all to see who could. There might be any number of reasons for any of these people to thrust music down their conductor's throat.

Matthew raised his hands again, the choir ruffled and settled, and then began ensuring that Ahab would perish, by singing '*he shall perish*' a great number of times.

Phryne stopped analysing and started singing.

CHAPTER NINE

*If once a man indulges himself in murder, very
soon he comes to think little of robbing: and
from robbing he comes next to drinking, and
Sabbath-breaking, and from that to incivility and
procrastination.*

Thomas De Quincey
'On Murder Considered as One of the Fine Arts'

The rehearsal ended with a resolutely cheerful Matthew telling
them that they had tried really hard, which was not, as the
alert noticed, the same as saying that they had produced anything good. Aunty Mark gathered his acolytes and prepared
to take them back to the Windsor, where he was staying. As
were John Wilson and Rupert Sheffield, who met the group
at the door.

Thinking that this ought to be an interesting encounter,
Phryne hung back far enough to clearly see each face. John,
a good fellow, merely nodded, smiled, and passed on to the
lantern projector. Rupert stared straight into Mark's eyes. Both
of them were very tall. Mark was muscular and Sheffield was

slim. Phryne was just about to comment when the rest of the choir came up beside her.

'My money's on Aunty Mark,' whispered Calliope.

'Every time,' agreed Tabitha. 'I've just been reading about male displays of dominance and aggression.'

'And you are looking at one right now,' murmured Oliver. 'Who will crack first?'

'I really can't tell,' answered Phryne. They were both very dominant personalities.

'If it's the Pommy bloke, you pay for dinner,' said Matthew to Phryne.

'That presupposes that I will dine with you,' Phryne returned.

Someone laughed. The tension began to grow. Silence fell.

'If they were roosters, they'd be pecking by now,' Tabitha informed the group. 'If they were lions, they'd be biting the throat or belly.'

'With Aunty, that's not out of the question,' murmured someone behind Phryne.

'Sheffield,' called John. 'Can you see if these slides are in order?'

Sheffield, summoned away, lowered his eyes. The choir let out their held breath.

'I still think Aunty would have won,' said Matthew.

'You know,' said Phryne, impressed, 'I agree with you. Therefore, dinner is on me. Just wait a moment, I need to speak to someone.'

She moved down the hall to linger near the projector. John looked up and smiled at her. Sheffield finished leafing through slides to glare.

'Hello, m'dear,' said John. 'So, they're all right, Sheffield?' he asked.

'Of course. They were in perfect order, as you should have known,' snapped Sheffield, and flounced off.

'He really does a wonderful flounce,' sighed Phryne. 'He could give lessons.'

'Good dancer, too,' said John. 'You're a singer, Phryne?'

'Just for this *Elijah*. Are you dining with me tonight?'

'No, m'dear, Sheffield and I have an engagement in St Kilda. The mayor.'

'Can I give you a lift?' she offered.

'Thank you—at about nine, then? Are you driving?'

'Mr Butler is coming back for me,' Phryne assured him.

'Oh, good.' John tried not to sound too relieved.

'Right, see you then,' Phryne told him, and went back to the group at the door.

'Sorry, can't dine tonight,' she said. 'Are you going to the Windsor with Aunty?'

'No, we'd love to, but he always insists on paying, and we feel . . .' said Oliver, blushing.

'Oh, I see. Well, off you go, here's a retainer for your help with Mendelssohn; drink one for me and I wish I was coming with you.'

She allowed herself to rumple Matthew's golden hair, which felt like Lin Chung's best silk, and stuffed some money into his hand. She waved away his protest.

'I will find a manner in which you can repay me,' she told him.

His eyes widened. He smiled.

The choristers went to the door and Phryne went backstage. A little snooping would definitely while away the time more pleasurably than listening to the science of deduction again. Like Tinker, she had got lost at 'The Science of Deduction'.

Snooping yielded little new data. A member of the choir

had a taste for barley sugar. Someone else read Sexton Blake and had left their copy behind. There was also a lost hat and a score. Phryne unlocked the conductor's room and left the score, marked Chloe in pencil, on the desk. The desk bore three blunt pencils in a cup, a clutter of ink nibs and a pen, a clean new blotter, some slide fasteners in a chain and some old tram tickets. And a lot of dust. Which also cloaked the back of the chair and a coat hung behind the door. Twopence and some cough lollies in the pockets. Probably belonged to a singer.

Nothing of interest. A burst of applause indicated that Sheffield had finished and Phryne locked the door, replaced the key in its absurd hiding place, and went out into the auditorium.

John was waiting at the door and limped ahead, down to the kerb where Mr Butler awaited in the Hispano-Suiza. Sheffield was already there, examining the hub cap. It might have occurred to him as to just how close he had come to falling under that big black car the other night.

In any case, he did not make any comment, but got in next to the doctor. Phryne accepted John's hand and climbed in.

'Do you need to change into evening clothes, gentlemen? We can wait for you,' she offered.

'No, my dear, His Worship said quite informal, and Rupert is always well dressed,' replied John.

Did Phryne see a faint tinge of rose on that porcelain cheek? Vain as a girl, thought Phryne. Well, vain as this girl.

'He is a poem in summer-weight worsted,' she agreed. Yes, that was definitely a blush. Hmm. 'More Keats than Wordsworth,' she added. John looked confused. Sheffield turned his face away but not before she saw his smile. 'A thing of beauty is a joy forever.'

'I have no idea what you are talking about,' said John. 'But never mind.'

'Yes, off we go, Mr B, if you would be so kind. St Kilda, ho!'

'Indeed, Miss Fisher,' said the chauffeur.

He allowed the big car to slide into the roadway. Collins Street was always busy, and trucks and motorbikes jostled for space with bicycles and even horses. Not to mention the pedestrians, who at this hour were rare, endangered and outnumbered. Mr Butler drove very well, smoothly, without stops and starts which might jar the elegant machine's feelings. They were held up on the corner of Spring Street when Phryne felt a sharp tug at the brim of her hat, registered that a shot had been fired, and stamped on Mr Butler's accelerator foot.

The Hispano Suiza screamed in protest but leapt away, narrowly missing a truck, a couple of pedestrians and a traffic policeman. She had registered the *putt-putt* of a motorbike, though this one sounded more like *potato-potato*. The rider, disguised in flying helmet and goggles, dragged his machine upright and hared off down a lane.

'We'll never catch him,' said Phryne. 'So sorry, Mr B—I hope I didn't hurt your foot. John? All right?'

John had flattened Sheffield beneath him and now was struggling to sit up. Mr Butler pulled the car off the road. Phryne leapt into the back seat, grabbed John by the back of his coat and hauled him into her arms.

'You've been making a regular habit of flinging yourself in front of bullets,' she remarked amiably. 'It's really not a good custom. Curb this tendency to self-immolation. Hurt?'

'Felt it pluck my shoulder,' John gasped.

The ruffled Sheffield seated himself again, smoothing down his suit, reshaping his elegant hat.

'Was that necessary?' he snapped. 'Really, John, you do panic.'

Phryne's voice approached absolute zero.

'Oh, panic, was it? Examine this.' She snatched off her hat. There was a neat hole in the brim.

Rupert touched it. 'A large calibre,' he remarked. 'Probably a .45.'

'And if you would care to look at the fortunately padded shoulder of your friend's suit?' she demanded.

Sheffield turned John towards him, gently. There was another hole. Large calibre. It had carved a furrow through the shoulder padding of John's old-fashioned suit. Phryne saw Rupert calculate angles, sines and cosines, basic ballistics, the height of the shooter, and where he had been before John had thrown him out of the line of fire. He swallowed abruptly.

'That shot,' Phryne told Rupert, 'would have gone straight through your pretty head. Now, thank the man nicely for saving your life, again, and decide if you need new clothes. The Windsor or St Kilda? John has had a shock. He needs hot sweet tea, a bit of mending and a little rest.'

'What about you?' snarled Sheffield.

'Oh, I'm used to it,' said Phryne brightly. 'I'm always just very happy that my assassins have such poor marksmanship. And you?'

'I was in no danger,' said Sheffield. 'John? Are you coming with me?'

'You go on,' said John. 'Don't worry about me. I'll be all right after a bit of a rest. I'll join you later.'

'Right,' said Rupert. He left the car and strode away.

'Home, Mr B,' ordered Phryne. 'Dot can mend your suit, John, and I can spring you for a cab to the Mayor's.'

'Thanks,' gasped John Wilson, reflecting that his life

already contained far too many instances of close encounters with missiles. It wasn't as though he was looking for trouble. But somehow it always found him. 'And you seem to have developed a habit of gluing me together again,' he commented to Phryne.

'And I'll stop doing it the very moment you no longer need paste, stitches or arnica,' promised Phryne.

'Agreed,' said John Wilson.

Phryne occupied the journey home by considering the many really satisfying ways by which she could murder Rupert Sheffield without a trace. She had reached thirty-five—cyanide distilled from apple pips, and there were plenty more on the list—when they arrived, and Phryne escorted John Wilson inside for some repairs to his health, spirits and attire.

She sat him down in the parlour. Dot selected matching threads to repair his coat, Jane asked about the damage to his leg occasioned by sudden movement, Mrs Butler brought him hot tea and passionfruit biscuits, and Phryne fumed. Sheffield was a callous beast with not an iota of gratitude in him. John was hopelessly devoted to the creature, and kept saving his life at risk of his own. And her hat was ruined. It was a smart bleached straw with raffia asters in it. And now it had a bullet hole in the brim. She had really liked that hat.

Presently, John professed himself recovered, Mr Butler rang him a taxi, and he limped away.

Phryne asked for a very large emergency cocktail and went to the telephone. Fanshawe had told her that there would be someone at this number at all times. That shooting had been a direct and unequivocal attempt on the loathsome Sheffield's life, and needed to be reported. What appalling enmity had the little tick dragged after him all the way from Europe to Australia?

The phone was answered by Fanshawe himself. He sounded delighted to hear from her.

'Is this line secure?' asked Phryne, using her identifying phrases.

'It is,' replied the calm public school voice. 'What's happened?'

'Two more attempts on Sheffield's life,' said Phryne, and outlined the facts quickly and clearly. 'I am concerned for my friend John. Can you put a guard on that mathematical automaton?'

'No,' said Fanshawe. 'He's seen us. He'd remember. He's very acute.'

'I know,' said Phryne. 'Any joy from your knitting decrypter?'

'She's still working. Looks like he really annoyed that gun-running ring. The remainder threatened him with all manner of deaths. Two missing: a man called Mitchell, an Englishman—we never caught him or even had a clear idea of what he looked like. Supposed to have retired to Australia. And an Italian, Guido Calvi. Very nasty piece of work. We're trying to trace him now. So far no sign of him. Anything more you can tell me about the shooting?'

'Large calibre—in fact, one bullet may even now be buried in my precious coachwork. I'll have it dug out. Probably a .45. War souvenir, perhaps; there are a lot of them around. The rider was slight but strong. No idea of colouring because of the helmet and goggles. But the bike made an unusual noise. Instead of "putt-putt" it had a broken rhythm, more like "potato-potato".'

'Harley,' said Fanshawe. 'Only Harley-Davidsons sound like that. Expensive bike. We might have a brief trawl around the Elizabeth Street motorbike shops. But they hang together pretty well, those chaps.'

'Well, do the best you can,' encouraged Phryne. 'I'll try to keep John alive until you catch someone.'

'You mean Sheffield,' said Peter Fanshawe. 'Keep Sheffield alive.'

'Do I?' asked Phryne, and hung up.

•

Phryne occupied the evening following Beecham's *Elijah* with her score. Excerpts had been released on disc. Tinker appointed himself her record changer and winder. He seemed to like the music.

'You like this stuff, Tink?' she asked.

'Never heard anything like it before, Guv,' he replied. 'Angel music.'

'So it is,' Phryne agreed.

'Guv?' he asked, in the interval between taking off one record and putting on another.

'Mmm?' asked Phryne, musing on angels.

Tinker looked worried. 'Guv, you got shot at. Who's after this Sheffield bloke?'

'That I don't know,' said Phryne. 'But I'm beginning to think it is time I found out. John ought to be safe enough tonight. Tomorrow, I am going to make some enquiries.'

'Who with?' asked Tinker.

'Everyone,' replied Phryne. 'Part two, please,' she said, and he wound the gramophone again and placed the needle very carefully.

More of them angel voices. Grouse.

•

The morning brought Jack Robinson, traffic summons in hand and face lined with care and woe.

'Someone shot at you!' he exclaimed.

'Yes, I noticed,' Phryne returned. 'Tea?'

'*Shot* at *you* from a *motorbike* in *Collins Street!*' elaborated Jack Robinson.

'Not at me, I think,' said Phryne soothingly. 'I suspect it was aimed at the very annoying Rupert. And in any case, he missed.'

'Only because his bike slid on a patch of oil,' said Robinson. He mopped his brow. He drank tea. 'And you almost ran down five members of the public and a traffic officer, plus nearly colliding with a truck.'

'There were only two people, I missed the truck and the policeman, and I thought we came out of it rather well. Except for my poor car. She has an appointment at the garage to have her bullet removed this morning, poor girl. And if I catch who did this they also owe me compensation for the ruin of a rather nice hat.'

'Is this connected with the murder of the conductor?' asked Jack, drinking more tea in a fraught manner.

'No, it's connected with Sheffield, who seems to have brought his enemies with him,' said Phryne, settling down to a cosy gossip. 'I am absolutely not allowed to tell you any of this, Jack, so I'd better only tell you all about it once. And you really can't tell anyone else. Are you willing to hear it within those constraints?'

'Yes,' said Jack.

'All right, then. Rupert Sheffield was a code-breaker in the Great War. Stationed in Greece. I happen to know the man who was in charge of that section, and I sent him a telegram asking about our Rupert.'

'How do you happen to know the head of Intelligence in Athens?' asked Jack.

'Another story for another time. Or ask Tinker to lend you some Sexton Blake stories. Suffice it to say that I was never bored when acquainted with the man—I'll call him C.'

'I can just see you as Mata Hari,' chuckled Jack.

'Don't be ridiculous. I was nothing like Mata Hari,' said Phryne, insulted.

Jack backtracked and apologised. 'No, of course not, I didn't mean . . .' He faltered.

'She got caught,' Phryne told him. 'Anyway, C told me that Sheffield had done some fieldwork, and would let me know about people who might prefer him to be titled Rupert Sheffield, deceased. Apparently there is a list.'

'Not as if we didn't have enough criminals of our own,' said Jack wearily. 'Some Pommy bastard has to import more.'

'Yes, I know, coals to Newcastle, eh? I do not care about Sheffield, though apparently he is a fine mathematician, but we really can't have spy versus spy enacted in our nice clean streets.'

'Or even in the filthy ones,' said Jack. 'What can I do to help?'

'I need to find—so far—a man called Guido Calvi and another called Mitchell, who must have retired here, who might be connected with crime—after all, it is their speciality. They were gun-runners, but that's rather a dying trade at the moment.'

'Not a big market,' agreed Jack. 'So what would they be doing instead?'

'Import/export covers a multitude of sins,' suggested Phryne.

'I'll get on to a bloke I know,' said Jack. 'And you'll get on to your two red-raggers?'

'Of course,' said Phryne. 'I'm expecting them any moment.'

'Good-o. Better stay off the phone, then?'

'You pick things up very quickly,' said Phryne in admiration.

'I have to, just in order to keep up with you,' said Jack Robinson. He kissed her hand gallantly, and was escorted out by Mr Butler. The detective inspector noted that Mr Butler was limping slightly, and assumed it was rheumatism.

●

Bert and Cec came into the house through the kitchen as was their custom. That way they got a taste of whatever Mrs Butler was baking, a brief summary of Phryne's problem, and could collect beer without bothering Mr Butler. That worthy was, most unusually, sitting down with one bare foot on a chair. Jane was rubbing arnica into a bruise on his instep.

'Jeez, mate, what happened to your plate?' asked Cec, tall and concerned.

'Miss Phryne stood on his foot,' said Jane.

'She's no more than a featherweight,' responded Bert, short and scowling. 'She musta landed on you from a height.'

'She stamped,' said Mr Butler.

'You really musta annoyed her.' Cec rumpled his blond Scandinavian hair.

'It was a rather difficult situation,' said Mr Butler. 'Beer in the refrigerator, gentlemen.'

'She's dived into the soup again,' said Bert resignedly. 'Don't move, Mr B, we're soldiers, we can always carry our own beer.'

'And these cheese crisps,' said Mrs Butler approvingly. 'And ask Miss Fisher if she would like a drink.'

'Never known her when she didn't,' responded Bert. 'All right, Cec, you grab the ice bucket and I'll take the beer and bikkies, and we're set. You're doin' good work there, Janey.'

'I just can't imagine how she managed to bruise his Achilles tendon,' worried Jane.

'I bet she's got a kick like a horse. Come on, Cec.'

'Right,' said Cec.

They found Phryne reading through a long list and grimacing.

'Gidday,' said Bert. 'C'n I interest you in a cheese bikkie, a couple of wharfies and a strong drink?'

'Always,' said Phryne, not looking up.

Cec mixed the drink, Bert opened the beer bottles, and they both sat down.

One of the things Phryne really liked about Bert and Cec, who had managed a whole war and an eventful career on the wharves without undue damage, was their patience. It was probably a function of having been snipers. Snipers had to still their excitement, slow their reactions, never take their eye off their target and fire between breaths. That took immense self-control. The two of them were gulping beer and munching cheese crisps and talking quietly about Cec's intended and how they could organise some fine linen for her hope chest. Admittedly, 'organise' meant 'steal'. Phryne didn't expect them to be angels. But if a threat eventuated, that moment, in that parlour, they would be on their feet and reacting sensibly before the second shot shattered the window.

Phryne did not wonder where her images were coming from. She really did not like being shot at. She put down the list and handed Cec her ruined hat. Bert poked a finger into the hole in the brim.

'It's a .45,' said Bert. 'Eh, Cec?'

'Too right,' agreed Cec. 'Pity, it's a nice hat.'

'I thought so too,' said Phryne. 'And the head inside it is also nice and I'd like to keep it that way.'

'So, who's after you?' Bert leaned forward, fists on knees. 'Anyone we know?'

'No,' said Phryne. 'Someone's after Rupert Sheffield, and that someone is probably connected with his past.' She outlined as much as she knew of Rupert's intelligence work.

'It's no use,' said Cec slowly, 'asking you to stay away from this doomed bloke? I mean, just asking.'

'No,' said Phryne.

'Thought so. Right, we're looking for import/export of the dicey kind—or are we talking real bad?'

'Probably real bad,' said Phryne. 'It took a lot of daring, shooting at a car in Collins Street.'

'Did you get a squiz at the gunnie?' asked Bert.

'No—overall, helmet and goggles, with matching Harley-Davidson,' said Phryne, taking a sip of her drink. Cec evidently believed that half a pint of gin was needed to soothe her nerves. He might be right, at that. Two of Cec's offerings and she would be soothed into unconsciousness.

'Harley,' said Bert.

'Yes, the engine made this odd noise, and I was told that only Harleys sounded like that.'

'So they do,' said Bert in a voice of lead.

'What?' asked Phryne, putting a hand on his arm. Bert looked concerned, which was a very bad portent.

'There's a bloke . . .' Bert drank a long gulp of beer. 'Bad bastard.'

'Very bad bastard,' agreed Cec.

'He uses blokes on Harleys. Good way to kill someone. Fast.'

'Yes, it was,' said Phryne. 'If the bike hadn't hit a patch of oil and spilled the rider, he would have been gone and someone would have been dead. And he zoomed off down the lane. Melbourne's full of lanes, though I'm betting he ended up in the bike shops in Elizabeth Street. Ride into the workshop, ditch the disguise, warehouse is full of bikes anyway. And out into the street as an innocent citizen.'

'Yair,' said Bert.

'Bert, you sound unhappy.'

'This bloke . . .' he began.

'The bad bastard?' asked Phryne. Cec was resembling a Viking who had just been told of an enemy fleet in sight. Keyed up. If he was a dog, his hackles would have been rising.

'Yair, him. Name's not Mitchell, but. And he isn't a dago. English. Got that lah-di-dah voice what makes you want to belt him with a brick. You know?' asked Bert.

'Oh, I do,' agreed Phryne.

'If he's after this Pommy pal of yours, then he's got a big problem.'

'Yes? Cec, why don't you ring for some more beer?'

'I'll go get it, save poor old Mr B's plates of meat,' offered Cec. 'Bert can tell you about Ratcliffe.'

'All right, Bert, tell me about Ratcliffe.'

'Why did you stamp on Mr B's foot, anyway?' asked Bert.

'It was between me and the accelerator. As I informed Jack, I also missed the two pedestrians, the truck and the traffic policeman. I had to get us out of the immediate vicinity of the shooting.'

'Always a bonzer idea.' Bert rubbed his eyes. 'Look, we don't know much about this Ratcliffe, and some of it's probably furphys, right? But he's got phizz-gigs on the docks telling him which cargos he wants to pinch, and somehow they always go missing. Cec reckons one of the gangs worked for him, all of the blokes in that gang. But now there's the strike he must be working out of Willi and not Port. That means he's come up against Maginnis, and he owns Willi.'

'Oh,' said Phryne. She sipped her drink. 'That's . . . really not good. Mr Maginnis is notably touchy when it comes to his territory.'

'Yair. One of Ratcliffe's main blokes was pushed under a train last week. Then day before yesterday one of Maginnis's blokes fell into a crushing machine.'

'Oh, wonderful. A criminal feud. And throw the pestilential Rupert into the mix with a revenger's tragedy and you get . . .'

'Boom,' said Bert.

'Well, there it is,' said Phryne. 'We'll just try not to get slaughtered.'

'Always been my ambition,' said Cec. 'Beer,' he added, shoving a cold opened bottle into his mate's hands. 'You starting a war, Miss?'

'No, I'm trying to extract someone out of a war. All right. Don't do anything for the present; just keep an ear to the ground and let me know if you hear any whispers about Rupert Sheffield.'

'What's he to you?' asked Bert.

'Less than nothing,' admitted Phryne. 'If this had happened in another country I wouldn't have said a word or lifted a finger. But it's here and now and my dear friend John Wilson is likely to be shot for being an innocent bystander.'

'Oh,' said Bert. 'Yair, well, that's always been a dangerous occupation. You give your D the office?'

'Yes, so keep any delicate operations out of his way. And don't use the phone. Leave a message with the household if I'm not here.'

'Yessir,' said Cec. He put down his beer bottle and saluted.

•

160

Dot came into the parlour after the wharfies had gone home to gather up the beer bottles. She found Phryne staring at a piece of paper in what looked like wild excitement.

'I shouldn't have said that this wasn't about the conductor's murder, Dot,' she said.

'Why not?' asked Dot. 'I don't like this, Miss Phryne, shots fired and nice hats ruined and all.'

'No, I don't like it either,' Phryne said absently.

'Though I reckon Miss Ellen can fix the hat—curl up the brim and sew on another aster.'

'That would be pretty. Look at this, Dot.'

Dot looked. It was a list of singers. Phryne's forefinger had landed on one name.

'Luigi Calvi,' read Dot.

'Precisely,' said Phryne. 'It could be his father who is trying to kill Sheffield.' Her eyes sparkled as other women's eyes shone when contemplating their sleeping firstborn or the prospect of a dance and a new dress.

Dot wondered, as she did occasionally, what her life might have been like if she had not met Miss Phryne.

Probably very tedious, she reflected. But sometimes tedious was pleasant.

CHAPTER TEN

Mathematics possesses not only truth, but
supreme beauty—a beauty cold and austere,
like that of sculpture.

Bertrand Russell
'Mysticism and Logic'

Phryne reported the presence of someone who might be related
to Guido Calvi to Mr Fanshawe. Then she put herself resolutely to bed for an after-lunch nap. Tonight's rehearsal might
be testing, in more ways than just musically.

•

Rupert Sheffield sat in the smaller bar at the Windsor Hotel.
The larger one was filled with choristers, even at this hour of
the morning. None of them appeared to have been to bed at
all—not to sleep, at least. The Cricketers was loud with trained
voices singing very rude songs for the most part. Occasionally
they would segue seamlessly from 'Charlotte the Harlot' in
four-part harmony—which he had never heard before, admittedly—to achingly beautiful plainchant. Or a folk song.

Sheffield was considering the problem of John Wilson. He had never asked John what he had done in the Great War. Now it seemed that he had been a frontline casualty-clearing medical officer, at only twenty-two years old. He had been brave. He had, indeed, been a hero. And he was scarred in the way that many old soldiers were. He had injuries. He had nightmares.

Sheffield had seen the limp, had heard his friend scream himself awake in the next room. Why, then, would he voluntarily stay with Sheffield, when there was a chance of being shot again? Why hadn't he left for nice, safe London the moment that whoever it was had tried to kill Sheffield? Why had he thrown himself across Sheffield to protect him? His behaviour made no sense. Sheffield could not stand things that made no sense.

He sketched out the equations in a notebook. His pencil flew over the page. John lived with Sheffield. John was a hero. John was willing to risk his own life to save Sheffield, even though he knew what it was to be shot. John had sustained bruises pushing Sheffield out of the way of that car. John never asked for anything from Sheffield, except his occasional attention. John looked at him.

Hard to work out what loading he could give to the way that John Wilson looked at him. Not dotingly or anything sticky like that. Affectionately. In a kindly manner. John tried to save Sheffield's face, even when he didn't care what effect he had on other people. John stood between Sheffield and a considerable number of annoying humans with their annoying emotions. John had caught an enraged fist and twisted the owner's arm behind his back with remarkable speed and skill when one of the university's more effervescent associate professors had objected to Sheffield's annihilation of his ridiculous theory. And perfectly justified criticism of his pretensions to knowledge. John saw Sheffield as someone in need of his protection. Insufferable! High-handed! Outrageous!

Sheffield looked at the way his Venn diagrams were coming out. They were resolving to an unacceptable conclusion.

He tore out the page, screwed it up, and started again.

By the time John was due to join him for lunch, he had completed the equations three times. Each time, he had seen the same conclusion revealed by his very own system, which had utterly betrayed him. Sheffield drained his glass of soda and wished that he drank alcohol.

Now what was he going to do?

He sat quite still for some moments. John came in and saw him sitting there, looking like a marble statue of Saint Sebastian on receipt of the fourteenth arrow. When he caught sight of John, he grabbed his notebook and began scribbling again.

John went to order himself a drink. Mark sang 'Au fond du temple saint' with his accompanist so beautifully that Sheffield could almost forgive him for challenging him. John sat down opposite him. Ordinary, pedestrian, unimaginative John. Strong, blunt hands, pleasant enough features, undistinguished blue eyes, greying hair. Nothing surprising about Dr John Wilson at all. But he occupied an unduly large part of Sheffield's world . . .

Sheffield, mind whirling, sought for a new mathematics to describe his new universe.

•

Phryne woke, went downstairs and dealt with her household problems (one sock lost in the laundry and Tinker's destruction of a good pair of trousers by falling off his bike). She ordered the purchase of more socks and a new pair of trousers, asked

Dot to mend the old ones for disguise, inspected Tinker's healing skinned knee, admirably cared for by Jane, and went in to lunch with a feeling that she almost knew what she was doing, which was a refreshing change. Not enough to give her a damaging sense of complacency, of course. But better than 'utterly at sea', her previous option. If the bad men were in Australia, a combination of Fanshawe, Jack Robinson and Bert and Cec would find them. She did not look forward to any contact with Maginnis, a vile creature with nasty henchmen. Or with this challenger, Ratcliffe. Bandit gangs became more marked in their attentions and flamboyant in their demonstrations when they felt threatened.

What had Sheffield done to threaten them? Was this revenge? Or had he actually taken some action in Australia which had drawn attention to himself—and John? It was no use asking Sheffield. He would definitely not confide in Miss Fisher. He was, though he did not seem to recognise the emotion, jealous, or possibly envious, of Phryne. And by the way poor Fanshawe had flinched when recollecting Rupert's visit, Sheffield would not tell the representative of MI6 in Melbourne, who might be able to help him. So who would he tell? Should she sic Jack Robinson on him? Not after Rupert had scorned him. She had already involved him, informally, in matters which he ought not to know. If pressed, he might protect Rupert by trying to deport him. A nice idea, but that would not protect John, if he persisted in bone-headedly flinging himself between that gorgeous creature and danger, as though his own life was not a good deal more precious.

He might tell John, if John asked. That looked like Phryne's best bet, unless her own enquiries bore fruit. Meanwhile, there was tea and a soothing afternoon watching Tinker play chess with Jane, watching Dot embroider waratahs, watching Ruth read her cookbook as though dreaming of amazing dishes.

Phryne had books which needed to go back to the library, so she settled down with a glass of wine—poor Mr Butler would be back at his shaker soon, but Jane wouldn't let him walk around much yet—and read her latest. If only the real world conformed to Hercule Poirot's rules. It would be so nice. She would love to gather all the suspects together and state, on the authority of the little grey cells, exactly how each one could have been the murderer but wasn't, until she reached the last person, who was, and who always confessed instantly.

That must be so convenient.

However, back in 221B the Esplanade, St Kilda, matters were extremely complex.

Just before five, Bert arrived at the kitchen door with urgent news. Phryne then rang Detective Inspector Robinson and arranged a few trifling matters. Then she called a friend in the country. Tomorrow ought to be intriguing.

•

Phryne took her score and went to rehearsal. The choir gathered, flocking to the stage. Rupert and John had not arrived. Phryne found herself cornered by the old pianist, Professor Szabo. He had lunched and probably breakfasted on ruby port, and was trying to tell her about Beecham and about the airy lightness with which Mendelssohn had to be conducted. She agreed with him. It was always politic to agree with passionate alcoholics.

But now there was a new conductor. Phryne took her place next to Chloe and examined him carefully.

Mr Henry James. Stout; nice corporation beneath that flamboyant waistcoat, dark, thick black hair, brooding stare.

Trying to look like Beethoven, she diagnosed. Quite a good imitation, except he didn't look Germanic enough. The face was weak, the curves soft and undistinguished, the mouth small. Did Melbourne specialise in the dark, swarthy and brooding? The choir already had Luigi Calvi, who was trying to be Rudolph Valentino, and there was also Rupert Sheffield, whose hair was as black as a raven's wing. Phryne did not mind embonpoint in men; they were huggable, like Matthew. Making love to Rupert, a concept which she was not entertaining for one moment, definitely not, would lead to bruises from those sharp hip bones and elbows and knees. And while she had treasured bruises acquired in a good cause, pleasure being a very good cause, those wouldn't be. Really.

Anyway, the new conductor surveyed the choir without any expression, raised his baton, and they began the usual warm-up exercises. His beat was reliable. He had a habit of raising one hand and smoothing back his shock of hair, which Phryne could tell was going to get on her nerves fairly soon. He also licked one finger to turn the pages of the score. Very insanitary. This, too, might well begin to annoy after a while. Phryne gave it about ten minutes.

'We'll begin with part one. The chorus is "Help, Lord. Wilt thou quite destroy us?" Much better in German as *"Hilf Herr! Willst du gavertil gen?"* But since we are singing for a monoglot Melbourne audience, English it is. Pay attention to the dynamics. This isn't hard. If you can't do this, you shouldn't be singing Mendelssohn. I don't even know why you chose Elijah. Inferior to the *Messiah* in every way. But there it is. Sing!'

There was a murmur of protest, quelled by the descending beat. *'Help, Lord!'* sang the sopranos. *'Help, Lord!'* sang the altos. '*Help, Lord!*' echoed the tenors and basses. '*Wilt thou quite destroy us?*'

The baton cut them off. 'You shouldn't be singing Mendelssohn,' Mr James snarled. 'You shouldn't be singing "Baa Baa, Black Sheep". Revolting. Sops, you are sharp. Tenors, you are off-key. Basses, you sound like mud. And as for the altos . . .' He stroked back the magisterial hair in a manner which made Phryne long for a serviceable hedge cutter. 'Again.'

'*Help, Lord*,' sang the choir, this time with an edge which almost resembled prayer.

'Terrible,' snapped Mr James, cutting them short again. 'Those of you who can actually read music should endeavour to do so. The rest, try to keep up. Right, this time we are going all the way through.'

'We haven't learned the notes yet,' said Matthew, putting up a hand. 'We'll need to note-bash before we can sing this one all through.'

'Nonsense,' said Mr James, glaring at Matthew. 'I thought you were a semi-professional choir, or I would never have taken this position. All the way through, please,' he said, and they tried.

By the time James called a halt, Mendelssohn was revolving in his grave and the chorus was totally lost. The basses had taken the wrong cue and were more than half a bar ahead. They finished first.

'We won!' said Tommy triumphantly.

James glared at him. Tommy stared back. He, too, had been glared at by experts.

'Répétiteur,' ordered James. 'The soprano line, if you can manage it.'

Professor Szabo, his hands as steady as a rock though the

rest of his body was trembling with indignation, played the soprano line. Then the tenor line, the alto line, the bass line.

The errors in the next attempt at 'Help, Lord' were pardonable. Mr James did not pardon them. He castigated the whole choir and sent them off to their tea break indignant, tearful or depressed, according to personal character.

'Where did we get this bloke from?' asked Oliver, blushing with indignation. 'And can we throw him back? That's what I always do with slimy horrible fish.'

'We need a conductor and he was the only one who was willing to do it for that money,' said Tabitha. 'Unfortunately.'

'Why can't we just declare Matthew the conductor and get shot of this overbearing bastard?' asked Chloe, about to don breastplate and helmet and mount her white horse.

'He's got a following,' explained Tommy. 'People pay to see him.'

'I wouldn't,' muttered Caterina. 'That hair!'

'Just makes you long for a pair of secateurs, doesn't it?' asked Phryne. 'I wonder what he uses on it?'

'Axle grease,' declared Tabitha. 'And I'm not touching any score he's been spitting on.'

'Can't we find someone else? Aunty's not going to like this one,' protested Daniel.

'He called us eunuchs,' said Luigi, who had insinuated himself close to Phryne and spoke into her hair. She could feel his hot breath on her nape.

'That could never be said about you,' she replied, leaning back a little into his body. Unmistakable proof that Luigi was not a eunuch pressed into her hip. Oh dear, thought Phryne. This is not a subtle Valentino. He just keeps trying it on until someone succumbs. And it isn't going to be me. Such a seducer has a hide of brass. People keep rejecting him until some poor weak-willed or distracted girl accepts, and then wonders what on earth she was thinking of. Thus his success.

'*Ciao*,' she said to him, fairly confident that no one else— except the polyglot Matthew, perhaps, or Caterina, and they were both out of earshot—spoke Italian.

'*Bellissima*,' he breathed into her ear.

'*Sei un bel ragazzo*,' said Phryne, calling him a beautiful boy.

'*Non bello com sei*.' He was close now, almost embracing her. No one else would hear this conversation.

'*Forse, potrei venirlo a contatta in seguito, se te lo meriti*,' she whispered, suggesting a later meeting.

'*A zia Marco*, Windsor,' he promised.

Phryne drew herself away. She turned to look at him, smiled wickedly, and went to get some tea. Flirtation without attraction was very tiring. But if finding Guido meant flirting with Luigi, she could do it. The deceased Mata Hari should have taken lessons from Phryne. Especially in how not to get caught.

'I say, you ought to be careful of him,' Tabitha warned. 'He's a bad man.'

'I know what I am doing,' said Phryne, and sipped tea. 'And I've met bad men before.' She did not mention what she had done to them.

The second half of the rehearsal was as bad, if not worse, than the first. Mr James not only went in for blanket condemnation—'You are a pack of talentless amateurs'—but also specific—'Which soprano is flat? You, sing the note. No, not you. You, sing the note . . .' until he had found Millicent, the soprano who sang flat, and unceremoniously ejected her from the choir.

Phryne left with her and caught up with her backstage. Millicent was at the point of tears, flushed and humiliated.

'And he doesn't even like Mendelssohn!' she exclaimed.

'He's a pig,' said Phryne, offering her a cigarette. 'Right up there with the worst. Have a hankie,' she said, handing her one. Millicent sniffed and blew.

'What am I going to do? My boy is in this chorus! I don't want to leave it without him! And he really wants to sing this!'

'Then come back tomorrow,' advised Phryne. 'Mr Henry James doesn't look at faces. He's totally self-involved. I promise, if you come back next rehearsal he won't know that you were the one he threw out. Trust me,' she said, and Millicent nodded.

'All right,' she agreed. 'Are you going to Aunty Mark's soiree tonight?'

'Probably,' said Phryne. 'He's at the Windsor, yes?'

'Royal Suite,' said Millicent. 'He always takes the Royal Suite when he's here. The bath has gold taps. It's very . . . well, very suitable.'

'He really ought to have ivory, apes and peacocks,' agreed Phryne.

Rehearsal dragged to an acrimonious conclusion, Mr James stalked off to the conductor's room, and the choir grumbled their way into the street.

'Coming?' asked Millicent.

'I'll just wait awhile,' said Phryne. 'I'll see you there.'

She was, in fact, making sure that Mr Henry James snarled his way into his outer garments and left the assembly hall. The Scots Church wouldn't tolerate any more corpses on their nice clean floors, and the choir needed somewhere to rehearse.

She saw Professor Szabo leave, en route to the Windsor. She watched the choir join up into their groups and couples and pass through the main entrance as Rupert and John came in.

'Hello, hello!' said John, sweeping her into an embrace. 'Come to keep me company, my dear?'

'Alas, no,' said Phryne, with genuine regret. 'I have a party to attend, but it is at your hotel. The Royal Suite—shall I see you there?'

'Am I invited?' asked John.

'Of course,' said Phryne, and kissed him soundly.

There was a hiss behind her, such as is produced by a cat on whose delicate tail someone has just placed a chair.

'Miss Fisher,' said Rupert Sheffield. His beautiful face could have been carved out of ivory by someone wishing for a talisman against humanity.

'Delighted as ever,' said Phryne. She failed to take his hand. She stood on tiptoe and kissed his cheek, then sauntered out of the assembly hall without a word or a backward glance.

'She . . .' protested Sheffield to John. He raised a hand to his cheek. He could feel her mouth, as though she had branded him. He felt oddly helpless. John took out his handkerchief and wiped the lipstick off.

'Always been an enthusiastic girl,' rumbled John. 'She didn't mean any harm, my dear chap.'

Phryne walked on, aware that she had just kissed what was in all probability an entirely virgin cheek. Leaving aside his mother, nanny, or favourite dog. None of which she could imagine Rupert Sheffield actually owning or tolerating.

She giggled. Privately.

No one tried to kill her as she crossed the road, which was nice, and the Windsor was just as it always was. Plush, confident and luxurious. Phryne loved it. She had lived at the Windsor when she first arrived in Australia. It was flexible, in the manner of the great hotels. With courtesy and aplomb it coped with exigent guests, including the actress with the leopard cub, the drunken rugby players, the visiting politicians with their mistresses and demands for entertainment and eccentric food preferences, and the tantrums of spoilt princesses. It had even coped with Phryne nearly being arrested on the premises for drug-dealing. Though the manager had reproved her, gently, at that point.

She had never been to the Royal Suite. It occupied fully half of the top floor and reminded Phryne of the setting of a romance novel. Everything which was not scarlet plush was specially woven, taffeta, mahogany, gilt-edged or marble. The bathroom taps, in the spacious chamber, were gold. As advertised.

The parlour was draped with silk velvet. It included a dinner setting. On this was a selection of cocktail savouries. Next to it was a full-sized bar with its own cocktail waiter, whose strained smile indicated that he had not been at the Windsor long. He was engaged in pouring Pol Roget into, of all things, a punchbowl, which was a wicked thing to do to such a venerable wine. Phryne claimed a glass as it was poured. The '97. Superb. If Aunty Mark was intending to adulterate this champagne, she would report him to the authorities for Cruelty to Wine.

Mark himself was dressed in a luxurious costume, somewhat recalling the Turkish: loose trousers, blouson silk shirt and colourful waistcoat. He was so forceful that the clothes looked fitting on him, and not in the least feminine. He caught Phryne's eye and winked.

'*Salut.*' She raised her glass. 'Very good champagne.'

'Nothing but the best for all my chums,' he replied. 'Once a year I stop being respectable. I come to another city, and then it's celebrate, sing, celebrate, sing, celebrate, concert until—I have to go home and be respectable again.' He made a sad face and Phryne laughed.

'Your liver will last longer that way,' she said unsympathetically. 'Tell me, is this going to turn into an actual orgy? I made no preparations, even assuming I would be welcome.'

'No, no, dear, just a little fun. Risqué, perhaps, but not obscene. Not until the company has thinned rather a lot to invitation-only. Tell me, who was that gorgeous piece I met at the door yesterday? The one with the witch-finder's eye and the face of an angel?'

'That would be Rupert Sheffield,' said Phryne. 'Mathematician and unwise acquaintance.'

'Oh, I could tell that, dear,' said Mark.

'Inadvisable doesn't mean undesirable, I know,' said Phryne. 'But I would say he was not sexed.'

'Not in your playing field, dear Miss Fisher, but probably in mine. But I have no taste for such creatures. I prefer them short, blond and cuddly.'

'There is a lot to be said for blond and cuddly, I agree. Will you have a party every night until the concert?'

'Mostly,' replied Mark, pouring her another glass of champagne. 'Unless I feel like a cosy night in, with room service and . . .'

'Cuddly company?'

He smiled a wide, gleeful smile. Phryne liked him enormously. This was a man with relish and zest in a shabby, exhausted age.

'Just so, Miss Fisher,' he agreed.

'And your view of Henry James?'

Mark's face screwed up into a frightful grimace.

'No, really, they've got him? How perfectly dreadful. You won't have any trouble finding out who killed Henry.'

'No? He isn't killed yet, by the way.'

'The hour will produce the man,' prophesied Mark. 'And the answer will be—he will be stoned to death by the whole choir, though the altos and the basses will probably do the most damage. They're generally more muscular. Of course, it depends on the size of the stones.'

'He's that frightful?' asked Phryne.

'Oh, yes,' said Mark. 'Have another drink to take the taste out of your mouth and let me introduce you to my friends.'

Phryne had an agreeable half-hour meeting the rest of the choir, all of whom were mopping up free drinks with alacrity. She was discussing Mendelssohn versus Handel when someone eased through the throng to stand far too close behind her and press his enthusiasm into her back. It could be no one else.

'Luigi, *caro*,' she murmured.

'*Si, Principessa*,' he agreed.

'*Vieni con me*,' she told him, and led him by the hand to a secluded nook, of which the room had many. They sank down onto a loveseat, which ought to keep his manhood on his side of the sofa. Phryne had chosen this chair on purpose. Not only did it preclude having to knee Luigi, but it meant that she could watch his face as the door opened and allowed, with any luck, John and Rupert into the room. If Luigi Calvi was Guido's relative, then he would have to react. His face was responsive, dark eyes and mobile mouth. If he did react, Phryne would see it.

Just as she was getting very tired of fending off his advances, John came in. But no Rupert followed. Drat. Sheffield must be tucked up in bed with his nice glass of hot milk and his equations to keep him warm. Luigi looked at John with complete indifference. Experiment over.

'*Ciao*, Luigi,' said Phryne, leaping up and moving out of grabbing range. She took John's hand. He smiled down at her, a little disconcerted.

'Hello, my dear, this is a crush!'

'Have a glass of this champagne, it's superb, and allow me to introduce you to our host. A very fine baritone.'

'Oh yes, indeed—Mr Henty, my dear fellow, how very nice to meet you!' exclaimed John. 'Heard you sing in Sydney.'

'This is John Wilson, a dear friend of mine,' said Phryne.

'And with excellent taste in music,' beamed Mark. 'Have another drink!'

A glance passed between John and Mark. Like knows like. Phryne wondered if Mark was going to invite John to stay on afterwards, when the choristers had gone home.

'I heard you this morning,' said John. 'In the Cricketers bar. That was you singing *"Au fond du temple Saint"*, wasn't it?'

'It was indeed. Are you here alone?'

'No, I am travelling with Rupert Sheffield, the mathematician.'

'We've met,' said Mark flatly.

'He's a good fellow, really,' said John.

Phryne actually saw the moment that Mark put all the salient facts together. He gave John Wilson a sympathetic, manly pat on the shoulder, and moved along.

Phryne found her choristers and they took to John immediately. The languid medical student Bones shed his indifference and hung on his every word. John looked comfortable talking to the young. Phryne could leave him and circulate, meeting the rest of Aunty Mark's broad acquaintance and talking to the balance of the guests.

It was an interesting party. It included firemen, a few doctors, a plumber, a principal dancer from the Ballets Russes and a lot of singers. She asked about the new conductor.

The general choral opinion was that Henry James was a blighter, a bounder or a bloody bastard (Tommy, whose rugby days coloured his vocabulary). He had favourites, though he did not prey on the sopranos. Or any other voice. He seemed to hate altos, for some reason. As to his musicality, opinion was divided. Some thought that he was skilled and had a good ear; others conceded the good ear but protested that he made all composers sound alike, and an attempt to make Mendelssohn sound like Handel was doomed to be frightful.

'Not that the audience will notice,' commented Matthew. 'They come to see oratorios like they go to church: to be bored in a holy cause.'

'Tsk,' said Calliope, slapping his wrist.

'There must be good conductors,' said Phryne. 'I sang with one in England who was a darling. Preferred coaxing to abuse. We sang like a heavenly choir for him.'

'Oh yes, we know one,' said Matthew. 'But he's conducting in Ballarat. Patrick Bell. Good old Pat. It is such a pity he's busy. He never shouts, always praises, and after a while you sing your heart out because you can't stand the pained look on his face when you get it wrong.'

'But for the present, we've got good old Henry,' said Tabitha. 'And we're going to have to make the best of him.'

'How do you do that?' asked Phryne.

'Don't take anything he says personally,' Tabitha advised. 'I always imagine him the moment after his trousers and undergarments fall off in full view of the audience. Makes me feel much better.'

'Excellent idea,' said Calliope.

'Still, erk,' Caterina pointed out.

'In your imagination, just concentrate on his morti-fied face,' said Phryne. Caterina brightened. Her agate eyes softened with delight. She clasped her hands. A delicate flush appeared on her peach-blossom cheek.

'Oh, lovely,' she crooned.

Tommy gulped a lot of his drink at once and choked. Calliope pounded him on the back.

'I do wish you'd rein that in a bit,' remarked Tabitha. 'You know what an effect you have on him.'

'Sorry,' said Caterina. 'Wasn't thinking. Would it help if I kissed him better?'

'Yes!' choked Tommy.

Caterina drifted over to his side, kissed him very gently on the forehead, and wafted away again. Phryne laughed. She went over to the bar to get another drink and was instantly claimed by Leonard, eyes burning, who demanded, 'They've actually employed Henry James for this concert!'

'Yes,' said Phryne, directing her gaze to the hand which was clutching her arm.

Leonard looked down. He let her go abruptly.

'Sorry, I wasn't at rehearsal. I just heard, thought it couldn't be. I mean, Henry James!'

'Instead of, as it might be, you?' asked Phryne.

'Yes!' he almost shouted. 'Well, yes, of course, me—I've been studying the piece for months, I know all about Mendelssohn, why not me?'

'I don't know,' said Phryne, inspecting him. Sweating, almost panting, reddened eyes, chewed lips, chewed finger-nails, this one was a boiling-over bouillabaisse of emotions. A nice potential murderer, if he desperately wanted to be conductor. Could he have removed Tregennis, then had to go away to Albury and had thus not succeeded in getting his appointment? Would he now try to kill Henry James in order to take his place? Interesting. Leonard would bear watching. 'Why do you think Henry James got the job?'

'Influence,' growled Leonard, leaning closer than Phryne would consider pleasant. 'He's commercial. He's bribed all the newspaper critics. He's successful. He steals all the best singers from the church choirs, promises them roles, solos, anything. Then he just uses them as chorus. They can't go back. Anyone who's gone with James is a traitor. He's clever.' Leonard's voice sank to a whisper. 'He's got spies everywhere.'

'I see,' said Phryne, who did. 'Even here?'

'Of course,' affirmed Leonard.

'Point one out?' asked Phryne.

'I don't know,' said Leonard. 'If I knew them they wouldn't be spies.'

'Of course. Well, must go, it's been very diverting.' She moved through the crowd, looking for John Wilson. He was still with the choristers, discussing the superiority of Vaughan Williams over Elgar.

'Oh, dear, Len got you, didn't he?' asked Calliope with warm sympathy.

'How badly does he want to be a conductor?' asked Phryne.

Matthew was fastest on the uptake. His eyes widened with shock and then narrowed with calculation. He looked a little sickened by his conclusion. 'You don't think . . .'

'Ah, but I do,' she said, sipping the drink. She really must lay in some more champagne of this quality. 'There is nothing which is, per se, unthinkable,' she told him.

'But wasn't he somewhere else?'

'Something I shall be ascertaining when I get home and look at my notes.'

'Look, he's always had a bee in his bonnet about being a great conductor,' explained Matthew, now seriously worried. 'But he wouldn't . . .'

'Wouldn't he?' asked Phryne.

Matthew did not reply. The choristers looked at each other with what Keats would have described as a wild surmise.

'Oh, goody, it's Len,' said Tabitha. 'Now if he can only get rid of Henry James, it will be a better, brighter world.'

'Tab!' exclaimed Calliope.

'You've forgotten something,' Phryne reminded them.

'What?' asked Tabitha, who liked her reasons for optimism.

'If he does that, you get Leonard for a conductor,' said Phryne.

There was a general groan.

'Count your blessings, one by one,' said Caterina.

'Must go,' said Phryne. 'It's been such fun. John, are you coming or staying?'

'When you say "coming" do you mean coming back to your house with you?' he asked.

'I do,' said Phryne, smiling.

'I'm with you,' he said.

'Half your luck,' muttered Matthew.

CHAPTER ELEVEN

Camerado! I give you my hand.
I give you my love more precious than money,
I give you myself before preaching or law;
Will you give me yourself? Will you come travel
with me?
Shall we stick by each other as long as we live?

Walt Whitman
'Song of the Open Road'

John Wilson reclined in Phryne's bed. She was curled up beside him. It was a loud night in St Kilda. Drunks were shouting, policemen were whistling for assistance, even ships navigating the channel were blowing sirens and foghorns.

Inside it was quiet and dark. Phryne was not sleepy. Making love seldom made her drowsy. John seemed to be thinking about something. His free hand was clenched on her breast. Phryne took it in both of her own.

'All right,' she said. 'What is it? Having second thoughts about me?'

'What?' He was startled entirely awake. 'No! I mean, of course not. No, it's about Sheffield.'

Of course it is, Phryne didn't say. 'Tell me all.'

'I do go on about him,' muttered John.

'No, I'm fascinated—please.'

'If you're sure . . .' He hesitated.

Phryne knew a demand bid when she heard one, even though she refused to clutter her mind with the rules of bridge.

'I'm sure. Go on.' Phryne rearranged herself so she was sitting up. John put his head in her lap and she stroked his hair.

'I had the strangest conversation with him today,' John reported. 'I was just ordering a little lunch in the smaller dining room—you know, the one with the deco murals of the sunbathers?'

'I know the room,' said Phryne, who was not going to let him digress too far.

'And he came in and, without even sitting down, he demanded, "Why do you stay with me? It makes no logical sense." And I didn't know how to answer, so I told him that I was his friend. I also made him sit down. You know how tall he is, he looms and the rest of the diners were all looking.'

'I can imagine.' Phryne suppressed a chuckle.

'And my soup arrived, and he took my spoon and tasted it, as he always does, and then he said, "But you were in danger," and that's interesting, Phryne, because he's been telling me that there was no peril—not with the car, not with bullets—and my actions were quite unnecessary.'

'Yes, I heard him,' said Phryne, repressing 'that little tick'.

'So then he said, "I have no friends," and I told him, no, you have at least one, and that is me. And friends do not allow their friends to get shot if they can prevent it. He thought about that for a while.'

'While eating your soup?'

'Yes, he seemed to quite like it. Mushroom, very good. They do a very fine lunch table at the—'

'You were saying about Rupert,' Phryne reminded him.

'Yes, the conversation got stranger. He asked me if I was your friend. I said yes, we had been friends for many years. Then he wanted to know how we could be friends when we hadn't seen each other for ten years, and I had to explain that distance in time and place doesn't affect a deep friendship such as ours.' He turned his head to plant an affectionate kiss on Phryne's navel. He really liked that navel. It really ought to have a ruby. Or possibly a star sapphire. That would contrast beautifully with her skin.

'And how did he react?' asked Phryne, very interested. Her campaign might have just taken a giant leap forward.

'He asked me if I had a lot of friends, and I said I had been remarkably lucky and had several. I said . . .' He faltered. 'I said I hoped that I could count him as my friend, as well.'

'And what did he say to that?'

'I swear, Phryne, he blushed. Then he muttered, "Of course," and stalked off. What do you make of it?'

'I suspect that Rupert is realising how much you mean to him.'

'Really?' asked John. Hope was stirring in his voice.

Phryne put a quelling hand on his chest. 'Yes, but we must make haste slowly. A grab-and-kiss-him-senseless would not be the way to manage this situation; it is extremely delicate.'

'Why?' asked John.

'Because the object of your profound affection is an idiot,' Phryne told him. 'You must go on as you are; try touching him gently, patting his shoulder, that sort of thing, very manly. And you must leave the rest to me.'

'Phryne,' said John, extremely worried, 'if your plan should go wrong . . .'

'I understand what is being risked,' she assured him. 'Leave the matter confidently in my hands, and I shall have him in your arms in—oh, a couple of weeks.'

John shivered. Phryne hauled him up into her embrace.

'It will be all right, I promise,' she said firmly. 'Trust me.'

'I do,' he said. Then he repeated more firmly, 'I do. You must have been a very dangerous spy.'

'I was,' she said. 'How did you know I was a spy?'

'Sheffield told me. Someone from the Athens office—nice girl, apparently, Mlle Jeanne? Was your dresser? She told Sheffield how wonderful you were.'

'So she was, excellent seamstress and loose-tongued as ever. And I bet she failed to seduce Sheffield.'

'He has no interest in the flesh,' said John, evidently quoting Rupert.

Phryne laughed. 'We shall see,' she said. 'Now, would you like to have another drink, or get dressed and go home or back to Aunty Mark's party, or for me to do something mildly obscene to you to distract your mind?'

'Oh, only *mildly* obscene?' asked John. 'I was holding out for banned by the Lord Chamberlain, utterly filthy.'

'We can manage that,' Phryne assured him, laying him out flat. 'The Lord Chamberlain—' she kissed his shoulder '—is very—' she kissed his nipple '—easily shocked.'

Her mouth continued downwards. John Wilson's mind was comprehensively distracted.

•

At breakfast, in her boudoir, Phryne received a coded message which had been handed in at the door by a messenger who did

184

not stay for an answer. She allowed John to feed her nibbles of her croissant while she sipped her coffee. Her pencil flew across the sheet, transposing numbers and letters.

'I see,' she said, as John kissed the last crumb from her cheek. 'Right. John dear, I have several things to tell you. But I shall wait until you finish that plate of breakfast—my, tomatoes and sausages and eggs and bacon and mushrooms.'

'For some reason, sleeping with you gives me a real appetite,' said John, and Phryne screwed up message and translation and flipped them into the fireplace, lighting the ball of paper and crushing the ashes.

Then she went to her malachite bathroom for a wash. She dressed with her customary speed in an elegant purple cotton dress. With it she wore an extravagant Spanish shawl, embroidered to within an inch of thread tolerance with parrots and hibiscus. Her hat was broad, shady and loaded with bright orange hibiscus flowers. On Phryne, nothing appeared to be overstated. John thought of her dressed entirely in cloth of gold, crowned and hung with Byzantine gems. She would still be essentially Phryne, black hair, green eyes, personality vastly greater than someone of five-two ought to command. Phryne could lead armies, and would do a damn sight better job than General Haig.

'You look tropical,' said John.

'It's the weather,' Phryne replied. 'How was breakfast?'

'Excellent,' said John, buttering his last piece of toast, pausing, then marmalading it too. 'What news?'

'It appears that your Rupert's most persistent enemies are called Calvi and Mitchell. Mitchell is thought to have come to Australia. They are not on record as entering Australia, but then, they wouldn't be. No one has had even a sniff of them in Europe. They were not, regrettably, shot by either the

Turks or the Albanians, and they are not in jail in Greece, or in England.'

'Drat,' said John, crunching.

'I have a description of Guido Calvi which is so generic it could be anyone, and no description at all of Mr Mitchell.'

'Ditto,' said John. 'Excellent marmalade, this.'

'Made by Mrs Butler's sister. Have some more tea to wash it down. However, it seems possible that this Mitchell character is a new man in the local criminal arena. His name is Ratcliffe. Heard the name?'

'Apart from the Ratcliffe Highway and the Ratcliffe Highway Murders, no.'

'All right, but keep an ear out. If anyone called Ratcliffe writes to or talks to or calls on or telephones your Rupert, then stick with him. Especially if he hares off like the worst sort of Gothick heroine, burning the assignation in the candle and going out to the abandoned castle after dark in her nightdress.'

'Right,' said John, chuckling at the image presented to him. Rupert Sheffield would look amazing in a long lace nightgown.

'And you do still have that Webley, don't you?' asked Phryne. 'I remember giving it back to you.'

'Yes,' said John.

'Then I should take it along with me,' she advised soberly. 'I suspect things will be hotting up any time now. Two attempts have failed. They are probably getting quite impatient.'

'I expect so,' said John. Phryne saw his straight-out-of-bed languor depart and his military bearing return. John was a doctor, not a soldier, but he knew far too much about battles for any enemy's comfort. And he might give up on his own life, but never on Sheffield's.

'I have a trace on Calvi,' she told him. 'In the choir. It's not a common name. And there are people working on this problem at . . . well, let us say at all levels. If you get into police trouble, ask them to summon Detective Inspector Robinson. If you get into working-man trouble, mention that you're a comrade of Bert and Cec. In any case, call me. Clear?' she asked.

He nodded. 'Clear.'

'Then I'll see you . . . oh, I forgot.'

She leaned over him, running a finger down his neck. 'Yes, the line should be about here,' she said, and then, without warning, bit. She sucked in a mouthful of flesh and he distinctly felt the mark of her teeth. It was curiously unerotic. Moreover, it hurt. He flinched. Phryne let him go and inspected her mark.

'That ought to do it,' she said, kissed him on the cheek, and breezed away.

Dressing, John saw what she meant. The round, indented love bite was placed so that it just showed above his shirt collar. Not enough to be evident to all. Just to someone who was looking closely.

Wondering if he had strayed into a production of *Les liaisons dangereuses*, John found his shoes. His knee was quite recovered. He must tell young Jane what a good doctor she was going to make. And take his leave of her charming household. After he had shown Tinker how to tie a salmon fly.

Phryne picked up the telephone. She was plotting.

John went into the bathroom to finish dressing. He felt like part of the family. They knew John was an invert and no one had raised so much as an eyebrow, not even the highly respectable Dot Williams. And she was a Good Girl if ever he saw one.

Phryne had gone out by the time he had shaved, limped downstairs, and seated himself in the garden with Dot, who was embroidering, Jane, who was asking him medical questions, Tinker, who wanted to hunt fish on their own terms, and Ruth, who was feeding the family her newly compounded orange cake. Made with real orange juice. It was her own recipe and she was very proud of it. She had also got flour on her plaits again. John demonstrated the knot, watched Tinker loop and tie, and tasted the cake, even though he had hardly any room after all that breakfast. But he would not want to disappoint Ruth, who reminded him of his little sister, dead of tuberculosis so long ago. He bit into a slice.

It was delicious. Molly contributed some fur, a passing bird a feather, and John showed Tinker how to make his favourite salmon fly. Tinker asked and John told him about the roiling toffee-coloured waters on the River Dee at Minnigaff in the Borders, where the salmon schooled, diving upstream, and did not eat, so only the most cunning angler could snare them. Tinker swapped him stories of wrangling huge snapper on a four-pound line.

John considered his state of mind. He was contented. For the first time in a very, very long count of years. Living with his adored Arthur had made him feel like this. Not excited, not surprised. There was tea and gentle conversation about uncontroversial subjects. He was not violently engaged, though he liked his present company very much. He was, in a word, happy. Content.

'Miss Phryne's asking everywhere about who's trying to kill your Mr Sheffield,' Jane told him.

'Yes,' said John, wondering how much he ought to tell these children, or indeed how much they already knew.

'Everyone's looking,' Jane informed him. 'Mr Bert and Mr Cec, Detective Inspector Robinson, that man who sends telegrams. I'm sure it will be all right.'

'Are you?' he asked.

'Of course,' Ruth assured him, patting him on the arm

with a floury hand. 'We've seen Miss Phryne do things you wouldn't believe.'

'Oh?' asked John.

'She held up a boat almost on her own,' said Tinker. He had really liked the adventure with the boats.

'She solved a mystery and rescued a captive maiden,' said Ruth, who adored romances.

'She broke a chair over a man who was attacking her,' said Jane. She wondered about the tensile strength of the chair, and how much force would have been needed to smash it. Also about the density of the head of the victim, who had been silly enough to attack Miss Phryne. Really, the criminal classes needed remedial education. The Chinese had picked it up very fast, but they were intelligent people.

'She talked a man with a gun out of his weapon under the Eastern Market,' said Ruth. 'She found a treasure in Castlemaine.'

'She's on the side of justice,' Tinker reassured him.

'Luckily,' said Dot. 'I always knew she would come and get me. I was kidnapped,' she explained. 'They thought they had Miss Phryne but they only got me. Silly of them.'

'Indeed,' gasped John. And he had thought that Phryne had retired to Australia for a quiet life. He said so.

'Most of the time it's quiet,' said Dot with profound thankfulness.

'Except when it isn't,' agreed Tinker, who liked action.

'And then we all have to combine together, obey orders, and it all works out all right,' said Jane, with perfect faith.

'How did she meet all you useful people?'

'She collected us,' said Dot. 'I was out of work and desperate, Tinker wanted to come to the city, Jane was a mystery and Ruth came with Jane.'

'Together always,' said Ruth sentimentally. 'Eh, Janey?'

'Always,' said Jane with unwonted emotion, taking Ruth's floury hand.

'She met Detective Inspector Robinson when she broke a cocaine ring run through a Turkish bath, before we met her,' Jane told him. 'And Mr Bert and Mr Cec carried her to the Windsor from the docks and she brought an abortionist to justice for them. Also Mr Cec got to hit him. So they're in, whatever she wants to do. And they're wharfies, so they know everyone in the underworld.'

'And she helps the police?'

'If they ask nice,' said Tinker with a grin. 'She's like Sexton. She takes what cases she likes and she does as she thinks fit. That's his motto. I reckon it's Miss Phryne's too.'

'But what about . . . what about her . . . house guests?' John floundered.

'She likes you, she wants to make you feel better,' Dot told him. 'Mr Lin's away, and in any case she's his concubine, not his wife. I don't reckon she'll marry anyone, ever. Mr Lin won't mind. It's not his place to mind. Miss Phryne does as she likes. And you look better, since she's been comforting you.'

'I am,' said John quickly. 'I am better. She's a wonderful woman.'

'Good, so tell us about what she did during the war,' urged Ruth. 'She won't talk about it.'

'It was so awful that she doesn't want to give you bad dreams,' said John slowly. 'It was like hell.'

Dot gave him a speaking look and crossed herself.

John took her hand. 'I mean that literally. If I think about hell, I think about Passchendaele. Smoke, stink, blood, mud, horror, high explosives. And into that came Phryne with her ambulance, outrunning the creeping barrage. She never left anyone to die in no-man's-land alone. Sometimes all she could do was lie down in the mud with them and hold their hands. Yet she shot a trench raider dead—with *my* gun—and never turned a hair. She was remarkable. And she was so young. Not much older than you, young feller-me-lad.'

'Gosh,' said Tinker. 'So, knowing her, how did you end up with this Sheffield bloke?'

'My . . . lover . . . died,' said John, reasoning it out. How *had* he ended up with Sheffield? 'I was slowly dying of boredom. And grief. My friend said he knew I was looking for an apartment to share and this Rupert Sheffield, a mathematician, was looking for a roommate. They were very nice rooms, we have a housekeeper, and he warned me that he played the piano all night long, and didn't speak for days on end, and writes equations on the wall, and I didn't mind those things, because I was moody and still so sad, and angry, because Arthur had left me after only a few years.'

'He couldn't help it,' Ruth pointed out.

'No, but sorrow is not reasonable.'

John Wilson could see Jane filing away the statement for further consideration.

'All right, but you're best mates, not just sharing,' objected Tinker.

'He is . . . eccentric,' admitted John. 'I never know what he is going to do next. He fascinates me.'

'And he is extremely beautiful,' said Jane dispassionately. 'You probably like looking at him.'

'Er . . .' said John wildly. 'Er, yes, I do.'

'And listening to that lovely velvety voice,' she added.

'Yes, it is a lovely voice,' agreed John, far out of his depth and still sinking.

'Miss Phryne will fix it,' Ruth told him. 'But you have to

stay alive. I don't want to think about what she'd do to your Mr Sheffield if he gets you killed. She'll feed him to the sharks.'

'Really?' asked John, now ready to believe anything about Phryne.

All of them, including the sober and respectable Dot, nodded.

'Oh,' said John. 'Well, I'd better stay alive then, eh?'

'That'd be a bonzer idea,' Tinker told him. 'Have a look at this knot, will you, Dr Wilson? I've made a blue somewhere.'

John untangled the knot, wishing that he felt less disconcerted.

·

Phryne Fisher was about to start a fight. In a pub. In a boners pub. Boners were known for the sharpness of their knives and the touchiness of their tempers. They spent their days cleaving animal flesh from bones, and knew a lot of practical anatomy. This made her contemplated action really unwise. But she was there with the full knowledge and almost approval of both the Victoria Police and the local representative of the Communist Party. Bert had come up with a name. The woman who knew all about Ratcliffe owned the Prospect Hotel, known locally as the Bucket of Blood. Slaughterhouse workers drank there. Few other men would dare. A bar full of people who stropped their knives on anything wooden and who were used to carving mammalian tissue, eight hours a shift, made uncomfortable company.

Mother Higgins was a harridan. Her daughter Margery was a pretty, graceful, modest slip of a girl who had apparently attracted Ratcliffe's regard. Mother Higgins disapproved of Ratcliffe, but could do nothing about him. Her most passionate desire was to get her daughter away from him.

Bert had spoken to Mrs Higgins, and made a deal. If Phryne could get Margery safely away, Mrs Higgins would tell everything she knew about Ratcliffe. The difficulty was Ratcliffe's watchers, who never took their eyes off the pub. If Margery left, she would be followed, and if she went too far away, she would be snatched. Mr Ratcliffe was a man who did not take refusal lightly. Therefore a little legerdemain was essential, and therefore the need to start a fight in the Bucket of Blood.

She almost managed it by walking in the door. Visions of loveliness like Phryne did not happen in the Prospect. She allowed the door to swing shut behind her, waiting until her eyes adjusted to the gloom. Right. The bar was a long dirty length of what had been polished mahogany, now irregular in shape because the clientele had tested their knives on its edge. The air was thick with smoke. The stench of exhaled beer was almost palpable. The sawdust had not been changed for years. She refused to think about what she might be walking on as she advanced down the pub. Some things crunched and rolled under her soles and she hoped they weren't fingers.

In the end it was very easy. She blew a kiss to one brutish countenance, choosing the face most resembling something on a police noticeboard. Then she moved out of reach of his grab and blew a kiss at the next candidate for a Wanted poster.

They instantly collided. Someone threw a punch. In seconds it was on for young and old and the barman was ensconced below the bar, clutching the valuable bottles.

Phryne sailed through the resulting riot and walked to the kitchen, where a frazzled girl was crouched next to the stove.

'Up,' said Phryne, stripping off her shawl and then her purple dress. Margery tore off her overall and put on Phryne's clothes. Phryne tucked the girl's hair up under her shady hat, draped her in the parrot shawl, and Mrs Higgins shoved her daughter into the backyard.

'The car's waiting,' said Phryne. 'Chin up, back straight. Walk like you own the world. Mr Butler will take you to a safe place.'

'Mum?' quavered Margery. She was a pale, doe-eyed, gentle creature. She was shivering.

'You go on, girl. I'll see you soon,' said Mrs Higgins, giving her daughter a fast, fierce hug. 'Now, off you go, here come the cops.'

The clanging of a police bell announced the arrival of a car full of policemen. At the exact moment that Mr Ratcliffe's men would be most distracted, Margery Higgins walked out to Phryne's car and was driven away.

'I reckon you better put on Margery's dress,' said Mrs Higgins, surveying Phryne's silk underwear and stockings. 'You started a real good barney when you had all your clothes on. If they sees yer now they'll wreck the joint.'

'Good point,' conceded Phryne, and not only put on Margery's sad grey wrapper, but her cook's mob cap, which hid Phryne's trademark shiny black hair. Then she tied on a stained apron.

'Good-o,' approved Mrs Higgins. 'But how are you gonna get outa here? They'll think you're her, they'll follow yer.'

'By prior arrangement, I'm going to be arrested,' Phryne told her. 'And when I get out I won't be as you see me. Double bluff.'

Mother Higgins thought about it.

'That Bert, he said you was real smart.'

'That was kind of him.'

'You promise my Marge'll be safe?' Mrs Higgins gripped Phryne's arm with a gnarled hand. She was a hag, raddled and damaged, red-eyed, filthy and tough as nails, but she loved her daughter. Phryne patted the hand.

'I promise,' said Phryne. Even now, Margery was on her way to a certain fruit-growing cooperative in Bacchus Marsh, protected by strong-minded women, heavily toothed dogs and the approval of the whole community. The minions of a city crook like Ratcliffe would stand out in that apple-rich area like a series of badly wounded thumbs. If they caused any trouble, they would be compost. 'However, what is Ratcliffe going to do to you when he realises you have smuggled your daughter out from under his nose?'

Mother Higgins barked a short laugh. 'I'm not afraid of 'im,' she snarled, showing teeth yellowed by a lifetime's pipe smoke. 'I got enough knives in this pub to gut 'im like a steer. Yair, and skin 'im and quarter 'im and bone 'im. And I bloody will, if 'e gives me any lip. He knew I couldn't do nothin' while Marge was still 'ere.'

'Right. Now, tell me all. We've got about fifteen minutes until they come to arrest me.' Phryne took a notebook out of her bag.

Mother Higgins lit her pipe and took a long drink from a bottle of red wine. She wiped her lips.

'Three years ago that bastard comes 'ere, and old Grogan's men started to die. Accidents. Then Grogan was found dead, drowned, caught up in an anchor chain. Ratcliffe took over. I seen bad bastards before, and 'e's no worse. Until 'e set eyes on my Margie I could live with 'im bein' boss cocky. There's always a boss.'

'Too true,' said Phryne.

'Him and his lah-di-dah voice and 'is Pommy ways,' sneered Mother Higgins.

'He was on his own, then? He didn't bring an Italian associate with him?'

'Eyties? Nah, no dagos. Just 'im. And that's enough. He took over all old man Grogan's lurks.'

'Which are?'

'Rum, sly grog, smuggling,' mumbled Mother Higgins. It went entirely against her grain to tell anyone anything.

'Girls?' asked Phryne.

'Nah,' she said. 'Not to sell. He takes 'em to keep. He just wanted one more girl. My girl. Fuckin' bastard.'

'Right,' said Phryne. 'And what's he been doing lately?'

'Eyein' off Maginnis's mob and tryin' to take over Willi. Followin' a bloke called Rupert Sheffield. I never heard of 'im. I dunno why 'e's lookin' for 'im, neither. And if I was that bloke I bloody wouldn't want to be found.'

'Indeed. Any idea that Mr Ratcliffe might have been called by another name once?'

'Funny you should say that,' said Mother Higgins, gulping more cheap red wine and spilling some down her corded throat to soak into her stained bombazine bosom. 'One Pommy sailor called him Mitch and Ratcliffe backhanded him across the deck.'

'Where does he live and what does he look like?'

'Medium everythin',' said Mother Higgins. 'Brown hair, Pommy skin, bit taller than me—maybe five-eight—close-shaven. Poncy sort of bloke. Brown eyes like rocks. Lives in that big house in Port. Bert knows. Oh, 'e's gonna be sorry 'e ever tried to steal my girl.'

'Yes,' said Phryne. 'He will be sorry.'

Mother Higgins, well oiled by red wine and relief, looked up muzzily at Phryne wearing her daughter's clothes, and saw another pair of stony eyes. These shone like emeralds. Ratcliffe's were the Mohr hardness of chocolate fudge by comparison.

'Reckon 'e might be,' she conceded.

•

Phryne smiled charmingly on the arresting officers, was led into a police car, driven to the station and shown into Detective Inspector Robinson's office. She sank down into his office chair, tearing off her mob cap. An overnight bag was sitting on the desk.

'How did it go?' she asked, eyes gleaming.

'Very good. We broke the Russell Street record. Fifteen outstanding warrants in one pub.'

'Mother Higgins must be collecting felons,' said Phryne. 'Any sign of the watchers?'

Robinson grinned.

'They were three of the warrants. Shop-breaking, burglary and assault occasioning grievous bodily harm. The Magistrates' Court has had to call in reinforcement off-duty beaks. Nicely done, Miss Fisher!'

'I'm so glad you're pleased. Now, before I get out of these revolting garments, let me tell you all I have learned about Mr Ratcliffe.'

She talked. Robinson frowned.

'I knew there was something wrong with Grogan's death. He was an old sailor, never would have got caught in an anchor chain. So this is the new boss, then. Oh, good. And he's moving into Williamstown, where that—' he paused '—unpleasant person Maginnis rules supreme. Therefore, trouble and corpses and my own chief going crook. Oh, joy.'

'You can thank me another time,' grinned Phryne. 'Now, get some lowly constable to show me to the ladies so I can change into the clothes which Dot sent for me, and I shall be taking myself home. I really need a bath.'

'And this Margery's all right? You've got her stashed somewhere safe?'

'Safe as houses,' promised Phryne, picking up her bag. Jack Robinson didn't notice that she hadn't told him where Margery Higgins was, because she had kissed him very chastely on the cheek as she swept past. Contriving to sweep, even when wearing a skivvy's disgraceful wrapper and grease-spotted apron.

Jack Robinson smiled.

•

Phryne caught the train home. No one appeared to be following her, or even noticing her. Dot had sent Phryne some of Dot's own clothes. They were too large for Phryne and she looked suitably dowdy in them. She slipped in through the back gate and found Tinker tying salmon flies at the wrought-iron table. Molly sat at his feet, waiting for stray bits of sandwich. Tinker's fingers moved nimbly. The line was almost invisible in the sunlight.

'That's clever,' she commented.

'Dr Wilson taught me,' said Tinker. 'He's a real nice bloke, Guv.'

'I know,' said Phryne.

'But yer not goin' ter keep 'im,' said Tinker, reverting to his original accent.

'No,' said Phryne. 'It's not kind to hang on to someone who wants to be with someone else.'

'Why ain't yer jealous?' asked Tinker.

'I don't know,' Phryne told him truthfully. 'I must have missed out on jealousy lessons. Do not let this worry you,

Tink. Now, I'm going to have a bath, and then some lunch. Stay alert. I might have been followed home.'

'Right you are, Guv.'

Tinker flicked a finger at Molly, who padded to the gate, sniffed all around it, and then returned to the boy, sitting down at his feet.

'No one there,' said Tinker. 'Me and Molly will be watching, Guv'nor.'

'I trust you,' said Phryne and went inside, wondering what that conversation had been about. And when had he trained Molly to seek in that admirably silent fashion? Tinker was a very clever boy.

Now for that bath. When she arrived at the top of the stairs, it was all ready for her. The scent of chestnut blossoms hung in the air like a hot afternoon in Paris in spring.

'Dot, you are a gem,' said Phryne, stripping off her borrowed clothes and padding barefoot into the bathroom. She stepped down into the green water and lay back. 'Divine.'

'Did the girl get away all right, Miss?' asked Dot, gathering up her discarded garments.

'Clean as a whistle,' said Phryne. 'Old prison escape trick dating back to the twelfth century, with a hundred previous users. Worked like a charm. Oh, that is so nice. That pub, Dot, it was dreadful. This ought to take away the smell of blood and smoke and beer. But the licensee of said hostelry is a formidable woman. She hasn't acted against this Ratcliffe because of the threat to her daughter. With Margery out of the way, things ought to become quite uncomfortable for him.'

'How nice,' said Dot. 'He sounds like a nasty man. Mr Bert and Mr Cec are coming to lunch, Miss Phryne. Do you have rehearsal tonight?'

'No, thank God. One dose of that conductor is enough for

the present. Another unpleasant man. We seem to be specialising in them lately. What's wrong with Tinker?'

'Oh,' said Dot. 'You noticed.'

'I did,' said Phryne, stirring the eau-de-Nil water with one hand.

'Jane,' explained Dot.

'He's fallen in love with Jane?'

'I think so,' said Dot. 'She hasn't noticed.'

'Of course she hasn't,' said Phryne, chuckling. 'Can't do any harm, Dot. She's the first female who's ever been interested in him. It will wear off, hopefully before Jane does notice, because I don't think she'd be interested.'

'Not in him, or not in any boy?' asked Dot.

'The latter, I think. She's all intellect. But you never know. He'll be good,' Phryne assured Dot. 'So that's why he was asking me about jealousy. All is now clear.'

'All right, Miss,' said Dot. She laid out Phryne's most sumptuous house gown, of blue and green watered silk, and went downstairs considerably relieved.

Dried, slicked, powdered and scented and brushed, Phryne floated downstairs, a vision in aquamarine robes, and phoned Fanshawe's number. She told the comfortable female voice on the other end everything she had learned about Ratcliffe. She suspected that the telephonist was knitting while listening. She concluded with an account of the police action at the Prospect, was told to 'be careful, dear' and hung up chuckling.

Now for lunch, Bert and Cec, and—aha—an unexpected telegram. Phryne ripped open the envelope and gave the boy a penny from the jar on the hallstand.

'Stay out of my way'. No signature. Of course, she had been seen entering and leaving the Prospect and Ratcliffe knew that she was somehow involved in the vanishing of Margery.

A mouse had been spirited away from under the cat's paw. Even calm placid moggies got upset if someone stole their lawful prey. Good. A frustrated Ratcliffe might easily make mistakes. Must double the guard, restock the crocodile swamp and take the safety catches off the spring-guns, Phryne thought. She was now a target. In her own right.

She drew in a deep breath of contentment. Like Tinker, Phryne liked action. The household ought to be safe enough, with Tinker and Molly guarding the back gate and Mr Butler the front door. Kidnapping did not seem to be Mr Ratcliffe's modus operandi. He preferred assassination to solve any of his little difficulties. All she had to do was keep an ear tuned for that gasping 'potato-potato' of the Harley. And remember that a Hispano-Suiza, suitably steered, was a match for any motorcycle.

Lunch. Bert and Cec had arrived. She sat down for a conference which might easily turn into a council of war. Beer was provided. There must theoretically be an hour of the day or night when Bert and Cec didn't drink beer, but Phryne had never deduced it.

'You stirred up a real ants' nest,' said Bert admiringly. 'Blokes runnin' round like headless chooks. Maginnis's men belting Ratcliffe's men. Ratcliffe's blokes necking Maginnis's blokes. Mother Higgins geein' up her knife-men and barrin' the door of the Prospect to any of 'em. She let it be known that any standover bludgers come into her pub they get killed, skinned, gutted, jointed, trimmed and served for dinner.'

'Roasted,' said Cec.

'With Yorkshire pudding,' said Bert. 'And she could do it, too. She's not a bad cook, considerin'.'

'Too right,' said Cec.

They drank more beer. Phryne showed them her telegram.

Bert sucked in a breath. 'Told yer he's rattled,' he said.

'Yes,' Phryne agreed. 'What's his household like?'

'Posh,' said Bert, and drank the rest of the beer. He seemed to think he had said all that was necessary. Phryne needed more information.

'Posh, yes, good, but who lives with him?'

'His girls,' said Bert. 'Poor cows. No better than slaves. That's why Missus Higgins was so scared for Margery. He don't . . . behave nice with women.'

'If I rescue one, can she steal something for me?'

'What d'ya want?' asked Bert.

'A blank sheet of his stationery and a sample of his handwriting.'

Bert gave her a very narrow, considering look. 'I reckon you're planning something very nasty for Mr Ratcliffe,' he said slowly.

'I am, yes,' said Phryne. 'What about it?'

'My cousin Siegfried's niece Hildegard works in the house,' said Cec. 'My cousin's been after her to quit, but she's too scared. If you can give her the ticket to go visit her old grandma in Bundaberg, I reckon she'll do it.'

'Good. Count on me for a ticket to absolutely anywhere. It shouldn't be too dangerous, if she dusts the study or the library and empties the wastepaper basket anyway.'

'Yair, Hildy's a housemaid. All right, Miss. What else?'

'Who would take over Ratcliffe's gang, if Ratcliffe was removed?'

'That's a problem for another bottle,' said Bert, opening it. 'I got no notion. Cec, what d'you reckon?'

'Dunno,' said Cec. 'He's got rid of any bugger who could challenge him. Real cock on a dunghill, that bloke. If Ratcliffe's not there, I reckon Maginnis'd just mop up whatever's left.'

'Nice,' said Phryne. 'And the girls?'

'Dunno,' said Cec. 'You could get your sister on to them.'

'Good plan.' Phryne's sister Eliza ran a mission for almost any good cause available. She would be able to cope with unshackling the slaves. This Ratcliffe was sounding even more like an excrescence on the fair face of Melbourne than ever.

'And where does Ratcliffe have his working headquarters?' asked Phryne. 'In Port?'

'Yair, there's a couple of warehouses, empty, and an old sheet-metal shop. End of Bay Street. They're s'posed to be pullin' 'em down. Till then, that's where Ratcliffe keeps 'is court.'

'Right,' said Phryne. 'I don't want any of us going there—' she raised her voice '—especially you, Tinker. Come in and join us,' she invited, and Tinker and Molly slunk into the parlour. 'If you want to know what's going on, you can always ask,' said Phryne.

'Yes, Guv'nor, but will you tell me?' asked Tinker.

Cec grinned at him. 'She's your commanding officer, son,' he said. 'She'll tell you what you need to know.'

'S'pose,' said Tinker.

'I promise, Tink,' said Phryne. 'When it all gets exciting, you will be there.'

'All right,' said Tinker, and smiled.

CHAPTER TWELVE

How doth the little busy bee
Improve each shining hour,
And gather honey all the day
From every opening flower!

Isaac Watts
'Against Idleness and Mischief'

Phryne lunched with Bert and Cec, then went for a fast thinking walk on the beach. She was rather counting on no Harley being able to sneak up on her, as she understood that motorbikes did not do well in deep sand. Then again, if they were like dispatch riders' bikes, which continued to operate even in Somme mud, this might be optimistic. However, no riders careered across the dunes, and she and Molly had a pleasant walk, except for the moment that Molly sighted Mr Brown, she snarled and he ran away.

Which was rather invigorating than otherwise.

She returned to a light afternoon tea and the news that Dot was going to a dance with Hugh Collins, Tinker and Jane had started a marathon chess tournament, and Ruth was cooking dinner. Mrs Butler had allowed her free rein of her precious kitchen. Mrs Butler had a *tendresse* for Ronald Colman, and there was a new film.

So it was going to be a very quiet, studious sort of night. Phryne knew that she had to stay out of the kitchen, where Ruth would be touchy about visitors. She also knew that she had to stay out of the parlour, because Tinker needed to concentrate. Many skills have been acquired by men for love of woman, and chess looked to be Tinker's love-offering.

Couldn't hurt. But that left Phryne with her own rooms or the garden for the perusal of her plan to bring down Ratcliffe. She did not feel entirely secure from being seen in the garden, so she retired to her rooms until Jane should trounce Tinker and Ruth should announce dinner. Molly was on guard by the back gate and the front door was locked.

Phryne sat on her sofa, rolling a bullet round and round in her fingers. It had been extracted from the coachwork of the Hispano-Suiza. A .45, definitely. She wished there was some way to tell which gun a bullet had been fired from. She stared at the bullet. It remained uninformative.

She tossed it into a dish of hatpins and went down to the drawing room for a drink.

•

She had not heard from John Wilson all day. Phryne wondered if Rupert was keeping him close, or at least away from Phryne. A promising development, if so, but it left Phryne at rather a loose end.

She was just trying to decide on whether a gin and tonic—which would mean going into the kitchen for ice—or a glass of wine—which would mean going down to the cellar—would improve her mood more, when the doorbell rang and Phryne went to answer it, pistol in hand.

John Wilson seemed a little surprised by his reception. He put up both hands and dropped his stick with a clatter.

'I surrender,' he told her.

'Come in,' said Phryne, grabbing the cane and allowing him to lean on her shoulder. 'And let me listen for a moment.'

No sound of 'potato-potato'. No sign of a motorcyclist.

'Motorcycle?' asked John.

'You really are very quick on the uptake, John dear,' said Phryne. She took his hat and placed it on the hatstand.

'Not if you listen to Sheffield,' he answered glumly.

'Yes, but I don't,' said Phryne sweetly. 'Come in, have a drink.'

'Excellent notion,' said John, accompanying her into the parlour. 'Sheffield's dining with the University of Melbourne, and I begged off for the night. I really don't have anything to say to these mathematical chaps, you know. They're far more intelligent than me.'

'But you could diagnose beri beri?' asked Jane, looking up from her chessboard. 'Check, Tinker.'

'Of course,' said John.

'Know how many bones there are in a human skeleton?'

'Yes, two hundred and six,' said John. This girl disconcerted him.

'And you could name them?' asked Jane, touching a pawn and then biting the end of that finger.

'If I had to,' John agreed.

'Well, then,' said Jane. 'I bet they couldn't.'

'Er, no, perhaps not,' said John. 'Anyway, the scholars picked Sheffield up in a closed car and they'll deliver him back, so he doesn't need me for the night.'

'Good, I do. I have a mission of great peril for you,' Phryne told him.

He smiled. 'And that is?'

'Go into the kitchen and ask Ruth to fill the ice bucket,' said Phryne.

Jane was impressed. Ruth wouldn't throw anything really heavy at nice Dr Wilson. Miss Phryne was really adroit with people, a skill which Jane admitted she did not possess.

Tinker tapped her hand.

'Check,' he said triumphantly.

'So it is, how clever of you,' she murmured. 'I see I shall have to pay attention.'

Tinker glowed.

Ruth did not throw anything at nice Dr Wilson, because her preparations for the cold buffet were all complete and chilling nicely, her salad leaves were washed and her salad dressings made. The mayonnaise crisis had been averted with a timely ice cube, and she was about to offer the company drinks anyway.

So Dr Wilson carried the ice bucket and Ruth carried the jug of lemonade into the parlour. Phryne compounded a gin and lemon, tinkling with ice, and led her guest into the other room, so as not to disrupt the chess players. Ruth would be taking her romance novel into the garden, as was her wont, until the light failed.

'So, what developments on the assassin?' asked John.

'It does seem that Ratcliffe is Mitchell, and it does seem that he is after Rupert specifically. No sign of Calvi; he does not seem to have stayed with Mitchell. He may not be here at all. I just like to be thorough,' said Phryne, sipping. 'Ratcliffe is trying to take over in Williamstown, and the warlord in charge of it will not give up easily. Their minions have taken to killing one another. This will keep him suitably nervous and distracted.'

'God, Phryne, by coming here I've precipitated a war,' said John, looking thunderstruck.

'Not you,' Phryne told him, patting his cheek. 'This was happening before you and Sheffield even landed in Australia. There's a strike on the waterfront, so a lot of the cargo is going out through Williamstown. Ratcliffe rules Port Melbourne, which is now idle. Therefore . . .'

'Oh, I see, we have warring tribes.'

'Exactly. It's all getting a little intense. How Rupert is involved with all of this I cannot imagine. Except, of course, that Mitchell wants to kill him.'

'That is a rather exceptional exception, Phryne,' said John.

'Yes, it is. Has he said anything at all about what he has done since he got here? Where have you been apart from Melbourne?'

'Brisbane and Sydney. We were going to go to Canberra but it isn't really set up for visitors yet. Nothing at all untoward happened in either city. Sydney University was delighted to see Rupert and he spent his time talking about mathematics. I did wander around a little. It's interesting, with that half-built bridge like claws across the harbour. It will probably be very impressive when it's finished. I went to the gallery; you know, traveller's pastimes.'

Phryne put down her glass and laid a hand on his good knee.

'Did you . . . sorry, I really need to ask this . . . did you find any agreeable company in either city? Someone who might, for example, have decided that they wanted to keep you and . . .'

'Followed me all this way in order to kill Sheffield and take his place?' John laughed. 'You give me too much credit, Phryne dear! I'm no pretty boy. I'm a crippled ex-army doctor with a broken heart and a hopeless infatuation. Definitely not the object of anyone's passion. And definitely not worth keeping, much less pursuing. And, no, to answer your question, I didn't go looking for agreeable company. I didn't meet anyone I wanted until I came to Melbourne and saw you coming up the steps. Never was more amazed and delighted in my life.'

'Or me,' said Phryne. 'Are we still friends? I had to ask, you know.'

'Of course,' said John.

'All right, so we can scrub a personal motive for assassinating Sheffield, unless he really got on someone's quince in Sydney or Brisbane.'

John sighed. 'He always does, but I can't think of anyone specific.'

'Right, then Mitchell/Ratcliffe it is, and we need to make a plan.'

'Are you going to use my irreplaceable Rupert as bait?' asked John in a rising tone. 'I forbid it!'

'Calm,' suggested Phryne. 'He only becomes bait if he offers himself up for sacrifice, and I promise it will not go that far. I have made arrangements. All you have to do if he goes out in response to a letter or a telephone call, refusing to explain and forbidding you to follow, is to first phone me—just with the word "go" if you haven't time—and then follow him. Take your service revolver and stick to him like glue. Can you do that?'

'Yes,' said John. 'Do I let him know that I am there?'

'As you like. I am pretty sure I know where he will be going, the dolt. Bay Street, Port Melbourne—right into the dragon's den. Then we shall conclude this and you can get on with your life without fear of imminent assassination.'

'That would be nice,' said John.

'Good. Are we agreed?' asked Phryne. 'What are your instructions?'

'On his departure in mysterious circs, I phone you, then follow him. I can do that,' said John. He leaned forward and put his hands on the chair back either side of Phryne's head, bringing his face down to hers. 'Try to keep him alive,' he said softly. 'I don't care about me, but I care most deeply about him.'

'I know,' said Phryne gently, and kissed his mouth.

Ruth announced dinner. All this high emotion had made Phryne very hungry.

•

John and Phryne sat in her parlour as, until Mr Butler got back, Phryne intended to guard the door. Not a bark had been heard from Molly in the garden, watching the back gate. Phryne was of the opinion that Ratcliffe was only slightly interested in her. He would suspect that it had been Phryne who had engineered Margery's escape. He would have a lot on his plate, what with Maginnis and now Mother Higgins and her slaughtermen. That telegram had just been an indication to Phryne that he knew who she was and where she lived. A warning. One she intended to heed.

She had coaxed John into talking about his life with Rupert and, as Rupert was always his favourite subject, John had been pleased to comply. She was listening with half an ear, because she had heard the back gate open. Molly gave a short, soft 'wuff' and Tinker left his chess game at a fast scramble.

He returned escorting Cec. The tall blond wharfie looked worried.

'I been hearin' your name,' he told Phryne. 'I been hearin' it from blokes who didn't ought ter know it.'

'Yes,' said Phryne. 'Mr Ratcliffe is not pleased with me.'

'Bastard,' said Cec. He held out a paper bag.

'What's this?'

'Handwriting and a piece of his own writing paper,' said Cec, grinning. 'Compliments of Sieg's niece Hildy. I just put her on the train to Queensland. You owe me three quid. She pinched a few sheets in case you want to practise, she said. She's a bright sheila, Hildy. I'm real glad she's out of it, but. That's not a nice house for a good girl. She says to tell you he uses dark blue ink, like a bank.'

'Take five pounds,' said Phryne, handing over a banknote. 'Thank you very much. Are you and Bert out of this firing line?'

'Yair,' said Cec, accepting a bottle of beer from Ruth. 'Thanks, Ruthie. You know the way to a man's heart. We never belonged to any gang but a stevedores' gang. Maginnis and Ratcliffe don't have nothin' on us.'

'I might need you, for the matters I described today,' said Phryne. 'Are you on?'

'Against Ratcliffe? 'Course,' said Cec. He drained the bottle, tipped his cap, and went away. Molly wuffed him out of the back gate.

'I just need to make a phone call,' Phryne told John, and went out into the hall. She riffled through the paper bag. Sieg's niece Hildy had done Phryne proud, and she hoped that the girl enjoyed her holiday in Queensland. Phryne held five untouched sheets of cream laid stationery with Ratcliffe's name and address on them, and a bundle of scrawled notes and drafts. Excellent exemplars.

She called the number again, and Fanshawe answered. Phryne heard children's voices in the background. This section of MI6 was charmingly domestic.

'Phryne here,' said Phryne, running through her identifying phrases. 'I need a forger.'

'Anything complicated?' asked Mr Fanshawe. 'Yes, yes, Daddy will be back directly. Isn't it time for you to go to bed? It's getting dark.'

'Suicide note,' said Phryne. 'I have the victim's stationery and handwriting samples.'

'Right. I shall send someone over in the morning to pick up the details—no, I'll come myself.'

'Listen out for Harleys,' Phryne warned him.

'I shall,' said Peter Fanshawe, and rang off.

Phryne went back to John. Their only shared memories besides were of the war, and she did not want to talk about that tonight. She wanted to look at John Wilson, with his greying hair and his limp and his shining righteousness, who did not think that, of Sheffield and Wilson, he was the one worth saving. And he did not need to go back to the Windsor tonight.

•

After breakfast, John left, and shortly afterwards Peter Fanshawe arrived. He was wearing a workman's dustcoat and had arrived in a plumber's van, requesting entrance at the back gate. It took Phryne's intervention to get him admitted to the house, over Molly and Tinker's strong exceptions. Molly especially didn't like the look of him. He smelt of a strange dog. A strange male dog.

'No, let him in, he's a friend of mine,' ordered Phryne.

'You sure, Guv?' asked Tinker, grabbing Molly's collar and hauling her back onto her hind legs.

'Sure,' said Phryne. 'But you are very good guards. Back to your posts, darlings. Come in, Peter.'

'You are doing a very good job,' Fanshawe told Tinker. 'No one's going to get past you. I'm glad Miss Phryne has sentinels.'

'That's us,' said Tinker.

Phryne led Peter into the parlour and offered him tea, which he did not accept. She showed him the exemplars and the blank sheets.

'All right, very good. Tell me about the man who is writing this suicide note.'

'No friends, no lovers. Uses dark blue ink like banks use. He hasn't any relatives here, or people he loves. This note ought to convey: "I've lost, I'm beaten, I'm not going to watch Maginnis take over my operation, so goodbye and I'll see you all in hell."'

'Ah, that sort of note,' said Peter Fanshawe.

'Can you do it?' asked Phryne.

'Me, no, but I know someone who can. I'll take those—' he put the papers carefully into his pocket '—and I'll be back before the end of the day. I have quite a journey ahead of me.'

'Bon voyage,' said Phryne.

'And if you're lucky, I'll bring you back some honey,' said Peter.

•

'That was odd,' said Dot.

'Yes, I know. One does not associate forgers with honey. But there we are. How was the dance?'

'Really good,' said Dot, blushing. Phryne surmised that she had spent most of the evening romancing a certain policeman and would not, if challenged, be able to name any of the tunes the band had played. So she didn't ask. She got on with checking the household accounts with Dot. Dot could add up pounds, shillings and pence in her head. Phryne was impressed.

•

Peter Fanshawe took the road for Eltham with a light heart. Matters had transpired on which he could do with advice, and in any case it had been ages since he had seen his mentor, retired MI6 Major Aloysius Tobit, who came to Australia because his asthma was so bad. Arrived, he found Australian asthma just as debilitating, but was cured by a folk remedy: the measured consumption of local apple blossom honey. Thereafter he had retired to the nearest source of apple blossom, Eltham, and indulged himself in innumerable bees.

Fanshawe could take or leave bees, but had a weakness for apple blossom honey. His wife always craved it when she was expecting. And he really wanted to talk to Major Tobit. Fanshawe was worried about Phryne Fisher and the operation she seemed to be running, on his ground, without discernible rules. Or, indeed, ethics. This suicide note for someone who wasn't presently aware of his fate being a case in point. But it was a nice day and the car was running through fields and then through woods. It was very pleasant to be out of the office for a change. He reached the small stone-built house with the green apple trees all around and took a deep breath as he got out of the car. He reminded himself that he must bring the children to visit, now that they were old enough not to grab at the bees.

They circled, lazily, full fed. This house always had bees. He knocked at the green front door.

Major Tobit's wife, Esther, welcomed him with a hug and an offer of scones, clotted cream and—of course—honey.

'He's just out talking to the hives,' she told him. 'Do sit down; let me look at you.' She was a dumpy, comfortable old lady in a pink hand-knitted jumper who had been a premier agent in her time. She still had uncommonly penetrating eyes.

'It's nice to see you, Mrs T.'

'And is all well with the children? Your wife? Good,' she

said. 'What brings you here? If it was just a friendly visit you would have brought your family.'

'Phryne Fisher,' said Peter, and Esther Tobit laughed out loud.

'Oh, indeed,' she said. 'I wondered when Phryne would do something to shake earth's foundations! She's been confining herself to crime—how has she dragged you into her whirlpool?'

'You know her?' asked Peter Fanshawe hopefully.

'Certainly, and so does Tobit. I believe she seduced him at some point. She does that. Before I met him and she doesn't mean any harm, you know.'

'No?' he squeaked.

'No, and you're in no danger. You're married. Phryne does have some standards. Ah, Ally, darling, guess who's been driving poor Peter round the bend?'

Major Tobit came in, having shed his beekeeper's overall. He only wore it because Esther objected to the sticky patches which amorous bees left on his clothes. Peter had seen him reach into a hive and have the bees crawl and settle all over his arms and face, kissing him and humming. Major Tobit just adored his bees, and the bees returned the sentiment.

'Peter, m'dear fellow.' Major Tobit shook hands. He was a chubby, rounded sort of man, just as Peter remembered him. 'How very nice to see you! There are such a large number of people who could be driving you round the bend, I cannot possibly choose between them.'

'Female,' hinted Esther.

'Lord, really? I wondered when Phryne would do something which would stagger humanity.' The Major chuckled. His three chins shook. 'What has she done to you?'

'Exacerbated a small war between two criminal gangs,' said Peter. 'Because one of them is an old client of ours.'

'Oh?' asked Major Tobit. 'Yes, tea, m'dear, and Peter will like scones with honey. She's been experimenting with making clotted cream, just as we used to eat it in Somerset.' He still had the remains of a burr in his voice. 'It tastes just as I remember it from my grandma's kitchen. Which of our previous clients?'

'Mitchell the gun-runner. Now called Ratcliffe. He's making a spirited attempt to kill Rupert Sheffield.'

'I can understand that,' commented Esther. 'The most insufferable young man I ever met. How Compton put up with him I do not know.'

'He was a superb code-breaker, and most of those mathematical chaps are a bit odd, you know,' said Major Tobit generously. 'Don't tell me Phryne's defending Sheffield? Not her type at all, I would have thought.'

'No, Sheffield has a friend of Miss Fisher's with him, one Dr John Wilson. Miss Fisher is very fond of Dr Wilson and thinks that Ratcliffe's attempt to remove Sheffield will invariably lead to Dr Wilson getting killed while trying to protect him.'

'That makes sense,' said Major Tobit. 'Phryne will go to extraordinary lengths to defend her friends. Tell me, you've seen her lately—how does she look now?'

'Small, thin, black hair cut in a cap, bright green eyes, very fashionable,' said Fanshawe. 'Reckless, I would have said, except she seems to make a lot of plans. Takes precautions. Intelligent. Flexible. She must have been a very good agent.'

'She was, until she got bored. Could go anywhere and be anyone. The stage lost a great actress in Phryne,' said Esther. 'However, she left us, went to stay at her father's house, arranging flowers and so on. Then she took off for Australia. We've been keeping a bit of an eye on her, of course. She knows a lot of secrets.'

'So, tell me, was she really a Mata Hari?' asked Fanshawe. Major Tobit snorted. 'No! Not at all! Peter, for shame!'

'Sorry,' Peter mumbled.

Esther leaned forward and put a hand on his arm. 'Mata Hari got caught,' she said, and grinned a wicked grin. It looked very out of place on her soft, elderly, female face.

'Ah,' said Peter.

'And now for some tea and scones and you can tell me all about Phryne's plans,' said Major Tobit comfortably.

Mrs Tobit brought in the tray. The scones were fresh out of the oven. The clotted cream was remarkable. The honey was golden and scented. Peter loaded and consumed one scone before he started to talk, to give him courage. He had no idea whether Major Tobit would reprove him for his actions.

Then Peter told him everything he knew about Phryne, Sheffield, Dr Wilson, the Ratcliffe/Maginnis contretemps and the vanishing of Margery from the Prospect Hotel.

Major Tobit chuckled. 'She's pulled that one before,' he said. 'Got it out of a medieval romance, she told me. Only works when there are a few uncontrolled entrances, or she can impersonate someone who is allowed in and out. Having herself arrested is a new twist. Very prettily done.'

'But it drew Ratcliffe's attention,' Peter protested.

'That wouldn't worry our Phryne. I bet you a jar of my best honey to a brick that her house is well secured.'

'Boy and dog at the back gate, Phryne herself at the front.'

'Indeed. Armed?'

'I expect so,' said Peter. He was feeling better, and it wasn't just the scones and the admirable honey. Major Tobit approved of Phryne. So did Esther. 'I asked Central, and they said every assistance. But it might get a bit . . . tricky.'

'You mean that she might kill Ratcliffe,' said Major Tobit.

'I know she is going to kill him,' said Peter. 'I have the means with me for you to forge his suicide note.'

'Ah,' said the Major. 'Well, we can do that. I trust her, and you can too. She will do as much damage as she feels necessary, and no more. And since Mitchell is Ratcliffe, he will be no loss. I'd love to get her a medal, but it really wouldn't do, you know.'

'Designing it would be a real challenge to the artist,' murmured Esther. 'Make sure you wash your hands before you begin, Ally. It won't do to have honey smears on a suicide note.'

'Right you are. What sort of ink does the fellow use?'

'Informant said dark blue, like a bank's.'

'And the tenor of the note?'

'To hell with all of you, I'm conquered,' said Peter.

'I'm not staying to watch your triumph,' said the Major.

'Quite.'

'No farewell to favourite wife or doggie?'

'No, he hasn't any of them,' said Peter.

'As I remember, Mitchell was an Englishman, went to university. So, educated English,' said Major Tobit.

'I suppose so,' said Peter.

'Right, I'll just go and wash my hands as my colleague suggests, and get on with it. You have another scone. Esther will get you some honey and some cream to take home with you. By the way,' said the Major, taking the brown paper bag in his clean hand, 'what happened to the other chap? Calvi, was it?'

'No sign of him. He isn't with Ratcliffe. Miss Fisher thinks she may have a line on him, too.'

'Admirable girl,' said the Major. 'Always thought so.'

'More tea?' asked Mrs Tobit.

•

An hour later, as Peter was being instructed in the making of clotted cream, the Major called them back into the parlour.

Mrs Tobit put down her ladle and wiped her hands on her apron. 'Yes, dear? How did you go?'

'I think this will do,' said Major Tobit, laying out a crumpled draft of a letter on the table, and showing a newly written suicide note. Peter gasped. The writing was not a perfect match, because that would be suspicious. It was a very close match. The handwriting was bold and had flourishes. The draft was a letter about coal supplies for a laundry. The suicide note said:

> *Vicisti, Galilaee! You've won. I'm not staying to watch you take over my concerns. I'll see you all in Hell. Soon.*

It was signed with the full Ratcliffe flourish.

'Beautiful,' breathed Peter.

'You do such nice work, dear,' agreed Mrs Tobit.

The Major flexed his fingers. 'I've never got arthritis, though my old dad had it something cruel. I put it down to the healing powers of—'

'Honey,' said Peter.

'Precisely!' said the Major, beaming and clapping him on the back.

Peter Fanshawe drove home with several pots of clotted cream and a dozen jars of honey. And a forged suicide note.

He delivered the note and one pot of honey to Miss Fisher's house and drove back to the garage to change clothes and vehicles, feeling profoundly pleased that he was in good favour, doing the right thing, and not an enemy of the Hon. Miss Phryne Fisher.

CHAPTER THIRTEEN

Since I am coming to that Holy room,
Where, with Thy quire of saints for evermore,
I shall be made Thy music; as I come
I tune the instrument here at the door
And what I must do then, think here before.

John Donne
'Hymn to God, My God, in My Sickness'

Rehearsal was frightful.

Not only was the conductor cruel, partial, and doing unpleasant things to Mendelssohn, wrestling him into the box marked HANDEL and chopping off the bits which didn't fit, the evening had started with a mad rummage to find the orchestral score.

'Sheer swank,' snapped Matthew, flushed and irritated. 'He doesn't need the full score to rehearse the choir. He just likes to show off.'

'Yes, but we still have to find it,' said Tabitha, practical as ever. 'Where did anyone see it last?'

'Conductor's room,' said Isabelle, fanning herself.

'It's not there now?'

'He says not,' replied Chloe.

'I'll go and have another look,' offered Phryne, as Mr James was working himself up to a full-dress snit. She took Matthew with her to the comically secured room, unlocked it, and found the score lying on the floor behind the desk, invisible from the door. It seemed a little damp; perhaps the roof leaked. But it was the score and Matthew bore it triumphantly back to the music stand.

The rehearsal started. The choir got through 'Baal, We Cry to Thee' without attracting too much criticism. Then they tried 'And Then Shall Your Light Break Forth' and were scorned.

'I will have to find a semi-chorus to sing this,' sneered Mr James. 'You can't manage it.'

'Not only does he push his revolting greasy hair back all the time, he licks his fingers every time he turns a page,' said Oliver. 'It's disgusting.'

'Répétiteur! You're off-tempo. Faster, if you can manage it,' ordered Mr James.

'It says *andante moderato*,' said Professor Szabo.

'You will do as I say or you will leave,' yelled James, and there was a pause. The choir looked wildly at each other. Where were they going to get another good pianist at this late date? Willing to play for ruby-port money? Finally, the melody was played again, at the tempo which Henry James preferred.

'Again, from B,' said James, and they sang again.

It was a relief all round when he finished the rehearsal early, scowled himself out, and the choir wound down by singing a folk song.

'*Oh the summer time is coming*,' sang the tenors.

'*And the leaves are sweetly blooming*,' sang the altos in answer.

221

'*And the wild mountain thyme,*' sang the sopranos.

'*Blooms amongst the blooming heather,*' sang the basses.

'*Will you go,*' asked the choir of each other, '*lassie/laddie, go? And we'll all go together, to pluck wild mountain thyme, all amongst the blooming heather, will ye go, laddie, go?*'

Phryne had never sung this before, but the tune was simple. It was also, overwhelmingly, suggestive. Each choir member had nailed down the object of his or her regard and was moving towards them.

'*I will build my love a bower, near the pure and crystal fountain,*' sang the sopranos.

'*And about it I will pile all the flowers of the mountain,*' sang the basses, '*will ye go, lassie, go?*'

Phryne felt eyes upon her. She turned, singing, and encountered the beautiful trout-stream eyes of Matthew the tenor, aflame with desire. '*And we'll all go together,*' she sang, '*and pluck wild mountain thyme, all amongst the blooming heather, will ye go, laddie, go?*' she asked.

He took her hand.

'Not yet,' Phryne told him.

'When?' he asked, pressing her palm to his lips. His mouth was open and hot.

'Soon,' said Phryne, and took her hand away.

'*If my true love cannot come, I will surely find another,*' sang the choir, '*to pluck wild mountain thyme, all amongst the blooming heather, will ye go, laddie, go?*'

Singing, they swept themselves out. They were heading for Aunty Mark's perpetual party. Phryne was intending to follow when she was stopped at the door by John Wilson. He looked worried.

'I say, Phryne, can we come to dinner tonight? Frightful cheek, short notice and all that.'

'Yes, of course—you mean both you *and* Sheffield?' she asked.

'His idea,' said John, clearly at a loss.

'Really? Very well. I shall just phone my house and warn them that there will be two extra for supper. The household dines early. We can take a taxi. I gave Mr Butler the night off. And yell if you hear a Harley-Davidson.'

'I will,' he promised.

Phryne went into the conductor's room and called Mrs Butler. Two more for one of her lavish suppers wouldn't strain the resources of her admirably well-stocked kitchen, but it was always a good idea to be polite to someone who could poison you, if they felt the need. She also arranged for Bert and Cec to pick her up. No sense in giving Ratcliffe a free hit. She then spoke to Dot.

Phryne occupied the rest of the lecture time in reading the notes to her Mendelssohn score. It sounded like her informants had been correct. Henry James's method was exactly the wrong way to conduct Mendelssohn. No wonder the old professor had gone out scowling. Poor old man. He would be climbing into a bottle tonight. Preferably one provided by Aunty Mark, who only served good wine.

Carried home with her guests without incident, Phryne showed them into the large parlour where Tinker, Jane and Ruth waited with Dot to greet them. Jane spent a considerable time staring at Sheffield. So much so that after a luxurious little supper and a few glasses of wine, John asked her how her chess was coming along and Rupert offered her a game. Jane looked at Phryne, who shrugged.

'Now, my dear fellow, be civil,' urged John.

Sheffield shrugged in his turn. Jane set up the board and held out her closed hands, a piece in each. Rupert did not touch her hand, as was the custom, but indicated the right fist, which Jane opened to reveal the black pawn.

'I'm black,' said Rupert.

'But comely,' said John.

Rupert flashed him a violet glance. Ruth and Dot returned to their discussion of meringues. Phryne sat near John and murmured, 'How have you been getting on?'

'Wouldn't let me out of his sight all day,' responded John. 'If he was a different person I'd say he was jealous. But he can't possibly be.'

'No?' said Phryne. 'His next ploy will tell you how he feels about you.'

'It will?'

'Watch,' said Phryne. 'And wait.'

Jane pushed forward a pawn in front of her king. Sheffield pushed out his own pawn opposite. Out came Jane's bishop three spaces. Sheffield's mouth turned down at the corners and he brought out his knight. Jane's knight came out to mirror his, and Sheffield's knight swept away Jane's pawn. Out came her other knight, and the black knight took that as well. A pawn in front of her queen captured the knight, and Sheffield, now actually frowning, pushed out his queen's pawn one square. Jane's face erupted into a delighted grin and her remaining knight took the pawn anyway. Now impassive, Sheffield calmly took the knight with his pawn. Straight away, Jane swept her slender arm across the board, grasped her bishop and took the pawn next to the black king. 'Check!' she said triumphantly. The ghost of a smile illuminated Sheffield's features, and he moved his king forward a square. Out came the other bishop. 'Check again!' Jane crowed, and Sheffield gently laid his king on one side.

'Very good,' he commented. 'Did you work that out for yourself, or did you read it somewhere?'

Jane looked affronted. 'I thought it up myself! Why, has somebody else thought of it too?'

Sheffield smiled again. Twice in one night, thought Phryne, looking on from a safe distance. Why, Mr Sheffield! Are you certain your face won't crack with the unaccustomed exercise? Better to keep this subversive thought unvoiced, she decided. Sheffield's long, elegant fingers began to reset the board. 'It is called the Boden Gambit,' he said softly. 'It is so rarely played I had quite forgotten it. Of course I should have moved my knight back at move four. If you thought of that yourself, you show promise.' He smiled for an unprecedented third time. 'And now you should give me a chance to play white.' He turned the board around and placed his queen's pawn forward two squares.

Fifteen minutes later, Jane turned over her king.

'I resign,' said Jane. 'Thank you for an instructive game.'

'You are . . . quite a promising player,' said Sheffield reluctantly.

'Thank you,' said Jane. 'I heard your lecture on the science of deduction. Would you perhaps explain the basis of your mathematical method to me?'

'Do you understand calculus?' asked Rupert. He was so pretty, Phryne thought, with his hand-tailored suit and tousled black curls. Pity he was such a cold-hearted monster. A mannequin. An automaton. All mind, no body.

Beautiful, though.

'No, I haven't done calculus yet,' confessed Jane.

Sheffield took out a sheet of plain paper and traced three straight lines without apparent effort using a thin pencil. He scorned such things as rulers. 'See this oblique line here? I want you to tell me the slope of this line.'

Jane glanced at the line. 'I'd say it was around two. It rises twice as high as it goes across.'

'Very well.' Now he leaned over the page again and traced a curve. 'What about this? It's a parabola now. What's the slope of this?'

Jane stared at the page. 'Wouldn't it depend on where you applied a tangent?'

'It would. Try here, where the x coordinate is two. This is a graph of the simplest quadratic, where the height is the square of the horizontal.'

Jane took up a hardcover book from the side table and laid it against the curve. She drew two or three tangents with the pencil and frowned. 'Is it a whole number?' she asked hopefully. Sheffield inclined his chin without speaking. 'I'd guess I was four. Is that right?'

'It is. Now try it where x is three.' He leaned over the page again and placed a small, decisive dot on the curve. He watched impassively while Jane drew a couple more tangents before finding one which satisfied her. 'Is it six?' she enquired.

'Yes. Now, what would you say if I asked for the gradient at one?'

Jane thought about it for a moment and put the pencil down. 'Two?' A short, decisive nod. 'Does that mean it's always twice the x coordinate?'

'Yes. Now you have the beginnings of calculus. I can prove it for you, if you wish?'

Sheffield took another sheet of blank paper and wrote a series of equations on it. 'As we make the width of our tangent smaller and smaller, the slope is equal to twice x plus the width of the line. As the width approaches zero, the slope approaches two x. Just be careful when dividing by very small numbers. It would never do to attempt division by zero.'

'So we're sneaking up on the answer?' Jane gave him a dazzling smile.

'We are.'

'I see,' said Jane. 'I will think about this.'

'If you can,' Rupert told her.

'Bedtime, darlings,' said Dot. 'Say goodnight to Mr Sheffield. Doctor. Miss Phryne.' She smiled on all three, and led the younger members of the party away. Jane paused at the door to rake Sheffield with a long, analytical stare before Ruth drew her away by the arm. Dot returned after a few moments and took up an unobtrusive place by the lamp, where her embroidery waited.

'That girl,' said John, 'scares me.'

'Indeed?' asked Sheffield. 'Why?'

'She's very clever, and completely unsympathetic. You saw her when she was massaging my leg. She could have caused me pain. The reason she didn't was not because she likes me, though I think she does. Or that causing pain is wrong. It was because she wanted those tendons and muscles back in the right order.'

'Also because I told her not to hurt you,' put in Phryne.

'Yes, that too, but mostly it was a rage for propriety. The muscles ought not to spasm, the bruise ought not be allowed to form. Therefore, arnica, and therefore, massage. I'm not explaining this well. But I am sure that she's a good girl, Phryne,' said John apologetically. 'And she'll make a very good doctor.'

'She wants to go in for forensic medicine. Professor Glaister's book has inspired her.' Phryne smiled at John. She was aware of Rupert bridling as she patted John on the arm.

'Well, that means she doesn't have to develop a bedside

manner,' said John, grinning. 'Her patients will never complain of lack of sympathy.'

'Fortunately,' responded Phryne. 'Jane had a very isolated and horrible childhood. She will learn love.'

'Is it something you can learn?' asked Sheffield abruptly.

'Of course,' Phryne said, pouring herself another glass of wine. 'We learn love from the people who love us.'

'John.' Rupert summoned him with an imperious wave. 'A word.'

John got up, with difficulty, and limped to where Rupert stood, staring out the window at the windy St Kilda night. There was a fast whispered exchange. John limped back to Phryne and delivered his message in a tone of absolute astonishment.

'I see,' said Phryne to Sheffield. 'You wish to wholly and intimately examine a woman. Surely you could hire one for the usual sum?'

The violet eyes shut briefly in pained distaste. Sheffield conveyed that satisfying his curiosity with a whore would induce instant nausea. Phryne was intrigued and not a little annoyed. That always made her reckless. 'Very well,' she said. Sheffield blinked. She had surprised him. Excellent. 'On two conditions,' she concluded.

'Of course there would be conditions,' drawled Sheffield. That drawl was beginning to really rasp on her nerves.

'Of course,' she replied, smiling sunnily into the beautiful face. 'One—' she held up her hand '—John comes too.'

'Phryne,' John began, deeply suspicious.

Sheffield cut him off with a wave of his long fingers. 'Agreed.'

'You strip as naked as you want me to be.'

This time he blinked and also paused.

'Why would you make a condition like that?' he asked. Phryne knew to the iota exactly how much he hated asking a question to which he did not know the answer.

'Power,' she said. 'The clothed have power over the naked. And while I have always had a soft spot for honest curiosity, I have no intention of allowing you to have power over me. Ever,' she added. 'You examine me, I examine you.'

'Sheffield,' said John, who had seen that sweet smile and heard that buoyant tone in Phryne's voice before, notably when she had shot that German trench raider. In the heart. To protect her wounded. 'I don't think—'

'Yes, I know,' said Sheffield offhandedly. 'And in that event, you shouldn't talk.'

Right, thought Phryne, that settles your fate, my boy. She had seen the slightly wounded but perfectly resigned look on her old friend's face. Ravishing this creature senseless so that he cried for mercy was probably a tad unfair, but it remained an option. The insult had caused John to cease protesting, which was all to the good. Phryne was about to take a risk to which the term Suicidal Insanity would be appropriate, and she didn't want John upsetting the razor-edge balance.

'Are we agreed?' she asked. Sweetly. John bit a fingernail. Rupert Sheffield accepted Phryne's hand and shook it.

'Agreed,' he said.

'Good, bring your magnifying glass and follow me. Dot, dear, no one is to come to my suite after Mr Butler brings a bottle of the good whisky, the usual accompaniments, and a bottle of cognac for me. Would you like a drink, Mr Sheffield?'

'I don't drink,' he said loftily.

'Of course you don't,' she said in a tone reserved by nurse-maids for children who have just dropped their rattle out of their cot for the fifth time. 'A jug of lemonade as well, if you would be so good, Dot.'

John Wilson's sense of unease was growing exponentially. But Phryne was fond of him and a woman of remarkable intelligence and courage. And Sheffield wanted to examine a clean and beautiful woman, which Phryne was, and he had accepted the conditions, and if it took watching Phryne seduce his dearest friend to see that dearest friend naked, then John could pay the price without regret.

Probably.

Phryne's boudoir, by the time they arrived there, had an elaborate drinks tray. John immediately poured himself a slug of the Glen Sporran, which was, he found as he glugged it down, just as good as he remembered it, an excellent single malt.

It did not seem to have an appreciable relaxing effect, so he poured another. Phryne was beginning to undress. She was beautiful, he thought, watching her sit down gracefully on her bed to remove her stockings, then standing to slide off the evening gown, the camisole and the lace-trimmed French knickers. She slipped the bandeau off her head and skimmed it across the room to her dressing table, where the peacock feather waved valiantly.

Then she went to her bathroom and came back with a hand mirror, and a selection of swatches of coloured silk. As Rupert Sheffield shed his clothes she flipped through them, trying to match the hue against his pale skin. As he removed his shirt she found the right colour.

'Ivory,' she said. 'Do you agree that this is a match for your skin tone?'

Sheffield took the mirror and considered the silk and his own bare chest.

'Yes,' he said indifferently. 'What is the value of the comparison?'

'That, I believe, you will perceive later,' said Phryne. She had the unselfconscious nudity of a cat, clad in its own skin. It is aware that its unadorned pelt is more beautiful than any clothing. She sat down cross-legged on her huge bed, stark white against the green silk sheets, and waited for her examiner to remove his undergarments.

And that made two cats, thought John Wilson, gulping down another whisky, a white tiger and a black cat. Sheffield was interested in Phryne, but there was no sign of any sexual arousal. He merely bent the whole of his attention on her, something which could reduce John to incoherence, but which was wasted on Phryne, who could outstare any feline. She smiled amiably and asked him where he would like to start.

'If you could lie down?' he asked, quite politely. Phryne obliged. Because of the width of the bed, Sheffield was obliged to stretch his length alongside her, on the green sheets, and the contrast between the man's porcelain skin and the verdant linen was almost too much for John. He dared not drink any more, and he wanted to look away, but he could not.

Sheffield was slim, with long bones and long muscles, supple and untouched. Not a scar on him, thought John. How could I think that he might want a battered old veteran like me? God, we're the same age. He looks so beautiful, lying alongside the decorative Phryne, only woman I ever desired. Naturally they would desire each other. But why bring me along to watch? Haven't I been tortured enough?

Apparently not. Sheffield started at Phryne's feet, picking up each one, pressing the toenails, flexing them, running a finger along the arch of her foot. He noted a wince and said uninterestedly, 'Oh, yes, the dancing,' and put her foot down.

'Sheffield, you're not going to hurt her,' said John firmly.

'No,' said Phryne, 'really he's not. Because you won't let him. Not dancing. You are pressing too hard. My bones are, as you might have noticed, gracile, being female. Continue, if you please,' she told Sheffield, and he did. He worked his way up to her knees, occasionally laying his cheek almost down on her skin, his dark curls sweeping and tickling. Phryne sighted down over her hip and reflected that of all the most gorgeous men she had ever been naked with, this was probably the most strangely undesirable. He was cold, even his fingers were cool on her body, and his lavender eyes might have belonged to an angel, or a demon, a creature unaware of earthly desires. Therefore, of course, unlikely to arouse her, which was to the purpose for what she had in mind.

Botticelli, she thought idly, would have adored him. He was definitely in the Mannerist tradition.

He reached the patch of dark coarse pubic hair, felt the quality of it between his fingers, then asked her to part her legs. Phryne did so. He did not caress her or react at all, leaving Phryne feeling vaguely insulted. Most people, reaching that goal, were at least conscious of the honour. She caught John's appalled gaze and winked at him.

John poured another glass of Glen Sporran. The dark curls were tickling her inside thighs now, and a cautious finger was parting the labia minora and majora with scientific curiosity. He identified, and unhooded, her clitoris. Phryne suppressed a giggle. Sheffield's head appeared above her belly, noted the giggle, and returned to his scrutiny.

He was kneeling up a little, and Phryne could see the sweet male slopes of his chest, belly and the scribble of hair around his entirely unaroused genitalia. Excellent.

He moved up again, examining her belly, tracing a scar which marked her smooth side.

'Shrapnel,' said Phryne. 'John and I were in the same raid and we all copped it. He saved my life,' she added.

'He saved *my* life,' said Sheffield, sounding affronted. He took a breast in his hand, weighed it meditatively, noted that the other breast was slightly smaller, then worked his way up, from breast to shoulder to neck, and then felt and even sniffed over her face.

'Floris Stephanotis,' she informed him. 'Coconut shampoo . . .'

'Champagne, Virginia tobacco, raspberries,' he told her. 'La Rose de Gueldy soap. Cognac.'

'Very good,' Phryne told him.

'Another scar,' he said. 'Here, under your hair. Not shrapnel.'

'Knife,' said Phryne.

He jolted a little, but did not comment. He ran a finger over her lower lip and tasted her lipstick. He made a face.

'John, a little lemonade for your friend,' Phryne ordered. 'He does not like the taste of lipstick.'

'Different if you taste it on her mouth,' advised John, entirely against his better judgment, which he seemed to have left downstairs. Sheffield made an interested noise, almost like a snort, then pressed his lips to Phryne's—entirely in the furtherance of science—which felt very strange.

Phryne was beginning to find this examination trying. His mouth was soft, his lips inviting, and she might have been kissing a doll. She took firm hold on her instincts and did not drag him into a bone-shattering embrace. John came to the bedside with the lemonade just in time. He had seen her fingers twitch.

'No, no, like this,' he told Sheffield, and leaned down to kiss Phryne. She curled her fingers around his collar and dragged him closer. Now that was a kiss, she thought, releasing him, and intercepting a violet-coloured Very light, full-on glare from the scientist.

Interesting indeed. John, as always, tasted of pipe smoke, his own flavour, and rather too much Glen Sporran. He had better knock it off or this really wasn't going to work.

'Why not light your pipe?' she asked him. 'You must be dying for a smoke.'

He retreated to the chaise longue. Phryne propped herself up on one elbow.

'What my learned colleague meant, Mr Sheffield, is that lipstick by itself is not pleasant. Kissing someone means that you also get their tastes and scent, as you must have got mine.'

'Yes,' said Sheffield. 'You taste of raspberries and cognac and, for some reason, smell like violets and cold water.'

'That is my signature scent,' Phryne told him. 'All humans have a scent and a taste. You taste of cream and a sharp herb: tarragon, perhaps, cut grass or rosemary. Something very green. Refreshing.'

'I was aware of the importance of scent,' said Sheffield, and continued his examination. He murmured over the strength of her hands and the calluses on her fingers, noted a small scar on her wrist, then asked her civilly to turn over. This time he began at her head, ruffling through her hair, rubbing a strand between thumb and forefinger as though he was classing wool. As soon as he had passed over her ears to her shoulderblades, Phryne asked John for a large cognac, with water and ice, and leaned up on her elbows to drink it. The Byronic curls were brushing the small of her back—he appeared to be counting vertebrae—and she shivered. In the mirror she caught the concerned glance which Rupert Sheffield sent towards John, who was now sitting at her side.

'Did I hurt you?' he asked.

'No,' said Phryne. 'Do go on. Fairly soon you will run out of me, and then it is my turn.'

Was it her imagination, or was the young man spending an inordinate amount of time palpating her buttocks and sniffing the inside of her knees?

Privately, Phryne grinned such an evil grin that John decided to stop looking into the mirror and go and light his pipe, as ordered. Phryne sipped her very good brandy until her last little toe pad had been closely scrutinised, then sat up cross-legged again.

'Have you all the information you require?' she asked politely.

'Thank you, that was adequate,' he said in that Irish coffee voice which ought to be used for charming John Wilson out of his undergarments. Adequate, eh? Phryne gestured, and Rupert Sheffield, displaying his first reluctance, laid himself out, flat on his back.

My Lord, he is so beautiful, thought Phryne, as John puffed out a cloud of smoke and tried to conceal a gasp. She began as he had done, picking up a long foot, aware of the bones in perfect order, close-cut toenails—he had been wearing well-fitting boots since childhood—and decided that she would state her deductions out loud. She considered calling John to sit beside her but there was a limit to anyone's endurance and he might be nearing it, what with this vision of loveliness laid out like a sacrifice. Agnus Dei, thought Phryne. Behold the Lamb.

That was such an odd notion that she shelved it for later consideration and began to speak in a dispassionate, vaguely pedantic tone, guaranteed to annoy her subject as much as possible.

'Here we see that the subject has been well fed and tended since infancy,' she intoned. 'There are no signs that he has ever run barefoot, no thickening of the sole, and no bunions or deformities of the toes to suggest ill-fitting footwear. No scars from stones or frostbite as one finds on the feet of the poor. Nails professionally cut.'

'As are yours,' said the subject.

'Indeed,' agreed Phryne. 'Be so good as to be silent, sir, unless you wish to disagree with my observations. I did you that courtesy.'

Rupert Sheffield snorted, but did not reply. John puffed another cloud which almost sounded like a chuckle. Phryne compared the feet, found a thickening in one which showed that a bone had been broken fairly recently, probably by having something heavy dropped on it. She said so. Rupert did not speak. But John said, 'Oh, yes, Phryne, that was on Dartmoor, a boulder. I had to haul him quite half a mile before we found some help.'

'Right. You, as my dear friend, on the other hand, are welcome to comment.' Phryne felt Rupert quiver under her hand. That 'dear friend' comment had got in among this pillar of rectitude. She grinned again. This was proving to be most entertaining, and she was mildly shocked to find that she had such a taste for torment. Ah, well. In a good cause, which made it more delicious.

'Strong calf muscles, he is a good walker and runner, lightly pitted kneecaps—gravel, I think, probably from the playing grounds of Winchester. Long bones, long thigh muscles, quite unscarred.'

Phryne leaned down and sniffed the porcelain skin of his upper thigh. 'Uses honeysuckle soap.' She allowed her falling hair to tickle the skin, and Rupert Sheffield shivered, but not with desire. He was dreading where her examination would next take her, but she switched her attention to his hands, examining them carefully.

'Telegraphs,' she said. 'I knew you were a code-breaker but you also sent telegrams. Look, John, telegrapher's thumb if ever I saw it. Otherwise, clean, well-kept hand, nails cut by the same professional, ink stain on this finger, pen callus on this, a writer's hands. And, of course, you play . . . what? Quite impressive musculature. No marks of overuse, no longer fingernails on the left hand—' she reached over his body to take the other hand '—so it must be piano. Keyboard of some sort.'

'He is a very good pianist,' said John dotingly. Rupert shifted uneasily under Phryne's touch. Her breast was pressing against his side. She seemed blithely unaware of this. John Wilson was not the only person who had never met anyone like Phryne Fisher.

And yet, and yet, she seemed unattracted by him. He was offended. Everyone said that he was beautiful. The fact that he did not indulge in foolish affections and desires meant only that he was superior to weak humans, who kissed and wept. This—all right, yes, facts are facts—beautiful, sweet-scented woman was touching him with hands as dispassionate as a surgeon's, and possibly with the same potential to maim.

It was not that he hadn't tried sex. People were lining up to educate him in his Intelligence days. The closest he had come to a lover was a Greek fisherman called Yanni. Yanni had laughed and kissed him and rumpled his hair and slept with him all one long cold night in a fishing boat off Piraeus. But Yanni had gone with the U-boat that killed him, and they never even found his boat, much less his body. And though he had felt pleasure, it seemed like too much trouble, when he could manage his infrequent uprisings of lust all on his own.

Now he did not know how he felt, and was fighting down the urge to look to John. John wouldn't let anything irreparable happen to him. John was always there. John was his friend. He shut his eyes but Phryne was moving again, this time paying attention to his chest, noting the lack of hair on it, until she leaned down over his belly and breathed on his genitalia. Her hair tickled him. She touched very lightly, said, 'Circumcised,' and moved on. Rupert released his held breath.

Now her gaze moved up to his face. She tilted his head to inspect his jaw, spent some time looking at his ears—'Long lobes, short cavum, quite the right proportion'—and then gazed down into his eyes as she ran a hand through his curls. He tried to look away but she had a firm grip on his hair.

'Most interesting eyes,' she said. 'Really, violet eyes. And in some lights—would you look to the left, please?—yes, see, almost silver. Remarkable.'

'They are,' rumbled John's blessedly familiar voice. 'I have never seen such beautiful eyes.' There, see, Rupert did not say aloud, John thinks my eyes are beautiful. I wish I had never agreed to this. I could have bought any whore's time, and I could have made her take a bath first. But this woman is so . . .

Phryne asked him politely to turn over, so he did, feeling less vulnerable. She had been right. The clothed have power over the unclothed. And those that do not care if they are naked or not have power over those who do. John, on the other hand, was there, fully dressed, and smoking his pipe (Robinson's Navy Cut as usual) and Rupert could smell his signature scent—thank you, the Hon. Miss Fisher, now I have a term for it—which at the moment was overlaid with Scots whisky, probably a single malt. Knowing Miss Fisher, fabulously expensive and only made to order in a small glen in the Highlands to some secret clan recipe. Cooked up in a *poit dhubh*. Which means 'black pot' in Scots Gaelic.

His mind was wandering. He was shocked. His mind never wandered! Rupert Sheffield's mind never lost its focus! What was happening to him? Concentrate. I am lying prone, a naked (!) woman is making observations about my spine, and John is watching. She's right about those scars, too. Curse her. Now John has seen them. I never meant him to see them.

'A flogging,' said Phryne, rather shocked and schooling her voice. 'Serious. Was he in battle?'

'Intelligence,' said John, sounding concerned. 'Never mentioned this. Contemporary with that time, at least. Ten strokes with a cane, I think, rather than a lash.'

John's hand, larger, warmer than the woman's, smoothed the shameful scars as though he wished he could erase them with his touch.

'Torture?' asked Phryne. 'You may speak, Mr Sheffield.'

'Landed on the wrong island,' he said into her pillow. 'Turned out to be Turkish, not Greek. Beat me on general principle, really. Then dumped me into the sea, from which I was rescued. When I got back Compton told me not to be such a bloody fool again or he'd send me back to England on a tramp steamer, tied in a sack. Which had previously held fish heads. He would have, too.'

'The salt made an instant scar,' said John, stroking the marks again. 'Must have hurt like hell.'

'I believe that I screamed, yes,' drawled Rupert. 'But I was lucky. If they'd kept me for another day . . .'

'Rape,' said Phryne with unacceptable bluntness. 'The Turks usually raped prisoners.'

John winced. Rupert merely agreed.

'That was on tomorrow's agenda. But they got bored with me, so I escaped a dreadful fate.'

'You never told me,' said John.

'Why would you want to know?' asked Sheffield, genuinely curious. 'It wasn't too bad,' he added, trying for some reason to comfort John, who sounded upset. 'Not after school. My fifth form Latin master could strike a good deal more shrewdly than that.' He expected to hear John laugh, but he did not.

Phryne's inspection moved downwards, stating that his buttocks were solidly muscular, confirming her views on his ability to walk and run. She worked her way down to his feet again and bade him sit up and drink his lemonade, as he must be thirsty. He did so and she sat facing him on the big bed, her female parts shamelessly displayed, looking at him very carefully. He had previously noted her very bright, very shrewd, very green eyes.

'Another experiment?' she asked. 'Since we are here?'

Rupert Sheffield had trained as a spy. He was constitutionally suspicious. But he knew that there was no one in the world more intelligent than he was. Phryne simply could not out-think him. It was impossible.

'Does it involve you touching me?' he drawled. Poor woman must desire him after all.

'No,' she said, surprising him again.

'Or me touching you?'

'No,' she said, with a hint of a smile.

'Very well,' he said. 'It may provide more data.'

'So it may,' she said softly. 'John?'

'My dear?'

Rupert disliked the way his John called her 'my dear' so effortlessly. John was not her dear. John was his. But John wasn't his in the same way as he belonged to her . . .

'You are overdressed,' said Phryne. 'Take off your coat and your shirt, please.'

'Phryne, do you know what you are doing?' he asked, even as his hands moved to his buttons.

'I do,' she said.

'If this does not work, you will break my heart, you know,' he said quietly, hanging his coat over the chair, removing his tie and taking out his cufflinks.

Phryne looked back at him with a steady gaze. 'I know. Trust me.'

'I do,' sighed John, and stripped off his shirt, turning to display his bare, muscular chest.

In a flash, Phryne had whipped the hand mirror out from under the pillow and shoved it in Rupert Sheffield's face.

'Look at your eyes,' she ordered. He looked.

'Four signs of sexual attraction,' she said relentlessly. 'Havelock Ellis's discovery. Dilated pupils. Are your eyes dilated?'

'Yes,' he said.

'Shortness of breath. Is your breath short?'

'Yes,' he gasped.

'Increased heartbeat.' Her cool fingers pressed on his pulse. 'Right. And finally—' she held up the silk sample against his chest and reflected them in the mirror '—arousal flush. You are now, at a guess, musk rose.'

'Yes,' whispered Rupert. He did not move. Phryne took the lemonade glass out of his hand. Rupert still did not move. Phryne sighed and walked to John, who knelt at the end of her bed, naked to the waist. She put a hand on his chest and bent to kiss him.

She was shoved out of the way by a flying Renaissance angel, who grabbed John Wilson, dragged him into his arms and kissed him fiercely, mashing their mouths together, until John's hand came up to run through the black curls and they slid down into a full body embrace. Interesting. Sheffield appeared to be trying to burrow inside John and nest inside his bones, like a worm in an apple. Phryne had never seen such a ferocious first kiss. Perhaps among tigers, say. The larger predators. Something with a lot of teeth.

Rupert's fingers were digging into John's shoulders, his long thighs were wrapped around John's waist, and he freed his mouth long enough to say, 'You are mine—mine! And I never thought I'd have a lover but I choose you. John? Now. Forever. John? Say yes, John.'

John was too stunned and overcome to speak. He breathed in the scent of Sheffield's hair and skin and almost wept with relief. His warm hand splayed out across the scars, obliterating them and their importance. He did not realise that he hadn't answered a question until a soft desperate whisper next to his collarbone said, 'Please?'

Phryne found her clothes and gown and collected the drinks tray and waited until she heard John Wilson say gently, 'Yes, my dear, yes, my love, yes, yes, yes.'

Then she withdrew into her boudoir, settled down on her couch, and poured herself a large drink. She felt that she deserved it. That had been, as the Duke of Wellington had remarked about a minor military engagement by comparison, a damn close-run thing. If she had not practically flung them into each other's arms, they would have spent the rest of their lives as they had been, Sheffield not noticing John's devotion but shamelessly relying on it, and John going down unkissed into his lonely grave.

A situation which could not be allowed to continue, but she had taken an enormous risk. Even now she was listening for a cry of horror or disgust from next door when Sheffield realised how entirely he had lost control.

If he came storming out, Phryne swore, she would trip him, tie him, sit on his chest and deliver him a scathing lecture on ingratitude, and proceed with the 'ravishing him senseless' which had been on her original agenda. And he would deserve it.

She took another sip. Really, she was shocked at herself. But she wasn't going to get dressed and see what was left of supper, though she was suddenly ravenous. These tentative lovers needed a guard, and in lieu of Cerberus, they had Phryne.

Which didn't mean she couldn't call Mr Butler for a tray of tidbits, so she did that. Razor-edge diplomacy made you hungry. No wonder all those ambassadors were so rotund.

•

John kissed Sheffield again, because he could, and felt the long-imagined soft lips yield beneath his own, the untaught mouth open, the tip of his tongue just tasting, withdrawing, returning. He was flooded with gratitude and lust in roughly equal proportions. He probably shouldn't do this, but he was bloody well going to, because Sheffield had leapt on him and kissed his mouth, Sheffield wanted him. And John hadn't said a word or made a move. Sheffield, astoundingly, marvellously, had seduced John. He might never get over this.

He wasn't sure that he wanted to get over it.

Amazement could go no further. If Phryne had ridden in on a unicorn he would merely have remarked on its elegant hocks and golden horn and suggested that she enter it weight for age at Flemington. Well, no, not a unicorn. Not Phryne. A dragon, perhaps. He was sure that she could tame a dragon. Look what she had done to Sheffield. His beautiful man, lying in his arms, squirming to get closer, closer. They were lying chest to chest, and he could feel the soft, smooth skin which he had often imagined kissing. Wonderful. If only this, utterly wonderful. But it appeared it was not going to be only this.

Rupert pulled at his belt.

'Too many clothes,' he complained.

'Quite right,' John agreed. He unlatched as much of Rupert as he could to allow him to remove his shoes and socks and garments, then allowed himself to be pulled back into the octopus embrace. Naked skin slid against his own nakedness. John wondered if he was actually going to swoon like a Victorian maiden. Excess of sensation was bringing him terribly fast towards a climax he did not yet want to have, in case, God forbid, this should be the only time Rupert Sheffield lay in his arms. He would have to talk to him. He would have to talk about whether Sheffield really wanted to do this.

Presently. After he kissed down that entrancing neck to the hollow of his throat, where a fast pulse beat. Later. After he sucked lightly at an earlobe and felt Rupert shudder. Any moment now. After Rupert had slid his hands down their joined bodies to his lower back and slammed them together. After which it was a confusion of kisses, caresses, and touches of such excruciating sweetness that he entirely forgot everything; except Rupert's mouth, his silky skin, the blaze of his lambent violet eyes.

When he recovered a little, he was lying in a tangle of limbs on green silk sheets with the most beautiful man in the world wrapped around him, as though John was a teddy bear. Rupert had fallen asleep. His sweet breath stirred across John's shoulder, cooling and drying his sweaty skin. Relaxed, he was a solid weight, not the ever-moving dragonfly he was when awake. John adjusted the position of his injured leg and

Rupert murmured a protest in his sleep and dragged him back again, pinning him down with those long legs.

He resigned himself. Sheffield was quite determined that John wasn't going to go anywhere, and that was that.

John Wilson smiled. He firmly rearranged Sheffield so that he was not lying on the scarred leg, and gathered him close. Rupert gave a small broken sigh and settled down again. It was so unbearably touching that John felt tears track, silently, down his face, and drip into the curly black hair.

He had the impression that the door had opened gently. Then it closed again, just as gently. Then he fell asleep, or possibly swooned. Like a Victorian maiden.

When John Wilson woke, he was so blissfully comfortable—more comfortable than he had ever been in his life—that he was disinclined to move. He allowed his eyes to rove. Nice room, lady's bedroom; of course, Phryne. Warm body next to him, for some reason lying heavily on his belly. Not Phryne. Black curls. A finger tracing the starburst of scar on his thigh, and moving up to touch the curved shrapnel fragments in his side.

'I want to know all of you,' said the Irish coffee voice of Rupert Sheffield. 'Every bit of you. John.' He said the name as though it was an endearment.

'Sheffield,' replied John. 'How do you feel?'

'Are you asking after my health, my state of mind, or whether I regret leaping upon you and claiming you as my lover?' he said clearly, still tracing shrapnel scars.

'All of those,' replied John. Sheffield was not going to stop being Sheffield just because he had dived headfirst into the lusts of the flesh. 'I want to know if you are going to push me away, scream that you have been violated, denounce me as a seducer, or say that this was some obscure experiment and we must never speak of it again.'

Rupert's face appeared above John's hip, eyes wide, mouth open.

'I hadn't even *thought* of some of those,' he said admiringly. 'But to answer the question, I am healthy, I feel wonderful, and I will never regret, never, taking you as my lover. Forever. You said forever,' he whispered in John's ear, throwing himself into the doctor's arms. 'You said yes.'

'I did,' John reassured him. 'You are everything that I want.'

'And I suppose I have to share you,' Rupert said, thinking about it. 'I don't want to share you.'

'Why would you have to share me?' asked John, puzzled.

'With her,' said Rupert. 'This is her bed.'

'But she won't expect me to lie in it again. With her, I mean. She's an old friend. She was comforting me . . .' John began to chuckle. Rupert felt his laughter through his cheek, which was pressed to John's chest. It tickled. He had not known that laughter tickled before.

'Why are you laughing? It feels strange,' complained Rupert.

'She was comforting me because of my hopeless unrequited and unrequitable love for a heedless asexual curly-haired genius with a talent for getting himself into trouble,' John said.

'Oh,' said Rupert.

'Yes,' said John encouragingly.

'That would be me,' he concluded.

'Indeed. You need a guardian. People keep trying to kill you. For some reason.'

'I know who it is,' said Rupert, silencing John's exclamation with another kiss. This lasted for some time.

When John reclaimed his mouth and his breath, he said, 'Who?'

'Oh, I broke up a rather promising arms-smuggling ring when I was in Greece with Compton. He told me there would be trouble about it. But I never expected it to follow me here.'

'Sheffield . . .' John's patience was wearing thin. Rupert slid a hand down his thigh, which distracted him. Really, this lovemaking was wonderful. Endless possibilities. There was so much of John which he did not know. If he had laid John out naked and examined him inch by inch he would have been lying in his arms a good deal earlier. A shameful failure in scientific method.

'We'll have to send a telegram tomorrow and ask what happened to the principals. I know that two were shot by the Albanians and one by the Turks and the rest should still be in jail in Greece. But there was an Englishman we never caught. Mitchell. He must have seen me here and thought I was coming for him—that the Science of Deduction was just a cover story. It's very funny,' said Rupert, and laughed in his turn.

'Sheffield, he's been trying to kill you!' protested John, sitting up. Rupert examined his face and put out one finger to soothe away the crease between his brows. His very own John whom he did not have to share with anyone.

'Yes, but he won't succeed, not while I have you with me. Isn't it time that you kissed me again?' asked Rupert, and John found that it was.

The kiss turned into lots of kisses, languorous, sleepy kisses, until Sheffield announced, 'I'm hungry.'

'So am I. I wonder what the time is? I had a watch somewhere.'

There was a knock at the door. Rupert dived beneath the green sheets. He had no intention of being seen naked by Miss Fisher ever again. John got up.

'Phryne,' Rupert heard him say, with that detestable note of familiarity. 'We ought to give you back your room.'

Rupert didn't hear the reply but he heard the laugh and a kiss. Then the door closed again.

'She kissed you!' he protested.

'Be charming,' John advised. 'Not only do we not have to move, she's sending up supper. A lady does not give up her bedchamber lightly. Mind your manners, my dear.'

Rupert glowed. That 'my dear' was the same easy affectionate 'my dear' he used to Miss Fisher. He resolved to be exceedingly charming. Especially since he was hungry, needed a wash, and never wanted to let John Wilson out of immediate grabbing distance ever again. He seemed to be magnetically attracted to his body. Some sort of electricity? He experimented with moving away, rolling over to the cool side of the bed, and was struck with a very unpleasant isolated sensation, so he rolled back and embraced John again. That was right. Close. John chuckled and kissed his neck.

Presently Miss Fisher came in with the supper trolley. She was presented with a memorable sight.

Rupert Sheffield, smiling like a minor deity, was wrapped around her old friend John as though he never meant to let him go. The contrast of John's stocky muscularity with the porcelain skin and the violet eyes was striking. They would make a very good painting, quite in the art deco style, of a soldier and his guardian angel. Rupert would look lovely with rainbow-coloured wings. Though guardian angels probably didn't have that glutted, sated, utterly debauched, smug smile. At least, not since Botticelli got so involved with Savonarola. She had never seen John Wilson look so dazedly content.

'Supper,' she said. 'Do eat, darlings. You need to keep up your strength. The bathroom and WC are through that door. Breakfast downstairs at eight, when I need to reclaim my room.'

Rupert let go of John and leaned out of his embrace to take Phryne's hand and kiss it. Phryne smiled at him. He was softened by love, violet eyes glowing, lips swollen with kisses. He looked like Canova's Eros.

'Thank you,' he said. 'For giving me my John.'

How much did that overactive mind actually deduce about what Phryne had done? Who was the player, and who had been played? Impossible to tell. Phryne leaned down and kissed his cheek, told him it was her pleasure, and went out.

Mrs Beeton always advised that any hostess who wanted to run a comfortable house should spend a night in her own guestroom. Phryne always kept an overnight bag in a spare room, in case of eventualities. And the narrow little bed was very comfortable, considering. Ember, shut out of her boudoir, joined her for the remainder of the night, sleeping decoratively on her pillow. As males in her bed went, he was undemanding and very, very pretty.

CHAPTER FOURTEEN

Poison grows in this dark.
It is in the water of tears
Its black blooms rise.

Wallace Stevens
'Another Weeping Woman'

Breakfast, Phryne considered, might easily be sticky. She had ordered the lovers to come down by eight, and by eight they were indeed ensconced at the breakfast table. They were freshly rinsed and looked chipper. John was tucking into a variety of things and Sheffield was eating scrambled eggs with slow relish.

'There is a *cuisine de famille*,' he told Ruth. 'And this is part of it. These are really quite adequate eggs.'

Ruth was about to bristle when Jane put a hand on her shoulder. From Rupert, that was a compliment. The two of them were warm and easy together. Phryne was pleased. She did not feel up to delivering blistering lectures this early in the morning.

'Have some of this honey for your toast,' she advised John. 'Apple blossom, it's really delightful.'

'Excellent,' agreed John. Phryne was looking at the side of his neck. Where her own delicate love bite had been was another, covering and obliterating it. Someone with a bigger mouth and a lot more suck had bruised John Wilson afresh over that token which Phryne had put there. The extra bruising meant, quite unequivocally, Mine.

They ate, drank tea, and farewelled their hostess. John kissed her on the mouth for the last time. It was a sweet kiss. She leaned a little into his stocky body, his warmth. Then she released him into other custody. Rupert, to her astonishment, also gathered her into his arms. He was slim and muscular and his body was almost vibrating under her hands.

'*Je vous en prie*, Madame,' he whispered into her hair, '*embrasse-moi?*'

'*Avec plaisir*,' Phryne told him. She kissed him. He tasted of green herbs and sex.

They smiled at her and left, John leaning on Rupert's arm. That limp was going to be a great advantage when they wanted to touch in public.

Fortunately today was laundry day, and Phryne went up to gather her sheets before they shocked Dot. Who would, indeed, have been horrified by their state. Phryne smiled. Goodbye, then, to Dr Wilson. It had been so nice while it had lasted.

But there were other options available. Though before she could choose one, she needed to solve the murder of the conductor. Which was proving difficult.

Oh, and bring down the loathsome Ratcliffe, of course.

For that she needed another cafe au lait. And perhaps a nibble of that scrambled egg dish of which Rupert Sheffield had condescended to approve. She tasted.

For *cuisine de famille*, it really was something special.

In an attempt to protect the choir from their conductor, Matthew had called an informal rehearsal, quite voluntary, no need to tell Henry James about it at all, for which Phryne had offered to pay. She had received a phone call that informed her that the Guido Calvi in question was indeed her Luigi Calvi's uncle. He had not emigrated to Australia with his brother in 1919, and no trace of him could be found. Phryne thought it would be easier just to ask Luigi.

The assembly hall was noisier during the day, but the choir had relaxed. Matthew was conducting from an ordinary choral score. The prof had not woken from his daily port-induced swoon, so the notes were being picked out by Daniel the giraffe boy, with Josephine to turn pages for him. Phryne had hopes that he might notice her, now that she was standing so very close to him that if he turned his head he would be nose-to-breast. He was an adequate pianist for note-bashing and the choir was getting the gist of the chorus '*Baal, We Cry to Thee!*'.

'*Heed the sacrifice,*' they sang. '*Heed the sacrifice we offer!*'

Just as Baal's attention should have been well and truly caught, the altos got lost and the sopranos, using the wrong note for their cue, went flat.

'Try again,' urged Matthew. 'This is sounding really quite good now.'

Baal was supplicated again, this time with more accuracy. Had there been a Baal, Phryne thought, he would have at least heard them. Whether he replied was always problematical, with gods. Elijah was defying them, saying there are a lot of you, calling on your god, there is only one of me, but I'm calling on the real God. The one with a capital letter.

'*Let thy flames fall and extirpate the foe!*' the people implored.

Now that had never worked. Any extirpating was going to have to be done by the people themselves. They had got themselves into this.

'*Hear us!*' cried the choir. '*Hear us!*'

From the door, Elijah replied, '*Call him louder! For he is a god. He talketh, or he is pursuing, or he is on a journey, or peradventure, he sleepeth. So awaken him, call him louder!*'

'Go on!' said Matthew, and the chorus ventured on the quartet, gathering confidence from Aunty Mark's presence.

'*Hear our cry, O Baal!*' rumbled the basses. '*Hear our cry, O Baal!*' sang the tenors, '*Hear our cry, O Baal!*' added the altos. '*Hear our cry, O Baal!*' the sopranos came in, with heavy emphasis on their G entry. '*Baal, now arise! Wherefore slumber?*'

'*Call him louder,*' sang Elijah scornfully. '*He heareth not! With knives and hatchets cut thyselves after your manner; leap upon the altar ye have made: call him and prophesy. Not a voice will answer you. None will listen. None heed you!*'

'*Baal!*' the bass voices burst out. '*Baal!*'

The chorus surged on. They knew this one, and it was coming together seamlessly now that the recit had been added in. They were singing for Aunty, who was now leaning on the conductor's podium, concentrating. Phryne thought him very handsome. But she always found intellectual processes intriguing. This was an expert singer listening to the chorus like a mechanic listening to an engine, trying to locate the (metaphorical) knocking noise which interrupted the smooth operation of the motor. And he himself was part of that operation. Who is the singer, and who the song?

Singing in a choir feels good, Phryne thought. The voices, the deep breathing, the exhilaration of listening to the parts fitting together, like a musical puzzle, like the music of the spheres (which would have to be four-part harmony). '*Mark how the scorner derideth us!*' sang the people, seconds before they had to change sides and become Israelites.

'*Draw near all ye people,*' sang Mark. '*Come to me!*'

As Elijah sang his prayer, Phryne examined all the faces she could see. None were angry. Even Leonard was listening to Aunty with admiration. Aunty Mark was a universal favourite. Then why did Phryne feel uneasy? Everyone loved Mr Henty, the celebrated baritone. She shook herself and paid attention to her score.

'*Lord God of Abraham,*' sang Mark, '*Isaac and Israel, O hear me, O hear me and answer me—*' He coughed. He stopped. He waved at Matthew. 'Sorry. You go on: "Cast Thy Burden".'

The one chorus in this oratorio which everyone liked and everyone knew was "Cast Thy Burden" and the choir segued into it easily. '*Cast thy burden upon the Lord, and he shall sustain thee,*' they sang, almost note-perfect. Phryne thought of all her soldiers, and hoped that they too were sustained: all the lost and injured and shell-shocked and mad. After all, if you have to cast a burden on someone, why not the Lord? Wasn't that what he was for?

'*He never will suffer for the righteous to fall: he is at thy right hand.*'

She hoped this was true. Things were about to become rather perilous, what with a sadistic warlord attempting to kill people of whom she was fond. And me, of course, she added to herself. This really was beautiful music.

'*Let none be made ashamed that wait upon thee!*' declaimed the choir.

Matthew let his hands fall and the choir relaxed, grinned, laughed with relief.

'That was really good!' said Tommy, sounding amazed. 'Of

course, we aren't supposed to be singing it, it's a quartet, but that sounded really good! Maybe he'll let us sing it.'

'We've got it,' said Calliope.

'Tea break,' announced Matthew. 'That was good, friends. If we can manage the rest of the work as well as that, we will have done a very good thing.'

'Tea,' said Mark. 'I never drink the stuff. Ruins the voice. A good working champagne is what a singer needs. I didn't know you were rehearsing—why didn't you tell me?' He sounded a little hurt.

Matthew hastened to explain. 'We were just note-bashing. James is so—'

'Much of a bastard,' put in Tommy.

'That we thought we'd better be prepared for him.'

'I'd use an axe, myself,' commented Mark. 'Or you could think about stoning him to death. That ought to add an edge to the work. "*Take all the prophets of Baal . . .*"' he sang and the choir joined in with fervour.

'*Let none of them escape you!*'

'See?' He grinned. He did not accept tea but drank hot water.

Phryne noticed that Daniel had taken Josephine's hand and kissed it. Nice. Really, she could choir-watch for hours. They were so volatile.

Someone pressed against her from behind. Ah, her constant ithyphallic admirer.

'*Ciao*, Luigi,' she said, without turning her head.

'*Ciao, bella!*' he replied into her neck.

'*Dove é Zio Guido?*' she asked.

'*Zio Guido é morte,*' he replied. He was surprised, but he did not remove his hot hand from her hip. Phryne wriggled a little to dislodge it. She turned and looked into his face and saw nothing but relatively uncomplicated lust in those liquid brown eyes.

He was just about to ask how she knew Zio Guido when they were back onstage and Mark led into the next chorus.

'O Thou, who makest thine angels spirits, thou whose ministers are flaming fires, let them now descend!'

The choir answered with such force that Phryne expected to see the score burst into flames. Another fugue: alto and soprano together, bass and tenor. They were the faithful people witnessing a miracle which would save their prophet's head. They put the *fuoco* into *allegro con fuoco*.

'The fire descends from heaven!'

Phryne wouldn't have been more than half surprised if it had. And wouldn't the Scots Church be annoyed. What would their insurance company say? Act of God?

Phryne went home for a little rest, some honey and lemon, to which she added a judicious quantity of whisky, and a round-up of the day's news. Nothing out of the way had happened, which was pleasant. She felt at a loss. Her lover had moved on, Lin Chung wasn't back from Hong Kong for another fortnight, and she felt vaguely restless. Her body had become accustomed to a pleasant and engrossing lover every night. Now her bed was empty. She almost wished that Ratcliffe would make his move.

'Drat it all,' said Phryne, and took Molly out for a walk. She was passing peaceably along the footpath, trailing her sunshade, the picture of innocence. A picture that positively cried out 'Shoot me now!'

She was quite pleased when she heard the 'potato-potato' of the Harley. As the assassin approached, slowing markedly— she surmised that he had a pistol and thus needed to get quite close—she stepped aside, thrust the steel-shafted umbrella into the spokes and gave him a strong push. The bike shuddered and the engine screamed. The rider fell hard. Phryne pounced. She dragged him off the road and dropped onto his chest with both knees. Molly stood next to his head, snarling.

She ripped off the flying helmet and goggles and stared down into a pair of terrified eyes. Male, spotty, young.

'Are you going to tell me why you were trying to kill me, or am I going to let Molly tear out your throat?' she asked affably.

Obligingly, Molly snarled again. She really did have excellent teeth. Primal terror transfixed the assassin. Mammalian ancestors shrieked at him to run, climb, hide from the dire wolf. He did not even think of grabbing for the pistol on the lanyard round his neck.

'You . . . you can't . . .'

'Oh, but I can,' Phryne assured him warmly.

'You wouldn't . . .'

'Ah, but I would,' she said.

'No!' he wailed.

Phryne thought that she had better conclude this before he collapsed from terror.

'I'm going to let you up,' she said, climbing off his body and souveniring the pistol, which she levelled at his head. 'You're going to pick up your bike and go away. And you're going to tell Mr Ratcliffe, from me, that if he comes near any of my household—or me—again, I will destroy him. Repeat the message.'

After a few false starts, the assassin managed to repeat it, word for word.

'Off you go,' said Phryne. 'Oh, and tell him he owes me three pounds. That was a very good sunshade.'

He pulled his bike back onto its misshapen wheels, removed

the mangled sunshade, and limped away, pushing the machine. Molly barked him out of sight.

'That was instructive,' Phryne told her. 'Good dog!'

She felt much better.

•

Rehearsal that night was worse than the night before. Phryne was impressed. She hadn't thought he could get any worse. But there was Henry James the conductor, shoving back his black hair, licking his forefinger, snarling at the choir. Even the chorus that they had got right during the day lost focus and died under his ferocious baton.

'You're useless, every one of you!' he yelled finally. Phryne thought he looked rather green—surely they hadn't been that bad? And again he finished the rehearsal early. He rushed out into the street, leaving the choir to finish their tea in disconsolate silence.

'Perhaps we should just abandon the concert,' suggested Julia, clasping her hands. 'And it was my chance at singing in the quartet!'

'No, dammit, we're not going to allow that bastard to upset us like this,' stated Matthew. 'Come on, let's sing something to cheer ourselves up, and then we can go on to Aunty Mark's. "Come again!"' he sang.

The others looked at each other, but the gravitational pull of the song was too strong.

'Come again! Sweet love doth now invite! Thy graces that refrain, to do thee due delight . . .'

Phryne loved this one. The voices chiming in exactly on time and in key made her shiver with a sensual pleasure which also belonged to scented hot bath water, a lover's mouth, or green chartreuse.

'*To see,*' sang the sopranos.

'*To feel,*' sang the altos.

'*To touch,*' sang the tenors.

'*To kiss,*' thundered the basses.

'*To die!*' they sang, a musical orgasm. '*With thee again, in sweetest sympathy.*'

'*Come again! That I may cease to mourn, at thy unkind disdain, for now lost and forlorn . . .*'

'*I sit,*' sang Julia.

'*I sigh,*' sang Calliope.

'*I weep,*' sang Josephine, looking at Daniel.

'*I faint,*' sang Luigi, staring at Phryne.

'*I die, in deadly pain, and endless misery,*' sang LobeliaandDavid, to each other.

'*Gentle love! Draw forth thy wounding dart. Thou canst not pierce her heart. For I that do approve . . .*'

'*By sighs,*' sang Tommy to Caterina.

'*And tears,*' sang Millicent to Luke.

'*More hot,*' sang Geneva to Luigi, who was distracted from Phryne for a moment.

'*Than are,*' sang Oliver to Chloe.

'*Thy shafts,*' sang Jenny to Bones.

'*Do tempt, while she, while she for triumphs, laughs.*'

On cue, Caterina laughed.

There was a moment's silence, and then they all joined in. God bless Dowland, thought Phryne. She hoped he was very happy, swapping tunes with Mozart in heaven.

She was following the choir out of the hall, en route to one of Aunty Mark's little soirees, when she found the score on a bench. That score. It had the requisite pages torn out. It was not marked with a name. The cover would never take fingerprints and, in any case, any member of the choir would have a right to handle it. Another dead end. Drat again.

She put it back where she found it.

Just ahead of her, Leonard was arguing with Professor Szabo. 'He's the conductor, he rules the choir,' he said. 'Unhappily.'

'He is a butcher,' said the old man. 'He has no respect for the music. Neither does your Elijah.'

'No, really, Prof, he's singing it beautifully,' protested Calliope. 'You didn't hear him sing the recit in "Baal, We Cry to Thee" today. Scornful. Perfect.'

'He interrupted the music to sing the Pirate King,' said the old man stubbornly. 'No respect.'

'Have it your way,' said Calliope. 'Are you coming with us to the party?'

'No,' said the old man. 'I go home.' And he went.

'Not like him to turn down free booze,' commented Tommy.

'Never mind,' said Calliope comfortably. 'He's upset. Come along,' she said, and the choristers went down the steps.

Phryne was in two minds. Party? Singing? Go home and spend a blameless evening and a chaste and pure night?

Only one mind, really. She set off after them.

•

Aunty Mark had the best parties. She was briefly drawn into a consultation with Gawain.

'I worry about him,' said Gawain. His plain face was concerned.

'Why?' asked Phryne. Aunty Mark was singing, glass in hand, the picture of Dionysian splendour.

'He's so bold.' Gawain shivered. 'He takes risks.'

'Only in trusted company,' said Phryne. 'But, look, here's my card. If he gets into any trouble, ring. I'll come right away.'

'Oh thanks,' said Gawain with real gratitude. 'Thanks. That's very kind of you.'

'Pleasure,' said Phryne, and went to get another glass of wine.

Now that Luigi was staying away from her he was unwearying in his pursuit of Geneva—such a relief—she had time to sip excellent champagne and appreciate caviar and sing rude songs. Not that they were all rude. Some, of course, detailed the adventures of the young apprentice in the chandler's shop, the regrettable hirsuteness of the Mayor of Bayswater's charming little daughter or spoke of remarkable engineering achievements involving reciprocating wheels, but others were just songs, sung with the heartiness of people who knew how to sing and had abolished any shyness with alcohol and good company in about equal quantities.

'*Fine knacks for ladies! Cheap, choice, brave and new! Good penny worths, but money cannot move,*' sang Aunty Mark, a creditable falsetto.

'*I keep a fair but for the fair to view,*' replied the choir. '*A beggar may be liberal of love.*'

Then, all together, they sang, '*Though all my wares be trash, the heart is true, the heart is true, the heart is true.*'

'*Great gifts are guiles, and look for gifts again,*' sang Luigi to Geneva. '*My trifles come, as treasures from my mind.*'

The song went on. Aunty Mark had a fair soprano and was enjoying the song immensely. When they reached the last verse, Phryne found herself standing near Matthew. His face was slightly flushed, his lips soft and red, his eyes trout pools where sensual fishes lurked.

'*But in this heart, where Beauty serves and loves,*' sang Matthew to Phryne.

'*Turtles and twins, courts brood a heavenly pair,*' sang Phryne to Matthew.

Dowland was doing a lot of the talking in this gathering.

'*Happy the man who thinks of no remove, of no remove, of no remove.*'

He really couldn't be a murderer, Phryne was telling herself, shifting closer. Just as she had decided to kiss now and think about it later, the door banged open and Leonard ran into the room. He was manic, dishevelled, and panting.

'Henry James is dead!' he cried. 'Now I get to be conductor!'

•

After that there was not a lot of point to continuing the song. They gathered around Leonard, glasses in hand, firing questions at him.

'Dead? Are you sure?' asked Calliope.

'Yes,' said Leonard. 'I went to his hotel room to . . . to have a discussion about what he was doing to poor Mendelssohn, and the door was open and he was there on the floor.'

'Dead?' asked Chloe.

'Really dead?' squeaked Julia. Phryne noted that Tommy had stationed himself behind her in case she fainted. He was the Harmony Choir designated Julia-catcher. She was far too interested to faint.

'Henry James dead?' demanded Mark, in his booming Elijah voice.

'Yes. I saw him,' babbled Leonard. 'Now I have to be conductor.'

They all looked at him.

'I have to be,' he insisted, his voice taking on an hysterical edge. 'It's my turn!'

'Be that as it may,' said Phryne, pushing to the front of the group, 'what have you done?'

'Me?' asked Leonard, quailing a little.

'Yes. About this death. Have you called the police? An ambulance? Told the management?'

'No, I came straight here to tell you that I have to be—'

'Right,' said Phryne. She exchanged exasperated glances with Matthew and Aunty Mark. 'Mark, you keep him here. Give him another drink. Bones, Tabitha, come with me. What is his room number?'

Leonard told her. Someone thrust him down into a chair and shoved a drink into his hands. They were trembling.

'I understand why you're taking him, he's a medical student, but why me?' asked Tabitha, nevertheless putting down her drink and her young man and joining Phryne at the door.

'You're a vet,' said Phryne. 'You're not squeamish. And I want a couple of irreproachable witnesses if matters are . . . as I think they might be.'

'What do you think?'

'I don't know, I haven't thought it yet,' said Phryne. 'Come along. He might only be terribly ill, and that idiot left him on the floor.'

But when they reached the conductor's room, it was clear that Leonard might be an idiot in many ways, but he knew dead when he saw it. Dead, horribly. The floor bore witness to the violence of his vomiting. The room stank. Tabitha and Bones watched from the door as Phryne tiptoed in and touched the dead throat.

'Newly dead,' she said. 'He's still warm. But definitely deceased. Let's shut this door, and we'll tell the management and get them to ring the police.'

'Why do we need the police?' asked the medical student. 'That death could have had many causes.'

'And the most obvious one?' asked Phryne, raising her eyebrows.

'Poisoning,' said Tabitha. 'Do keep up, Bones! A strong poison, at that. Not strychnine. Perhaps digitalin? Most poisons produce vomiting and purging; the system tries to rid itself of the agent. That's why they're so bad in horses, who can't vomit.'

'Right,' said Bones faintly.

'You go back to the party and sit down,' said Tabitha kindly. 'We can do the rest.'

Tabitha was so sensible and bracing and she was excellent company when one had to go and advise the management of a very prestigious hotel that one of their guests was (probably) the victim of either a homicide or a suicide.

They took it as well as could be expected.

Tabitha and Phryne went back to the party, which had toned down a lot. Aunty Mark consulted Phryne with a look as she returned and shut the door. She nodded. He immediately announced, 'Now is the time for a good solid lament. "Weep, O Mine Eyes".'

Matthew took up a spoon and began to conduct.

'*Weep, o mine eyes, weep, o mine eyes, and cease not,*' they sang.

That John Bennet must have been really cheerful company, thought Phryne, mind racing. Who had killed Henry James? The trouble was there were so many possibilities. If possible, he was even more hated than Hedley Tregennis. Even Phryne had forced her homicidal feelings down, though she would never have resorted to poison. She just wanted to shoot him where he stood, abusing the répétiteur. That would have been nice.

No one stood out, except the loon presently getting stuck

into his second glass of gin and grinning. Would Leonard kill Henry James for the chance to conduct? It did appear likely.

The song moved into Mozart's *Ave verum corpus*, one of the most agonisingly beautiful laments he ever wrote.

'*Ave verum corpus*,' sang Tabitha at her ear, '*natum de Maria Virgine . . .*'

Phryne kept thinking, singing without concentration, until the music swelled into the '*in cruce pro homine*'. Then she stopped thinking at all.

●

It was to a grave and solemn *Requiem aeternam* that Detective Inspector Robinson arrived at the crime scene, though he was by no means sure that it was even a crime. But the initial search of the room had found no poison, and no box, bottle, paper or glass which could have held poison. And when he saw Phryne Fisher emerging from the musical room his heart sank.

'So it is a murder, then,' he said to her.

'Yes, I expect so,' she replied. 'I suggest you have a very serious word with Leonard Match. He really, really wants to be conductor.'

'Seems like a minor motive for two murders,' demurred the detective inspector.

'It's not,' said Phryne. 'And we've known murders done over tuppence and a funny look.'

'So we have,' he said heavily. 'Right. Let them keep singing, and I'll interview them one by one. Don't want your Leonard to bolt.'

'Any idea how long he's been dead?'

'Only hours,' said Jack Robinson.

'Because he was looking a bit green at rehearsal and he finished it early,' said Phryne.

'So he might have eaten or drunk it at your rehearsal?' asked Robinson. Singers. He hated talking to singers.

'We didn't see him eat or drink anything, and he rushed off before tea. So if it was there, he must have brought it with him.'

'Well, well, maybe he's a suicide—but we haven't found a note.'

'He would have left one,' Phryne was certain. 'Something like "what an artist is lost in me".'

'Nero,' returned Jack. 'Last words.'

'You never cease to surprise me, Jack,' Phryne told him.

CHAPTER FIFTEEN

Like a rose rabbi, later, I pursued,
And still pursue, the origin and course
Of love, but until now I never knew
That fluttering things have so distinct a shade.

Wallace Stevens
'Le Monocle de Mon Oncle'

Phryne had returned home late and alone. Questioning choristers had been as fruitless as Robinson knew it would be, but
he had grimly done it anyway. The result was a lot of people
who alibied each other in a vague way—'There were five tenor
voices in the semi-chorus of "He Spoke the Word"'—which
added up to a large amount of nothing much.

The police were searching the Scots Church hall and the
hotel room for anything which might have contained poison,
and so far were not finding it. Leonard Match had voluntarily,
for a strict sense of the word, emptied his pockets and revealed
handkerchiefs and loose Dr McKenzie's Menthoids and some
paper which might have contained a white powder, which
he could not currently explain, being drunker than several

skunks. Robinson had filed him in the holding cells for the night, until he became a little more lucid.

Would anyone really kill two conductors to take over a choir?

It seemed unlikely. But Miss Fisher was involved, and that always saw the Unlikeliness Quotient rocket sky high.

Robinson took himself home for four hours' sleep, Mark calmed the choristers and sent them away, and Phryne went home by herself. There were places she could have gone, things she could have done. But she wasn't in the mood for indelicate delights. What she really wanted was a cup of cocoa, a bath and a soft bed.

When she came in all the household was fast asleep. Only Molly gave a formal 'wuff' of greeting and then lay down again with her head on her paws. Phryne walked slowly upstairs, forgot the cocoa in favour of a tot of brandy, and put herself to bed. She was exhausted.

And so, she did not sleep immediately, but allowed her mind to rove freely over the available evidence. She considered the death of Tregennis: his mistress had drugged him, but an adventitious passer-by had stifled him with that torn-out music from a choral score. An unmarked choral score. Not one of the two that were missing. Then Henry James: a cruel and stupid man with no manners or mercy and a list of enemies that must far outweigh his friends. Both men were such very good candidates for murder, and—what did one make of Leonard Match? Did he want to be conductor so badly that he would kill for it? The murder of Tregennis had been a matter of seizing an opportunity, but the murder of James had required planning. Arsenic, for example, might have been the poison, and that had to be signed for in the Poisons Book. This was a legal requirement for any poison sale. The medical examiner was doing an analysis. Soon Robinson would know what had caused James's demise. And he would tell Phryne.

So all Phryne had to do was go to sleep, and the morning would bring answers. She embraced a pillow, hugging it to her body, and snuggled into her clean sheets. She fell asleep at last, and dreamed of music.

•

She was awoken by Dot bringing coffee and her croissant and the news that Detective Inspector Robinson wanted a quick word.

'I'm staying in bed this morning, Dot; I promised myself a lie-in. If he just wants a quick word, he can come up here.'

'Well, you're decent enough, Miss,' agreed Dot. Phryne had donned an extravagant red silk gentleman's dressing gown over her nightgown. It was rather too large for her, but it presently smelt of John Wilson, and Phryne liked the scent. Dot liked the golden dragons.

Dot relayed the message via the house phone, and poured Phryne another cup of coffee. Presently Jack Robinson plodded up the stairs.

'How goes it?' Phryne asked.

'Examiner reckons an acute dose of an irritant poison, probably arsenic,' he told her. He slumped down into an armchair and Dot poured him coffee, too. He looked as though he needed it.

Jack Robinson was only familiar with coffee from a Bushell's Coffee and Chicory Essence bottle with a genie on it. The real thing came as something of a shock to his tastebuds. Then he gulped.

'So, antimony, arsenic, rat poison, something like that?' asked Phryne.

'Yair,' agreed Robinson. 'You sure he didn't eat or drink while he was with the choir?'

'Yes,' said Phryne. 'He was in my direct line of sight the whole time. He was unusually unpleasant to the sopranos—usually he has it in for the altos—and I'm a soprano, so I was watching him closely. For my cue. Also, trying to work out where to stick a stiletto for maximum efficiency,' she admitted. 'Another murder victim who has been positively begging for an unpleasant death, though possibly not this unpleasant.'

'Yair, it was nasty, all right,' said Robinson. He leaned back in the soft chair and closed his eyes. Just for a moment.

'Dot, ring down for another pot of coffee. Jack, you're falling asleep, and you don't want to do that until you can sleep for more than a few minutes.'

Dot obeyed. Phryne let him drift until the fresh pot of coffee came. 'Dot, would you pour the detective inspector a cup of black coffee with a lot of sugar? Drink it down, Jack dear, and your eyes will just pop open.'

'Jeez,' observed Jack Robinson, having absorbed the black, bitter, oversweet liquid. 'You're right. Now, where was I?'

'Asking if I was sure that he didn't eat or drink while with the choir.'

'Yair, I remember.' Robinson was dealing with a rush of caffeine into his bloodstream. It felt very strange. But good. He'd have to find out how to make this sort of coffee. It was only a matter of time until it became an illegal drug. 'You're sure?'

'Certain. But he did begin to get sick while I was watching him. He turned green, finished the rehearsal early with curses all round, and ran out.'

'Then where did he get the stuff?'

'Perhaps he wasn't feeling well from natural causes. He looked like a man who liked good food and wine. He might have lunched too well, felt ill, and rushed back to his hotel to take some patent remedy—which had the poison in it.'

'Yair, except there's no sign of it in the room.'

'Then the murderer took it away. He hadn't been dead long when I saw him, Jack. He was still warm. But no pulse, no respiration.'

'You don't think he could have still been alive?'

'No,' said Phryne, wrapping the dressing gown closer around her thin frame. 'I know death when I see it.'

Jack Robinson believed her.

'All right. Any bets on who did it?'

'If it wasn't Leonard, I can't imagine who did it. They all hated him. But poison's difficult. The murderer can be miles away when the actual murder happens.'

'Yair, it's a bastard all right. Anything on the . . . other front?' he asked.

'I warned off a young thug on a Harley yesterday. Since then I haven't heard a thing.'

'You didn't injure him?' asked Jack, getting up.

'No, I just threatened to allow Molly to tear out his throat. I must say she played up to it splendidly. Some dogs do have a sense of theatre, I find. Why?'

'Harley and rider found in the river this morning,' Jack told her. 'Fouled a chain-link ferry. Cut throat.'

'Not me,' promised Phryne, crossing her gold-embroidered dragon with a wet forefinger.

'Right. Just asking,' said Jack.

'But here,' said Phryne, reaching into a drawer, 'is his gun. It was on a lanyard round his neck. British Army-issue Webley Mark VI. I borrowed one during the war.'

'There must be thousands of 'em kicking around,' observed Jack.

'I expect so,' said Phryne. 'You'll let me know about the autopsy?'

'Yair,' said Jack and went away, slightly dizzy with caffeine.

•

Phryne lay back in her bed and sipped her own coffee. Mr Ratcliffe was a stringent employer, and clearly had never been told that it was unwise to shoot the messenger. Fewer people would now be willing to bring him bad news, and warlords needed to know what was happening.

She had ensured that young man's death as surely as if she had shot him herself.

As she was willing to do that, she did not allow the notion to upset her. Instead, she found her copy of *Bleak House*, adjusted her pillows, and read herself back to sleep, until Dot woke her at noon with the news that her bath was run and she had a visitation of choristers.

'Which ones?' she asked sleepily.

'They gave their names as Matthew, Calliope, Bones, Caterina, Tommy, Tabitha and Oliver,' said Dot, consulting her list.

'Right, well, they are welcome, and they can wait until I've finished my bath. Offer them some refreshments, Dot, and I shall be down directly. I don't feel like doing anything energetic today so I shan't dress. And tell Mrs B that was very good coffee. Her coffee would raise Lazarus.'

Dot looked pained at the blasphemy. 'Miss,' she protested.

'All right, tell her that it raised a partially unconscious policeman,' Phryne offered. 'Poor Jack. Nothing but problems. Tell me, Dot, any sign of watchers? Any trouble?'

'No, nothing,' said Dot, crossing herself. 'Thank the Lord.'

'And what is everyone doing?'

'Tinker and Jane are playing chess in the garden, Molly is keeping an eye on the back gate, Ruth is in the parlour making a scrapbook of recipes, and I'm here,' said Dot. 'Ember is in the kitchen, because Mrs Butler is making fish pie.'

'I love that fish pie,' said Phryne, shedding her dressing gown. The scent would fade within a few days, and that would be the end of John Wilson in Phryne's life. She would miss him.

'So does Ember,' said Dot meaningly. Ember was an expert snatch-and-run bandit. Mrs Butler had better keep a heavy pot lid over her cooling fish.

Phryne bathed in a leisurely fashion, dressed in her aquamarine gown, and went down the stairs to find a knot of choristers too excited to sing, which was an index of how excited they were.

'The cops think Leonard did it!' exclaimed Matthew.

'And what do you think?' asked Phryne, sitting down. Her blue-green dress flowed around her. Matthew found her distracting.

'We . . .' He faltered. 'We don't know.'

'You mean, "I don't know",' snapped Tabitha. 'It's a silly idea. Even though he has got one of those French things about conducting . . .'

'An *idée fixe*?' asked Phryne.

'Yes, one of those. About being a great conductor.'

'Is he a good conductor?' asked Phryne.

They all exchanged glances.

'No,' said Tommy.

'In a word, no,' agreed Calliope. 'He cares about it too much. He has to examine the history of every note and why it is where it is. Nothing ever gets done and he can't forgive the slightest error.'

'So, not destined to be a great conductor?' asked Phryne again.

'Never,' said Matthew sadly. 'It's a pity.'

'But, as I was saying, he isn't a murderer,' insisted Tabitha.

'How do you know, Tab?' asked Oliver, rubbing a hand through his unruly red hair.

'I just do,' she stated.

'That isn't actually evidence, you know,' observed Bones. 'People with an obsession will do anything to get what they want. I haven't done psychiatric practice yet, but that's what the textbook says. I looked it up,' he added.

'Yes, but really! The two murders aren't the same. One was just because someone walked past and found Tregennis dying. The other must have needed planning,' argued Tabitha.

'Precisely what I told Detective Inspector Robinson this morning,' said Phryne. 'There are two explanations. One is that there are two murderers.'

'There are enough people who would want James gone, if not actually dead and gone,' agreed Caterina.

'But that means there are two murderers in the one choir!' protested Oliver. 'That's really unlikely!'

'The whole situation is really unlikely,' said Matthew. 'Unlikely doesn't mean impossible.'

'True. Use the Sherlock Holmes maxim and what do you get?' asked Phryne. 'Either two murderers with entirely different motives in the one choir, or one murderer who might have just found Tregennis lying on the floor, probably with his mouth open, and stuffed music into it on impulse. And then, he knew he could kill. So the same murderer planned the death of James. When my policeman comes back I shall know what sort of poison was employed. Which thesis do you consider most probable?'

'One killer,' conceded Matthew. 'Two really is pushing probability further than it will go.'

'All right, now if it isn't Leonard, then who is it?' Phryne paused as Mr Butler brought in the tea trolley. The choir poured tea and milked and sugared and tasted the petits fours and thought.

'Who hated James the most?' asked Tommy.

'Everyone, really,' answered Calliope. 'He nagged and cursed all of us. He usually played favourites, which was always embarrassing, especially for the favourite. You know, call as it might be Caterina out of the choir, tell everyone they ought to be able to sing as prettily as she can, make her sing the soprano part, abuse the sopranos for not being Caterina.'

'And make Caterina wish she wasn't there,' said Caterina feelingly. 'But he hasn't had time to pick out the favourites with this choir.'

'He's just been sticking to generalised abuse,' said Bones. 'He doesn't like altos. Maybe an alto killed him.'

'Very funny,' replied both the altos present.

'We really don't know,' confessed Bones. 'I still think that it could be Leonard. In which case he really isn't fit to plead, and will spend the rest of his life in a nice comfortable bin, conducting the lunatics' choir.'

'You really are a cold-hearted bastard, aren't you?' asked Calliope.

'He's a medical student,' explained Phryne. 'He'll get his compassion back once he's dealing with people.'

'Or?' asked Matthew, who was quick.

'Or he'll become a surgeon,' said Phryne. 'Let us consider anyone with medical expertise. How about you, Bones? Could you lay hands on anything like antimony?'

'God, yes, there's a jar of it in the lab,' replied the student.

'Arsenic, too. Strychnine. On the open shelves. But, as it happened, I didn't.'

'And you?' Phryne looked at Tabitha.

'It's in rat poison,' she replied. 'So I know how to treat animals that have been poisoned. But I didn't, and I wouldn't. Thanks for asking,' she added, and took another petit four.

'Matthew?'

'No, it wasn't me. I don't know anything about poisons.' He looked quite unmoved by the accusation.

'Calliope?'

Calliope flushed red with anger. 'No! How can you ask? I don't even use rat poison. I just acquired a serviceable cat. He's called Orion, the mighty hunter. Oh, and here's another . . . I bet you're a great big dangerous rat killer, eh, beautiful boy?'

Ember, foiled of his attempts to get at the fish, had hopped up onto the garden table to see if anyone had a little milk or possibly even cream to spare. He nosed agreeably at Calliope's cheek as she leaned down to talk to him. He knew that tone. It meant food and devotion. He liked both.

Calliope could not possibly have poisoned James, thought Phryne, watching her carefully scooping the cream off her apple tart and feeding it to Ember, lick by lick.

'Tommy?' continued Phryne.

'I don't know nothing about poisons, and if I wanted to kill James, I would have thumped him.' This was self-evident, and in the event James would have stayed thumped.

'Oliver?'

'God, no,' he said.

'Caterina?'

'It wasn't her,' said Tommy instantly.

'Let me speak for myself,' said Caterina, pushing Tommy's

protective hand from her shoulder. 'No, it wasn't me. I'm Italian but my name is Caterina, not Lucrezia.'

'Indeed. And it wasn't me,' Phryne told them. 'Are you going on with the concert?'

'Probably,' said Matthew. 'We really need the money. I can carry on as rehearsal master until we get a new conductor. We're getting quite good,' he added hopefully. 'And Aunty Mark has come down from Sydney specially for this concert, as well.'

'And your new conductor isn't going to be Leonard? I mean, even if he didn't kill the previous conductors?'

'No,' said Matthew. 'Poor chap. He'll be so disappointed.'

'Well, keep me informed,' Phryne told him. 'And, listen, Matthew—be careful. Someone doesn't like your conductors. I think you are . . . charming—' her voice held a world of promise '—and I don't want harm to come to you.'

'All right,' Matthew told her. 'I'll be careful.'

'Good,' said Phryne, and had them ushered out. Something was itching at a corner of her mind, and she wanted to think.

•

Twenty minutes' hard thinking just got her a memory of a Renaissance portrait of a pale, sad lady. Bugger, thought Phryne, and decided that she needed distraction.

Unfortunately there was no one around who seemed likely to provide it. She was not good enough at chess to understand the game Tinker and Jane were playing. Mrs Butler was busy. Finally she joined Ruth in the parlour, cutting out the recipes which she had saved from newspapers and magazines as Ruth glued them into her scrapbook and spoke excitedly of feasts to come. Phryne found her company soothing.

•

John Wilson sat in his own room, trying to gather his wits. It had been a fascinating but shattering couple of days and he felt as though he had been broken into small pieces, pieces which had then been jumped up and down upon by elephants and then reconstructed with strong glue in an unexpected form. He had lost a lover, Phryne, and found a lover, Rupert Sheffield. He felt honoured and terrified in about equal proportions. Now Sheffield had him, John Wilson, what would he do with him (John Wilson)? Had Sheffield ever had a lover, of either gender, before? If so, what had he done to them? Were bits of them scattered in some foreign field? How could he ask? He didn't have the words. But he really needed to know. When Sheffield said—insisted on—forever, how long was that? Next week? Next year? Until Rupert got bored? Until Rupert got them killed?

More likely to be until Rupert got him, John, killed. But that didn't matter. He still needed to know. He had told Phryne that if she calculated incorrectly and Rupert rejected him, she would break his heart. He wasn't at all sure that it might not now be exploded into a thousand pieces, now that he knew what lying all night in Sheffield's arms felt like.

It felt like he had died and gone to heaven.

But John reminded himself that he was a doctor and had survived the Battle of the Somme and was supposed to fall with his face to the foe, and all that. Humming 'Land of Hope and Glory', not entirely ironically, he stood up to open the communicating door between their rooms and found Sheffield standing on the other side, hand out to grasp the handle.

'Ah,' said John, taking the hand in both of his own.

'Come in,' said Sheffield. 'Are you having second thoughts? This isn't going to be easy. We are an illegal relationship. We will have to watch every public move.'

'I know,' said John. 'No, I have no second thoughts.'

'But you have questions,' said Rupert. The violet eyes flicked over his face. 'Ask, and I'll answer.'

'I think I'd like to sit down,' said John. His injured leg was threatening to collapse under him. Sheffield locked the communicating door and the room door and lay down on his bed. He extended his arms. 'Come here,' he said quietly.

John lay down. He arranged their limbs so that he could look into Rupert's face.

'Ask,' said Rupert.

'When you say "forever", my dear, what do you mean?'

Rupert arched an eyebrow. 'Really, John, I thought English was your native tongue . . .' he began. 'I mean forever, until we both die, until the end of time,' he said calmly. 'You are mine, I am yours.'

'What if you get bored?' asked John, frantically trying not to exult.

'I won't,' Rupert assured him. 'You are endlessly fascinating.'

'But, Rupert, have you ever had a lover before?'

'There were people who wanted me,' he answered slowly. 'But I did not want them. A girl kissed me, a French kiss, her *tongue* was in my *mouth*—and I felt sick. In fact I seem to remember I *was* sick. I was sixteen. I never tried that again. Women are . . . squelchy. Swampy.'

'So, not girls. What about boys?' asked John.

'Several people in Athens tried to seduce me,' said Rupert coldly. John felt instantly very sorry for them. They probably swore off sex for life. Nunneries. Monasteries. That response would have sent me straight off to Mount Athos as soon as I could get a ticket, John thought. 'Then I was captured,' he said. For the first time his voice broke. John embraced him and Rupert buried his face in John's shirt front for a moment.

'They talked about what they were going to do to me. I realised that I had never had a lover, and after they had finished with me, I never would have. So when they got bored . . .'

'There was more to it than that, wasn't there?' asked John, stroking the curly hair.

'Yes, all right, yes,' said Rupert, his voice ragged. 'I fought. I bit and clawed and shrieked curses; I fought like a mad thing, like an animal, and I got loose and I ran straight into the ocean. I didn't care if I drowned. I swam out to sea. My back hurt, I was cold, I was weak, I started to sink. I remember looking up at the stars. Cold, distant, beautiful. Then a Greek fisherman called Yanni picked me up. He pulled me out of the sea into his little boat. He called me a merman, *thallasandros*. He dried me and put olive oil on my back and gave me wine and when he put a hand on my thigh and said, *parakalo*, please, I said, *ne*, yes. Because I could still die and I didn't want to die without finding out what love felt like.'

'And what did it feel like?' asked John, very gently.

'It was cold and I was in pain but it felt . . . pleasant. He ruffled my hair and called me *thespoinis*. Maiden. He only had one blanket and we lay all night off Piraeus, waiting for the tide to turn. He kept me warm. I was shocked and shaking. Yanni liked me. He called me *adelphemou*, my brother. In the morning he took us into harbour, and Compton was very cross with me.'

'What happened to Yanni?' asked John, filled with tenderness.

'He was killed. A U-boat. I never saw him again.' And Rupert Sheffield laid down his head and wept for Yanni the fisherman, while John stroked his hair. 'And I felt so sad that I thought, never again. If this is love, the pain is much greater than the pleasure. So I decided not to do it again. Until I met you. And until I saw you with your Miss Fisher.'

'Did she make you jealous?' teased John.

'Hopelessly,' agreed Rupert. 'You're mine.'

'And I have a big bruise on my neck to prove it,' said John.

Rupert loosened his collar and exposed his throat, a gesture strangely like a wolf signalling submission.

'You can bite me, if you wish,' he said in his cut-glass accent.

'That won't be necessary,' John told him.

Rupert opened his violet eyes wide. 'If I ask politely?' he said. 'Please will you bite me?'

Overcome by primitive emotion, John grappled him. John pinned Rupert flat on his back, knelt over him, growled, 'And you're mine!' and bit.

Rupert Sheffield laughed out loud. Marked. John, unlike Miss Fisher, was biting his throat at the junction with his shoulder. This token of possession was not meant to be generally seen. Only John would see the marks of his teeth on Sheffield and know that he was his.

John thought of everything. He must be protected at all costs. Mitchell remained a threat to John because John would die to protect Sheffield, and Sheffield could not allow that situation to continue. Mitchell thought that Sheffield had recognised him and was about to seize him and turn him over to the authorities for treason.

Surely when Sheffield offered him a deal—his silence for John's safety—then he would agree. It would be a rational outcome.

And John must not know. He would worry. He would interfere. Sheffield could handle this small matter of negotiation all on his own.

CHAPTER SIXTEEN

I help myself to material and immaterial
No guard can shut me off, no law prevent me.

Walt Whitman
'Song of Myself'

Since no one had actually died on the premises, the Scots Church allowed that night's rehearsal to go ahead. Matthew was conducting. Leonard was still in police custody. Fortunately, he had lost his temper with the arresting officer and punched him. That meant he could be charged with assaulting an officer of the law, and his lack of bail money meant that he was staying where he was.

The choir were trying to show decent regret, and not doing very well. So they were singing, instead. 'He Shall Give His Angels Charge Over Thee'. It was even beginning to sound beautiful.

Mendelssohn did a really good angel, Phryne considered. That was Tinker's opinion, too. Angel music. 'That they should protect thee in all the ways thou goest.' This was usually sung as a double quartet but the Harmony Choir had, by tradition, always sung it as a chorus. 'So everyone gets to sing the pretty bits,' Matthew had explained it to Phryne.

'Nice,' said Matthew. 'Now, we need to get "Yet Doth the Lord See It Not" right. Just take it slow and watch the dynamic, it ought to flow, gently.'

'It's *allegro vivace*,' said Professor Szabo.

'Quite right,' said Matthew. 'But let's try it slowly to start with, all right? Then we can speed it up. We've got to put in all the notes.'

'Mendelssohn,' grumbled Caterina. 'Too many notes.'

'At bass entry—from the top,' ordered Matthew, and the basses growled, '*Yet doth the Lord see it not!*'

No wonder Leonard wanted to be a conductor. The power. Raise hands and everyone sings. Make the cut-off gesture and everyone falls silent.

Matthew, however, was not at all interested in power or dominance. Phryne found that very attractive. Matthew just wanted the music to sound beautiful. And his devotion was catching. The choir, disrupted, grumpy and scratchy, began to calm and to sing out. Music did have charms to soothe the savage breast, thought Phryne, puzzling over the soprano entry, and then deciding just to go along with Chloe. She had a strong, sweet voice and she never missed a note.

Chloe, as the widow, led into the soprano solo, '*O man of God, what have I to do with you?*' singing while buffing her nails, easily, her voice creamy and accurate. When she finally donned her breastplate and mounted her horse, her Valkyrie would summon heroes into her arms before they could ask, 'What hit me? Oh,' which were most heroes' last words.

The widow implored Elijah for the life of her only son.

Then Chloe realised that she was singing alone. Elijah was still sleeping off his hangover, probably in very tasty company.

'Sorry,' she said, breaking off and flipping through her score.

'No, that was lovely,' said Matthew. 'Really. But if we could get on with "Blessed Are the Men—'

'Hear, hear,' murmured Phryne. Tabitha chuckled.

'—Who Fear Him",' concluded Matthew firmly. 'Right?'

He raised his hands. They sang. After an hour's hard work, they could sing *allegro* quite enough to be going on with *vivace* for 'Yet Doth the Lord', and even Professor Szabo was pleased. The choir went to get tea and the professor began to play.

He was wonderful. Phryne forgot about tea and sat where she could see him, the hunched, elderly, drunken gnome, his miraculously undamaged fingers flowing over the keys, a Liszt piece of hideous difficulty. Even on the rehearsal piano, a cranky old grid, the music was remarkable.

'He's such a good player,' murmured Matthew at Phryne's ear, offering tea. 'Such a pity.'

'What drove him to drink, when he had music like that in him?' asked Phryne, accepting the cup. Milk and one sugar. Just as she liked it. How lucky, or observant, of Matthew. Both qualities were useful.

'The grog got him,' said Tommy sadly. 'Poor old bloke. Orchestras need pianists who come to rehearsal sober. I think he got sacked a few times, then he got a job "tinkling the ivories" on a cruise ship, came to Australia, and liked it here. He can't stand the cold. That's what he said, anyway.'

'You like him,' said Caterina.

'Yair,' said Tommy, blushing and shuffling his feet.

'I think that's very kind of you,' Caterina told him.

Tommy stammered but Caterina caught the cup before he could spill hot tea all over his trousers.

Calliope smiled. 'He only plays when he's happy,' she told Phryne. 'And that isn't very often, poor old man. We must have pleased him.'

'Well, Matthew is just conducting Mendelssohn to the written tempo and dynamics,' said Oliver. 'That's how Mendelssohn wrote it. The prof's a Mendelssohn purist.'

'And a good thing, too,' observed Tabitha. 'I hate all these experiments. The composer knew what he was doing.'

'Hear, hear,' said Tommy.

The professor finished the Liszt and began on a Chopin étude. He played for the whole break, and when the choir were again in place and Matthew announced 'Open the Heavens and Send Us Relief' he segued into it without pause.

This occupied the rest of the time allowed. When they finally got it right and sang it through not only without a mistake but *andante sostenuto*, there was a loud crash overhead, and it began to rain.

And the choir began to laugh helplessly, leaning on each other, sobbing with mirth, and Professor Szabo sat at the keyboard and laughed until he wept.

•

It was a cheerful party who stood at the door and looked at the rain pouring down without cease. Behind her, someone began to sing the boy's solo. It was Caterina, and to the sound of the rain it was startlingly effective, the last word rising to a high surprised squeak.

'Behold! A little cloud ariseth now from the waters. It is like a man's hand. The Heavens are black with cloud and with wind: the storm rusheth louder and louder!'

And the choir sang, *'Thanks be to God for all his mercies,'* beginning with the awed whisper of those who had seen a miracle, then swelling to a triumphant shout. '*Thanks be to God, he laveth the thirsty land!*'

'*The waters gather, they rush along!*' sang Phryne, as the gutters filled and pedestrians ran for cover. '*The stormy billows are high, their fury is mighty!*'

They sang through to the end.

'Thanks be to God,' said Matthew. 'He laveth a thirsty land, you know. Now, who's got an umbrella? And are we all going to Aunty Mark's party?'

There were five umbrellas in all. The choristers ferried one another to the Windsor Hotel, singing an ironic, damp, but entirely cheerful round called 'Sumer Is I-cumen' In'.

Phryne still didn't know who had suffocated Tregennis, and she definitely didn't know who had poisoned Henry James (though choristers did seem like the obvious suspects), but for the moment she didn't care. If it had been Leonard, as seemed likely, he was in safe custody and that meant Matthew was safe. Phryne wondered if the Harmony Choir would find it difficult to persuade another conductor to risk this perform-ance of *Elijah*, which seemed to be comprehensively cursed.

Still, she had sung in a scratch production of *The Gondoliers* in France, where the theatre had been shelled just when the Duke of Plaza-Toro had entered into his patter song. He had kept singing. Bits of roof had rained down on the audience. This was not a possibility in Australia. Thanks be to God.

Exhilarated by racing through the rain, they were singing silly songs. It was a silly song sort of evening.

Aunty Mark, enthroned on a large armchair probably meant for a visiting monarch, began, '*Be kind to your web-footed friends . . .*'

'*For a duck may be somebody's mother,*' rejoined many voices.

'*Be kind to your friends in the swamp, where the weather is always domp (to rhyme with swamp)*' explained the tenors.

'*You may think it's the end of my song, well it is, but to prove that I'm a liar,*' sang the altos.

'*I'm going to sing it again, and this time I'm going to sing it even higher,*' boasted the sopranos.

Phryne enjoyed the resultant cacophony. Fortunately the Royal Suite had no floors above it. Even the Windsor might find this level of noise a little hard to tolerate in a lower room.

Finally the song reached its logical conclusion. '*You may think it's the end of my song, well it is.*'

Complete unison, absolute silence. Then they laughed and started talking again. Aunty Mark announced that tomorrow night he would have a quiet night in, with just a few drinkies and a good book. Phryne cynically doubted that he would be reading much. His friend Gawain blushed.

Phryne walked out to get a taxi not terribly late, kissed Matthew goodbye, and took herself home. When she arrived there was a message which asked her to ring Fanshawe's number.

The soothing voice of Mrs Thomas greeted her. 'Ah, yes, Miss Fisher, have you had a nice sing? Ratcliffe is preparing his warehouse for something. One of his men bought ammunition today: .455.'

'A Webley,' said Phryne.

'In all probability. Now, you take care, dear. Ratcliffe has eight thugs always with him. And he killed one of his motorcycle assassins because—'

'Yes, I heard,' said Phryne. 'Pulled out of the river. With the bike, which seems wasteful.'

There was a sigh. 'These criminals,' said Mrs Thomas.

'Mr Fanshawe says, anything you want, whenever you need it. Any idea what you'll need, or when?'

'I will probably need a couple of armed men, probably near that warehouse, and knowing this sort of power-mad lunatic, probably soon.'

'No, they don't generally have a lot of patience, those bad sorts. I'll station two men near that warehouse, dear. Your identifying phrase is Black Cat. They can help, and they can also clean up a bit if things become messy.'

'Thanks. I'll try to keep the scene as clean as I can.'

'You do that, dear. Someone on this line all the time—you call if you need us. Take care of yourself, my dear.'

'I shall, thank you. Happy knitting,' said Phryne, and rang off.

Among the mail, there was a note from John Wilson, asking her to lunch at the Windsor on the morrow. Phryne grinned. She would certainly go. She was very tempted to take Jane, who had beaten Sheffield at chess, or Ruth, who would love the food, or Dot for the decor or Tinker for the shock value. But only her name was mentioned, so she would be lunching without domestic support.

This gave her an agreeable freedom of action. And the Windsor's food was always worth eating.

Bed, thought Phryne. Bathed and changed, she rootled out Lambie from the bottom of her wardrobe, and took him to bed with her. But when she dreamed, she dreamed not of John Wilson, now irretrievably lost (but gone to a good home). She dreamed of Matthew. And woke feeling that the day was full of promise.

This feeling persisted through the morning. Dot reported that no watchers had been seen and no suspiciously vegetable-sounding motorcycles had been heard. Tinker said that Molly had slept through the night on the foot of his bed without twitching an ear. Dot was taking the young persons to the zoo. Phryne declined to accompany them. As she paused at the door, Dot looked at Phryne and said, 'You will be careful, Miss?'

And Phryne embraced her and told her, with not a single qualm, that she would.

'You go to hell for lyin',' observed Bert, who had come in through the kitchen as was his wont. He had slightly startled Phryne.

'I'll save you a seat,' she snapped.

'Deal, Comrade. Oughta be real cosy down there. Meet all our old mates again,' said Cec. 'We brung them plans.'

Phryne repented her rudeness. 'Good, have a seat, the family has all gone to the zoo. Dot likes the monkeys, Tinker loves big cats, Ruth loves feeding the bears and the elephant ride and Jane adores snakes.'

'I mighta guessed it,' grunted Bert. 'I hope that Sailor ain't up to his antics, or Dot won't know where to look.'

Phryne had once attracted the attention of the infamous Masturbating Monkey, and giggled a little at the thought of what poor Dot would do. Sailor was a mandrill who reserved his most impressive performances for when there were women in the audience. One either admired his brightly painted behind or his . . . well, yes, the less said the better about what you could see in his fist when he turned around. Still, it was a patriotic behind. Red, white and blue, as Phryne remembered. PG Wodehouse had commented when he saw one, 'That chap's wearing his school colours in the wrong place.'

'Show me the plans,' requested Phryne, as Mr Butler brought in the beer.

'Bay Street,' said Bert, running the hand not holding his bottle down the street. 'Here's the warehouse. Something's been happenin' in the second one. Far as anyone knew, it was empty. Now he's moving there—men, or maybe cargo. No one's talking, and they're all jumpy.'

'This gate, it's wire?' asked Phryne.

'Yair, cyclone wire. Padlock. This one's wood. Old wood, you could bash through it—though not in that pretty car of yours.'

'Nice idea, but I forgot to order a tank,' responded Phryne. 'Guards on the gates?'

'Couple of 'em, all the time. Guns. When the local Ds see 'em, there's gonna be trouble,' prophesied Bert.

'Did you see anyone watching this factory?' asked Phryne.

'One bloke with a pair of binoculars. I caught the flash from the lens,' said Cec. 'Dunno who he's working for.'

'Me,' said Phryne. 'There should be two of them. If you encounter them, use my name. It's Black Cat.'

'Suits yer,' said Bert, holding out a hand without looking for another beer. Cec put one into his grip. They really had the most remarkable partnership. She was pretty sure they could read each other's minds. Meeting on the hot cliffs at Gallipoli had that effect. Herodotus's Spartans, fighting to the last man at the Hot Gates, Thermopylae, must have been much the same. *At first they resisted with their weapons, and when they were broken, with their hands and their teeth, until they were overcome by a new army coming from behind, and they fell and left a name that will not be forgotten.*

Phryne swallowed down a sob. The Great War never really went away, however much she tried to forget it. She hoped that she was better at strategy, in this little tiny war, than General Haig had been in his great big one. Then she snorted. The veriest schoolchild would be better at strategy than General Haig. And Phryne had left school a very long time ago.

'All right,' she said. 'This is what we will do.'

Bert and Cec listened and approved.

When her household came home, full of buns and artificial lemonade, telling of bears and taipans and extremely rude monkeys, Phryne knew what to tell all of them. They had parts to play. They knew them. And Tinker, particularly, was very pleased at being included.

John Wilson should have his lover. And his life. Phryne had made up her mind.

•

Phryne and Lambie slept the sleep of the entirely innocent, which was hardly fair.

The morning might have dawned fair and bright, as it tended to do in Australia in summer, but Phryne did not see it. She was in a languid mood. She bathed sumptuously, lay about impersonating an odalisque all morning, and then dressed and went to lunch at the Windsor. Her life did seem to be concentrating about this part of the city, these days.

One glance at Rupert and John revealed that they were one. At last, Phryne thought. John was glowing. He looked like the John Wilson Phryne had met on the Somme, when she had dragged him into her ambulance, though cleaner and less shell-shocked. Younger, in some senses. Happier. Some sort of *éclaircissement* must have been reached about what Rupert meant when he said 'forever' and 'mine'. And if she had not been able to deduce that just from looking at Rupert, there was the bruise on John's neck.

Rupert looked exactly like Ember who had just polished from his whiskers the very last of the crème Chantilly. A bowl of crème Chantilly, moreover, which had been carefully placed on a high shelf out of the reach of the most athletic of cats. He had something he wanted, he had consumed it, and it was too late for anyone to demand its return.

Phryne made a point of leaning down and kissing Rupert. His skin was as white as porcelain and strangely cool under her lips.

'My dears,' she said, and beamed at them.

John beamed back; Rupert looked away.

'Lunch,' said John.

A waiter appeared with menus and advice about wine. Phryne ordered briskly. Rupert ordered for John.

'I say, Phryne, is it your choir that's been singing in the Royal Suite? Lovely voices,' said John.

'That's my choir, and we have been plagued with murders, the latest being a poisoning death—arsenic—on your floor. Henry James. A man who had so many enemies that finding who killed him is going to be testing for the local police. There are so many candidates, including me. Horrible man.'

'Aren't you going to help them?' asked John. 'When I first met you again, after so many years, you said—'

'My small talents are at their disposal,' said Phryne, and Rupert Sheffield actually smiled. He looked like an angel approving of Good Deeds Amongst Mankind.

'Your talents, Miss Fisher, are not small.' Rupert had won the perceived contest, and felt magnanimous. Phryne thought that was nice of him. She supposed.

'Arsenic?' said John. 'Silly poison to use in these modern times. We can test for it, you know.'

'Marsh's test,' said Phryne.

'Indeed. And we can tell from the deposit in the hair shaft how long the person has been poisoned. I gather this was a bit sudden?'

'Yes, he was ill one hour and dead the next.'

'So, acute arsenical poisoning. It dissolves quite easily in a weak acid—lemon juice, say, or hot tea.'

'I know, but there was no bottle or flask, no means of delivery that anyone can find. I can only assume that the murderer brought it with him and took it away when he—or, of course, she—left. But this is not a nice topic for a luncheon table. Are you enjoying your stay at the Windsor?' asked Phryne.

'I think it will always be one of my favourite hotels,' responded Rupert. 'Despite the singing. Then again,' he added, as John frowned at him, 'I have seldom heard "The Sexual Life of the Camel" sung with such skill and fervour.'

'It is one of our favourites,' admitted Phryne.

Lunch proceeded through tomato soup, a rather good *boeuf en croute*, and an Australian delicacy, a pavlova, for dessert. During which Sheffield was called away to the phone.

'I think this might be it,' said Phryne. 'Don't take your eyes off him tonight. That isn't too harsh a task,' she added.

John leaned over and grabbed her forearm. His knuckles turned white. Phryne knew that she would have a bruise on that arm. She did not move but instead took his free hand in her own. He knew that clasp. It meant safety. The dying lads in no-man's-land had felt that grasp. 'Don't let him get killed,' he said fiercely. 'Promise!'

'I promise,' said Phryne. 'Remember your instructions. Don't let him out of your sight, and call me. I have it all arranged.'

'All right,' said John.

'Now let me go, he's coming back, and you're creasing my sleeve,' said Phryne, and John laughed. He dug into the confection of meringue, fruit and cream and he and Phryne were discussing tropical fruits amicably when Sheffield came back from the telephone. He was tight-lipped. Lunch concluded shortly afterwards.

When Phryne got home, she stayed within hearing of the phone. She was waiting for trouble. Which didn't mean that she allowed anyone to miss dinner. Dot, who was not formed for combat, was given the code words and the phone number to call Fanshawe if Phryne was not home before morning. She resolved to sit up and sew. What with Mrs Thomas knitting and Dot sewing, they ought to have the matter stitched up in no time.

Because everyone was nervous and no one could concentrate, Phryne played a noisy game of snakes and ladders with her household until, at about eight o'clock, the phone rang.

It was John Wilson, and all he said was: 'Go.'

'Right,' said Phryne. 'Minions, it is time to don your disguises. I have to ring Bert and Cec and Fanshawe and Dr MacMillan. Now, darlings, stay calm, stay detached, and stay out of the way of any stray ordnance. Clear?'

'Yes, Guv,' said Tinker.

'Yes, Miss Phryne,' chorused Ruth and Jane.

Phryne made her calls. Then she went upstairs and changed her clothes. Bert drew up outside in the taxi. Cec drew up in a battered van which had once belonged to Jno Clarke General Carrier. Or possibly still did. Cec might have borrowed it. Phryne kissed Dot and got into the van. The minions got into Bert's taxi. And they drove away.

Dot sat down in the comfortable armchair, found her embroidery and moved the light. It was going to be a long night. Before she started sewing, she took out her rosary, and began praying for Miss Phryne's intention.

CHAPTER SEVENTEEN

The TRUMPET'S loud Clangour
Excites us to Arms,
With shrill Notes of Anger,
And mortal Alarms.
The double double double beat
Of the thund'ring DRUM
Cryes, 'Hark the FOES come;
Charge, Charge, 'tis too late to retreat.'

John Dryden
'A Song for St Cecilia's Day'

Rupert Sheffield had left John asleep in their mutual bed; an after-dinner snooze. He had kissed him goodbye and was sure that he would see him again soon. Mitchell had called and requested a meeting. Rupert could tell him that he didn't know who Mitchell was, that Mitchell was perfectly safe, and to call off his dogs before Rupert went to the local authorities. Mitchell would then do so, and Rupert would come back. He was sure that he would be home before John woke up.

As soon as the door clicked shut, John leapt up, dragged on his clothes, found his service revolver and cracked open the door. He could see Sheffield just ahead of him. He followed, as silent as a famished wolf who had been short of fresh lamb for a very long season of winter.

He lurked until he heard Sheffield tell the doorman, 'Bay Street, Port Melbourne.' Then he telephoned Phryne with the code word from the lobby telephone, and was soon in his own taxi, in pursuit.

The taxi driver was chatty. He might not have entirely believed the reasons that John gave for his visit to the most dire portion of Bay Street, but money was money, and the fare was an affable bloke and very sound on cricket. And he was very nice about Bradman, considering he was a Pom.

Arrived, John saw the last flick of Sheffield's coat as he rounded a shabby warehouse, and caught up with him.

'What are you doing here?' hissed Rupert.

'I'll always be here,' said John. 'At your back. Bare is man's back that is brotherless.'

'I'm just going to talk to the man,' said Rupert. 'You shouldn't be here.'

'Oh, yes,' said John, sliding a hand around Rupert's jaw and holding him so that he had to look into John's eyes. 'This is what "forever" means, my dear. You don't walk into danger on your own. Not anymore.'

'Oh,' said Sheffield. 'I hadn't thought of that.'

'Think of it now,' said John.

'My aim was to keep you safe,' said Rupert.

'And if you get killed doing so, I shall follow,' said John. 'Promptly.'

Rupert ran a finger down John's neck to the love bite. One flesh.

'All right. Let's go,' said Rupert, and John followed, his Webley in his hand, hoping frantically that Phryne's plans were sounder than those of General Haig.

The warehouse, when they forced the rusted doors open, was dark and quiet. But some sort of noise—shouts and thuds—was happening at the other side of the building. John was alert for sentries and spies and danger, but couldn't see much in the dim light. Of course, this Mitchell bloke—Phryne had called him Ratcliffe—would give orders that Rupert should pass unmolested. That didn't mean that marksmen weren't hidden in this infernal gloom.

'Mr Sheffield,' said the man from the darkness of the warehouse.

'Mr Mitchell,' said Sheffield. 'I do not know you and I do not need to know you. What you are doing here is no concern of mine. You can forget about me. You do know that I have never seen your face?'

'Let's keep it that way,' said Mr Mitchell. A very educated English voice.

Sheffield's mind raced. 'Born in Leeds, probably a working man's child, went to a local school, won a scholarship to a public school—Eton, I think—and thence to Cambridge. Sciences,' drawled Rupert. 'Main motivation: money.'

'Money is power,' said Mitchell.

'A certain sort of power, yes,' agreed Sheffield. 'Well, here I am. What do you want with me?'

'I'm going to kill you,' said Mr Mitchell.

'I rather thought it might be that,' responded Sheffield. 'Would you like to know why?'

'I rather think I know,' said Rupert. 'The arms business—not a lot left of your organisation after Compton and I finished. Your chiefs are all dead or in jail. And I've heard that Greek jails are really quite uncomfortable.'

'That, yes,' agreed Mr Mitchell. 'But the reason why I am not just going to shoot you cleanly, but spend some time on your demise, is a man called Andreas Katzis. Do you remember Andreas?'

'Yes,' said Rupert, who never forgot people who tried to strangle him with a fishing net. Anyway, so far, Andreas occupied a set of one element.

'You killed him,' said Mr Mitchell, his Cambridge accent fraying back to its roots.

'I might point out that he was trying to kill me at the time,' said Rupert evenly.

'Doesn't matter!' yelled Mr Mitchell. 'He was my son!'

Rupert did not reply.

'Aren't you going to lie, and say you're sorry, to save your miserable life?' screamed Mr Mitchell.

'If you like,' said Sheffield calmly. 'But since there's just you and just me, as you promised, there doesn't seem to be a lot of point.'

'I didn't come alone,' said Mitchell.

'Oddly enough, neither did I,' said Rupert. He stepped swiftly into the shadows. 'Are we going to re-enact the Gunfight at the OK Corral?' he asked. He sounded only mildly interested. He was listening for the other men breathing. To his left, he knew, it was John. There, to the right—high up—a sniper? Surely not. But someone had shifted his feet. This was beginning to look like a major miscalculation. He should have enlisted some soldiers of his own. But that would have meant asking either the loathsome Fanshawe or Miss Fisher. He had not reasoned that he would need help.

'First, Sheffield, I will shoot your friend John Wilson. He knows your mind. He is an honourable man and I can't imagine how he tolerates you. It's always good business practice to exterminate any potential avengers. Then, you. It will be such a pleasure. You killed my son and you drove me out of my business. I retired to Australia, as far away as I could get, and what did I see? You.' Mitchell's voice was gluey with passion.

'And the cream of the joke,' Rupert replied, 'is that I was not looking for you and I don't know you by sight. But you do not need to shoot Dr Wilson. He knows nothing at all about my Intelligence days. I only met him after I retired and went back to pure maths. You could still walk away from this.'

'No,' said Mitchell slowly. 'It is just unfortunate about Dr Wilson. You ruined me, and I am going to kill you. Slowly. Beginning with the gut,' he said consideringly. 'That will take ever so long to kill you and every moment will be agony.'

He lifted and aimed the gun.

'No,' shouted John Wilson. Too late to shoot and stop that finger on that hair trigger. He leapt for Sheffield and threw himself between his lover and the gun just as it went off. Rupert Sheffield caught John's body full in his arms. Then he looked up into a face he had never seen before and waited to die.

He heard an exasperated snort above him. Then a boy in trousers, unravelling jumper and cap, dropped down from above and kicked the semi-invisible Mr Mitchell very hard in the testicles.

'These megalomaniacs are *so* boring,' the boy said. He grabbed the gun and shot the man in the temple. He was speaking as the boom and crash died away to echoes. 'If you'd just shut up and killed Sheffield, this could all be over now,' he told the corpse. 'But you just had to gloat. Now you are dead and it serves you right.'

Sheffield, frantically investigating John for injuries, felt a small hand grab him by the hair, compelling his attention. Green eyes burned into violet eyes.

'Get up!' said Phryne Fisher. 'Pick up John—I think he's

299

fainted. He really hates being shot. You idiot. This is all your fault. And I shall expect you to be grateful for your rescue.'

Grief and horror had not derailed Sheffield's mind. He stood up, gathering John into his arms. John was moaning. He was bleeding!

'How . . . ?'

'Tell you later, darling.' She dropped a folded white paper on the dead man's lap. Then she wiped the gun and placed it carefully in his hand, closing the fingers around it. 'Grab John and let's go. I have some friends distracting the others but that can't last forever. This way.'

Rupert slung John's unconscious weight over his shoulders into a fireman's lift, holding on to one leg and one arm, and ran after the boy in the cap into a yard, through a tall gate and into the back of a tradesman's van, which instantly began to drive. Rupert sat down with John's body in his arms and lolling head supported by his shoulder while Phryne opened his coat. There was some blood, but not enough to indicate a serious wound.

'All right,' said Phryne. 'For a blithering idiot, a pair of blithering idiots, both of you have got off very lightly. He will live to blither again. Press here. You might as well have his blood on your hands literally as well as figuratively.'

'Why did you intervene?' asked Sheffield, feeling blood well up hot from the much-loved flesh, aching with the idea that John would be in agony when he woke. The sensation was strange. And novel. And extremely painful. He bit his lip on something that might have been a sob. Phryne took off the boy's cap and shook out her hair. She lit a gasper, which filled the van with the sweet scent of Virginia tobacco, overlaying wool, sugar and rubber, which had been its previous cargos.

And, dreadful, the coppery butcher's shop scent of John's blood. On his hands.

Phryne's voice was incisive, as though she needed to get some information to Sheffield before John recovered consciousness. 'Because John is my friend and for some reason he adores you, and you are so pretty together, and you were going to get him killed,' she said, blowing a smoke ring. 'You walked open-eyed and alone into a trap, you madman.'

'I didn't know John was there until later,' said Rupert.

'Where else would John be? You said "forever", I heard you.'

'With me,' whispered Rupert Sheffield, pressing his cheek against John's forehead.

'Right. And instead of asking for help, you march into a warehouse in a city which you do not know without telling anyone, offering yourself up for . . . sacrifice . . .' Phryne remembered her vision of that alabaster body laid out on her bed. Agnus Dei. She sucked some more smoke and wished she had thought to bring a flask. 'Who do you think you are—Sexton Blake?'

Rupert Sheffield stiffened and was about to take offence when John moaned and reached for his free hand, and he kissed the fevered cheek.

Phryne Fisher, clad in boy's clothes, one hand flourishing her cigarette and the other tapping Sheffield's knee for emphasis, was unforgettable. And impossible to ignore. He knew every inch of that body. And he knew nothing at all about her. A valuable lesson. Stay away from women in future. They were incalculable. She was talking. He was listening.

'You can't leave John behind ever again; he's part of you now, and however much I might want to slap you until you weep, he can't live without you, and if he dies, how long are you going to survive him?'

'Oh! Yes,' said Sheffield, who hadn't thought about this before. 'I don't believe . . . I would want to live without him. In fact, it was a relief, looking into that gun barrel. If John was dead, I wanted to die with him. Most illogical.'

Phryne snorted and clipped him lightly across the ear.

'Idiot! Right. So I needed to make sure that your Mr Mitchell, who is my Mr Ratcliffe, set his ambush, then spring it before he killed anyone valuable, and then I had to take care of his future threatening behaviour.'

'By?' asked Sheffield, feeling John begin to shiver. He was going to need warmth and treatment soon. Phryne stubbed out her gasper and lit another.

'Making sure he didn't have any future. Though I may have to review my previously scornful opinions on the Sexton Blake sort of villain. That man really did spout the same sort of twaddle; he really did delay your death until he could get through his speech, giving me time to shoot him.'

'Nature and art,' said Sheffield.

'Which you need not tell John. He already thinks I'm some sort of monster.'

'No,' said John as he swam into consciousness, lifting his head from Sheffield's chest. 'No, I really don't, Phryne.' He sat up a little, wreathing an arm around Sheffield's neck with perfect trust. 'Did you kill him?'

'Certainly I killed him. Did you want to spend the rest of your honeymoon being hunted by a not-quite-retired-enough arms dealer?' said Phryne waspishly. 'Good. We're here. Dr MacMillan will be waiting. I'll just scout a little . . .'

Rupert saw her jump lightly out of the van, and look right and left. In both cases she caught some sort of signal. Then she waved them out, Rupert supporting John, and hustled them into a nice little garden. The van took off. The garden gate closed. There was a strong scent of cut grass, full-blown roses, water and blood. John was taking some of his own weight and asked Phryne as she opened the door of a small, tidy house, 'Where are we?'

'This is where Dr MacMillan grows her roses and lays her blameless head. Come in, sit John down. Here's a chair. John, don't bleed on the carpet.'

Dr MacMillan came in calmly, ordered Sheffield to bring John into the back garden, and laid him out on a scrubbed, draped table in the summerhouse. It was overgrown with the dark red roses called Black Boy after King Charles the Second, and the scented petals dropped all around as the mannish woman—the best kind, Sheffield decided—laid the wound bare, cleaned it with gentle hands, put in a lot of iodoform powder and stitched it shut. Eleven stitches, and every one felt as if it had gone through Sheffield's flesh as well. Then she sat John up to wind a bandage around his body, pressing a pad against the wound. She watched for a moment. No staining was evident. She administered morphine by injection. She began to scold him in her soothing Scots voice as she directed Sheffield to carry him again, into the house and into a nest of soft blankets on a couch.

'The shirt is for the fireback,' she told him. 'You daft great gowk, puttin' yerself in the way of harm after all this time out of a war. Pining for the battlefields, is that it? Now, your friend will go into my bathroom there and wash his hands, he will be back directly, and I shall see about tea.'

Rupert Sheffield, scrubbing John's blood from his hands with a nailbrush and hospital soap, swore that this was the last time, the very last time, that he would have to do this. John's blood was on his shirt. He ripped it off and threw it to the floor.

When he came back Phryne was perched on a chair in the parlour, sipping whisky and combing her hair with her fingers. He sat down bare-chested on the couch, wrapping himself and John in the blankets, and felt his friend lean gratefully on his chest as Rupert's arms closed around him. Then Rupert raised his head and stared into Phryne Fisher's eyes.

'I promise,' he said, 'that I will never endanger John again.'

'Or yourself . . .' she prompted.

'Or myself. And I have to thank you,' he added. 'For our lives.'

'Pleasure,' said Phryne. 'On the understanding that if you do this again I will personally shoot you in the head.'

He did not doubt her sincerity. Or her marksmanship.

'If this happens again and it's my fault, I will let you. Indeed, I will beg you.'

'Deal,' said Phryne. 'And if you break his heart, I will cut you into bits. No one will ever find them. Because they will be such very *small* bits.'

'That, too,' agreed Sheffield.

'The local sharks see my wharfie friends as good providers,' she elaborated.

'Agreed. But what if he leaves me?'

'He won't,' Phryne replied. 'He has a true and faithful heart. Or, rather, he had it. He gave it to you. If you die, he'll die.'

Sheffield felt John shift and snuggle in his embrace and acknowledged the truth of this remark. He could not imagine his John ever leaving him, except in death. He suddenly and desperately sought for something else to think about.

'Will you tell me how it was arranged?' asked Rupert. 'You seem to have a very efficient organisation.'

'I borrowed a couple of men from Fanshawe,' Phryne told him.

'Fanshawe is a fool,' said Rupert.

'He's really not,' Phryne commented. 'He's useful. About time you learned the difference, my boy. Shall I go on?'

'Please,' said Rupert.

'I wanted them in case we needed to have official sanction. They were my reserve; I didn't need them, as it happened. My wharfie mates staged a scene at the gate, refusing to let Mr Ratcliffe's minions in. Backed up with a shotgun. A sobering weapon at close range. My adoptive children were my lookouts. Cec drove the van. Bert was in the warehouse, ready to carry anyone who was hurt. He was also armed. We had at least three alternative plans. Luckily Plan One worked well and here we are.'

'And that fetching jumper?' asked John, surfacing on a cushion of morphine, chuckling.

Phryne stood up with one elegant hand on her hip, turning to the audience like a mannequin exhibiting a striking new gown.

'Isn't it just the peak of the mode? I borrowed it from Tinker. He'll be cross, it's got a bit more unravelled.' She pulled at a sad, grey-blue thread. 'Do you think I can I call them in, Elizabeth?'

'Indeed, any danger of pursuit should be over. If they followed, they will have gone haring after that van, and Cec is very good at losing followers,' said Dr MacMillan.

'And, in any case, their chief has killed himself,' observed Rupert.

'As you say,' said Phryne.

'That takes the impetus and ambition out of most gangs,' observed Rupert.

'That is true,' said Phryne.

'And the suicide note is right there in his hand.'

'Yes, I saw it,' said Phryne.

'And naturally the handwriting will match any samples available,' insinuated Rupert.

'Of course it will,' said Phryne.

'Shot through the temple. The right temple,' mused Rupert. 'So he must have been right-handed. And his fingerprints are on the gun, still clutched in his hand.'

'Right again,' said Phryne.

'And if it was expedient that he should disappear, that would have been managed also?'

'Concrete pour tomorrow morning two factories away,' Phryne told him.

'I asked Compton about you,' said Sheffield.

Phryne grinned. 'Did you now? What did he say?'

'The most dangerous woman in the world,' quoted Rupert. 'And what did he say when you asked about me?'

'Idiot savant,' said Phryne. 'Emphasis idiot. Emphasis savant.'

'That sounds like Compton,' said Rupert.

'Was he wrong?' asked Phryne.

Rupert looked down at John lying on his chest, injured because of him, smelt a faint after-scent of copper, swallowed, and said, 'No, he was right. On both points. And about you.'

'So kind,' said Phryne, and went to the front door to call in her family. There was a scatter of feet and Rupert stared at the lookouts.

Boy, one, ragged, evident source of that disgraceful jumper as he was wearing a beige version of same. Bright eyes, filthy tweed cap. Two, female, long legs in a too-short, too-small dress, crammed on sun bonnet which concealed her face, plaits. Basket. Three, also female, hauling a large sugar bag, overlarge dress and apron, scarf. The third put down her sack and Phryne dived on it, extracting some garments and a pair of sandals. She bent to take off the heavy boots and winced from her bruises. Instantly the boy knelt to undo the knotted laces. Miss Fisher's minions served her, thought Rupert, out of love. He could understand that now. Phryne patted Tinker's cheek as the boots and ragged socks were removed, and wriggled her toes as if she was glad to see them again.

'Nail down those filthy socks, Tink,' she told him. 'God knows what they'd do if they escaped.'

'Right you are, Guv'nor,' said Tinker, grinning up at her. Phryne shucked her trousers and went into the bathroom, tossing aside her jumper as she went.

Rupert noticed that her undergarments were of her usual silk. Anyone undressing that particular boy would have been in for a surprise.

And a bullet in the head, of course. Or at the least a boot in the testicles.

'She is, you know,' murmured John sleepily into Rupert's collarbone.

'She is?' asked Rupert.

'The most dangerous woman in the world,' said John, and fell asleep again.

'That's true,' said the girl in the candle-snuffer bonnet, bending so her friend could haul it off her head. It gave with a ripping of seams. 'We're just lucky that she's on our side.'

'Which side would that be?' asked Rupert.

Jane looked at him as she found her own and Ruth's clothes in the sack and handed the rest over to Tinker.

'Miss Dot says she's on the side of the Light,' she replied. 'A religious concept.'

'I am familiar with it,' Rupert told her.

'Otherwise you could say that she is ethical,' Jane said, removing her scarf and fluffing out short blonde hair. 'For instance, when she rescued me from a mesmerist, we told her she couldn't take me and leave Ruthie in a terrible place, so she took the two of us.'

'And she got me from Queenscliff on approval,' Tinker told him, stripping unaffectedly and putting on respectable shorts and a shirt with no holes in it. Suddenly he had become a nice public school boy home for the holidays. Rupert blinked.

'I have seen you before,' he told Tinker.

'Yes, you have,' said Tinker in his best 'polite' voice. 'Too right, mate,' he added, in his original accent.

'And you,' he told Jane. 'I played chess with you. You were quite promising.'

'Thank you,' said Jane. 'You seem different.'

'How?' asked Rupert.

'Softer,' said Jane, before her sister elbowed her in the ribs. 'No, I'm not being rude, Ruthie,' she protested. 'Look for yourself. You know Miss Phryne says we should observe carefully.'

'Only if it isn't impolite,' said Ruth primly.

'He won't mind,' said Jane. 'He's been observing us. Fair's fair.'

'So it is,' said Sheffield. In Jane he had met a nature as direct as his own, though she had learned manners much earlier. 'Well? What are your deductions?'

'I can't use a mathematical proof,' said Jane. 'But when we saw you before you were arrogant, and you didn't like people. Not just us. You were jealous of Miss Phryne. You were unhappy, and you tried to make everyone else unhappy as well. And you needed us to know how much more intelligent you were than anyone in the world.'

'Jane!' cried Ruth.

'He asked me for my deductions,' said Jane mulishly.

'And I bet he's sorry he did,' said Ruth.

A tender heart, thought Rupert. I used to think that was a contemptible weakness. What an idiot. Compton was right.

'Go on,' he told Jane.

'Now, you're not snarling, you're not telling us how clever you are. You never touched anyone before. You wouldn't even touch my hand when I held out the chess pieces. You're touching Dr Wilson, you're embracing him, skin to skin. As though you love him.'

'And he's snuggling into your arms as though he loves you,' said Ruth, clasping her hands. 'It's just like a romance except it's men.'

'Jeez,' said Tinker, who had a limited tolerance for romance.

'Dr MacMillan has tea in the kitchen,' said Rupert out of a merciful impulse, and Tinker left. Sheffield recoiled a little as Jane approached and stared straight into his eyes. Her own were blue and very sharp.

'Yes,' she said coolly. 'Softer. The underlying musculature has relaxed a little, the overall definition of flesh over bone is more—'

'Sculptural,' said Phryne, coming back wearing a green linen shift dress which might indeed have been at the peak of the mode. 'What are you doing to Mr Sheffield, Jane?'

'He *asked*,' said Jane, wounded by all these people who misunderstood her motives. 'He asked for my deductions.'

'I did,' affirmed Rupert.

'More, Jane?' asked Phryne, smiling. That pitiless, uninvolved gaze scanned him again. It was like staring into a searchlight.

'There's a blue shade under his eyes; he's had a shock. His hand has just the remains of a tremor, and he's scrubbed that hand very hard. Did it have blood on it? Not his blood, he's not hurt. Dr Wilson's blood. An enemy's blood wouldn't worry him. No gunsmoke on his arm, either, so the person who did the shooting was Miss Phryne.' Jane took Phryne's hand. 'And not your usual Beretta, it must have been a bigger handgun. You've pinched the webbing between thumb and forefinger.'

'And can you guess who I shot?' asked Phryne.

'The bad man,' said Jane, smiling up at Phryne with perfect faith. 'Of course.'

'And that will do,' said Dr MacMillan, allowing Tinker to wheel in a tea trolley. 'Tea. You will make a great diagnostician, nae doot, my hinny, but you need tae improve your bedside manner.'

John woke and drank extremely sweet tea in a room which contained Phryne and her family and, of all the most unlikely and wonderful things in the world, Rupert Sheffield holding the cup for him to drink. He drank all of it, not objecting to the sweetness. Rupert took the cup away and kissed him gently.

He closed his eyes.

●

When he awoke again he was disoriented and in pain.

'The morphine has worn off,' observed Rupert. 'John? Do you know where you are?'

'You're here,' said John with vast relief. 'I thought I was dreaming.'

'No, you're in Dr MacMillan's house. You've been—'

'Shot,' groaned John. 'I know how that feels. It feels bloody awful, in case you are still collecting information. I remember. The warehouse. You're unhurt?'

'Entirely. If I put my arm behind your shoulders can you

sip some water and take these pills? The doctor left them for you. She said you'd wake in pain.'

'She was right. How long have I been asleep?'

'Four hours. It's early morning. You should sleep again.'

'It was worth a wound,' said John, groping for Rupert's hand, 'to have you with me.'

'No,' said Rupert sharply. 'Nothing is worth your being wounded. How can you say such a thing? There's a slice out of your side; I felt your blood pulse under my hand. Never say that again.'

'All right, my dear,' John agreed. He drank the water and swallowed the pills. Morphine, he knew that bitter taste. 'These pills will take half an hour or so to work,' he told Rupert. 'Until then, would you . . . would you lie down beside me? The thing about pain,' he went on, 'is that it makes you feel rather lonely.'

Sheffield removed his shoes and his outer garments and crept into bed beside him, wincingly careful not to jolt or touch the bandage. John lay on his side and Sheffield embraced him very gently. John, who had been chilled, relaxed into his warmth. The wound burned. But he had endured worse, and not in such precious company.

'Talk to me?' he asked, for distraction and the pleasure of hearing Rupert's beautiful voice. Irish coffee, Phryne had called it. Now, only when speaking to John, it was Irish coffee made with pure whisky and dark chocolate and cream.

'What would you like me to talk about?' asked Rupert, close to John's ear.

'What did you make of Phryne's children?'

'Remarkable. The boy is just a boy. Fisherman. Has a black and white dog. Poor parents, missing father. Wants to be a policeman, I think, and is a devotee of Sexton Blake, which is why he calls Miss Fisher "Guv'nor" and why he's called Tinker.

'I doubt that's the name with which he was christened, if he was christened. Ruth, the girl with plaits, has a gentle heart and is probably a good cook. Flour on one of her plaits. Strong hands from kneading and whisking. Reads a lot of romances. She thought we were a pretty sight. And the one called Jane is going to rule the world someday. She deduced your injury from the way that I had scrubbed my hands.'

'Clever,' admired John. He caught his breath at a minor movement, then said, 'You liked her?'

'Scared me to death,' confessed Rupert.

'She has that effect on me, too.' John tried not to chuckle.

'Not one of them thought there was anything wrong or even strange about us being together,' said Rupert. 'Well, Tinker went out to the kitchen, but that was dislike of sentiment, not . . . not . . . loathing.'

'Any child who lives in Phryne's house,' said John, 'is guaranteed a very liberal education. If their brains don't explode in the first couple of weeks, then they're probably immune to any surprise.'

'Pity mine was not so liberal,' observed Sheffield. 'I thought all sexual desire was both wrong and sinful and love was a sign of weakness.'

There was a pause in which John winced again. The house was quite silent. John could hear a clock ticking two rooms away. He was never going to be reconciled to the idea of being shot. But it was just a furrow in his flesh. No ribs had been broken. He would heal, with another scar for Rupert to memorise. And the splendid Rupert, who loved him, John, forever, he was untouched. His mind was wandering away. Rupert took his hand.

'I am so sorry,' said Rupert desolately. 'I have made major errors and I nearly got you killed.'

'Yes,' said John. 'Yet here we are.' He grunted a laugh and regretted it instantly. He squeezed Rupert's hand.

'Isn't the drug working yet?' asked Rupert anxiously. 'Shall I fetch the doctor?'

'It will work soon, and I'm not going to arouse our Lisbet from her lawful bed. She gets very sarcastic when woken without cause. I'm wounded already. I'll be all right in a little while,' said John, leaning back into Rupert's arms, feeling his lover's body heat saturating every cell. 'Stay with me. Be here when I wake again?'

'So, you forgive me?' asked Rupert into John's hair.

'Yes, my love, yes, my dear,' said John, sliding into sleep. 'Yes, yes, yes.'

CHAPTER EIGHTEEN

*Was this the face that launched a thousand
ships?
And burnt the topless towers of Ilium?
Sweet Helen, make me immortal with a kiss!
Her lips suck forth my soul: see where it flies!*

Christopher Marlowe
Doctor Faustus

Phryne and her minions did not get home until a scandalous three o'clock in the morning. While Tinker, Ruth and Jane told Dot all about it, rummaging for provender in the American Refrigerating Machine, Phryne reported to the imperturbable Mrs Thomas the whole story. She tutted, wondered what the world was coming to, reported that the carefully arranged suicide had been just the thing, and that Maginnis's men were now battling the disheartened remains of Ratcliffe's in the warehouse in Bay Street, whence they had been summoned by a Mysterious Message through—possibly—communist channels. Local police had been alerted and were on their way.

'Nice, neat operation, Miss Fisher,' said Mrs Thomas. 'I think the stories I've heard about you might be true.'

'Please,' said Phryne, who felt that some informality was called for, 'call me Phryne. Convey my best wishes to Mr Fanshawe in the morning. Goodnight,' she said.

'Goodnight, dear, sleep well,' said Mrs Thomas cheerily.

When Phryne got to the kitchen there was really quite a lot of egg and bacon pie left. She ate two pieces before Tinker scoffed it all.

•

The whole household slept in. Breakfast was a merry meal more akin to lunch. When the doorbell rang, they all stopped and waited until Mr Butler returned with an enormous box of Haigh's superfine chocolates and a huge bouquet of orchids. They were blooming, varicoloured, strangely scented, and rare. Phryne arranged them in a glass bowl.

Ruth read the card. 'To the Fisher family. From John and Rupert. Heartfelt thanks.'

'Very proper,' said Phryne, and awarded everyone the chocolate of their choice.

The household scattered to their usual tasks. Phryne, who had just remembered the portrait of the sad Renaissance lady from her cogitations before Sexton Blake had taken over her life, took down the *Encyclopaedia Britannica* and turned to B. She read while she ate her cherry liqueur chocolate.

Half an hour later she was ringing Jack Robinson. An hour after that she had alighted from the police car sent to fetch her, at the Medical Examiner's office.

'What gave you the idea?' he asked.

'You couldn't find the container for the arsenic. All the cups and glasses in both places tested clean. And you're thorough,

315

Jack, you wouldn't have missed anything. That seemed odd. Then a member of the choir,' said Phryne, 'told me her name was Caterina, not Lucrezia. In connection with me asking them about poisons. Arsenic was very popular in the old days, when there was no forensic science and no Professor Glaister. Inheritance powder, they called it. Pure, deadly, white, dissolves in any weak acid.'

'What's a weak acid when it's at home?' asked Jack Robinson.

'Tea is tannic acid, vinegar is acetic acid, orange juice is citric acid; there are a lot of acids about in general use. Lucrezia Borgia, of whom I am sure you have heard, had a hollow ring which she could use to deposit arsenic into a drink. It could be mixed with, say, lard as a base, and rubbed into leather to make poisoned gloves. It's an adaptable poison, and in the old days people died quite frequently of typhoid and cholera. Same symptoms. Can be used long term to produce a chronic toxicity . . .'

'And you're doing my work for me again, Phryne?' asked the spry and elderly Dr McLaren. He was an emeritus chemistry professor at Melbourne University and called in when forensic problems were beyond ordinary knowledge. In person he was another gnome, small, shrunken and bald. But Professor McLaren was vibrant with purpose and bright of eye. As a hobby, he bred Siamese cats.

'No, no,' said Phryne, who had great respect for the old man. 'Just a few preliminary notes.'

'Fine puzzle you've set me,' said the old man, with relish. 'Though I believe Lucrezia Borgia to be a much maligned woman. What could she be but what her father and brothers made her? They married her off at the ripe old age of thirteen—the first time. Poor girl. However, as my learned colleague Miss Fisher was saying—' he led the way into his laboratory '—arsenic use was widespread. Now that we have a reliable test for it, it is not so much used, homicidally. But it's reliable and, of course, the fact that there is a test for it doesn't mean that the death will be seen as suspicious. If no one tests, it might as well be one of those Sherlock Holmes colourless, odourless, undetectable South American poisons.'

'Granted,' agreed Jack. Laboratories made him nervous. He always felt that sooner or later they would blow up. His experience at school—where an overenthusiastic application of sodium metal to a sink full of water had taken out the sink and the ceiling—had confirmed this view.

The full orchestral score lay on the metal bench. Professor McLaren put a hand on it.

'Now, you say this vanished?'

'Yes,' said Phryne. 'For up to twenty-four hours.'

'And when you found it again, it was a little damp?'

'Indeed.'

'And your conductor used to lick his finger before turning the page?'

'That was his disgusting and invariable habit,' she confirmed.

'Right. I suppose I can't just cut up the score?' he asked hopefully.

'Not yet, but you can cut the ends off a few pages. They wouldn't have had to poison the whole score. Just the top right-hand corners. That was where his wet finger landed.'

'Well, we'll see,' said the professor, taking out a scalpel and slicing a number of corners off the score.

'What is this all about, Miss Fisher?' asked Robinson.

'Borgias,' said Phryne, watching the little bits of paper bubble away in an Erlenmeyer flask with an attached glass

317

condenser. The professor had placed it in a fume cupboard. 'They rather specialised in poison. Drinks, knives, gloves and books. One nasty method was to send someone a pornographic book, and poison the pages so that when the reader, aroused and careless, licked his finger to get to the next page to find out what happened to the lovers, he would get a small dose of poison. Depending on his libido, he would either be slowly poisoned or would get an acute dose. In either case, he would be dead. Arsenic is cumulative. It stays in the system. This is Marsh's test for arsenic.'

'All I can see is bits of paper in clear fluid,' said Robinson.

'Oh, but wait, my dear sir. The distilled water is free of all contaminants. Look at that glass surface,' said Professor McLaren excitedly.

'It's clear,' said Jack. 'Or, no, wait, it's going smoky. Like a stain.'

'Indeed, dear boy,' said McLaren, who had never really left the lecture theatre.

The thin smoky stain deepened and widened. It was a brownish charcoal colour with a shining metallic disc in the middle.

'There is the mirror,' said Phryne.

'That is arsenic?' asked Jack.

'Arsenic or antimony, they are both Group Five semimetals. Both are inimical to life. But with the addition of a weak solution of chlorinated lime, we shall see.'

He poured in another clear fluid. Jack was going to steer clear of transparent fluids for a while. Beer seemed a good substitute.

The blackish mirror cleared as if by magic.

'Arsenic trioxide, without a doubt,' crowed Professor McLaren. 'Thank you so much for this, my dear.' He kissed

Phryne on the cheek. 'I haven't been so amused for ages. I had no idea we had such inventive murderers in these parlous days.'

'How much arsenic is in that score?' asked Jack.

'Oh, grains and grains, my dear sir—enough to kill an elephant. Several elephants. Though where your murderer got pure arsenic I don't know. Commercial arsenic is coloured with either soot or indigo. There's no trace of any colouring agent. And no trace of any admixture, either.'

'Not rat poison, then?' asked Jack.

'No,' said Professor McLaren. 'Now, it's been such fun, but I must get on. Princess the Lady Regina of Alphington is about to kitten. I must be there to support her.'

'Right,' said Jack.

They went back to the police car. Phryne made a note that the choir needed a new orchestral score. Allen's would provide.

'So, how did he do it?' asked Jack.

Phryne waved a hand. 'Oh, simple enough. Nasty, though. Shows a very vindictive spirit. One would take the score home, dilute your arsenic in hot water and lemon juice, then just paint it onto the tops of the pages. Might take a while because you'd have to wait for each page to dry. That probably explains why it was a little damp when I found it.'

'Who could have done it?' asked Jack. 'You know these people.'

'The whole choir,' replied Phryne. 'I think your best bet is to find the arsenic. Pure arsenic is used in a lot of industrial applications—paints and dyes and glass-making. Someone must be missing an oz or two.'

'Blimey,' said Robinson, and slumped in his seat.

•

Phryne was conveyed home. That was inventive, she considered, and Jane was most impressed when Phryne told her about the Borgia feast and how it should be avoided.

'But what does it taste like?' asked Jane.

'It's pretty tasteless, or so I have been told,' answered Phryne. 'I direct your attention to the encyclopedia. And I utterly forbid you to try rat poison. That wouldn't be a good test, anyway, as it's a combination of poisons.'

'And we don't have any,' Jane told her, sounding disappointed. 'Mrs Butler won't have poison in the house. Ember catches the rats and mice, and she keeps out the black beetles with bicarb and flies with oil of mint and mosquitos with citronella.'

'Never mind,' said Phryne, and went to lie down. She needed to think. If this was Leonard's doing, he had displayed a breadth of imagination which she did not think he had. Were there history students who might have read about this method and decided to try it on James? If he stopped licking his fingers and turning pages, if he abandoned this repulsive habit, then he would not be poisoned. If he persisted in it, he would die.

As a lesson in manners, it seemed a little extreme.

•

Rehearsal was pleasant, without Henry James. His ghost was not heard as the choir worked on their full-dress choruses. 'Then Did the Prophet Elijah Break Forth Like a Fire'. It was a little scrappy, but adequately *moderato maestoso*. Matthew was pleased and Professor Szabo played minuets for the tea break. Most of the choir began to dance.

Phryne felt someone take her hand. It was Matthew.

'May I have this dance, beautiful lady?' he asked. 'Less energetic than the Charleston.'

'Certainly,' said Phryne and walked, moved, dipped, through the set piece, which was clearly designed to allow everyone in the room to see who was dancing with whom and what they were wearing. It was soothing. Various versions of an actual minuet were being danced. But they were all decorative, even if they were not canonical. Phryne saw that Caterina was coaxing Tommy through the steps with admirable patience. They were very sweet together. Daniel was dancing with Josephine. Both of them were concentrating hard, which made the disparity in their height less ridiculous. DavidandLobelia, however, were dancing the wreathed-together, swaying embrace known as 'the nightclub shuffle', usually only seen when both parties needed to lean on someone because they were too drunk to stand up on their own.

They went back to rehearsal, and managed the final chorus, 'And Then Shall Your Light Break Forth', with the last words of the oratorio: *'Lord, our Creator, how excellent thy name in all nations! Thou fillest Heaven with glory,'* and then an Amen noticeable for its brevity. They stopped and drew breath. They were pleased with themselves.

'Good!' said Matthew. 'Right, it's Aunty Mark's night in, so everyone go home and do the same. We are really improving, friends. And the good news is, Pat Bell's Ballarat engagement is finished, and he's coming Wednesday to take over.'

'Oh, wonderful,' said Calliope. 'He's such a nice man. But you've been very good too,' she told Matthew.

The choir applauded as he left the dais for the last time. He gave them a graceful bow.

'Are you sorry?' asked Phryne.

'Me? God, no,' he said, transparently honest relief washing over his broad face. 'It's a huge responsibility, getting it right. Hearing all the parts, trying to slot them together. Finding out where the mistakes are. I'm handing us over with a reasonable chance of getting up to concert pitch by the time of the performance. That's enough for me!'

'So it is,' said Phryne. 'What a very nice man you are.'

'Er . . . thanks?' he said.

'I'm so sorry that I can't take you home with me and ravish you,' Phryne told him. 'But I still have to find out who murdered two conductors. You should be safe now; you're out of the spotlight.'

And she went away, leaving Matthew feeling as though someone had carelessly nailed him to a wall. With hot, gold nails. *What* had she said?

Phryne had already gone. He would ask her to elaborate on Wednesday. Or maybe not. That was a lady who knew her own mind. And they still didn't know who had killed Tregennis and then killed Henry James. General opinion was that it was Leonard. But he had not been arrested. And that policeman was still making enquiries.

Matthew reminded himself that Gran would be cross if he was late in cooking her dinner. When she was cross, she was very unpleasant. And he had his pets to feed.

So he took the tram to Carlton, very agreeably confused.

•

When Phryne arrived home to a light supper, more tributes had arrived. There was a modest but expensive bunch of gardenias from Peter Fanshawe. A fiendishly valuable flask of Attar of Roses, without its import/customs duty stamp, directed to Officer, Commanding. An obviously hand-picked sheaf of garden roses tied up with a bandage from Dr MacMillan—she really did grow beautiful roses. They were Black Boy, the roses which covered the bower in which she had operated on John

Wilson. They smelt intoxicating. The note said *such pretty boys* and probably didn't refer to the roses. Now, unless Rupert had utterly gone back on his word and somehow damaged John, in which case she would shoot him in the head, however beautiful, things ought to work out well between those two. It still worried Phryne that Rupert did not appreciate what an altogether excellent person John was, but that would come in time.

It had better.

Supper was delicious, and she and Lambie slept well. The morning brought a host of household tasks, which Phryne managed; a hairdresser's appointment, a sister alight with indignation and a worried policeman.

'Phryne!' exclaimed Eliza. 'Comrades Bert and Cec brought me three women they said came from a man called Ratcliffe's house.'

'Yes,' said Phryne. Eliza was her opposite. Phryne was small, thin, dark and heterosexual. Her sister was tall, bosomy, fair and a devout Sapphic. Despite which they got on very well.

'Yes, I told them you might be able to look after the freed slaves.'

'Do you know what that beast did to them?' demanded Eliza furiously.

'No,' said Phryne. 'And you don't need to tell me, I can guess. My memory is already well-stocked with horrors. Can you find someone to care for them?'

'Yes,' said Eliza.

'And a small donation might be acceptable?' added Phryne, reaching for her purse.

'Of course,' said Eliza. She eyed Phryne narrowly. 'Comrade Bert said that Ratcliffe is dead. Is that true? These girls need to know. I've never seen . . . slaves really is the best

323

word . . . so terrified. They are sure he is going to recapture and punish them.'

'He's dead,' said Phryne, pressing a banknote into her sister's hand.

'How do you know he's dead?' demanded Eliza.

'I killed him,' replied Phryne.

Eliza did not even blink. 'Jolly good,' she rejoined. 'Well done. I only wish that you could bring him back.'

'Why?' asked Phryne, startled.

'So you could kill him again.'

•

The policeman was exhausted and discouraged.

'This case has got me stumped,' he confessed.

'Me, too,' said Phryne. 'We know "how", which ought to mean we know "who", but I really can't think that Leonard Match thought out that Borgia trick. I doubt he reads anything but music. And the history student who might know about it, Caterina, is the one who used the name Lucrezia. She didn't particularly have it in for Henry James. And I suppose the two murders are connected.'

'Maybe they aren't,' offered Jack accepting a tea cup. 'Thanks, Mr B. What if the Tregennis smothering was some passing chorister who just hated him for a moment, and then sort of forgot about doing it? Pure spur of the moment thing? And the James murderer had been planning it for months?'

'Can't have been; we didn't know we'd get James until after Tregennis was killed. But, all right, what if James had a deep and passionate enemy amongst the choir, who, once James was actually in his power, decided that his long-nurtured plan could now be carried out? I'm saying "his" for convenience. Poison does tend to be a female weapon.'

'That could happen,' agreed Jack. 'Still too many people who hated the nasty coot.'

'Yes,' said Phryne. 'What about the source of the arsenic?'

'We've been looking,' Jack told her. 'But almost everyone in paint or dye uses it, and they're real careless with it. Couple of foundries, you could walk in and help yourself to a pocketful of the stuff and no one would notice. They use it so commonly they forget the blasted stuff is lethal. And that's just the white powder, the arsenic trioxide. Chemists keep a poisons book for the commercial arsenic. No names we know, so far.'

'I'm still watching,' said Phryne. 'Something will break. I'm going to sing in this *Elijah*; it is going to be very good. And we've got a new conductor coming tomorrow. His name is Patrick Bell and apparently he is well known as a sweetie. That will be a nice change.'

'I bet,' said Jack. 'Be careful,' he added, and took his leave. 'By the way,' he said at the door, 'you didn't have anything to do with that riot in Bay Street last night, did you? Where Ratcliffe killed himself and Maginnis got cut up by Mother Higgins's slaughtermen? The riot squad is still finding bodies—the fight spread out into a sheet-metal shop as well.'

'Me?' asked Phryne, clasping both hands to her breast.

Jack Robinson smiled grimly. 'I thought as much,' he said, and Phryne closed the door.

Phryne decided that she would attend Aunty Mark's party. She might also have a word with Rupert Sheffield, if she saw him, about the immense value of his lover. Rupert had not seen John as Phryne had seen him: courageous, exhausted, gentle with the injuries which he could not treat, swift and skilled with scalpel and needle.

He was not, however, with any luck, likely to see anything like that.

Phryne decided to have a nap. Tonight she needed to watch everyone in the choir, and that would prove tiring. Lambie was waiting for her faithfully in her bed. Wrapped around him was Ember. Phryne snuggled up to them both.

•

The Windsor really was coping with Aunty Mark's perennial party very well. On her magnificent way up the main staircase, she encountered John Wilson.

'How are you, my dear?' she asked, not touching him.

He took her hand. 'I'm not really damaged, Phryne, it was just a bit of a scrape. Scared poor Rupert, though.'

'So it did,' said Phryne. She hoped it had scared him into a suitably humble frame of mind.

'He's hardly let me out of his sight. I just needed a little air. Going for a walk in that park over there. I left him asleep. You look gorgeous,' he told her. Phryne posed. She was wearing a trailing dark-blue and gold brocade gown. Her fillet held a peacock feather. It just about suited her, thought John.

'I'm going to Aunty Mark's,' she told him.

'Have a lovely time. We're almost underneath, in seventeen, as you know. Try to sing some madrigals. Rupert likes madrigals.'

'All right,' said Phryne, and watched him limp away. He was favouring his side, but not too much. Those stitches must be pulling. But he was healthy. He would heal. And now he had his lover. A good result all round, thought Phryne, and continued up the stairs.

She was intercepted and offered an arm by Tommy, who had Caterina on his other arm.

'Between two beauties,' he said joyfully. 'A thorn between two roses.'

Phryne and Caterina smiled at one another. They knew they were beautiful. And Tommy was a thoroughly nice chap. If Caterina wanted him, she could have him.

At the second staircase they met Rupert Sheffield, who had woken up without his John. He looked worried and almost dishevelled.

'He's gone for a walk in the park,' Phryne told him. 'Just across the road.'

It was a measure of Rupert's improvement in manners that he stopped, took Phryne's hand, kissed it, and murmured, *'Madame est magnifique,'* before he hurried in pursuit.

Aunty Mark had decided on an Ancient Greek theme, and was draped in a very revealing tunic and a chlamys made of a bedsheet. He sat on his throne and ordered his 'slaves' to sing songs for his amusement. The slaves were delighted to comply as long as the champagne held out. Someone had leaned out of the window and hauled in a rope of ivy to crown the participants. A bacchanal. How delicious.

'Marcus, I am feeling overdressed,' she said to him.

'That can be remedied.' He grinned wolfishly. 'You would have no shortage of volunteers to assist you in disrobing.'

'Perhaps later,' promised Phryne. 'Can we have some madrigals, Your Majesty?'

'Mad wriggles? Indeed!' he agreed. 'Come along, slaves, it is the month for Maying.'

While they started to sing, *'Now 'tis the month of maying, when merry lads are playing . . .'* Phryne got herself a drink and sat down by the window. She looked out into the well-lit street. And there, coming past the statue of General Gordon, were John and Sheffield. John was leaning on Sheffield's arm. They were well dressed and polite and obviously gentlemen, and no policeman would ever think that the reason John was holding on so tightly to his friend's arm was that he adored him immeasurably with a totally illegal passion. 'You see, but you do not observe,' murmured Phryne to herself.

'Hmm? What are you looking at?' asked Mark, manifesting himself beside her.

'Lovebirds,' said Phryne.

'Oh,' he said. His mobile mouth formed a perfect O. 'Well, isn't that the haughty piece and his shadow? They've come together, haven't they? How very agreeable.'

•

The party went on. Phryne spoke to all of the choristers in turn, even Julia, and gleaned no useful information. Professor Szabo told her that Matthew had been quite a good conductor, and he didn't know about this Patrick Bell. Several voices put in that Pat Bell was an excellent musician, and a good fellow besides, but the professor seemed unconvinced, and reminded them of the almost godlike conducting of Thomas Beecham. At which point, they stopped listening, as usual.

Phryne was about to finish her gin and tonic and take her leave, pleased but not enlightened, when there was a hubbub. She was grabbed bruisingly tight by the arm. It was Gawain and he was beside himself.

'Quick!' he shouted at her. 'It's Mark!'

He dragged Phryne through a throng of discomfited singers to the magnificent bathroom, where Mark, in his tunic, lay in the huge tub. His ivy-leaf crown was still on his head. He seemed to be asleep. But his face was under the water.

Phryne took charge. 'Tommy, Oliver, get him out. Shoulders and feet, hurry up! Gawain, run down to room seventeen, it's almost under this one, and bring John Wilson here. Tell him

I sent you. Go. Run!' she ordered, and he ran. 'Everyone else, please get back. We need some room.'

'Shouldn't we put him on the couch?' asked Tommy, who was bearing the weight without any strain.

'No, floor—he's got water in his lungs. We need to get it out.'

They laid him down.

Phryne touched his neck. A pulse throbbed beneath her fingers, thready but present. 'He's still alive. Where is Gawain with that doctor?' She dropped to her knees beside Mark and opened his mouth with her finger. A little fluid trickled out.

She leaned forward and locked her mouth on his, breathing some life into him.

Nothing happened. His chest rose and fell and was still again. Why couldn't she remember what to do? She breathed for him again. Rise, fall, stop. Rise, fall, stop.

Then someone thudded down beside her and said, 'Keep going, Phryne dear, good work. You two boys, take his arms. Now move them out and up, then in and down. One, two, one, two. Good lads. Keep going.'

John, thank God. Gawain, jealous and frantic, shoved her aside and took over the breathing. Phryne blindly put out a hand for someone to help her to her feet and found that she was being embraced by Rupert Sheffield, who was watching John work with absolute fascination. Phryne was breathless and dizzy. Rupert held her with perfect sureness, but all his attention was fixed on the lifesaving scene at his feet. John was exhorting, encouraging, dragging everyone in his orbit into the rescue.

He had always been able to do that. Phryne remembered him in a battle, rallying the less injured to care for the more gravely injured. And he had persuaded them, too, while the sky exploded overhead.

329

Rupert asked, 'Was he like that in his casualty clearing station?' and she answered, 'Just so. Sorry to lean on you, I'm feeling a little unsteady,' and he said absently, 'Not at all. I had not realised that he was so . . . charismatic.'

'Only when saving lives,' said Phryne. She could have straightened up but she was also fascinated, and she liked embracing Rupert Sheffield. He was quite strong, though so slim. He was only wearing a loose shirt and trousers, not his usual suit. He and John must have been interrupted in preparation for bed.

'I can see why you dragged him into your ambulance,' he murmured.

'He told you about that?' she asked, surprised.

'No secrets,' said Sheffield. 'Not anymore.'

'There, that's a good lad,' said John with satisfaction.

Mark dragged in a breath all on his own, was turned on his side, and water gushed out of his mouth, staining the carpet. He heaved and choked.

'You're all right, my dear,' John told him. 'You passed out in the bath. But Phryne was here and she saved you.'

'Actually, it was Gawain, Tommy, Oliver and mostly John,' said Phryne.

Rupert gave her an absent-minded squeeze of approval.

'Now let's get you cleaned up a bit, my dear chap. You'll be all right, I promise. Someone phone down for some hot tea, honey and lemon.' John sat Mark up against his arm. He put his ear to the wet tunic and listened. 'Good. No nasty sounds. You can't have been under long. Where's his bedroom?'

Oliver and Tommy made a chair and carried Mark to his bedroom. He was already recovering, giving a little royal wave as he was borne from the room. Gawain, Phryne and Rupert followed. John excluded the others.

'Strip off that rag, rub him dry and warm,' ordered John, and Gawain obeyed.

When Mark was re-clad in startling purple silk pyjamas, sitting up against a pile of pillows and sipping hot tea, John said, taking his wrist and feeling for his pulse, 'You really shouldn't bathe when you're too tiddly, you know. That could have been serious, if Phryne hadn't got you out.'

'I didn't,' protested Mark. 'I seldom bathe in my clothes.'

'Then what happened?' asked John. 'You had a lot of water in your lungs.'

'I don't know. One minute I was ducking into the bathroom for a quick pee, the next I was kissing Gawain with a couple of louts hauling on my arms. Felt like an elephant was sitting on my chest, too,' answered Mark querulously.

'Ah,' said Phryne.

Rupert exchanged a glance with her. Green eyes met violet eyes.

'John, have a look at the back of his head,' said Rupert.

John felt through the curly hair. His fingers stilled. There was a lump.

'A nasty little blow?' hazarded Phryne. 'Just hard enough to knock him out for as long as it took to load him into the tub and run a bath?'

'How did you know?' asked John. 'How did you *both* know?' he clarified.

'Observation,' said Rupert. 'He says he doesn't bathe in his clothes. His eyes are a little unfocused. He's a big strong man, it wouldn't be easy to persuade him to lie down and be drowned.'

'Thank you, precious,' said Mark. He was definitely recovering. 'And it's true. I would not like being drowned at all.

331

And only select persons gain admittance to the royal bathing chamber.'

Gawain giggled, mostly from relief.

'But he wasn't drowned just in water,' said Phryne.

'Indeed?' asked Rupert.

'Extra data,' she told him, apologetically. 'I started the breathing process, so I kissed him first. Sorry,' she said to Gawain. 'And the taste in my mouth was champagne.'

'You had been drinking it,' said Rupert, testing the hypothesis.

'No, I was drinking gin and tonic. Quite a distinct taste. Not only champagne but the Pol Roget. An unforgettable wine.'

'Which I'm rapidly going off,' murmured Mark.

'Which means,' said John, 'that someone dotted him a good one, shoved him into the bathtub, ran the water, then opened his mouth and poured champagne into it until he drowned.'

'That's it,' said Rupert. 'Any idea who might want you dead?' he asked Mark.

'I really can't think of anyone,' he said sadly. 'I thought I was among friends.'

'You'll have a headache,' said John. 'But you aren't concussed. Take some aspirin. Rest for the night. If you don't feel better by morning, call me. I'm in room seventeen.'

'Take two aspirin and call me in the morning?' said Mark, and began to laugh helplessly. Gawain joined in, wobbly giggles.

'Just so,' said Rupert, and escorted John from the room. He was already whispering into John's ear as they left the gathering.

'That's it for the night, darlings,' Phryne told the party. 'Aunty Mark needs her beauty sleep. Why not take a bottle home? And package up all this food, it's too good to waste.'

'You can all come back to my place,' offered Tommy. 'Just down the street. My dad's away.'

Slowly, gossiping, the choir scavenged the feast with the thoroughness of ants at an unguarded picnic and went away. Phryne saw them all leave. None of them had the wet arms and shirtfront which the murderer must have had. Phryne made sure that the rooms were empty and saw herself out.

That had been interesting. Someone had tried to kill Mark, who had no enemies. And wasn't a conductor. And Leonard was still in jail.

But she had been privileged to see John Wilson at work again. And so had Rupert. He would never look at his lover in that dismissive way again.

On the whole, a good night. Everyone, at least, was still alive.

CHAPTER NINETEEN

Is death in hell more death than death in heaven?

Wallace Stevens
'For an Old Woman in a Wig'

'So,' said Robinson, 'the murderer must have left early. None of the people you saw were or had been wet.'

'No. It was early in the night so they were all clothed . . . no, I am not going to elaborate. Clothed in what they had worn to the party.'

'Right,' said Jack, grinning at what Phryne was not going to elaborate on.

'Only Mark was wearing a costume. A tunic and a sheet. He was still wearing the tunic when he was in the bath. He had been hit over the head, then rolled into the tub. The assailant needn't even have had to be very tall. Or very strong. There's a knack to moving an inert body. I have it myself.'

Jack Robinson suppressed another smile.

'I can see how that might be handy,' he told her. 'But I

don't reckon you could manhandle a hundred and fifty-odd pounds of bloke that far all by yourself.'

'Lie on the floor,' ordered Phryne.

He looked at her. She was serious. He did as she ordered, lying flat on his back. He hoped that Phryne's family would not come in.

They came in, of course—Dot, Jane, Ruth and Tinker. They stopped. They stared. Jack tried to sit up.

'Stay still,' said Phryne sternly. 'You have just been hit on the head and rendered momentarily unconscious. I have to move fast, so I can drown you before you start to wake up. Imagine that sofa is the bathtub. Are you imagining it?'

'Yes,' said Jack, aware of four sets of fascinated eyes riveted on the scene.

'I can't dead-lift you; you're too heavy and I'm not strong enough. So I use your own body to move you. Here is a rigid lever, knee to hip. So I use that . . .' She forced his knee down and to one side, and pushed. His body rolled with it. 'Then I use your shoulder and spine—they're all attached, see, your skeleton is a frame—and do this.'

Another shove, and he rolled onto the sofa. The minions applauded.

Jack sat up. 'All right, I was wrong. Where on earth did you learn to do that?'

'Loading stretchers on the Western Front,' said Phryne. 'It's called a *point d'appui*. A point of balance. So, as you see, the murderer might be anyone. I just need to find out who left that party early. They must have been wet. Someone might have noticed, though choirs do tend to be wrapped up in each other.'

'How did you do that, Miss Phryne?' asked Jane. 'Can you show me?'

'With your knowledge of anatomy it should be a cinch,'

Phryne told her. 'But not now, and not with poor Detective Inspector Robinson. He's embarrassed enough to be going on with.'

'No, really,' said Jack, blushing to show that he wasn't embarrassed at all. 'Do you think this attempted murder might be . . . might be because Mr Henty is . . .'

'An invert?' asked Phryne. 'Surely not. Anyone meeting him for more than seven seconds would know that. If they objected they wouldn't go to his party. Probably wouldn't be in the choir, either. It's well known that he is a general favourite.'

'But that method, that opening his mouth and pouring champagne down his throat, that's . . .'

'Personal?' asked Phryne. 'Yes, it is. And he hasn't any rejected lovers floating around. I asked specially.'

'What if he approached some bloke who doesn't bat for that team, and the other bloke took . . .'

'Belated, elaborate, vicious revenge?' asked Phryne. 'It's possible. Just not very likely. Aunty Mark's usually pretty specific in his tastes. He wants someone who wants him in return. He wouldn't ask anyone of whom he wasn't pretty sure. He'd be too easy to blackmail. Look what happened to Oscar Wilde. They all walk a knife's edge every day. Anyway, the evening hadn't got to the invitation-only part. But I shall think about it.'

'Good,' said Jack. 'Can I get up now?'

'Of course, my dear,' said Phryne, extending a hand. 'We may now consider you thoroughly drowned.'

Ruth, at this statement, threw herself into Robinson's arms. 'Just don't drown for real,' she sobbed.

Jack patted her. 'What's the matter with you, now, Ruthie?' he asked gently. 'What's come to my good girl?'

'I just saw you drowned when Miss Phryne said that. I could see how it might happen. And I like you,' said Ruth.

Jack hugged her. 'I like you too,' he told her, offering her his handkerchief. 'Wipe your eyes now. I promise not to get drowned.'

'Never?' she demanded blurrily.

'As far as I can manage it,' he assured her.

Jane, rigid with disapproval, had withdrawn to the parlour. Tinker didn't know where to look so sent Molly over to lick Ruth better. Molly obeyed and Ruth laughed as the warm tongue washed her face. Then Dot took Ruth away for some tea and iron tonic.

Jack let her go. Phryne fanned herself.

'What was that about?' asked Robinson. 'Poor little thing!'

'She has a gentle tender heart, poor girl, and she imagined you drowned rather too vividly,' explained Phryne. 'And she likes you, so she was upset. You reacted correctly, Jack dear. But I and my family are really putting our backs into embarrassing you today, aren't we? Need I apologise?'

'For you manhandling me and then having a pretty girl cry over my corpse?' asked Robinson. 'No fear!'

'Nice,' said Phryne. 'Tea or beer?'

'Better be tea,' said Robinson. 'Or maybe some of that coffee?'

'Coffee it is,' said Phryne. 'I'll have some too.' And Mr Butler withdrew.

'Thing is,' remarked Robinson, 'that this is the third murderous assault connected with that choir. Shouldn't they just abandon this concert?'

'If they do that, we will never find out who is doing this.' Phryne sipped her drink. Homemade lemonade and ice, lovely.

337

'We have a new conductor tonight. Patrick Bell. I shall arrange a guard for him.'

'But you can't trust any of the choristers!' objected Jack.

'I know two who are completely innocent,' said Phryne. 'And one more who probably is. None of them would have attacked Aunty Mark. And they are the requisite Big Blokes. If they shadow him at all times, he should be safe enough, and we might catch the killer. Otherwise they will have to disband, and that would be a pity. Besides, I want to sing this oratorio.'

'Have it your own way,' sighed Robinson. 'Keep me posted.'

'I will,' said Phryne.

Robinson drank his coffee. It was real good stuff. And it was nice to know that someone would weep at his funeral.

•

'Right, let's get started,' said Patrick Bell. He was a middle-sized, rangy welterweight with cropped brown hair and an easy manner. Phryne was disposed to approve of him. He was conducting from the choral score, for a start. He had no floppy hair to push back and so far he had shown no signs of licking his fingers.

His deep blue eyes flashed briefly over the choir. 'I don't know what you've been doing with this work so far, but here's how it looks from where I'm standing. You're a small choir, and I'm told you are really good singers. So while we don't have the forces to do a huge Sir Thomas Beecham production number out of this, that doesn't matter.' His thin lips curved in a momentary grin. 'Because I don't think that's what Mendelssohn wanted. This is a work of light and shade. You may have noticed, for instance, that the recitatives are very spare and filled with silences. If he'd wanted to do Handel-style recits with first inversion chords with the left hand, he would have written them. He knew how to. He just didn't want that. I've had some of the soloists clenching their fingers in mock anguish while they sang them, and that's not good. You have to sing the silences in Mendelssohn. There are moments of comedy, there are moments of savagery, and there are choruses of angelic bliss. I want you to sing "He Shall Give His Angels", and "He That Shall Endure to the End" as if you were little angels flapping your heavenly wings. Barely any vibrato, please: just a little bit of colour on top. And if you can sing them the way I think Mendelssohn wanted, then I'll consider giving you "Cast Thy Burden" as well. That's usually done as a bravura quartet, but I'd like to see it as another angelic chorus. So let's hear you sing "He That Shall Endure", please.'

Fair enough. Another Mendelssohn purist. The chorus picked up their scores, took a deep breath, and began to sing.

Matthew had done well to take them over the lumpy bits over and over again. The entries were still a little ragged, but the bulk of the notes were there and in the right place. The conductor stopped them seldom, always to go back over a large chunk of music, so that the alterations merged into the whole and made sense. He did not swear. He did not abuse them. He did not yell. At most, he winced occasionally. His beat was as clear and regular as a metronome. He knew exactly what he wanted, and meant to get it.

Yes, Phryne approved of Patrick Bell. So did the professor. He played Schubert lieder for the soloists to sing during tea break. Tabitha and Caterina sang 'The Brook' to general applause.

'Hello,' said Patrick Bell to Phryne. 'You're the famous Miss Fisher, aren't you? Pleased to meet you.'

'Delighted,' said Phryne. She was, too.

Phryne shook hands. Tommy and Oliver flanked the

conductor, who was beginning to look a little beset, even overshadowed.

'You chaps couldn't find something else to do for a moment, could you?' he asked.

'Miss Fisher said to stay with you,' said Tommy. 'So I'm staying.'

'And me,' said Oliver. 'We always do what Miss Fisher tells us.'

'I did,' Phryne told Patrick Bell. 'Because you are a very good conductor and we don't want you to go the way of the other two.'

'I heard about that,' said Patrick.

'So,' Phryne rejoined, 'you have a bodyguard. They are responsible for your body, and not for anyone else's, and while you're with us, you aren't going anywhere without them.'

'Oh,' said Patrick. 'That's very kind of you, Miss Fisher, but I can take—'

'Care of yourself?' she finished. 'So could Tregennis and James. And Mark Henty.'

'God, don't say anything's happened to Aunty Mark?' gasped Bell. 'Best voice in Australia. Nice chap, too. Even though he's "so". I was looking forward to his Elijah, it ought to be tremendous. He's a treasure. That baritone with a tenor, almost clarinet quality!'

'He's all right,' soothed Phryne. 'But someone tried to kill him last night. And he's another big strong man who can take care of himself.'

'I get the point, Miss Fisher,' conceded Bell.

'Good, because the next time I was having to say "big strong man" it was going to be "big stwong man" and no one wants me to do that,' she told him. 'Scorn is not good for the voice.'

'Neither is getting murdered,' observed Tommy.

'Too right,' said Oliver.

Together they constituted a wall of muscle and it might take a siege engine to get through them to Bell. And Phryne doubted her murderer had brought a ballista with him. She noted that Leonard was back, looking nervous. No one was talking to him. He bustled up to Patrick with a sheaf of notes about Mendelssohn and entered into a ferocious discussion. Discussions raised no welts. Leonard was unarmed and either Tommy or Oliver could flatten him like a bedsheet with one blow of a mighty fist.

Rehearsal began again. Bell stopped the choir.

'No, no,' he said. 'You want to sound round, round vowels. Not back country Australian,' he drawled. 'You must have respect for the language you are singing.'

'Then why aren't we singing it in German?' sniped Leonard. 'It was written in German.'

'Because we want the audience to understand the message,' replied Bell. Leonard didn't seem to have any effect on him at all, though Leonard drove Phryne up the wall. 'The message is faith and love and truth and peace shall conquer. No one who lived through the last war would associate peace, truth and love with German.'

There was a clash of notes as someone slammed both hands down on the piano keys. Then Professor Szabo staggered out from behind his instrument. A long, sharp dart fell from a blowpipe in his grasp. He shuffled forward, fell on his knees at Patrick's feet, and took his hand. Oliver and Tommy moved closer. Phryne broke ranks to kick aside the weapon and draw her little gun.

'I couldn't kill you,' wept Professor Szabo. 'You understand Mendelssohn.'

Rehearsal, after that, was abandoned. Patrick Bell, rather

shaken, sat down with Professor Szabo while several choristers went to find a telephone to summon Detective Inspector Robinson from his cosy home, where he was doubtless enquiring after the state of health of his orchids. He would want to be in on this. Phryne kept the little gun to hand. Professor Szabo might be peaceable enough at present, but if he had managed to kill both Tregennis and brought down the 'big stwong' men all by himself, then he had to be closely watched. Phryne would back her Beretta against anything, however big or strong.

The old man was so unthreatening. He was shrunken and drunken and running out of years as fast as a mayfly runs out of days.

'Tell me, Professor,' she said, patting his hand. 'You found Tregennis already dying—I understand that; the man was a pig.'

'I just stuff the music down his throat. He never bother to learn it properly. I take the pages out of my own score. I know this music in my bones. I don't need a score,' said the old man.

'Right, and I am sure that Henry James was a cruel and stupid man, which is a bad combination, I agree.'

'He butchered the music,' snarled the professor. Some of the choir stepped back onto the toes of those behind. Suddenly, they were beginning to believe that the old prof might be a murderer after all.

'Yes, he did,' said Phryne in a voice as smooth as cream. 'Where did you get the arsenic?'

'I work a while in a glass factory when I came here,' he replied, still holding Bell's hand. Tommy was watching him very closely. If he produced a knife or something, Tommy could stop him. Tommy liked feeling brave. 'I keep a little arsenic, in case things get too bad for me. They tell me all about how dangerous it is. So I borrow orchestral score, and I paint it on pages. If he stopped licking, then he goes free. Until I think of something else. But he didn't, he was a pig, and—'

'All right,' Phryne commented. 'I understand. But what had Mr Henty done to you? He's a great singer.'

'Pervert,' snarled the old man. 'He made fun of the oratorio with his Pirate King. And he was going to sing the prophet, the holy man! Elijah is a prophet of God! This is holy music. And he had his parties and his friends and his . . . his . . .'

'Success,' prompted Phryne. 'His admirers.'

Professor Szabo showed the stumps of yellowing teeth.

'What right had a pervert to admirers? People love him! And he would corrupt the music, the divine music!'

'So you knocked him out, stuck him in the tub, and poured champagne down his throat?' asked Phryne. Patrick Bell was beginning to feel beset again. The old man's clasp on his hand was hot and his pianist's fingers were very strong.

'I did!' said the old man. 'I did it and I am proud—proud! But you,' he said to Bell, 'you understand. I was going to fire that dart into you. No one would have known where it came from. Then the concert would be cancelled. No one would be able to lay filthy hands on my Elijah.'

'But you liked my conducting,' said Patrick Bell.

'Yes! You understand Mendelssohn. The silences. The angels.'

'So you couldn't kill me,' said Patrick steadily.

'No,' confessed Professor Szabo. He burst into tears.

•

Jack Robinson arrived, was apprised of the situation, and took the professor away. The choir sat in the hall and sang rounds and madrigals. *'Aprille is in my mistress' face,'* sang Tommy to Caterina. *'But in her heart, but in her heart a cold December.'*

They smiled at each other.

Singers, thought Phryne. Well, that concludes that puzzle, and neither Rupert nor I could solve it. The prof had left Mark's party, covering his wet shirt with his coat, before the alarm had been raised. And everyone was so used to his unexpected arrivals and abrupt departures that they didn't even notice him.

Calliope was weeping. She was being consoled by Bones.

'It's all right,' said the young man. 'It's like I told you. He isn't fit to plead.'

'That's not why I'm crying,' she informed him. 'But never mind. I would like a hug anyway.'

Bones obliged.

'Oh, Lord,' sighed Matthew, burying his head in his hands.

'What seems to be the problem?' asked Phryne.

'Now we don't have a pianist,' said Matthew. 'We can manage all right for the rehearsals, but who's going to play the piano in the concert?'

'There is,' Phryne told him, 'a concert-level pianist presently in Melbourne who owes me rather a large favour.'

'Will he need to be paid?' asked Matthew.

'He already has been,' Phryne told him.

•

Phryne telephoned the Windsor and told John Wilson that she had to see him and Rupert at once.

'Very well, my dear. Is this another medical emergency?'

'No, it's the solution to the murders, and Rupert didn't deduce it, and neither did I. You will want to see his face as I tell him and I want to ask him for a favour.'

'I do and you shall,' replied John. 'Would you like to come up to our room?'

So quickly had it become 'our' room.

'I'll be right there,' said Phryne. 'Order me a very large gin. And maybe a little tonic. If you insist. The choir will be flocking over soon, so prepare for a noisy night.'

'I'm prepared,' chuckled John.

•

'Before we go to Aunty Mark's—' Patrick halted the general movement to the door with the conductor's raised hands; obediently, everyone stopped '—we have to decide what to tell him. About the murders.'

'What should we tell him?' asked Tabitha.

'That a mad man tried to kill him because he mocked Mendelssohn with his Pirate King,' said Bell, looking at them all in turn. Heads nodded. Tutts were tutted. No one wanted to flay Aunty Mark with Professor Szabo's blistering hatred.

'But . . .' Leonard started. The entire chorus turned as one and glared at him. He struggled. 'The truth . . .'

'Leave the truth to Mendelssohn and God,' said Bell.

'But . . .' Leonard was wriggling.

Tommy dropped a meaty hand on his shoulder. 'We aren't going to hurt Aunty Mark's feelings,' he told Leonard. 'Because if we do, he won't sing for us. And we want him to sing for us. Also, we really like him. Am I making myself clear?'

'But . . .' Leonard's voice was a whisper. Holding in a piece of information this juicy would give him an ulcer, he knew it.

Tommy leaned down so that he could speak into Leonard's ear.

'If,' he whispered, 'Aunty Mark learns about this from you, I will pound you into putty.'

'And I will help him,' whispered Oliver into his other ear.

'Really smooth putty,' elaborated Tommy. 'Like they use to fill cracks between floorboards.'

345

'All right!' squeaked Leonard.

'Not a word, gesture, lifted eyebrow, pursed lips, grimace, knowing smirk, hint, allusion or written communication?' demanded Isabelle, who worked in a lawyer's office.

'No!' squealed Leonard.

'Good,' said Patrick. 'You know, I could really do with a drink. Several drinks. Big ones. Are your rehearsals always this exciting?'

•

When she reached their door, John let Phryne in, Rupert handed her a very large gin to which a little tonic had been added, and both escorted her to a chair.

'You solved it?' asked Rupert. His voice was quite even, but a little rancour was leaking out at the edges.

'No,' confessed Phryne, who had much less invested in always being right. 'I didn't have a clue, it was a complete surprise.'

Rupert relaxed a little. 'Not enough data?' he asked.

'Precisely, and a very interesting series of misdirections, the first of which was, of course, that in Tregennis's case there were two murderers.'

'*Novus actus interveniens*,' said Rupert. He looked like a large, well-fed cat, lounging on this untouched bed—this must be the room they weren't sleeping in—and plumping a pillow for John, who needed to rest his leg. Without being asked. It would be strange having a lover who could anticipate one's every wish. Intoxicating, in fact. Like this drink. She felt she had to translate.

'Which, learned colleague, is Latin for "a new act intervening". If the violinist had been the only murderer, then we would have found Tregennis on the floor, an obvious victim of a heart attack from chronic ingrained bad temper, and it would not have been investigated,' said Phryne. 'He might not even have been examined.'

'Possibly,' murmured Rupert. 'If the medical examiner was busy.'

'Indeed,' agreed Phryne. 'Then there was James. A noxious individual. Plethora of enemies. Hosts of them. It would be hard to find anyone who *didn't* want to kill him. But then there was Mr Henty. A darling. Everyone loved him. And that attempted murder seemed more personal, more vicious, more—'

'Manic,' supplied John. 'An outburst of crazy hatred.'

'Exactly. The act of a fanatic. I could not imagine who it was; and neither could you, Rupert?'

'No,' he admitted abruptly. 'I could not deduce. Too many variables.'

'Quite. So all I could think of was to provide my new conductor with bodyguards, Tommy and Oliver, both huge, as a wall between him and the killer. It would take time to dig a hole through either of them and someone was bound to notice.'

'A good notion,' agreed John. 'So what happened?'

'I shall a tale unfold,' said Phryne with relish, and unfolded it.

She was pleased with the result. John and Rupert gradually, perhaps without noticing, drew closer and closer together, until they were actually embracing, shoulder to shoulder, backs against the headboard. John had commented as she spoke, calling upon his God repeatedly, but Sheffield had not said a word. Phryne finished her drink.

'You could not have found him,' said John. 'You didn't have enough clues. Either of you.'

'Insufficient data,' agreed Rupert. 'They hate us,' he added flatly.

'Some of them,' agreed Phryne. 'Especially if you limit your search to deranged Hungarian maniacs with an obsession for Mendelssohn. This is a small set,' she told him, smiling.

'I suppose so,' he replied, and smiled in return. He was more beautiful, now. More present. The Sons of God, she recalled, who descended to earth and fell in love with humans. Rupert was definitely one of them.

'And now, I have a favour to ask,' she told him.

'Ask,' he said.

Phryne asked.

•

In the morning Phryne woke with a headache and a sense of a job well done. Or at least, done. And neatly packaged in brown paper, tied with a ribbon, and posted to the correct address. Dot brought her coffee and croissant and she sipped and nibbled with pleasure.

'Detective Inspector Robinson, a huge bloke who said to call him Tommy, and Hugh are downstairs,' she told her employer.

'Not a new problem, Dot? I'm out of solutions and I have a headache,' said Phryne.

'Here's your aspirin, Miss, and they're just sitting down to breakfast. You've got time to recover a bit. You must have got home late,' said Dot.

'Yes, it was a rather wild party. Did you hear the end of the mystery?' asked Phryne, taking the powders and drinking down a large glass of water.

'Yes, Miss, Hugh told me. That Mr Sheffield didn't work it out, either, Miss.'

'As long as it was resolved, Dot, I don't care who worked it out. At least it's over.'

'Yes, Miss, it's over. The prisoner killed himself last night in the holding cells. He had arsenic concealed in a coat button. He's dead.'

'That's that, then. Poor old man. A Borgia plot and a Borgia death. I think I had better have a coolish shower. That ought to set me up for the day. Wait, Dot—if Szabo is dead, why are Jack and Hugh here with Tommy? Apart from the pleasure of our company, of course.'

Dot blushed. 'The old man's room. He's left all his property to this Tommy. And Hugh says that Detective Inspector Robinson wants a stickybeak.'

'So do I,' replied Phryne. 'Back in a tick. Find me some easily washed clothes suitable for poking around sordid places,' she added as she vanished, naked, into the bathroom.

When she came back Dot gave her a cotton skirt and loose coat in dark blue, which Phryne had never much liked, and a faded blush-pink blouse.

'Good,' said Phryne, flinging on her garments. 'If this ensemble gets destroyed, it will be no loss. See you later, Dot dear.'

●

Collins Street, thought Phryne; my life has lately revolved around this bit of Collins Street. The room was, as she had predicted, sordid. The landlord of number eighty-eight was lounging in the doorway, eyes alert for easily abstracted valuables. Robinson ordered Hugh to go downstairs with him and pick up anything he might have taken from this room 'for safekeeping'. The landlord sighed. Cops. He had better hand over the engraved watch, the two pounds ten and the cufflinks.

But he was keeping the odd seven and threepence. A man had his pride.

The room stank of old alcohol and perpetual misery and unwashed socks. Tommy, exerting his strength, broke through eight layers of paint and hauled the window open. The clanging of trams drifted in with the smell of ozone.

The floor of the room was largely carpeted with bottles. Tommy, a tidy soul, was packing them into a box so that no one turned an ankle. The bed was indescribable. Professor Szabo had not gone in for laundry. Phryne found a clear space in the nook which held clothes and dropped into it the sheets, a filthy shirt, some appalling underwear, threadbare socks, dreadful trousers. The only thing actually hung up in this wardrobe were his concert clothes, safely enclosed in the cleaner's paper bag. The only pair of shoes on the floor were concert shoes, polished shiny and worn through, their soles complemented with cardboard.

Otherwise there were bottles. Jack took the drawers of the dressing table out and laid them on the stained, denuded mattress.

'Hello, hello,' he said. He had found a small shagreen case.

'A medal?' asked Phryne. Jack opened it. The hinge broke. This hadn't been opened in a long time.

'I don't know that one,' said Tommy.

'*Eisernes Kreuz*. It's an Iron Cross,' whispered Phryne. 'And here's his citation.' She puzzled through the German which described the feat for which the honour had been awarded. 'He was a doctor,' she told Tommy. 'He rescued the wounded under fire. On the Western Front. That's how he knew how to move unconscious bodies. His name was Maximilian Schneider.'

'Tailor,' said Robinson. 'That's what Schneider means.'

'And so does Szabo,' said Phryne. 'He ran away from the

Great War. He had been a concert pianist with Beecham and then he joined up. And we know what that war did to people.'

'Poor old bugger,' said Tommy. 'I should send this back to his people. Any letters or anything? Did he have any people?'

'I can't see anything else. Here are concert programs, more concert programs—yes, see, here's his name. He did play with Beecham. Maximilian Schneider. I think he's kept every one.'

'Put them in this bag,' said Tommy. 'I'll look after them.'

Phryne packed the carefully preserved paper into the cloth bag. 'And here's a letter. Read a lot; look at the wearing in the folds. A love letter, perhaps, to be so treasured. Oh,' she said.

'To a very fine pianist, with thanks for a superb performance,' Tommy read over Phryne's shoulder.

'It must have been with this,' said Hugh, who had retrieved the landlord's loot. He opened the back of a gold watch. '*To Maximilian Schneider, a fine pianist, Beecham.* Gosh,' added Hugh.

Phryne was flooded with a sense of the limitless tragedies of the world, which was soaked in bitter tears. She shook herself.

'Right, nothing else here but razor and toothbrush and cheap soap. You?' she asked Robinson.

'No, just some newspapers—no letters, no passport. He must have jumped ship. Left his old life behind.'

'But he couldn't leave music,' said Tommy. 'You can never leave music behind.'

This was such a profound comment from someone whom Phryne had considered simple that she stared at him.

'I can understand what Caterina sees in you,' she told him.

'Yes, well, anyone got time for a drink?' he asked, blushing. 'I've got two pounds ten.'

'And I'll get the rest of the money from that landlord on the way out,' said Jack.

CHAPTER TWENTY

Just as my fingers on these keys
Make music, so the selfsame sounds
On my spirit make a music, too.

Music is feeling, then, not sound;
And thus it is that what I feel
Here in this room, desiring you,

Thinking of your blue-shadowed silk,
Is music.

Wallace Stevens
'Peter Quince at the Clavier'

John knew that the task would be hard, but he was resolved to go through with it anyway. Whatever Sheffield might say about the matter, Phryne had given them each other, and therefore her favour must be repaid. He was firm. He was determined. Rupert had never seen him like that before. He agreed.

But that didn't mean he had to like it.

'The creaky old heap of strings will be miserably out of tune,' he protested, as they went in the front door at the Town Hall. The piano was on stage. It was a highly polished

Bechstein Grand. And the piano tuner was just playing a brisk Irish jig to test the tuning.

'Wrong,' said John, with relish. He so seldom got to say that to Sheffield.

The piano tuner, led by his little daughter, tapped his way down the aisle. He stopped near Rupert. The little girl whispered something. The piano tuner said, "Scuse me, mate,' took Rupert's hand, spread it over his own, and pinched the base of the thumb. Rupert, unused to Australians, was at a loss and did not move, frozen with outrage. 'Yair,' said the old man. 'You'll be bonzer. Beaut piano. Nice hands.'

The little girl smiled shyly at John and led her father away. Rupert scrubbed his right hand down the side of his trousers to wipe off the contaminating touch.

'He was just being friendly,' John told him. 'He's blind, he couldn't just look at your hands. Come along. Play me a song.'

'I am sadly out of practice,' protested Rupert. 'I probably won't be able to remember how to play.'

'Try,' insisted John. 'I'm not critical.'

He knew that was exactly the wrong thing to say, which was why he said it. Rupert bridled, pulled up his cuffs, and laid hands on the keys. He played a C chord. Then he played all the notes on the keyboard, one after another, a long ordered tumble of sharps and flats.

'Adequate,' said Rupert.

He closed his eyes and instead of the loud, flashy thing with a lot of chords which John expected, he played a little music box tune by Couperin. It was charming.

'Nice,' said John. 'Play some more, love?'

'Requests?' asked Rupert. He flexed his hands. Nice hands, the blind man had said. It had been far too long since he had touched a keyboard. And now he could play for John. That was an unexpected pleasure.

'You're one with culture,' said John. 'Mozart? That Russian feller?'

'Mozart is the king,' said Rupert, and began to play, from memory, the piano concerto he loved the most, K 595. The last movement. He found the fact that he loved Mozart and now loved John interesting. Loving John did not mean that he loved Mozart less. Curious. He was not, however, intending to add anyone else to his portfolio. Mozart and John would do nicely.

John listened. No such decorative creature had sat down at the piano since Liszt died, he thought. Tall, slim, tumble of raven curls, pale skin, elegant profile. Rupert was completely focused on the music. His violet eyes were open and tranced. His hands flew. The music built all around him, like the golden ladder which took Jacob to heaven.

Other people had drifted into the auditorium, attracted by the music. Cleaners docked their brooms, the ticket seller left her box, the carpenter put down his tools. Twenty musicians left their backstage rehearsal to lurk in the wings and listen with appreciation.

'This bloke, who is he?' asked French Horn of Trumpet. 'Why haven't we heard of him before?'

'He's that mathematician the Harmony hired to do their *Elijah*,' said First Violin, unconsciously straightening her skirt and combing back her hair. First violins are always well informed. 'He's come to try out the piano. The door keeper told me.'

'Jeez, he's bloody good,' said Percussion. 'How do Harmony rate him? He's concert level.'

'Lucky,' said First Violin. 'I suppose. We'd better get this *Elijah* right.'

354

'Yair,' agreed First Clarinet. 'I don't think he'd like it if we messed it up. Someone go and get Greg. P'raps we ought to have a bit of a rehearse with this bloke. What's his name?'

'Sheffield,' said First Violin. 'Rupert Sheffield. Gosh, isn't he gorgeous?'

'Good player,' agreed First Clarinet.

First Violin whispered, 'That wasn't what I meant, Jimmy,' as the concerto came to an end. Rupert shook his hands and wiped his hair out of his eyes, and became aware that he was being applauded.

He scowled. Then he stood up and bowed to the cleaners and the carpenters. And John. John returned the bow.

'God, that was marvellous,' he enthused.

'I'm a little rusty. Eleven wrong notes and one transposed phrase.'

'I never heard one note out of place,' said John enthusiastically.

'And neither did we,' said First Violin, who had ventured out onto the broad expanse of empty stage, unsupported. 'Hello,' she added, quailing a little under the violet gaze. 'We're the orchestra.'

Seventeen, if that, female, violinist (callus under jaw), nervous, Australian, prodigy, lonely, poor, orchestra is her family, thought Rupert.

'Only one of you?' asked Rupert. He smiled. John exhaled the breath he had been holding. Being loved had had a wonderful effect on Rupert's manners.

'There's twenty of us,' she explained as the others came onto the stage.

'So I see,' said Rupert.

'And this is our conductor, Mr Kale.'

'Mr Kale,' said Rupert politely.

'Heard you playing,' said Greg Kale, a short, perspiring,

355

plump man with sandy hair. 'Lovely. You played with an orchestra much?'

'No,' said Rupert, concealing the fact that he had never played with an orchestra at all.

'Right, right, you were recital, weren't you? Suppose we do a run-through of *Elijah* now, and we get the feel of playing with you.'

'I don't have the piano score,' said Rupert.

'No worries, mate, here she is,' said Mr Kale briskly, plucking the score from a pile of them. 'Now, Pat Bell will be conducting the actual performance, due to me losing to him when we cut cards for it—I reckon he's got a dodgy pack; I always lose to him. But my boys and girls are good. Some of 'em are bloody good. And I won't have 'em forgotten for a lot of bloody screechers hogging the limelight. So we need to get this one right.'

Rupert sat down again. John rose and stood beside him. He couldn't read enough music to know when to turn a page, but he and Rupert had devised a system of nods so they worked very well together. The only real difference in their partnership, John thought, as he propped his stick so that he could easily lean on it and turned to the first movement of *Elijah*, was that now I can tell him how much I love him, and he can tell me.

'Sheffield?' he asked, under cover of the orchestra dropping music stands, swearing, and accusing each other of stealing their favourite chair. (The mystery of how the timpani sticks ended up in the cello case never did get solved.)

'John?' breathed Sheffield.

'I don't think I've ever been so happy in my life.'

'Nor me,' said Rupert, and very gently laid his hand on John's thigh.

First Violin saw this gesture, as she came to the piano for her tuning notes, and sighed.

John heard her, and looked up into her eyes. 'What's your name, my dear?' he asked.

'Jasmine,' she replied, tightening a string.

'There'll be someone for you, Jasmine,' he told her.

'How do you know?' she demanded in a fierce undertone.

'Because there was someone for me,' said John. 'When I never thought there would be.'

She smiled. Rupert murmured an agreement.

Jasmine took her bow and played a long, clear, heartfelt A.

•

From 'As God the Lord of Israel Liveth' through 'He Shall Give His Angels Charge Over Thee', from 'Baal, We Cry to Thee' through 'Them That Shall Endure' all the way to 'And Then Shall Your Light Break Forth', everyone agreed that the concert was a triumph.

It had been sold out, as news like Rupert Sheffield and Mark Henty got around in musical circles. Jack Robinson had quite enjoyed it, especially since his killer was caught, the murders all explained, and the poor old man who had done them was safely in the morgue and had no need to worry about being hanged. No doubt he was now explaining his actions to Satan, who was reputed to enjoy a good tune.

Dot liked the sacred quality of the libretto, and Tinker loved angel music. Ruth liked the way that they all looked, the ladies in long black skirts and white shirts, the gentlemen in black trousers and white shirts. The soloists in liturgical colours: Chloe (soprano) in green, Caterina (soprano) also in green, but darker, Tabitha (alto) in purple, the bass Oliver with a gold rosette, and the tenor Matthew with a white one.

Jane was uninterested in music. She wondered if Dr Wilson was straining his stitches and overexerting his injured leg by standing so long next to Sheffield, turning the pages. Why turn pages? Couldn't someone invent a device like a piano roll, which scrolled the music past the player's eyes? That would mean no one would have to stand there and turn pages. They could sit down and not hurt their sore leg.

Wasted effort made Jane cross. On the other hand, her chess opponent looked very handsome in his beautiful black suit. Savile Row again, she assumed. Jane could hear the ladies around her, discussing not the music or the execution of it, but how very delectable Sheffield was. Jane rolled her eyes. Sheffield was spoken for. Couldn't they see how his eyes were resting on his page-turner? No one else's approval mattered to Rupert Sheffield.

The choir and the orchestra grinned at each other, light-headed. 'We got away with it' could have summed up their mood. 'We just sang way above our usual ability! Where did *that* come from?'

The orchestra felt the same. No one had lost their place, those tricky entries were always marked with a good downbeat from this Bell bloke, who wasn't a half-bad conductor, and the choir had mostly kept up. The piano had been close to faultless and Jasmine had played as though possessed by the spirit of Paganini.

Everyone bowed. The applause went on. The soloists walked off. The clapping continued. The soloists came back. Phryne heard Mark say, 'Three curtain calls, darlings, then I'm off to the party.'

He was right. Three curtain calls, and the soloists walked off and did not come back. Followed by the orchestra. The conductor bowed one last time and stepped off the stage. Followed by the choir.

'That ought to keep us for the winter,' Matthew remarked to Oliver. 'We sold out the Town Hall!'

'Some of it's down to that Pommy bloke,' conceded Tommy. 'And that little girl with the violin.'

'And some of it is down to us!' cheered Calliope, embracing Oliver. 'And Pat!' She embraced him, too. It was an embracing sort of night. John, who felt the need to sit down for a bit, fended off questions from Jane as to how badly his leg hurt.

'Nothing at all, I'm just a bit tired. Wasn't that a marvellous concert? Haven't heard better in London.'

'John, are you all right?' asked Rupert anxiously.

'I'm just sitting down for a bit, my dear chap. You played very well.'

'I have never played with an orchestra before,' confessed Rupert. Jane noted that his curls were damp. It was hot under the lights. 'Exhilarating! I kept expecting something hideous to happen.'

'But it didn't. It sounded fine!' said Phryne. 'Rupert, John, your taxi is waiting to carry us to the hotel in style. Jane, Ruth, Tink and Dot, your taxi is waiting to ferry you to St Kilda. I shall be home late. Come along, darlings,' she said, ushering them effortlessly out of the Town Hall and into the street. 'Good night.' She waved and her family was driven away. Cec opened the car door and allowed Rupert to help John in. Somehow he didn't mind as much as he had used to that Rupert knew how crippled he was. Phryne planted herself in the front seat next to the driver.

'Windsor, Cec dear. Did you enjoy the music?'

'Beaut,' commented Cec, the hand-rolled cigarette never moving from the corner of his mouth. 'They did real good in that tricky chorus, where if you ain't careful it sort of sounds like a waltz. "Thanks Be to God, He Laveth the Thirsty Land". Mendelssohn ain't sugary. Bloody good work. And the orchestra was first rate, especially that little girl and her fiddle and your mate on the piano.'

'Thank you,' said Rupert faintly. He would never get used to Australia.

'And this ride's on me,' said Cec, stopping outside the Windsor. 'Thanks for the ticket.'

'My pleasure,' said Phryne. Cec let John alight at his own pace, then slammed the door and took off. Rupert took John's arm.

'You'll want to wash and change,' said Phryne.

'I will, this suit's like a sponge,' said Rupert. He had become human.

'But will you come up to the party later?'

'Certainly,' said John.

'Indeed,' replied Sheffield. 'I would like to congratulate Mr Henty on his noble performance.'

'See you then,' said Phryne and ran up the stairs, moving through groups of choristers, alight with success, and probably a bit short of oxygen. Phryne had a party in prospect, a drink and a few of the Windsor's celebrated cocktail canapés, and then she would be taking Matthew home with her. The murderer was dead, the case closed, John had his Rupert and all was gas and gaiters.

•

Aunty Mark was enthroned again. The choir milled about, intoxicated with their performance. The only sign of tension was in Gawain, who had nearly lost Mark and didn't intend to let him out of his sight ever again. He certainly would never bathe alone in the future, though that would not worry either of them.

Phryne collected a drink. She noticed that Mark had changed his brand of champagne to Veuve Clicquot, quite Phryne's own favourite. Understandably, he had lost his taste for the Pol Roget '97. Excellent wine though it was. Caterina was elated, climbing onto Tommy's shoulders and singing, *'Free from wards in Chancery, up in the air so high, so high,'* while Tommy hung onto her legs with an expression of baffled devotion which simultaneously brought tears to Phryne's eyes and made her giggle. Free indeed! Free to find another lover, free of anxiety, free of care altogether.

Which called for another drink. She turned in her concert white and black, anonymous in the crowd, and someone offered her a frosted glass.

Matthew. Oh, he was good-looking. Snub nose, broad face, golden hair which begged to be tousled—so she tousled it. Trout-pool eyes, warming into hope. Red mouth begging to be kissed.

So Phryne kissed it. Then she kissed it again. Then she drank the drink.

'Will you go home with me?' she asked.

'I would go anywhere with you,' he answered.

'A very good reply,' said Phryne. 'Agreeably unconditional.' She patted his chest and grinned at him.

A stir at the door announced the entry of Sheffield and John Wilson. There was a cheer. Rupert slid through the well-wishers to congratulate Mark. Aunty put his head on one side, suppressed a laugh, and congratulated Sheffield on his 'performance'.

John laughed and found a seat. He was instantly supplied

with drinks and food by elated choristers. Here was an audience member who could tell them how good they had been.

And John did. It was his honest opinion, which warmed their hearts.

'*Tu as joué du piano comme un ange.*' You played like an angel, said Phryne to Rupert.

'*Et tu as chanté comme une ange.*' You sang like an angel, he rejoined, violet eyes glowing.

'*Qu'en est-il de Jean?*' And what of John? asked Phryne.

He laid a hand on her shoulder, a voluntary touch. '*Tout ira bien pour Jean,*' he said. All will be well with John.

'*Pourquoi?*' asked Phryne, mesmerised.

'*Parce que John est un ange incarné.*' Because John really is an angel.

'*Tu l'as remarqué?*' Oh, you noticed? asked Phryne, patting the hand.

'*On me l'a signalé.*' It was drawn to my attention, said Rupert, and smiled a conspiratorial smile.

•

'Sing for me,' John suggested. 'I would like that.'

He was running out of compliments. They ringed him. Phryne, Matthew, Calliope, Caterina still mounted on Tommy, Oliver, Miriam, Lydia, Chloe, DavidandLobelia, Isabelle, Irene, Bones and Tabitha, Alison, Millicent, Annie, Mary, Geneva, Luke, Ophelia, Aaron, Emmeline, Maisie, Daniel Smith and Josephine, Leonard, Luigi and Julia (that's going to be an explosive mixture, thought Phryne; light the blue touch paper and retire immediately), Helen and Jenny.

'What shall we sing?' asked Matthew.

'Whatever you sing when you're happy,' said John desperately.

Sheffield rescued him. 'I heard you sing Laudate last night,' he suggested. 'Christopher Tye.'

'*Laudate nomen Domini, vos servi Domini*,' they sang, the four parts meeting and melting and joining in an entrancing way. '*Ab ortu solis usque ad occasum ejus. Decreta Dei iusta sunt, et cor exhilarant! Laudate Deum, principes, et omnes populi!*'

So they did. Praise the Lord, princes and all people. John and Rupert smiled, drank a final toast, and went back to number seventeen and their shared rhapsodies.

Thereafter the party slipped into rude songs, ruder songs, and positively obscene songs. There seemed to be no end to their repertoire.

All of which, Matthew noticed, Phryne knew. Even the one about the wheel. Even the one about the protected status of the hedgehog on shipboard. He had edged closer to her and was standing at her side when she put out a hand and asked, 'Coming?'

And he followed her, as he had said he would.

If Phryne had a plan, she always carried it out unless it was a really unwise plan, when she might think about it again. This was a good idea that needed no further consideration. Matthew was whisked through the night, admitted, and conducted through the silent house, up a flight of stairs, and into a lady's boudoir such as he had never seen.

She turned his shoulder so that he saw his face in the mirror. The reflection was crowned with ivy leaves.

'Are you a bacchante?' he asked. She kissed him in reply.

All previous, fumbling, not really sure which way to turn his head to fit that mouth, nose-banging episodes in his past were forgotten. Phryne knew exactly what she wanted. So did Matthew.

'Buttons,' she said, both hands at the front of his shirt. He tried to undo the ones on her concert shirt. They were dressed exactly alike. They resisted his fingers. Phryne flicked them open, shedding the shirt and the camisole under it. Breasts.

He had never got enough of breasts. These were perfect; they fitted into the palms of his hands. They felt indescribably lovely.

'Matt,' she breathed. 'Just remember this. I don't belong to you. I don't belong to anyone. And you don't belong to me. I just want to make love with you. Agreed?'

'Agreed,' he whispered. Of course she didn't belong to him. No one this . . . divine could belong to anyone but herself. But, oh, she was dropping the skirt, kicking off her shoes, rolling down her stockings. He grappled with his obdurate garments. Why did anyone put so many buttons on trousers? What use were they? Had he ever *asked* for buttons? Finally, he managed to divest himself of every impediment, and flung himself down on Phryne's bed, where she was waiting for him.

Naked, she was beautiful and curious. She rolled him over and studied his back, licked a line down his spine, turned him back again and threw herself onto him, like an amorous cat, sliding and purring. He grabbed a thigh and a handful of buttock and ground himself closer to her soft flesh, her smooth skin. Then he found himself engulfed in warmth, and stifled a groan in her kiss. Nipples scraped his chest. Fingers caught in his hair. He felt the strangest internal series of muscles clutch and close like a hot, wet, velvet-gloved hand. He cried out.

He found himself flat on his back, wet, panting, astounded, while Phryne nibbled meditatively on his earlobe.

'That was good,' she drawled.

'Yes!' he said.

'For a beginning,' she told him. '*Baise-moi!*'

•

When Matthew woke in the morning to the censorious glare of a black cat, which wasn't one of his black cats, his world had utterly changed. For the better.

Phryne liked happy endings.

GLOSSARY AND NOTES

'SO' accompanied by a gesture, the hand held bent from the wrist with the little finger crooked, was a universally recognised sign for a homosexual man. As was the term 'playing for the other team'. Before the useful phrase 'Are you a friend of Dorothy?', which allowed gay men to safely identify each other. There were, of course, other markers <g>, but these ones seem to have been in use since Oscar Wilde's time. Male homosexuality was illegal and punishable by imprisonment until very recently. Practitioners of the 'love that dare not speak its name' walked the edge of a razor every day, and had to be careful. Contemporary documents use both the term 'queen' and 'quean', which seems to have been pronounced differently, perhaps 'quaine'. An incomplete limerick I found in some collected letters—the first lines of which are 'There once was a pretty young quean / his suitors were often in pain'—leads me to this conclusion, though I wish the irritating person who scribbled it in a margin had scribbled the rest. How did it end? Gain, Main, Deign, Fain, Again, Vain? Rats. I have ventured to finish it in the 'naughty' style of many 1920s limericks:

There once was a pretty young quean
His lovers were often in pain
He demanded they kiss
Some of that, some of this
Again and again and again.

But it isn't history, of course. Quean was a word in the Guid Scots Tongue for a flaunting woman. One sees the attraction of the term. I would give a lot for a tape of the '20s equivalent of the 'Omi Palone' homosexual dialect of Soho, but until someone invents a reliable time machine, I am not going to get one (and the same goes for dropping in at the Library of Alexandria with a large skip)—sigh.

VERY LIGHT: a very bright starshell, sent up to guide the gun-aimers to their target. Accounts say it was a bright, bluish, very hot light, similar to lightning. Thunderstorms would later trigger shell-shock episodes in returned soldiers who had been exposed to it. Some of them were my relatives, so I am sure about this. I can't understand how anyone on the frontline got through the Great War even passingly sane.

TRENCH RAIDERS crept across no-man's-land to kill soldiers in the opposing trenches. They did not use firearms, but clubs and knives, aiming to strike silently and slide back without being detected.

PRIVATE EYE is not a modern term; see Pinkertons' emblem, the open eye, with their motto 'We never sleep'. This dates to the nineteenth century and was in common use. A common phrase for a private detective in the 1920s was private dick, which I don't like for many reasons, and 'tec', which sounds too much like 'tech' to modern readers. Just saying.

LEVITICUS AND SCRIPTURE I refer you to Luke 7 for the story of Longinus, and to Galatians chapter three for the statement that Old Testament Law is no longer applicable to those of the new Faith (ie, Christians). I too sat for long hours in church and read the Bible, and came to some of these conclusions all on my own (and for the others thank Professor Dennis Pryor, who spoke fluent Ancient Greek). The soldier who thrust a spear into Christ's side might have been called Gaius Cassius Longinus, but 'Longinus' just means 'the tall bloke', so it might have been a common name. He isn't a saint in the Catholic church but he is in the Eastern Orthodox, though there he might be spelled 'loginus', which resembles the Greek word for 'the word', 'logos'. Or the man whose lover had been healed by Christ might have found himself promptly martyred for saying that Jesus was indeed the son of God. It is now impossible to tell whether he existed or what his name was if he did.

Paul went on to make severe remarks about homosexuality, but that was flesh-hating Paul of the 'better marry than burn'. I prefer him in Galatians.

PHIZZ-GIG: an informer.

FURPHY: a rumour. In the Great War, water was carried in tanks marked Furphy and Co. They were naturally centres of gossip.

COMPTON MACKENZIE was head of British Intelligence for the Mediterranean during the Great War. He has left extensive memoirs, for one of which he was prosecuted in 1934 for breaching the Official Secrets Act. He says that British Intelligence Melbourne had an office in Collins Street but doesn't tell me where, which considering what he does impart, is annoying. I've put it at the Parliament end, rather than the legal end, for no other reason than it fitted nicely with the Scots Church Assembly Hall and the Windsor Hotel, and I have always loved those unassuming, delightful, brass-plate-decorated shops. (When I was a child I met an apricot poodle called Andre there and had orange crush at a white-painted outside table while wearing a new dress. A highlight of my youth.) *First Athenian Memories* and *Gallipoli Memories* are still valuable insights into that part of the Great War. Anyone who picks up a sly ref to a TV show on which I doted in my youth is not wrong.

Sherlock Holmes and me (a love/hate relationship)

I read all of the works of Arthur Conan Doyle as a child, including *The Lost World* and Professor Challenger, his appearances in the cross-correspondences after death, the Brigadier Gerard stories, and all of the Sherlock Holmes stories. I was mildly annoyed while I was fascinated, because what Holmes was doing—his Science of Deduction—was a common female skill and, like all female skills, was awarded no applause and even sneered at as 'women's intuition'. Picture the scene: my mother and I are working in the kitchen when my brother staggers in, white as a sheet where he isn't green, and collapses to the floor doing a very good imitation of a dying child. My mother gave him one raking, comprehensive look and said, 'I told you not to eat those apricots.' When he started throwing up it was clear that he had, indeed, climbed the apricot tree and eaten a lot of green ones, which he had been strictly forbidden to do. I was relieved. I am fond of my brother. And I was also impressed. I demanded to know how my mother knew that he hadn't been stabbed in the stomach or was dying of beri beri or the Black Death (you can imagine my reading at the time). She had to think about it, then she rattled off, all in one breath, 'Scuffs on his shoes, bark in his hair, juice stains on his T-shirt, sap on his front, bark in his fingernails, drying juice around his mouth. And he was guilty.'

That is Sherlock Holmes's deduction at its best. The basis of Holmes's method is exceedingly close observation. He needs to use deduction on criminals because they won't tell him the truth. Had my mother demanded of my brother what he had been eating, he would have denied eating anything, for the same reason as any other law-breaker. Women have deductive method because they need it. As the gatherers in hunter/gatherer societies, and the providers of the bulk of the food, they have to be able to keep an eye on everything, while grabbing the straying toddler and trying not to walk on thorns. It's an unfocused, all-encompassing, panoramic attention. It's special.

Which is why Sherlock annoyed me. As the Duchess says in Dorothy Sayer's novel *Clouds of Witness* (at page 106), 'My dear child, you may give it a long name if you like, but I'm an old-fashioned woman and I call it mother wit, and it's so rare for a man to have it that if he does you write a book about him and call him Sherlock Holmes.'

I actually wrote a Sherlock Holmes homage and pastiche story for a collection of food-related mysteries which I wrote with Jenny Pausacker, *Recipes For Crime*. It was called 'The Baroness' Companion', and was a fair working Sherlock Holmes story. Conan Doyle plots very well, but he writes not very brilliant Victorian prose, not hard to imitate if you leash the adverbs and severely limit the use of adjectives. And employ occasional Victorian metaphors like 'the wind cried like a child in the chimney'. The experience of writing it was illuminating. I knew his methods, (Watson). I employed them.

Then people started making movies. Basil Rathbone was good, but his Watson was too bumbling—not like the man of action in the books. Jeremy Brett was a marvellous canonical Sherlock, the best there will ever be. His Watson was a very Conan Doyle Watson. Then a movie was made which emphasised the almost homoerotic edge of Sherlock and Watson. I had already thought about this because of a novel called *My Dearest Holmes* by Rohase Piercy, where they finally got together after the Reichenbach Falls. Touching. The original allows such an interpretation. 'It was worth a wound; it was worth many wounds; to know the depth of loyalty and love which lay behind that cold mask.' 'I am here to be used.'

The BBC then decided to rethink Sherlock Holmes for a modern technological age and it is mind-boggling (though I'm not altogether sure that I wanted my mind to be boggled this much). BBC Sherlock is a borderline Asperger's prodigy, amazingly rude to everyone (which the original Sherlock never is), his PTSD army doctor Watson is beyond excellent, and his Moriarty is not the Victorian Capitalist Villain of the original but a genuine psychopath. 'I'll burn the heart out of you.' I've met murderous psychopaths in my legal practice and BBC Moriarty is exact. Also, Benedict Cumberbatch is astoundingly, strangely, beautiful. I still haven't been able to watch him fling himself off the top of St Bart's Hospital.

I saw half of one episode of *Elementary*, where Sherlock is in America and his Watson is a woman, and it's silly. The BBC Sherlock possesses the imagination.

But I can't write a psychopath. I have to get inside a character to put them in a novel and I have enough nightmares as it is. Really. Those uninterested eyes—the same if they are looking at an apple, a chair or a dying woman—frighten me even in retrospect. So my villain at least has reasons for doing what he does, and my Sherlock-type character is a mathematician. His companion is a Great War doctor. During that obscenity of a conflict, the British Army did drag students out of the medical schools to run casualty clearing stations. Even for wars, that is unbelievably cruel. What they were doing is now called triage. God knows what that experience did to them. Actually, I have a pretty good idea. So, me and Sherlock. I naturally own no rights in any of the incarnations of the divine detective. And if I met the original, I would be hard pressed as to whether I would kiss him, or belt him over the head with a brick.

Possibly both.

On choirs

Music has always been important to me. Everyone in my extended family could sing, and one was a singer with the D'Oyly Carte Opera Company and sang *Invictus* before King George. That was my great Uncle Gwilym, who had that 'baritone voice with a tenor quality' shared by my Mr Henty. I was a singer as soon as I could speak. So naturally I joined choirs, and became a very part-time amateur folkie for a while. Choirs are important. Even mediocre singers manage university choirs, because everything they sing is note-bashed until the veriest tone-deaf tyro can sing it. I love singing in choirs. Listening to the way the music builds, diminishes, folds, where the parts slot into the whole, is fascinating. And when a choir actually performs the piece they've been rehearsing, and it works—and for some reason such things always work, even when the choir doesn't deserve it—it is magical. A fine natural high. I met most of my enduring friends by singing with them. Anyone who thinks they recognise themselves in this work probably does, though some people are compilations. And my conductors are definitely not portraits, but rather a vicious and spiteful combination of everything that has annoyed me about conductors over the last forty years. So there. A soprano's revenge may be long in coming, but when it arrives, let the wicked tremble.

BIBLIOGRAPHY

Songbooks and music

Mendelssohn, Felix, *Elijah* (recording) Bryn Terfel with Renée Fleming, the Edinburgh Festival Chorus and the Orchestra of the Age of Enlightenment, conducted by Paul Daniel, Decca, 1997.

Mendelssohn, Felix, *Elijah* (vocal score), New Novello Choral Edition, Novello & Co. Ltd.

The F4 Compendium (songs) (ed. David Greagg).

The Monash University Choral Society Songbook (compiled by Alistair Evans, Gudrun Arnold and Ximena Inglesias, with Carolyn Edwards, Andrew Scott, Anneliese Wilson, David Young and Winston Todd; illus Bill Collopy), 1996.

Books

Abrahams, Gerald, *The Chess Mind*, Penguin Books, London, 1960.

Doyle, Sir Arthur Conan, *The Casebook of Sherlock Holmes*, Penguin Books, London, 1927.

The Epic of Gilgamesh (trans. Herbert Mason), New American Library, New York, 1970.

Glaister, (Professor) John, *The Power of Poison*, Christopher Johnson, London, 1954.

Hoffnung, Gerald, *The Symphony Orchestra*, Souvenir Press, London, 1955.

Homer, *The Iliad* (trans. EV Rieu), Penguin Classics, London, 1950.

The King James Bible

Mackenzie, Compton, *My Life and Times* (series), Chatto & Windus, London, 1964.

——*Gallipoli Memories*, Panther, London, 1965.

——*First Athenian Memories*, Cassel & Co., London, 1931.

Pausacker, Jenny and Greenwood, Kerry, *Recipes For Crime*, McPhee Gribble, Melbourne, 1995.

Piercy, Rohase, *My Dearest Holmes*, Gay Men's Press, New York, 1985.

Sayers, Dorothy, *Clouds of Witness*, New English Library, London, 1962.

Willet, Graham, Murdoch, Wayne and Marshall, Daniel (eds), *Secret Histories of Queer Melbourne*, Australian Lesbian and Gay Archives, Parkville Vic., 2011.